The Tom Blake Thrillers

ADRIAN WILLS

ISBN: 1546738398
ISBN-13: 978-1546738398

For my wife, Amanda, and my boys, Oliver and Thomas,
for all your unending support..

Deep Sleepers

Chapter 1

A gang prowled the dimly lit room like hunting dogs stalking an injured calf; their attention focussed on a figure collapsed in a chair with his hands bound behind his back. A potato sack had been pulled over his head and his T-shirt ripped open from his throat to his stomach.

Tom Blake, sprawled on his front with his eye to a hole in the floorboards, counted four men. Three were lithe and wiry with hard faces, dark clothes, and tattooed arms. The fourth was short and fat, with a belly that hung over his belt, and rolls of flab that rippled down his neck where his head morphed into his shoulders.

'Names!' the fat man screamed.

The figure in the chair muttered something inaudible and his interrogator swung a clenched fist so hard into the knot of his stomach that Blake winced.

'Who are you working for?'

'No one.'

'I don't believe you.'

'It's the truth.'

The interrogator sighed and hung his head. 'Okay,' he said, quietly.

He nodded at one of his henchmen who stepped out of Blake's narrow field of vision. Blake concentrated on controlling his breathing, trying not to move, fearful that a creak from the rotten floor would give him away. He detected the faint smell of smoke. Not the bitter, chemical-infused odour of a cigarette, but the pungent aroma of burning wood. Blake sniffed the air, and frowned as he heard the sound of coals being raked.

The man who'd disappeared returned with a metal rod glowing red hot at one end, pulsing in waves of radiant orange and white in the darkened room. The fat interrogator examined the flattened tip at arm's length before thrusting it at the exposed chest of the man in the chair, who bucked violently as if he'd been plugged into the electrical mains, his screams echoing through the empty building, shattering the silence and startling a kit of pigeons roosting in the roof. Skin sizzled, and the nauseating stench of burning flesh hit Blake at the back of his throat.

He rolled onto his back, and stared at the exposed rafters trying to block out the howls, wracked by the guilt that he'd failed the man whose life he'd vowed to protect. What was worse, he had no idea who the abductors were nor how they could have possibly discovered that Ben Proctor was an impostor.

Proctor's abduction had been as efficient as it had been unexpected. The gang had screeched to a halt in a battered old Vauxhall, grabbing him from the street as he neared his flat. They'd bundled him into the boot, and driven to an abandoned Victorian railway station on the edge of the city where, presumably, they thought no one would hear his screams. Blake, who'd been discreetly following Proctor, had witnessed it all. He'd clambered onto a precarious canopy over the old platform, and slipped into an upstairs room from where he could observe through a tennis ball sized gap in the floorboards.

'Take him outside!' the fat man shouted.

Two men lifted Proctor, and dragged him out of the room with his feet trailing. Blake scuffed across the filthy floor and was about to climb out of the first floor window when the men appeared from around the side of the building. They carried Proctor to the edge of the platform, and stood him with his toes hanging over the drop as Blake retreated into the shadows.

The fat interrogator approached Proctor from behind, and said something in his ear that caused Proctor's head to jolt back and his body to tense. He tried to move away from the edge, but he was held tightly, lacking the strength to overcome the powerful grip of the three men.

'Please, no!' His muffled cry of anguish a desperate plea.

Blake's puzzlement lasted only a moment before he realised their intentions. It was a cheap psychological trick he'd seen once in a film. Blindfold a man, put his feet on the edge of a low drop, and tell him he's standing at the top of a tall building. His imagination would cripple him with fear and guarantee he'd spill every dark secret he'd ever taken to his heart.

But it didn't quite play out like that. The interrogator placed his hand between Proctor's shoulders and shoved hard. Proctor fell forward, his scream knocked from his lungs when he hit the ground a second later, disappearing into the undergrowth that had swallowed what was left of the old railway track. The gang burst into cruel laughter and sloped away, leaving Proctor whimpering and gasping.

Cars doors slammed, an engine rattled to life, and tyres crunched over the hard ground. When he was sure they'd gone, Blake eased himself through the glassless window, dropped onto the canopy and down onto the platform.

He quickly located Proctor, who was lying awkwardly across the rusty tracks with his legs tucked up to his chest and his hands twisted behind his back. Blake lifted him to his feet, like an older brother dusting off a sibling after a playground scrap, and removed the sack from his head. Proctor's eyes were red and swollen, his lips puffed and a trickle of blood ran from his nose.

'I'm sorry,' Blake muttered under his breath.

Proctor tried to open his eyes, but the effort was too much. He allowed Blake to cut the cable tie from his wrist without question.

'Let's have a look at that burn,' said Blake, teasing back

the ragged shreds of Proctor's T-shirt.

Even in the gloom, Blake could make out an angry, crimson welt. At its centre, a white blister was already starting to form.

Proctor stumbled, his legs weak. Blake caught him under his arms and walked him slowly back to his car, hidden in a scrub behind a disused signal box. As Proctor settled into the passenger seat, his eyes peeled open and he stared at Blake with faintly disguised contempt.

'Who are you?' he asked, coming to his senses.

'Never mind,' said Blake. He closed the door, walked around the bonnet and slid in behind the wheel.

'What do you want?'

Blake slotted the key in the ignition and fired up the engine. He was about to pull away when Proctor's hand fell on his wrist, gripping it tightly.

'I asked you a question. Who are you?'

Blake sighed. 'Listen, I can explain everything. Right now we need to get you sorted out.'

Chapter 2

Colonel Harry Patterson replaced the phone in its cradle and swivelled in his chair. Through the bare branches of the trees opposite, he watched a pleasure boat drifting along the river with a dozen hardy tourists scattered along its top deck. But his mind was elsewhere.

Blake's call had been a major concern. Ben Proctor was an experiment on which they'd staked their reputations. He was supposed to be the perfect spy, a new breed of undetectable sleeper agent. There were few logical explanations for his abduction beyond the unthinkable fact that his cover had been blown.

Patterson's desk phone gave a short trill, and he snatched up the handset.

'Yes?'

'The deputy director general is asking if you have a moment.'

Patterson checked his watch. 'Tell him I'll be there in five minutes. Thanks, Heather.'

He flipped the lid of his laptop closed and grabbed his jacket from the back of the door. The DDG wasn't a man to be kept waiting. He bounded up four flights of a grand stone staircase that wound through the centre of Thames House, the headquarters of the British security service, MI5, racing to the top floor under the watch of former prime ministers and agency director generals in their gilt-edged frames.

He announced himself to a secretary and took a seat outside floor-to-ceiling wooden doors. Exactly four minutes later he was ushered into a spacious, cold office where Sir Richard Howard, a small man with rimless glasses over crystal blue eyes and thinning, silvery hair parted neatly to one side, was sitting behind a desk in front of a large window hung with greying net curtains.

He waved Patterson towards a strategically low chair in the middle of the room, placed deliberately at a distance from the desk. All part of the power games to remind visitors of their lowly status in the presence of one of the most powerful civil servants in the country, the man who ran international and domestic counter-terrorism operations for MI5.

'Feeling at home with us yet?' Sir Richard asked, replacing the top on his fountain pen and looking up from his paperwork, his thin smile unnerving.

'I'm still getting used to your civilian ways of doing things, but I think I'm finding my feet.' Patterson said, smoothing out a crease in the leg of his the Savile Row suit that had cost him a small fortune. He'd chosen a sombre navy pin-stripe he thought befitted an intelligence officer in the secret service, but preferred his comfortable army fatigues and well-worn desert boots.

It had been less than a year since Patterson had left the Army after his black-ops intelligence unit, Echo 17, had been terminated. The unit had specialised in covert overseas missions using experimental hypnotic techniques to extract information from high-value targets. But with a growing budget deficit, the Ministry of Defence had announced Echo 17 would be deactivated.

With his career on the line, Patterson had pulled some strings to secure an unlikely meeting with MI5's counter-terrorism chief and made a compelling case for the unit to come under the security service's wing as a non-military operation. He had proposed the creation of a Deep Sleepers programme, using Blake's skills honed as a warfare psychologist, to infiltrate suspected terror organisations with undercover agents. With their subconscious controlled by Blake, they could be embedded in key positions and become virtually undetectable.

Sir Richard had agreed to a pilot scheme with the one condition that Blake, who would continue to work in the field, would become a deniable asset. He had to exist as a ghost and have no direct contact with anyone in MI5 apart from Patterson who would run the unit from an office in its headquarters. And so Patterson had engineered Blake's death. His Army records documented that a Taliban sniper in Afghanistan had fatally wounded him. Patterson even went as far as having Blake's empty coffin returned to Britain for a full, military funeral, and personally oversaw the obituary that was released to the press.

'How's Blake getting on?' asked Sir Richard, almost casually.

They both knew that the Deep Sleepers programme was a test of Patterson's competency and effectiveness.

'Fine. He's reporting very positive things with our deep sleeper.'

'Proctor? Is he making any progress?'

Patterson paused just a little too long, and the pitch in his voice was a little too high when he answered. 'Absolutely. The leadership appear to be totally convinced that he's genuine. He's ideological, dispossessed, and reliable. And he's in deep, exactly where we wanted him.'

'They believe his cover story?'

'Without doubt. He's fitting in well with the grassroots membership, and I'm sure it won't be long before he's able to provide some decent intelligence on what's really happening on the inside.'

'Good, good,' said Sir Richard, sitting back in his chair and steepling his fingers. 'But I'm afraid we're going to need to accelerate the programme. We don't have the time we thought we had. Proctor needs to start delivering results.'

'But you said this was a low-level operation to test the programme,' said Patterson, feeling the sweat build on his brow.

'Well, things have changed.' The DDG took a file from a drawer and pushed it across the desk. 'Take a look.'

A set of grainy black and white photographs sat on top of a pile of papers.

'The latest intelligence we've pulled on the BFA.'

Patterson flicked through the pictures. They'd all been taken with a long lens, and although the faces were blurred and indistinct, it was clear they were all of the same man. 'Ken Longhurst?'

Sir Richard nodded.

'Where were they taken?'

'Blackburn. Luton. Bristol. Dover. That last one was in Coventry just two weeks ago.'

'All at British Freedom Alliance marches?' Patterson studied the pictures closely. In each one, Ken Longhurst, the charismatic, recently appointed leader of the BFA, was wearing a hooded top or baseball cap pulled low over his face. He was surrounded by the same muscled, sour-faced hard-men with their shaven heads and Nazi tattoos.

'Every one of those protests ended in violent attacks on the black and Asian communities.'

Patterson raised an eyebrow. 'And you think Longhurst was orchestrating it?'

'If he wasn't orchestrating it, he was at least complicit.'

'Well, that goes against the grain.'

'Less than five months ago, he was vowing to clean up the party and root out the racists, bigots, and troublemakers, to paraphrase his own words. He promised to turn the organisation around and make it electable. The prime minister's fear is that the people are beginning to believe him, and all the indications show they could make ground in the next round of local elections. They already have representation in Europe. Before you know it, they'll have a seat in the Commons and then where will we be? Far be it for us to involve ourselves in the muddy world of politics, but I don't like the smell of this. Longhurst's not what he purports to be. And I want to know what's going on.'

'Why not release the pictures to the press? They'd have a field day.'

Sir Richard sucked a sharp breath through his teeth. 'That's not the way we do things here.'

'We'll see what Proctor can find out.'

'There's more I'm afraid. Take a look at the print-outs.'

Under the stack of photos were several loose sheets of printed A4 paper with columns of figures, certain numbers circled in pen. Most were five or six figure sums.

'The numbers highlighted show single deposits made into the BFA's bank account,' said Sir Richard.

'These are big sums. Where are they coming from?'

'We don't know, but we suspect an anonymous benefactor. The payments started shortly after Longhurst was appointed leader. They've grown steadily, and have swelled the BFA's modest balance considerably. We need to know who's making those donations and why.'

'Can't you trace the payments back to source?'

'We've tried. Each donation has come through a series of complex transactions via offshore accounts and Swiss banks. In short, they're untraceable.'

'And you want Proctor to find out?'

'He's our best hope.'

'Perhaps they're just stockpiling cash for a big election push?'

'Maybe they are. But maybe they're planning something else. Whatever it is, I want to know. Money is power, you know.'

'Of course.'

Sir Richard held out his hand across the desk and Patterson passed him back the file. 'How long before Proctor can achieve some results?'

'Maybe six months, possibly a year. It depends how long it takes him to infiltrate the management structure.'

'He has six weeks.'

'It's impossible -'

'Six weeks. You promised when you first came in here begging me to save your career that Blake could deliver something special. Now's the time to prove it.'

'I understand.'

'And keep me up to date with developments.' The DDG picked up his pen, removed the cap, and turned his attention to a heap of paperwork on his desk, indicating to Patterson his audience was over.

Patterson shuffled out of the office and pulled the enormous doors closed behind him, scuttled down the stairs, and slipped into his office, dialling a number on his mobile phone.

'Blake, it's me,' he said, quietly. 'We have a problem.'

Chapter 3

Proctor woke with a start. His eyes sprung open and his breath caught in his throat. He was still fully clothed, lying on the couch and wrung out with sweat. A siren wailed past the window, an eerie caterwauling carrying across the still, night air. Empty beer cans littered the floor, and cigarette butts were piled high in an ashtray. The smell of stale tobacco smoke hung heavy in the dreary room.

He had no idea how long he'd been asleep, only that he'd fallen into paracetamol-infused alcoholic slumber when fatigue had finally caught up with him. He glanced at his watch. Not yet eleven. Early by his standards. He swung his feet to the floor, and sat up too quickly. A pain shot through his head and a metallic sourness flooded his mouth as if he'd been sucking on coins. His tongue darted over cracked lips, and he fished at his feet for a beer, hoping to find a half-finished can, but discovered he'd drained them all.

It had become a regular pattern since his abduction. Sleep came to him only through alcohol or drugs. Even then, it wasn't a fruitful, energy-reviving sleep that refreshes the soul, but a fitful dormancy punctuated with dark nightmares. Neither was his mental state greatly improved when he was awake. He'd been gripped by a fear of leaving his flat, and the limit of his capabilities was a hurried visit to the store at the end of the road to stock up on dwindling beer supplies.

Proctor was worried he'd lost his nerve. He'd never been afraid of anybody before the attack. He'd always been defined by an unwavering self-confidence that some interpreted as arrogance. It was an attitude that said to hell with anyone else; from the way he walked, to the look in his eyes. Those dark, menacing orbs that burned with venom and loathing. He looked like trouble. The sort you crossed the street to avoid.

His slight build accentuated his height. He was whippet-thin but sinewy and loose-limbed, nimble on his feet and born with a swagger that suggested an underlying violence. He kept his hair closely cropped and wore only black. Two Nazi SS bolt tattoos were prominent on his forearm, and a white-power clenched fist visible on his upper arm when he rolled up his sleeve.

The blank screen of the television flickered in the corner of the room. Below it, a DVD player hummed and clicked at the end of the film Proctor had been half-watching. He grabbed the remote and replayed his favourite scene, the one where Stallone rips out the throat of a Burmese solider with his bare hands.

He lit a cigarette, and squinted through the smoke at the graphic images, imagining what he'd do to the men who'd jumped him in the street, and playing out in his mind the revenge he'd exact. Maybe he'd slash open their bellies and let them watch their steaming entrails slop out on the floor as they died.

You know who you are, what you're made of.
When you're pushed, killing's as easy as breathing.

Proctor intoned the words under his breath. He crossed the room and yanked his hunting knife out of the plasterboard, walked back to the couch, and wiped the blade clean on his leg. Willem Dafoe was on his knees, head thrown back, his body riddled with the bullets of a chasing Vietcong pack of guerrillas. Proctor aimed for his throat. The knife whistled through the air and struck the poster through the two dog tags that replaced the 'o's in

Platoon, lodged in the wall with a twang and stayed there.

Proctor winced. Painkillers had taken the edge off the worst of the pain in his chest, but every time he moved, an agonising twinge reminded him of his injury. He still didn't understand why he'd been targeted. They'd accused him of being some kind of impostor, but he had no idea what they were talking about. Probably mistaken identity. Not that that was any excuse. They'd still pay the price.

Proctor's fingers drifted to the wound where it felt as if a colony of ants was marching over his skin. Through his T-shirt, he scratched at the edges of the dressing trying to relieve the awful, crawling itch. But the more he worked at it, the more intolerable it became.

He jumped from the couch, and slouched into the bathroom with its avocado-coloured bath and basin, cracked tiles and mouldy ceiling. He tugged on the light, splashed cool water over his face and stared at the gaunt reflection in the mirror. His eyes were ringed with dark circles like bruises, his skin pockmarked with acne.

He balanced the smouldering cigarette on the edge of the basin, and tugged his T-shirt off over his head. His chewed fingernails picked at the edges of the surgical tape until the dressing sucked away from the sticky lesion beneath.

Proctor drew a sharp breath as he prodded at the inflamed skin, unable to draw his eyes away from the ugly wound. He peered at it more closely, turning to catch the light, but unable to comprehend what he was seeing. The fluid-filled blister had formed into a definite, familiar shape. It looked like the letter 'P' dissected with a horizontal stroke.

The shrill tone of his mobile phone broke in on his thoughts. He hurriedly reapplied the dressing, pulled his top back on, and tossed the remains of the cigarette into the toilet bowl.

He answered without checking the number. 'Hello?'
'It's Mike.'

'What's up?'

'Nothing. Why?'

'You sound - is everything okay?'

'Yeah, of course. Listen, are you in? I need to talk to you.' He paused. 'It's quite urgent.'

'Yeah, I'm here. Come over.' Proctor knew he wouldn't be sleeping for a while, and welcomed the company as a distraction from the dark thoughts clouding his mind.

'Be there in ten minutes.'

His friendship with Mike Clark had been cemented after they'd marched shoulder to shoulder at Proctor's first BFA protest rally. The day had ended predictably in a series of sporadic brawls as the right wing extremists were confronted by anti-fascist counter demonstrators. Proctor and Clark had found themselves isolated, surrounded by a gang of young Muslims in a back alley, and facing a vicious kicking. Until Clark pulled a knife. A gleaming seven-inch blade he'd had hidden in his waistband behind his back. The snarl on his lips convinced the gang he was crazy enough to use it, and they'd fled in fear. Afterwards, the two men collapsed in fits of jubilant laughter, congratulating each other like young warriors who'd seen off an entire army.

Clark arrived at Proctor's flat precisely seven minutes after his call. He pulled back the curtains, checked the street below left and right, and back again, while Proctor fetched two cans of lager from a fridge yellowed with age. He threw one across the room. Clark caught it one-handed, snapped it open, and emptied half the contents down his throat in one go.

Proctor fell onto the sofa and drew a Marlboro from a depleted pack. The flame from a plastic lighter crackled and hissed. As he took a deep draw, he watched his friend pace the room.

'What the hell's wrong with you? Sit down, will you,' he said. 'You're making me nervous.'

'Can I have one of those?' Clark nodded at the

Marlboros. Proctor tossed the packet over with the lighter.

'What's happened, Mike?'

'Nothing really.' Clark fixed his friend with a long, hard stare, as if he were working out whether he could trust Proctor with what was on his mind. 'Something happened a couple of nights ago. I wanted to tell you before but - '

Ash fell from Clark's cigarette like dirty confetti.

'Tell me.'

'Some arseholes jumped me, managed to get me in the boot of their car, and took me off.'

Proctor puzzled over the look on his friend's face. Not quite embarrassment. Shame, maybe.

'I had to tell someone.' As Clark dragged hard on the cigarette, Proctor noticed his hand was trembling. 'They did something awful.'

'You can tell me, Mike,' said Proctor, but he suspected he already knew what was coming.

Clark slipped off his jacket, pulled his T-shirt over his head revealing an angry welt, red and inflamed in the middle of his chest. 'Look at what they did.' There were tears in his eyes.

'Yeah, I know,' said Proctor, softly. He stubbed out his cigarette, pulled up his own top, and ripped off the dressing. 'Same here.'

'What the hell? They came for you too?'

'I think we've been branded, like cattle.'

'But - why would anyone do that?'

'I don't know, but I sure as hell intend to find out.'

Chapter 4

At precisely eight o'clock, thirty mobile phones chimed with the delivery of an identical text message. Trent Garside threw back the remnants of his mug of tea, and read the brief instructions.

'Queen's Head. Chichester Road. Fifteen minutes.'

He gathered up his notebook, threw a few coins on the table to cover the bill, and left the comfort of the all-night café for the frigid night air, setting off at a brisk pace as the pub was a good ten-minute walk.

A jostling scrum of reporters, photographers, and cameramen had already gathered in front of two thickset men in ill-fitting black suits who were trying to manage the melee. One held a clipboard in massive hands laden with gold sovereign rings. He was checking off names, and waving through those on an approved list.

As Trent took his place in the queue, raised voices caught his attention. One of the bouncers was arguing with *Daily Tribune* reporter, Harry Coles, a slight man, with greying hair swept back from his brow. His checked jacket had the crumpled look of someone who had slept in his clothes. He was no physical match for the thug with the teardrop tattoo under his eye.

It was apparent that the disagreement had arisen over Coles' name being missing from the list. Unwilling to enter into a discussion about the situation, a second bouncer took matters into his own hands. He grabbed two handfuls of the reporter's jacket, lifted him clean off his feet, and threw him across the road still clutching his notebook. His yelp was pitiful.

Coles tried to stand, still protesting his rights, but was kicked to the ground. Two or three photographers fired off a few snatched frames, none keen on attracting the wrath of the two brutes. Besides, none could afford to miss the press conference and have the ignominy of calling their night news editors to explain why.

When Trent saw that it was Coles who'd been thrown out of the line, he wasn't surprised. His paper was a liberal left-wing national that had printed a series of exposés on the British Freedom Alliance and its leader, Ken Longhurst, the former used car salesman with an oily charm who'd been hailed by the party as a reformer with serious ambitions to win electoral representation at all levels. He claimed to be on a mission to cauterise the unsavoury elements of the party that had left it languishing in the political wasteland for so many years, and had even employed a slick publicity machine to convince the nation that Longhurst wasn't a racist.

Not that the *Daily Tribune* saw it like that. It portrayed Longhurst as a violent bully unprepared to tolerate anyone who threatened his view of how British life should be. They'd spoken to anonymous party activists who claimed Longhurst ruled by fear, bullying, and intimidation, and whose private desire remained the reclamation of the country for British whites.

It had made uncomfortable reading for the BFA, but Longhurst's response had been to keep his head down, issue a brief denial of all the allegations, and refuse all media interviews. Yet the longer he had remained out of public view, the bigger the story had grown, until it had become one of the most discussed talking points of the week. The BFA's claims of political legitimacy had been debated on chat shows and news hours across television and radio. And so when selected journalists finally received an invitation to a press conference, there was a clamour of excitement. A robust rebuttal from Longhurst would certainly give the story legs for another few days.

As Trent reached the front of the queue, he felt a pang of guilt. Harry Coles had picked himself off the floor and dusted down his clothes, but was visibly shaken. Trent pretended not to have seen him.

'Name?' asked the bouncer with the sovereign rings.

'Garside. Trent Garside. Freelance.'

'Press card?'

The bouncer studied the plastic identity card Trent produced from a worn wallet, and waved him inside.

The Queen's Head was a dingy, working class pub with faded red carpet sticky from spilt beer, its faded wallpaper and ceilings tinged a tobacco yellow.

The lounge was already filling up. Journalists, photographers, and cameramen were arranging themselves around wooden tables, glared at from the bar by a dozen menacing-looking men with arms streaked with discoloured tattoos. A stage at the front was partially obscured by a red velvet curtain.

Trent pulled up a stool and shook hands with the man already at the table, Pete French, a former colleague who still worked at the *Newham Gazette*.

'This is all a bit odd, isn't it?' said Trent, pulling a dog-eared notebook from his bag. Two television crews were setting up their cameras on tripods to their right, while a row of photographers had settled on the floor with their cameras clutched to their chests.

'Yeah, but I wouldn't have missed it for the world, not after Longhurst has been playing the invisible man all week,' said the Gazette reporter.

'What do you reckon? Think he'll announce his resignation?'

'I'm not sure Longhurst knows the meaning of the word.' Both men smiled at the joke. 'Anyway, it's been a good week for them, hasn't it?'

'Are you kidding?' said Trent. 'He's been hung out to dry by pretty much every news organisation in here.'

'Yeah, but money can't buy the sort of exposure they've had. Their profile's gone through the roof. Keyes must be rubbing his hands with glee.'

A hush fell over the chattering reporters as a smartly dressed man appeared from the wings.

'Good evening, Ladies and Gentlemen, and thank you for coming,' said Michael Keyes, the party's director of communications, and the man largely credited with the turnaround in the BFA's fortunes. 'Apologies for the secretive nature of the invitation, but as you know, some disruptive elements seem hell-bent on making trouble for us.'

Keyes was well-known by most of the reporters for a number of high-profile public relations positions he'd held in government, and it had come as some surprise to most of them when he was unveiled by the BFA as their spin-doctor-in-chief. His brief was simple. To rebrand the party and make Ken Longhurst electable.

'As you all know,' Keyes continued, 'we've been the subject of a number of vindictive slurs in recent days, accusations that are absolutely without foundation. We thought it was one rogue paper with its own peculiar vendetta. We tried to ignore it and let it blow over, but I'm afraid you're a bit like sheep, aren't you? What started as an insignificant - and largely fabricated - series of lies, dressed up as journalism, has sadly snowballed into mainstream news. I know many of you wanted interviews with Ken, but we hoped the fuss would die down. That clearly hasn't happened, so tonight we wanted to set the record straight once and for all.'

Keyes paused between each sentence, sweeping the room with his gaze, making sure each and every reporter felt he was speaking to them individually.

'So I've asked Ken here tonight to answer all your questions, and hopefully put some perspective on this so-called story. I trust we'll see some positive coverage in tomorrow's papers?' He checked his watch. 'I make it less than two hours for most of you to get your copy filed for tomorrow's editions so, without further ado, it's my great pleasure to introduce the leader of the BFA, Mr Ken Longhurst.'

Like a compere at a second-rate talent show, Keyes took a step to his right and gestured to the curtain over the stage. The BFA thugs at the bar clapped and cheered. Someone whistled.

Ken Longhurst appeared theatrically; a wide grin fixed on his face, and was immediately drowned in a sea of photographers' flashes. Television cameras whirred into life, and reporters lifted their pens in anticipation. Longhurst looked good. An open-necked white shirt under a tailored black suit accentuated his tan. Black hair, peppered grey, was combed neatly into place, and his shoes were polished to a glossy sheen. He grabbed a microphone from a stand.

'Good to see so many of you could make it tonight. As Michael has explained, we thought it would be useful to set out our stall after all the lies that have been written and broadcast this week. I'm sure you all have plenty of questions so let's throw it open. Put up your hands, and when we come to you, remind us of your name and who you represent.'

A sea of hands shot up as the clamour for answers began, and Ken Longhurst settled in for a long evening.

Chapter 5

The last glimmer of sunlight had already faded as the rows of shops and cafés along the high street were closing for the evening. Handfuls of last minute shoppers were meandering home as traders fastened shutters and bolted doors. In the shadows, Blake kept his eyes fixed on the building opposite. He was trying to look inconspicuous, his hands shoved in his pockets and his shoulders sloped, leaning against a wall between an estate agent's office and a hardware store under the cover of a small arcade. Through a window of Proctor's flat, he could make out the flickering light cast by a television, and occasionally he caught a glimpse of a shadow moving around inside. Proctor was obviously at home, but Blake needed to be sure he was alone.

He'd been watching from the same position for almost an hour when a middle-aged man with a grey beard stepped out of the hardware store and locked up with a bunch of keys on a bungee cord attached to his trousers. If he noticed Blake, he did a good job of ignoring him. A few minutes later, the lights in the estate agent went out and two loud women in business suits swept out, laughing and joking. One caught Blake's eye. She returned his smile with a glint in her eye, then grabbed her colleague by her arm and they disappeared giggling down the road.

Another twenty minutes passed before the door to Proctor's flat opened. A thin, pale figure dressed in black slid out and scurried away with his eyes to the ground and his shoulders hunched. Blake knew that Proctor hadn't

21

ventured far since his run in with the gang who'd abducted him. He suspected Proctor wouldn't be gone for long so he moved fast.

He pushed off the wall, and loped across the road, feeling in his pocket for a key. In a single fluid movement, he had the lock to Proctor's front door open and let himself into a narrow hallway. Ahead, a steep flight of stairs rose up to the first floor flat. Blake paused to listen for movement above. Through the wall to his left, he heard the dull clatter of dishes from the Chinese takeaway, but upstairs was quiet.

He took the stairs two at a time, and found the flat in darkness. The television was still on in the corner and the sodium glow from the street lights outside filtered through the window giving him enough light to see by.

An unpleasant, musty odour of sweat and stale tobacco smoke hung in the air, and Blake noted a pile of dirty dishes filling the kitchen sink. Empty beer cans were strewn across the floor, and a tabloid newspaper had been left open on a pine dining table. Blake picked his way across the floor, turned off the television and settled into an armchair facing the top of the stairs.

Less than four minutes later, he heard a key rattle in the lock, followed by footsteps bounding up the stairs. Proctor emerged into the gloom, feeling for the light switch on the wall. The room was suddenly bathed in bright, white light.

'How the hell did you get in here?' Proctor dropped a blue plastic carrier bag as he spotted Blake rising from the armchair. The bag landed with a thud, and six cans of beer rolled out.

Blake noticed his hands had balled into tight fists by his sides. 'Relax, Ben, it's only me.' He made it across the room in three easy strides, and placed a reassuring hand on Proctor's upper arm. 'You're safe. I'm not here to cause you any harm.'

'Who are you?' Proctor's voice wavered, and his face crumpled in alarm.

Blake tapped Proctor's shoulder three times. 'Sleep now, Ben.'

Proctor's eyelids fluttered and his chin rolled onto his chest. Blake guided him to the sofa and laid him down with his head on a cushion. When he was sure Proctor was in a deep trance, he drew the curtains, grabbed a dining chair, and pulled it up close to the younger man's head.

'My name is Tom Blake, and you work for me and the government. That means you'll do everything I ask of you, without question. When you awake, you will not recognise my face, but when you see me again you will understand that I am not a threat.' Blake spoke slowly and deliberately, drilling into Proctor's psyche. 'How do you feel?'

'Fine,' said Proctor, the emotion filtered from his voice so that he sounded like an automaton, lacking pitch and tone.

'I want you to tell me about the night you were abducted. Do you remember what happened? It's important you give me as many details as you can recall.'

Proctor screwed his eyes tight and rocked his head back as if reacting to an unpleasant smell. 'They jumped me in the street; put me in the back of a car blindfolded. I didn't know where we were going.'

'Okay, that's good, Ben. What else? Did you see their faces?'

'No, they put a bag over my head. I didn't see anything.'

'What about their voices? Did you recognise any of them?'

'No.'

Blake stretched his legs and took a moment to assess Proctor's physical condition. His face was drawn and pale. An angry red spot was erupting on the side of his neck, and unkempt wisps of facial hair sprouted from his chin and cheeks.

'So no idea who they might have been?' asked Blake.

'No.'

'What did they say to each other?' Blake tipped his head

back, and traced the intricate patterned swirls of the yellow-tinged Artex ceiling.

'Nothing.'

'This is important, Ben. Delve deep into your memory and try to remember.'

'They didn't say anything.'

'They must have said something.'

'Only when they were asking me questions.'

'Do you know where they took you?'

'No.'

'I followed them. They took you to an old railway station.'

'They tied me to a chair and screamed questions at me.' Proctor's face creased. 'Then they...' Proctor's words drifted away.

'I know, Ben. I saw what they did to you.'

'They branded me with a hot iron.'

Blake sat up straight, not sure he'd heard correctly. 'What did you say?'

'They branded me.'

'What do you mean?'

'They burned a letter onto my chest, but I don't know what it means.'

Blake had dressed the wound in the dark as best he could, and given Proctor a handful of powerful prescription painkillers he kept for emergencies. In his haste, he'd not paid that much attention to the injury itself.

'I want to take a look. Can you take off your T-shirt?'

Proctor's movements were slow and imprecise as he rose from the couch and stripped off. He stood swaying on the spot with his eyes closed as Blake peeled back the dressing. He studied the raised blister for a brief moment, nodded, and handed Proctor back his top.

'Any idea what this symbol means?'

Proctor opened his mouth to answer, but was interrupted by the trill of a ringing phone coming from the back pocket of Proctor's jeans.

'Take out your phone and hand it to me,' said Blake, after two rings.

The caller's identity was blocked. Blake answered the call and held the phone to his ear without speaking.

'Listen carefully to what I have to say,' said a rough male voice, muffled in a way that suggested the caller was trying to disguise it. 'You performed well the other night. I want to congratulate you. We've been impressed with everything about you so far, and now the time has come to invite you formally to join us as a reward for your loyalty. Four men are on their way to collect you. Don't resist them, and do exactly what they tell you. They have been instructed to bring you to me. When you arrive, I'll explain everything. But time is pressing. My men will be with you any moment. Please be ready.'

Blake was about to mumble an answer, hoping to pass off as the younger man, but the line clicked dead.

He stared at the phone in his hand, then at Proctor, still deep in a trance. The heavy rattle of a diesel engine grew louder and came to a halt outside the flat. Doors opened, slammed shut, and heavy boots thudded on the pavement.

Chapter 6

Blake pulled back a corner of the curtains. A beaten-up, blue Transit van had pulled up on the pavement directly beneath Proctor's flat. So much for the advanced warning. Someone hammered hard on the front door, an insistent banging, which echoed up the stairs.

'Some men are about to force their way into your flat,' said Blake, in Proctor's ear. 'They're going to take you away. It's important you don't resist. I don't know where they're going to take you, but I think we're both going to find out more about what happened to you the other night.'

Proctor didn't react. His eyes remained closed, his breathing slow and easy.

'I'm going to wake you now. You'll return to being Ben Proctor, a trusted and valued member of the BFA. You'll remember nothing about this conversation or that I was even here. Start counting backwards from ten, and when you reach one you'll be fully awake.'

The front door splintered open, and feet clattered up the stairs. Blake dived for the landing and the door into Proctor's bedroom. He vaulted the bed, and slid underneath, pushing aside crumpled cardboard boxes and a battered suitcase that had seen better days. He spread himself flat on the dusty floor and froze.

An indistinct voice carried through from the front room where he expected the gang had found Proctor in a waking daze. He hoped Proctor's post-hypnotic disorientation would be explained away as the shock of being suddenly woken from a deep sleep.

'What do you want?' said Proctor.

'You need to come with us.'

Hesitation. Blake pictured the stand-off in the next room. Proctor with his fists clenched, his brain wavering between fear and the sub-conscious instinct to comply that he wouldn't quite understand.

Blake suppressed a sneeze as a cloud of dust particles tickled the sensitive membrane in his nostrils.

Another voice spoke, closer and clearer. 'I need a pee. Back in a minute.'

The bedroom door flew open, and a pair of boots appeared. Black leather Doc Martens, scuffed on the toecaps, mud on the soles.

Blake caught his breath and held it. The boots planted themselves in the doorway.

Come on, this isn't the bathroom, idiot.

But the feet didn't shift, and Blake had an uncomfortable feeling. His mind raced, retracing his last steps, wracking his memory for any mistakes he'd made. He couldn't think of anything, experience and training having made him ultra-cautious. It had become second nature after a lifetime of covert missions. But something wasn't right.

A head and shoulders peered under the bed. Sharply-chiselled features and a close-shaven scalp. Eyes darted left and right. Blake, hidden behind the boxes, focussed on holding in a sneeze as his throat tightened. The man was so close that he could smell stale garlic on his breath.

Not a muscle in Blake's body twitched, save for his heart, which was racing so fast that he was convinced its violent pounding would give him away. One finger at a time, his hand closed around a wire coat hanger. With the element of surprise, it could be used to inflict some horrific damage, especially to the exposed, fleshy parts of the man's face. Blake bent the wire out straight between his finger and thumb and readied himself.

'Hey, Jack, what you doing? Come on, we're going,' said a voice from the hallway.

'Yeah, yeah. I'm coming.' The man stood up.

Blake watched the boots march out of the room, and let go of the breath he was holding. He listened to feet clump down the stairs, and the front door slam shut. An asthmatic engine coughed into life and someone hit the accelerator hard, over-revving to keep it from stalling.

Blake rolled out from under the bed, and sprinted into the abandoned living room. Proctor was gone. From behind a crack in the curtains, he watched as the van pulled away. It arced across the road, and sped off in the direction from which it had come, spewing an oily plume of exhaust fumes in its wake. He made a mental note of the registration plate before springing down the stairs in pursuit.

His car was parked in its usual spot in a nearby residential street. He pulled away from the kerb with tyres screeching, swinging the leather steering wheel left and right through a series of tight turns down the familiar back roads, eventually pulling up at set of traffic lights stuck on red at a junction with the high street.

The lights remained static for what seemed like an eternity, and when they finally changed he jumped on the accelerator, gunning through the crossroads and emerging onto the main road more than a hundred yards behind the van.

Blake followed through the suburbs, maintaining a discreet distance, passing grimy Victorian terraces and then beyond into the leafier, more expensive conurbations. Eventually, the road widened into a fast-moving dual-carriageway that swept through the outskirts of the city and out onto a busy motorway heading south.

The van appeared to be in no particular hurry, cruising at a steady sixty-five in the inside lane, occasionally sweeping around a slow-moving lorry before resuming its position in the slow lane.

Blake dialled a pre-programmed number on his phone connected to a hands-free system, and Harry Patterson's voice boomed through the car's stereo speakers, 'What's happening?'

'I think Proctor knew his attackers,' said Blake.

'What makes you say that?'

'Because they hid their faces and their voices. The logical conclusion is that he knew who they were.'

'So they were from the BFA? Does that mean his cover has been blown?'

'I'm not so sure.'

'What other explanation is there?'

'He was being tested. They wanted to see if he would crack.'

'Why?'

'I took a look at the injury on his chest earlier. I should have done it before, but I wasn't thinking straight. I thought it was about loosening his tongue, but I was wrong. They've branded him. The welt's come up quite clearly. It's like a symbol or something; I just don't know what it means.'

The van turned off the motorway and joined a single carriageway. Blake kept his distance, watching the brake lights flicker as the driver took a series of turns at speed.

'You debriefed Proctor?'

'He's as confused as we are.'

'So where are you now?'

'Proctor's been picked up again. They're taking him out of London into the country. I think it could be the same men. But this time they called ahead. I'm following to see what happens.'

The brake lights ahead flashed as the van took a sharp turn right onto a narrow lane, its rear end fishtailing as its skinny tyres struggled for grip on the damp asphalt. Blake slowed and made a more controlled turn.

'What did they say?'

The lane was narrow and twisting, barely wide enough

for a car to pass. Through the tight corners, the van had vanished. Blake feathered the accelerator, and gripped the steering wheel tightly. 'Harry, I've got to go. I'll call you when I know more.'

'Where are you exactly?'

'Not sure. Somewhere in Sussex I think. Seriously, Harry I've got to go.'

Blake battled to keep the car on the road as he sped through a sharp corner that kept tightening. He damped the brakes, and as the road straightened hit the accelerator hard again.

Suddenly the van was dead ahead, having come to an almost complete standstill, its taillights blindingly bright in the darkness as it turned onto a rutted, muddy track through a thick wood. Blake stamped on the brakes, locked the wheels, and the tyres squealed in protest as the car slewed out of control across the road in a straight-line skid.

It flashed past the van, missing its scratched, rear bumper by less than an inch, ending up with its bonnet buried in a hedge.

Chapter 7

The van quickly shot out of sight, bumping through the trees, and vanishing into the darkness. Blake swore under his breath at his lack of concentration. It was a stupid lapse. He'd risked blowing the operation wide open and signing Proctor's death warrant in the process. He needed to take more care.

He eased the car out of the hedge, thankful there was no obvious damage, and drove on until he found a layby, pulled a hasty three point turn, and retraced his route back to the wood.

The track was pitted with deep, muddy puddles more suited to a 4x4. The saloon, with its sporty low-profile tyres and low clearance, struggled, and it was brought to a snail's pace with Blake's body jolted in every which way by the unpredictable camber. Fearful of being seen, he tried killing his headlights and navigating by the light of the moon, but ancient knotted trees with boughs like deformed arms formed a thick canopy overhead. And when he almost crashed the car into the gnarled stump of a fallen horse chestnut, he abandoned the vehicle in a clearing behind a tangle of bushes and opted to continue on foot instead.

He grabbed a Stormwalker jacket and retrieved a Glock 26 from a hidden compartment in the boot, a smaller weapon than his favoured Browning, and which slipped more neatly into the waistband of his trousers. He chose a route parallel to the track, picking a path through the undergrowth, brushing through brambles and using the trees for cover. The only sounds, the screech of owls and the creaking of ageing branches high overhead.

After a ten-minute march Blake picked out lights ahead. As he circled closer, he saw the van parked with its headlights blazing, illuminating a dilapidated farmhouse with gaping holes where its doors and windows used to be. On its southern flank, a single-storey extension had fallen into decay, and although its walls stood resolutely, the roof had collapsed, leaving exposed and rotting beams like the skeleton of a beached whale protruding through putrid flesh. At the north-western corner of the plot, a barn had better withstood the ravages of time, and looked remarkably unscathed by nature's onslaught.

Blake tucked himself behind the trunk of a towering oak, and scanned the site. Three men were standing around the van, smoking and chatting casually. He counted three other vehicles; off-roaders caked in mud, and suspected there must be more men. Another two figures stood shoulder-to-shoulder silhouetted by the headlights in front of the farmhouse. The man on the left was recognisable by his height and build. Ben Proctor was standing ramrod straight with his eyes focussed ahead. The man next to him was shorter and partially obscured.

Blake rushed low and fast to his right, and fell to one knee behind a tree twenty yards farther on. Now he could see that the man beside Proctor had a neatly trimmed goatee beard and a jutting jaw. Mike Clark, one of Proctor's closest associates in the BFA.

A figure emerged from the darkness of the house, and the chatter that had carried on the still, night air suddenly ceased, and cigarettes were hastily stubbed out. At first, it was no more than an indistinguishable shadow with a tall, domed head. Blake squinted into the gloom, wishing he'd remembered to bring a pair of night-vision glasses. Then the figure stepped out of the gloom into the glare of the van's headlights. Proctor and Clark stood rigid. From the size and shape, Blake determined it was a man, but it was impossible to be sure, as he was wearing an elaborate, hooded robe made of sumptuous red velvet decorated with curious-looking symbols stitched in gold thread that concealed his face and body. The material flowed over his feet, brushing the ground, and gave the appearance he was floating.

He extended an arm from a voluminous sleeve, and beckoned the two men to kneel. Proctor and Clark bowed their heads in supplication, and dropped to the ground as the figure began a low incantation, like a religious chant. In fact, the whole scene had taken on a sacred reverence, which made Blake shudder. He didn't have much time for religion in any of its guises.

The robed man placed a hand on the head of each of the men kneeling before him, but from his position, Blake couldn't make out any of his words. He needed to be closer. He rose slowly from his crouch, and calculated that, with all eyes on the scene being played out, he could make it safely to the barn by skirting behind the van.

He drew himself to his full height, but caught movement in the periphery of his vision. A branch snapped with a loud crack that splintered the nighttime still. Blake reached for the gun in his waistband, but reacted too late. Cold, hard steel pressed roughly into the bone behind his skull, and a voice hissed in his ear.

'Stand up slowly! And no sudden moves.'

Chapter 8

Blake raised his arms. 'No problem,' he said, trying to sound relaxed.

'What's your name?'

Blake shuffled to his right, and twisted from the waist, cocking his head as if he'd not quite caught the question. In reality he wanted a clear view of the gun. He was in luck. Nothing more than a farmer's shotgun. Heavy, cumbersome and slow firing, but on the other hand you didn't need to be the world's greatest shot to make it count.

'Sorry, what's that?' said Blake, feigning ignorance.

'Stand still or I'll blow your bloody head off. Now who are you? What are you doing here?' The questions barrelled off the gunman's tongue.

Blake noticed his finger coil tightly around the trigger of the double-barrelled Winchester, but it was apparent from the awkward way he was holding it he lacked familiarity with the weapon. The stock wasn't quite in his shoulder. His hands a little too far apart. An amateur, probably handed the gun and instructed to patrol the perimeter as a look out scout while the ceremony with Proctor and Clark took place.

'Look, I don't want to cause any trouble,' said Blake, in his most disarming tone. He lowered his arms and turned slowly, gambling that the scout didn't have the balls to shoot.

'I said stand still,' he screamed, taking two steps back as Blake knew he would, a natural instinct to put himself out of harm's way. It was also precisely the wrong thing to do.

Blake jabbed with his elbow, knocking the barrel away from his body, and in a single motion, dropped into a crouch, and with his leg hooked the gunman's feet from under him, knocking him flat on his back.

Blake wrestled the gun from his grasp, tossed it into the undergrowth, and fell on his chest. He was a burly man with a round head, thick neck and arms matted with coarse, black hair, his breath sweet with the tinge of alcohol. Blake wrapped his hands around the man's throat, and squeezed hard with his thumbs pressed into his larynx. The man's eyes bulged from their sockets, and his face flushed red as the supply of blood was cut to his brain, his lungs starved of air.

In a blind panic, the scout snatched at Blake's wrists but his efforts only hastened the inevitable as he used up the limited oxygen in his bloodstream. He bucked like a wild mustang, but Blake pressed harder, refusing to let go, until eventually the scout's body went limp, and his brain shut down.

When he was sure the man had lost consciousness, Blake checked for a pulse. It was weak, but steady. He'd be out for the count for a while, but shouldn't suffer any lasting effects. Blake found a length of vine coiling across the damp woodland carpet and used it to tie the scout's wrists and ankles. Then he dragged the body deeper into the wood and hid it under a cover of fallen branches and leaves.

Proctor and Clark were still on their knees when he returned, the robed figure gesticulating with expansive gestures above their heads, like a high priest in a weird cult, speaking words in a low monotone that Blake couldn't catch. Needing to move closer to hear what was being said, he darted away to his right on a circuitous route away from the farmhouse bringing him to a copse on the northern edge of the site. He broke the cover of the trees, and sprinted across open ground towards the barn, aiming for a section where the wall had collapsed, leaving a hole large enough to drive a car through. He clambered over the fallen rubble, and stumbled inside.

He picked his way over the remains of a few hay bales, past a rusting red tractor with cracked and deflated tyres, and towards a low window in the wall that overlooked the farmhouse. A wooden shutter hung loose from its hinges, leaving a gap that allowed Blake a perfect view of the courtyard, allowing him to examine in detail the elaborate robes the priest figure was wearing.

The material had been beautifully embroidered with gold trim and swirling emblems. But one symbol stood out, prominent on the front of the gown. A symbol that Blake had seen before. It looked like the letter 'P' dissected horizontally, but crafted with spiralling flourishes and curls. It was the same symbol that had been branded on Proctor's chest. The symbol of the Phineas Priests.

The priest's voice rose to a crescendo as he placed a hand on the men's heads, and urged them to stand. As they rose, he took the edges of his hood and pulled it back, letting it fall over his shoulders.

From inside the barn, Blake had a clear view of his face bathed in the bright light of the van's headlights. The wide grin and rich-man's tan. The black hair peppered with grey.

Ken Longhurst extended his arm and shook each man warmly by the hand.

Chapter 9

Trent Garside rubbed the sensation back into his fingers, and continued to study the computer screen. It was so cold in his flat that he'd contemplated heading for a nearby café, until he'd considered the bitter wind and drizzle outside. Now his back was aching from leaning over the low coffee table where he'd set up his laptop, and he was becoming increasingly frustrated with the lack of progress in his investigation.

The internet was choked with information about every conceivable subject apart from the one that gripped his interest. Various articles widely documented that Ken Longhurst was a former businessman turned politician, and there was plenty about the BFA's humble beginnings in the 1980s when it had been set up with the explicit aim of repatriating Britain's immigrant population. But there was next to nothing of significance on Longhurst's life before the BFA. And the less Trent found, the more intrigued he became. If the party was being bankrolled by an anonymous benefactor, he was sure Longhurst's past would hold the key.

He sipped at a mug of strong, black coffee and returned to the entry for the British Freedom Alliance in an online encyclopaedia, hoping to discover something he'd missed first time around. He pored over every line, and double-checked each reference, but drew the same blank. Finally, he decided to try revising his search.

He typed "Ken Longhurst BFA businessman" into a search engine, which returned more than three million results in less than a second. Most of the entries were articles he'd already read, but on the third, he discovered an article from a local newspaper he'd not previously seen.

He smiled when he saw the byline. His old friend and colleague, Pete French, the chief reporter at the *Newham Gazette*. It was a position Trent imagined he'd hold until they carried his lifeless body to the grave. Trent skimmed the story without much hope or expectation. It was a human-interest feature about local characters. A fairly dry and predictable filler piece with a large picture of a suited and grinning Longhurst.

Trent made it halfway through the article, and was about to give up on it when he found a reference that caught his eye. It was a small, almost insignificant nugget of information, but nonetheless something new. A crumb of a lead.

He found Pete's number in his phone, and dialled. The call was answered after two rings.

'Trent, what's up? Still obsessing with the BFA?'

'It's called research, Pete. I'll give you a lesson one day.' He fell back into the soft cushions, and ran a hand over his tired eyes. 'But to be honest I'm struggling. There're so many question marks over the BFA, I can't even begin to fathom out the answers.'

'What do you need to know, other than they're just a bunch of racist fanatics? That's it.'

Trent could hear the familiar background hubbub of his old newsroom. A mixture of chat, ringing phones, and the clatter of computer keyboards.

'A bunch of racist fanatics who happen to be snatching power across the country. Listen, until Longhurst came along I'd have agreed with you. They weren't worth bothering about. But they've got cash now, and they're gaining quite a following. I'm seriously worried about this country. Before you know it, we'll have sleepwalked into the BFA having become the acceptable face of modern politics. Doesn't it worry you?'

'It's clever marketing, that's all. A new logo and a poster campaign have given them a bit of a boost. It'll blow over. It always does.'

The BFA's marketing strategy had begun with a rebrand, which included the toning down of its traditional demand for the repatriation of immigrants, although it remained in the small print of its manifesto. Longhurst had then cleverly focussed attention on the country's deepening economic crisis, repeatedly taking a stand on the government's failure to tackle rising socio-economic problems, and sidestepping awkward questions about the BFA's own questionable policies.

'I don't know, Pete. This thing's building momentum.'

'Longhurst's a charismatic guy. People like him. He tells them what they want to hear, and he speaks his mind. That makes him different and appealing. Plus he has a top-notch comms team. People will lose interest though. They'll see through him.'

'You know they're still committed to removing all non-whites from Britain? And even Longhurst talks about the dark spectre of Islamic extremism. I want to dig deeper, Pete. I want to find out what's really going on inside the belly of the beast.'

'Well, be careful, Trent. I don't want to be writing your obituary. You know what they'll do if they find you poking about.'

The BFA retained a firm of hotshot city lawyers poised to launch legal proceedings against any journalist who claimed the party was racist. A number of newspapers that had made such insinuations had already been forced to pay undisclosed sums of damages when they discovered the burden of proof was against them. But as Trent had found, obtaining evidence to prove such allegations was beyond difficult. Party gatherings were held in secret, and policed by hired muscle. Trent knew of at least two journalists who had infiltrated the BFA, but were exposed before obtaining any usable material. One was still learning to walk again, after what Michael Keyes later described as a 'regrettable accident'. The other had been beaten and hospitalised after being unmasked.

'Thanks for the concern,' said Trent.

'I mean it. Now was there a reason for the call?'

'I want to find out who's putting up the cash. I found an old interview you did with Longhurst a while back.' Trent ran a finger across the computer screen and read out the date of the article. 'You mention something about a failed used-car business that Longhurst ran. Don't suppose he mentioned the name of it by any chance?'

'Maybe. I can't remember. Hang on, let me look my notes out.'

Trent remembered that Pete French kept his old notebooks in a cardboard box under his desk, dated in bold black pen.

'Here you go,' said Pete, his voice muffled as if he was holding the phone under his chin while he flicked through his old shorthand notes. 'It was called Diamond. He said he ran it with a partner, but wouldn't elaborate. He didn't want to talk about it as I remember, so we moved on.'

'Any inkling who this business partner might have been?'

'Sorry, he wouldn't say.'

'Where were they based?'

'Somewhere local I think. Why? Do you think it's relevant?'

'It might be, but at the moment it's the only lead I've got.'

'Trent, sorry I've got to go. I've got another call coming in. Let's speak soon, and please be careful. I mean it.'

'Thanks, Pete. I owe you a beer.'

Trent hung up and dropped the phone on the sofa. He rolled his neck to stretch out his muscles and dived back into the computer, his fingers flying over the keyboard with a new found energy. A lead at last. He knew he could rely on Pete.Insert

Chapter 10

Trent Garside studied the dozen skeletal figures lined up in vinyl-covered armchairs around the edge of the lounge. Each one a shadow of their former selves, living out their days waiting for the inevitable cold hand of death. God's waiting room, he thought. He stood with a milky tea in a chipped, porcelain cup, and was reminded of his mother's slow deterioration in a home not unlike Sunny Bank. It was the smell that brought back the worst memories. A peculiar combination of stale urine and biscuits. The fragrance of the Grim Reaper lurking.

An old television set was blasting out in the corner, the volume set so loud the speakers were distorting. Above the din came the clatter of dishes from another part of the building, as staff prepared lunch for the residents.

A nursing assistant who'd met Trent when he'd arrived, and who looked barely old enough to be out of school, appeared with an elderly man shuffling on a walking frame.

'Here you go, Bob,' she said.

'Mr Longhurst?' said Trent, as the old man slumped into a chair, his mop of white hair carefully combed into place, apart from a rogue tuft that stubbornly stood on end at the back of his head. 'My name's Trent Garside. I'm a journalist.'

'Sit down, sit down,' he instructed, with a wave of a hand speckled with liver spots.

'I wanted to talk to you about your son. I'm writing a piece about his success. They say he could eventually win a seat in the House of Commons,' said Trent, finding he was shouting to be heard over the noise of the television.

Ken Longhurst's father nodded sagely. 'Yes,' he said. 'His mother and I are very proud of him.'

Trent had discovered Ken Longhurst's mother had died from cancer more than eight years previously, but let the comment go. They'd lived for more than thirty years in a prim semi-detached house in Croydon, but when Trent had visited he'd found the house empty and the garden overgrown. A neighbour had told him that Bob Longhurst had been moved into a care home and scribbled its name on a scrap of paper. Trent wasted no time in arranging a visit. It was a shot in the dark but he hoped the old man might be able to reveal a few untold secrets about his son.

'Can you remember what he was like as a child?' Trent raised his pen to his notepad in expectation of a coherent answer.

'He was a good boy. Gave his mum and me the run around sometimes, but that's children, isn't it?' The man laughed and induced a phlegmy coughing fit. 'Now what was your name again?'

'It's Trent, Mr Longhurst.'

'I've not met anyone called Trent before. Is it foreign?'

'No. My mother just had a strange taste in names.'

'And who are you working for?'

'I'm a freelancer, but if I can get the information I need, I'm hoping to persuade one of the national newspapers to take the story.'

'I see,' Bob Longhurst replied, but Trent wasn't sure that he did.

'Does Ken have any brothers or sisters?'

'No, he was an only child. We couldn't have any more even though we'd have liked a brother or sister for him.'

'And where did he get his interest in politics, Mr Longhurst? From you?'

'I can't bear politics. Bloody politicians are all the same aren't they? Can't be trusted.'

Trent smirked at the irony. 'From where then?'

'He's always had a way with words, even at school. He managed to get all the bigger boys on his side when he was being bullied, and they looked out for him. I suppose he had a natural talent for these things.'

'I see.' Trent continued to scribble shorthand notes. 'And before he went into politics he was a successful businessman. I think he had a used-car company.'

'Well, he made a mess of that, didn't he? But I blame that so-called business partner of his. He took everything my boy had worked hard for.'

Trent raised an eyebrow. 'Remind me of the name of that business partner.'

'Samson. Gary Samson. How could I ever forget after what he did. Don't know why Ken ever got involved with the man. He was trouble from the start.'

Trent waited for the old man to continue, but his attention had been drawn to a quiz show that had started on the television.

'Henry the Fourth!' Bob Longhurst yelled across the room.

'But he recovered, didn't he, Mr Longhurst? I mean, he's a rich man now.'

'What? No, he hasn't got any money. You don't think he'd leave me in here if he was rich?' Bob Longhurst nudged Trent's arm, and laughed a throaty laugh.

'So how's he affording the Bentley? The big house? The expensive suits?'

Bob Longhurst laughed again. 'Mr Garside, I might be old, but I'm not going to fall for that one. Ken might have a heart of gold, but that's about it!' The laugh turned into another spluttering cough.

Trent rested his pen on his pad and frowned. 'Yes, I must be thinking about someone else.'

The smell of boiled cabbage wafted through the room, and some of the residents began to rise unsteadily from their seats and tramp out.

'Lunch time,' said Mr Longhurst. 'Are you staying to

eat?'

'What? No. Thank you but I can't.'

'Right-o. Well, very nice talking with you, and good luck with the article.' Bob Longhurst dragged his walking frame close to his chair, and pulled himself up. 'I hope I've been some help,' he said, as he joined the slow-moving exodus.

'Yes, thank you, Mr Longhurst. It's been very enlightening.'

Chapter 11

Gary Samson was hunched over a copy of the *Racing Post* on a stool beneath a bank of television screens. He didn't seem to notice Trent Garside appear in the doorway. Neither did the only two other people in the bookmaker's; a thin, grey man in tracksuit trousers and a scruffy bomber jacket watching a race, and a bored-looking cashier flicking through a magazine behind a glass security screen.

Trent sauntered up to the counter and spoke through the glass. 'I'm looking for someone. I wondered if you could help?'

The cashier looked Trent up and down. Tiny arteries had fractured under her skin leaving unsightly blotches on her cheeks. 'Depends,' she said, pulling a thin cardigan around her shoulders.

'His name's Gary Samson. I was told he comes in sometimes.'

The cashier nodded towards a man with thinning, blond hair huddled over his racing paper and returned to her reading material.

'Thanks,' said Trent.

He took a stool next to Samson, and grabbed a betting slip and stubby blue pen from a Perspex box. 'Any good tips?'

'What?'

The belt straps from Samson's dirty, cream raincoat dangled against his leg.

'I wondered if you had any good racing tips?' Trent nodded at Samson's newspaper where he'd highlighted races and horses in swirling black ink.

'No, not really.'

'Come on, you must have one you can share,' said Trent.

'Who are you?'

'The name's Garside. Trent Garside,' he announced, presenting his hand. 'You're Gary Samson, right?'

'Do I know you?'

'I wanted to talk about Ken Longhurst. I'm trying to find out some information about him, well, about the British Freedom Alliance really. I think you know him - or at least you did.'

Samson's face darkened. He banged his palms on the counter and eased off his stool. Trent followed as he approached the cashier, betting slip in hand.

'I've no idea what you're talking about.'

'I think you do,' said Trent. 'You were in business with him. You ran Diamond Cars together. What happened, Gary? I need to know what went wrong.'

Samson passed his betting slip with a wedge of notes under the security screen.

'Fifty quid on Modern Romance in the three-thirty?' said the cashier, counting out the cash.

'Please, Jean.' Trent watched over Samson's shoulder. 'Are you the filth?'

'I'm a journalist. I'm writing a piece about Ken Longhurst's rise to power in the BFA and, more to the point, where the party's getting its money. And I have a feeling you might be able to help,' said Trent.

Samson turned from the counter and put himself toe-to-toe with the reporter, their faces inches apart. Trent forced himself to hold his ground, determined not to crumble under the test of nerves.

'Okay. But not here.' Samson brushed past Trent's shoulder and headed for the door. He threw it open, and lumbered out onto the street with Trent following a few paces behind.

He led the reporter to a nearby park, found an empty bench overlooking a boating lake, and the two men sat at opposite ends.

'First things first, I want assurances my name's kept out of this,' said Samson, wrapping his coat around his chest.

'Of course. It goes without saying. I take the protection of my sources extremely seriously.'

Samson nodded. 'Stitch me up and I'll come after you. Clear?' There was a menace in his tone that left Trent in little doubt that he meant the threat.

'You absolutely have my word. But I'm coming up against the proverbial brick wall on this Longhurst backgrounder. I need someone who knows him.'

Samson snorted. 'He's a man who's got a lot to hide. What do you want to know?'

'Let's start with how you met.'

'We've known each other since we were knee high to grasshoppers at school. We always used to hang around together, right through to when we went to the same comprehensive. It was always us bunking off to smoke fags around the back alley and chasing the same girls.'

'What about the car business? When did that start?'

'After we left school. We bought a couple of old wrecks, did 'em up, mainly in my dad's garage, and flogged 'em for a decent profit. At first, it was a hobby, just selling to mates, you know cash in hand, but then we started to make some serious cash. Then we found premises, and set up Diamond Cars.'

'So what went wrong?'

'We were making so much money we couldn't spend it fast enough. We were young and carefree. No commitments, no ties. We bought houses and fast cars, and blew the rest on booze, girls, and fancy suits. Then Ken got greedy. He started fiddling the books, creaming off the profits behind my back. The next thing I knew we were filing for bankruptcy, and the business was finished.'

'Embezzlement?'

'He took the whole bloody lot and left us with nothing. And I never saw it coming.'

'But you went to the police?' asked Trent.

'Don't be stupid. We wasn't exactly playing by the rules in the first place, you get me? If the police had been involved we'd have both gone down. Don't go printing that though.' Samson wagged a finger at Trent.

'No, sure. So what did he need the money for?'

'I wish I knew. We were making plenty, but it wasn't enough for him.'

'I don't understand. The guy's positively rolling in it now. And he's injected a shed load of cash into the BFA.'

Samson shrugged. 'Who knows? I've not spoken to him in years. When we fell out, he dropped off the radar for a while. I heard he went to America and when he came back, he was loaded. The next thing he's involved with this bunch of neo-Nazis. What d'ya call them? The BFA? It makes me sick every time I see him on the news.'

'So you were surprised when you heard he'd turned to politics?'

'Sure. He'd never shown any interest in that sort of thing when I knew him. All he ever cared about was number one. I doubt much has changed, despite the appearances. Look, that's about all I know. I hope it helps with whatever you're planning to write about him, but seriously, keep my name out of it, yeah?' Samson stood and shoved his hands in his pockets. 'And don't contact me again.'

Across the lake, a flock of seagulls launched themselves in the air, spooked by a small child chasing towards them as Samson walked off without a backwards glance, affirming the interview was over.

Trent slid his notebook away, and sat for a while contemplating the new information. No wonder Longhurst had been at pains to keep his past under wraps. It was the sort of scandal that could bring a politician down. But Trent sensed it wasn't the full story. It was a good start, but he knew there were many layers still to unravel in the Ken Longhurst narrative.

Chapter 12

Captain Felipe De Santos was contemplating a mountain of paperwork on his desk. A pile of petty cases. Theft. Robbery. Assault. Even the odd neighbour dispute. But nothing of unusual concern. He smoothed a hand over his stomach sub-consciously flattening the material of his shirt over his middle-aged spread. The second helping of feijoada - a stew of black beans, sausages and cuts of pork - he'd taken for lunch was sitting heavily on his stomach. And in the rising afternoon heat, sleep was circling like a ravenous vulture. He could close his eyes just for a moment. No one would know.

He was jolted out of his short-lived siesta by the sharp ring of a phone. He snatched up the handset 'De Santos,' he snapped, as he bolted upright.

'Sir, there's something I think you should look at.'

'What is it, Prieto?' He asked, recognising the voice of the young desk sergeant from the front counter at the Brazilian Federal Police station in Obidos.

'It's a bag. Two fishermen brought it in. They hooked it out of the river about ten miles south-east of here. They thought there might be a reward.'

'Can't you deal with it?'

'I really think you should look at it, sir. It looks new and it's full of clothes. There's also a passport. British.'

De Santos sighed. 'Okay, okay. Leave it in the conference room. I'll take a look in a minute.'

A ceiling-mounted fan rotated slowly, punctuating the air with a rhythmic hum, but had little effect countering the oppressive heat in his small office. The police captain wiped away a bead of sweat from his brow, closed a paper inside a green cardboard file, and set it on the pile to his right. The completed pile. It was about an even height with the "still to do pile" on his left. Sometimes he wondered if he'd ever clear the backlog. As soon as one case was closed, it seemed to be replaced with at least two more.

He pushed himself away from his desk. The casters of his chair rumbled on the tiled floor. He picked up the finished paperwork and filed each report in metal filing cabinets that ran along the length of one wall at the back of his office. When he was done, he pulled open the door and strode down the corridor.

The bag turned out to be a bright red rucksack with grey straps, and apart from a few scuffs appeared to be brand new. As promised, the desk sergeant had left it on a table in the middle of the conference room. It had suffered remarkably little damage from having been submerged in the river as the two fishermen had claimed.

De Santos unclipped two catches securing the bag closed and emptied the contents onto the table. The desk sergeant had diligently compiled an inventory, which was clipped to a board next to the bag. De Santos mentally ticked off each item as he came to it. Two plain T-shirts, one white, one red. Both pressed and folded neatly as if they had come straight off the shelf of a clothing store. A pair of canvas shorts, barely worn. Four pairs of cotton boxer shorts and three pairs of white sports socks. A torch with four fully charged batteries, a silver compass in a leather pouch, and some foiled-wrapped ration packs. Strangely, there was no wash bag or soiled clothes.

Lastly, he found the passport zipped into a separate compartment and wrapped in a protective plastic bag. A burgundy cover with a gold leaf coat of arms. A unicorn and a crowned lion standing proudly either side of a crest under the motif: 'United Kingdom of Great Britain and Northern Ireland.'

The police captain flicked through a number of blank pages until his thumb came to rest on the final page. He examined the photograph of a young man with blank eyes, short dark hair, and a glazed, emotionless expression. No more than early twenties he speculated without checking the date of birth. Someone's son. No doubt one of the hordes of young backpackers who chose the adventure of the Amazon after finishing school and before committing to a lifetime of employment drudgery.

Finally, he checked the name. He read it twice to make sure he wasn't mistaken. The name was familiar to him. He was sure he'd seen it somewhere, and then remembered. He snapped the passport shut and hurried back to his office to double-check.

Chapter 13

Captain De Santos ran his finger down the page of the report he'd hooked out of the filing cabinet at the back of his office, and found the number he was looking for. He glanced at his watch, made a quick calculation, then picked up the phone and dialled the number.

'Hello?' A woman's voice. Soft and suspicious.

'Mrs Lucy Chapman?'

'Who's this?'

'My name is Captain Felipe De Santos of the Brazilian Federal Police. It's about your brother, Nicholas.' De Santos hesitated, trying to find the right words. His English was excellent but he struggled with how to break the news. 'We've found some of his belongings.'

De Santos was a fastidious man who liked to do things the right way. With more than twenty-five years' experience, he'd earned the respect of his fellow officers for his attention to detail. His uniform was always immaculately pressed, and his thick head of hair well groomed. On his desk, he kept his pens in a neat line, and couldn't abide stray sheets of paper and folders left strewn about. The product of a dysfunctional mind, he told himself. Similarly, the loose ends of an unsolved mystery unsettled him, poking and needling him like a petulant child craving attention from a parent.

It was therefore with some relief that he recognised the name in the back of the passport. He matched it almost immediately with the file on a man who'd been reported missing some months previously.

He'd opened the file at his desk, and examined the photograph stapled to the inside cover to compare the likeness. It was a close enough match to satisfy him that it was the same man. Nicholas Richards, a twenty-year-old from Britain.

A report in the folder described how he had set out to trek along the Amazon alone during a gap year from university, but had disappeared without trace. He had been scheduled to phone home when he landed at Rio de Janeiro, but the call was never made. The authorities had carried out enquiries around the airport, and at hotels and hostels. They had checked mortuary records for unaccounted bodies, but nothing turned up. Every line of enquiry proved fruitless. It looked as if he had simply vanished.

As a matter of routine, a missing person file had been sent to police stations around the country, and had ended up on De Santos' desk for filing. The captain had assumed on an initial inspection that the Briton had most likely disregarded advice to avoid Rio de Janeiro's sprawling slums, and probably been mugged and killed for his wallet or camera. A sad but inevitable case.

There was a long silence on the other end of the line.

'Mrs Chapman?'

'Yes, sorry - I'm here.'

'Nicholas' rucksack was brought in by two fishermen who found it in the river yesterday morning.'

'In Rio?'

'No, I'm phoning from Obidos, on the Amazon river. The rucksack was found floating in the water.' De Santos paused to allow the man's sister to process the information. 'We looked inside and found a few of his things. There wasn't much I'm afraid. Some clothes, a torch, and a few accessories. And, of course, his passport.'

'And Nicholas?' the voice on the line asked weakly.

'No sign, I'm afraid, although I'm sending two of my men to the spot where it was found to look for clues. But I have to warn you it's a remote area, and the river is particularly fast flowing at that point, so I'm afraid we don't hold out a great deal of hope. I'm sorry.'

'Of course. I understand. Thank you. But at least that's some proof, I guess. If you found Nicholas' rucksack in the Amazon then he must have made it out of Rio.'

'Yes, I suppose - '

'So he must have arrived safely in Brazil. We just need to work out how he reached the Amazon. Somebody must remember something.'

'Well, yes but - '

'And just because you found his rucksack doesn't mean he's dead, does it? He could have lost it. Perhaps he was robbed. And without his passport he'd be completely stuck. What about his wallet?'

'There was nothing else in the bag.'

'He could have found a job and earned some money to keep travelling.' Her voice faltered as she spoke. 'Maybe he injured himself and he's being looked after in one of the villages along the river. There are hundreds of remote communities out there aren't there? I was looking on the map.'

'Mrs Chapman, I think we need to be realistic.'

'You need to widen your search, Captain. Can you put some more men on the case?'

'Your brother's been missing for weeks. He could be anywhere. Do you have any idea how big the rainforest is? He could have fallen in anywhere along the river, and his bag could have been carried for miles. I'm sorry, but I don't have the resources to carry out that sort of search. The best I can do is issue a description to some of the riverside villages, but I think you need to prepare yourself that Nicholas is probably dead.'

De Santos immediately regretted his bluntness. He could sense that his words had stung her. He should have realised that news that Nicholas' belongings had been found would have given her a moment's belief that her brother could still be alive.

'I understand. I just thought - ' Her words trailed off.

'Mrs Chapman, I'm very sorry.'

'Yes, well thank you for phoning. I'm sure you're very busy.'

Captain De Santos heard the line click dead and hung up. He closed the missing person report, and smoothed his hand across the cardboard folder. He knew there was virtually no chance of the body being found. If it hadn't been washed away, then it had surely fallen prey to the many predators that roamed the rainforest. He stood up and replaced the file in the metal cabinet.

Case closed.

Chapter 14

Lucy Chapman banged hard on the door until her mother, tea towel in hand, answered.

'They've found Nick's rucksack. I wasn't going to tell you, but I thought you'd want to know,' she said, gunning out the words.

Her mother sighed and walked back into the house, leaving her daughter on the doorstep.

'Some fishermen on the Amazon found it near their village,' Lucy persisted. She stepped over the threshold, and was hit by the familiar smell of beeswax and wood smoke. 'I had a call from a policeman.'

Lucy hurried into the kitchen after her mother. Since Nicholas' disappearance, she'd imagined a hundred and one scenarios to explain why he'd vanished, but none involved his death. She wouldn't even contemplate the idea. The discovery of the rucksack confirmed in her mind that he must still be alive.

'Don't you see, Mum? If they found his rucksack, then he must have made it to Brazil and out of Rio. I told you, didn't I?'

'Darling, please don't do this. Nick is dead. Why can't you accept the facts?' Emily Richards said, standing with her back to her daughter, her hands resting on a worktop. 'I find it as hard as you do, but we have to move on. 'When she spun around, her eyes were red, her cheeks streaked with tears. 'Don't you see? We can't live the rest of our lives in the past. Now, I don't want to hear any more about it.'

'Well I need to know the truth, even if you don't. We owe him that much.'

'Lucy, they found his rucksack, that's all. It had to turn up at some point. It doesn't change the facts. Nick is gone, and he's not coming back.'

'Mother, you can be so infuriating. How can you write him off so easily?'

'He'd changed, Lucy. You must have seen that.'

'Of course I did, but - '

'I didn't recognise him anymore, and neither did you. I don't know who he was or what he wanted out of life. He'd moved on from his family - from us - and there was nothing we could do about it. He made his own choices.'

Although Lucy was older by six years, she and Nick had been close as children. In retrospect, it was probably a natural reaction to their father leaving when they were small. It was only in their teenage years that they'd drifted apart as their interests varied. And after Nick had fallen with their mother, he'd cut her out of his life too. She often wondered whether she could have tried harder to reconnect, and the guilt of not doing so haunted her. But she'd been newly married, and starting a business. She had lots on her plate, her own life to worry about.

His announcement that he was off to Brazil had come as a shock to both of them. He'd never shown any interest in travelling before. The farthest he'd been was to France with the school.

'We could have tried harder to get through to him,' said Lucy.

'You mean I could have tried harder?'

'No, Mum, I didn't mean that.' Lucy pulled out a chair at the kitchen table where they had shared so many happy meals together. It seemed a lifetime ago.

'I thought it was just a phase, and that if we gave him some space he'd get over it, and we'd get him back again. When he phoned to say he was sorry for everything, I really believed it. And then he announced this ridiculous trip to South America.'

'We thought it would do him some good, remember?' said Lucy. 'And that maybe we could start afresh when he got back.'

'You know I believed him when he said we'd sort our differences when he came home.' Her mother wiped away a tear. 'I told him I forgave him for everything.'

'I know, Mum. But something must have happened to him in the airport. He promised he'd call the moment he landed. We have to find out what went wrong. What if he's lost and trying to get home?'

'Stop it, Lucy. I don't know what happened, and neither do you. But it's time to let go.'

'I'm not giving up on him, Mum.'

'I'm being realistic, Lucy, for Christ's sake. What do you suppose happened to him? He was in the wrong place at the wrong time in a country he had no idea about.' The venom in her mother's voice surprised her. 'He met the wrong people, maybe they wanted money, his camera, his passport, I don't know. And knowing Nick he tried to fight back or argue his way out of the situation.'

'But what about his rucksack? If it was found in the Amazon, then he made it out of Rio!'

'Rio, the Amazon, Timbuktu. It's all the same. The wrong place, the wrong time.' Lucy's mother slammed her fist on the worktop to emphasise her point.

'So it's easier for you to believe he was murdered so you can start living your life again? Well, I'm not ready to accept his death quite so easily, thank you. I know he's still alive somewhere, and I'm going to find him, whatever it takes.'

Lucy realised they'd both raised their voices to the point that they'd ended up screaming at each other. God knows what the neighbours must have thought.

'Mum, I'm sorry, I didn't mean to upset you. I only came because I thought you'd want to know about the rucksack.'

'Thank you, but it's probably best if you left now. I have things to do.'

Her mother had started fussing over the dirty worktop and clearing away dishes on the draining board, turning her back on any problem life threw up, just as she always did.

'Mum?'

'Just go please.'

Lucy stood, and slung her handbag over her shoulder. 'I'll call you later then.'

'Yes, you do that.'

Chapter 15

Lucy Chapman and her husband arrived at the Brazilian Embassy fifteen minutes before her scheduled appointment with the ambassador. But she had to wait more than thirty minutes before a lean man in a neat suit ambled down the corridor to meet them. He introduced himself as Miguel Alves, the ambassador's private secretary, and ushered them to his office where they took seats in comfortable, high-backed leather chairs around an ornate, marble coffee table scattered with glossy magazines.

'I'm so sorry for keeping you waiting,' said Alves, with an apologetic smile. 'I'm afraid the ambassador is very busy today and won't be able to see you personally, but I hope I'll be able to help.'

Lucy shot her husband, Peter, a look as if to say "I told you so." Having encountered so many obstacles in her efforts to find her missing brother, when the embassy finally responded to her barrage of letters demanding assistance, she could hardly believe their offer of a meeting was genuine.

'We appreciate you taking the trouble to meet us,' said Peter, ignoring his wife.

'I understand you wanted to talk about your brother, Nicholas?' Mr Alves crossed his legs and placed his fingertips over his lips.

'I suppose you know the background to the case?' said Lucy.

'Yes, I understand that your brother left the UK to

travel in Brazil, but inexplicably disappeared and despite a widespread search in the city, no leads have been discovered.'

'It was a crazy idea,' said Lucy. 'He wasn't much of a traveller, but he came up with this half-baked idea to go exploring around the Amazon. But something happened to him when he arrived, and the police in your country don't seem to be taking his disappearance very seriously.'

'I see.' Alves looked thoughtful as if weighing up a great problem. 'Tell me, how much planning had gone into this trip, Mrs Chapman?'

'Well - ' Lucy hesitated. The truth was she had no idea. She'd not spoken to her brother for many months after the row with their mother. His call to announce he was making the trip was a surprise to them both. She suspected it was an impetuous decision, and that any planning had been minimal. 'He'd been talking about it for ages,' she lied. 'It was somewhere he always dreamed of visiting.'

It was Peter's turn to shoot his wife a look, and her chance to ignore him.

'Perhaps you can tell me exactly what his plans were?' said Alves.

'I don't know why you're asking me. It should all be in the file. He flew from Heathrow to Rio, and was going to make his own way to the Amazon from there,' she said.

Alves stood, and walked to a leather-topped desk at the other end of the room, his footsteps cushioned by a rich, deep-pile carpet, scooped up a cardboard file, returned to his seat, and started leafing through the papers inside.

'Do you know how Mr Richards was planning to travel from Rio to the Amazon, Mrs Chapman?'

It was an innocent question, but Lucy was scalded by the accusatory tone. She looked down at her hands, and realised they were trembling.

'I don't know,' she said, quietly.

'I see. And where was he staying?'

'I don't know. He didn't discuss that with us.'

'You said yourself that your brother wasn't very well travelled. Is that correct? In fact, according to records supplied by your government, he'd hardly been out of the country before.'

Lucy felt her anger boiling. Alves made it feel as if Nick was responsible for his own disappearance, and that she was somehow culpable. 'He made a rash decision to go, okay? I don't suppose he did plan the trip as he should have done but that doesn't explain what happened to him. But your country has done virtually nothing to find him, and I want to know why. All I know is that he arrived in Rio, and that was the last we heard of him. Please, I'm begging you, all I want is answers, and for you to take it seriously. My brother is missing - dead for all I know - but you want to lay the blame on Nick.'

'Believe me, Mrs Chapman, we're taking this case seriously. Very seriously.' Alves narrowed his eyes as he spoke. 'Let me ask you one more question. Is it true Mr Richards had cut all ties with his family shortly before he disappeared?'

'What's that got to do with anything?' asked Peter.

'Maybe nothing. Maybe everything,' Alves replied, enigmatically.

The insinuation was obvious to Lucy. Nicholas had been on the verge of being thrown out of university because of his lack of application and subsequent poor grades. He was in debt on an eye-watering scale, and his life was spiralling out of control. Their mother was furious when she found out he'd squandered his education, and when she refused his pleas to bail him out of his financial woes, they'd ended up in a vitriolic argument. She ordered him out of the house, and told him she never wanted to see him again after the names he'd called her. And she'd regretted it ever since. They only heard from Nick once more. A solitary phone call to say he was sorry, and to announce his expedition to South America.

'We came here today to get some movement on the

case,' said Peter. 'I want to know what investigations have been carried out so far. We don't even know if Nicholas is alive or dead.'

Lucy dabbed at her eyes with a tissue as her tears burned hot down her cheeks. Peter gave her hand a reassuring squeeze.

'You're right. We don't know if he's still alive - but to be honest, Mr and Mrs Chapman, we don't know that your brother even arrived in Rio.' He dropped the bombshell so casually that it took a few moments for the couple to comprehend what he was saying.

'I beg your pardon?' said Peter. 'Of course he arrived in Rio.'

'But no one heard from him in Brazil. We've studied CCTV footage from the airport from the time his plane landed, but he didn't show up. It's possible he caught an internal flight from the airport, but none of the airlines have a record of your brother flying. So we checked whether he boarded a coach or bus from Rio, but again, nothing.'

'But what about his rucksack?' said Lucy. 'Some fishermen found it in the river near Obidos. It had his passport in it. He must have made it somehow.'

'That's a bit of a mystery, for sure. But we've double-checked with the immigration service and they confirmed what we suspected. They have no record of your brother passing through border controls. I'm afraid we don't believe Nicholas Richards was ever in Brazil.'

'What? Are you mad?' screamed Lucy.

'And that means it ceases to be a matter of Brazilian concern.'

Chapter 16

A cold, dank mist wrapped its icy tendrils around the arthritic fingers of the bare branches of the trees. Most of the leaves had fallen, and the park had succumbed to autumnal greys and browns, apart from one oasis where a tangle of evergreen bushes with waxy leaves shimmered in the dull afternoon light.

Blake checked the map on his phone again. It showed that he was right on top of the entrance to the underground bunker. Still it eluded him.

'Come on, this way.' He hadn't seen Patterson approaching and the sound of his voice made him jump.

The colonel breezed past, swinging a leather attaché case cheerily. He turned off the path, and into the clump of bushes. He pulled back a few branches to expose a painted metal door, daubed with faded swirls of graffiti, set into an algae-stained concrete block, no larger than a flatbed truck. With a large key he pulled from his pocket, Patterson sprung the lock, heaved the door open, ushered Blake inside, and slammed the door closed behind them.

They stood briefly in total darkness until Patterson found a light switch on the wall. An overhead strip light illuminated a narrow hallway, and a flight of steep, concrete steps that disappeared into the darkness below.

Patterson led the way down into a damp, musty room buried deep beneath the park. He found another light switch, and three low hanging light bulbs flickered into life. The floor was littered with indistinguishable scraps of faded paper, rat droppings, and inexplicably a coil of electrical wire.

'What do you think?' Patterson asked.

'Nothing a lick of paint couldn't improve. Nice suit, by the way.'

'Pinstripes are all the rage with the MI5 top brass.'

'So what is this place?' asked Blake, screwing up his nose at the musty, damp odour.

'Exactly what it looks like. An old nuclear bunker built during the Cold War and forgotten about. It was supposed to be used as a temporary base for civil servants to deal with the aftermath of an attack. Far enough away from parliament if it had taken a direct hit, but close enough to walk to.'

'I'd have rather taken my chances elsewhere,' said Blake as he paced out the claustrophobic perimeter. 'So what are we doing here?'

'I know how much you hate the thought of meeting at headquarters so I decided this would do nicely. Out of sight, and no one to eavesdrop.'

'How thoughtful.'

'I found reference to it in some old papers, and it wasn't too difficult to requisition a key from the Ministry of Defence vaults. I doubt whether anyone will ever notice.' Patterson picked up a chair that had been knocked over, and set it upright in the middle of the room. He wiped the seat with his hand, and sat down. Blake grabbed another chair, and placed it opposite his boss.

'Not quite the Ritz is it? But I suppose it serves a purpose.'

'So tell me about Sussex.'

'Very illuminating,' said Blake. He gave Patterson a detailed account of Proctor's evening from being collected from his flat to the encounter with Ken Longhurst in the woods.

'Some kind of initiation ceremony?' asked Patterson.

'Almost certainly. I think Proctor was abducted by members of the BFA who branded him as a sign of allegiance. The ceremony was to complete his enrolment in a sub sect within the organisation called the Phineas Priests,' Blake continued.

'Yes, I asked Marty to see if he could find out anything about this priesthood.'

Marty Price, a former Special Forces intelligence specialist who'd been assigned to Echo 17 before it was disbanded, now ran his own private intelligence company providing services to governments, corporations, and wealthy individuals.

Patterson laid his attaché case on his lap, and hooked out a slim, cardboard file. He read from the contents inside. 'Marty says the Phineas Priests are an extremist movement based in the States, with no evidence, until now, of any activity in Europe. However, it's a fairly chaotic organisation with no known leadership or membership process as such.'

'Is that it?'

'No, there's a bit more. It's primarily a Christian movement that takes a hard-line stance on inter-racial marriage, homosexuality, and multi-culturalism. The name, Phineas Priest, originates from the Israelite Phineas, who, in the Old Testament, killed an Israelite man who'd slept with a Midianite woman. The story goes that he killed them both with a spear, and in doing so, ended a plague sent by God to punish the Israelites for their sexual excesses with the Midianites.

'And as a reward for his actions, God granted Phineas a "covenant of peace" and gave him and his children everlasting priesthood. They take it literally, and use the story as justification for violence against inter-racial marriages and other perceived immoralities. They also believe that God's chosen people are all white and the black community are non-human. Plus they have an ingrained hatred of Jews.'

'Justification for violence?'

'They've been responsible for a number of terrorist

attacks on targets including abortion clinics, banks, and even FBI buildings,' said Patterson.

'Any fatalities?'

'A few serious injuries, but murder's not on their rap sheet yet. They're known by a single symbol -'

'Let me see,' said Blake, snatching the file from Patterson's hands. 'It's the same mark they branded on Proctor's chest. It was on Longhurst's robes too.'

'That makes sense. So now we have evidence of a definite link between the BFA and far-right extremism. The question is what are they planning? We need Proctor to find out.'

'I still have to debrief him after his little excursion. Let me find out what Longhurst had to say.'

'I have a bad feeling about this, Blake. There's also the small matter of those donations to the party coffers. The DDG wants Proctor to start digging around their finances. Get him to find out who's writing the cheques. Longhurst makes me nervous, but we need to tread carefully. He's a public figure, and we can't go wading in with all guns blazing.'

Blake shrugged. 'Relax, we're onto him, and he has no idea. He's an egomaniac, but Proctor is right by his side. Give it time, we'll nail him.'

Chapter 17

Blake peered around the door-frame, and was almost bowled over by a black rubbish sack that came tumbling down the stairs. From the flat above, tinny pop music was blaring from a radio.

Blake eased up the stairs, and found an ample-bosomed woman in the kitchen. Her long, raven hair streaked with grey was tied in a ponytail that hung halfway down her back. She was standing on a step-ladder in cheap black leggings that emphasised her fat legs, scrubbing the insides of the cupboards.

'Have you seen Ben?' said Blake, over the din of the radio.

The woman stopped cleaning and glanced over her shoulder. 'Jeez, you half scared me to death,' she said.

'I'm sorry,' said Blake. 'I was looking for Ben Proctor?'

'Well tell me when you find him, will ya?' The woman dropped the cloth in a bowl of water, and stepped down from the ladder. She lit a cigarette from a pack on the worktop and exhaled a stream of hazy smoke. 'Who's asking for him?'

'I'm a friend. When did you last see him?'

'Months ago. I got a call last night saying he was off. No apology, no forwarding address, and no bleedin' rent either.'

'I see,' said Blake.

'Is he in trouble?'

'No, nothing like that. Was his rent up to date?'

The landlady laughed. 'I've had nothin' for two months.

So I says to him I either gets paid or he's out. You sure you're not a copper?'

'I'm just a concerned friend, but I've not heard from him in a while. I was worried.'

'You don't much look like the type he usually hangs around with.'

'No,' said Blake. 'I guess not. I'm a sort of uncle figure. I look out for him. It was something I promised his mother.'

'Is that right? Well, I can't help. This mess is all he left.' She waved a hand at two half-filled rubbish sacks and sprinkled a fine confetti of ash over the floor.

'Would you mind if I had a little look around? He might have left a clue about where he was going.'

The woman shrugged. 'Please yourself, but I've cleared most of his mess up.' She stubbed out her cigarette, wrung out the cloth, and began scrubbing again.

Blake started in the bedroom where the doors to a free standing cupboard were wide open, and an assortment of empty wire hangers were suspended from a silver rail. Under the bed he found a single black sock, but the suitcase and cardboard boxes had gone, and a white chest of drawers was empty apart from yellowing newspaper that lined the bottom of each drawer.

In the bathroom, flecks of toothpaste peppered the sink and a grey tidemark ran around the bath. He raked through a small bin under the basin, but found only a blunt razor blade, an empty deodorant can, and several screwed up tissues stained with blood.

'Find anything?' the woman asked, as he emerged onto the landing.

'No, nothing.'

Blake moved into the lounge where the mutilated Platoon poster was still stuck to the wall and the carpet was stained with suspicious black marks. He jammed his fingers between the cushions of the threadbare sofa, where clumps of dust and the odd low denomination coin had found a home, and checked behind the curtains. Nothing. For some unknown reason Proctor had gathered up his few belongings and moved out. And Blake didn't have the first idea where to start looking for him.

He collapsed on the couch, attempting to hold his rising panic at bay. He stared at his reflection in the dust-coated screen. Knees together, shoulders back. A military posture that was hard to shake after more than twenty years. His eyes drifted to the landing, and fell on the two bulging sacks. If Proctor had left any clues, it was most likely that's where he'd find them. A familiar tune came on the radio, a popular hit from the nineteen eighties, but the name of the band wouldn't come to mind. Blake sighed, resigned to the unenviable task of getting elbow deep in Proctor's garbage and pulled himself up.

'Can I take these bags for you?' said Blake.

'Don't worry, I can manage,' said the landlady, who was pouring the dirty water from her bucket down the sink.

Blake plucked a crumpled newspaper from the top of the nearest bag. It was a three-day-old tabloid that had been well thumbed. He flicked through the first half a dozen pages scanning the headlines, and was about to toss it back in the sack when something caught his eye in the top right hand corner of page seven.

'Can I take this paper?'

'Take what you like. I was only going to chuck it out,' the landlady said.

'Thanks,' said Blake, who was already half-way to the stairs.

He spilled out onto the street, hurried left, and jogged back to his car, which was parked in its usual place around the back near a block of council flats.

A gang of boys loitering nearby fell silent as he approached. Street kids with mean looks and a defiant attitude, blocking the pavement as if they were waiting for trouble. Blake fished in his pocket for a twenty pound note, and held it folded between his thumb and forefinger.

The eldest boy broke into a gap-faced grin, and his sour expression dropped from his face. He pushed past the other boys, and plucked the note from Blake's hand.

'Thanks, Shay,' said Blake. 'Make sure you share that out with the others, and don't spend it on booze and fags. Understood?'

'As if we would,' said the boy, feigning indignation.

'Right, now go and do something useful and stop scaring old ladies.'

The boys ran off laughing down the street. Blake checked there was no damage to the Audi, but true to their word, the boys had kept a safe eye on it. He had little doubt that if he'd not paid for their services, the car would have lost its wheels by now. It was that sort of neighbourhood.

Blake unlocked the vehicle with a button on a remote control key fob, and removed a computer notebook from the glovebox. He settled behind the driver's wheel, called up an internet search engine, and checked the newspaper he'd taken from Proctor's flat. Circled in blue ink was the word "Nutwick". Immediately below it "Stoneleigh", heavily underlined.

Surprisingly, there was only one Nutwick in the whole of the country, and it was less than sixty miles away. Blake started up the engine and made a mental note of the directions. With luck, he could make it in a little over an hour.

'So, we're off to Sussex again, Ben. Now what an earth are you doing there?' he asked himself as he pulled away.

Chapter 18

Nutwick was a quintessential English village with chocolate box charm. At its heart was a handsome Norman church with a graveyard of lopsided headstones enclosed by a stone wall. Blake parked in the adjacent village square, which was bordered on one side by a terrace of Georgian townhouses and a row of pretty cottages on the other.

The aroma of burning wood hung in the air, and it didn't take him long to identify the source as a red brick pub called the Red Lion. Inside, the air was warm from a roaring log fire in a corner of a compact lounge that was all but deserted. He approached the bar where the landlord was wiping the surfaces clean with a towel. Blake ordered a pint of local ale with a quirky name and pulled up a stool.

'Is it always this quiet?' Blake asked.

'It is these days. It's not like it used to be.'

Blake estimated the landlord to be in his late sixties, but he might have been younger. A drinker's nose, bulbous and reddened with broken blood vessels, aged him considerably.

'I'm sorry to hear that.'

'Here on your own?'

'For the time being,' said Blake. 'We're thinking of moving out of town, and fancied something more rural. I'm spending a few days exploring the area.'

The landlord looked disapproving. 'Not many places left the locals can afford,' he said.

Blake drank deeply from his pint, ignoring the faintly veiled criticism. 'It's a lovely village. Just what we're looking for.'

'A bit too quiet at times.'

'Have you lived here all your life?'

'For the best part of thirty years. But they've only just accepted us as locals.' The landlord laughed at his own joke.

'You know the area well then? Would you help me get my bearings?' asked Blake. He'd brought the computer notebook with him, and placed it on the bar. When he flipped open the lid, the screen slowly revealed a satellite image of the village, grey blocks of buildings surrounded by green squares of fields and countryside. 'We're here, right?'

Blake pointed at the screen. The church, graveyard, and square were easily identifiable at the centre of the village.

The landlord slipped on a pair of reading glasses that had been hanging on a chain around his neck, and squinted at the imagery. 'Yes, that's right.'

'And opposite, of course, is the church.'

'St Mary's, yes. That's where the village shop used to be.' The landlord ran a stubby finger across the screen. 'But, of course, that's been converted into a house now.'

'And this building behind the church must be the old rectory?'

'Still owned by the church for the moment, and it's probably worth a small fortune if they ever decided to put it on the market.'

'And most of the land around the village is farmland as far as I can see. Is it all owned by the same farmer?'

'No, there're two families. The Harpers have this bit,' the landlord poked his finger at the screen again. 'And the Goddards own this bit.'

'And I heard about a place called Stoneleigh. Do you know it?'

'Stoneleigh Cottage? Rosie Thomas' old place? I'm afraid you're a bit late. They've sold it already.'

'That's a shame,' said Blake, feigning disappointment. 'It was on my list to check out.'

'Rosie was living there on her own right up to the end. Ninety-two she was. Refused to have any home help, I heard. No real family to speak of neither, although somebody said she had a son in London.'

'And the house has been sold already?'

'It was on the market for ages, but it only sold a few weeks back.'

'Any idea who bought it?'

'Not that I've heard.'

'Can you show me on the map?' asked Blake. 'Out of curiosity.'

The landlord pointed to a small square a mile or so outside the village, surrounded by fields on three sides, a wooded area to the rear, and a meandering track leading to it from the main road.

'I hope the new owners have deep pockets. It'll need a bit of work. Don't think Rosie had a thing done to it since Stan died, and that must be getting on for fifteen years. You want a refill?' The landlord nodded at Blake's empty glass.

Blake ordered a pint of the same, and a plate of pie and mash from a menu on the bar.

'The only way in is via this track from the main road, is it?' he asked.

'That's right. Like I said, it needs a bit of modernising really.'

Blake stared at the satellite image a little longer, making a mental note of the geography surrounding Stoneleigh Cottage and assessing the terrain before snapping the notebook closed.

'Do you have any rooms? As I said, I'm here for a few days and I could do with a decent bed for the night.'

'Only a few, but you're in luck. Tonight you can take your pick.'

Blake woke early the next morning, feeling refreshed from a decent night's sleep, which he attributed to the country air and the unusually dark night. No light pollution this far from London.

He reached for a lamp on the bedside table. It threw a yellow light across the room and illuminated a walnut chest of drawers and a wicker-backed chair where he'd laid his clothes out the previous evening. He swung out of bed and took a shower. The water came out tepid and at little more than a slow trickle, but was sufficient to cleanse his body and invigorate his senses. He threw on a pair of canvas trousers and a heavy-duty cotton shirt over a long-sleeved base layer, and slipped out of his room.

The pub was silent. Blake checked his watch. Evidently, no one else had stirred so early. He padded across the landing in his woollen walking socks, carrying his boots and let himself out of a back door that opened into a small courtyard.

Outside, the air was thick with early morning mist and the aroma of the countryside. A pungent blend of mud and manure. The sun was weakly filtering through heavy cloud providing just enough light to see, and after checking his bearings, Blake headed off in the direction of a footpath he'd noted earlier on the map.

The muddy path cut along the edge of a sheep field, and after two hundred yards, turned due south, over a stile and into a second pasture where the wild grass had grown tall and was thick with dew. It left Blake's trousers soaked from the knee down. The village quickly disappeared behind him, hidden by hedgerows tangled with brambles and old dog rose heavy with puckering red hips.

The wood behind Stoneleigh Cottage came into view as Blake crested a hillock, the tips of tall Scots pines reaching for the sky. He noticed a curious symmetry about the trees, which had been planted equidistant from each other so that no matter at which angle you looked, they appeared to be arranged in arrow straight lines. Under the canopy of their branches, the temperature was a degree or two warmer and the ground was covered in a carpet of dead pine needles where no vegetation grew other than few grotesque mushrooms sprouting from the base of some of the trunks. The silence was eerie. Nothing stirred, not even a gentle breeze. Blake shuddered and pressed on, making a beeline for the cottage at the far side of the copse.

He found it on a bearing to his left, and congratulated himself that his sense of direction had brought him within twenty yards of the house without a map. Stoneleigh was a simple, regular shaped two-storey building with a slate-tiled roof and an unkempt garden of brambles surrounded by a low, crumbling stone wall. A rectangular porch, tacked onto the rear, looked as though it was a later addition.

Blake crept to the edge of the wood and, knowing he was well hidden in the gloom, scanned the building for signs of life. Drab curtains hanging from the upstairs windows hadn't been drawn, which indicated it was either unoccupied or Proctor was sleeping in a room at the front. No lights were on, so Blake assumed that if Proctor was living there, he was probably still asleep.

He scouted through the cover of trees to his right for a better perspective on the house, and noted a red hatchback car parked at an angle in the drive. It was an ageing, indistinct Renault splattered with mud and with a window on the passenger side left open a fraction. Blake made a mental note of the number plate, and stepped out of the shadows. He jogged across the open ground, trying to keep low, and was half way to the stone wall when he noticed movement behind the glass of the porch door. Someone was reaching for the handle. He heard the click of the latch, and the door swung slowly inwards.

Blake stood, and sprinted hard with legs and arms pumping. If he didn't make the cover of the wall he'd be spotted the moment the door was fully open. Four yards out, he dived onto his stomach and crashed through a patch of wild undergrowth. He hit the wall with his shoulder, and pressed his body flat into the ground, his heart pumping and his senses wired.

The porch door slammed shut, and feet trotted along a concrete path. Blake held his breath, listening for any clue that his noisy arrival had raised an alarm but it was evident that whoever had come out of the house was walking in the opposite direction. Blake pushed himself up on his arms, and peered over the top of the wall. A lumbering figure was sauntering towards the Renault. His head was close shaven, and his arms adorned with tattoos. But even from behind, it was clear to Blake that it wasn't Ben Proctor.

Chapter 19

As he turned towards the car, Blake saw Mike Clark's face. Pinched and narrow. On his upper arm, an Aryan eagle with its wings spread was tattooed in dark ink. He was whistling to himself and swinging a car key around his finger. Clark opened the driver's door and jumped in behind the wheel. The engine caught on the second attempt, rattling into life on what sounded like three cylinders. Clark crunched the gears, and hit the accelerator hard, spinning the front wheels in the mud until they gained enough traction to send the car hurtling through a tight turn and along the track to the main road.

Blake noted the time, and gave himself fifteen minutes to finish what he'd come to do. Clark could return at any time. He stepped over the wall, picked his way through the overgrown garden, and let himself into the house through the porch.

Immediately before him, a narrow staircase rose steeply up to the first floor. To his left was an empty room he guessed had been a dining area. Worn patches on the patterned carpet revealed where a table and chairs had stood for many years. Beyond it was a kitchen with dirty dishes piled in a stained, metal sink. Generations of cooking smells and grime clung to every surface.

Blake stole back to the hallway, and poked his head around a door to the right of the stairs. Another empty room, which looked as if it might once have been a lounge. He wandered towards a window overlooking the drive, and pulled back a net curtain discoloured with age. The paint around the frame was flaking, but the window seemed to be in working order. Blake flipped a catch open and peered through the filthy pane in the direction the Renault had disappeared.

When a floorboard creaked above Blake's head, he froze, listening for movement, and then crept back to the bottom of the stairs where swirling floral paper lined the walls. The elevation was so steep it was like looking up the face of a mountain, and Blake wondered how the old lady had managed them in her later years. Perhaps she hadn't and for a moment he was distracted with the thought of the fragile frame of the elderly Rosie Thomas curled up on a couch living out her days on the ground floor.

Blake took the stairs slowly, pausing on each one to listen. When he reached the landing, he found three closed doors, and chose one at random. It was in darkness behind heavy, closed curtains. A crumpled heap of bedclothes was laid out under the window, and the rancorous stench of body odour and stale cigarette smoke saturated the air. Empty beer cans were scattered around the floor, and a yellow, plastic lighter was balanced on a pack of Marlboro red tops next to an overflowing ashtray and a pile of dirty clothes; a pair of jeans, a black T-shirt, and a dark fleece jacket. Proctor's clothes.

From another room, he heard the sudden rush of water. A toilet being flushed. Blake returned to the landing as an adjacent door flew open. Proctor appeared semi-naked and bleary-eyed from a dingy bathroom. He was wearing only a crumpled pair of boxer shorts that hung from his narrow waist. A gold triskelion swung from a chain around his neck, just above the wound where he'd been branded on his chest by the Phineas Priests, angry and inflamed against his pallid skin.

Blake was across the landing in three strides. In his sleep-induced haze, Proctor hadn't even registered the intruder. Blake tapped him three times on the shoulder. 'Sleep now, Ben,' he said, softly.

His words seeped into Proctor's subconscious mind like fine sand flowing through a sieve. His muscles softened, his eyes rolled closed, and his chin dropped onto his chest. He allowed Blake to escort him back to his room without protest, and lay down on his makeshift bed.

Blake sat on the floor with his back against the wall and pulled his knees up to his chest. 'I thought you'd deserted me, Ben. You certainly took some tracking down.'

Proctor was lying with his hands resting on his stomach, a passive expression on his face.

'But now I've found you, I need a copy of your door key, please. I'm sure Mike won't be so generous in leaving the door open in future.' Blake grabbed Proctor's fleece, and fished in the pockets until he found a silver key on a metal ring. 'This it? In the pocket of your top?'

'Yes,' said Proctor, in a monotone.

Blake held it between the tips of his index finger and thumb, and used his phone to take a three dimensional scan that he would later send to Patterson to create a replica.

'Now, I need to know what you've been up to, Ben.' Proctor's chest rose and fell in a slow rhythm. 'Who were those men who picked you up from the flat?'

'The Phineas Priests.'

'Why did they take you to that wood?'

'It was a ceremony to welcome us into the priesthood,' said Proctor, his eyes flickering behind their lids.

'I was watching from a distance. Do you understand? I saw Ken Longhurst. He was talking to you both. What did he say?'

'He wanted to reward our commitment. He told us it was an honour to be accepted into the priesthood, and that we'd be given extra responsibilities now he knew he could trust us.'

'It's excellent progress, Ben. You've done a fantastic job getting accepted into the inner circle. Did he elaborate on what extra responsibilities he wants you to take on?'

'We're -' Proctor hesitated.

'Go on, Ben. What is it?'

'He said we weren't to talk to anyone about it. We're not even allowed to speak of the existence of the priests.'

'I understand, but remember you don't work for Longhurst. You work for me, and for your country now. It's your duty to tell me everything you learn about the BFA and their connection with the Phineas Priests. Is that clear?' Said Blake.

'Yes.'

Blake rose to his feet, and pulled back the curtain a fraction to confirm they weren't about to be disturbed by the return of Mike Clark.

'What did Longhurst tell you the purpose of the Phineas Priests is?'

'To fight the threat from foreign migrants and to secure Britain for the British,' said Proctor.

'How?'

'By any means necessary.'

'That's what Longhurst said?'

'Yes. He wants us to fight the immigrants and the Islamists.'

'Did he say why?'

'They're threatening our way of life. They're envious of our freedoms, and they want to destroy them. They've taken our jobs, and threaten our communities, but most of them can't even speak English. They don't want to live by our rules, and they're trying to drive us out of our homes.'

'That's what Longhurst told you?'

'Yes.'

'Has he given you any specific instructions or orders?'

Proctor's brow furrowed. 'He says we have to take direct action to show the country won't lie down and pander to the liberal left. He wants us to take the fight to them.'

'What about this house? What's with the move to Nutwick?'

'The house belongs to the priests.'

'I guessed that but what's wrong with London?'

'It's somewhere where we can keep our heads down,' said Proctor.

'Why do you need to keep your heads down?'

'In preparation for our assignment.'

'What assignment, Ben?'

Before Proctor could answer, they were interrupted by the sound of a car door being slammed. Blake sprang to his feet, and pulled the curtain back. Mike Clark was striding towards the house with a smouldering cigarette between the fingers of one hand and a carton of milk in the other.

'We don't have much time. Mike's back, so keep your voice down. I need to know what assignment you've been set.' Blake knelt at Proctor's side and placed his ear close to his mouth.

Proctor spoke quietly as instructed. Blake's eyes opened wide as the enormity of what he was being told struck him.

'Where?' asked Blake. But Proctor didn't have an answer.

Mike Clark's voice hollered up the stairs. 'Oi, Ben, you lazy git. You up yet?'

'Ben, you need to wake up now. You won't remember this conversation, and you'll forget that you've seen me in the house. You are Ben Proctor, and you are a valued and trusted member of the Phineas Priests.' Blake helped Proctor to his feet, and manoeuvred him out onto the landing. 'Start counting backwards from ten, and when you reach zero you'll be wide awake. Then go down stairs and keep him in the kitchen for the next five minutes. Understood.'

Proctor nodded, and started counting under his breath.

'Ben? Are you there?'

Blake slipped back into Proctor's room, silently closed the door, and prepared his escape.

Chapter 20

Blake had already determined there was only one option if he had to leave in a hurry. It was the window and a short drop onto the drive or nothing. He drew back the curtains, and let the early morning daylight flood into the room through glass encrusted with a film of dirt. It looked as if the sash window hadn't been opened in years, but with a little effort it gave way an inch, and a blast of cold air swept in, washing away the stale fug inside.

Below, he heard two male voices, deep and low. No urgency. No alarm. Proctor was doing his job keeping Mike Clark occupied, although he would have no conscious idea that he was following Blake's instructions. Blake forced the lower sash open wider until he was able to jam his shoulder under it and drove through his thighs, dislodging years of dirt and grime that had virtually welded the window shut. He stuck his head through the opening and assessed the drop. A clump of bushes immediately below should break his fall.

He listened again, but noticed the voices had fallen silent, and then he heard the resonant thud of boots plodding up the stairs and echoing through the building.

Blake threw a leg out of the opening, ducked under the sash, and lowered his body out of the house until he was dangling from the frame by his fingertips. He calculated that it reduced his fall to less than four yards, and lessened considerably his risk of turning his ankle, or worse.

He broke his fall with a commando roll, and sat up in a crouch beneath a ground floor window. When he heard no sounds from the house, he stood and ran for the cover of the woods. He vaulted the low stone wall, and sprinted for the trees, not daring to look back until he was safely hidden in the copse.

Within twenty minutes, he was back at the pub. He changed out of his soiled clothes, and took breakfast alone in the bar, washed down with strong, black coffee. When he was finished, he returned to his car that was covered in a light film of dew, and checked his phone. No signal. He needed to find higher ground.

The road out of Nutwick meandered along a valley lined with trees, and fields intermittently filled with sheep and cattle. Eventually, Blake found a remote layby on a road that had climbed steadily for several miles. He pulled in, and tried his phone again. The signal was patchy, but better than in the village. He dialled Patterson's number.

'Blake, where've you been?'

'Trying to find Proctor. He's moved out of the London flat, but I've tracked him down to a cottage in Sussex.'

'Okay, so what's going on?'

'He was sent by the BFA, or more specifically the Phineas Priests, to keep a low profile. I think they own the cottage. It was sold recently, but could you check it out for me? If there's a paper trail back to the BFA, it connects Proctor and Longhurst.'

'Slow down,' said Patterson. 'First of all, have you spoken with Proctor?'

'Yes,' said Blake. 'I carried out a full debrief. He confirmed what we suspected. Longhurst has recruited him as a Phineas Priest. He told Proctor the aim of the priesthood was to close Britain's borders to new immigrants, and declare war on non-Whites living in the country.'

'So they're effectively acting as the BFA's secret military wing?'

'I hadn't thought about it like that, but yes, I guess so. Proctor says they're trying to keep a lid on the whole thing, and Longhurst's forbidden them from even acknowledging the existence of the group.'

'Okay, it's a worry, but good news that we have a man on the inside. But realistically, what are we talking about, half a dozen brainwashed thugs looking to stir up trouble at the odd political rally?'

'It's more organised than that, I'm afraid. This isn't a band of lawless vigilantes.' Blake paused for effect. 'Proctor's been instructed to plant a bomb.'

Patterson's sharp intake of breath was audible even on the poor mobile connection. 'You're absolutely sure?'

'It's the last thing he told me before we were disturbed and I had to end the debrief. The problem is I don't know how serious to take the threat.'

'Any mention of a target?'

'Not yet. They've told Proctor to keep his head down and wait for further instructions.'

'Anyone else involved?'

'He's been teamed up with Mike Clark who's staying at the house too. So you see, if we can prove that Longhurst owns the cottage, it directly connects him with the plot,' said Blake.

There was silence on the other end of the line.

'Harry? Are you still there?'

'Blake, I need to call this in. It's a credible threat to national security. I can't sit on this kind of information.'

'Not yet, Harry. You have to give me time to find out what they're planning. Look, there's no bomb and no plot. Just two guys who've been told to go away and wait for further instructions. If you raise the alarm now, we risk losing control of Proctor. He's my responsibility. I have to keep him safe. We owe him that much. Let me use him to find out what's going on so we can reel in Longhurst and the rest of them. Once they've identified a target, we'll call it in. I promise. But give me a few more days. A week at least.'

'Alright. One week, then we'll review it. But I want

regular progress reports, understood? And for God's sake, don't let Proctor out of your sight.'

'Of course. Thanks, Harry. I appreciate it.'

'So what's your next move?'

'I'm going to ground to keep an eye on the house, but there are some things I'm going to need. Do you think you'd be able to get them together for me and have them couriered over to where I'm staying?'

'I'll do my best. What do you need?'

Chapter 21

After studying a map of the terrain around Nutwick, Blake came up with a plan. Ben Proctor had disappeared once already and he wasn't about to let that happen again. He needed twenty-four hour surveillance, a job usually requiring a dedicated team of at least half a dozen men. But there was only one of Blake. No back-up to call on. No one to trade places with after a four-hour block. But Blake relished the challenge. It was what was he was trained to do.

He drove back to the village, and slowed to a crawl as he approached the entrance to Stoneleigh Cottage, craning his neck for a glimpse down the track to the house, but the building was hidden behind thick bushes and invisible to anyone passing. So he accelerated away, out of the valley and onto a car park he'd identified half a mile farther on.

The car park, laid with loose stone chippings and edged neatly with pine timbers, was deserted. Blake pulled up under the branches of an immature horse chestnut and locked the Audi remotely with a key fob he slipped into his pocket. He crossed the road, and vaulted a wire fence into a rolling green field that clung to a steep hillside.

He set his sights on a grove on the crown of the hill, which consisted mainly of oaks and elms, their leaves a spectacular riot of russets, yellows, and burnt reds. When he reached it, he was breathing hard from the exertion, and sweat plastered his clothes to his skin.

The grove marked a point where three fields converged and comprised no more than forty trees, which sat starkly against the skyline. Blake hustled through a tangled carpet of dead leaves, fallen branches, and sinewy brambles until he emerged onto a ridge on the eastern flank, overlooking a pasture of cattle and, more importantly for Blake, Stoneleigh Cottage to the southeast.

It was the perfect location for an observation post, on high ground, and with the trees for concealment. Blake dropped onto his stomach, supporting his body on his elbows, and studied the cottage, noting the mud-splattered Renault was still parked outside with its bonnet angled in towards the house, the only indication that anyone was at home.

Satisfied he'd found his spot, Blake shuffled backwards into the cover of the grove and brushed himself down. He located a hollow between three close growing trees and concluded it would suffice for a camp. Ideally, he'd have used a tarpaulin strung up between the trunks to make a shelter, but he'd not planned on sleeping out when he'd left London in a hurry and had to improvise using his rusty survival skills.

He found a straight length of fallen timber and hooked it into the crook of an overhanging branch, then supported shorter branches along its length like ribs fused along a spine. He finished the roof with interwoven ferns, to keep out the worst of any rain, and laid the floor with green leaves. Weather permitting, it would hold up for at least a couple of weeks and had the advantage of being camouflaged from all angles.

When he was done, Blake crawled back to the ridge, made himself comfortable, and fixed his sights on the cottage. He cleared his mind and slowed his breathing, concentrating on entering a kind of hibernation in which he could sustain himself immobile for hours on end. It was a technique that had ensured his survival during countless undercover missions for Echo 17, the now defunct black ops unit, whose specialism was in operating covertly in hostile environments, waiting for days or weeks to target selected individuals for interrogation, often under the noses of their enemy.

It had been uncomfortable, mind-numbing work punctuated by sudden, intense bursts of activity in extremely volatile situations. Blake had quickly learnt to control his mind and body so that he could blend into the background, hidden in ditches and foxholes without being detected for as long as the mission required. Psychologically, the demands were as tough as any physical challenge the SAS had thrown at him, even considering the hell of 'Selection', abandoned on a rain-scarred mountain in Wales with a fifty-five pound Bergen strapped to his back and days of endless route marches in the freezing cold with feet blistered raw.

Mental toughness was a pre-requisite, but Blake found he had a natural aptitude for the job. While others struggled with the isolation, Blake thrived on the solitude the role demanded. He never considered himself a recluse, but found the company of other people a drain on his energy, and was never happier than when left alone with his thoughts.

The weak, autumnal daylight was fading rapidly and the temperature dropping fast when Blake finally checked his watch. Throughout his entire five-hour vigil, not a soul had stirred in the cottage. He edged away from the ridge and stood stiffly, stretching all his major muscle groups and rubbing sensation back into those parts that had long gone numb.

He picked his way through the gloom back to his car, and turned the heater up to full as he drove back to the village square, the streams of warm air reviving his frozen extremities. He made a mental note to pack warmer clothes and a pair of gloves. If he was going to survive any length of time out in the open at this time of year, he needed decent kit.

The pub was empty when Blake walked in.

'Good day?' asked the landlord, emerging from a room

behind the bar.

Blake nodded, not in the mood for small talk. He ordered food from a greasy menu and took a table in the corner near the fire.

'Almost forgot,' said the landlord, pouring Blake a pint of beer. 'Parcel came for you earlier. It's in the office when you're ready.'

'Thanks. I'll grab it when I've eaten.'

The food was nothing special, a reheated meat pie with lumpy mashed potato and a selection of vegetables, which had had most of their nutrition boiled out of them. But Blake was determined to enjoy it. He knew it might be his last decent meal for days.

He collected the parcel on his way back to his room. It was wrapped in brown paper with a white envelope taped to the top, addressed to Daniel Jackson, the name he'd used when he'd checked in.

Inside the envelope was a single sheet of paper. A solitary line of text printed on it: *"As requested. Keep safe. HP"*

The package was filled with hundreds of multi-coloured polystyrene chips that spilled out when Blake cut open the top with a pen knife. Buried amongst the packaging were six plastic containers, which Blake lined up on the bed. At the bottom of the box, swathed in bubble wrap, was a miniature electronic monitor and a high-powered, military grade sighting scope and tripod.

He packed all the items in a rucksack with some warm clothing, and placed the bag by the door with his boots. He set an alarm on his mobile phone, lay on the bed, and closed his eyes.

Chapter 22

Blake woke at one minute to three in the morning, sixty seconds before his phone sounded a shrill alarm. He rose without hesitation, letting his eyes adjust to the dark. He splashed his face with cold water, threw on a thick jacket, and sneaked silently out of his room with his rucksack and boots. He stole around the front of the pub to the square, and from the boot of his car, retrieved a few essential items he always carried in case of emergency. A military sleeping bag, one that was actually guaranteed to keep out the cold, a selection of foil ration packs, a camping stove, billy can, tin mug, four spare mobile phone batteries, and a two litre bottle of water. He packed the rations, batteries, and camping equipment in the rucksack and threw it on the back seat with the water and sleeping bag.

It took precisely four minutes to drive to the car park on the far side of the village. Blake parked in the same spot under the horse chestnut tree and headed to the grove on top of the hill, guided by a bright moon hanging low in a cloudless sky.

He stowed his equipment in the shelter, repacked the rucksack with the six plastic boxes, and returned to the ridge where he could see Stoneleigh Cottage in darkness. He slipped over a wire fence and into the cow field, turning his feet sideways to stop himself sliding down the hill. Through the misty murk, he could make out the indistinct shapes of dozing cows, lowing mournfully, and as he picked his way through the long grass, slippery from recent rainfall, he was careful not to disturb the sleeping herd. The last thing he needed was a stampede in the middle of the night.

The field levelled off at the point it adjoined an overgrown garden on the blindside of the cottage. Blake stepped over a green and decaying wooden fence and trod carefully through the weeds, conscious that bruising the vegetation would give away that someone had been trespassing.

With his body pressed against the brickwork, he sidestepped around the cottage towards the living room, aware that Proctor was asleep in the room directly above. The old sash window gave way an inch when Blake tried the lower casement, and with a second effort grudgingly opened wide enough for him to slip inside.

He checked his watch, and noted the time displayed by the luminescent tips of the hands. Time was of the essence. He gave himself fifteen minutes to be in and out. Not a second longer. It was good discipline. From his trouser pocket, he pulled out two sachets he'd taken from a hotel during a recent stay in Prague and fitted the transparent shower caps over his boots to protect the carpet from his muddy footprints. From his jacket pocket, he took a head torch and pulled it on.

Inside, he scanned the room, following the white torch beam as it floated across the wallpapered walls. He found an electrical socket low down to the floor, its faceplate yellowed with age. Kneeling on the carpet, he removed one of the plastic boxes from his rucksack, together with a tool kit rolled up in fabric and secured with black ribbon. Blake selected a medium-sized flathead screwdriver, and removed two long screws securing the electrical plate to the wall. It came away easily enough, exposing a mass of coloured wires extending into the brickwork.

From the plastic box, Blake took a metallic disc, the size of a low denomination coin, and slotted it into the socket before screwing the faceplate back into position. Then he moved into the dining room and kitchen, and repeated the procedure at sockets in each of the rooms.

When he was finished, he returned to the hallway at the bottom of the stairs and popped out the bulb hanging from a length of wire from the ceiling, replacing it with an alternative from another one of the boxes. It wasn't identical in shape to the original bulb, but close enough that Blake doubted Proctor or Clark would notice.

Eight minutes had already elapsed, and downstairs was supposed to be the easiest part of the operation. He still had two more audio listening devices to fit in the bedrooms where Proctor and Clark were sleeping.

Blake took the stairs slowly, judging his weight on each step to avoid the creaks, and made it onto the landing. A nasally rumble of snoring was coming from Mike Clark's bedroom. It was a good sign he was sleeping deeply, but Blake decided to leave the room until last.

He turned off the torch, and eased opened Proctor's door. The agent was wrapped up tightly inside a heap of bedclothes beneath the window, lying on his side with a pale, tattooed arm hanging out of the covers, his breathing deep and slow. The curtains had been only half pulled closed, allowing enough light from the bright moon for Blake to locate an electrical socket near the door. His fingers moved quickly and efficiently, by now warmed up to the task, and the two screws spun out easily. He fitted another bug and had the faceplate back in place within a minute.

With one last check that Proctor hadn't been disturbed, he backed out of the room and pulled the door closed. Four and half minutes left to complete the job and clear the house. Still on track, but he'd have to hurry. Now he regretted leaving Clark's room until last. His hand hovered over the handle of the door as he noticed that Clark's snoring had stopped.

Blake froze as he heard a groan followed by the creak of floorboards. Just Clark rolling over in his sleep, Blake tried to reassure himself. He waited with his heart rattling in his ribcage. But there were more sounds. The shuffle of bedclothes, Clark clearing phlegm from his throat, and the floorboards creaking again. Someone was moving about in the room. Blake retreated and watched in horror as the handle turned and the door began to swing open.

He flung himself down the stairs, almost tumbling as the plastic shower caps on his feet slipped on the worn carpet. He hit the hallway with a thud, and hurled himself into the lounge where he clung to the wall and waited for the sound of pursuing footsteps.

But they didn't materialise.

Blake waited for what seemed like several minutes, but logic dictated could only have been a few seconds, before he heard a noisy stream of water. Clark relieving his bladder. Then the sound of a toilet flushing, echoing unusually loudly through the silent cottage.

Blake's instinct was telling him to get the hell out while he could, but his brain was arguing the toss. He'd installed four audio listening bugs in the sockets and a visual device in the hallway light. It was probably enough. But it left a major blind spot in Clark's room. Any phone calls or conversations in there would be missed. It wasn't acceptable. Blake knew he had to finish the job. So he waited, knowing that if Clark decided to head downstairs instead of returning to his room, he was in real trouble. He'd find the window open in the lounge, and then stumble on Blake hiding in the shadows.

There was no way of knowing how he would react, but Blake had a pretty good idea.

Chapter 23

Trent Garside prised open one eye and focussed on the digital display blinking the time at him. It was still early by his standards, but he resisted the temptation to roll over and drift back into his dreams. He had work to do. He gave himself a count to ten, swung his legs out of bed, and was struck by a chill in the air and the realisation that his ancient boiler must have cut out in the night.

With bleary eyes, he dragged his drowsy body into the kitchen and hit the reset button, listening with satisfaction to the muted roar of gas igniting and the clunk of pipes. It would take a while for the flat to heat through, but he denied himself the luxury of returning to the delicious warmth of his duvet. Instead, he threw on a chunky wool sweater over his T-shirt and flicked on the kettle. A hot mug of tea would soon revive his senses.

He'd been up late trawling the web for information that would link Ken Longhurst with America, but had run up against a familiar blank. Determined not to be defeated, he returned to his laptop, tea in hand, and with a renewed vigour brought on by a decent night's sleep.

The screen of his laptop flashed on, and Trent navigated straight to his e-mails, which had filled up overnight with the usual unsolicited communications offering everything from cut price broadband to cheap insurance and pills for sexual potency. He hit the delete button with gleeful abandon, but hesitated when he came across a message with the subject title "Ken Longhurst." It had been sent from an address he didn't recognise, and he opened it with an excited anticipation, hoping at last it might be a breakthrough.

The message was short and to the point.

'I thought you might find this interesting,' it said.

It was signed, 'Gary Samson.'

Trent clicked on a hyperlink pasted into the body of the e-mail. It opened a web page showing a facsimile of an American newspaper called the *Beaumont Messenger* from ten years earlier. One article dominated the page with a monochrome photograph across six columns. A smiling group of men and women bunched together in the sort of picture local newspapers specialised in.

Above the picture was a bold headline: 'Christian Conference Attracts Record Numbers.'

The article was an uninspiring read about an inaugural conference of a quasi-political religious organisation called the Christian Morality Campaign. There was no mention of Ken Longhurst or even the British Freedom Alliance. Trent scratched his stubbly chin and re-read the story line-by-line, absorbing the content in case he had missed something important.

A Christian conference held in Beaumont this weekend was attended by almost 300 people, far in excess of the organizers' expectations, writes Jeff Rogers.

Oil tycoon, Larry Hopper, who was pleased but not surprized by the turnout, established the Christian Morality Campaign.

He told the Messenger: 'People are looking for an alternative voice and we're offering that alternative. They're disenfranchised and disillusioned with our increasingly liberal politicians, and they want to see a return to the traditional values.'

Mr Hopper, one of the region's leading oilmen, said he founded the CMC after an increasing frustration at what he described as the failings of modern society.

The organization is opposed to abortion and has an open anti-homosexuality policy.

'We just want to give like-minded individuals the chance to get

together to discuss what's on their minds,' said Mr Hopper.

Following the success of the conference, the organization hopes to hold an annual event in the city.'

Trent's eye wandered to the photograph that accompanied the piece. Around twenty delegates had been lined up for the picture outside an anonymous-looking building. At the centre of the group, an avuncular man with a thick beard and wearing a traditional Texan Stetson was grinning widely. A caption confirmed Trent's assumption that this was Larry Hopper.

He guessed that the key to deciphering Gary's cryptic message was in finding out more about the oilman. And so he began a furious web search and discovered that, unlike Ken Longhurst, background information on Hopper was not difficult to come by.

Trent leapt from the sofa and bounded across the room, startling his middle-aged cat, Tabitha. She lifted her head wearily and shot Trent a puzzled look as he grabbed his briefcase, discarded on the floor near the front door, and rummaged around inside for a notebook and pen.

When he returned to his computer, he absentmindedly gave Tabitha a gentle stroke on the top of her head, causing her to arch her neck, drinking in the attention of her owner. Trent scribbled the name Larry Hopper in bold capitals along the top of a page of his notebook and set about furiously scribbling notes.

After two hours, his eyes began to sting. Glancing up at the clock on the front of the oven in the kitchen, he found it was already late morning.

'Time to get dressed I think, Tabs.' He gave the cat another stroke as he headed for the bathroom to fill the bath. As the cold stream of water lethargically turned hot, he returned to his laptop and the article from Beaumont.

The image of Larry Hopper was already haunting him. He had a sense that the photograph had some deep significance that he failed to grasp. He hit the print button and closed the page. Across the other side of the room, a wireless printer jumped to life as ink cartridges launched into a staccato dance across a blank sheet of paper.

The bath was close to over-running. Trent tested the water with his elbow and inched his pasty body into the tub. He submerged all but his head and his knees, then closed his eyes. Images of Larry Hopper filled his head as he drifted into a light sleep, his muscles eased by the warm water.

He awoke ten minutes later with the uncomfortable sensation that he was getting cold. He sat up, washed his face, and dried himself with a thin towel. He wiped steam from a mirror and tackled a small, white pimple on his cheek with the care of a surgeon. Feeling suitably cleaned and groomed, he wandered back to the printer, gritty crumbs sticking to the soles of his bare feet.

A single sheet of paper was waiting for him. Trent snatched it up, again studying the picture of Hopper and the crowd of delegates. With fresh eyes, he noticed something that had escaped him before. It was the clue he had spent all morning searching for, and yet it had somehow eluded him.

'Gotcha,' he gasped. Tabitha uncurled her head from her body and stared at him through narrow eyes. 'Now that could explain an awful lot.'

Chapter 24

The phone had already rung three times, and on each occasion Professor John Sturridge had glanced up from his marking and glared at the unfamiliar number. The fourth time he snatched up the handset.

'Yes?'

'Professor Sturridge? My name's Trent Garside. I really need some help. I'm researching the rise of far-right politics in Britain for an article I'm writing - '

'My specialism is in American politics,' the professor said, interrupting Trent. 'I'm probably not the best person to speak with. Why don't you give my colleague - '

'No, Professor Sturridge, it's exactly your expertise I need,' Trent continued. 'It's about Larry Hopper. You know who he is, of course. Well, I have a suspicion he's bankrolling the far-right in the U.K., and possibly has connections with the British Freedom Alliance too.'

Trent hoped the allegation would peak the professor's interest.

'An interesting accusation, Mr Garside.'

'Would you meet me?'

'I'm quite tied up -'

'It shouldn't take long.'

'Let me check my diary.'

'I'm already in Oxford. I can be with you in half an hour.'

*

Trent sank into a well-worn leather chair as Professor

Sturridge pulled up an armchair on the other side of a low coffee table scarred by coffee mug scorch marks.

'I really don't have long. I can give you twenty minutes before my next tutorial group. You wanted to know about Larry Hopper?'

'I appreciate your time,' said Trent, taking out a notebook and pen from his briefcase. 'I understand that you've met him in person?'

'A few years ago.'

'But you spoke to him for a research paper?'

'Like you, I needed some background on his early years, so I approached him for an interview.'

'Well, I've read as much as I can on the internet, but I'm not sure I'm getting the whole story. What's he like?'

'My honest opinion?'

'Of course.'

'He's a bigoted narcissist who poses a grave threat to the stability of the United States.'

Trent wondered if he was joking, but the professor's face was stony serious. 'Can we start with how he became involved in the oil industry?'

'It was a family business. It was supposed to have been handed down to the eldest son, Isaac, but he wanted nothing to do with it. But his second son, Larry, was different. He yearned to please his father and thought it was a good way to prove himself. He was right. He was a quick learner and showed a natural talent for business.

'When he took over, it was a small-scale operation comprising a couple of medium-sized oilfields, but Larry had ambitions for greater things and started to expand. Within a few years, he'd mopped up a dozen or so independent operations in the region until the Hopper enterprise had become one of the largest and most powerful in southern Texas.'

'That's impressive,' said Trent.

'Maybe. The speed and scale of his ambition was certainly unprecedented, but there were question marks over his methods.'

Trent looked up from his note taking and raised an eyebrow.

'Most of the businesses he acquired were bought at prices well below their market value,' said the professor. 'Now how do you think he managed that?'

Trent shook his head. 'He was a hard negotiator?'

'Undoubtedly, but there's widely held suspicion that most of those firms were coerced into selling.'

'What do you mean coerced?'

'I mean, Larry Hopper used intimidation, fear, violence even, to get what he wanted. In those early years, nothing stopped him when he set his sights on an acquisition.'

'Is there any evidence to back that up?'

The professor laughed ironically. 'Nothing that would hold up in a court of law. I think he was careful to make sure no one could testify against him, but there were plenty of accidents and mishaps.'

'Accidents?'

'Nothing that was directly attributable to Hopper, of course, but it's surprising how many of his business rivals and their families had a terrible run of luck around that time. You can look up the details yourself, but there were a whole litany of fires, floods, car crashes and apparent Acts of God. And one by one, they all agreed to sell up.'

'Did you ask him about it?'

'I'm an academic, Mr. Garside, not a reporter. I wanted to find out what motivated him to go into politics. I wasn't looking to grill him about how he'd built his business.'

'Okay, so how did he - or rather why did he - get into politics?'

'You have to understand that, like his father, he was, and remains, a devout Christian. He claims he had a desire to give something back to the community. But what sparked his interest in politics in particular was an incident in a neighbouring town when a young black girl fell pregnant after being raped by a white boy. Her doctor refused to carry out a termination on moral grounds, and when her parents went to the press, the ensuing storm divided the community. It inspired Hopper to become involved with the pro-life campaign, and he became responsible for organising a series of protest marches and rallies across the state.

'But as with so many things with Larry Hopper, there was more to it than met the eye. The way he described the incident to me made me quite uncomfortable. Of course, as a Christian, he had strong feelings about the sanctity of life, but it struck me that the issue was just as much about race. If that poor child hadn't have been black, I doubt he'd have shown the same interest.'

'You don't paint a very flattering picture,' said Trent.

'You wanted to know what I made of him. I'm telling it as I saw it.'

'So you're saying he's a racist?'

'There's another story from around the same time about a young black man and his family who were forced from their home by a lynch mob after he was convicted of a fairly minor theft offence. They burned the house to the ground, and literally ran them all out of town. And who do you think was credited with inciting them?'

'Hopper?' said Trent.

'Well, it certainly fitted with the strong-arm tactics he'd learnt in business.'

'What about the Christian Morality Campaign? How did that come about?'

'That was a direct spin-off from his pro-life campaigning. What started as an issue about the rights of the unborn child, soon became a demand for what he called a return to core American values and a traditional moral fortitude. He found his words were like opium to the impoverished masses who bought into his God-fearing rhetoric without question.'

'It gave him the idea of creating a political movement and at a conference he organised to address several hundred die-hard supporters, the idea of the Christian Morality Campaign was born.'

'The conference in Beaumont?' asked Trent. 'I heard about that.'

'He famously gave a speech deriding the breakdown of American society, and called on every citizen to fight back against the country's moral decline. I guess that set the tone for the future of the party. Incredibly, support for the CMC grew rapidly. It initially gained a foothold in the south, but eventually its popularity spread across the country. He openly condemned abortionists, mixed marriages, gay weddings, and spoke out about the growing tide of illegal immigrants. And for whatever reason, this brand of fundamental Christianity struck a chord with many ordinary Americans.'

'I see,' said Trent, scribbling furiously.

'Now, let me ask you something. You said on the phone that you suspect Larry Hopper is bankrolling the far right in the U.K.?'

Trent sat back in his chair and closed his notebook. 'It's not much more than a theory at the moment, but I think Larry Hopper could be diverting funds to the BFA, yes.'

'Do you think Hopper is pulling the strings of the BFA? If so, that's a dangerous allegation.'

'Dangerous?'

'Do some research on the Phineas Priests.'

Trent flipped open his notebook and wrote down the name.

'I doubt you've heard of them, but in the States they've been behind a number of terrorist attacks, and although their campaign started fairly low key, they're getting more audacious. What began with the firebombing of an abortion clinic, and an explosion at a gay wedding, quickly became a plot to bomb an FBI building. And you remember the flight to Mexico that exploded in mid-air last year? That was later claimed by the Phineas Priests. Relatively few fatalities so far, but each time the attacks have become more serious.'

'What does that have to do with Larry Hopper or the BFA?'

'I'd stake my reputation that Hopper's behind the Phineas Priests, and if Hopper has links to the BFA over here, it's going to end in bloodshed. I just hope you're wrong.'

Trent rummaged in his briefcase for the printout of the *Beaumont Messenger* report he'd printed from the internet. He straightened the piece of paper on his knee and offered it across the coffee table. 'I think you'd better have a look at this.'

The professor studied the printout for a moment, and shrugged. 'It's a report on that first conference in Beaumont. So?'

'Take a closer look at the photograph. Recognise the face over Hopper's left shoulder?'

The academic peered intently, drawing the paper closer to his face. 'Ken Longhurst?'

'Younger, but definitely him. Proof at least that there's a link between them.'

'So it seems,' said the professor.

He handed the paper back to Trent as a loud knock on the door interrupted the interview. The professor glanced at a clock on the wall. 'Just a minute,' he called out. 'I'm afraid that's my tutorial group arriving.'

Trent gathered his belongings into his briefcase. 'I appreciate your time,' he said. 'It's been an education.'

'My pleasure. So what next?' asked the professor, as he stood and showed Trent to the door.

'I'm not sure yet.'

'You know Larry Hopper is due in the country?'

'Really?' said Trent, his eyes lighting up. 'When?'

'Next week. He's been invited to speak at the Oxford Union.'

Chapter 25

Pete French was still at the office typing up a late story with only the cleaner for company, when the phone rang. 'Trent. What's up?'

'You still in the office?'

The cleaner flicked on a vacuum, and began poking about under the desks at the far side of the newsroom.

'I'm on a late breaker and wanted to get it filed before I left.'

'Pete, I'm onto something really big with the BFA. I'm pretty sure they're being funded with American money. Ever heard of an oilman called Larry Hopper?'

'That bloke from the Christian campaign group?'

'The Christian Morality Campaign. He's bankrolling the whole U.K. operation.'

'Wow, can you prove it?'

'I'm getting close. But there's more. Hopper's also connected to a right-wing extremist group called the Phineas Priests. The FBI's been investigating them because of their involvement in violence against minority groups.'

'Slow down, Trent. Who are the Phineas Priests?'

'No one really knows, but lots of people in the States suspect that Larry Hopper is behind it all.'

'Hang on, are you suggesting that because Larry Hopper is funding the BFA, these Phineas Priests are going to start launching attacks in Britain?'

'I don't know, but it's a possibility don't you think?' Even over the phone Pete could sense Trent's excitement, as if he was on the verge of something massive. 'I know it's a big leap, but that's why I want to pick your brains. Can you think of any recent incidents that the BFA might have been behind, I mean anything that's overtly racially or morally motivated?'

Pete watched the cleaner run the vacuum effortlessly around the floor. He pulled a forced grin as she glanced up at him, conscious of a pair of eyes watching her at work. 'Nothing springs to mind.'

'Well, let me know if you think of anything. Maybe I'm wrong, but I have this really bad feeling that something's going on. Did you know Larry Hopper's in the country this week? He's going to speak at the Union. I'm going see if I can get along.'

'Now you mention it -' Pete scrabbled around his desk for a copy of the *Evening Standard*. He flicked through the pages until he found the picture story he'd remembered. 'His yacht arrived in London yesterday. It's moored in Canary Wharf. There's a picture in today's Standard if you can get your hands on a copy.'

'Does it say if Hopper was on board?'

Pete scanned the few lines of copy to the right of the photo. 'It says he's due to fly into the country and will join the yacht later. He uses it as his floating home-from-home because he hates staying in hotels when he's abroad. How the other half live, eh? There's not much more information, I'm afraid.'

'No, that's great. Thanks, Pete. I might see if I can get an invite on board.'

Pete laughed at the joke, but when Trent hung up he had a terrible feeling that his friend had been deadly serious.

*

Blake made himself as comfortable as he could in his shelter, and tried to grab a few hours' sleep, cosseted in his thick Army sleeping bag, and with a woollen hat pulled tightly over his head and ears. He managed two hours, and rose at five to boil a saucepan of water on the camping stove for a brew, and to heat up one of the ration packs.

After eating, he crawled to his observation point on the ridge, and flicked on the monitor he'd left set up in the grass. The picture on the screen flickered and stabilised. It showed a black and white image of the hallway in Stoneleigh Cottage. A fish-eye lens captured the front door, the bottom of the stairs, and a section of the dining room.

Then he unwound a set of headphones from his pocket, and plugged them into his smartphone, which was picking up feeds from the three audio devices in the electrical sockets. He tried them all in turn, starting with the two downstairs, and then switching to the device in Proctor's room where he heard the rustle of bedclothes and the slow breath of his agent sleeping.

Blake was still annoyed that he'd not been able to place a bug in Mike Clark's room. But he reminded himself it was better than being caught red-handed in the cottage and blowing the entire operation. Against the odds, Clark had decided not to return to bed, but had tramped downstairs after waking in the middle of the night. Blake hadn't waited to find out why, fleeing from the house and quietly closing the window behind him. As far as he could tell, Proctor and Clark were none the wiser that he'd ever been there.

Blake flicked through his phone to a map of the vicinity, showing the cottage at the centre of the page surrounded by fields and the village away to the southeast. A blue dot was flashing near the house, marking the position of the red Renault thanks to a device Blake had attached under a wheel arch that would track it's movement.

Happy that all the devices were working correctly, Blake grabbed the scoping telescope, and set it up angled towards the cottage. Then he took a deep breath, prepared himself mentally, and settled in for a long wait.

Chapter 26

Harry Patterson moved slowly through the security checks in the reception of Thames House feeling as if he was being strangled by his tie, and resolved to remove it the moment he was behind his desk. After flashing his pass to a security officer and pushing his way through a controlled barrier, he ducked through a side door and took the back stairs up to the first floor, fiddling to release the top button of his shirt. The stuffy formality of his new clothes was symptomatic of the claustrophobic environment in which he now found himself. It was ironic that he yearned for the freedoms of the military, where no one had questioned his motives or methods as long as he delivered results. By contrast, his masters in MI5 wanted to keep a tight rein on his operations, with constant demands for reports and methodologies. He was swamped under a flood of e-mails and dossiers.

His personal assistant, Heather, had already unlocked his office; he wasn't allowed to keep a key. The door swung open on well-oiled hinges, and he headed straight for the coffee machine, dropping his attaché case by his desk. The coffee was strong and black. A Columbian brew in a pot that was never allowed to run dry. That was one of the few perks he enjoyed these days.

At his desk, he fired up his laptop, and prepared himself for the deluge of e-mails and memos he knew would be waiting for his attention. Intelligence updates dropped into his inbox throughout the night, providing a detailed analysis of political developments and crises around the world, prepared by an unseen army Patterson imagined were slaving away in an airless underground bunker somewhere deep beneath his office. He was supposed to read each briefing note in detail, but in truth he skim read the ones that caught his fancy and deleted the others.

The computer screen lit up, and Patterson pulled up his chair with a sigh. He yanked off his tie, and shoved it into his top drawer as he scanned through the latest missives. One in particular stood out among the rest. Although he recognised the name of the sender, it was the subject line "Holiday Cottage" that caught his attention.

Patterson opened it without hesitation.

Hi Harry,

Thought I'd drop you a note about the cottage. I've had a good look around, and I'm sure it's going to be perfect for you. I checked the sockets in the living room and kitchen, and took a look at the light fitting in the hallway. Everything seems to be working fine.

Blake's coded message was unambiguous to Patterson. It meant he'd successfully fitted the audio bugs in two rooms at the cottage where he'd located Proctor, and installed a video circuit in the entrance hall.

The socket in the first bedroom is also fine, but access to the second bedroom was problematic. It was a hurried job in the end, but all is fine. The council remain unaware.

That was an issue. If one of the bedrooms was unconnected, Blake's surveillance operation would be severely curtailed. It was unlike Blake not to finish a job, but he'd known the man long enough to know that he must have had good reason.

I took the liberty of servicing your old car. It needs a little work, but I'll keep track of progress.

Best wishes
Dan

At least Blake, who'd written under his alias Daniel Jackson, had managed to fit a tracking device to Proctor's red Renault. Patterson didn't bother with a response. He was about to delete the message when the phone on his desk rang.

'Colonel Patterson, the deputy director general would like a catch-up.' The way his PA enunciated her words reminded Patterson of his school matron.

'Thank you, Heather.'

Sir Richard had insisted on being kept personally updated on the Deep Sleepers programme ever since he had sanctioned it. It had become his pet project and that meant Patterson had to provide a running commentary on developments, even if there were none.

'I checked your diary and told him you would be free at ten-thirty this morning.' Having access to the diaries of all six of the intelligence officers she'd been assigned, Heather took pride in keeping them organised.

Patterson sighed inwardly. It left less than ninety minutes to pull together a briefing note on Blake's progress. Ninety minutes to compose something coherent enough to keep his boss happy, but without compromising Blake's operation. He dare not mention the bomb plot that Blake had spoken of. Sir Richard would have to be content with an anodyne report about Proctor's unexpected move to the country. Patterson opened a blank page on his computer and began to type.

Chapter 27

Settled in the back seat of a taxi streaming along a busy three-lane highway on the outskirts of Rio de Janeiro, Lucy Chapman and her husband, Peter, were lost in their thoughts. A string of beads swung hypnotically from the rear view mirror as they darted through the traffic, dodging cars, lorries, and vans heading towards the high rise blocks of the city looming large on the horizon. The air in the cab provided a cool relief from the stifling heat that had struck them when they'd landed at the airport, a stark contrast to the chilly, damp weather they'd left behind in London twelve hours earlier. They'd arranged the trip on the spur of the moment, hastily arranged after the news that Nick's luggage had been discovered on the Amazon, and undeterred by the lack of assistance from the Brazilian embassy.

'You here on holidays?' their driver asked, breaking the silence and jolting Lucy out of her reverie. He was a middle-aged man with a paunch that strained at his Hawaiian shirt, and a bald spot that he'd tried to cover over with strands of greasy, black hair. He was gripping the steering wheel lightly with one hand, the other arm resting on the back of the passenger seat.

'Hmm?' said Lucy, sensing his gaze on her. She found a pair of tired brown eyes staring at her in the mirror.

'It's a nice place to stay,' the driver repeated. 'You come before?'

Lucy turned to her husband for support, unsure how to respond. He smiled sympathetically and took her hand.

'We've actually come to look for somebody,' said Peter, sparing his wife the awkward conversation she didn't want to have.

The driver's eyes flicked from the road back to the mirror. 'Who you lost?'

'Lucy's brother. He travelled to Brazil, but he's not been seen since he left London. We don't know what happened to him after he got off the plane, so we're here hoping to find some answers. But to be honest, we haven't a clue where to start.'

'Why he come to Brazil?'

Peter leaned forwards to hear the driver over the noise of the engine and hiss of the air conditioning. 'He was travelling.'

'A backpacker?'

'Yes, that's right. We think he was planning to explore the Amazon.'

'Lots of backpacker in Brazil,' said the driver. 'But no so many take taxi. Too much expensive.' He rubbed his finger and thumb together in the universal sign for money.

'Yes,' said Peter, slumping back in his seat.

They sat in silence for the rest of the journey to their budget hotel near Copacabana Beach, where the driver pulled hard on the handbrake and swung around in his seat.

'I help you,' he said. Two large sweat patches were spreading from under his arms despite the coolness of the cab. Several of his teeth were missing. The few that remained were no more than black stumps. 'I help find your brother,' he repeated, as Lucy stared blankly at him.

'Oh, I see,' said Peter.

'I have friends who might know what happened. You have picture?'

'Yes, of course.' Lucy snatched up her handbag and scrambled through the contents.

'You go to hotel and I wait for you here. You bring picture?'

'Yes, thank you. That would be great. Give us five minutes and we'll be right back.' Lucy slipped out of the car and was immediately struck by the oppressive heat.

Peter paid the driver and included a large tip for helping to unload their bags.

'My name is Eduardo - Eduardo Oliveira,' said the driver, shaking Peter's hand enthusiastically and grinning like a maniac. 'Pleased be at your service.'

An hour later, Lucy and Peter were back in the taxi, stuck in traffic, surrounded by a cacophony of car horns and angry shouting. The way ahead was blocked by a procession of vehicles struggling to make their way through a tiny back road that snaked through a densely populated shantytown. Eduardo was leaning out of his window and had joined in the shouting match, berating some unseen culprit. Every few seconds, he slammed the heel of his hand into the horn in the centre of the steering wheel.

Eventually, they crept forward until they passed an open-backed truck, which had pulled up in the narrow street, leaving barely a car's width to pass. Two men were struggling with an unwieldy wooden wardrobe. As the taxi inched by, Eduardo screamed a torrent of abuse in Portuguese at the men who stopped momentarily to argue back.

Clear of the obstruction, they drove deeper into the city, where scruffy-looking buildings crowded the streets. A spaghetti tangle of electrical cables criss-crossed between the houses, and lines of washing were strung from balconies.

'Is it much farther, Eduardo?' Lucy shouted, over the whine of the engine.

'Just up here.' Eduardo had promised to take them to meet an acquaintance, who ran a popular backpackers' hostel and who had recognised the description of the young Briton.

They pulled up outside a nondescript townhouse next to a shop selling fruit from tables laid out on the pavement.

'We here,' Eduardo announced, theatrically.

He stabbed a stubby finger at a plastic doorbell at the side of a wooden door set into a white rendered wall. It was answered by an overweight man in his late forties, who greeted Eduardo with a broad smile and a friendly handshake. They exchanged a few enthusiastic words in Portuguese before Eduardo introduced the couple.

'This my good friend, Miguel Barros, who owns hostel,' he said.

'We're hoping you can help me find my brother,' Lucy blurted out.

'Yes, of course,' Barros replied, waving them inside. A stubby cigarette was burning between his fingers, and tufts of coarse hair poked out from around the top of a vest that might once have been white.

They followed him in single file along a short corridor to a reception desk hidden under piles of old newspapers and discoloured coffee cups.

'Did you bring a picture of your brother?' Barros asked.

Lucy produced a dog-eared photograph of Nick from her bag. It had been taken in the year before he'd left for university when they'd spent the day in the park with a hastily purchased picnic of bread and cheese, washed down with a bottle of warm Chardonnay. She remembered how excited Nick had been at the prospect of starting college. Like a seven-year-old on the night before Christmas, she'd joked with him.

'His name's Nick Richards. Nicholas.'

Barros took the picture and sucked on his bottom lip. 'Yes, I know him. He was here for two days only.' He spoke without looking up. 'It's definitely him.'

Lucy glanced at her husband, hardly daring to believe what she was hearing.

'How can you be so sure?' said Peter.

Barros looked up from the photo, and seemed to notice Lucy's husband for the first time. 'I remember because he was a nice guy. Quiet. Kept himself to himself,' he said.

'Did he tell you why he was here? Where he was going?' Lucy fired out the questions.

Before the hostel owner could answer, footsteps sounded on the stairs at the end of the hallway. Two young Australians chatting noisily appeared from the stairwell and squeezed past. Lucy watched as they let themselves out and slammed the front door behind them.

'We talked a little when he arrived,' said Barros. 'He was going to the Amazon, but was in Rio for a few days before he left. I remember him because he paid for five nights, but left after two.'

Lucy's eyes widened, the blackness of her pupils swallowing her bright blue irises. She grasped for her husband's arm, waiting for Barros to elaborate, but didn't register the fleeting glance between Barros and Eduardo.

'He told me he was going to visit Pao de Acucar, but never came back.'

'Sugarloaf Mountain?' said Peter.

'Yes, he was going to take the cable car to the top. I told him it has the most wonderful views.'

'So when did you realise he was missing?' asked Lucy.

Barros shifted in his chair. 'I think it was a day or so later. I found his room empty.'

'Did he leave any of his things?'

'No. Everything was gone.'

'Everything? Even his rucksack?' Lucy frowned.

'Yes, he'd even made his bed before he left.'

'Why would he pack and take his rucksack for a sightseeing trip up Sugarloaf Mountain? It doesn't make any sense,' said Lucy, turning to her husband.

Peter shrugged.

'I'm afraid that's all I can tell you.' Barros rose from the chair. 'Good luck in finding your brother. He was a very nice man.'

Eduardo took the cue. 'Thank you, Miguel. Very helpful.' He ushered Lucy and Peter to the front door.

'Just one more question. Please?' said Lucy.

Eduardo hesitated as Lucy resolutely refused to move. His eyes flickered towards Barros.

'I was wondering if you called the police when you realised Nick was missing?'

'People come and people go all the time. I didn't think it was necessary. I'm sorry.'

Eduardo became insistent that they needed to leave, and Lucy allowed herself to be shepherded back down the corridor by his firm hand on her shoulder.

'I hope you find him,' Barros shouted after them.

Lucy stumbled onto the humid street, her mind churning. Two young boys wearing the golden-coloured football shirts of their national team bumped past, screaming in joyful delight, but she barely noticed. She settled into the back seat of the taxi with her forehead furrowed.

'Shall we go to Sugarloaf?' asked Eduardo.

'Yes, I guess so.' Peter looked to his wife for agreement.

'Just bloody drive will you?'

Chapter 28

'I think we need to be realistic.' Peter Chapman was standing at one end of a cable car with his wife ascending Sugarloaf Mountain with a gaggle of excited tourists who were drinking in the stunning panorama. 'Hundreds of thousands of people come here every year. What are the chances of someone remembering Nick?'

They were rapidly approaching the top of Urca Hill, the mountain's midway point where they would have to transfer onto a second car to reach the summit.

'Peter, don't start, please.' Lucy was clutching the picture of her brother, absentmindedly flicking the corner of the photo with her thumb.

'What if, by some miracle, someone does remember seeing him? What then?'

'Peter!' Lucy startled herself with the ferocity of her tone. 'You know why I've got to do this.'

'Yes, I do understand, but...'

'But what?'

'I'm worried we're on a wild goose chase. Maybe Nick did come here before he disappeared. So what? So does almost every other tourist visiting Rio. Just look around at the number of people.'

'What else are we supposed to do? We don't have any other leads. I can't sit back and do nothing. But you've never supported me over this have you?'

'I'm here, aren't I?'

'You're here, but you think it's a waste of time.'

'And money,' Peter muttered under his breath.

'Is this what it's all about? Money? My brother's not worth it, is that it?' Lucy raised her voice, ignoring the scowls from the other passengers.

'That's not fair.'

'You and your precious bank balance. It's always money, isn't it?'

'Well, there's not going to be much of it left the way we're going through it.'

'What do you mean?'

The cable car slowed to a halt and the tinted glass doors slid open. Lucy and Peter filed out onto a viewing terrace with scenic views of the city and its beaches below.

'Come on - what are you trying to say exactly?' said Lucy.

'We're spending a small fortune without achieving very much.'

'I don't know what you mean. We've hardly been here five minutes.'

'Well, our enthusiastic taxi driver has cost me over five hundred quid already.'

Eduardo had dropped them at the entrance to the mountain and insisted they head for the summit while he parked the car. He promised to quiz staff on the lower station and said he'd meet them in two hours.

'Five hundred?' asked Lucy, raising her eyebrows. 'You must be wrong.'

'It's what he's demanded so far, in cash. He doesn't have any idea what happened to Nick, and I don't think he really cares. He's playing us for mugs.'

'Don't be so ridiculous.' Lucy fought angry tears as she turned her back on her husband, leaned over metal railings, and stared at the tiny buildings below. Everything looked so small and insignificant from the mountain; the trees, beaches and flotillas of yachts and boats buzzing around the harbours like miniature replicas of the real thing. Another cable car made its slow journey up the mountain and deposited its complement of visitors on to the viewing platform.

'Lucy, I'm sorry, but I don't want you getting hurt. The money doesn't matter. But what are we doing here?'

'You heard what Miguel said. Nick left the hostel to come here, so someone must have seen him.'

'I know what he said. But I'm not convinced Nick...' Peter's words trailed away.

'Not convinced what?'

'That he was even at that hostel. What if Eduardo fed Miguel a story that he knew you wanted to hear?'

'Why would he?' Lucy snapped.

'For money? You said yourself it makes no sense that he'd come here with his backpack and all his stuff when anyone else would have left it in their room.'

Lucy scanned her husband's familiar face, trying to make up her mind about whom she believed. He was right; it did seem implausible that Nick would abandon the hostel with no good reason. But why would they lie to her? 'Peter, I need your support. I can't do this on my own. I know you never cared about Nick, but do this for my sake?'

Peter threw his hands up in submission. 'All right, let's not fight. Let's start asking around. Have you still got that photo?'

Lucy kissed him on the cheek and trotted towards a row of shops and restaurants under a white canopy. Peter followed begrudgingly, a few paces behind, watching his wife move from shop to shop, greeting each assistant with a wide smile, and handing over the snapshot. Each time the reaction was the same. They would carefully scrutinise the picture with a look of concern and hand it back with a shake of their heads.

Eventually, they exhausted all the outlets and every member of staff they could find. They rode a second cable car to the summit in silence and repeated the process, questioning shop assistants and café staff, but none remembered Nicholas Richards.

'Lucy, we'd better get back down again,' Peter said, gently, tapping his watch. 'Eduardo will be expecting us at the bottom in fifteen minutes. Maybe he's had better luck.'

Lucy nodded reluctantly. They squeezed into a waiting car and started the slow descent, blind to the breath-taking views through the windows. A second car delivered them back to the foot of the mountain, through a dirty, grey concrete ground station. Lucy trudged down the steps onto the street, scanning for Eduardo.

'I expect he's gone to check on the car,' said Peter.

'Go and find him, I'm parched. I'll grab a drink over there.' Lucy pointed to a café on the opposite side of the street. 'Come and get me when you find him.'

She crossed the street, dodging a slow moving stream of traffic, glad for a few moments of solitude to gather her thoughts and wrestle with her doubts. She took a seat at a table on the pavement, and ordered two Cokes from the waiter. While she waited, she replayed recent events through her head.

'Obrigada,' said Lucy, as the waiter returned with two red cans and two scratched high-ball glasses that had been filled with little round ice cubes.

She drank hungrily, and the cold liquid burned her throat. Across the road, Peter was striding towards her with purpose. As he drew closer, she recognised the look of concern on his face.

'What is it?' she asked.

'Eduardo. He's vanished.'

'I expect he's gone to fill up with petrol or something.'

Peter pulled out a chair and took his wife's hand across the table. 'No love, he's gone. There's no easy way to say this, but he's taken our money and cleared off.'

Chapter 29

Home and alone, the battle-weary sergeant ran the images through his head, replaying every graphic frame. He gulped down the last mouthful of beer, and threw the empty can across the room. It missed the bin and clattered across the floor like an expended NATO round. It was his last can, but the alcohol had done little to numb the pain. So he hauled himself to his feet, picked up his wallet, and ventured out of the warmth of the flat for resupplies.

The corner shop was a short walk away, illuminated brightly in a dark row of houses. It smelled of washing powder and newsprint. He headed directly to a chiller cabinet at the back, hooked out a pack of strong lager, and paid without speaking to the man behind the till, who glanced up only briefly from his crossword puzzle.

As he staggered out of the shop, he failed to notice the gang of three young men loitering in the shadows, watching in silence. Had he observed the scene as he was trained to do, he would have seen one of them, awkwardly tall, rocking from one foot to the other, cobalt-black eyes staring from under a hooded-top. But his thoughts were elsewhere, in another time and place, as he crossed the road and ventured up a side alley lit only by the glow of a sodium street lamp.

The gangly youth followed silently, and quickly closed the distance, slipping his hand behind his back, his fingers closing around the cold, hard handle of a carving knife in the waistband of his tracksuit trousers. He dropped his right shoulder, and barged past the soldier with a force that knocked him off his stride.

'Sorry, mate,' hissed the youth, whirling around and ramming the point of his knife into the soldier's chest. 'Now give us your wallet.'

The sergeant stood square, glanced down at the weapon and back at his attacker with contempt.

'Come on, I'm not mucking around. Give us your wallet. Now!' screamed the young man, trying to steel himself, and checking nervously for the reassurance of his two companions on guard at the end of the alley.

'Piss off,' said the soldier. He dropped his carrier bag of beer and snatched the youth's arm with both hands. He wasn't going to be pushed around by a young upstart on his own doorstep, knife or not.

He tightened his grip around the thin wrist and twisted, trying to wrench the weapon free, but lost his balance and stumbled. His eyes widened as he slumped forward, his face pale, the blade slicing through the muscle in his stomach as easily as a fruit knife through a peach.

The youth pulled his hand free with panic in his eyes. His hand covered in warm, silky blood, bright crimson even in the amber glow of street lamp. He stared; disbelieving what he'd done, then dropped the knife and ran.

The soldier fell to his knees with a terrible gasp, clutching the gaping wound as if trying to hold in his guts. Blood seeped through his fingers, pooling on the pavement, and he knew he was in trouble. A dull throb began where he'd been cut open and quickly became an intense pain. He wanted to run. To scream. And he was back in Afghanistan again.

He fell face down, his strength deserting him, and a creeping chill washed over his body. He felt so cold, his life slowly pumping out onto the street in a vivid scarlet puddle. All he wanted was to curl up and sleep, to make the hurt go away.

Through a dull haze, he heard a voice. Someone lifted

his head. He prised open his eyes and recognised the man who'd taken his money in the shop.

'Can you hear me? Hold on, it's going to be okay. You're going to be alright. Help! I need help here!'

But it was already too late.

The soldier died on the spot where he had been stabbed, cradled in the arms of a stranger in a cold, dark alley not so far away from home.

Chapter 30

The sleek outline of the Bell 222 helicopter appeared over the horizon, stark against the azure sky. Inside, Larry Hopper was being treated to a spectacular view of London where the River Thames cut a swathe through densely populated streets.

'What's the big white tent?' the Texan asked, his deep southern drawl crackling through the communications system.

'That was the Millennium Dome, sir. It's a concert venue now,' said the pilot.

They slowed as they approached the towering office blocks that dominated the old Victorian dock site, and where thousands of panes of glass now glistened in the low, autumnal sunshine. The pilot brought the aircraft to a virtual standstill over the river, with the rotor blades whipping up rippling peaks and gently nudged the chopper over land. With minute adjustments to the controls, he countered the buffeting crosswinds and landed with the gentlest of bumps on a helipad at the water's edge.

A black Jaguar with darkened windows rolled out from behind a nearby hangar and drew up close. A chauffeur in a charcoal suit and peaked cap jumped out and held open a rear door for Hopper as he sauntered from the aircraft with his personal assistant trailing in his wake.

The journey to his yacht, moored in the heart of the city's Docklands, took a little more than seven minutes. The *Clara Barton*, a 200-foot Italian-built superyacht had sailed in several days earlier, in preparation for Hopper's arrival on account of the businessman's refusal to stay in hotels when he was away from home. He hated their unfamiliar beds, obsequious tip-demanding staff, and tedious décor, and avoided them whenever he could. With its crew of twelve seasoned and trusted sailors, who Hopper insisted dressed immaculately in maritime whites, it was an expensive luxury, but one that the Texan could well afford. Besides, the yacht, with its sleek lines and tinted glass, made a bold statement, a declaration of his power and wealth.

The Jaguar delivered Hopper to the gangplank guarded by two muscled men in wrap-around dark sunglasses, where he was greeted by the yacht's captain, a tall Scandinavian with leathery skin.

'Good trip, sir?'

'Is Longhurst here yet?' Hopper snapped. Despite travelling in business class for his flight to Britain, the effects of jet lag were taking their toll on his humour.

'He's waiting in the conference room,' said the captain, with a slight bow.

Hopper marched on board and headed through a luxurious lounge with thick, cream carpet, a pristine white sofa, and white lilies on a coffee table, towards a conference room at the opposite end of the yacht. He crashed through the doors and startled Ken Longhurst, who sprung from a leather chair around an oval table.

He beamed at the Texan with an impossibly white set of teeth. 'Larry,' he said, with his hand outstretched.

'Been waiting long?'

'No, no,' Longhurst lied, subconsciously glancing at his watch.

'You've seen the papers today?' Both men sat, and Hopper beckoned to his assistant who had taken a seat at his side and pulled out a tabloid newspaper from a briefcase. Hopper glanced at the headline before sliding it across the table. 'War hero killed in race attack? Are you kidding me?'

Longhurst scanned the story, which had been carried over from the front page and covered almost the entirety of the fourth and fifth pages. 'I know, it's depressing,' he sighed.

'Depressing? This guy was a hero. He fought in Afghanistan, for your country, and was butchered like a dog in an alley on his doorstep. He should have been on a pedestal for what he did. He didn't deserve this.'

'The police are saying it might have been a mugging that went wrong,' said Longhurst, weakly.

'Mugging? Really?' said Hopper, with disbelief. 'You know it was a gang of Asians? The guy who found him saw them running off. It's pretty clear to me they knew he was a soldier and they hunted him down.'

'But why?'

'It's obvious. He was fighting the Taliban to make their God-forsaken country a better place to live. And this was his reward. Revenge. Pure and simple.'

'But the papers -'

'Ken, the police are covering up the facts. That's what's wrong with this place. Everybody's scared to tell the truth. It makes me sick. And you know what, I can guarantee they'll be folks claiming to be Brits, who've got the passports to prove it, rubbing their hands with delight. You know why?'

Longhurst shook his head.

'Because these kids who did this,' Hopper jabbed his finger at the newspaper, 'claim to love your country, but they don't want to play by the rules. They want Sharia Law and our women to be covered from head-to-toe. They sit around conspiring against us in mosques we allowed them to build. And you have to ask yourself, if they hate our way of life and what we stand for so much, why don't they just leave? You should be ashamed to have let this happen.'

'But nobody saw this coming,' Longhurst stammered

'I saw it coming. I've seen it coming for a while.' Hopper slammed his palm on the table. 'Your immigration controls suck. This country's given refuge to every waif, stray and bleeding heart from every hellhole around the world for years, but they have no respect for our freedoms or our way of life. Your governments have consistently let them all in without question because your politicians are lily-livered and weak, too afraid to stand up and make a difference, to defend what made this country great in the first place. I've seen it happen in the States and now it's happening here. The thing is, what you going do about it?'

'We're getting the message out, and people are listening to us, but it takes time. We're seeing real progress with getting representation at local council level, and I'm sure it's only a matter of time before we secure representation in the Commons.'

'But you don't have time. You need to act now. Stem the tide, put a block on immigration, and start destroying the cancer festering in your communities and eating away at your democracy. The time for politics has passed. We're at war. The front line might be in some desert in Afghanistan, but the battles need to be won at home. They've brought the fight to our front door, and we can either stand back and be cowed into surrender, or we can do something about it. We need to take direct action and the sooner the better.'

'What did you have in mind?' Longhurst looked intently into the Texan's rheumy eyes.

'Have you put the preparations in place like I told you?'

'I have two very capable men ready and willing.'

'Warriors, Ken. Soldiers of peace. I'd like to meet them. Bring them here, but be subtle about it. It's important they're not seen here.'

'Of course,' said Longhurst. 'I'm ready to do whatever it takes.'

Chapter 31

Blake had quickly settled into a routine, waking early for a small breakfast from his rations, before checking the electronic listening devices, each programmed to begin recording when triggered by movement in the house. On the whole, he found that once Proctor and Clark had taken to their beds, they didn't stir until late morning.

By six, he was in position on his stomach on the ridge overlooking the cottage, monitoring the men's movements and conversations throughout the day. Their exchanges remained frustratingly banal, as if they were killing time. They talked very little about the BFA and never about the Phineas Priests or any bomb plot.

Their routine was equally mundane. After taking a late breakfast, they usually spent their mornings watching daytime TV on a portable in Proctor's room. Occasionally, one of them would drive into Nutwick for milk, cigarettes, or a newspaper. Sometimes, they would head farther afield to a supermarket in a retail park on the outskirts of a nearby town, and Blake would watch the little blue dot on the screen of his smartphone snake its way along the back roads, stop for an hour, and wind its way back again. They returned with bulging carrier bags that revealed to Blake that they were living on a diet of ready meals, crisps, Coke, and beer.

Their afternoons varied little from their mornings, watching TV and taking the occasional nap, and by the early evening their drinking began. The more they drank the louder and more boisterous they would become, until they passed out some time after midnight.

Blake grabbed meals when he could, and focussed on building a mental picture of the inside of the cottage. He slept only when he knew Proctor and Clark had turned in, and made sure he was back in position well before they surfaced.

After five days, a regular pattern had established, but on the fifth evening, everything changed.

During the day, Blake detected a nervousness in the men's behaviour. Their conversation was muted and their language terse. Neither man took a drink, and by early evening, they disappeared into their own rooms. Although the television in Proctor's room was on low, it was unusual not to hear the men's raucous laughter and obscene jokes.

That evening, Blake remained at his observation post, and shortly after midnight watched the grainy images on his monitor of the men emerging down the stairs and into the hallway. They left the house through the porch, and jumped into the red Renault. A moment later, the engine rattled into life and bright headlights illuminated the hillside, almost blinding Blake as he observed through the scope. The car pulled away and disappeared along the drive towards the main road, its taillights blinking.

Blake jumped up and ran through the wood, batting aside loose branches, and crashing through the undergrowth. He sprinted headlong down the hill, struggling to keep his footing. He vaulted the wire fence at the bottom, and reached his car out of breath, fumbling for the keys in his pocket.

There was no sign of the Renault on that stretch of road, which indicated to Blake that it must be heading north east, through Nutwick, towards the motorway. His suspicions were confirmed when he checked the blue dot on his phone.

He caught up with the car a few miles beyond the village. It was cruising along at a steady pace, well below the speed limit. Not too fast, but not too slow. Easy on the corners, cutting through the rolling countryside with its headlights dipped.

Blake kept his distance, ensuring the Renault's taillights remained just within sight, constantly checking the blue dot on his phone. He drew a hand over the six-day growth on his chin, and realised in the comfort of his car how grubby he felt. He was wearing the same clothes he had thrown on five days earlier. They were stained with mud, and covered in fragments of decaying leaves. Beneath his woollen hat, his scalp itched, his greying hair matted to his head. His feet were uncomfortably hot inside his boots, and his eyes felt like someone had rubbed sand into them. He blinked the discomfort away and concentrated on the road.

The A-road eventually turned into a motorway, where they encountered the first traffic since leaving Nutwick. Mostly lorries on early morning delivery runs, and passengers and airport staff heading for the first flights out of Gatwick. Blake slotted in behind a seven-and-a-half ton box van that was trundling along in the inside lane, and monitored the movement of the Renault through his phone. Although it was travelling faster on the motorway, it rarely ventured above the speed limit, smoothly changing between lanes to overtake slower moving vehicles. Nothing to warrant the attention of a bored police patrol.

After twenty minutes, the Renault pulled off into a roadside service station with a backlit billboard advertising a fast food outlet and a coffee chain. Proctor followed, slowing along the access lane and into a large car park. He noted the Renault pull up in an empty space in a section marked out by low hedges a short distance from a single storey building housing restaurants, cafés, shops, and toilets. Blake drove past, and found a space a little farther on, killed his lights, and watched the Renault in his rear view mirror.

Proctor and Clark remained in the vehicle, but in the low light, it was impossible to tell what they were doing. It occurred to Blake that they'd discovered the bugs in the cottage and taken the car to talk in private. But it was a long way to travel for assurances they weren't being listened to. They'd driven nearly twenty miles. They could have pulled up in a layby much closer.

Blake had his answer a few moments later when a pair of dazzling headlights appeared in his mirrors and an expensive-looking black Bentley pulled up alongside the Renault. Proctor and Clark climbed in the back, and no sooner had the doors closed than the car pulled away sharply with a throaty roar.

Chapter 32

The Bentley had already vanished into the traffic when Blake hit the exit slip road onto the motorway. He floored the accelerator, and slotted into the slow lane ahead of a fast moving lorry, which flashed its lights at him as a rebuke. With a check in his mirror, Blake switched into the middle lane and watched the speedometer rise to a hundred. The Bentley was a short distance ahead cruising in the fast lane and sitting low on its wheels, humming along at a deceptively high speed. Blake noted the number plate. KL99.

The motorway ran out at an intersection with the M25, London's orbital highway. The Bentley swung through the junction, following an arcing loop heading east towards Kent, with Blake trailing behind, trying to keep up without being noticed. In a few hours, the motorway would be congested with commuters, tradesmen, and lorry drivers, but for now, it was unusually clear and both cars hurtled through the early morning traffic unhindered.

The Bentley eventually turned off onto a dual carriageway that led through the leafy suburbs of Greenwich and the Blackwall Tunnel beneath the Thames. It re-emerged on the Isle of Dogs, where the skyscrapers of Canary Wharf looked down on the city below, lights twinkling from the windows of a thousand empty offices.

The island had once been the beating heart of British trade and industry, with streets thick with the exotic aromas of imported coffee, spices, and rum, the evocative smells of far-off lands. Now it was home to more than fourteen million square feet of office and retail space as the island was reborn as one of London's most significant financial centres.

Open carriageways gave way to residential streets, and the Bentley finally slowed to a more pedestrian pace, with Blake trying to maintain a discreet distance through the tight network of roads.

Its taillights rose and fell as it floated over a lifting bridge with vast girders straddling the carriageway like a great, iron portal. A few seconds later, Blake rumbled over the same strip of road and the Millennium Dome appeared to his left, lit up like an alien spacecraft that had dropped from the skies. To his right, a deep-water quay reflected multi-coloured lights from the high-rise buildings that surrounded it, and three gunmetal cranes stood to attention side-by-side, with their redundant arms pointing to the night sky in perfect symmetry.

The Bentley hooked right through a small roundabout and disappeared in a series of residential back roads. Blake eventually caught up with the car as it slowed on a narrow lane, with its headlights reflecting off a looming white wall between two brick buildings. Blake pulled over, killed his own lights, and stared into the darkness trying to make sense of what he was seeing. The wall was peppered with oval, black holes and he realised it was the fibreglass hull of a large boat moored in the quay.

When the rear doors of the Bentley opened, and Proctor and Clark emerged, Blake threw his car into reverse and made a U-turn. He retraced his route, back to the blue lift bridge, swung hard left onto a gravel track past a storage warehouse, and skidded to a halt at the water's edge. A sleek, white superyacht was moored on the opposite side of the quay, beneath a block of smart flats. She looked like a playboy's toy, with crisp lines, polished metal handrails, and tinted windows, an opulent fusion of high-speed motor cruiser and ocean-going hotel. She was easily two hundred feet long, and reared up over five decks. Blake counted at least three sundecks on different levels, and above the bridge a vast array of navigational bulbs and masts were mounted on a radar arch.

Blake grabbed a pair of binoculars from the passenger foot well and scanned the boat for activity. The stars and stripes of the American flag hung limply from a pole on one of the upper decks that was bathed in a yellow glow from hidden down lighters. Her name had been painted half way along her superstructure, just below the bridge. It sounded familiar to Blake, but he couldn't immediately place it.

Movement on an aft deck caught his eye, and he steadied the binoculars to focus on a thin man with a shaven head. Ben Proctor. A pace behind was Mike Clark. They were confronted by two security guards who appeared from the far side of the vessel, significantly taller and broader than the other two men, with dark jackets and crisp white shirts, which strained against their necks and shoulders. After frisking them for weapons, the guards waved Proctor and Clark inside a cabin and Blake lost sight of them.

He dropped the binoculars in his lap and snatched up his phone. His fingers glided across the screen and found the number he was looking for.

'Marty, I need your help,' said Blake, when Marty Price answered.

'Blake, it's two in the morning.' The intelligence specialist sounded groggy from sleep.

'You know I wouldn't call if it wasn't important.'

'What's up?'

'I need some information.'

'Can't it wait until a more sensible time in the morning?'

'Not really. It's about a boat, called the *Clara Barton*.'

Marty sighed. 'Hang on a minute; I need to get to the computers.'

Blake imagined his friend and former Army colleague swinging out of bed and padding across the wooden stripped floor. 'Is this something to do with the Phineas Priests?'

'The Phineas Priests?'

'Yeah, Harry called a few days ago. Said it was something you were working on.'

'Possibly.' Blake heard the hollow tapping of a keyboard.

'The *Clara Barton*? As in the founder of the American Red Cross?'

'I thought I knew the name, but I couldn't place it.'

'Well, she was only one of the most honoured women in American history, Blake. A nurse in the American Civil War before going on to found the American Red Cross if I remember rightly. So what is it? A ship?'

'A superyacht. Expensive-looking.'

'Well, no great mystery. Let me guess - you're sitting in the middle of Canary Wharf looking at it right now?'

'How did you know?'

'It says in the *Evening Standard* that she sailed in two days ago. There's a nice picture of her, too. She's a beauty. Belongs to the Texan billionaire, Larry Hopper, who's in town to talk at the Oxford Union. You know, Blake, you really could have looked this up yourself. You do have internet access on your phone.'

'But it's always a pleasure chatting with you, Marty. Tell me about Larry Hopper. I've never heard of him.'

There was a pause on the line as Marty delved into his databases and cross-referenced with the World Wide Web. 'Are you familiar with the Christian Morality Foundation?'

'Sounds vaguely familiar. Couldn't tell you much about it though.'

'It's a big Christian Right movement based in the States. And Hopper's the main man behind it. He's supposed to be something of a character, and popular too. The organisation's growing at rapid rate in middle America.'

'Is he legitimate?'

'What do you mean?'

'Any suggestion of criminality?'

'Not that I can see.'

So what was he doing inviting two thugs from the BFA on board his luxury yacht in the middle of the night, Blake mused. 'Anything else?'

'I can do a full report, but the headline is that he made his money in the Texan oilfields before turning to God.'

'Hang on, Marty. Something's happening. I've got to go.'

Across the still waters of the quay, Blake had been watching another figure moving purposefully towards the *Clara Barton*. He was wearing a long raincoat and carrying a briefcase. Although it was late, Blake thought it was feasible it could be a businessman making his way home after staying late to complete an important deal. That is until he appeared on the aft deck waving his arms excitedly at one of the dark-suited guards.

Blake trained his binoculars on the rear deck. The man was tall and slim, and gesticulating with something in his hand. It was clear from his manner that he was remonstrating with the guard who was trying to shoo him off the boat. Eventually, the man turned as if to walk away, but whatever he said as a parting shot seemed to work. The guard beckoned him back on board and ushered him down a flight of steps to a lower deck, and inside the vessel.

Chapter 33

The galley was starkly functional, with pale walls, polished chrome work surfaces, and industrial-sized extractor fans. Trent laid his briefcase flat on the nearest worktop and studied the room with his hands on his hips. He had been surprised at how easy it was to bluff his way on board with a hastily concocted cover story and fake identity card that he'd knocked out on his computer. The guards had tried to turn him away, but he'd been insistent that while Larry Hopper's yacht was moored in U.K. waters, the law entitled him to carry out an environmental health inspection. Finally, the threat of having the vessel impounded did the trick. Reluctantly, one of the guards escorted him along a narrow walkway and through a discreet door in the hull that led to the staff quarters and service areas.

Trent turned a slow circle, surveying the layout of the galley, and was disappointed to find the guard still in the doorway watching with suspicion and clearly irritated at the disturbance in the middle of the night. Trent sucked the air through his teeth and gave a disapproving shake of his head.

'I'll need to see your certification, including all your health and safety documents. Your IO163, your VT88, for example' said Trent making it up as he went along. 'And of course your FDT30-21, which should be on display here somewhere.' He made an exaggerated show of looking for the imaginary certificate.

The guard's eyes narrowed then widened. Trent forced

himself to hold the challenge of his glare until the guard eventually relented with a huff. 'Wait here,' he said.

Trent listened to his footsteps recede, crooked his head out of the doorway, and, satisfied that the guard was gone, grabbed his empty briefcase. It was only as he set off along a poorly lit passageway that he realised he had no idea what he was doing or where he was going. His efforts had been so concentrated on finding a way onto the vessel that he'd given scant regard to what he might achieve if he were successful. He'd come with the hope of finding some evidence to connect Hopper with Ken Longhurst, but with no idea of what that might be he was navigating blind.

His initial thought was to find Hopper's living quarters and with the galley clearly below the waterline, he guessed he needed to ascend a few decks.

He reached a junction between two intersecting corridors, and on a whim, chose to turn right, along a corridor lined with closed doors and illuminated by low-level emergency lighting. The passageway ended at the foot of a wide spiral staircase that appeared to run up through the centre of the yacht, which Trent presumed was used by the staff and crew to service the living quarters above.

Trent stopped at the bottom of the stairs and listened. With the silence punctuated only by the low drone of a generator and the regular slap of waves against the hull, he took his chances and began to ascend. The stairs ended in a spacious hallway, from which, another corridor, lined with thick, cream carpet, extended. There were six doors, three on each side. Trent pushed at each one with light fingers. The first two were locked, but the third was ajar. He eased it open and found an empty, bijou cabin with a double bed under a porthole overlooking the quayside. The bed was undisturbed, with a thick duvet smoothed neatly over a mattress. Trent scanned for luggage, but the room seemed to be unoccupied.

He started to back out of the cabin when he heard an unexpected sound. Muted voices, indistinct under the drone of the generators. Silently pulling the door closed, he listened with head cocked. The sound was coming from the far end of the corridor, and although the life-preserving part of his brain was screaming at him to walk away, his curiosity won over.

Trent tiptoed to the end of the passageway where another corridor crossed it at right angles, and pressed his ear against a door opposite. The voices were clearer. Several people were in conversation, talking in low tones. Trent considered that it might be members of the crew, but dismissed the idea as readily as it occurred to him. At this early hour of the morning, he expected everyone apart from essential staff, such as the security guards, to be asleep. His excitement and trepidation grew as he considered that it might be Larry Hopper himself behind the door.

He shifted his position, and with his legs apart, placed his ear lower down the door, hoping to make out the words being spoken. He laid his hands flat on the smooth oak, and used them to support his weight, balancing precariously, which meant that when the door suddenly swung inwards, Trent stumbled into the room, only just catching himself from falling flat on his face.

'What the hell?' shouted the man behind the desk, jumping to his feet.

Trent's eyes opened wide as he recognised Ken Longhurst. On either side, he noticed two shaven-headed thugs with sneering scowls closing in on him.

'Who are you?' snapped Longhurst.

'Environmental health?' offered Trent, as he regained his balance and tried to reverse out of the room.

'What?'

'I was inspecting the kitchens, but lost my way,' said Trent, his mind working double time on how to escape, regretting the mess his curiosity had landed him in.

'Don't I know you?' Longhurst's eyes narrowed.

'I don't think so,' stammered Trent, a hot flush washing

from his feet to the top of his head. He wiped a sheen of sweat from his brow.

'You're a journalist. I've seen you before.'

'No,' said Trent, suddenly aware of a fourth figure in the room. A portly man was shuffling in his seat in the shadows.

'A journalist? What the hell is he doing on my boat?' Larry Hopper's voice boomed in an American drawl.

The Texan had aged considerably since his photo had appeared in the *Beaumont Messenger*, but he was unmistakable. As he leaned forward into the light, Trent recognised his hoary features. His grey hair was swept over his head, and his thick beard was almost white.

'Deal with it,' Hopper hissed, as he fell back into his chair.

Longhurst snapped his fingers at the two thugs looming at Trent's side. 'Get rid of him,' he ordered.

Chapter 34

A fist to his stomach and a chopping blow across his neck, brought Trent to his knees. He slumped to the floor with the taste of bile in his mouth, fighting a clouding darkness that threatened his vision. Hands grabbed him under the arms, pulled him to his feet, and dragged him from the room. He was aware only of passing along the corridor and descending into the bowels of the yacht.

They dumped him in a chair in a cold, dark room filled with shelves laden with provisions. Mike Clark slipped outside, while Ben Proctor crouched on his haunches in front of the journalist, his eyes bright with a menacing cruelty.

'Who are you? What do you want?' Proctor sneered in Trent's face, his breath musky.

Trent quickly decided that playing ignorant was his best hope of surviving the situation. His eyes fell to the ground, trying to avoid Proctor's intense scrutiny.

'We don't like people who stick their noses in where they're not wanted.' Proctor grabbed Trent's face and squeezed his jaw in a powerful grip. 'What were you looking for?'

With Proctor's hand clasped around his mouth, Trent couldn't answer even if he'd wanted to. He looked beseechingly at his captor, with an expression he hoped conveyed his innocence.

'Tie him up. Let's see if we can loosen his tongue,' said Proctor, as Clark returned to the room.

Clark grabbed Trent's arms and bound his hands

roughly behind his back, pulling the rope so tight that it chaffed the skin around Trent's wrists. Trent tried to pull his arms free, but found the knots were solid and he was completely at the mercy of the two skinheads. Proctor regarded him as a child might consider an ant on a stone. It was almost as if he was contemplating whether to crush him or toy with him. Either way, Trent knew he was in deep trouble.

'What are doing on this boat?'

Trent shook his head and let his chin slump onto his chest. Proctor took a step forward, and drove the heel of his boot down hard on the top of Trent's foot. A lightning bolt seared up his leg and through his body. Trent howled in agony.

'I asked you a question,' Proctor screamed in his face. 'Who are you, and what are you doing on this boat?'

'Nothing,' Trent muttered, trying to fight the pain that consumed every sense.

The heel of Proctor's boot struck again, and Trent was sure he heard the crack of bone in his big toe. His vision blackened and his head swam.

'Let's not play games.' Proctor paced around the chair in a casual circle. 'What's your name?'

'Trent Garside,' he gasped, his short-lived spirit of resistance deserting him.

'Right. Not so difficult was it?'

Mike Clark was propped up against a wall watching with an impassive expression, as if he'd seen it all before.

'What are you doing here?'

'Environmental health.'

'Really?'

Trent nodded, not daring to look Proctor in the eye. He didn't want to antagonise Proctor any further and thought if he kept to his cover story, they'd have to let him go.

'I don't believe you. Perhaps you need a little encouragement to remember the truth.' Proctor snapped his fingers at Clark who looked up, puzzled. 'See what tools you can find in the kitchen.'

Clark jumped off the wall and left the room with a grudging lumber.

'The question is what sort of encouragement do you need.' Trent's pupils grew wide. 'We don't want to leave any visible marks, so that rules out the face. What about the knees? Do you think that would be persuasive enough?'

Before Trent could answer, Proctor drove a clenched fist into his stomach with such force that the chair scraped backwards across the polished floor. Trent coughed and spluttered, gasping for breath.

'Will this do?' asked Clark, as he reappeared whistling nonchalantly and holding up a wooden chopping board and a silver steak tenderising hammer.

'Perfect.'

He handed the items to Proctor and untied Trent's arms.

'Now, which is it to be, pinky or ring finger?' said Proctor, with a sickly smile, as Clark twisted Trent's wrist so that his hand lay flat on the chopping board Proctor had placed on the journalist's thigh.

'Please, God, no,' Trent sobbed.

'Stop being a baby.' Proctor reached for the tenderising mallet and raised it up to his shoulder. With his free hand, he spread Trent's fingers.

'I'll tell you everything you want to know,' Trent blurted. 'I'm a journalist investigating the BFA -' The rest of his sentence stuck in his throat.

'Keep talking,' said Proctor.

'I'm trying to prove a link between the BFA and Larry Hopper.'

Proctor looked blankly at him. 'Who's Larry Hopper?'

Trent frowned, momentarily thrown by Proctor's ignorance. 'The guy who owns this yacht? You were in the room with him just now.'

Proctor shrugged and lowered the mallet. Trent sucked in a lungful of air, relieved that the threat to his hand had receded.

'Well, that wasn't so hard, was it? Now, I think your co-operation deserves a little drink,' said Proctor, sweeping out of the room.

Trent twisted in the chair, clutching his hand. He watched Proctor return with a cheap bottle of cooking brandy. He opened the bottle with his teeth and spat out the cork.

'It'll have to be brandy. It's the best I could do.' Proctor snatched Trent's jaw and prised his mouth open. 'Come on, open up.'

Clark stood behind Trent, and held his head steady with two meaty hands clamped over his ears. Proctor forced the glass bottle between Trent's lips and manipulated his jaw to stop him clamping his teeth shut. The alcohol burned as it hit the back of Trent's throat, causing him to cough and splutter a mouthful over Proctor's T-shirt.

Proctor wiped spittle from his face and attacked Trent's jaw with renewed vigour, ramming the bottle forcefully into his mouth. 'Drink!' he yelled, tipping up the bottle.

Trent gulped the liquid down, trying to ignore how it seared his gullet on its journey to his stomach. Twice he suppressed a compulsion to gag, knowing it would only incense the two thugs.

'Swallow it,' Proctor shouted in his ear, until the brandy dripped from Trent's mouth and stained his shirt.

When he choked on the liquid for a second time, and sprayed brandy across the floor, Proctor punched him in the sternum, knocking Trent's breath from his lungs.

'There's still some left,' said Proctor, holding the bottle up to a strip light on the ceiling. It was still at least half-full. 'Aren't you thirsty?'

It took another ten agonising minutes for Trent to consume the whole bottle. When he was done, his eyes had glazed and his head lolled languorously on his shoulders as the alcohol coursed through his veins. At least it had numbed the pain in his foot, but now a wave of nausea swept through his body, and he couldn't stop himself retching, vomiting a foul pool at Proctor's feet, disappointed to see the skinhead step out of the way just in time.

'Get him some fresh air,' said Proctor. Rough hands pulled him from the chair and dragged him out of the room.

A door opened and a wall of air hit Trent in the face, cool and refreshing after the stuffiness of the storeroom where the odious smell of alcohol-laced vomit hung like a vile fug. He breathed it in through his mouth, momentarily revived as he submitted to the will of the two men dragging his semi-conscious body along a damp gangway.

They came to a halt and stood Trent upright. He swayed and stumbled with no idea or little care as to where he was. He heard water lapping against the hull of the yacht, but was conscious of very little else until he felt hands lifting him off the ground and over a hard edge.

Suddenly, he was plummeting, his heart shocked into working double-time by a spike of adrenaline. His body hit the icy water with a noisy splash, enveloping him in its darkness. His arms and legs thrashed in an uncoordinated effort, driving him farther down into the frigid depths. He forced his eyes open, but in his drunken confusion had no sense of which direction to find the surface.

The pressure on his lungs grew ever stronger, urging him to draw a watery breath until a vice-like grip squeezed his chest and crushed his sternum and spinal column. Eventually, his resistance failed, and his eyes bulged as he drew water deep into his lungs, regretting too late the agony of the liquid drawn deep in his chest. Starved of oxygen, his body became limp and he sank slowly to the bottom of the quay.

Chapter 35

He was standing knee-deep in a lush field of cornflowers, a cool breeze ruffling his hair. Alpine mountains rose like giants, their snow-capped peaks glistening in the rising sun, while wisps of clouds drifted through the azure sky above. At his feet, Trent heard the chirrup of a contented cat. He scooped up a thin tabby tangling herself around his legs.

'Tabitha, what are you doing here?' The cat purred and arched her head to rub against his cheek.

Suddenly, darkness threw its cloak over the day and the fields and mountains vanished. Trent dropped the cat onto the old red carpet of his childhood bedroom. Familiar thick curtains were drawn across the window, but a bright moon allowed his eyes to pick out the furniture; a bookcase full of dog-eared paperbacks, a wardrobe with its handle missing, and his bed with its inviting heap of crumpled bedclothes.

'Trent? Is that you?' His father's voice called from the landing.

'Dad? I'm here -' His mouth formed the words, but he made no sound.

His arm shot above his head, and with a sharp tug, he was pulled upwards, floating up through the ceiling and into the night air where the stars winked and shimmered, out of focus and indistinct.

His head broke the surface of the water, and a strong arm gripped him around the chest and under his arm. A deep chill penetrated him to the core and he felt death's cold breath on his neck.

Something dug into his back as he lay asleep. It woke him from his dreams, but when he tried to roll over, he was overwhelmed by the feeling he was suffocating. He gagged and vomited hard, coughing up lungfuls of water. Trent sucked in a gulp of air, which prompted a further bout of coughing.

Above him, a figure hovered, holding his head, his face a blur. He tried to focus, but the blackness took him again.

Strips of light flashed past with mesmeric regularity. Trent prised open his eyes. He was lying on the back seat of a car, wrapped in a woollen blanket that scratched his neck. It reminded him of childhood, driven in his father's old Jaguar on the long journey home from a trip to his ageing relative. Street lamps scrolling by threw strange shapes over the seat in front, slowly elongating into curious shapes before vanishing.

His head was thumping, and he shivered despite the warmth of the blanket, fighting to suppress the nausea, which came in waves rising from his stomach as his face flushed hot and sweaty. It wasn't helped by the overpowering factory-fresh smell of new plastic and oil. His eyes fell on the silver buckle of a seatbelt, watching as it reflected lights and shapes of unknown objects whistling past and, for a moment, he felt quite calm.

When Trent's eyes flickered open, he found he was in a sterile white room, lying under white sheets and with a wooden veneer table bridging his legs. He tried to push himself up on the pillows, but his ribs were sore and he was connected to an intravenous drip with a looping, transparent tube flowing into a needle protruding from his right hand.

'How are you feeling?' A voice spoke softly from the far side of the room.

'Where am I?'

'You had an accident. You're in hospital.'

Trent squinted at the stranger, who stood and walked towards the bed. 'Who're you?'

'That doesn't matter right now,' said Blake. 'Do you remember anything about last night?'

'Are you a doctor?'

'I pulled you out of the water after you fell from a boat in Canary Wharf. Can you remember anything about it at all? '

Trent shook his head and licked his lips. A memory slowly surfaced. 'The *Clara Barton*?'

'Why were you on board?' Blake poured water into a plastic cup from a jug and handed it to Trent.

'The last thing I remember is hitting the water when they threw me overboard.'

'You were lucky.'

'I don't feel very lucky.'

'You didn't die.'

'I suppose not.'

'So what were you doing on Larry Hopper's yacht?'

'Why all the questions? Are you a copper?'

'I work for the government. It's really important that you try to recall the details.'

'So secret service then?' Blake didn't reply. 'And the fact that you were staking out the yacht means you have the same concerns about Hopper.'

'What concerns?'

'Hopper and the BFA. They're in partnership. You didn't know?'

'Mr Garside, you're an investigative reporter who was unlawfully on board a yacht belonging to an American national in British territorial waters. You were also risking a highly sensitive intelligence operation. I need to know what you were doing and what happened on board, or there could be serious consequences.'

'So what's your interest? Larry Hopper? Or the BFA?'

'We could always arrange to have your body found

floating in the quay as they originally planned and nobody would be any the wiser. I saved your life last night. In return I'm asking for a few straight answers.' Blake dragged the armchair to the side of the bed and sat down. 'Or there are alternative methods I could employ.' The threat was implicit in Blake's tone. Trent swallowed hard. 'You obviously know that the *Clara Barton* is owned by Larry Hopper but what were you hoping to achieve by sneaking on board?'

'Okay, I'll tell you. But it goes no further, right? This is my scoop. I was trying to prove that Hopper is funding the BFA. It's common knowledge that they've benefited from a large injection of cash, right, but the donor's remained anonymous. If it's Hopper, and he's pulling Longhurst's strings, then the public has a right to know. I needed a paper trail, something that links him with Longhurst. So I told the guards I was an environmental health officer to get on board. It was pathetically easy really.'

'Except they caught you before you found anything.'

'That's not true,' said Trent, beginning to enjoy himself. 'I stumbled across Hopper in a meeting, and guess who he was entertaining?'

'Longhurst?'

'It was late, so I was surprised they were still up. I've no idea what the meeting was about, but it doesn't matter. The fact that Longhurst was on that boat is all the proof I need that they're working together.'

'Not necessarily.'

'Come on, it's incontrovertible. Listen, if you like, I can quote you in the piece. What's your name?'

'You can't publish any of this,' said Blake, folding his hands in his lap.

'To hell with you. You can't tell me what I can and can't publish.'

'I can draw up a D-Notice if you want to make it official.'

'This isn't a security issue. Unless you think Hopper's

orchestrating something more than a pay cheque to the BFA?'

'All I'm saying is it wouldn't be helpful right now for Hopper to find out that his friendship with Longhurst is public knowledge. If you wait until I give you clearance to publish, I'll give you the full inside story,' said Blake.

'Seriously? The whole inside track?

Blake said nothing.

'Okay, it's a deal. I'll hold off, but only on the understanding that I get the exclusive later.'

'I'll be in touch,' said Blake, rising from the chair. 'Right now, you need to concentrate on recovering.'

Blake pushed the chair back into the corner of the room and returned to the side of Trent's bed. 'Just one more thing.' He leaned in close and spoke in Trent's ear.

A moment later, the journalist's head slumped onto his chest as he fell into a deep hypnotic trance.

'When you wake up you'll have no recollection of our conversation and no memory that I was in your room. When you're discharged from hospital, you're free to continue your investigations into the BFA, but you won't publish any information about Ken Longhurst or Larry Hopper. Start counting backwards from ten, and when you reach zero you'll be fully awake and feeling refreshed.'

Trent counted down slowly and opened his eyes. He was in a sterile white room, lying in a hard bed under crisp sheets and with a drip attached to the back of his hand. He eased himself up on his elbows, surveyed the empty room, and wondered where the hell he was.

Chapter 36

A veil of low cloud hung over the horizon, showering the landscape with a persistent drizzle and coating the roads with a greasy sheen. The wipers on Blake's Audi swept the windscreen with a metronomic beat, but the screech of rubber on glass was lost among the soft notes and epic crescendos of Faure's Requiem blasting from the speakers. Blake, navigating his way back to Sussex on autopilot, was pre-occupied pondering on the BFA, Larry Hopper, and the information provided by the journalist who'd been captured on board the Texan's super-yacht.

At first, he didn't register the flash of red that hurtled around a blind bend, threatening to spill onto the wrong side of the road. The car was rolling on its suspension, its wheels rumbling over the cat's eyes in the middle of the carriageway.

Blake, whose speed had crept well over the limit, jumped on the brakes and flicked the steering wheel with no panic, training and experience sub-consciously kicking in. The incident would have been a small blip on an otherwise uneventful journey, but for the fact that in the damp conditions, his rear end slid out onto the wet verge, and as the tyres lost traction, the Audi was thrown into a sideways spin. Blake steered expertly into the skid, and with a squeal of protesting tyres, the car came to a juddering halt across the carriageway. A small hatchback flashed past without slowing, accelerating away with black smoke belching from its exhaust, the driver seemingly oblivious to the accident he'd almost caused.

'Idiot!' Blake slammed his palm against the steering wheel.

Instinctively, he noted the number plate, which was partially obscured by mud and dirt, and realised it was the red Renault from Stoneleigh Cottage. He'd expected Proctor and Clark to be lying low at the house, not tearing around the countryside drawing attention to themselves. Something was wrong.

He hit the accelerator hard and set the Audi's front wheels spinning. He over-revved the engine and crashed through the gears, and within a mile had caught up with the Renault. He followed discreetly as it approached a small town and settled into a crawl through heavy traffic.

It pulled up in a narrow space in the half-empty car park of a train station. Proctor emerged in a black top with a hood covering his shaven head. Blake parked and followed him into the concourse, where Proctor bought a ticket from a dispensing machine and caught the next train into London. Blake slipped unseen into the same carriage and chose an aisle seat where he could see the back of Proctor's head.

Proctor sat silently throughout the journey, staring out the window at the changing landscape flashing past, and eventually jumped off at London Bridge, where he was swamped by a crowd of businessmen, students, and tourists. He headed through a ticket barrier onto the Underground and followed signs for the Jubilee Line. Blake trailed him at a distance as he skipped down a slow moving escalator and onto a near-deserted northbound platform.

Blake hung back, waiting for the rush of hot, dirty air from the tunnels that signalled the arrival of a train, and joined an adjacent carriage to where Proctor had slumped into a seat. He kept an eye on his agent through a scratched, square window between the compartments, while hanging onto an overhead strap.

They passed through Waterloo, Westminster, and

Green Park, where an ebbing tide of passengers flowed on and off the train like waves on a beach. Through Bond Street, the crowds eased, but Proctor stayed seated until Dollis Hill, where he finally alighted.

He turned out of the station and onto the corner of a residential street, sauntering past rows of Victorian terraces with a spring in his step that gave the appearance he might actually own the road. His fists were clenched as if in a perpetual rage, and he held his like a libidinous cockerel. A young mother with a pushchair and a toddler in tow deliberately crossed the road to avoid him. There was no doubt about it, Ben Proctor looked like trouble.

He crossed a metal footbridge over a railway line and through a park into a residential estate, then slipped through a gate and into an allotment, a large expanse of open ground where hundreds of plots were meticulously tended.

Blake ducked behind a wooden shed and watched as Proctor pulled out his phone and made a call. He chatted briefly and hung up. Less than a minute later, a man in scruffy jeans, a misshapen woollen jumper, and curls of ginger hair spilling from under a peaked cap appeared. He reached out a hand to greet Proctor, and as they turned to walk away, Blake had a clear view of him.

He was surprised that there was a familiarity about the shape of the eyes, the angle of his nose and the cut of his jaw. Age and a wispy beard had altered his appearance since the last time Blake had seen his face, but he was sure he wasn't mistaken. The only question was what Martin Kelly was doing in the heart of the British capital meeting with a representative from the British Freedom Alliance.

Chapter 37

Proctor remained oblivious to the suspicious looks from a scattering of mud-caked gardeners as Martin Kelly led him along a gravel path through the allotments. With his hood down and his sleeves rolled up revealing a gallery of neo-Nazi tattoos, he looked every part the right-wing fanatic. By contrast, Kelly seemed in his natural environment in his grubby jeans and earth-blackened fingers. Blake had assumed the former IRA bomb maker was long dead. The fact that he was alive and well came as less of a surprise to him than that he had apparently moved to England and was living in obscurity under the noses of the security services.

Kelly remained on MI5's most-wanted list in connection with his suspected part in a number of high profile bombings on the British mainland during the height of the troubles in Northern Ireland. Blake had last seen his picture as a young undercover officer at the start of his Special Forces military career, when his team had come close to locating the explosives expert on at least two occasions, although never close enough to allow the notorious killing squads, whose existence the Army vehemently denied, to target him. As the peace process gained ground and other threats to Britain's security came to prominence, the appetite for bringing Republican terrorists to account waned, and the hunt for Martin Kelly had been quietly forgotten.

The willowy Irishman looked ravaged by years of living on the run, but he still dragged his right leg as he walked, an injury said to have been the legacy of a mishap with an incendiary device that had detonated in his lap. His unmistakable gait was well known by the men who hunted him as a distinguishing feature that couldn't be disguised.

The two men, chatting casually, turned left along a track between a line of plots. They stopped outside a shed with windows masked by sheets of yellowing newspaper. Kelly produced a key from his trouser pocket, and after checking no one was watching, unlocked the door and let Proctor inside.

Blake hunkered down behind an overgrown patch of weeds and long grass and waited. Less than five minutes later, the shed door swung open, and Proctor emerged clutching a sports bag. He looked around nervously, swung the bag over his shoulder, and strode purposefully out of the allotments. Blake gave him two minutes head start then followed at a distance as Proctor retraced his steps back to the Tube station.

At Dollis Hill, Blake jumped on the same carriage as Proctor, fearful of letting his agent, and more importantly the sports bag, out of his sight despite the risk of being recognised. He tried to relax, scanning a discarded copy of a free newspaper that had been abandoned on an adjacent seat, while Proctor sat stony-faced with his back straight and the bag on his lap.

The train swelled with passengers as it edged closer to the centre of the city, but at Baker Street, a bored-sounding voice crackled through the speakers to announce the service would be terminating at the next station because of an unspecified incident on the line. The news was greeted with a collective moan. Blake made a quick calculation that they'd need to pick up the Central Line to Bank and switch to the Northern Line to make it back to London Bridge station. A simple detour, but one that meant mingling with crowds, and an increased risk of losing his mark.

When the train rolled to a halt at Bond Street, Proctor

was quickly on his feet. He pushed his way out of the carriage, and hustled towards an exit signposted for the Central Line, with Blake fixed on the back of his head bobbing above a throng of confused passengers.

The crowds made it impossible to rush, and Blake was able to keep Proctor easily within in his sights as he shuffled through a network of tunnels and escalators to reach a platform swarming with passengers. Two trains arrived within minutes of each other, filling until they were fit to burst with people crammed into every space. Proctor and Blake made it onto the third train, jostled onto the same carriage more by luck than judgement.

When the doors glided closed, Blake strained to see around the sweaty bodies and spotted Proctor at the far end of the compartment, standing with his neck crooked under the curve of the ceiling, and clutching the bag tightly to his chest.

By the next stop, the heat generated by so many bodies packed into such a confined space had become unbearable. The air was heavy and beads of sweat dripped down Blake's back. He planted his feet firmly on the floor to brace himself against the constant lurching as the train slowed and accelerated through rapid turns, but a tangle of strangers' legs and bags prevented him from repositioning more comfortably. He counted down the seconds until they reach the next station, when the doors would openly briefly and provide a burst of cooler air. His only consolation was that he could see Proctor clearly, and remained close enough to the door to hop off if Proctor made a dash for it.

Eventually, the train slowed and came to a halt at Oxford Circus, where the station was lined at least five deep. Blake gripped an overhead leather handle and held himself upright as the momentum sent a crush of people falling on him. The door against his shoulder grumbled open and he was hit by a refreshing breeze. A few hopefuls waiting on the platform attempted to push their way on board, but were rebuffed with militant bad humour. The doors sighed closed and the train moved off again.

The same thing happened at the next station, and again at Holborn where the despairing faces of those waiting looked at those shoehorned into the carriage with envy. Blake's eyes fell on a blonde woman at the back of the platform with a faraway look in her eye. The merest hint of make-up cleverly amplified her natural beauty, and Blake found himself transfixed.

As if sensing his gaze, she looked at him briefly, but glanced away as she caught his eye, finding interest in scanning the length of the train instead. Her focus fell on the mid-section of Blake's carriage where Proctor was standing. She stared intently, her mouth dropping open and her expression changing. The faraway serenity Blake had read a moment before faded and her eyes widened, her previous calm composure evaporating. Then, as the doors banged closed, she lunged forward, pushing and shoving her way through the crowd, screaming a piteous howl that cut through the rattle and hum of the train pulling away.

Inside the carriage, everyone turned to stare, but quickly lost interest. The seasoned London travellers had seen it all before, and worse. Just another crackpot losing their grip on reality. They were only glad it wasn't their problem.

The woman's palm slapped the window by Blake's head, and she was knocked sideways off her feet, crashing into a bemused family of Japanese tourists. Blake tried to make out the words she was screeching but all he heard was a pitiful howl and then the train was plunged into the darkness of a tunnel and her screams faded away.

Chapter 38

Lucy Chapman rubbed her eyes and succeeded only in making them sorer. The air in the carriage was thick with the dirt from the city, and she remembered why she usually avoided the Tube. At least she had managed to find a seat and hadn't had to endure standing huddled against a stranger's sweaty armpit.

A young black woman, with ludicrously long, painted fingernails and her hair in elaborate plaits sitting opposite, was tapping away at a mobile phone. She was plugged into a pair of earphones that produced a fast, tinny beat and never once looked up until the train pulled up at her stop.

Lucy absentmindedly touched the handle of her flight case by her feet, and wondered what her husband was doing. The previous two days they'd barely spoken, and sat in an uncomfortable silence on the long flight home, both bearing the sort of seething resentment that buried into the soul. She had stormed off at the airport shortly after their return to the U.K.

The trip to Brazil had been a disaster. It had cost them a small fortune, and although Lucy hated to admit it, Peter was right. They had been conned by their taxi driver, and hadn't found a single genuine clue about her brother's disappearance. The stress it had put on their marriage had exposed the fragile cracks in their relationship. The tension between them had finally exploded in an almighty row in their hotel room forty-eight hours earlier. Not the sort of row that cleared the air, but the sort in which home truths, better left unsaid, were hurled around like emotional bombs, and which had only served to deepen their resentment of each other.

After landing at Heathrow, Peter had made an attempt at a reconciliation, but Lucy was tired and emotionally spent.

'Lucy, I'm sorry if I've upset you. Let's talk about it,' he had implored, as they stood at a luggage carousel watching the slow procession of other people's battered cases.

'I think we're probably past talking,' she had hissed back at him.

'Come on, it doesn't have to be like this.' He had tried putting his arm around her shoulder, but she had shrugged it off like a petulant child. 'Just...don't!'

'I want to find Nick as much as you do, but you have to be realistic.'

'Do you, Peter? Do you really want to find Nick as much as I do, because you sure as hell don't act like it.'

'Of course I do, it's just - '

'It's just what? Costing you too much? Taking up too much of your precious time?'

'Of course not. But we've got our lives to live too. We can't put everything on hold to find Nick when he might well be - '

Peter had stopped himself saying it, but they had both known what he'd meant. He broke his wife's gaze and scanned the conveyor belt for any sign of their cases.

'When he might well be dead?'

'It's a possibility, but not one that you're even willing to contemplate. I'm sorry, it's an awful thing to have to think, but you have to accept it, for your own sanity, if nothing else.'

'Screw you, Peter!' Lucy had screamed at her husband, before grabbing her cabin bag and marching off towards the arrivals hall.

'Lucy! Where are you going?'

'I can't be around you right now. I'll stay with mum or something. Don't try to get in touch.'

She had left him standing like an abandoned puppy, with his big, doleful eyes staring after her. She had been surprised he hadn't put up more of an effort to stop her going, but she realised now that she had made her feelings quite plain.

The arrivals hall had been bustling with passengers loaded up with bags, but nobody had noticed the petite, blonde sobbing quietly to herself in a corner. They all had places to be, loved ones to greet, lost in their own personal worlds, with no time or inclination to worry about someone else's problems. Lucy fished out her mobile phone from her bag and called the only person she could turn to.

'Are you back? How did the trip go?' The sound of her mother's voice triggered more tears. 'Lucy, darling, what's wrong?'

'Can I come home for a few days and stay with you?' she sobbed down the line.

'Of course. What is it, sweetheart?'

'Nothing, mum, - I'll tell you when I see you. I'll be there in a few hours.'

Three noisy youths joined the carriage and fell into the seats beside Lucy, laughing and joking crudely. Perched on the edge of her seat, she counted off the stations.

Earls Court.

Gloucester Road.

Knightsbridge.

Hyde Park Corner.

The boys finally stood up and disembarked at Green Park, much to Lucy's relief. A middle-aged man and woman quickly took their seats. He was dressed in a sombre blue suit and cream raincoat. She was immaculately turned out in a long, flowing dress.

Piccadilly Circus.

Leicester Square.

Covent Garden.

One more stop. By now, the train had filled to bursting as they swept through some of the city's most famous landmarks.

As the train pulled into Holborn, Lucy struggled up with her flight bag and forced her way through a throng in the doorway. She slipped out onto the platform, straightened her dress, and followed signs for the Central Line as the train rumbled away behind her.

She was disheartened to find her platform crammed solid with people, and the mood turning ugly. She watched four trains stop, each packed tightly with passengers gasping for air as the doors opened and closed a few seconds later. But she was in no rush, and hung towards the back of the platform, unwilling to join the crush. Announcements kept coming, apologising for the busy trains, and explaining about a problem at Green Park, but it did little to quell the mood of frustration.

By contrast, Lucy felt an unexpected calm. She had needed time alone and, ironically, being in the centre of a large crowd gave her the isolation to think things through. There was nothing quite like a horde of strangers to focus the mind and allow a certain introspection.

She checked her watch and considered her options. She could take a taxi, but she was short on cash. There was always the bus, but she had no idea which one to catch, or even where to find the right stop. She could walk to another station, maybe even pick up another line, and try a different route. But that would mean dragging her bag through the crowds. So she resolved to give it another ten minutes.

Another train arrived and departed taking with it a few lucky individuals who managed to squeeze on board. Three more trains, she told herself, then she'd give up.

Lucy peered at the faces looking thoroughly miserable. If anything, there was less room than on the previous train. She accidentally caught the eye of one man who was staring her way. He was tall and rugged, with dark brooding eyes and an impassive expression.

She looked away quickly, glancing along the rest of the carriage with morbid fascination at the desperate expressions. The mid-section seemed worst. Passengers' necks were craning around each other's arms and the windows dripped with condensation. Pressed into the door was a man with a shaven head holding a sports bag to his chest. He rolled his neck as if to ease the tension in his muscles, and she saw his face in profile. A familiar face. He turned to look out onto the platform. Their eyes locked for an instant, and Lucy felt as though an arrow had struck her in the chest.

'Oh my God,' she muttered under her breath as the train lurched forward. 'Nick!' she cried out.

She dropped her bag and threw herself into the melee of ill-tempered passengers, fighting and bustling her way forwards.

'Nick! Nick! Nick!' she wailed like a banshee.

The crowd parted in horrified bewilderment. She reached out for the carriage, not really knowing what she was doing. Her hand slapped the glass and she was pitched sideways, thrown to her knees.

When she picked herself up, the train was already disappearing into the tunnel, its taillights twinkling in the darkness, and from deep within her chest, a heart-wrenching sob rose up.

Chapter 39

A roll of posters poked out of the bag slung casually over Lucy Chapman's shoulder. It was early evening, and large numbers of people were coming and going through Holborn Underground station in the Kingsway. Many were distracted by their phones, either staring into their screens or talking with the device clamped to their ear, all lost in their own little worlds, somehow negotiating their way without looking or talking to each other.

Lucy stood at the side of a kiosk selling newspapers and confectionery, watching people's faces, and wondering where to begin. She had planned to put up posters around the station, but her middle-class self-consciousness rendered her temporarily paralysed. She didn't even know if it was legal to put them up on the streets of the capital. Mind you, there were plenty of others around, torn and faded, mostly advertising nightclubs and live music events. At least hers would be for a worthwhile cause. She decided to take her chances as the crowds seemed to thin momentarily.

She stepped assertively across the pavement, and approached a building adjacent to the station with granite walls that towered high above the tree-lined street. She placed a poster over a defaced purple notice advertising DJs she'd never heard of, appearing on dates that had long since passed. She fixed it in place with four strips of sticky tape and stepped back to check it was straight.

'Excuse me, madam.' The voice over her shoulder made her jump.

She whirled around ready with her excuse, fearing she was about to be chastised, and was surprised to be confronted by the grinning face of a tall man in a bright yellow jacket and dreadlocks tucked up inside a knitted beanie hat.

'How are you this evening?' he asked, with a wide smile. She noticed he was clutching a clipboard. 'You know, you remind me of someone. You look just like Gwyneth Paltrow.'

Lucy stared at him with bemusement, wondering if he was making a pass at her.

'Yeah, you know you've got her eyes.' He leaned backwards, and to one side, as if to better gauge the contours of her face. 'Yeah, definitely, man. You're a dead ringer.'

Lucy coyly tucked a strand of blonde hair behind her ear and looked down at her shoes.

'Now let me ask you, do you donate to charity because we're out this evening talking to people about this really special work that's being done to combat cancer.'

'I beg your pardon?'

'Did you know that for just three pounds a month - ' His voice trailed off. 'Hey, what's that?' He pointed to her poster.

'That?' said Lucy, blushing. 'I'm looking for my brother, Nick. I saw him on the Tube the other day, and I thought someone might know where he is. It's stupid really, but...'

She had scanned one of favourite pictures of Nick into her computer and enlarged it to fill up most of an A4 side of paper. Above Nick's face, she had typed 'MISSING' in a bold font. Underneath, she had added, 'Can you help find my brother?' and included her name and her mobile number. She had worried about publicising her contact details in a city that had its fair share of cranks and creeps, but decided it was a risk worth taking.

The man with the dreadlocks took a step closer to examine the poster more thoroughly.

'Oh, man - that's tough. How long's he been missing?'

'Several months. We thought he'd gone travelling in Brazil, and they tried to tell me he was dead then - . Sorry, this sounds so silly now I say it out loud, but I saw him on the train. I didn't know what to do. I've put some adverts in the Standard but that's turned out to be quite expensive. You probably think I'm mad.'

'Bummer. You must be out of your mind with worry?'

There was an uncomfortable silence between them, which Lucy eventually found the need to interrupt. 'I'm sorry about the charity thing, I can't really afford - ' Lucy began to apologise.

'Hey, no worries. That's not important compared to this. The name's Rory.' He held out a hand by way of introduction.

'Lucy.'

Rory nodded to her bag. 'You want a hand with the rest of those?'

'No, really, it's okay,' she said, not really meaning it.

'Come on, it won't take half as long if we both do it. Here you go,' he made a grab for the roll of posters, and she didn't resist.

'Hey, Letitia,' he called to a woman dressed in a similarly bright jacket hovering around the entrance of the station. She wandered over and listened with interest to the story of Lucy's missing brother.

'Right, give me some of those,' she said, taking a clutch of posters. 'Have you got some tape?'

Lucy handed Letitia the roll, and watched as she fixed Nick's image to the side of a redundant red telephone box.

'This really is terribly kind.'

'Don't mention it. To be honest, it's a welcome break,' said Rory.

Within fifteen minutes, Nick's face had been plastered over most of the available surfaces immediately outside the station. In a couple of places, Letitia had even created a montage, putting the posters into a large rectangle, four across, and four high.

As Lucy stood back to watch Rory hang the last poster, she was overcome by the spontaneity of their help. For the first time in a long while she didn't feel alone, and with so many images of Nick's face now visible around the station, she felt certain it would only be a matter of time before he was found.

Chapter 40

The return journey to Sussex on the over ground train was far less stressful. The carriage Proctor found was a little more than half-full, with plenty of free seats. Blake sat four rows back, stretched out his legs, and lifted his face into the stream of cooled air pumped out from a vent over his head. He could have easily fallen asleep, allowing the gentle rocking to send him into a deep slumber as they picked up speed through the outskirts of the city and into the countryside. But he daren't let his eyes slide closed, even for a second.

Twenty minutes into the trip, Proctor rose from his seat. He collected the sports bag from under his legs, and stumbled along the gangway. Blake pretended to be absorbed in the view from the window. He counted to ten and followed as Proctor walked the length of three carriages and ducked into an empty toilet cubicle. As he tried to close the door, Blake barged in and they fell clumsily into a tiny bathroom that was hardly big enough for them both. When Blake straightened up, he found himself nose-to-nose with Proctor.

'Hello, Ben,' he said, with a disarming grin, pulling the door closed.

'What the hell?'

'Sleep now.' Blake tapped him three times on the shoulder, and his eyelids fluttered shut. 'You're safe here. Nothing bad is going to happen. Relax and sleep deeply.'

Proctor's head rolled onto his chest, and Blake sat him on the toilet bowl.

'We don't have much time.' Blake made himself as comfortable as he could, perched on the edge of a small basin. 'I need to know what's in the bag.' The holdall had fallen to the floor, and Blake prodded it with his foot.

'My bag,' said Proctor, through a sleepy haze.

'I know, Ben. I need to take a look inside.' Blake bent over awkwardly and hooked it off the floor. He placed it on Proctor's lap and opened the zip. It was packed with ten rectangular blocks, like children's modelling clay, wrapped in clear plastic. He raised an eyebrow and held one of the blocks under Proctor's nose. 'Semtex?'

Proctor nodded wearily.

'Now what would you be wanting with Semtex, Ben?'

'For the ferry,' said Proctor, his voice devoid of emotion.

Blake blinked hard, unsure if he'd heard correctly. 'What ferry?'

'The one to France.'

'Where?'

'Dover.'

Blake sucked the air through his teeth. 'Who's idea was that?'

'Ken wants us to do it. He said it was time to act after the soldier was killed. We have to do something to make people realise our controls on foreigners are a joke.'

Blake carefully replaced the block of Semtex and closed the holdall. 'When did he give you the orders?'

'On the boat.'

'In Canary Wharf?'

Proctor nodded.

'You realise what he's asking you to do? If you go through with this, you'll kill hundreds of innocent British nationals. How does that help the BFA's cause?'

'Dover's the soft underbelly of immigration. Ken says we have to make the people understand before it's too late.'

'He's insane.'

The men were suddenly pitched into darkness, and the carriage shuddered violently. Proctor's limp body rolled to one side, and Blake braced himself against the walls as a change in air pressure pressed against his inner ear. The shadow of a train passing in the opposite direction flickered past the window, the rush of air and clatter of metal filling the bathroom with noise. And then it was gone.

Blake sat Proctor up straight. 'Tell me what happened on the *Clara Barton*, the boat in Canary Wharf.'

'Ken wanted us to meet him there.'

'Was anyone else on board?'

Proctor screwed up his face as if he was struggling to recall. 'An American.'

'Did you find out his name?'

'No.'

'Well, what did he look like?'

'He was big, I mean not tall but fat. With a bushy beard, and a weird accent, as if he was from the Deep South.'

'Larry Hopper,' said Blake.

Proctor didn't react to the name. He wasn't surprised. It was unlikely that Longhurst would have risked revealing Hopper's identity to his two henchmen.

They were interrupted by a loud rap on the door.

'Just a minute,' Blake called out. 'So what's the plan for getting the explosives on board the ferry?'

'We have to plant a bomb in a car and drive it on board. Martin Kelly told me how to pack the Semtex around the wheel arches and showed me how to set a timer.'

Blake caught his own reflection in the mirror above the sink, and noticed his gaunt expression. Too little sleep. Too much stress. He rubbed a hand over his face. 'You've done really well, Ben. One last thing. Do you have a date for the attack?'

Proctor shook his head. 'Ken will tell us when he's

ready. We have to wait.'
   'Wait for what?'
   'I don't know.'

Chapter 41

'Heather, can you fix a meeting with the deputy director general. As soon as possible.'

'I'll see if he can fit you in later this week.'

'I mean right now,' said Harry Patterson. 'I'm on my way up there now. It's urgent.' He slammed the phone down, shut his laptop, and grabbed his jacket from the hanger on the back of his door. He took the stairs two at a time, pulling on his jacket as he went.

Twenty minutes later, he was sitting in the DDG's office in the strategically-placed chair in front of Sir Richard's desk.

'This had better be worth it, Patterson,' said Sir Richard, adjusting his cuffs. 'I've just walked out of a meeting with our French counterparts.'

'I've heard from Blake and I thought you'd want to know straightaway.'

'Go on.'

'He's found evidence of a credible plot being planned on British soil.'

'How credible?'

'They're planning to target a cross-Channel ferry. They've already acquired enough Semtex to blow open the bow, and now they're waiting on a date to strike.'

Sir Richard sat back in his chair and blew out his cheeks. 'Who's behind it?'

'The order's come specifically from Ken Longhurst.'

'It doesn't make sense. If they hit a ferry, they'll likely take hundreds of British lives. It would be a massive own goal.'

'Not if the Phineas Priests claim responsibility. Longhurst will condemn the attack, of course, but will use it to demand that the government tightens up border controls. No doubt, the home secretary will feel compelled to come out on the defensive, but Longhurst will be the one sympathetically whimpering about lost lives and the imperative to protect the rights of British citizens. You can see how this could propel him further forward in the opinion polls, while the Home Office is left squirming on the back foot.'

'Are you sure about this? It's a monstrous idea.'

'Blake's evidence is unequivocal, I'm afraid. But there's more. We believe the BFA and this plot in particular is being funded and co-ordinated with American finances.'

The DDG's eyes opened wide. 'Can this get any worse?'

'Longhurst has been holding meetings with Larry Hopper, the Texan oilman. It appears that he's co-ordinating the action and has approved the attack in the Channel. Our inside man was in the room when the order was given.'

'What's an American oilman doing getting involved with this sort of business?'

'He's suspected of co-ordinating similar attacks in the U.S. He's on the FBI watch list although no one's ever been able to pin any charges on him. This could be our chance to nail him.'

'We'd better alert the FBI,' said Sir Richard, reaching for the phone on his desk. 'Any idea of how long we have to stop them? If we can round them up and bring them in - '

'Sir, please don't make that call right now. Blake says the date's imminent, but they're waiting on the word from Longhurst. We need a little time to extract our man. We have to come up with a plan without blowing his cover.'

Sir Richard replaced the handset and took a moment to

consider. 'I understand. But the moment you get the merest hint of a date for this thing I want to know. Is that clear? In the meantime, we'll put surveillance on Longhurst and Hopper.'

'Hopper's due to speak at the Oxford Union in a couple of days. Not exactly keeping a low profile.'

'The Union? Christ, they'll let anyone speak there these days. This is good work, Patterson.'

'Thank you, sir, but most of it's down to Blake.'

Chapter 42

Larry Hopper gripped the edges of a wooden lectern tightly, trying to ignore the beads of perspiration on his brow. He had already run the gauntlet of protesters gathered outside the Oxford Union, but had expected the reception inside the chamber to be warmer. He was disappointed that the students were treating him with what could at best be described as coldness and at worst downright hostility.

'We are a society that has lost its way,' he had begun, only briefly glancing at his notes. 'We have lost sight of our guiding principles, and that is why Christians are finding their voice again.'

The debating chamber was packed, but it wasn't the numbers that made him uncomfortable. He was used to large crowds, but in the States his speeches were usually greeted with an evangelical fervour. Here his words were being met with stony expressions.

He'd been asked to speak about the Christian Right, and the reason for the momentum it had gained in America, a subject in which Hopper was well versed, and a fine opportunity to spread the word to an audience across the Atlantic.

'Our nation's founding fathers built our laws and standards for American society based on the principles laid out in the pages of the Bible.' Hopper delivered his words slowly, taking long pauses for effect.

Although it was the first time he'd spoken outside America, he'd been delighted to accept the invitation to appear at the Union, the world's most prestigious debating society. Founded in 1823 as part of Oxford University, it had proved a unique training ground for many of Britain's politicians and prime ministers. Its regular debates dated back to the 1870s and have been held under the watchful eyes of former prime ministers Edward Heath and William Gladstone who are immortalised in stone busts in a red-walled hall off Cornmarket Street where audiences sat in rows of dark wooden benches finished with plush red leather.

International names from politics, religion, science, sport, and even Hollywood have been invited to speak, often to great media fanfare. Former American presidents Richard Nixon, Jimmy Carter, and Ronald Reagan, actors Johnny Depp and Clint Eastwood, footballer Diego Maradona and even popstar Michael Jackson had all spoken at the Union. And it was with the weight of this knowledge that Hopper spoke with the gravitas he believed his subject deserved.

'The U.S. has developed into the most powerful country in the world - a utopia of democracy and high living standards that has become the envy of the world. But the dreadful attacks perpetrated on American soil on nine-eleven opened our eyes and made us see that all was not well, that there were individuals willing to take the most extreme actions to destroy our way of life, to crush our ideals and beliefs - the ideals and beliefs that have made America great. It taught many ordinary Americans, the good folk who live their lives abiding by the law of God that things had changed under their very noses. We recognised that Liberal leftism had opened a door that allowed the enemy to walk right into our living rooms.'

As the Texan's voice boomed and echoed around the hall, he surveyed his audience, observing the hundreds of pairs of eyes staring back at him.

'Franklin D Roosevelt once famously said that the only thing we have to fear, is fear itself. But we had become paralysed by fear - the fear of admitting that we were Christians and proud of it. But let me say again that our great country was founded on the Bible - the Bible that built America. And you, the future leaders and opinion makers of England and Britain, with whom we have such strong bonds, should sit up and take note because I see the same attacks that I've witnessed on America's foundations happening here.'

Hopper paused, trying to evoke a sense of drama. But the eyes in the room looked back at him only with scepticism. The Texan took a spotted handkerchief from his trouser pocket and mopped his brow.

'In your very own country, I have read stories of good, decent Christians who have been banned from wearing their crosses - the ultimate sign of goodness. In what sort of world can that be right? And yet this is a country where Muslim teachers are allowed to be covered from head to foot with not even their faces visible. Why? Because Liberal politics tells you that you can't stand up for what you believe in - that in a free society it's simply wrong to allow women to be subjugated, no matter what their beliefs might be in their own societies. If they want to live in a free democracy they must fall into line with a free democracy's beliefs.'

At the precise moment, as Hopper began to get into his stride, he sensed the audience bristle. There were mutterings among small groups towards the back of the hall, but he pressed on.

'The Bible is the cornerstone of our society, our Christian principles, and our very way of life. It shouldn't be threatened as it has been. Without the principles of the Bible, who is going to defend the rights of the unborn child against the murdering abortionists?' Hopper slammed his palm on the lectern, but it failed to drown out the sound of a collective drawing in of breath. To his left, the chairman of the Union was looking decidedly awkward.

'And who is going to protect the sanctity of marriage?

We, in the Western World, are a multicultural society built on many different colours, and we welcome everyone with open arms.' Hopper's eyes fell on a young Asian woman in a hijab. She looked at him with daggers, and Hopper quickly glanced away to check his notes.

'But we as Christians say that if you come to live with us you must live by our laws, by our standards, by our principles without favour or prejudice! And those governing principles are sacrosanct. We will not tolerate abortion. Every child from the moment of creation is a gift from God, and only God's will has the power to take that child from this earth. Marriage between a man and a woman is at the heart of a decent family, and we contest the only institution fit for raising our children. We absolutely reject gay marriage as an abomination.'

From somewhere near the back of the room, an unseen figure began to heckle. 'Nazi! Get off!'

Hopper pressed on. 'And it starts by bringing our educational system back under our control. Children should be taught a Christian curriculum, and books with anti-biblical language banned.'

'You're no better than Hitler!' another voice piped up, receiving a few muted expressions of support.

'Without God, there is no right and no wrong,' Hopper tried to continue, but more and more voices began shouting out. Hopper stood resolutely, his chest pumped out.

'Racist!'

'Bigot!'

The chairman rose to his feet to plead for calm, urging the students to allow Hopper to continue, but the insults continued to be hurled. Then a few disgusted individuals stood and walked out.

'Please, calm down. Show some respect for our guest!' the chairman shouted, but his voice was drowned out by a slow handclap, which had started to the right of Hopper and spread through the hall, gaining volume and resonance as it went. For a few seconds, the oilman stood rooted to the spot, unsure how to react. The chairman gave him an apologetic look, but the situation was rapidly getting out of control.

'Out! Out! Out!' a chant rose above the hand clapping.

Two thick-set minders took that as their cue to intervene and marched in to usher Hopper out. And as he reached the exit, a loud cheer rose up.

Hopper was whisked out of a rear entrance, surrounded by his security men, to where a black people carrier was waiting with its engine already running. Hopper collapsed into the back seat next to Ken Longhurst.

'Well, that didn't go so well,' said Hopper, as the door slammed shut and the car pulled away.

The driver had no choice but to take them through the group of protesters who were still gathered at the front of the building. Although they couldn't see Hopper and Longhurst in the back seats through the one-way glass, word had already spread that the speech had been abandoned and that Hopper had fled. They knew it was his car and as it slowed to give way to traffic, they surrounded it, banging on the roof and windows. Snarling faces pressed up against the window, their eyes full of anger and hatred.

'Get us out of here, driver,' Hopper demanded, and the car sped off into the night.

Chapter 43

A grainy image appeared on a flat-screen television on a wall at the end of a darkened room. Six pairs of eyes watched as the camera moved unsteadily like a poorly shot home movie.

'Are you picking this up?' Blake's voice hissed through the speakers.

'We're seeing pictures, Blake, and hearing you loud and clear.' The DDG, two senior anti-terror security officers, and two Met Police officers in uniform had joined Patterson around a conference table at MI5 headquarters.

As Blake steadied his phone, the camera picked out a number of greasy tools laid out on a bench inside a garage workshop. Wrenches, spanners, and industrial-looking containers of fluids, illuminated by the light of Blake's head torch.

'As I'm sure Harry's explained, we tracked the two Phineas Priest suspects to this garage where we believe they have been preparing two vehicles in readiness for an attack on a cross-Channel ferry.' Blake spoke in a hushed whisper.

As the senior team had assembled in the briefing room, Blake had been breaking into the garage through a bathroom window at the back of the building, located in a rundown industrial estate on the outskirts of Crawley, a stone's throw from Gatwick Airport. White walls supported a pitched roof clad in corrugated asbestos that had been blackened by the elements, and two ancient-looking fuel pumps stood on the forecourt below a towering sign displaying the price of diesel and unleaded.

Once inside the bathroom, Blake had picked his way into an office where two desks were buried under swathes of oil-stained paperwork. An internal window ran behind the farthest desk and overlooked an adjacent workshop. A glass-panelled door marked 'staff only' had been left unlocked.

An overpowering odour of paint fumes hung thick in the air of the workshop. Blake fixed his head torch and switched on the camera on his phone before making contact with Patterson via a Bluetooth earpiece.

'This evening, the first suspect, Ben Proctor, left the BFA safe house carrying the sports bag he collected from the IRA bomb maker, Martin Kelly,' Blake continued. 'We have evidence that it contains in the region of two kilos of Semtex. His accomplice, Mike Clark, has been missing for around three days, whereabouts unknown.'

Apart from Patterson and the DDG, no one else in the room was aware of Proctor's identity as an MI5 undercover agent. For Proctor's safety, Blake was keen to keep it that way.

He turned to his right, and the pictures blurred momentarily as the lens struggled to keep up with the movement.

'The first of the two vehicles we think they intend to use is this Mercedes Sprinter van, which has recently been resprayed.' Blake touched the bodywork with his index finger, and turned his hand over to show the camera, the tip of his finger stained with a reddish smear.

At his feet, he focussed the camera on a coil of cable attached to a spray gun. Then he gave his audience a three hundred and sixty degree tour around the vehicle.

'Unfortunately, all the doors are locked so I can't check inside, but I'll take some pictures so everyone can ID the van later.'

'We're getting that very clearly,' said Patterson. 'What about the number plates? Have they been replaced?'

'The screws look intact.' Blake read out the registration plate number for Patterson to take a note. 'I'm assuming it's stolen so it should come up on a police database. But this is possibly the more significant vehicle.'

Blake pointed his phone at a nine-year-old blue Ford saloon that had been raised off its front wheels on jacks.

'I suspect this is the car they're planning to use for the bomb. It's a Ford Mondeo, and as anonymous as they come. There must be thousands of cars like this one on the road.'

Its paintwork was scratched and faded in keeping with a vehicle of its age, and unlike the van, there had been no attempt to alter its appearance. Blake tried the handle of the passenger door, but found it locked.

'This is interesting,' said Blake, the excitement in his voice apparent even through his whispered tones. He pointed the camera at the ground, and when the image focussed, the men watching saw a discarded sports bag lying in the corner by a pile of old tyres.

'The bag Proctor picked up from Kelly?' asked Patterson.

'It looks like it.' Blake scooped it up one-handed. 'The last time I was able to take a close look, it was full of Semtex. It's empty now,' he said, tipping it upside down and shaking it to prove his point.

Blake dropped to his knees and shone his torch under the chassis of the car, training the camera along its beam. Then he examined the front of the car where the wheels had been removed, the circular brake drum and rusty suspension coils clearly visible.

'Here we go,' said Blake. 'I count five blocks. Can you see?'

He turned the camera towards the clay bricks that had been neatly packed into the wheel arches. Blake reached up and prised one of the blocks free. It was heavier than he had expected, and when he turned it over, he discovered that a large magnetic block of metal had been buried in it.

He re-attached the block and scanned the others for a detonator. He found it attached to the middle brick. A coil of wire was taped neatly along the inside of the bodywork and disappeared inside the engine housing. He shuffled around to the passenger side, and found five more bricks in the other wheel arch with another wire snaking up through the front end of the vehicle.

Inside the car, blue plastic sheets had been draped over the seats to protect the fabric. Blake's torch beam picked out the glove compartment, which had been open. He could just make out thin wires protruding through the opening, their ends attached to a mobile phone in a cradle on the dashboard.

'It appears that they've rigged up a rudimentary detonation device that's triggered by a mobile phone signal. My guess is that it requires a call or text message to set off the blast,' said Blake.

'Excellent work, thank you, Blake,' said the deputy director general, speaking for the first time.

Blake glanced at his watch. He'd been in the workshop for a full twelve minutes. He'd given himself fifteen minutes to be in and out. It was time to leave.

'I don't want anything going wrong on this operation to jeopardise the good work that's been done in the field already,' said the DDG in Blake's ear. 'I want these bastards nailed.'

'Sir, I need to get going,' Blake interjected, heading back towards the office and checking he'd not left any evidence of his visit. But a noise outside caused him to freeze and kill the torch. The screen on the wall in Thames House went blank.

'Blake?' said Patterson. 'What's going on?'

'There's someone coming.'

It sounded as though a car had pulled up outside the workshop. Blake heard a door open. He clicked off his phone and shoved it in his pocket.

Footsteps tapped across the forecourt, and keys rattled

in a lock. Blake scuttled around the van looking for a place to hide, realising if someone came into the workshop he'd be discovered in an instant. With nowhere to take cover, he opted to crouch behind the rear of the vehicle and watch the office from the shadows.

The main door to the office was thrown open and the overhead lights buzzed on, flooding the room in stark, white light. A man headed for one of the desks, and Blake watched him rifle through some papers. He whistled a familiar tune that Blake couldn't place, and turned his attention to a row of filing cabinets along the back wall.

Blake edged backwards, deeper into the darkness until he bumped into a workbench. When he put a hand out to steady himself, it fell on a sheet of vinyl, cool and smooth to the touch. His hand recoiled as the office lights went out and the office door slammed shut. A car door opened, thudded closed, and an engine coughed into life.

As Blake listened to the vehicle pull away, he felt the tension ebb from his body. He flicked on the torch and shone it on the workbench where his hand had fallen. It was covered in colourful sheets of letters and numbers that he'd not paid attention to before. They looked like decals used for sign writing on vehicles. And a dawning realisation hit him.

Chapter 44

The Rose and Crown was an old-fashioned type of pub, with no jukebox and absolutely no fruit machines with their irritating tunes and flashing lights. It was exactly the sort of place Pete French was drawn to, especially as they knew how to keep good beer. It had become his regular haunt, near the newsroom and on his way home. Trent found him at the bar hunched over a newspaper, nursing a half-finished pint. Trent hobbled over, laid his crutches on the floor, and eased himself up onto a stool.

'Thought I'd find you in here.'

'It's where I usually am,' said Pete, glancing up from his paper. 'What happened to your leg?'

'It's a long story.'

'Anything to do with the BFA by any chance?'

'Is it that obvious?'

'So you've made some progress then?'

'A little,' said Trent.

'And Hopper?'

'I've had the pleasure of his company, albeit rather briefly.'

'You've met him?'

Trent pulled a knowing grin. 'I managed to get on board his yacht.'

Pete folded his paper closed and gave his friend his full attention. 'How?'

'You know, a little improvisation, a dash of imagination.'

'You managed to blag your way on board Larry

Hopper's super-yacht in the middle of Canary Wharf? Genius! So what went wrong?'

'I got caught and they threw me over the side.'

Pete laughed hysterically, but stopped when he realised his friend wasn't seeing the funny side. 'You're okay now though? I mean, apart from the leg?'

'It'll heal.'

'Christ, Trent, you're lucky they didn't kill you.'

'I think that was actually the idea,' said Trent.

'And you confronted Hopper?'

'More like I stumbled across him. He was entertaining a friend.'

'Don't tell me Longhurst was on board too?'

Trent nodded and took a gulp of beer.

'You're kidding?'

'They were holding some sort of conference. I accidentally barged in and that's when it turned nasty. There were a couple of BFA heavies who forced a bottle of brandy down me, broke a couple of bones in my foot, and chucked me overboard.'

Pete's mouth hung open. 'Wow. Seriously?'

'Yeah. They said at the hospital I was lucky that someone saw what happened and dived in to save me. Not that I can remember much about it. Anyway, on a positive note, at least I now know for sure that there's a connection between the BFA and Larry Hopper.'

'Proof that Hopper's financing them?'

'I have a suspicion there's more going on than that.' Trent checked the barman wasn't listening. He was at the back of the bar checking his mobile phone and well out of earshot. 'I think he's here to orchestrate some sort of attack. They think he's behind a number of incidents in the States, and my guess is that he's here to incite Longhurst to do something similar.'

'An attack?'

'They'll probably be looking to target a mosque or something. Low-level stuff. I don't know really, maybe something bigger.'

'That's a serious allegation, Trent. You got enough to publish?'

'Not yet. I want to know exactly what they're planning first, and maybe get some harder evidence. As far as they know, I'm fish food at the bottom of the wharf so that should make my life a little easier for now.'

'Trent, be careful. You can't muck about with these guys. They didn't kill you last time, but they won't make that mistake a second time.'

'It's fine. Anyway, I think I've found a way into the BFA. You're not going to believe this. 'Trent pulled out a folded scrap of paper from the pocket of his jacket and smoothed it out on the bar. 'I found this earlier. There're loads of them plastered around Holborn station.'

'A missing person's poster? How's that help?'

'It's some bloke called Nick, but I swear this is one of the BFA guys who was on Hopper's yacht.'

Pete frowned as he scoured the poster, Nick Richard's beaming face staring back at him. 'Really?'

'Trust me; he got up pretty close and personal. I'd recognise him anywhere. He's lost a bit of weight, and he's shaved his head, but it's definitely him. Look, if I can get hold of his sister and put them in touch, it could be my way into the organisation,' said Trent.

'You're forgetting one thing. He's missing, and you have no idea where to find him.'

'I'll find him. How hard can it be? I can check all the regular BFA places. He's bound to turn up somewhere.'

'Are you going to tell his sister that he's run off to become a neo-Nazi then? That might come as a bit of a shock, don't you think?'

Trent hadn't considered that. He'd been so caught up with the excitement of recognising the man in the poster that he'd not taken into account the ramifications of tracking him down. 'What's the worst that can happen?'

'That they actually manage to kill you this time?'

'Don't be so melodramatic, Pete.'

'Please be careful. I'm serious.'

'I'll be okay. I'm like a cat with nine lives.' Trent managed a half-hearted smile.

'I nearly forgot. I've got something for you.' Pete grabbed his briefcase from the floor and flipped open the catches on his lap. 'You might find this interesting,' he said, handing Trent a single sheet of paper.

'What's this?'

'I was doing some digging around Longhurst's business background after you called me the other day. It's from the Land Registry. I discovered he's a director in a property management company called Montrieth. Companies House says he runs it with a couple of other directors. Didn't recognise their names though. Their account returns are pretty basic, but what's interesting is that they've received a number of fairly substantial lump sums deposited on a regular basis. Several hundred thousand pounds worth of lump sums each time.'

'Donations from Hopper.'

'Could be,' said Pete, with a shrug. 'It would be an easy way for party donations to be hidden. I'll send the accounts over to you when I'm back in the newsroom.'

'So what's this?' said Trent, waving the slip of paper.

'It looks as if the company used some of the cash to purchase a house in Sussex a few months back.'

'Isn't that what a property management company does?' asked Trent.

'It's the only property they own, Trent. It's a cottage in the middle of nowhere. A place called Nutwick. I looked up the pictures on the estate agent's website. It's pretty rundown. Not the sort of place you'd expect Longhurst to be buying for an investment.'

'Holiday home?' ventured Trent.

'If he wanted it for his personal use why purchase it through the company? Trent, in my humble opinion, and I'm no expert, but it looks to me as if they've tried to conceal the purchase. Maybe he's bought it on behalf of the BFA.'

'What would they want with a cottage in Sussex.'

'You said yourself they were planning some kind of attack. Perhaps they're using it as an operational base. It's certainly out of the public eye.'

'Bloody hell, Pete. Do you really think so?'

'I don't know, mate. It's just a hunch.'

'There's only one thing for it, then,' said Trent, downing the remnants of his pint of beer. He slipped off the stool and picked up his crutches. 'I'll go and have a snoop around, just as soon as I've had a chat with this woman about her missing brother.' He folded the poster back into his pocket and limped towards the door. 'Cheers, Pete. I owe you another one.'

Chapter 45

Trent had already finished a large cup of black coffee when Lucy Chapman walked into the café. He instantly knew it was her from the uncertain way she stood in the doorway scanning the tables.

'Lucy?' Trent asked, rising from his seat and beckoning her over to his table.

Lucy smiled as a prospective employee might greet a manager at a job interview. Her straight, blonde hair was pulled back in a ponytail, and she clutched a large bag, which dangled on the floor. Her bright red raincoat fell open, revealing a figure-hugging charcoal dress, which clung to her petite frame. 'You must be Trent?'

Trent noticed how cold her fingers were as he took her hand. 'Nice to meet you,' he mumbled, a little fazed by being in the company of a beautiful woman. As he sat down, he busied himself rearranging cups, napkins and a sugar pot, unable to hold her gaze.

'Coffee?' he asked, catching the eye of young waiter clearing a nearby table.

'Cappuccino, thanks. You said you know where my brother is?'

'I said I'd seen your brother.'

'Where?'

Trent ran a finger nervously around the rim of his cup. He had never considered himself much of a player, and envied the type of man who could walk up to a woman in a bar and strike up a conversation. The woman sitting opposite was well out of his league, and he felt a little embarrassed to be monopolising her time. He reminded himself why he'd called in the first place.

'I need to explain why I wanted to meet face-to-face. I'm a journalist, working freelance, for different publications, but mostly investigative work.'

'I see,' she said, but he could tell that she didn't. The waiter brought a cup on a saucer and placed it on the table. A sprinkling of chocolate had begun to melt into the foamy topping of milk.

'I'm investigating the British Freedom Alliance.'

Lucy showed no reaction.

'I'm trying to work out who's financing them. The guy in charge, Ken Longhurst - '

'I'm sorry, you said you had information about Nick?'

'Yes, I'm coming to that. You see, in recent years the BFA has come into quite a lot of money and I think it's down to an individual rather than a lot of smaller donations.'

'I'm sure that's all very fascinating, Mr Garside, but what does this have to do with Nicholas?' She fixed Trent with her unblinking cold, blue eyes.

'Bear with me. I've been trying to stand up this story that someone's funding the BFA anonymously because I think the public has the right to know that it's happening and who it is.'

'Are you deliberately trying to waste my time? Either you've seen Nicholas or you haven't. Which is it, Mr Garside?'

Trent threw back the last of his cold coffee and pondered his reply. 'I think I've seen him, yes.'

'You think? Where?' There was a strained emotion in her voice.

'The thing is, and I'm sorry to be so blunt, but I think he's joined the BFA.'

'Don't be so ridiculous!'

'I've seen him with Ken Longhurst. He's working for him as a sort of minder. You know, like a bodyguard or something.'

'What utter nonsense. You're sick, you know that? You've dragged me halfway across London to play games with me, is that it? ' Lucy stood up so forcefully that her chair almost toppled over.

'Hear me out, please. I met him, and he tried to kill me.'

'Nick doesn't have a violent bone in his body, and as for the BFA, he would deplore everything they stand for.'

'I know it sounds ludicrous, but I was as close to him as I am to you now. Please, sit down,' Trent implored.

'What is it with you people? All I want is to find my brother. I've had some odd people contact me since I put those posters up, but this is off the scale.'

Trent pulled the folded poster from his pocket and flattened it on the table. 'I don't know what he's done, or why or how you came to lose him, but I swear to God this is the man I saw. Of course, he doesn't look much like that anymore. For a start, he wears his head shaved and doesn't do much smiling.' Lucy was already heading for the door. He had to stop her. 'I can take you to him,' he blurted out

Lucy stopped in her tracks. 'You know where he is?'

'Yes.'

'Where?'

'I can show you. I'll take you there.'

'And why would you do that?'

'Please believe me, I'm not lying. I need to talk to him about the BFA, and I think he'll listen to me if you're there.'

'Goodbye, Mr Garside.'

'The thing is - this picture isn't a terribly good likeness is it? For a start, it doesn't really show his cleft lip.'

Lucy froze halfway out the door.

'It's healed well, but the scar is obvious when you get close.'

Lucy cast a glance over her shoulder, a look of uncertainty on her face. 'Alright, prove it. Take me to him.'Trent had already finished a large cup of black coffee when Lucy Chapman walked into the café. He instantly knew it was her from the uncertain way she stood in the doorway scanning the tables.

'Lucy?' Trent asked, rising from his seat and beckoning her over to his table.

Lucy smiled as a prospective employee might greet a manager at a job interview. Her straight, blonde hair was pulled back in a ponytail, and she clutched a large bag, which dangled on the floor. Her bright red raincoat fell open, revealing a figure-hugging charcoal dress, which clung to her petite frame. 'You must be Trent?'

Trent noticed how cold her fingers were as he took her hand. 'Nice to meet you,' he mumbled, a little fazed by being in the company of a beautiful woman. As he sat down, he busied himself rearranging cups, napkins and a sugar pot, unable to hold her gaze.

'Coffee?' he asked, catching the eye of young waiter clearing a nearby table.

'Cappuccino, thanks. You said you know where my brother is?'

'I said I'd seen your brother.'

'Where?'

Trent ran a finger nervously around the rim of his cup. He had never considered himself much of a player, and envied the type of man who could walk up to a woman in a bar and strike up a conversation. The woman sitting opposite was well out of his league, and he felt a little embarrassed to be monopolising her time. He reminded himself why he'd called in the first place.

'I need to explain why I wanted to meet face-to-face. I'm a journalist, working freelance, for different publications, but mostly investigative work.'

'I see,' she said, but he could tell that she didn't. The waiter brought a cup on a saucer and placed it on the table. A sprinkling of chocolate had begun to melt into the foamy topping of milk.

'I'm investigating the British Freedom Alliance.'

Lucy showed no reaction.

'I'm trying to work out who's financing them. The guy in charge, Ken Longhurst - '

'I'm sorry, you said you had information about Nick?'

'Yes, I'm coming to that. You see, in recent years the BFA has come into quite a lot of money and I think it's down to an individual rather than a lot of smaller donations.'

'I'm sure that's all very fascinating, Mr Garside, but what does this have to do with Nicholas?' She fixed Trent with her unblinking cold, blue eyes.

'Bear with me. I've been trying to stand up this story that someone's funding the BFA anonymously because I think the public has the right to know that it's happening and who it is.'

'Are you deliberately trying to waste my time? Either you've seen Nicholas or you haven't. Which is it, Mr Garside?'

Trent threw back the last of his cold coffee and pondered his reply. 'I think I've seen him, yes.'

'You think? Where?' There was a strained emotion in her voice.

'The thing is, and I'm sorry to be so blunt, but I think he's joined the BFA.'

'Don't be so ridiculous!'

'I've seen him with Ken Longhurst. He's working for him as a sort of minder. You know, like a bodyguard or something.'

'What utter nonsense. You're sick, you know that? You've dragged me halfway across London to play games with me, is that it? ' Lucy stood up so forcefully that her chair almost toppled over.

'Hear me out, please. I met him, and he tried to kill me.'

'Nick doesn't have a violent bone in his body, and as for the BFA, he would deplore everything they stand for.'

'I know it sounds ludicrous, but I was as close to him as I am to you now. Please, sit down,' Trent implored.

'What is it with you people? All I want is to find my brother. I've had some odd people contact me since I put those posters up, but this is off the scale.'

Trent pulled the folded poster from his pocket and flattened it on the table. 'I don't know what he's done, or why or how you came to lose him, but I swear to God this is the man I saw. Of course, he doesn't look much like that anymore. For a start, he wears his head shaved and doesn't do much smiling.' Lucy was already heading for the door. He had to stop her. 'I can take you to him,' he blurted out

Lucy stopped in her tracks. 'You know where he is?'

'Yes.'

'Where?'

'I can show you. I'll take you there.'

'And why would you do that?'

'Please believe me, I'm not lying. I need to talk to him about the BFA, and I think he'll listen to me if you're there.'

'Goodbye, Mr Garside.'

'The thing is - this picture isn't a terribly good likeness is it? For a start, it doesn't really show his cleft lip.'

Lucy froze halfway out the door.

'It's healed well, but the scar is obvious when you get close.'

Lucy cast a glance over her shoulder, a look of uncertainty on her face. 'Alright, prove it. Take me to him.'

Chapter 46

Blake was frozen to the core. He had spent an uncomfortable night sprawled on his stomach on the damp ground on the ridge overlooking Stoneleigh Cottage. Somewhere above a buzzard screeched as it soared out of the trees and up into the gloomy morning sky to begin its hunt for breakfast. The sun had risen, but was hidden behind a thick blanket of low cloud. In the dip of the valley below, a veil of mist clung to dew-covered tufts of grass.

He had been in position for seven straight hours, waiting for Proctor and Clark to return, but the house had remained empty overnight. The red Renault was missing, and its tracking device had ceased transmitting. With no idea where the men were holed up his concern was growing. He wiped his nose with the back of his hand, and checked his watch. It was just before eight. He pulled out his phone and dialled a pre-programmed number. It rang twice.

'Where are you?' Patterson's voice sounded strained.

'Back at Stoneleigh, but Proctor and Clark are missing.'

'What about the car?'

'It's gone, and the tracker's failed. Did you have any joy with the sets of plates from the vehicles at the garage?'

'Both stolen as we suspected, and there's nothing to link them directly to the BFA,' said Patterson.

'The truck's being converted to look like a removal van. It'll say County Removers on the side. I think it's their getaway vehicle, which means one of them will attempt to take it to France in the next few days, then we'll know for sure the game's on. Notify the port and ferry companies, and you'd better warn the Border Force too. But let them know they mustn't be stopped. If they think we're onto them, we'll lose them both.'

'Why would they take the van to France in advance?'

'So they have a vehicle inside the port to make their escape once they've set their bomb. If we can find out when it's booked to return, that'll give us a rough idea of the date of the attack. I suspect they'll attempt to book the Mondeo late onto the same ferry as the van returning from France.'

'We've checked out the garage by the way, but we drew a blank. No known criminal connections or links to the BFA.'

'Get it under surveillance. When they move the vehicles we need discreet eyes on them.'

'A team's on standby. There's another ready to pick up Martin Kelly. What about you? What are you going to do now?'

'I'm going to have a poke around the cottage. Phone me the moment you get anything on those vehicles.'

Blake hung up and eased himself to his feet. The muscles along his back, shoulders, and legs all protested. He shuffled back to his makeshift camp, boiled up a mug of coffee, and prepared himself for the trudge down the hill to the cottage.

*

The sash window in the lounge lifted without protest, and although it jammed a third of the way open, the gap was wide enough for Blake to squeeze through. With shower caps on his boots, he moved quickly through the hallway and into the kitchen, which was suspiciously clean. No dirty dishes. No leftover takeaway cartons. Not even so much as a mug left to dry on the draining board.

Blake bounded up the staircase and stormed into Proctor's room. Apart from the stench of stale cigarette smoke, there was no other evidence that anyone had been living there. The bedclothes that had been heaped underneath the window had gone, and the ashtrays and beer cans cleared away. Clark's bedroom was the same. In the bathroom, the only sign of recent habitation was a chalky residue of toothpaste in the basin and a toilet seat left up.

It looked as if the cottage had served its purpose and Proctor and Clark had no intention of returning. Blake cursed himself for a wasted, unpleasant evening watching over an abandoned property. He sat at the top of the stairs and pondered where the men might have taken refuge. Probably another BFA safe house. Most likely near the garage where their vehicles were being prepared. Blake had hoped for another opportunity to debrief Proctor before the attack. There were still key details he was unsure of, let alone a plan to extract Proctor in due course.

The sound of a vehicle approaching interrupted his thoughts. He heard tyres splashing through puddles on the driveway and the low drone of an engine. Finally, the red Renault was returning, Blake thought.

He jumped up, sprang into Proctor's room, and approached the window, keeping in the shadows. A white taxi was pulling up outside, and a man he recognised emerged. A woman stepped out from the back seat, and together they took a moment to survey the outside of the house.

Even though he had been expecting it, the knock on the front door echoed around the empty house and made Blake jump. He weighed up his options and their outcomes, and after a second knock made a decision. His only course of action was to confront the journalist and nip his curiosity in the bud.

'Yes?' said Blake, opening the door.

Trent took a step back, seemingly surprised that Blake

had answered. 'We're looking for someone,' Trent stammered.

Blake took a good look at the woman who was standing slightly behind Trent. He noticed her piercing eyes and slight frame, and wondered if she was Trent's photographer. But she had no camera equipment, and besides, he decided she was too smartly dressed.

'I see. Well, can I help?'

'I'm looking for my brother. Does he live here?' the woman piped up.

'Sorry,' said Blake, offering his best apologetic look.

'His name's Nicholas Richards. Nick,' the woman persisted.

Trent tottered forward. 'I've been helping my friend track him down. He's gone missing, but she thought she'd seen him on the Tube.'

'So what makes you think he's here?' asked Blake.

'I'm not sure - ' said Trent.

'Like I said, I don't know anyone called Nick. You must have the wrong house.' Blake took a step back to close the door.

'Hang on a minute, do I know you?'

Blake froze.

'Your face is familiar. I think we might have met.'

'No, you're mistaken, I'm afraid,' Blake said, without conviction.

'And you don't know anything about this woman's brother? He's with the BFA.'

'If you know anything about Nick, please, you must tell me,' Lucy Chapman pleaded, her eyes imploring.

She looked so vulnerable, so desperate.

'I need to know if he's alive. Mr Garside's been trying to tell me that he's involved with the far right, but it seems so out of character. Please?'

There was something about the look in her eye that touched Blake. It was a sadness, not of someone grieving, but of someone who was battling with the painful conflict of loss and hope. She must have contemplated that her brother was dead, but without proof, she would have been clinging to belief he was still alive. Either way he was lost to her. It was a pain Blake could empathise with. Ever since the disappearance of the only woman he had ever loved.

It had been a long time since his fiancée had disappeared. She had simply vanished as if the ground had opened up beneath her feet. There had been no signs of a forced entry or a struggle at their home, and none of her belongings were missing. It was an impossible conundrum. Suspicion had initially fallen on the IRA, and that maybe she'd been abducted in retribution for his job in Northern Ireland. But then there were so many people who would have wanted to see him suffer that the list of suspects was long. An investigation had been carried out by a Special Forces unit. Informants had been squeezed, and suspects pulled in for interrogation, but there had never been any real leads. No one had ever claimed responsibility and, of course, no one saw anything. It was a revenge of the cruellest kind.

The hunt was eventually scaled back, and Blake was told to face the probability that she was dead. Without knowing what had happened to her, he'd never been able to grieve. He often contemplated her death, but still clung to the hope that she would be found alive and they could carry on with their lives as they had once planned.

'He's alive, but he's not here,' said Blake, at last.

'Oh my God!' Lucy's knees buckled and she threw her hands to her face. Trent grabbed her elbow.

'He's fine, but as Mr Garside quite rightly said, your brother does have an involvement with the British Freedom Alliance, although it's not quite as straightforward as it seems. I'm afraid I can't tell you anymore. I'm sorry.'

'Where is he? Can I speak to him?'

'Not at the moment. I don't know where he is, but he's

involved in something extremely serious. Look, I work for a government agency that is investigating the organisation. Maybe soon we can arrange for you to see him, but I need to know I can trust you first. We're talking about a matter of national security.'

'What do you mean?'

'I can't tell you anymore. I'm sorry.'

'He's my brother. I have a right to see him.'

'And you will. But not right now. You wouldn't recognise him right now anyway.'

Trent had remained silent, taking it all in. 'You're with MI5 aren't you? Right, well I want to be there when they're reunited and I want the full background story too. It's the least you two owe me.'

'You'll get the exclusive, but you have to stop digging around the BFA. I'll tell you everything you want to know, but only on that agreement. Give me your numbers and wait for my call. Be ready to move quickly. I won't be able to give you much notice. I'll give you a location and I'll bring your brother to you. Go home now. Sit tight, and wait for my call.'

Lucy seemed about to say something else, but thought better of it. They rattled off their contact details, which Blake plugged straight into his phone.

'Come on, let's go.' Trent ushered her back to the waiting taxi, and Blake watched them leave.

When the car had disappeared down the drive, he stepped back inside and closed the door. He checked around for any incriminating sign of his presence then slipped out the front window. He drew it closed behind him, and set off back up the hill to the copse on the ridge.

Chapter 47

The journey home to London passed in a blur. Lucy sat in the back of the taxi watching the world flash by as Trent made small talk with the driver. She was buzzing with questions, but when she tried quizzing Trent, he seemed reluctant to talk, almost paranoid about being overheard. When they arrived in the city, she tried one last time and suggested they went for a drink. Trent hesitated, then proposed going to his flat.

It was cold and gloomy and tainted with cooking smells. He left her standing awkwardly by the front door while he fussed about clearing dirty dishes and sweeping up newspapers and scraps of A4 paper scrawled with spidery handwriting. Finally, he poured her a large Pinot Grigio into a smudged glass from an open bottle in the fridge, before hobbling into his bedroom with a mumbled apology.

While she waited, Lucy inspected a shelving unit filled to overflowing with books of all sizes, mostly obscure biographies about people she had never heard of and fat historical tomes from a range of eras. But interestingly, no fictional works. A towering metal CD holder that arched and twisted like a piece of modern sculpture stood next to the bookcase with scores of albums stacked in slots that looked like teeth. She scanned the spines, but struggled to find more than a few bands that she recognised.

A cat brushed against her leg, as she was halfway along the rack, curling her body around Lucy's calves and flicking her tail. When Lucy knelt to caress the back of her head, she was rewarded with an excited purr.

'I see you've found Tabs,' said Trent, returning the room.

'Tabs?'

'Tabitha. She lives here with me.'

'Actually, she found me,' said Lucy, standing.

Trent shuffled into the kitchen dragging his leg. He took the wine bottle from the fridge, topped up Lucy's glass, and poured one for himself.

'I guess I ought to thank you,' said Lucy.

'It's okay.'

'How did you know about Nick? Until a few days ago, I was beginning to believe he was dead. I've travelled halfway around the world looking for him, probably at the cost of my marriage. Then, out of the blue, I find out he's not only alive, but he's caught up with some fascist lunatics. Where did you see him?'

Trent hung his head and stared into his glass. 'I can see this has been a bit of a shock for you.'

'There's an understatement. I always had a feeling that Nick was alive, but this is something else. Please tell me what you know about him.'

'I don't know where to start.'

'Try the beginning. You said earlier that you were investigating the BFA. Why?'

'Because a few years ago they were nothing but a small time bunch of bigoted thugs. Now they're a highly-organised political force threatening to steal power at all levels across the country.'

'So what?'

'Something must have changed. They're still a bunch of bigoted thugs, but now they have money, which has paid for a fairly unconvincing makeover. I wanted to know where the money's coming from,' said Trent. 'So I went digging. You ever heard of Larry Hopper? He's an American billionaire.'

'The guy who was heckled at the Oxford Union?'

'I think he's the one with the big chequebook.'

Lucy unzipped a pair of knee-length black boots and sat on Trent's old sofa, curling her legs up under her body. He noticed she had carefully painted each one of her toenails bright red. 'So what's this got to do with Nick?'

Trent explained how he'd managed to trick his way on board Larry Hopper's yacht. 'But I got caught,' he said, sloshing the remnants of his wine around the bottom of his glass. 'And that's when I saw your brother.'

'On the yacht?'

'Look, Lucy, you're not going to like this, but you need to hear it. From what I can tell, your brother is acting like some kind of minder for Longhurst. I stumbled into this meeting, and Nick and this other guy dragged me off, took me below deck and - '

'And what exactly?'

'Well, how do you think I did this?' Trent nodded to the cast on his foot. 'Your brother broke it in two places because I wasn't quick enough telling him my name.'

The colour drained from Lucy's face. 'Nick did that to you?'

'And worse. He threatened to smash my hand with a meat mallet, then force-fed me with a bottle of brandy and threw me overboard expecting that I'd drown.'

'Except you didn't, obviously.'

'No. I thought I was going to die, but...'

'And you're quite sure it was Nick, because it doesn't sound like him at all,' said Lucy.

'He looks different now, but he was right in my face. There's no mistake, I'm sorry.'

'That MI5 man said Nick was involved in a matter of national security. What was he talking about?'

'That's what I'd like to find out. Presumably they have some intelligence on Longhurst and Hopper.'

'Yes, I expect so,' said Lucy. She brushed her fringe out of her eyes. 'You only called me because you thought I was your ticket into this story, didn't you?'

'Of course not,' Trent protested. 'Well, maybe a little. I thought if I could reunite the two of you, you could persuade Nick to talk to me, to tell me what was going on in the BFA.'

'You bloody journalists, you're all the same. Never mind what I might be going through.'

'It's not like that.'

'So what is it like?'

'Lucy, I want to help.'

'When I thought I'd lost Nick it was as if someone had stolen a little bit of my soul. But I couldn't grieve because I clung to this hope that he was still alive. And now this. What am I supposed to do now?'

'Lucy, I'm so sorry. I didn't really think.'

'No, you didn't, did you?'

'At least you know he's alive, and you'll see him again soon. That's good news isn't it?'

'Maybe. Who knows? All I have is what you've told me, and the word of some spook who says he's investigating Nick for his involvement in the BFA. What's he going to be like when I do meet him? They must have brainwashed him. He might not even recognise me.' A tear rolled down Lucy's cheek, leaving an inky black trail of eyeliner.

'It's going to be alright,' said Trent, sitting and taking her hands in his. 'You should be happy. We've found your brother.'

'It's too much to take in.'

'Tell me about him.'

'Nick? What do you care?'

'Tell me about when he went missing.'

'To this day, I don't know much about it. He was at university, but he was struggling, trying to live in my shadow when he should have been doing his own thing. We asked too much of him.'

'We?'

'Me and mum. She wanted the best for him, but he wasn't academic. Not really. He fell in with the wrong crowd, spent most his time and money out drinking, and at the end of his first year he failed most of his exams. Mum read him the riot act as if he were a six year old. But you know, ever since dad died, she's been on her own and doing her best to bring up two kids. It was tough on her too. I guess Nick thought he'd earned some freedom when he went off to college and didn't appreciate mum sticking her nose into his business. It ended in a horrible row, and Nick stormed out, telling us not to bother trying to contact him again. And that was it. Mum stopped funding him, and we never saw him again.

'We both thought it would blow over. You know, he and mum can both be a bit hot-headed, but he cut off all ties with both of us and made it quite clear he didn't want to be contacted.'

'And you never heard from him again?' asked Trent.

'Only the once. Several months later, he called out of the blue to speak to mum. He said he was sorry for everything and that he was going travelling to sort out his head. He had a ticket for Brazil and was due to fly to Rio the next day. He promised to call when he landed, to let us know he was safe. But he never made the call.'

'What did you do?'

'We tried everyone we could think of; the Foreign Office, the police, the Brazilian authorities, but no one was that bothered about helping us. You know, a few people made sympathetic noises, but that was it. The trail went cold and we never found out anything else. They told mum to prepare for the worst, and that he was probably dead. She seemed to be able to cope better than me, and accepted that we'd never see Nick again.

'That day I saw Nick on the Tube, I'd just returned from Rio, but it was a wild goose chase. I spent most of my time rowing with my husband.'

'I'm sorry,' said Trent.

'Don't be. I dumped him at the airport, but we'd been having problems for months. It just brought it to a head.'

'So you didn't make any headway in Brazil?'

'No, and the weird thing is that we couldn't find any evidence that he had ever even arrived.'

'That's odd.'

'We had a meeting at the Brazilian Embassy before we went, and they were adamant that Nick was never in the country. But we checked with the airline, and they say they have records that he was definitely booked on the flight. And now he turns up in London. I'm so confused.'

Lucy leaned across the sofa and rested her head on Trent's shoulder. Unsure how to react, he reached up and stroked her hair, drinking in the smell of her perfume.

'It's going to be okay, you know. We'll sort it out. Don't worry.'

Chapter 48

Walking into the reception of an anonymous-looking hotel on the outskirts of Dover, Blake was conscious that he looked a wreck. He'd come straight from the cottage in Nutwick, and couldn't remember the last time he'd showered or taken a bath. His hair was matted and his face was covered in thick stubble. The receptionist, wearing too much make-up and her hair scraped back tightly in a bun, looked him up and down as if weighing up whether he was a vagrant chancing his luck. Blake flashed her a broad smile.

'Good afternoon, sir. May I help you?'

'I need a room for a few nights.' Blake pulled his wallet from his pocket and flipped it open so the receptionist could see the assortment of credit cards lined up inside. 'And to be honest, I'm desperate for a bath.'

As the receptionist tapped Blake's details into a computer, he noticed her long fingernails, painted a deep maroon and looking suspiciously fake. She handed him an electronic credit card shaped key wrapped inside a little folder and directed him along a corridor past the lifts.

The room was identical in layout to a hundred he had stayed in before. A simple bathroom led off a short hallway, opposite a wooden wardrobe. The bedroom was small but functional. There was a desk with a chair, a luggage stand, and trouser press fixed to the wall. A comfy-looking double bed had been made up neatly with a green floral bedspread.

Blake dropped his travel bag on the stand and ran a

bath, savouring the thought of the warm water easing his tired muscles as the tap gurgled and spluttered. While he waited, he laid out a razor and shaving foam by the sink then stripped out of his dirty clothes. He wiped the steam from the mirror with a fluffy white towel and examined the weary face staring back at him. His cheeks were sallow and his eyes sunken in deep, dark pits.

When the bath was only half-full he eased himself in, wincing as the scalding water stung his skin. He left the tap on and turned it off with his toes only when the level threatened to spill over the top. Then he laid his head back and let the heat penetrate every sinew, ligament, muscle, and bone until he began to feel human again.

He remained motionless for almost thirty minutes, by which time the water was growing cold. He dried himself with a towel and wrapped it around his waist while he shaved. The hairs on his chin had grown so long that they snagged on the razor and twice he nicked the skin. He ambled back into the bedroom and collapsed on the bed.

It was dark when he woke, startled by a loud trill. He glanced at the red numbers on the alarm clock by the side of the bed.

2:53am.

He sat up, rubbed his eyes, and snatched his mobile phone as it vibrated across the desk.

'Yes?'

'We've got a crossing for the van,' said Patterson. 'It was booked within the last hour. The ferry company alerted us.

'When?'

'Lunchtime.'

'Today?'

'Yes. They're on the 12:55 ferry.'

'When is it booked to return?' Blake was suddenly aware that his exposed chest and upper arms were cold, chilled by the air conditioning that had kicked in while he was asleep.

'First thing the day after on a boat that's due in at around eleven,' said Patterson.

'What about the vehicles? Have they been moved?'

'Not yet. They're both still in the garage. There are teams surrounding the building and they've reported positive IDs on Proctor and Clark.'

'Any booking for the Mondeo?'

'No, but the ferry companies have been given the details. They'll flag it the moment a booking's made. We should know very quickly.'

'What about tactical teams?'

'All in hand. The South East Counter Terrorism Unit has been fully briefed, and will have armed officers covering the port when we need them. I'm assured they can provide a ring of steel.'

'I'll still need to get Proctor out, unharmed.'

'Do you have a plan?'

'I need a car. Something nondescript and non-traceable left near the port. Can you sort it?'

'Of course. What about Clark?'

'Once he's on board, I'll pick him up, but I'll need a diversion to get Proctor out.'

'I'm sure we can think of something.'

'It's imperative that the police don't get him. We have a duty to extract him safely.'

'Do you think I don't know that, Blake? While you've been playing action man in the field it's me who's been taking the heat.'

'Just don't screw this up.'

Chapter 49

Through the deep haze of sleep, a noise pervaded Lucy's dreams. A relentless throbbing that wouldn't stop. She forced open an eye, and realised she had no idea where she was. The lank curtains with dated floral patterns were as unfamiliar to her as the striped duvet. Her mouth was dry, and the distant pounding of a white wine hangover surfaced from deep inside her head. She rolled over. Trent was sleeping deeply, perfectly at peace and totally unmoved by the noise.

She scrambled around the discarded items of clothing on the floor and eventually found her phone, but didn't recognise the number that flashed up in the display. 'Hello?'

'Mrs Chapman?' She felt a pang of guilt at hearing her married name. 'This is Tom Blake. We spoke yesterday at the cottage?'

Lucy sat bolt upright, clutching the duvet to her chest. Trent stirred. 'Yes, yes. What is it?'

'If you want to see your brother, you need to head for Kent. Wait in the services at Gillingham on the M2.'

Lucy shook Trent's shoulder. As he slowly roused into consciousness, she repeated the instructions aloud.

'Be there in two hours. Wait for me and don't move. Is that clear?'

'Absolutely. We'll be there.'

*

Blake dropped his phone into the pocket of the dark overalls that hung loosely over his muscular frame even when they were pulled over his body armour. It was a standard one-size fits-all design finished off with a yellow fluorescent vest so that he fitted in with the other dockers around the port. From his position in the cab of a forklift truck, he had a good view across an expanse of hard standing where the lanes were marked out with solid white lines and numbered sequentially from his left to his right. Queues of cars, vans, and lorries were parked facing the towering steel stanchions that indicated each of the ferry berths. Two ships were already in port. Blake had watched with fascination as each one manoeuvred into its moorings with inch-perfect accuracy and minutes later spewed out a flow of traffic.

A handheld radio crackled on the dashboard of the forklift, next to Blake's Browning 9mm.

'Blake, are you there?' said Patterson.

'In position near the back of lane one-three-two.'

'We're set and ready, just waiting on the arrival of Proctor and Clark. We have eyes on Proctor's ferry. It's making its approach to the harbour and should be offloading within ten minutes. Standby.'

Blake threw the radio back onto the dashboard and grabbed a pair of binoculars from by his feet. He watched the funnel of the ferry move slowly from the Channel into the horseshoe-shaped harbour. Then he scanned the rooftops of the surrounding buildings and counted at least a dozen police snipers in position with their rifle sights trained towards the moorings. They were exposed to anyone walking along the top of the famous White Cliffs, but it was unlikely Proctor or Clark would spot them. Blake also knew that there were scores of undercover officers scattered throughout the port, and teams of uniformed rapid response units in marked cars hidden out of sight. On his command, the whole port would light up with law enforcement officers armed to the teeth.

It was only a matter of being patient and waiting for the right time.

*

Inside the port control room on the eastern harbour arm, Patterson could almost reach out and touch the ferry as it drifted lazily past. The control tower was a four-storey construction with angled windows that gave three hundred and sixty degree views of the Channel, the port, and the cliffs. A row of desks groaning with banks of computer screens relaying real-time information about shipping movements, weather, and tides faced the sea.

'Well, this looks like it. Hope your man's got his facts right,' said Assistant Chief Constable Clive Smitherman-Banks who was leading the South East Counter Terrorism Unit.

'In many ways I hope he's got it wrong,' said Patterson.

'Well, quite. At least we're ready for them.' Smitherman-Banks was a trim man with a twinkle in his eye and more than twenty-five years' experience. Something of the old seadog about him, thought Patterson.

The ACC picked up a radio to address the response teams on the ground. 'Standby everyone. The *Dawn Spirit* is making its final approach into the harbour. Remember, we're looking for a maroon van and a single white male. I want a positive ID. Await my command for further instructions.'

As he replaced the handset on a desk, he spoke with a port controller sitting at one of the computers. 'And news yet on the Ford?'

'It's not checked in yet,' he said.

Smitherman-Banks shot Patterson a look, which the colonel ignored. 'Maybe your man's wrong after all.'

*

The Tom Blake Thrillers

The *Dawn Spirit*'s final approach seemed to take an age. Blake had driven the forklift close to a service ramp and waited as the captain edged the ferry into its berth, while dockers and ferrymen scurried around tying off ropes and preparing the vessel for a quick turnaround. Eventually, the first of the vehicles appeared and rolled onto the harbour apron.

First came a convoy of articulated lorries, which thundered and rattled across the gangway, mostly foreign-registered trucks from Poland, Holland, and France, although some had travelled from farther in Europe and even the former Eastern Bloc. A handful were British vehicles returning home.

Once the lorries had been cleared from the decks, a slow procession of cars and vans followed, a ragtag assortment of vehicles of varying age, size and colour. There were businessmen travelling in smart saloons, older couples in campervans, families with luggage boxes strapped to their roofs, and an array of commercial vans. But no sign of the maroon Mercedes van.

Blake jumped down from the forklift with a growing sense of unease, fearing he'd missed Proctor as the last of the vehicles rolled down the ramp and disappeared. He slipped the Browning into a holster under his overalls, grabbed the radio, and jogged up the ramp.

'Is that all of them?' he asked the first crew member he found.

'Yep,' the man said.

'I was looking for a maroon van. Are you sure that's not still on board?'

'Let me check, hang on.' The man spoke to a colleague by radio. Blake heard the response for himself. The ship was clear and getting ready for the next crossing. On the apron, a woman in an oversized fluorescent jacket waved a queue of cars forward.

'Patterson, it's Blake,' he shouted into his radio. 'The

214

van wasn't on board the *Dawn Spirit*.'

'Are you absolutely sure?' Patterson's disembodied voice hissed over static.

'Positive. Can you double check that the van cleared the border controls in Calais.'

'I'll get back to you.'

Blake returned to the cab of the forklift truck, dodging the fast flowing stream of cars rolling up the ramp onto the ferry. He began to ponder the possibility that Proctor had switched vehicles in France to avoid detection, and cursed himself for not thinking of the possibility earlier.

'Blake, this is Patterson. We have confirmation that Proctor and the van cleared border controls in France. He must have missed the boat for some reason.'

'Right, okay.' In the background, Blake could hear phones ringing amid an excited hubbub. 'What's going on up there, Harry?'

'I'm not sure. Something's going on.' Patterson fell silent.

'Harry, are you there? What's going on?'

Silence.

'Harry? Talk to me.' Blake had a bad feeling in the pit of his stomach. 'Harry, for Christ's sake answer me.'

'Blake, it's not good. Something's kicking off. They're pulling all the response units out. We're on our own.'

Chapter 50

It was late morning when Lucy and Trent arrived at the motorway services. A taxi dropped them near the entrance, and while Trent paid, Lucy ambled inside out of the cold. She was wearing the previous day's clothes, and although she had managed a tepid bath at Trent's flat, she still felt grubby. Her hair was pulled back in a ponytail and needed a wash. Two paracetamol had eased her hangover, but her stomach was unsettled. She checked her watch and waited for Trent, who hobbled in swinging himself along on his crutches.

'Coffee?' he said.

She nodded and helped him climb a set of steps to a burger restaurant that bridged the motorway. Lucy sent Trent to find a table and ordered for them both. When she returned with two steaming cardboard cups, he was staring out the window at the traffic below.

'Listen, about last night,' he said.

'It's okay, you don't need to say anything.'

'I didn't want you to think I was trying to take advantage.'

Lucy reached across the table to take his hand and saw him notice the platinum rings on her left hand, an uncomfortable reminder for him that he had spent the night with a married woman. As if either of them needed reminding.

'You didn't take advantage. It wouldn't have happened if I hadn't wanted it to,' said Lucy, but she couldn't help but think it wouldn't have happened if not for the two bottles of wine they'd polished off.

Trent nodded. 'Fine,' he said. 'So what did the MI5 guy say exactly?'

'To meet him here and not to move.'

'Do you think he'll bring Nick?' asked Trent, raising his eyebrows.

'Who knows? We're in his hands now though, aren't we?'

They sipped their coffees watching the traffic flow in steady streams, caught in an awkward silence, which was finally interrupted by a sound from Trent's pocket. He grabbed for his phone, grateful for the distraction. Lucy watched him screw up his face in concentration. 'Lucy, something's going on. Twitter's going mad about some incident in Canterbury.'

'That's not far, is it?'

'Less than an hour away. I wonder if this has something to do with your brother.'

'Why do you say that?'

'The cathedral's been cordoned off and there's a big police presence. Hang on, someone else is saying smoke's coming from inside the building.'

'What's that got to do with Nick?'

'I don't know, maybe nothing. But the MI5 guy said Nick was involved in something to do with national security. Maybe he meant a terrorist attack?'

'Are you mad?'

Trent placed his phone on the table and rubbed his eyes. When he looked up at Lucy, she saw something in his expression that chilled her to the core. 'Trent? What is it?'

'There's something I've not told you.'

'What do you mean?'

'Your brother, Nick, there's no easy way to say this.'

'For pity's sake, spit it out, Trent.'

'I think Nick is involved with a secret sect that's working for the BFA, called the Phineas Priests.' He tried to take her hand, but she pulled it back. 'It's a group that started in America, linked to Larry Hopper. The FBI suspects they're responsible for a number of attacks in the States, and I think MI5 are looking at the possibility that Nick is involved in something similar here.'

'You're insane.'

'And what if that something similar is an attack on Canterbury Cathedral? It would all make sense. They were planning this attack all along.'

'You don't know there's an attack on the cathedral. It's probably just a coincidence.'

'With that many police? I don't think so, and I reckon Nick's behind this. Lucy, I don't have all the answers, but right now, my gut instinct tells me I'm onto something. Look,' he showed her his phone. 'It's going crazy. Some people are saying there was an explosion. That's got to be a bomb.'

'Stop it.'

'Come on,' Trent stood up and grabbed his crutches. 'Let's go.'

'Go where?'

'To Canterbury. This is going to be massive. We've got to be there.'

'No.'

'What?'

'Trent, I'm not going.'

'Why not?'

'Because the instructions were quite clear. We weren't to move from here whatever happened.'

'Well, of course they'd tell us that. Look, they probably want us out of the way. I have to get there. This could be a huge story. Do you understand?'

'Not really, but do what you want. I'm staying here. If there's a chance I can see Nick again I'm not going to blow it on your hunch. I'm sorry.'

'Suit yourself. I'll see you later.'

Trent hobbled back towards the entrance, struggling with his crutches, and leaving Lucy cradling her cup. She watched him hop down the stairs and disappear out the door. Then she turned her attention back to the traffic and let out a deep sigh.

*

It seemed as though everyone in the control room was on the phone barking instructions.

'What's happening?' said Patterson, as Smitherman-Banks ended one call and before he could answer another.

'We're in the wrong place. This was a diversion. Several devices have been found in Canterbury Cathedral. That was the real target. The bomb squad's on the way, but I'm diverting the response teams there immediately. I'm sorry.'

'What about the blue Mondeo?'

'Still no sign. Looks like it was all part of an elaborate hoax, I'm afraid. Don't beat yourself up about it. Nothing you could have done.' Smitherman-Banks' phone rang again. 'I'm sorry, I need to take this.'

Patterson stared across the harbour as another ferry edged out of the port, a plume of black smoke rising from its stumpy funnels. Around him, members of the police Gold Command team were hurriedly packing up their belongings. Patterson spoke into his radio handset. 'Blake, are you there? It's Patterson.'

'Harry, what news?'

'It's not good, I'm afraid. There's been an attack on Canterbury Cathedral. Multiple devices have been found. They think the ferry plot was a diversion. Proctor and Clark must have been onto us.' There was silence at the other end of the line. 'Blake?'

'It's not a diversion. I'm absolutely sure of it. Canterbury is the hoax,' said Blake. 'You have to stop them leaving.'

'I don't think I can. They're hell bent on getting out.'

'Do your best, Harry, it's all I ask.'

Blake watched helplessly as the sniper teams packed up their kit and stood down. From all directions, scores of men dressed in blue overalls and fluorescent jackets were jogging towards the terminal building. On the far side of the port, lines of lorries were parked up, either waiting for later ferries or preparing for their onward journeys. If Proctor had managed to slip into Dover, Blake was sure that was where he would be parked, hidden among the trucks, waiting for Mike Clark. It had to be worth a check. He stamped on the accelerator and the forklift truck shot forward.

He trundled along the first line of lorries, suspiciously viewing the drivers who were either checking over their loads, smoking or chatting. There was the odd commercial van, but nothing that remotely resembled the Mercedes Proctor and Clark had had modified. At the end of the line of trucks, he swung the forklift through a wide arc and weaved back between a second row.

Eventually, Blake ended up at the far side of the port and drew to a halt. He watched through a chain link fence as the last of the marked police cars sped out of the port with their sirens wailing and knew he'd missed his chance to stop them.

'Harry? Is that everyone gone?' he asked, over the radio.

'I'm afraid so, Blake. Sorry. Any sign of Proctor?'

'I don't think he's made it back yet. When's the next ferry?'

'I can see one about ten minutes out. According to the controllers she's due in at 11:55.'

'Which berth?'

'Three.'

'I'll go check it out.'

'Just a minute.' The radio crackled and hissed.

'What is it, Harry?' There was no reply, just white static noise.

After a brief pause, Patterson's voice said, 'It's the

Mondeo. The control tower's been notified that it's checked into departures and they have a positive on Mike Clark.'

Chapter 51

The intricate operation to bring a 40,000-ton ferry into port started all over again. The ship's movement was so slow and controlled that it was almost impossible to tell when it had actually berthed. Dockers and crew worked frenetically to secure her so the turnaround could begin. Metallic clangs and rattles signalled that unloading was underway, and a parade of heavy goods vehicles proceeded down a short ramp with their exhausts belching thick diesel smoke.

The numbers of cars queueing in the boarding lanes was constantly being swelled by a trickle of vehicles from a service road. Blake kept a close eye out for Clark's car, but his view was suddenly obscured by a procession of lorries pouring out of the newly arrived ferry and cut in front of him. He counted at least fifty lorries disembarking before the first of the cars was allowed off. While most of the trucks were foreign-registered, almost all the cars had British number plates. Among them were campervans and commercial trucks, but no dark-coloured removals van.

'Blake, do you have a visual on Proctor yet?' said Patterson.

'Negative.'

But as Blake tossed the radio onto the dashboard he saw a flash of maroon at the top of the ramp. A Mercedes van rolled down the ramp and hit the apron trailing behind a mud-splattered, silver Land Rover. As it passed, Blake took a good look through its passenger window, and saw Proctor behind the wheel. He recognised his distinctive frame, his dark, short-cropped hair, and the vivid tattoo exposed on his shoulder.

'Harry, it's Blake. Correction. I now have a visual on Proctor. Repeat, Proctor has arrived.'

*

A small crowd of journalists had already gathered when Trent arrived at the cathedral. They were standing at the edge of a police cordon on the wrong side of an ancient stone gateway, waiting in anticipation for any nuggets of information. Inside the cathedral grounds, visible through the archway, was a white Army bomb disposal truck and a number of uniformed police officers bustling around.

Trent pushed his way through hordes of curious onlookers with his press pass clenched between his teeth, and took his place at the back of the reporters. He sidled up to a young, blonde reporter who looked barely old enough to have left school. She was clutching a notepad in one hand and a ballpoint pen poised in the other. 'Have the police said anything?' he asked, without introduction.

'They're due to give a statement in the next ten minutes,' she said, with a nervous smile.

'Anyone manage to get into the grounds before the cordon went up?'

'No, I don't think so.'

Trent was disappointed. In his early days as a cub reporter, he'd have never let a police cordon stand in the way of him landing a scoop.

He watched with mild interest as a television reporter straightened his tie and muttered lines to himself as he prepared a piece-to-camera. Alongside him, an enthusiastic radio reporter was carrying out rapid-fire interviews with any eyewitnesses who could be persuaded to talk, the bright red sponge on the end of her microphone rammed under their noses.

'Are they going to give us any access inside?'

'I don't think so, no,' said the reporter, stepping away from Trent.

From the other side of the cordon, a middle-aged woman in a yellow fluorescent jacket three sizes too big approached the journalists and informed them that the officer-in-charge, Assistant Chief Constable Clive Smitherman-Banks, would shortly give them an update on the situation.

A few minutes later, the officer appeared from the cathedral precincts, trailed by a woman in a smart trouser suit, a uniformed inspector, a fire officer, and a soldier in Army fatigues.

Smitherman-Banks introduced himself briefly, as microphones were thrust at him and cameramen jostled for the best position. He cleared his throat. 'I have a short statement. A few minutes before eleven this morning, multiple explosive devices were found inside the cathedral by staff. The building was immediately evacuated, and an Army bomb disposal team was dispatched. At the moment, that team is working to make the devices safe. As you can imagine, it is a slow process, but we are doing everything we can. Major Collins?'

The soldier stepped forward, and spoke with a grim expression. 'To elaborate slightly, we are currently dealing with up to five devices, which we are treating as credible. We're using a remotely controlled robot, but I'm afraid at this stage there's not much more I can say. We hope to be able to give you more information later.'

'Has anyone claimed responsibility?' Trent called out.

'Not at the moment,' said Smitherman-Banks.

'Well, any idea who might be behind it then?'

'Not yet.'

'Can you confirm that you're investigating a possible link with the British Freedom Alliance?' Trent continued to probe. He noticed Major Collins cast a nervous glance at the police commander, but Smitherman-Banks' face gave nothing away.

'It wouldn't be right to speculate about any suspects at this stage. I'm sure you understand,' he said.

'Do you know when the devices were planted?' asked one of the television reporters.

'It's too early to say.'

'Is it right that one of the devices was emitting smoke?' asked Trent.

Smitherman-Banks deferred to the Army officer. 'We can confirm that smoke has been detected in the building, but it's unclear whether that has come from one of the devices,' said Major Collins.

'Ladies and Gentlemen, thank you very much for your time. We hope to give you an update in a couple of hours.' Smitherman-Banks turned on his heel, and strode towards the cathedral gate, followed in procession by the other officials.

'Hardly a full and frank explanation of what the hell's going on,' said Trent, catching up with the young reporter.

'I suppose there's nothing for it but to hang around and wait for the update,' she said, slipping her notepad into the pocket of her coat.

'I suppose so,' said Trent. But he had no intention of hanging around.

*

Blake observed from the bottom of the ramp as a long line of cars was waved on board towards teams of crewmen in hard hats and high visibility jackets who were directing the drivers into parking spaces, spreading the load evenly throughout the lower decks of the ferry. He was nervously watching for Clark in the blue Ford, hoping the port controllers had made a mistake and that he was due on a later ship.

'Harry, any joy yet getting those response teams back?'

'I'm working on it,' said Patterson, over the radio. 'I need more time.'

'We don't have time, Harry. If Clark boards this ferry, we don't have a plan to stop him.'

'I'm well aware of that, Blake. Do you have eyes on him yet?'

'They started loading the ship a few minutes ago, but I can't see him. I guess he's in one of the queues, but it's really busy down here.'

'You'll have to find a way of stopping him on your own. We can't let him drive on board with the explosives if we don't have armed back-up,' said Patterson.

'Negative. We have to let him on board.'

'Blake, listen to me. Don't let Clark get that ferry. That's an order.'

'If I try to stop him, or he thinks he's been rumbled, there's every chance he'll detonate the bomb. I can't take that chance, Harry. There are too many people around. I need him out of the car and incapacitated. I think he's planning to abandon the vehicle on the car deck and slip off the vessel before it departs. That gives me a small window of opportunity to stop him.'

'And if you fail?'

'Then it's not worth thinking about.'

The first line of cars cleared and an adjacent queue was waved forward. Blake scanned the vehicles and spotted an old blue Ford ten cars back. 'I think I can see him.'

'Blake, confirm; do you have eyes on Clark?'

As the cars crept slowly forwards, Blake stared through the windscreen of the Ford, squinting against the light reflected off the angled glass. As it drew closer, he recognised the familiar figure of Mike Clark behind the wheel. He looked relaxed, driving with one hand on the wheel, his right arm out of view, and his eyes never wavering from the car ahead. The Mondeo hit the metal ramp with a clatter, and was swallowed up into the body of the ship.

'Clark's on board,' said Blake. 'Do you copy?'

'Roger that, Blake.'

'I would suggest we need those response teams. Now.'

*

A pair of wooden gates that hung between two crumbling stone pillars was all that stood between Trent and the cathedral precincts. It was one of few unguarded entrances into the grounds and hadn't taken him long to find. A mere ten minutes hobble from where the press pack had been penned safely out of the way. The only problem was that they were at least six feet high and topped with a protective ridge of iron teeth.

Trent waited for a gaggle of teenagers to pass, laughing and giggling in their school uniforms, blissfully unaware of the drama in the cathedral. He feigned interest in the window of an adjacent shop, and when they were gone seized his chance. He tossed his crutches over the top, and hauled himself up onto a wheelie bin, which wobbled under his weight. With a final check that nobody was watching, he grabbed the top of the gate and dragged his body over. He winced as the metal teeth dug into his ribs, but the discomfort was nothing compared to the agony that shot up his leg as he landed on his broken foot. Fighting the urge to scream, he bit hard on his lower lip.

Eventually, the pain subsided and he was able to sit up, drawing in deep, restorative breaths. He retrieved his crutches and stood awkwardly, assessing his surroundings. He was on a gravel drive at the rear of the cathedral. It swept past the ancient flint and ashlar Archbishop's Palace with its exquisite mullioned and transomed windows, which in any other setting would have been a grand and handsome building. But in the shadow of the Caen stone cathedral, Trent thought it looked rather plain.

Keeping close to a long wall opposite the palace, he shuffled towards the cathedral's South West entrance where he had expected to see large numbers of police officers. But the area was deserted. Beyond the entrance, the white bomb disposal truck was parked up. Several men in Army fatigues and navy blue berets were standing at its rear end talking anxiously and examining a small screen. He imagined they were watching a video feed from a robot deployed inside the building.

He was about to move forward for a better view when a flicker of movement caught his eye, and an over-inflated figure in a green-padded suit waddled out from inside the cathedral. He inched slowly towards the white truck, pulling off an oversized helmet. Three soldiers ran across to help. They chattered in excited voices, and although Trent couldn't make out their words, he had the definite sense that something significant had occurred.

*

'Sir, there's an urgent call for you.' A young constable held out a mobile phone to Smitherman-Banks.

'Who is it?'

'Colonel Patterson, from MI5. He's still in Dover.'

Smitherman-Banks snatched the phone. 'Yes?'

'You're in the wrong place. Proctor arrived on a ferry just after you left. Clark checked in shortly afterwards. You must have passed him as you all left. We need response teams down here urgently. Blake's on his own.'

'Hang on a minute, Patterson. I told you, it's a diversion. We've got multiple devices here at the cathedral. The bomb disposal teams are inside at the moment. I don't think we need to worry about Proctor and Clark anymore.'

'With respect, sir, the cathedral is the diversion. An attack is imminent here at the port.'

The ACC was momentarily distracted as the door to the command centre he'd set up in one of the diocesan buildings flew open. Major Collins strode in with an anxious look on his face. 'Look, what am I supposed to do? I've got five bombs here and God knows, there may be more.'

'Excuse me, sir, I need to a word.' Major Collins caught the ACC's eye and raised a finger to emphasise his need to interrupt.

'Hang on a minute, Patterson. What is it, Major?'

'The devices are hoaxes. They're not even terribly sophisticated. A bit of modelling clay, a few wires and a digital clock face. To the untrained eye they look the business, but they're most definitely not viable.'

'Are you sure?'

'One hundred per cent.'

'Oh Christ! Patterson, are you still there?'

'Still here, sir.'

'I'm scrambling the armed response teams. They'll be with you in twenty minutes. Keep me posted.'

*

In his heavy, steel toe-capped boots, Blake reached the car deck with his thighs burning. He jogged between the tightly packed lines of vehicles, bumping past passengers wrestling with children and luggage, and with a cacophony of noise ringing in his ears. The hubbub of shouted commands, the hum of engines, and the echo of car doors slamming. But Blake ignored it all, focussing on finding Clark. He spotted the blue Ford parked in a left-hand lane, near the bow of the ship.

An ideal location for a bomb because of its proximity to the bow doors. The explosion would rip a hole in the hull like punching through a wet paper bag, with catastrophic consequences. Sea-water would flood onto the deck and capsize the ship within minutes as the rising waters caused the ferry to become unstable.

Clark was already out of the car, reaching into the back seat. He pulled out a blue bag, which he threw over his shoulder, and locked the car remotely with an electronic key. Blake ducked behind a campervan as Clark turned and joined a column of passengers trudging towards the stairs to the upper decks. Blake followed discreetly, filing up the narrow stairs behind an elderly couple and a family with two teenage boys.

When they emerged onto the passenger decks, Clark angled right towards the stern, and walked purposefully towards the men's toilets halfway along a central passageway. Blake slipped into a noisy video games arcade opposite and spoke quietly into his radio.

'Harry, are you there? I'm on board with a visual on Clark.'

'Blake, I'm here. Where's the car?'

'Parked on the main deck near the bow doors. I've followed Clark onto the passenger deck. He's got a bag with him.'

'I've alerted the terrorism unit, and they're turning around the response teams. They should be here any minute.'

'Well, tell them to come quietly. Any sign of flashing blue lights and the game's over.'

*

Trent, propped up on his crutches, could only watch and speculate as police officers appeared from nowhere running in all directions. The commotion was followed by the ear-piercing noise of sirens and a pulse of flashing blue lights. Something had definitely happened, and it looked as if the police teams were pulling out. Maybe they'd located another bomb. Trent tried to check his Twitter feed, but the signal in the cathedral precincts was too weak. He shoved the phone back in his pocket.

An unmarked blue saloon screamed up outside the cathedral offices with lights flashing behind its front grille. As it skidded to a halt, Smitherman-Banks appeared at the door. A uniformed officer shot out behind him, and opened the rear passenger door so the ACC could slide into the back seat. Then the car swung around in a tight arc and sped off. The white bomb disposal truck followed a few moments later, and within five minutes, all activity within the cathedral grounds had vanished. The police and army had moved out and abandoned the scene.

Trent shifted his weight from one arm to the other. It made no sense that everyone had pulled out so quickly. Unless the cathedral devices were a hoax and a diversion. Maybe the real story was kicking off elsewhere. He hobbled out of the shadows and wondered where he could find a taxi as the sound of sirens wailing disappeared in the distance.

*

Blake scrubbed his hands in a chrome basin while scanning the toilet cubicles in the mirror. All the doors were closed, but only one was occupied, a small square of red indicating the lock had been engaged. He ignored two men who walked in, and headed for the urinals, keeping his eyes fixed on the door behind him, and wondering how long he could keep up the pretence of washing.

Eventually, the bolt on the cubicle door shot back, and Mike Clark emerged wearing a high visibility vest over a set of navy blue overalls, a docker's uniform identical to the one Blake had on. He had an identity card embossed with an authentic looking logo and a passport photo hanging around his neck. He stopped to check his appearance in the mirror and caught Blake watching. Nothing for it but to bluff it out. Blake nodded a friendly greeting as he hoped one docker might acknowledge another, and returned his attentions to his hands. Blake shook them dry and approached a wall-mounted hand-drier as Clark turned for the exit. Blake noted he had lost the sports bag, but was carrying a mobile phone in one hand. The device he presumed Clark would use to trigger the bomb.

Blake counted to five and followed Clark out. He looked left and right along the passageway, which was flooded with meandering passengers walking in twos and threes, and spotted the back of Clark's head a short distance away. He marched quickly like a man with a purpose, and dived back down the staircase to the car deck below. Rather than returning to the Mondeo, he walked in the opposite direction, towards the open stern where a low sun was flooding the deck with hazy light.

He kept tight to the central bulkhead, dodging around the door mirrors of vehicles, with the mobile phone clutched tightly in his left hand. Blake watched from the bottom of the stairs and, realising where Clark was heading, dived through a door into the deck on the opposite side of the bulwark. He sprinted as fast as his steel-capped boots would allow, and pulled up where the metal divide ended no more than ten yards from where a handful of crew were busy parking the last few cars and vans.

As Blake waited, hidden from the adjacent deck, he sensed a gentle vibration that had been almost imperceptibly reverberating through the ship intensify. It built into a deep, low throb that rattled and clanked through every rivet as the ferry's four massive diesel engines were called into duty. Blake tensed and waited. He started to count to ten, but only made it to six before Clark's weaselly figure breezed past.

Chapter 52

'Hey, buddy,' said Blake, springing out behind Mike Clark.

Surprised by the unexpected voice, Clark did exactly what Blake had anticipated, and as he turned his head, Blake caught him with a fearsome punch that connected with his jaw and stung Blake's knuckles.

Clark was sent wheeling off balance. He pirouetted on one foot and collapsed, sprawled across the bonnet of a car. The sudden jolt set off a series of ear-splitting blasts from the vehicle's horn, which echoed around the cavernous hull and alerted the crewmen, who froze on the spot to watch. Blake grabbed the back of Clark's collar, hauled him upright, and delivered a second blow, jabbing his dazed victim square in the face and shattering his nose. It exploded in a mess of cartilage and blood. Clark's legs buckled, and he slumped to the floor, propped up against the wheel arch of a car.

Blake stood over him, drawing deep breaths. Clark wiped a sleeve across his face, smearing blood and snot across his cheek. His fingers twitched around the phone still in his hand, and he shot Blake a sickly grin.

'It's over. Give me the phone,' said Blake. He was all too aware that if Clark hit the trigger, they'd both die in the close-quarters blast. But that was the least of his worries. The ship was fully loaded, and many innocent lives would also be lost if Blake didn't stop him.

Clark met Blake's gaze, his face expressionless.

'I said give me the phone,' Blake repeated.

'You want it, try taking it,' said Clark, as he lifted the hand holding the phone.

Blake was poised, and at the first flicker of movement aimed a steel toe-cap at Clark's wrist. His aim was good. The phone spilled from Clark's grasp and clattered away under the wheels of a white Transit van. Clark screamed in agony, his wrist shattered.

But, at the same instant, Blake felt the sharp blade of a knife pierce the muscle of his thigh. With his attention focussed on Clark's left hand, he'd not noticed him palm a weapon in his other. At first, there was no pain, only the fearful knowledge that he'd been stabbed. He staggered backwards as the strength in his leg drained, catching the back of his head against a metal stanchion. Colour drained from his vision, and he could only see in monochrome shades of grey, as if he was looking down the cloudy lens of telescope.

Blake concentrated on holding onto consciousness, aware that Clark had rolled onto his stomach and was scrambling on the floor, hunting frantically for his phone. But he went in the wrong direction, and popped up again empty handed. Blake tried to stand, but his leg was in a bad way, refusing to take his weight.

Clark moved away, heading towards the bright daylight coming through the open stern. Then he was running, heading full long towards the white gates that had been closed behind the last cars on the deck. Two crew hands backed away as he approached, their eyes wide in terror as the sight of the bloodied man pitching towards them.

Blake shook his head to clear his vision. The famous white cliffs of Dover were shifting slowly to their left as the ferry's giant propellers bit hard in the shallow water, and eased the ship away from its berth. He shuffled on his backside towards the nearest car, grabbed its overhanging wing mirror, and hauled himself up. Clark was building up speed, tucked up in a full out sprint. Blake's hand searched inside his overalls and grasped his Browning in the holster under his arm. He pulled it out in a smooth motion, steadying himself against the bonnet of the car and aimed for the top of Clark's back at a point between his shoulders. With his arms locked, he squeezed the trigger and fired two rapid shots as the ship lurched sideways, knocking him off balance. The crewmen dived for cover as two deafening cracks echoed around the car deck.

Clark stumbled as the ship righted itself, losing his momentum, but the bullets had sailed harmlessly over his shoulder and ricocheted off the ironwork. He glanced back at Blake and set off again, head down and arms pumping. Blake tried to take another shot, but the flow of blood from his leg had left him weak. He levelled his weapon, but didn't have the strength to keep his arm steady. He let the Browning drop as Clark vaulted the gates and tottered on the rear lip of the deck, alternatively glancing down at the churning water below, and the concrete berth they were leaving behind.

Blake realised with horror that Clark intended to jump, but the gap was already several yards. There was no way he could make it. Suddenly, Clark launched himself with his arms and legs flailing, and disappeared out of Blake's view.

By the time Blake had managed to drag his injured body to the stern, the ferry was already picking up speed and negotiating its way out of the harbour towards the Channel. His first expectation was that by some miracle, Clark had made the jump, but there was only a crowd of dazed dockers standing on the berth looking down bewildered into the water. Blake followed their gaze towards the seething mass from the ferry's thrusters, which made it look like the sea was boiling. Where the foam should have been white, it was churning up a gruesome pink, the remains of Clark's pulverised body.

'Are you in contact with the bridge?' Blake demanded of one of the crewmen who was standing ashen-faced to his right.

The man nodded, his pupils dark and wide.

'Then raise the alarm. I'm with the security services. Tell the captain he has to turn the ship around and get it evacuated as soon as possible. There's an explosive device in one of these cars. Do you understand?'

The crewman nodded again, looking far from reassured. He lifted a radio and started gabbling into it. Satisfied he was doing as he he'd been asked, Blake collapsed on the floor to inspect his leg. His trouser leg was stained dark crimson, and a black handle of a knife was protruding alien-like from his thigh.

He slipped his arms out of the overalls and stripped off his shirt, which he tore into long strips. He laid them on the deck then he grabbed the handle of the knife firmly with both hands. After taking a moment to compose himself, he drew out the blade in one quick motion.

His scream reverberated around the deck, a blood-curdling yell that filled the air as sticky blood began to ooze from the wound. Blake bound it tightly as best he could with the fabric strips, hoping he'd put enough pressure on his thigh to stem the flow.

Using both hands, he pulled himself to his feet and retraced his steps to where he'd fought with Clark, then, with a degree of discomfort, fumbled under the white van for Clark's phone. He'd made a mental note of where it landed and found it easily enough. It was an old style Nokia, only a few years old, but already out-dated in looks. The screen was locked by a four-digit passcode. Blake didn't even bother trying. He flipped the device over in his palm, slid open a rear compartment, and removed the slim lithium battery pack inside.

He placed the battery in one pocket, the phone in another, and breathed a sigh of relief as the wail of approaching sirens floated on the autumnal breeze. So much for subtlety, he thought to himself.

Chapter 53

Proctor was sitting behind the wheel of the Mercedes van watching his side mirrors, with two fake passports lying on the passenger seat. He had parked behind a Polish-registered lorry while he waited for the ferry he'd arrived on to depart. He checked the clock on the dashboard again. The departure was already fifteen minutes delayed, and he was getting anxious. Mike Clark should have joined him by now if everything had gone to plan. He contemplated slipping outside to see what was happening, but talked himself out of it. Their plans were quite specific. He was to wait in the vehicle until Clark joined him. There was no need to draw unnecessary attention to himself.

He tried to persuade himself that the delay had been caused by a mechanical fault, or late running passengers. He chewed on a fingernail and pondered how long he should give it before driving off. He had resolved to wait fifteen more minutes when the passenger door clicked open.

'Where the hell have you... ' His sentence was cut short when he realised it wasn't Clark.

'Hello, Ben,' said Blake. 'Relax, you know who I am, and that I'm not here to do you any harm.' He tapped Proctor on the shoulder.

'What are you doing?' Proctor's brow creased.

'Sleep now, Ben.'

Proctor's eyes fluttered closed and his head yawed left and right before his chin dropped onto his chest. Blake watched a short, fat lorry driver jump from his cab and start washing out a flask, but he paid no attention to the van.

'I want you to remember that you work for me, and that you will do everything I tell you. You won't recognise my face, but you will know when you see me that I pose no threat. Now listen carefully. Mike's not going to be able to meet you. So instead, you and I are going to drive out of the port together. You'll follow my directions precisely, and if anyone asks, tell them we're business partners returning from a trip to France. Is that clear?'

'Yes.'

'Now you're going to wake up. Count back from ten, and feel yourself waking slowly.' Blake touched Proctor on the shoulder again.

Proctor's eyes opened, and he struggled to focus as if unexpectedly woken from a deep slumber. He had a look of puzzlement across his face, like a man unsure of where he was or why he was there. Blake gave him a few minutes to become fully conscious then instructed him to start the van.

'Let's get you home. Follow the signs to the exit, and drive nice and slowly.'

As the van moved off, Blake fished in his pocket for his radio.

'Harry, it's Blake. Has the ferry been evacuated?'

'Blake? Are you okay?'

'I'm fine, Harry. The ferry?'

'They're doing it now. Most people are off, and armed teams are securing the ship. What happened to Clark?'

Blake glanced at Proctor, whose eyes were fixed on the road ahead.' You won't find much left of him. He tried to make a jump for shore, but fell into the sea and was dragged down by the propellers.'

'Right' said Patterson, after a pause. 'So where are you now?'

'I'm with Proctor. We need safe passage out of the port. I don't want to be stopped.'

'Don't worry, I'll see to it.'

'What about the switch car?'

'It's in place, as we discussed.'

'Thanks. I'll call later.'

'Good luck.'

Blake dropped the radio into the foot well and settled back into the seat, a searing pain throbbing through his thigh. The van swung through a narrow covered exit and they passed a large Customs inspections hall lit by a yellowish glow from overhead sodium lights. Blake scanned the buildings with their blacked-out windows, half-expecting an over-enthusiastic officer to order them to stop. But no one appeared. They sailed straight through without seeing a soul.

'Take a left at the roundabout,' Blake said, as they rolled out of the port and into the outskirts of Dover.

The road climbed and curved towards the White Cliffs. 'Watch your speed. We don't want to draw attention to ourselves.'

But Blake need not have worried. Proctor drove steadily within the speed limit as Blake fed him a series of instructions that took them into a respectable-looking residential area on the outskirts of the town consisting mainly of detached 1930s bungalows with tidy gardens and rows of Victorian terraces. They turned into a narrow alley, and pulled up outside a wooden shed with double doors secured with a padlock that had been left unlocked. Blake jumped out as the van came to a halt, and found an anonymous black saloon inside with the keys in the ignition.

'Get in - you can drive,' Blake said. 'Back to the motorway and this time, don't hang about.'

The car roared out of the shed, rattled along the alleyway and two minutes later, they were back on the main road heading towards London.

They drove without speaking, their silence punctuated only by the sound of tyres rumbling over the road and the wind rushing around the window seals. Proctor kept the saloon at a steady eighty miles-per-hour, putting Dover quickly behind them, and closing in on Canterbury.

As they approached the outskirts of the city, Blake pointed to a layby on their left. 'Pull in there,' he ordered.

Proctor did as he was told, slowing down alongside a green waste bin that had been filled to overflowing. He pulled on the handbrake, but left the engine running. To their right, over fields in the distance, the historic spire of the cathedral spiked the sky.

'Switch the engine off,' said Blake.

Proctor glanced at Blake with concern.

'Don't worry. Nothing to panic about. But I need to bring you up to speed on a few things.'

Proctor switched off the engine and waited. Blake tapped his shoulder, and Proctor fell into an instant hypnotic slumber.

'From this evening, Ben Proctor will be dead and you will resume your old identity. Your work for me is over. You will remember nothing about the last two years. When you wake, you will do so as Nick Richards. You will remember nothing about Ben Proctor. That name will no longer mean anything to you, and you will have no recollection of being involved with the British Freedom Alliance. Do you understand?'

'Yes.'

Blake took his time with the debrief, drilling deep into Nick Richard's subconscious, ensuring that the memories of the BFA and his involvement with the Phineas Priests were erased. Blake had created a monster, and now it was time to kill him off. The doctor slaying his Frankenstein. Plans were already underway to stage a road traffic accident. The getaway car would be found burned out, wrapped around a tree, and the body inside unrecognisable. Ultimately, it would be concluded that Ben Proctor had died fleeing from the scene of a failed terrorist atrocity that he had planned under orders from Ken

Longhurst and the BFA.

Nobody outside of MI5 would know the truth that Proctor was killed gently and painlessly in a nondescript layby in Kent.

'Nick, how you are feeling?'

'Fine.'

'Good. Now there's someone who I promised I'd take you to meet. It's time to wake up.'

Blake counted slowly. The man next to him gradually regained full consciousness. Nick Richards opened his eyes, blinked a few times, and looked around, dazed.

'Take your time, Nick, this is going to take a little bit of getting used to.'

Chapter 54

Lucy Chapman was on her fourth cup of coffee and feeling restless. She had the distinct feeling that she'd been stood up. It had been more than two hours since Trent had left, and there had been no communication from Blake. She was beginning to wonder if she was about to have her hopes dashed again.

A motorbike thundered along the motorway below, its engine screaming as it picked its way through lines of traffic. She watched it ride away until it was no more than a dot on the horizon and became aware of a presence at the table. When she looked up Blake was taking a seat opposite.

'You waited,' he said, more as a statement of fact than a question.

'Just like you told me to.' Lucy scanned the restaurant over his shoulder expecting to see Nick loitering, waiting to be called forward.

'I'm sorry, I would have been here sooner, but there were some unavoidable delays.'

'I see' she said.

'The journalist, Trent, is he here?'

'He went to investigate an incident at the cathedral in Canterbury.'

'He may be gone a while then.' Lucy thought she saw the shadow of a smile flicker across Blake's face.

'About my brother? You said you'd tell me what happened.'

'I promised I would reunite you.' Lucy could barely breathe as she heard the words. 'But I need to tell you a few things first.'

'Is he here?'

'You can see him in a minute, but it can't be a permanent reunion. I'm sorry.'

Lucy felt the bitter sting of disappointment. 'What do you mean?'

'He's not the man you knew. You need to prepare yourself for that,' said Blake.

'You said he was involved in something serious, and that I might not recognise him?'

'He's been working for the security service. We placed him undercover in the BFA.'

'A spy?'

'Keep your voice down,' said Blake. 'You're not supposed to know. You're meant to believe he's dead. They'd throw the book at me if they knew I was even talking to you. But I want you to know the truth. Can I trust you with that?'

'I've been trying to find out the truth for so long. Why now?'

'Because I think we owe it to you; because I know what it's like to lose someone and never know if they're alive or dead. This country owes such a debt of gratitude to your brother, but very few people will ever know what he's achieved. I'll tell what I can, but you can never mention a word of it. Can you agree to that?'

Lucy shrugged her shoulders like a sulky teenager.

'I met him while he was at university, when I was looking to recruit someone to take part in an undercover programme we were developing. We'd had our suspicions about the BFA and needed to place someone deep on the inside. Nick was young, intelligent and disillusioned. Most importantly he'd cut all his ties with his family,' said Blake.

'He told you that?'

'Obviously we ran some background checks.'

'Oh my God, you spied on us?'

'We had to be sure he was genuine. He was perfect. So we engineered it that Nick was introduced into the BFA, and with some guidance he quickly became integrated into the party and was able to feed me vital inside information. Of course, we had to eradicate his past. We changed his name, although we built his legend around his own personal history. Then we told him to make contact with his family one last time, and tell you he was taking a gap year to travel,' said Blake.

Lucy's mouth dropped open as the realisation struck her. 'You faked his death?'

'We couldn't take the risk that you would try to contact him. It would have put him in a lot of danger. The break had to be clean.'

'What about his rucksack? How did that turn up in the Amazon?'

Blake shook his head.

'That was you as well?'

'We had to tie up the loose ends for Ben's, I mean Nick's safety. As far as his BFA contacts were aware he'd dropped out of college to follow his interest in the far right. We let it be known by them that he was harbouring huge debts and had little prospect of getting a job. We created an opportunity for them to support him, to invest in him. That's how he gained their trust. At the same time, we had to make sure his family genuinely believed he was dead.'

'It's hard to take in. I mean, he's the least likely person I know to get involved with a group like that. He'd hate everything the BFA stood for. How did you do it?'

'I can't tell you that. His transformation was gradual, but by the end, he was totally convincing. We spent a lot of time and effort getting him to act and think like a neo-Nazi.'

'You mean you brain-washed him?'

'No, it wasn't like that. But look, it's all over. We've

pulled him out.'

'You said he was involved in something serious?'

Blake looked down at his hands folded on the table. 'You'll hear later today about an incident on a ferry at Dover. There were explosives packed into a car designed to kill and injure hundreds of passengers in the middle of the Channel. Thanks to Nick, a tragedy was averted. He played a crucial part in saving lives. He's a hero.'

'But you can't tell me what, right?'

'No. But thanks to Nick, arrest warrants are being carried out across the country to pick up some of the senior people in the BFA, including Ken Longhurst. But unfortunately, Nick's role will never be publicly recognised.'

'I don't understand why they wanted to attack a cross-Channel ferry.'

'Because they wanted to make a point, I guess. The BFA saw Dover as the soft underbelly of immigration into Britain.'

'That's madness.'

'Nobody ever claimed there was any sanity in terrorism.'

'Can I see Nick now?'

'Of course, but he may be a little disoriented. He's been through a lot, and we've just pulled him out of deep cover. He's spent the last two years with the belief that he would never see his family again, and now we're about to reunite you. But this will be a one-off meeting. A chance to say your goodbyes.'

'Goodbyes?'

'Nick will be given a new identity. And he'll be leaving the country for good, for his own safety and yours. He's responsible for the fall of some powerful people, not only in this country, but abroad, and the chances are they're not going to be too happy. I can't put you in danger by giving you any more information. You must write him out of your life. I know it's tough, but at least you know that he's alive and well.'

Lucy felt as if she was losing her brother all over again, even before they'd been reunited. A second death.

'Let me see him now.' Lucy wiped away tears with the back of her hand.

'You won't have long. I need to get him away tonight, but if you're ready, follow me.'

Blake eased himself from the seat and winced, the bandages around his leg drenched with blood.

'Are you alright?' Lucy asked, with genuine concern. 'You're bleeding.'

'I'm fine. Come on.'

Lucy followed Blake into the car park. He led her to a far corner where a black saloon was parked. A figure was sitting in the driver's seat. Her heart skipped a beat. Blake hobbled up to the vehicle and rapped on the window. A tall, gaunt figure stepped out, raised himself to his full height, and turned slowly.

'Nick, there's someone who wants to say hello,' said Blake.

Lucy could barely recognise her brother. His skin was a pallid grey, his hair cropped short, and his eyes bloodshot.

'Nick?' She had thought for so long about how it might be when she was reunited with her brother. Now the moment had arrived she wasn't sure it met her expectations. There was something different about him, as Blake had warned her. It wasn't only his physical appearance. He stared at her through a stranger's eyes, as if processing her features and trying to recall her face.

'Lucy?'

'What's happened to you?' She took a few tentative steps forwards, tears rolling down her cheeks. Nick looked to Blake, as if for reassurance.

'I've explained everything to Lucy. She's here to say her goodbyes,' said Blake.

Nick smiled sheepishly. 'I'm sorry, Lucy.'

It was the smile that did it. Lucy launched herself at her

brother, and almost knocked him off his feet. She threw her arms around his body and hugged him tightly, surprised that there seemed to be little more to him than sinew and bone.

Nick stood with his arms outstretched, unsure what to do. It had been a long time since anyone had shown him any affection. All he had known in recent months was hatred and anger. Slowly he closed his arms around her.

'They tried to tell me that you were dead, but I never believed it for a minute.' Lucy gripped him vice-like as if she would never let go.

Nick tried to speak, but the words choked in his throat.

'Do you remember that day in the park before you left for college? I took a picture of us lying on the grass. I always kept that with me. I knew one day I'd find you.' She finally released her grip on him to look at his face.

'I remember,' he whispered. 'We ate bread and cheese and drank wine.'

'That's right.'

'How's mum?'

'She didn't take the news of your death too well, but you know, she's fine.'

'You know you can't tell her, don't you?'

'I know,' Lucy sniffed. She was struggling with mixed emotions. The anguish of knowing she would never see her brother again after the elation of finally finding him gnawed at her heart. And how was she supposed to keep this secret from her mother?

'Time's nearly up I'm afraid,' said Blake, as two cars rolled around the far edge of the car park. They came to a halt behind the black saloon.

A tall man in an expensive-looking white shirt, jeans, and mirrored sunglasses stepped out of an Audi and handed Blake the keys. Then he jumped in behind the wheel of Proctor and Blake's getaway car.

'What's happening?' asked Lucy, fearing she already knew the answer.

'We need to stage an accident with the car,' said Blake.

'You're going to kill him off again?'

'As far as the police are concerned Nick was partly responsible for the plot to blow up a cross-Channel ferry. They'll be looking for him as part of their investigation. They'll soon find the van we abandoned, and it's only a matter of time before they trace this car. They'll find it run off the road and burned out. They won't easily be able to identify the body, and our people will see to it that the dental records are doctored. As far as they will know, Ben Proctor was behind the wheel and he died trying to escape from the port.'

Lucy said nothing as the saloon reversed out and drove for the exit back onto the motorway, followed by the SUV.

'Are you sure the police will be convinced?' Lucy finally asked, as the cars vanished.

'These guys are professionals. They know what they're doing. Now I'm afraid it's time to go. You need to say your goodbyes.'

'Wait. Where are you taking him?'

'You know I can't tell you that.'

'I know, but you said you were sending him abroad. That means you're taking him to an airport, right?' Blake looked at her impassively. 'Let me come with you, I mean to the airport. You owe us that much. What harm can that do?'

Blake thought for a moment, looking off into the distance as if contemplating whether the decision could land him in any more trouble than he was probably in already. 'Come on then, get in. You'll get me sacked.'

Lucy yelped a squeal of delight before jumping into the back seat of the Audi next to her brother.

Chapter 55

Lucy's phone jigged across the wooden bar, threatening to topple her glass of Sauvignon Blanc. She glanced at the screen. It was the sixth time Trent had rung in the last hour. Each time she toyed with the idea of answering, but concluded it would complicate things. Better to ignore him for the time being.

'Aren't you going to answer that?' The voice made her jump. She grabbed the phone, rejected the call, and slid it into her bag. Nick pulled out a stool and sat down.

'I ordered a bottle of white for old time's sake,' she said, ignoring his question. He took a tentative sip.

'Can't remember the last time I drank wine.' Nick looked at his sister as if seeing her for the first time. She grinned, hardly daring to believe that he was back from the dead.

He had changed out of his clothes. Blake had bought him a smart blue shirt, dark jeans, and a V-neck cashmere jumper. Long sleeves hid the tattoos that would later be laser removed, but he still looked gaunt, and Lucy hated his hair so closely cropped. However, it was a vast improvement on his appearance in the service station car park.

'What will you do when I'm gone?' he asked.

'What can I do? I can't tell anyone. Besides, who'd believe me? I can't even tell mum. What would I say? That her only son is alive and well? That his death was faked and that I found him after a chance encounter on the Tube, and he's disappeared on a fake identity and we'll never see him again?'

'I really don't know what to say to make this better.'

'Why did you do it, Nick?'

'What?'

'Why did you let us think you were dead?'

'I didn't think I had much choice.'

'I know you had your differences with mum, but how could you leave us like that? And to let us think you'd died in some slum somewhere on the other side of the world?'

'It wasn't like that.'

'So how was it?'

'I didn't know what they'd told you,' he muttered into his glass. 'They just said they'd sort it out. I felt like a failure. I couldn't live up to mum's expectations, to your expectations. I wasn't you, Lucy. I wasn't academic, I was never going to achieve what you had, and it felt as if whatever I did mum could never be proud of me.'

'So you gave up on us both?'

'I thought mum hated me. The last time we argued there was such, I don't know, disappointment in her voice. It was as if she despised who I was. We both said things we probably shouldn't have done. I wanted to lead my life my way. Look, I had no money, no prospects, and after that row, no family to turn to. Then I was offered a job I couldn't refuse.'

'Did you know who Blake was? Who he worked for?'

'Not really. He wanted me to do some undercover stuff for the government, and in return, he promised he'd sort me out for life if I did alright. It sounded exciting. I thought it was my way out.'

'And did he tell you that it would involve cutting your family out of your life forever?'

'I thought I'd lost you already.'

'Christ, Nick, it nearly broke mum's heart. I've never seen her so happy as when you phoned her before you supposedly left for Brazil. Then when the police arrived with the news you were missing she was devastated. We all were. You have no idea what that did to her. It was awful. It was as if a little piece of her had been stolen.'

'I thought you'd be glad to be rid of me. I'd been such a pain in the arse.'

'Don't be so bloody self-pitying.'

Lucy snatched up her glass and took a large gulp of wine. Small groups of weary travellers were camped out around tables in the airport bar. Nick looked around, conscious that they had both raised their voices, but no one was taking any notice.

'You said something about seeing me on the Tube?'

'I saw you once. At Holborn. I was on the platform. It was packed with people. A train pulled up but there was no room to get on, and as it was leaving I thought I saw your face. In fact, I was convinced it was you. Of course, the irony was that I was on my way home from Brazil, where we'd been looking for you.'

Nick furrowed his brow as he tried to recall the incident. 'I didn't see you.'

'You looked me straight in the eye, but you had a faraway look, like there was something on your mind. I could tell you didn't recognise me.'

'But you still managed to find me?'

'Can you believe I put up missing posters, like I was looking for a lost cat,' Lucy snorted a half laugh. 'It was the most embarrassing thing I've ever done. I covered the outside of Holborn station with your ugly mug. They were literally everywhere. I used that picture I took in the park before you went to Uni.'

'And someone recognised me?'

'A journalist who'd been investigating the BFA. He thought your face was familiar. He called me, but I didn't believe him when he said you were involved with them. I couldn't believe that you'd get involved with something so... so ghastly.'

Nick hung his head.

'I knew it wasn't true. He claimed he'd met you on a

yacht in Canary Wharf, and that you'd done something awful to him.' Lucy looked her brother in the eye, tears welling.

'Lucy, I don't remember. I don't know how to explain it, but it was as if I was living inside someone else's head. I don't have any memories of who I was or what I did.'

'How can you not remember?'

'I don't know. I feel like I've woken up from a dream and the harder I try to grasp hold of the memories, the further they slip away.'

Lucy took her brother's hand from his lap. 'Nick, what did they do to you?'

'I don't know.'

A large brown envelope dropped over their heads and landed on the bar with a slap.

'Your new life, Nick,' Blake said, looming over them. 'Your new name, passport, driver's licence, and bank account details. The money we agreed has been deposited, and will be available to you from the moment you land. But please wait to open it until you're in the departure lounge at least.' He dropped a second envelope on top of the first. 'And that's your ticket. Again, I'd ask you to refrain from opening it for the moment. Lucy, you understand that today must be a clean break? For Nick's safety and for yours.'

Lucy dipped her head in acknowledgement.

'I'm sorry to break up the party, but we've got to get you on a plane. The sooner you're out of the country the better for everyone. Time to say farewell.' Blake walked away and waited at a discreet distance.

'Well I guess this is it, Sis,' said Nick, standing.

Lucy's eyes were bloodshot. 'Don't leave,' she sobbed.

'I don't have a choice. You know I don't. If I could turn back time and make a different choice, I would. But I can't.' His words choked in his throat.

Lucy threw her arms around him, and burrowed her face into his neck. 'I love you, Nick.'

'I love you too. Who knows, one day they might let me come back. Never say never.'

'Don't ever forget me.'

'How could I?'

Lucy dived into her handbag with one hand, wiping tears with the back of the other. 'I want you to take this.' She produced the dog-eared photo she'd used on the missing posters. Nick stared at the picture silently before tucking it into a pocket in a leather travel bag by his feet.

'Lucy, I am so, so sorry for everything.'

'I know,' she replied, composing herself. 'You'd better go. You've got a plane to catch. Goodbye, Nick.'

'Goodbye, Lucy.'

They stood for an uncomfortable moment, looking at each other as if waiting for some further revelation that didn't come. Eventually, Lucy picked up her handbag and walked determinedly away.

When he was sure that she had gone, Nick scooped up his cabin bag and found Blake waiting outside. They walked together to the check-in terminals, Nick clutching his two envelopes tightly.

'I guess this is where I find out where my new life begins?' Nick ripped open the smaller envelope, and pulled out the one-way ticket. He smiled to himself as he checked the destination. 'Really?'

'We've set you up in a rented apartment for the first six months. All paid for in advance. The details are all in the second envelope. What you decide to do after that is up to you.'

Nick tore it open and tipped the contents into his free hand. Among the documents was a maroon passport. He flicked it open to the back page, and found a younger-looking photo of himself against a name he didn't recognise.

'Your new identity,' said Blake.

'That's going to take some getting used to.'

'It won't take as long as you think. Now come on, we need to get you checked in.'

Nick slumped off in the direction of the rows of queues snaking towards a line of check-in desks, bag slung over his shoulder. When he returned, Blake walked with him to the departure lounge.

'This is it, Nick. The start of your new adventure. Thank you for everything you've done, and good luck.'

An hour later, Nick was sitting on a plane, a seatbelt strapped tightly across his lap, staring out a small window at the damp runway. A middle-aged businessman wearing overpowering aftershave and a crumpled white shirt settled in beside him.

'Is it your first visit to Brazil?' he asked, peering past Nick to see through the window.

'Yes,' he replied, not feeling at all inclined to strike up conversation with a stranger.

'Well, Rio is beautiful at this time of year. I'm sure you'll love it.'

'I'm sure you're right.' Nick smoothed out the photo that Lucy had given him on his knee. He traced the features of her face with his finger, recalling how the sun had warmed their bodies as they lay on the cool grass, enjoying the alcohol buzz from the wine.

The roar of engines accompanied the sensation of bumpy movement forward. Nick closed his eyes and let his head fall against the back of the seat as the aircraft rumbled across the runway, gathering speed. And then he felt the seat punch him in the back with the acceleration of the plane. In less than a minute, the tyres lifted from the ground, and they were away, powering free from the earth's pull and soaring high into the sky.

The Armageddon
Virus

Chapter 1

Tom Blake shook the rain from the sleeves of his coat and combed the moisture from his hair with his fingers. It was a grey, autumnal afternoon that had dampened his mood long before the message had chimed on his phone and intruded on his day. The instruction was unequivocal. Drop everything.

His decision to use public transport had been a mistake. The mortuary was on the far side of town but the fug of stale carbon dioxide on the Underground had made his head buzz and his eyes sting. All he wanted was to lie down in a darkened room. It didn't help that he knew what was waiting for him behind the double doors. A soulless square room, tiled in white under unforgiving strip lights. And the smell. The sweet, rotten stench of corporeal mush. The memory of it from medical school made him feel green.

He took a deep breath and crashed through the doors.

The body was lying on a cantilevered table under a thin sheet with only the feet, head and shoulders left uncovered. A cardboard tag with a name scribbled in black ink had been tied with string to the big toe. It was the body of a man, a little older than Blake, maybe in his early fifties. His hair was bitumen black, receding over a dark skull. A rash of salt and pepper bristles masked sallow cheeks. His skin was puffed and bloated. Someone had arranged his arms at his sides and his legs out straight so his feet fell away at the ankles. Blake stepped closer with his top lip curled and his nose wrinkled, like he was inspecting the remains of an animal at the side of the road.

'Who was he?' he asked.

The pathologist on the other side of the slab stretched his back. He looked tired, like he'd worked through the night and been called back to cover the next day's shift.

'You don't know?'

Blake shrugged. The message said to take a look at the body but he wasn't sure what perspective he could bring. Anatomy wasn't his speciality. They knew that. But a twenty year military career had left him pre-programmed to follow orders without question.

The pathologist unhooked a metal clipboard and read from a handwritten form. 'Javed Rahimi. Forty-eight years old. Five feet eight tall. One hundred and eighty-six pounds.'

'Cause of death?'

'Multiple organ failure and severe internal bleeding. He had haemorrhaging around his lymph nodes, heart, kidneys, stomach and intestines.'

'What's your supposition?'

'That he was poisoned.'

'Murdered?'

The pathologist's eyes flitted over Blake's shoulder to the woman standing at the back of the morgue. She'd been waiting in the corridor when Blake arrived and followed him in. No welcome. No introduction. But he had a pretty good idea who she was.

'It looks suspicious,' said the pathologist. 'His white blood count was incredibly high although toxicology came back inconclusive. No trace of anything in his blood, urine or tissue samples.'

'You don't think an external trauma could have caused the haemorrhaging?'

'Possible but improbable. We found no bruising. I would speculate it was something he either ingested or inhaled.'

'So why do you need me?'

The pathologist looked at him blankly. 'I've no idea who you are or why you're here,' he said. 'I was told to give you the facts. That's all.'

The click of high heels echoed off the tiled walls as the woman stepped forwards.

'He was a political refugee.' Her voice was deeper than Blake had expected and carried an authority he found appealing. 'He came here five years ago from Iran seeking asylum after being arrested and tortured for his involvement in protests following the disputed election of President Ahmadinejad. When he was released he fled the country, made it across Europe and into Britain clinging to the axle of a lorry.'

'So?' said Blake. He caught a breath of perfume as she breezed past. It was subtle and expensive. He wasn't sure why he was surprised that an MI5 field agent should be wearing scent.

'For the last three years he'd been working as a cleaner for the Prison Service.' She stopped on the opposite side of the table so Rahimi's body was between them. She had delicate features, paper-thin, almost translucent skin and tight, corkscrew hair the colour of autumnal oak leaves.

'So call the Met,' said Blake.

She gave him a weak smile. 'A few weeks ago the Pentagon issued a general alert through their Iranian Directorate after intercepting a series of calls made from the UK. They were placed to an agent on their radar.'

'And you think Rahimi made them?'

'We don't know for sure. The Americans say the calls were made from inside the prison.'

'Where he worked?' Blake raised an eyebrow.

'The Prime Minister's furious. God knows how GCHQ missed it. There'll be an inquiry, of course, but for now he's demanding a quick investigation and whatever was being planned shut down.'

'So Rahimi was murdered?'

'We don't know but it seems a likely explanation. It

would help to find out if he made those calls.'

'Why would he?'

'We don't know.'

'What do you know?'

'That he had a good job as a computer programmer in Iran but took a cleaning position here to make ends meet.'

'And now he's dead. Do you have any evidence he made the calls?'

'Not specifically but the facts are straightforward. A series of phone calls made to an Iranian agent were intercepted and an Iranian cleaner at the prison winds up dead.'

'People die all the time. Doesn't mean a thing.'

'Unexplained internal haemorrhaging and possible poisoning. You don't think that's even a little suspicious?'

Blake wiped his nose with the back of his hand. His skin was cool. Even on a dull autumn day it had been like walking into a chiller cabinet. 'It's still quite a leap of imagination.'

'But nonetheless a possibility we need to investigate.'

'Where was he found?'

'He rented a room not far from where he worked. A shared house, mostly occupied by other immigrants. They raised the alarm when they hadn't seen him for a few days.'

'Had he tried to get any medical help?'

'We don't think so.'

'Well, that's curious.'

'Why?'

'Because death by poisoning is a slow, agonising death. He'd have been cramped up in pain, possibly for days. If that had been you, would you have called a doctor?'

'Maybe he didn't have one? Or perhaps he became ill so quickly he didn't have the strength to call for help?'

'Maybe,' said Blake. He pulled the sheet covering the body down to expose a line of ragged stitches running from his sternum to his stomach where he'd been carved up in post-mortem. Blake grabbed a wrist. Lifted it to inspect the skin from the shoulder then repeated the examination on the other arm.

'Did you look for puncture wounds?' Blake asked. The pathologist had wandered to the far side of the room and was busying himself at a worktop. 'It's possible he could have been injected.'

'Of course, but we didn't find anything.'

With two straight fingers, Blake rolled Rahimi's head to one side, the stiffening effects of rigor mortis having long since vanished. He checked his neck on both sides then set his head straight again.

'No other marks or bruises?' asked Blake.

'Nothing out of the ordinary.'

'Anything in his stomach?'

'No.'

Like a plasterer checking his work for imperfections, Blake scrutinised every inch of Rahimi's skin. He pulled the sheet away from his legs and set it in a heap over his pelvis. He ran a careful eye over both legs then lifted his knees to check the back of his thighs.

'What's this?'

The pathologist shuffled back to the table, dropping a pair of wire-rimmed glasses onto his nose. He screwed up his face as Blake pointed to a tiny blemish. 'An insect bite. Probably a mosquito or a bed bug. Nothing more.'

'It's worth a closer look. You should carry out a biopsy.'

The pathologist took a step back and lifted his glasses. 'A biopsy?'

'Do as he says,' said the woman.

'Have you searched his room?'

'We didn't find anything,' the field agent replied.

'What about a mobile phone?'

'It was sent to the lab but they've already confirmed it wasn't used to make the calls.'

'Who did he last call?'

'It hadn't been used for more than a week before his

death.'

'I see,' said Blake.

'You think it's significant?'

'I've no idea, I'm not a detective. You should try CID.'

'We can't leave it to them. This is a matter of national security.'

'You don't know for sure.'

'We can't take the risk.'

'So what happens next?' The woman didn't reply, letting Blake work it out for himself. 'I need to know what you need from me,' said Blake.

But even as he formed the words he sensed he already knew the answer.

Chapter 2

Her car was parked in a leafy avenue a few minutes' walk from the mortuary. The paintwork of the sporty two-seater was so highly polished that it reflected the branches of the trees. She unlocked the doors remotely and Blake folded himself into the passenger seat with his knees up to his chest. Inside was immaculately clean. Almost obsessively spotless. It could have come straight from the showroom apart from the hint of perfume that hit him as he opened the door.

The woman smoothed out the legs of her trouser suit and adjusted her jacket as she climbed in beside him. She tucked a stray strand of hair behind her ear and checked her make-up in the rear-view mirror. When she slotted a key into the ignition, she left one hand on the wheel. No wedding ring. Not that it was unusual for MI5 agents to be single, particularly those who worked in the field.

'I'm Alex,' she said as she started the engine.

'Doesn't sound much like a spook's name. I thought you got to choose a pseudonym? I imagined you'd have picked something more sophisticated.'

'Like what?'

'I don't know. Eloise or Paris?'

A smile crept across her face. She checked over her shoulder and pulled out. 'What's wrong with Alex?'

'I didn't say there was anything wrong with it. Is it just Alex?'

'Mortensen. It's Danish, on my grandfather's side.'

'I'm guessing you already know my name?'

'Blake,' she said. 'Although I thought you'd have chosen something more sophisticated.'

'They tried to fix me up with a new name but I didn't like it.'

'When?'

'It's a long story.'

The car rumbled through the smart commercial districts of the city and swept over the River Thames, leaving behind the tourists and well-heeled businessmen on the north bank. They were heading for the ugly, post-war blocks of flats on the outskirts. Blake reached for the lever under his legs but found the seat was already pushed back as far as it would go.

'Is it far?' he asked, the dashboard digging into his knees.

'You're taller than I thought,' said Mortensen.

'What were you expecting?'

'The agency doesn't usually recruit tall guys. They tend to stand out in a crowd.'

Blake didn't consider himself particularly tall but even at a fraction under six feet he'd been a giant among the squat NCOs of the SAS.

'I'm not like you,' he said.

'What do you mean, not like me?'

'I'm not a spook.'

'Well, you work for MI5 and I think that's pretty much the only qualification.'

'You know what I mean.'

'I don't think I do. If you're not a spook, what are you?'

It was a good question. Blake's transition from the military had happened so quickly. When they announced his unit was being disbanded, it came as a complete surprise. A victim of a nervous government and budget cuts. Somehow his commanding officer, Harry Patterson, had convinced MI5 to bring the unit under the auspices of the service. Told the Deputy Director General straight that Blake's skills, honed as a military psychologist, would be an invaluable asset for an organisation battling against a mounting home-grown terror threat.

'Did Patterson send you?'

Mortensen ignored the question. 'I was told to meet you at the morgue and fill you in on Rahimi's background, that's all. They said you had some medical knowledge and that you might be able to help with the case.'

'I don't think I can.'

'Your boss has a different opinion.'

'So Patterson did send you?'

'He was confident your expertise would prove valuable.'

'With what exactly? A spurious link between a dead refugee and a supposed phone call the Americans think was made in the prison where he worked?'

Mortensen kept her eyes on the road, unmoved by Blake's outburst. They pulled up outside a Victorian terrace in a scruffy street stippled with litter. Weeds had woven themselves around an iron fence set into a low wall. A bored-looking police officer was standing with his hands clasped behind his back in front of a blue door. Its paint was cracked and peeling.

'I was told you'd have a unique perspective on the case and I was to offer as much assistance as you needed. That's it. Now do you want to take a look at Rahimi's bedsit or not?' said Mortensen, ratcheting on the handbrake.

Blake peered up at the building. 'How long did he live here?'

'For the last eighteen months. It's privately-rented, like most of the places in the area. They've mostly been converted into flats and filled with low income benefits claimants.'

Blake trailed Mortensen up five crumbling steps to the front door. Mortensen flashed an identity card and the police officer stepped aside. Rahimi's room was on the ground floor along a narrow corridor adjacent to a flight of stairs that disappeared up to a gloomy landing. The door was hanging off its hinges. The frame was splintered and sealed off with strips of blue and white police tape.

'Put these on.' Mortensen tossed Blake a pair of latex gloves and ducked into the room.

The foul stench of death hung in the air, lingering on nicotine-stained walls and the dirty carpet. Mortensen flicked on a light and disturbed a squadron of flies that had gathered on the exposed bulb hanging from the ceiling. The room was small. Big enough only to accommodate a bed, a wardrobe and a table. There were traces of white forensic powder on some of the surfaces. A pile of soiled bedclothes lay in a crumpled heap on the mattress. A grubby sink was tucked against the wall next to a uPVC door that led out to a concrete courtyard.

Blake was drawn to a faded photograph with dog-eared corners stuck to a wall over the bed. He peeled it off and studied the three smiling faces. An older woman, her head covered by a black headscarf, was flanked by two girls. One looked to be in her late teens, the other a few years younger. Each had lustrous brown eyes and thick lashes. No mistaking they were a mother and her daughters. The similarity between them was striking.

'Is this Rahimi's family?' asked Blake.

'His wife, Niyoosha, and his daughters. Alaleh's fourteen. The elder girl, Yasaman, is seventeen. Their current whereabouts in Iran is unknown.'

'He left them behind?'

'I guess he had his reasons.'

'Do they even know he's dead?'

'The embassy's been notified. It's up to them to pass on the information.'

Blake dropped the photo on the table and poked around a pile of books and newspapers. A plastic lighter was balanced on top of a packet of foreign-branded cigarettes. He picked out a stubby butt from a mound of ash in an overflowing ashtray and sniffed it like a connoisseur selecting a fine cigar. He pulled a face and dropped it. Moved lightly across the floor towards the wardrobe. Stopped to rock back and forth on a board that creaked under his weight. The wardrobe was pathetically bare. Three cotton shirts and two pairs of beige polyester trousers were hung from the sort of wire hangers given away at dry cleaners' stores. The sum of Rahimi's belongings swinging sparsely on a metal rail.

A limescale-encrusted razor and a can of shaving foam were lined up around the sink next to a toothbrush with splayed bristles and a dried sliver of soap. Blake ran his fingers around a mirror splattered with white toothpaste flecks, feeling for anything hidden behind it, then tried the handle of the patio door. It was locked and there was no key. Outside, concrete steps led into a shady courtyard pebble-dashed green with moss and algae. Blake shaded his eyes with one hand and peered out at dirty puddles that had formed in the depressions of a sunken patio.

When he turned back into the room, his gaze fell on the dishevelled bed. He fished under the cheap pine frame with a flailing arm and pulled out a canvas travel bag in a cloud of dust. He unzipped it, found it was empty and slung it back. He slumped to his haunches and peered around, looking for something, anything, he might have missed.

He was slowly rising to his feet when he heard it. Or maybe it was something that he'd felt. He wasn't sure.

'Listen,' he said.

'What?'

'Can you hear it? It's only faint.'

Mortensen cocked her head to one side. They listened together but heard only the drone of a frustrated fly trying to break out through the glass of the patio door.

Blake fell on his hands and knees, moving away from Mortensen. At the far side of the room he picked at a frayed edge of carpet until he'd teased a section free. He rolled it back to reveal a crumbling foam underlay hiding stained floorboards running the width of the room. One of the planks had been sawn through in two places. A knot the size of a large coin had fallen out leaving a hole just big enough for a finger. Blake tucked the carpet under his knees and was about to hook the loose plank free when he froze.

'What now?' asked Mortensen, leaning over his shoulder.

'It's stopped,' he whispered.

He jammed a thumb into the hole. Pulled out the plank and peered into the cavity between two joists. There was something in the darkness. A rectangular lump of plastic. He reached in and pulled out a mobile phone. An old model. Thick and heavy with an old-fashioned number pad. The screen was alight, bright enough to illuminate his hand and lower arm. It was displaying a message. Two words. Mortensen read them out loud.

'Missed call.'

Chapter 3

Blake tried the keypad, prodding at the buttons with a thick finger, but the device was locked by a passcode. The phone was like a technological relic. A brick designed only for placing and receiving calls, unlike the hand-held super-computers that now masqueraded as phones. It was no doubt a pay-as-you-go device. An over-the-counter purchase that could be bought without any documentation. Untraceable.

'We should get it over to the lab,' said Mortensen. The note of hesitation in her voice wasn't lost on Blake.

The lab could wait.

There are ten thousand possible permutations for a four digit code and the chances were high the phone would auto-disable after a number of failed attempts. But people rarely use random codes. Most choose numbers they can easily remember. Sequences with a personal significance.

'What's Rahimi's date of birth?' asked Blake.

Mortensen screwed her eyes shut as she tried to recall the information she'd seen on a file. 'March the twenty-third.'

Blake punched in the date as four digits.

2 - 3 - 0 - 3.

The phone chirruped. An incorrect code. He tried it in reverse.

3 - 0 - 3 - 2.

Wrong again.

'What about trying the month first, the way the

Americans write their dates?' Mortensen suggested.

Blake tried again. 0 - 3 - 2 - 3.

'No, that's not it either.' He looked around the room seeking inspiration. 'What year was he born?'

'Nineteen sixty-four,' said Mortensen, this time without hesitation.

Blake tapped in the numbers and the screen turned blue. A handful of icons appeared on the display.

'We're in,' he said. He navigated his way through a series of menus to the call register and was surprised to find no calls had been placed on the phone but there were two numbers in the list of calls received.

'Mean anything to you?' Blake passed the handset to Mortensen.

'No,' she said, frowning. 'But if this was the phone used in the prison then the times should match up with those of the intercepted calls. Come on, we really ought to get it over to the technical lab. Have you seen enough?'

Blake stood up and balled the latex gloves into his pockets. They'd made his hands sweaty despite the powder on the inside. 'Yeah, let's go.'

Mortensen's car had attracted the attention of a gaggle of greasy youths cooing over its sleek lines. They dispersed briefly when Blake shooed them away but re-formed as Mortensen fired up the throaty V6 engine. The bravest ones hollered a volley of wisecracks. Mortensen floored the accelerator and pulled away with a squeal of rubber which provoked a sarcastic cheer.

'What did the other tenants tell you about Rahimi?' Blake asked.

'He was a loner who left the house at around six every morning and was home after five. Regular as clockwork. He spent his free time on his own in his room.'

'When did anybody last see him alive?'

'Five days ago. One of the tenants passed him as he was going out. He said Rahimi was a little agitated but didn't think much of it.'

'And no one saw him after that?'

'Not in the house. It looks as if he took himself to his room when he fell ill and stayed there until he was carried out.'

'What about the prison? Didn't they notice anything suspicious?'

They pulled up in a queue of traffic on a bridge behind a red bus with a rattling engine spewing out dirty diesel fumes.

'We've not spoken to them yet.' Mortensen threw Blake an awkward glance.

'Why not?'

'Operational reasons.'

'I thought this was an urgent matter of national security?'

'Blake, you'll have to trust me on this, okay?'

'So, let me get this straight. You suspect Rahimi was making calls to an Iranian terrorist from inside the prison where he worked. A few days later he ends up murdered but you didn't think it was worth speaking with the prison staff?'

'We don't know he was murdered, or whether that phone belonged to him or even if he made the calls. It's all conjecture.'

'But I'm not getting the full picture, am I?'

'Everything will become clear in time, I promise.'

They were moving again but the traffic was heavy. They rolled on a few metres and stopped. Mortensen had the heater on, blowing hot air, trying to keep the windscreen clear. A nausea swelled from the pit of Blake's stomach. It was uncomfortably warm and he craved the taste of a cool, fresh breeze.

Another five metres. Mortensen jammed on the brakes, a little too sharply. They both jolted forwards in their seats.

Blake

Blake stared out of the window with dead eyes at the stream of shoppers drifting from store to store. Too many questions, not enough answers. It all felt wrong.

His left hand fingered the smooth plastic of the door handle.

If Mortensen was serious about getting to the bottom of Rahimi's involvement in some kind of plot, speaking to staff at the prison should have been top of her list. She was hiding something. He was sure of it.

'You're playing games with me,' said Blake.

The car crept moved forwards a few metres until the brake lights of the truck ahead flashed on and Mortensen stamped on the brakes again.

Blake let his right hand fall casually to his side and in one movement unclipped his seat belt. He was out of the car before Mortensen knew it, striding along the street with his hands in his pockets.

Mortensen swore under her breath, pulled off the road and mounted the kerb.

'Blake, wait!' she shouted as she jumped out of the car, forcing a white van to swerve. She mouthed an apology and ran after Blake, bowling through startled pedestrians.

She caught up with him as he was turning into a side street.

'Listen to me,' she said, grabbing his upper arm from behind.

He spun around on his heel. 'I told you, start talking straight or I walk away.'

'Just calm down, okay? Let's get this phone to the lab and I'll tell you everything I know. We'll find somewhere quiet to talk. Please, get back in the car.'

'Let's talk now.'

'Later.'

'Fine.' Blake found his phone and dialled a pre-set number. It rang twice before diverting to an answerphone. He decided not to leave a message.

'Who're you calling? Patterson? You know it was his idea for me to work with you.'

Blake hands balled into fists. His jaw was clamped so

tightly that a vein behind his ear began to pulse. Every instinct told him to keep walking. This wasn't how he operated. Patterson should have known better.

'You want to be reassigned?' Mortensen asked.

'Murder mysteries aren't really my thing.'

'Patterson thought we'd work well together. At least give it a chance.'

'He knows I work alone.'

'He said you could be a bit of a cold fish. Cantankerous I think he said. Maybe he knows you better than you think.'

'I work alone,' Blake repeated.

'You didn't operate solo in Echo 17 though, did you? Or did I get that wrong?'

'That's classified information. What do know about the unit?'

'A Special Forces deniable asset, acting under the direct authority of the Prime Minister?' said Mortensen. 'I read the files. The unit is still operational, only now it's run by MI5 under Patterson's direct command. Want me to go on? You're currently the only active operative...'

'Enough,' Blake snapped.

'Come back to the car. We'll find somewhere to talk.'

Blake's shoulders slumped, his will to protest evaporating. He trudged back to the car behind Mortensen like a defeated man.

'I was given special clearance to read those files, just so you know.'

'By who?'

'The Deputy Director General.'

'The existence of the unit is known only to a handful of people, and for good reason.'

'But it's not run by the military any more is it? It's an MI5 asset. Things change. Get used to it.'

'It's still a covert operational unit that has to stay off the grid precisely because of what I do.'

'And what is that exactly?'

Blake ignored the question, watching the road ahead snarling under the weight of traffic.

'Your job was never to work alone. So what changed?' Mortensen asked.

'I did.'

'Why?'

'I don't know.'

'Do you miss it? The Army, I mean?'

'I miss the unit as it used to be, before the Ministry of Defence shut us down and consigned a dozen good men to the scrapheap. One up to the accountants, but life goes on. I'm happy enough.'

'I read something about a Deep Sleepers programme. What is it?'

'I thought you'd read the files?'

'There were holes.'

'Probably for good reason.'

'Patterson said you can get inside people's heads. What is it, some kind of mind control?'

The cause of the heavy traffic revealed itself as a set of roadworks that blocked one side of the carriageway. Traffic flow was being controlled by temporary lights.

'It's not something I can talk about,' said Blake, crossing his arms. He wasn't supposed to have a history or a background beyond his supposed fatal shooting in Afghanistan by a Taliban marksman. He lived his life in obscurity. A ghost. The fewer people who knew of his existence the better.

Mortensen took the hint and sat in silence drumming her palms on the steering wheel.

When her phone rang it made them both jump. It was connected wirelessly to the car's stereo system so the sound reverberated through the speakers. Mortensen answered with a push of a button on the wheel.

'Can you get back to the mortuary urgently?'

Blake recognised the voice of the pathologist.

'We can be there in fifteen minutes,' said Mortensen,

glancing at a clock on the dashboard. 'What's wrong?'

'There's something you should see. I don't know how we missed it before.'

'We're on our way,' she said.

Chapter 4

The pathologist led them along a corridor to an office cluttered with paperwork and ushered them into chairs opposite a desk. Faded yellow paint was flaking from the walls and a florescent tube flickered overhead. A narrow window letting in virtually no natural light gave views out onto the dirty bricks of an adjacent wall. Three long shelves groaned with the weight of serious-looking medical textbooks on anatomy, surgical pathology and microbiology.

The pathologist sat down, gathering his lab coat around his body. With a frown he reached into a drawer and produced a plastic pot, sealed with a white screw-on cap.

'We found this after some further exploratory work,' he said.

He swept away some loose papers and set the pot on the desk. It contained a tiny sliver of metal. Blake picked up the pot and rolled the shard around.

'We found it in Rahimi's leg under the surface of the skin near a blemish we thought was an insect bite,' the pathologist said, lifting his glasses and perching them in a crop of sandy-coloured hair.

'What is it?' asked Mortensen, as Blake handed her the pot.

'A poison pellet, we think. Are you familiar with the Georgi Markov case?'

'The Bulgarian Secret Service assassination?'

'It has the hallmarks of a copycat killing,' said the pathologist.

'You think Rahimi was killed by someone with a poison-tipped umbrella?' said Mortensen. 'That's a bit fanciful.'

'But a plausible explanation at this stage. I'd like to run some more tests but it looks highly likely the pellet was filled with a powerful toxin and injected into his thigh.'

'I've pulled bigger splinters out of my thumb. Could something that small really have killed him?' Mortensen rolled the pellet one way and then the other.

'That's the interesting thing. It's actually less than two millimetres in diameter. A precision-engineered piece.'

'Which suggests we're looking at a sophisticated assassination,' said Blake. 'Do you have any thoughts on the poison they used?'

'Something fast-acting. My guess is ricin. It would certainly account for all the symptoms - the haemorrhaging and the high white blood count, for instance.'

'But the dose must have been miniscule,' said Mortensen.

'Even very small amounts of ricin can have fatal consequences once it gets into the bloodstream,' the pathologist said.

'It's exactly what the Bulgarians used in the Markov assassination in '78. He thought he'd been stung by an insect as he crossed Waterloo Bridge,' said Blake.

'And a few days later he was dead,' said the pathologist. 'And the thing about ricin is it's so easy to come by.'

'An extract from caster beans, if I remember rightly?' said Blake.

'Simple to obtain but deadly because it has two toxic elements. The first penetrates cells to create a passage for the second toxin which attacks the cell itself and stops it being able to produce proteins. The effect is the cells die off one by one leading to a painful and protracted death.'

Mortensen set the pot back down on the desk with a shudder.

'The question is, who's behind it?' said Blake. 'It would

have required highly-specialist laser-cutting technology to drill into a pellet this small. And it would have to be constructed out of a very hard material to stop it distorting when it was fired into the body.'

'I made a point of looking up the Markov case before you arrived. That Bulgarian pellet was made out of platinum and iridium, which are both biologically inert,' said the pathologist. 'They coated it with a wax that dissolved at body temperature allowing the toxin to be released. Very clever and brutally efficient.'

'And unless Rahimi sought immediate medical help, his death was inevitable,' said Blake.

'But not instant. The poor bugger would have been in agony for days.'

'The question is, who has the capability to produce something like this?' asked Mortensen.

'The KGB had labs working on this sort of thing at the height of the Cold War but who knows who they might have sold the technology to,' said Blake.

'The Iranians?' suggested Mortensen. 'They've always had a cosy relationship with Moscow.'

'True, and it would fit your theory that Rahimi was communicating with Iran.'

'But it doesn't explain why they had him killed. The PM needs to be informed.'

'That's your department, I believe,' said Blake.

'Of course, the coroner will also have to be told,' said the pathologist. 'There'll have to be an inquest.'

'How soon do you have to let him know?'

'It's a possible murder case. He already has the preliminary paperwork but I need to let him know about the pellet.' The pathologist swept up the pot and returned it to his desk drawer. 'It does somewhat change the complexion of the case.'

'Yes, of course,' said Mortensen, standing up. 'Just how soon would you let him know? Is it reasonable that perhaps it could take a few days for the information to filter down, if you catch my drift?'

'Are you suggesting I withhold information?'

'Not at all, I'm suggesting this is a serious matter of national security. If you could give us a couple of days to make some inquiries before the coroner is notified, that would be helpful.'

'That would be very irregular. If it was discovered I failed to disclose…'

'You won't be failing to disclose anything. You'll send your updated report to him, but not for a few days. We need at least forty-eight hours head-start. As soon as the coroner's office is informed there's a risk of the information leaking out. You do understand, don't you?'

The pathologist slammed the drawer shut. 'You don't leave me much choice do you? Okay, I'll hold off for two days. That's it.'

'Thank you,' said Mortensen, turning to leave the office.

Blake followed her closely out of the building. He caught her by the elbow as they stepped out onto the street.

'You promised me some answers,' he said, spinning Mortensen around.

'Not here,' she said.

'Then where?'

'My apartment's not far. Come back with me and I'll fill you in on everything I know.'

'Everything?'

'Everything.' Mortensen sighed. 'There's something else you really need to know.'

Chapter 5

Her apartment was on the third floor of a modern fortress of steel and glass on the banks of the Thames with views across the river. She showed Blake into an open-plan living space with white walls and sparse furniture.

'Make yourself comfortable, I'm going to freshen up,' she said. 'Help yourself to a beer. I'll be out in a minute.'

Blake found the fridge and grabbed a bottle of lager as the sound of a shower running drifted through from an adjacent room.

He stood by ceiling-height windows where rivulets of rain clung to the glass causing the lights opposite to shimmer and watched the ebb and flow of early evening activity. Tiny figures darting through the rain on the opposite bank and cargo-vessels struggling against the tide.

His warm breath fogged on the cold pane.

'Can I get your help for a second?' Blake spun around at the sound of Mortensen's voice.

She was framed in a door wearing a red dress that clung tightly to her slim frame. 'Could you do me up?'

She held the front of the dress to her chest with one hand and was half-turned with her back towards him, the material puckering open. Blake's eyes lingered on her naked skin, pale and unblemished save for a peppering of freckles across her shoulders. His eyes ran along the sharp prominence of her shoulder blades and traced the dual tracks of muscle that ran the length of her spine.

'Come on, I won't bite,' said Mortensen. Her face was glowing. 'I love this dress but it's so difficult - ' she said.

Blake's cheeks flushed.

'What's wrong?' Mortensen swept her hair away from her neck. 'I thought I'd treat you - to dinner, I mean,' she said. 'I thought it would be good to get to know each other better.'

'Not a good idea.'

'I thought you wanted to know about the Rahimi case, but if you've changed your mind?'

Blake looked up at the ceiling as if seeking divine inspiration. 'I'm sorry. It's just been a while.'

'Since a woman's asked you for help dressing for dinner?'

He walked across the room, grasped the silver zip between meaty fingers and inched it upwards, careful not to catch her skin.

'There,' he said.

Mortensen adjusted the tightness around her chest and floated back to her room. 'I won't be long.'

Blake noticed his own worn jeans and crumbled shirt. 'I'm not really dressed for going out,' he shouted.

'Don't worry, you'll be fine.'

They ate at an intimate Italian restaurant with red chequered tablecloths and wicker chairs. The owner, an avuncular man with pipe cleaner-long legs, tried to seat them in the window but Mortensen insisted on a table at the back with unobstructed views across the room.

'Routine caution,' Mortensen said, as she allowed Blake to pull out her chair.

She dropped a clutch bag at her feet. It hit the floor with a noticeable thud.

'We want you to go into the prison undercover,' she said as a young waiter stepped out of earshot with their order scribbled on a pad. 'Find out what you can about what Rahimi was up to.'

'Into the prison?'

'It's technically two prisons, a category-A jail for regular and remand inmates and a high security unit, mostly full of murderers and terrorists, within the compound. You'll have heard of a few of them thanks to the tabloids.'

'And that's where the calls were made?'

'Yes, but we don't know how Rahimi smuggled in a phone. Security is incredibly tight. The only access is through the main prison, passing through a series of gated entrances independently controlled by a central locking system overseen by a command hub. There are more stringent measures protecting access into and out of the unit, full body scans, physical inspections and banks of CCTV cameras. Frankly, it'd be easier to break into the vaults of the Bank of England.'

'So why didn't you tell me earlier you wanted me inside?'

'Patterson's decision. He wanted you to take a look at Rahimi's body and get a feel for the case first. He was adamant I wasn't to tell you.'

'What's the plan for getting me in?'

'We're still working on that.'

Blake swirled his wine around the inside of his glass, gripping its stem between his finger and thumb. He'd only seen the inside a prison once before. They'd hit it hard and fast. A standard four-man team tearing into the town in the dead of night under a plume of desert dust. They'd ripped the door off its hinges with blocks of C-4 and filled the bunker with assault rifle fire, quickly overwhelming the poorly disciplined Iraqi guards. Most had died before they'd reached their weapons. Those who'd been asleep died in their beds.

It took less than three minutes. In the haze of smoke and dust filtered green by their night-vision goggles they'd found the racked and broken bodies of prisoners lying on stone floors. More than twenty skeletal scraps on the verge of death, caged behind bars and with hopelessness in their eyes. Victims of one of Saddam Hussein's notorious hidden detention centres.

'Sir, you need to see this,' the message had crackled through an earpiece in Blake's ear.

At the far end of a corridor they'd found a room.

He recalled two of his men standing at the entrance with their rifles poised. The ground had been caked in blood, rusted shackles bolted to the walls. A metal bedframe had been placed in the middle of the room with scarlet-stained leather straps tied to each corner. Two electrical leads with crocodile-jaw metal clamps had been attached to a car battery next to a wooden chair.

Blake had ground his teeth and gripped his Carbine tightly.

'Sir, I've found al-Sadr,' said another voice in his ear. There'd been a pause, filled with static crunch, then, 'He's alive. Just.'

He'd been cowering in the corner of a dirty cell. His body bloodied and bruised. At least they'd reached him before he made it to the hangman's noose, the usual punishment for suspected informants.. He could barely stand, let alone walk so they'd carried him out on their shoulders. The best they could do for the rest of the prisoners was to set them free, smashing open their cell doors as they left.

'I still don't understand why you haven't talked to the prison staff, or the Governor at least,' Blake said, draining his glass and ordering another bottle of Tuscan red.

'You're assuming Rahimi's contact inside Marshside is a prisoner. But until we can prove otherwise everyone in that prison is under suspicion.'

'It doesn't make sense for a prison officer to be involved? Why would Rahimi risk smuggling in a phone for a prison officer?'

'We're not making any assumptions. I take it you don't have a problem with going in?'

'It's what I do. How soon can you make the arrangements?'

'We need a day, maybe two. You won't get much

notice.'

'Not a problem.'

'You don't have commitments?'

'No,' said Blake.

'Family?'

Blake finished a mouthful of pasta and wiped his mouth with a napkin. Folded it on his lap. 'No.'

'I thought you might be married, that's all. I don't think I'd appreciate it too much if my husband disappeared in the middle of the night without so much as a goodbye.'

'You're married then?'

'I meant it hypothetically.' Mortensen pushed her plate to one side. She had only picked at her food. 'No one special waiting at home?'

Blake shifted in his chair trying to think of a way to change the subject. 'No.'

'Wedded to the job?'

'Like I said, I prefer to operate on my own. Life's easier that way. Anyway, I don't make great company.'

'I don't think you're as cold as you like to make out.' Mortensen crossed her legs, brushing her foot against Blake's calf. He flinched. 'So which is it, never found love or bitten so badly you've told yourself you'll never love again? I bet it's the latter.'

'Not even close,' said Blake.

'So come on, who was she?'

'Who?'

'The woman who broke your heart.'

The restaurant was filling up and the noise of sociable chatter growing loud. Blake watched an elderly couple greeted by the owner with warm handshakes and kissed cheeks. He made such a fuss of them they must have been regulars. They took a table at the back, near the kitchen. Blake acknowledged their friendly smiles with a nod. They were easily in their eighties, dressed in their finest and still enraptured by each other's company. Blake imagined they'd enjoyed a long and happy marriage.

'Stop being coy,' Mortensen said.

'Can we talk about something else?'

'I was right. There was someone.'

'A long time ago.'

'So how did you manage to let her go?'

'It doesn't matter. Anyway, what about you? You must have plenty of admirers?'

Mortensen feigned embarrassment although the glint in her eye suggested she was pleased by the suggestion. A waiter moved in to clear their plates before she could reply. 'It's complicated. Currently single and enjoying it.'

'Dessert? Coffee?' said Blake.

The waiter stood poised with a pencil hovering over his pad.

'Just the bill,' said Mortensen. She watched the waiter move away. 'Come back to mine for a nightcap.'

'Is that a good idea?'

'Of course.' Mortensen leaned across the table with wide eyes full of innocence. 'We should discuss how we're going to get you into Marshside.'

'Do you ever think of anything other than work?'

Mortensen rocked back in her seat and laughed. 'Come on, let's go.'

Chapter 6

It was a cool night, fresh from the earlier rain. Mortensen took Blake's arm as they walked along the riverbank. Like two lovers on an evening stroll. Her dress accentuated all her best features. Tight in the right places, pinched at the waist and short enough to show off toned legs. They fell into a natural rhythm, matching each other's stride.

They stood side-by-side in the lift up to the third floor of Mortensen's apartment block, staring at their distorted reflections in the polished metal doors. It came to a halt with a gentle bump, and as they slipped out into the corridor, Mortensen gave Blake an encouraging smile.

Her apartment was in darkness. Blake's hand hovered over the light switch but she stopped him, her fingers falling over his.

'Leave them. I like to watch the river at night. It's better in the dark. Sit down, I'll fetch us a drink.'

Blake fell onto a sofa and watched Mortensen float around in her bare feet. She had the poise of a ballerina, her back arched and her toes pointed. As she leaned into a sideboard, the hem of her dress rose high up the back of her thighs.

'Whisky?' she asked, producing a bottle of single malt and two glasses.

Blake caught himself gazing at her thin waist and the swell of her calves. He chastised himself, stood and moved to the window. Somewhere outside a siren wailed and through a break in the cloud a luminous moon appeared.

'Amazing views,' said Blake, as Mortensen handed him

a glass filled perilously full.

'Are you trying to get me drunk?'

'Now why would I want to do a thing like that?'

They chinked glasses and Blake took a large gulp, the liquid burning the back of his throat.

Blake noticed for the first time the colour of Mortensen's eyes. Emerald green. They seemed to sparkle in the moonlight, drawing him in. He leaned closer until their heads were almost touching. Her breath on his cheek was warm and sweet. He moved a hand to her waist but Mortensen turned away with a knowing smile. She drifted to the sofa. Smoothed her dress under her.

'Come, I want to know more about you. You're an enigma,' she said.

He sat so their thighs touched, drinking in her perfume, like jasmine on the morning rain. 'What do you want to know?'

'Who is Tom Blake?' she whispered.

He raised the back of his hand to touch her cheek and blinked hard.

He couldn't focus on her face.

Her delicate features swam around her face, lost in a blur. His head felt light and he struggled for breath. He leaned forwards to put his glass on the table but misjudged the distance. It fell to the floor, splattering the carpet.

'Don't worry, it's okay,' Mortensen said, her voice pulsating in his ears.

'I don't feel so great. I need to….' But he couldn't finish his sentence. Searing pain shot through his brain. He flushed hot and cold, a sweat breaking out on his brow. The room was spinning. The brush strokes of an abstract painting on the far wall swirled and merged into a hideous maelstrom of colour.

'You look a little pale,' Mortensen's voice sounded distant, like she was calling to him from the far end of a tunnel.

He heard another voice beckoning him. It was a

woman he recognised from a long time ago, buried in the recesses of his memory. But when he turned to look there was no one there.

He tried to speak but the words came out of his mouth only as strangulated noises. He needed air. When he tried to stand his legs buckled. He slumped in a heap on the floor, clattering against the edge of the coffee table.

'Let me open a window.' It was Mortensen's voice but he failed to comprehend her words. 'You'll feel okay in a minute.'

He tried to move his leg, an arm, a hand, but nothing worked. It was like the connection from his brain to his muscles had been severed. His cheek was pressed into the deep pile of the carpet, soft and coarse at the same time. He couldn't see anything other than the weave of the carpet and the tacks that pinned the fabric to the sofa.

His breathing came quick and shallow. 'Help me….' he croaked, his eyes flickering wildly, his pupils wide opals.

Mortensen moved across the room. He heard a rattle of a key turning in a lock and the sounds of the city rush in. The hum of traffic sounded loud after the tranquility of Mortensen's apartment. A salt-crusted breeze washed in from the river, cooling Blake's back.

'Alex?' he groaned.

Darkness was crowding his vision, creeping around the periphery of his sight. A thin, needle-like pulse ticked rapidly in his wrist and under his jaw, quickening as he fought unconsciousness.

And then all hell broke loose.

The door splintered in its frame and the windows flew open. The floorboards shuddered with the weight of heavy boots and screaming voices filled Blake's head.

'Get down! Stay where you are! Don't move!'

Over his shoulder, a table was tossed to one side and a heavy hand grabbed his collar, hauling him over. His eyes opened wide and his jaw fell slack at the sight of a dozen masked men. They wore dark jumpsuits and helmets, balaclavas and respirators concealing their faces. The barrels of twelve Heckler and Koch MP7s were trained on his body.

A boot kicked an arm away from his body. He glimpsed Mortensen by the window where a curtain was billowing. Her arms were crossed, her face unreadable.

'Right, get him up,' a gruff voice barked. Two of the gunmen slung their weapons over their backs and dragged Blake to his feet.

Blake focused on Mortensen's face.

'I'm sorry, Blake' she said. 'Get him out of here.'

Chapter 7

Blake woke in the back of a van. His head struck the jagged edge of a wire mesh, rousing him from semi-consciousness, his mouth dry and his brain dull like it had been stuffed with rags. He raised a hand to his temple to check for blood and found his wrists were cuffed. He blinked sweat from his eyes and tried to focus as the vehicle lurched on its axles through a tight corner.

He was inside a cage. Trapped like an animal. The air was a bitter fug of urine and stale sweat. Through a darkened window he glimpsed unfamiliar buildings flashing past in a blur.

They passed through gates in a high brick wall. Came to a halt with a jolt. Boots hit the ground. Two men in uniform threw open the rear doors, grabbed him by the arms and marched him through a walled courtyard. They dragged him into a dreary reception area that smelled of disinfectant, checked his details against a computer, bagged his clothes and inspected his hair for lice.

They made him change into jogging bottoms and a grey t-shirt. White socks and a pair of black shoes with self-fastening straps. Two prison officers with stony faces escorted him through a bewildering labyrinth of corridors of white painted walls, steel gates with solid locks, high ceilings and polished floors. They emerged into a quad formed by the towering walls of the surrounding buildings. It was open to the elements apart from a wire netting that formed a protective ceiling below the second-storey windows. Cameras were mounted on poles and powerful floodlights turned night into day.

The High Security Unit at Marshside was a squat hexagonal building on the far side of the courtyard. Blake sensed the hopelessness as he was led inside.

'Blake, Tom. Remand prisoner. Awaiting trial,' said one of the guards to a man behind a counter.

Cold adamantine eyes drilled into Blake. 'Remand?' He said it like it was a novelty word.

'Recommendation of the Home Office, Sir.'

'Tough guy are you?'

He stepped out from behind the counter and stood eyeball-to-eyeball with Blake. Ramrod straight. So close that he could smell the coffee on his breath. Blake recognised the air of military authority. Maybe a former sergeant major. They tended to end up in places like this at the end of their Army careers.

'Whoever you are and whatever you've done outside, forget it right here. You've just walked into the dragon's den and home to a nastier bunch of bastards you wouldn't want to meet. Unpleasant men, aggressive men who've done unspeakable things and are paying their dues. They're in for the duration and they don't care about life because no one's given them a reason to care. That makes them worse than dangerous. Stay out of their way and don't upset them. Don't share your business with anybody and don't ask them theirs. Do you understand?'

Blake wondered what Patterson had let him in for.

'My domain and my rules,' the officer continued, 'whether you're here for life or waiting for trail. I don't care.'

He drove a tightly-clenched fist into Blake's stomach. A deft blow he didn't see coming. It doubled him over, forcing the air from his abdomen and made his lungs feel like they were collapsing.

'Keep your head down and your mouth shut and you'll get along fine.' He stretched his fingers and rubbed his knuckles.

They passed Blake's shoes through an X-ray machine and shoved him under a security arch. They prised open his mouth and peered under his tongue with a penlight torch. They checked the soles of his feet and the palms of his hands. Just like Mortensen had said. Security tighter than the Bank of England.

His cell was at the end of a corridor alive with night-time babble. Men restless in their beds. Snoring, coughing, chattering and whimpering. Bed frames squeaked and pipework clattered.

There wasn't much to his cell. Brickwork and concrete with just enough room for a metal sink, toilet bowl and a bed fixed to the wall. The door slammed behind him and bolts snapped into their housings. He tried the mattress. The sheet was thin and the blanket coarse but they smelled clean enough. He folded a pillow under his head and lay down. He didn't bother to undress. His eyes were sore and his head still spinning from the effects of whatever Mortensen had slipped into his drink. All he wanted to do was sleep.

It came easier than he'd imagined but was less restorative than he'd hoped. His dreams were filled with vivid images. Rahimi's body laid out on a slab, his eyes wide open. Thousands of flies pouring from a wound in his thigh, filling the room with the drone of sibilating wings. Three women hovering over his body wiped tears from their eyes with the loose ends of their headscarves. Their wailing soared to a crescendo until Blake had to cover his ears.

He woke with a start drenched in sweat as electric lights pulsed into life. He sat up and realised there were no windows and no natural light. The day was regulated by an automated flick of a switch. Under the stark reality of a fluorescent tube, his cell looked even less inviting than it had in the dead of night. And smaller. Barely ten paces long and half as wide. Thick paint slapped on brick walls and a ceiling that was oppressively low.

A metallic clunk followed a short buzz as the lock on the door was released. The cell filled with the sounds of a prison block waking. Shuffling and banging. The chatter of early morning banter and cat calling. Blake swung his feet off the bed and ran his fingers through his hair. Rubbed his eyes with the balls of his hands. The few hours of snatched sleep had done little to revive his senses. Full-consciousness seemed out of reach somewhere in the back of his mind.

The sound of the door thudding open against a rubber stopper caused him look up. He'd expected visitors. Maybe not so soon. Word would have travelled of a new inmate. They'd want to check him out. Put him in his place.

He forced himself to remain seated on the bed. Tried to look relaxed. Calm. If he was going to earn status he needed to set his stall out early. Show no fear. Stand his ground. Let them see he wasn't afraid.

'Where's Ray?'

Blake stared at the diminutive figure who shuffled into the cell. Thinning grey hair fell over his shoulders and his clothes hung limply from his skeletal frame.

'Who are you?' said Blake.

'What are you doing in Ray's room?' If he'd have been standing, the man would have barely reached his chest. 'What have you done with him?' he hissed. 'Cat got your tongue?'

He skulked to the sink, ran a bony finger around the bowl and licked it like a chef tasting a sauce. Smacked his lips. Pondered for a moment looking to the ceiling, then cocked his head as if he'd reached an important conclusion.

'Why did they put you in here?' he asked.

Blake didn't have a cover story. His entry into the prison had been so sudden he'd not had the chance to think it through. No good making one up either. Patterson must have arranged a pretence. He decided to say nothing.

'You don't say much do you?'

'I don't have much to say,' said Blake.

'Ah, it speaks!' The man stepped towards the bed. Leaned in close, nose to nose, violating Blake's personal space. His breath was like sour milk. The man snatched a towel folded on the end of the bed and ran a bristly cheek across it. Held it to his nose and breathed in its fragrance. Put it down and reached for Blake's prison-issue toiletry bag.

'Touch that and I'll break your arm,' said Blake. He tried to sound matter-of-fact. Didn't want to start a fight but had to lay down some authority.

The man pulled back his hand like he'd been burned. 'Think you can touch me? I'll kill you! I'll fucking kill you!' he screamed, his pupils growing large and black. Thick veins pulsed on his forehead. 'I'll snap you like a puppy's neck!'

Blake rose from the bed. Drew himself to his full height and pushed the man away.

'Don't touch me!' the man howled.

'Leave my things alone,' said Blake, shooting a glance at the door. The rest of the block would find out soon enough they had a new neighbour. No good getting them all excited so early in the morning.

'Okay, okay, I'm fine,' said the man, panting.

Blake let him catch his breath, watching his chest rise and fall as he brought his anger under control. It disappeared as quickly as it had flared. 'I meant what I said. I could kill you right now if I wanted.'

He perched on the end of the bed. Turned to Blake and held out a bony hand. His fingernails were long and yellow. 'Name's Walt,' he said.

'Blake,' said Blake, refusing to shake his hand. 'Been in long?'

'Fifteen? Twenty? I forgot. But they're never letting me out. So what's the point in trying to remember?'

'What did you do?'

Walt noticed his hand still hanging in mid-air. He

withdrew it with a slight shake of his head and tucked it into his lap.

'Shouldn't go asking people their business. Didn't the guards warn you? No ask, no tell.' He looked Blake up and down. 'They'll like you, you know.'

He gave a phlegmy laugh, reached over and squeezed Blake's bicep. 'Strong too. Do you have kids?' His eyes opened wide.

Blake shook his head.

'Pity. I miss the sound of them playing most of all.' His eyes fluttered shut. 'Chasing around with their chubby arms and pink knees, smelling of talc.'

He licked his lips and wiped a globule of spittle from the corner of his mouth.

'Did you do something to a child?' Blake's blood ran like ice through his veins and revulsion rose from the pit of his stomach. He wanted him off his bed and out of his cell.

'As if they'd let you anywhere near children again, you filthy nonce.' The voice came from the corridor. A giant with glistening ebony skin filled the doorway. A bleached-blond Mohican brushed the top of the frame. Bulging shoulders and rippling biceps glistened where he'd ripped the sleeves from his t-shirt.

Walt jumped up and cowered in the corner.

'Get back to your dirty little hole,' said the man in the doorway, raising a hand as if to cuff Walt on the back of his head as he scuttled past.

'They found the bodies of six kids in his loft,' he said when Walt had gone. 'Cut out their hearts and livers once he'd had his fun. They reckon he cooked them up and ate them.'

A second man squeezed into the cell. If anything he was bigger than the first. Blue veins ran like the tributaries of a river down the length of muscular arms. His hands, the size of plates, fell at his side. He had piggy eyes set into deep sockets and the skull of a Neanderthal. Round and thick and heavy.

Blake suspected he knew the reason for their visit. Time for an education in the rules. No doubt prison was like the military. It had its own order. And right now the new guy needed putting in his place. Make sure he realised where he stood in the food chain. Right at the bottom.

Only Blake wasn't ready to take a pasting. With only a few days to find out what Rahimi had been up to he was banking on fast-tracking his status application. He stood relaxed, running the scenarios through his mind and plotting his moves.

The cell was cramped and his only exit was blocked. But in his favour the two men in his cell were all vanity muscle. Pumped up on steroids and serious hours in the gym. They looked tough but that didn't make them fighters. Blake had training and experience on his side.

He set himself so that he was comfortably balanced on the balls of his feet, ready to react. He relaxed his hands at his sides and rolled his head to loosen his neck. He made a bet with himself that the white guy would come first, charging like a rhino, all power and no finesse. The Mohican would follow with fists swinging wildly, using brawn over brains.

He waited.

He looked the men in the eye, watching for the inevitable flicker that would signal the launch of their assault.

They stared back but didn't move.

Then the Mohican spoke.

'There's someone wants to meet you,' he said.

Chapter 8

They led Blake from his cell and along the corridor with their rubber soles squealing on the tiled floor. Haunted-looking men lining the route fell silent as they passed. Men with abandoned hope in their eyes, more irritated than intrigued by the new arrival disrupting their pointless daily routines.

The Mohican pushed Blake into a cell where a man naked from the waist up was sitting on a bed. He was the size of a bear with a barrel chest and a plump stomach, a man whose youthful muscular frame had been lost to middle-age. His head was hairless, smooth and round, his torso covered in tattoos, elaborately-scrawled words and enigmatic hieroglyphs.

He looked up as if from a trance, noticed Blake and beckoned him in.

'Come,' he said in a low murmur.

The cell was stale with sweat. It was identical to Blake's apart from a table with a melamine top and metal legs. On it lay a gilt-edged bible longer than Blake's forearm and thicker than his fist. It was open at one of the books from the Old Testament.

The man on the bed drew a deep breath and let it go slowly, straightened his spine and stared at Blake with black, impenetrable eyes.

'Are you a killer?' he asked.

'I've not been convicted of anything,' said Blake, 'I'm on remand.'

'Don't lie to me. The wing doesn't take remand

prisoners.'

Blake shrugged. What was that accent? He put it as mid-European, maybe Slavic. 'I was caught up in something, that's all. It's a misunderstanding.'

'So you're innocent? Join the club. Everyone's innocent in here, Mr Blake,' he said with a phlegmy laugh.

'You know my name?' said Blake a little too urgently and instantly regretted it.

'I make it my business to know what's going on.'

'Then you have the advantage over me.'

'Dragoslav.'

'You're a Serb?' Dragoslav's eyes narrowed. 'The tattoo,' said Blake, nodding at the man's neck. The emblem was a black scorpion with a barbed tail and pincers poised to strike. Blake knew it from a long time ago but it hadn't lost its power to repulse him. The symbol of the feared paramilitaries who'd operated a reign of terror during the Balkans War.

The Scorpians were the most of brutal of soldiers in a conflict that had plumbed new depths of inhumanity. Torture, rape and mutilation were their weapons of terror. They'd first risen to prominence in the besieged town of Srebrenica, butchering their way to notoriety and slaughtering more than eight thousand Muslims under the noses of United Nations peacekeepers. Their killing was indiscriminate. Men, women and children all suffered at their hands. The foreign correspondents coined the term 'ethnic cleansing' to describe it, managing to sanitise in pithy journalese the horrors Blake had heard about in appalling first-hand testimonies from those who'd survived. He'd been part of a coalition hunter-killer unit made up of British and American Special Forces tasked with bringing as many of the perpetrators to justice as they could find. But in six months they'd located less than fifty men. The rest had vanished back to their previous lives protected by people who either loved them or feared them too much.

To find one sitting an arm's reach away twenty years later but still untouchable was a blow that hit Blake hard.

'A distant memory of my past,' said Dragoslav, touching his neck lightly where the tattoo was fading.

'Were you at Srebrenica?'

Dragoslav replied with an almost imperceptible nod and Blake willed himself to remain calm.

'So you were at the massacre?' His throat tightened and he swallowed hard.

'It was necessary for the future of my country and my people.' His mouth turned up in a malevolent grin.

Blake tried to look impressed, against his instinct to step forwards and throttle the life out of him. 'So how did you end up in Britain?'

'My wife was British. I'm a UK citizen now.'

'Was British?'

'She died,' Dragoslav said without emotion or elaboration. 'Enough questions about me. I'm interested to know about you. Tell me, what's it feel like when you kill?' He steepled his fingers over his stomach.

'What makes you think I'm a murderer?'

'I can see it in your eyes. It's intoxicating, don't you think? That moment when you hold the absolute power of life and death in your hands?'

Blake had been a soldier for most of his life. There were times he'd had to be a cold and ruthless killer. But only when it was necessary to preserve the lives of others. Never for pleasure. 'I don't know what you're talking about.'

'Everyone is a killer in here. A wing of men who delight in the suffering of others. But let me give you some advice. Trust nobody. Understand?'

'I can take care of myself.'

Dragoslav grimaced. 'I've heard that before. He bled dry before the guards found him.'

'You're trying to intimidate me?'

'There are more than thirty men on this wing. Vile

creatures locked up together twenty-four hours a day. What do you suppose they do for amusement? We're one of a kind, you and I. We should be friends.'

Dragoslav rose from the bed with a supple fluidity that seemed unlikely for a man of his size. He padded across the floor and flicked through the pages of the bible.

'Are you a religious man?'

'Not really,' said Blake.

'You don't believe in one omnipotent being who controls our fate and judges our lives?'

'I believe we hold our fate in our own hands.' Blake had formed an early view that life was for living. Live it hard and live it well. But when it was over, it was over. There was nothing else. No heaven and no hell. When it was time to go, there wasn't much religion or a god was going to do about it.

'This book used to give me peace but now, I don't know. I believe true omnipotence comes from being able to decide who lives and who dies. What could be more powerful than that?' Dragoslav looked up from the page, stood still for a moment like he was running an internal dialogue through his head.

'I want to show you something.'

He banged on the door twice with his fist. The Mohican appeared.

'Fetch him,' Dragoslav said, before turning back into the cell and sweeping up the bible.

He laid it on the bed, pulled the table up to the sink and unfolded a face cloth. Soaked it under the tap. With a powerful twist of his hands, Dragoslav squeezed the cloth dry, straightened it out and soaked it again.

The sight and sound of running water reminded Blake of his raging thirst and his throbbing head. He licked his lips. They were cracked and dry.

The door crashed open and a slight figure with terrified eyes bulging from their sockets was thrust into the room, half carried by the Mohican who had an arm across his chest and a hand clamped over his mouth. The Neanderthal was behind them.

'Hemingway,' said Dragoslav. Blake could smell the man's fear.

The Mohican lifted Hemingway off his feet and dropped him on his back on the table so his head fell over the sink. He fought against their attempts to pin him down with erratic twists and jerks. A pathetic plea for mercy escaped from the back of his throat. Not a full-bodied cry but a whimper muffled by the wet cloth Dragoslav draped over his face. It moulded to the point of his nose and cratered over his mouth. His breathing came quick and fast through his nostrils like a steam train building speed. Every muscle in his body went taut.

Dragoslav fetched a bucket from under the sink, filled it with water and held it over Hemingway's head. Slowly he poured a stream of water over the cloth that covered the man's face. It wasn't much more than a trickle, hitting him between the eyes and around his nose. It ran down his neck and drenched his t-shirt. It seeped into his throat and sinuses and leached into his trachea. Hemingway kicked and bucked like a wild stallion, as with each ragged breath, he drew the fluid down into his gurgling lungs. Sensing he was drowning, an uncontrollable panic racked his body and a primeval instinct to survive kicked in. It took all of the strength the two giant men to hold him down.

Dragoslav kept pouring, prolonging the agony, until the bucket was empty. He threw it to the floor and grabbed a handful of Hemingway's hair, hauled him and ripped the cloth from his face. Hemingway sucked in gulps of air. He coughed and spluttered, stalactites of spittle oozing from his mouth.

'First and final warning. Next time I'll take an eye,' said Dragoslav, running the back of his hand along Hemingway's cheek. 'Get your affairs in order by the end of the week or face the consequences.'

Hemingway slumped from the table in a trembling

heap and was dragged out of the room. Dragoslav wiped his hands dry on a towel and calmly folded it over a rail under the sink. He smoothed out the creases and checked it was hanging straight.

'Are you familiar with the method?' he asked. 'I'm told it's widely used by American interrogators.'

'So I've heard,' said Blake. He knew all about waterboarding. But the thought of ever using the technique to elicit information sickened him.

He'd seen it used once before, by CIA interrogators at an American safe house on the outskirts of Islamabad when he'd been a guest of a unit of US Navy Seals. They'd arrested a young man, not much more than a boy, suspected of running messages for insurgents. The CIA agents were tired-looking men with blood-shot eyes, thick beards and leathery skin who stripped the boy naked, blindfolded him and strapped him to a sloping wooden board. For three days they repeatedly took him to the point of drowning, using a running hose and a cloth over his nose and mouth until he was ready to confess to just about anything.

It was horrific to watch and produced nothing more than an unsafe confession from a youth barely old enough to shave. Later Blake had questioned the interrogators, intrigued by their reliance on such a seemingly barbaric practice. They explained that carried out correctly the technique brought on a controlled death that could be repeated over and over to great effect. And if done incorrectly? Terminal hypoxia, the brain fatally starved of oxygen, they said.

'The Americans don't consider it to be torture but a legitimate interrogation method,' said Dragoslav.

Blake shrugged as if he didn't hold an opinion. 'So what was that all about?'

'I deal in personal insurance. Hemingway defaulted on a payment.'

'A protection racket?'

Dragoslav sucked in a breath through pursed lips. 'An ugly description. I provide security services.'

'And you want to make me an offer?'

'I have a straightforward proposal. There will be no negotiating or cutting deals. A one-time only offer. For two hundred a month I guarantee you'll not be harmed while you remain with us at Marshside.'

'You're having a laugh, right?'

'Do I look like I'm joking?' Dragoslav's face clouded.

'Nobody has access to that sort of cash locked up in here, surely?'

'Most are sitting on sizeable bank accounts, even if they can't access them while they're inside. And they can always ask for help from friends and family. It's a small price. I expect one payment into a specified account every month. No defaults and no excuses.'

'And if I refuse?'

Dragoslav straightened himself to his full height and stepped up close to Blake so his enormous bulk bore down on him. Blake stood his ground, focusing on a vein in the Serb's neck pulsing with a slow and regular rhythm.

'A one-time offer, Mr Blake. Be careful you make the right decision.'

'I'll pass. Thanks all the same.' Blake turned to leave.

'Maybe I'm not explaining my proposition very well,' said Dragoslav, his cheeks flushing crimson. He pushed past Blake reaching for the handle of the cell door, as if he meant to pull it open and summon some assistance.

It was time to seize the initiative. Three against one in the tight confines of the cell was not a fight Blake relished. He dipped his shoulder and sprang forwards, catching Dragoslav with full-force between the shoulder blades. The Serb's head catapulted forwards and thudded into the steel. His legs buckled and he dropped to the ground.

Chapter 9

Blake held his breath, listening for movement outside the cell. He counted to ten but no one came. Dragoslav groaned and rolled onto his back. Blake could have finished him off. Wrapped an arm around his neck and snapping his spinal cord with a quick jerk of his skull. Game over. But he wasn't a murderer. He needed to make a statement of intent. That's all. To earn some respect, a little status to move freely around the prison without interference. And no better place to start than with the guy running a protection racket.

Dragoslav sat up on his knees, a wounded and dangerous animal. A lump on his forehead was swelling into an ugly bruise. Blake stood back and let the big man haul himself up, watching as he rose unsteadily, swaying from side to side. Dragoslav shook his head to clear the haze behind his eyes.

Blake reminded himself of Srebrenica and relaxed his shoulders.

With a roar, twenty-five stone of fat and under-used muscle shot across the cell. Blake stood his ground. Waited. Let the Serb build up a momentum and at the last moment sidestepped, letting Dragoslav fly into the wall behind, jabbing at his head with a wasp-sting punch as he went.

The Serb spun around, his face red. 'Stand and fight like a man,' he growled.

'You're slow and weak, old man. I doubt you could fight your way through a wet tissue these days.'

He came again, pawing the air with enormous fists, under the misapprehension his size and longer reach gave him the upper hand. But when he drew back his right arm it was with such exaggeration that his intention was hopelessly transparent. He was looking to land a wild right hook that could probably lay a man out for a week. But he was too cumbersome. Too obvious. Blake ducked under his fist and countered with blows to the Serb's torso, pounding the soft tissue of his liver and kidneys through a thick layer of loose muscle.

Dragoslav fell back. Came again. Throwing flailing punches while Blake bobbed and parried.

'You're nothing but a washed-up has-been,' said Blake. 'Without those two heavies out there you're pathetic.'

Dragoslav mumbled a reply. It could have been, 'Go to hell.' It might have been something else. It didn't matter. His bare chest, glistening with sweat, was heaving. He was flabby and unfit and despite his size, no physical match for Blake.

'Come on, is that all you've got?' Blake put on an expression of mock disappointment.

Dragoslav opened his mouth to speak but his words made it no further than his throat. Blake swung an elbow in a looping arc towards the Serb's head. The sharp tip of bone struck his skull like a hammer blow and sent him stumbling backwards. He recovered quickly, wiped the wound with the back of his hand and examined a sticky smear of crimson with disgust.

'You filthy dog,' he said, before launching an avalanche of uncoordinated punches Blake had no difficulty blocking.

As the lactic acid from the exertion seared his muscles, the Serb's arms sagged below his waist, his energy levels temporarily sapped. Blake whipped a sideways kick from his hip striking the Serb's ribs with the power of a baseball bat hitting a home run. He heard the bone crack. Dragoslav ignored the pain. The Serb saw the move coming. He wasn't quick enough to block the shot but managed to pluck Blake's ankle from the air. Twisted and pushed in the same movement and sent Blake sprawling across the floor, the wind knocked from his lungs as he landed heavily on his back.

The Serb was on top of him in a flash, hands grappling for his neck. Hot fingers gripped the cartilage below Blake's chin, squeezing and tightening, pressing harder and harder so Blake could neither swallow nor breathe. The edges of his vision clouded, losing his grip on consciousness. A few more seconds and he would be out cold. A minute more and he'd be dead.

Blake tried breaking the Serb's grip but his hands were vice-like around his throat, his face contorted in a grotesque snarl. In a last desperate attempt to save himself, Blake scrambled for Dragoslav's ears, took a firm hold with his fingers and jammed his thumbs into his eyes. He squeezed for all his life was worth, the soft orbs squelching and deforming under the pressure. Dragoslav howled, released his grip and allowed Blake to buck his hips and roll the heavy Serb away. Blake crawled across the floor gulping for air. Bright lights flooded his vision as he sat gasping with his back against the door, each strained breath a mixture of agony and relief.

The respite was temporary. Dragoslav recovered his senses and stood. His eyes were narrow, red slits. He lunged with a new-found energy, throwing a jab that missed its mark by an inch. Blake snatched his wrist as it whistled past his ear and twisted the Serb's arm until it was almost wrenched out of its socket. Blake kicked him across the room with a foot planted in the small of his back. Dragoslav stumbled, fell against the bed and smashed his face on its concrete base.

'Tell me when you've had enough and we can renegotiate the terms of your deal. Let's say five hundred a month and I won't come back and kick your ass again. I'll give you the details of my account,' said Blake, wiping sweat from his brow.

Dragoslav spat blood on the floor. His mouth was a pulped mess. 'Who are you?' he gurgled through the gap where his front teeth had been.

'Don't worry about who I am. Worry about what I'm capable of.'

'Keep your eyes open because you'll need to be looking over your shoulder for the rest of your life. I guarantee it.'

'Your threats don't wash, old man.'

Heavy, impatient footsteps stomped in the corridor and both men glanced at the door as if expecting it to be thrown open. Dragoslav seized the distraction and threw himself across the cell. Blake turned too late, felt the cold sting of a blade slicing through flesh. A lucky strike that caught him on his bicep a few inches below the shoulder.

He caught Dragoslav's wrist, ploughed his elbow into his nose and slammed the Serb's hand into the brickwork. Dragoslav dropped the improvised weapon with a howl and it clattered to the floor. A razor blade embedded into the handle of a toothbrush he'd secreted under his mattress and palmed when he'd fallen by his bed. Blake kicked it away and glanced at his wound. A deep gash the length of his hand oozing sticky blood down his arm. But the cut was clean. It should stitch up no trouble.

Blake slipped his uninjured arm around the Serb's neck, jumped on his back and squeezed hard, using his free hand as a lever to exert maximum pressure. Dragoslav thrashed and kicked, smashing Blake into the walls. But Blake's resolve only hardened. Through gritted teeth he hung on and, ignoring the agony from the wound on his arm, pulled tighter. It would have taken wild dogs to have dragged him off.

Eventually the Serb's movements slowed and his body went limp. Blake let him crumple to the floor and laid him out along the length of the cell. The Serb's mouth was a gaping mess and his nose bloodied and flattened where Blake had broken it with his elbow. He didn't look pretty but it was nothing that should cause any lasting damage. He'd be off the wing for a few days in a hospital bed. Out of Blake's way. The injuries a warning to anyone else looking to cause the new arrival any trouble. Job done. Almost.

Blake slumped on the bed, letting his heart rate come back under control. His blood-smeared hands were shaking. The after-effects of the rush of adrenaline. It would pass soon enough. Drips from the tap at the sink caught his attention. The steady plip-plop of beads of water forming and falling in a regular beat. Cool, refreshing water. Blake ran his tongue over dry, cracked lips. Jumped up from the bed, stepped over the body and turned the tap on fully. He gulped down hungry mouthfuls, hardly noticing the metallic tinge from the prison's network of pipes. He splashed a handful over his face and the back of his neck, washing away the sweat and blood. Rinsed the wound on his arm, cleaning off the caked blood, testing how deep the cut ran. He made a bandage from a strip of bedsheet, wrapping it tightly around the wound. Grabbed the towel from under the sink and dried his mouth as he turned back towards the door.

It was wide open. The Mohican and the Neanderthal were standing rigid staring at Dragoslav's body, their jaws slack at the horror they saw. Blake followed their gaze to the mess that had been the Serb's face. Splashes of blood stained the floor and the sheets were streaked red. The cell looked like a house of horrors. Blake folded the towel and hung it on the rail.

'Why are you standing there gawping? He needs medical attention. Get him out of here, quickly.'

One man grabbed the Serb's ankles, the other slipped his hands under his arms and between them they half-carried and half-dragged him out of the cell.

The corridor was alive with the sounds of men chatting and grumbling. But a hush descended over them when they saw the beaten, unconscious body of Dragoslav.

'Put him down,' said Blake.

'But you said...' the Neanderthal tried to protest.

'I said put him down.' The look Blake shot him was sufficient to quell the protestation. Blake drew back his shoulders, held his head high and scanned the length of the wing, making sure he caught everyone's eye. A hunter posing with his spoils.

'Is he dead?' someone called out.

Blake scanned the faces but wasn't sure who'd asked. 'He'll live. But he'll be sore for a few days.'

Blake had anticipated the sight of Dragoslav bloodied and defeated would attract a crowd. That they'd all want a close look, to see how he'd vanquished the bully who'd ruled over them with intimidation and fear. But none came. Even laid out cold, the Serb seemed to hold a power over them. For a while, the only sound was Dragoslav's burbling breath as he drew air through his blood-soaked mouth and nose.

Halfway along the corridor one of the prisoners emerged from his cell, a small man with slicked black hair and an eye half-closed in a permanent squint under hooded brows. His footsteps on the tiled floor sounded hollow. When he saw Dragoslav, he broke into a jog, fell to his knees and tilted back the Serb's swollen head

'What have you done? He's half dead,' he said, holding an ear over his mouth.

Blake peered at him through squinted eyes. His arm was throbbing and his head was light.

'Guards! Guards!' the prisoner shouted. He checked Dragoslav's breathing and hunted for a pulse. 'Medics!'

Blake felt as if he was drifting towards the ceiling, looking down on himself from above. His eyes were heavy and there was a dull ache in his back. He needed to sleep. He stepped over Dragoslav's body and headed towards his cell, his steps falling subconsciously one in front of the other. He ignored the calls of alarm from a scrambling force of prison guards. The sound of keys rattling in locks was distant and dull as though he was in the aftermath of a close-quarters explosion that had dampened his hearing. He had only one thought in his head, of collapsing onto his bunk, letting his eyes close and falling into a deep sleep.

Two sharp stabs in his back jolted him back to the moment. A sharp pain between his shoulder blades where two tiny barbs had pierced his t-shirt and attached themselves to his skin just out of reach no matter how far he stretched his arm.

'Stand still!' a voice barked.

A crackle of electricity signalled a jolt of nerve-twisting agony that ran through the length of Blake's body, cramping his muscles and clawing his hands and toes. His teeth clamped down on his tongue and he tasted the sweet, metallic flow of blood trickle down his throat. He collapsed to his knees and, unable to control his muscles, collapsed headfirst, his convulsing limbs dancing to the tune of fifty thousand volts. He imagined his inner organs being cooked and his brain being fried. He fought with consciousness, sensing it eluding him, until his eyes fluttered and fell closed.

Chapter 10

The isolation cell was a cold and damp windowless box with a low ceiling and concrete walls. There was a dirty mattress on the floor and a slop bucket in one corner. Standing in the middle of the room Blake could almost touch both walls at the same time. A light behind a plastic cover never went out making it almost impossible to sleep or to delineate the day. With twenty-four hour artificial light, days and nights were impossible to distinguish. It was enough to drive some men mad.

But not Blake. He was well-versed in surviving isolation, a skill honed from days tucked up in concealed dug-outs on observational duties. He'd learned how to combat the boredom by surviving in a trance, like a computer in sleep-mode ready to spring to life at the touch of a button. He kept his mind active by solving imaginary maths puzzles, designing architectural plans for buildings he knew well or challenging himself to list countries and their capitals in reverse alphabetical order.

For the first few hours he'd tried to sleep on the thin mattress but he was sore all over and no matter which way he turned he couldn't find a comfortable position. He tried lying on his back, with his knees drawn up, but his muscles still fizzed from the electrical charge they'd tasered through his body. His tongue was swollen and tender and his head swam from a lack of food and water.

'You'll be best off in here for a while, for your own protection,' said one of the guards as he'd shoved Blake into the cell.

'I don't need protection,' Blake had protested.

'Trust me, you do. Let Dragoslav and his cronies cool off for a bit.'

'For how long?'

'Depends on the governor. Maybe when the excitement's calmed down on the wing and you're no longer considered to be a danger to anyone else.'

Food was delivered through a horizontal serving hatch in the door. His first meal was an inedible-looking pile of brown mush served on a plastic plate with a beaker of water and a brittle, plastic fork. An evening meal appeared five hours later.

'Hand me your dirty dishes,' said a voice through the hatch.

Blake's tray was snatched away. It was replaced by another that contained a half-full plate of slop and a mug of tepid, milky tea.

'Thank you,' said Blake.

'You're welcome.' The voice sounded familiar.

'What is it?'

'Stew, I think.'

'Another culinary triumph. What's your name?'

'I can't talk to you,' the voice whispered loudly. 'The food's supposed to be punishment rations. Sorry,' it said as an afterthought.

'I've eaten worse.' Blake recalled the countless packets of Army rations he'd survived on. At least the prison meals were warm. 'My name's Blake.'

'Everyone on the wing knows who you are.'

'I like to make a first impression that lasts.'

'I've got to go.'

'Stay a minute. Please?'

There was a pause. Blake sensed the man on the other side of the door was keen to chat. After all, Blake must be the talk of the block after what he did to Dragoslav.

'If they catch me, they'll throw me in the box next door. I'm Sweeney.' A hand shot through the serving hatch. Blake grasped it. It was warm and calloused.

'I'm going mad in here on my own,' Blake lied. 'It's good to hear another voice.'

'It's not supposed to be a holiday camp.'

'You been inside long?' Blake drank thirstily from the mug of tea. It was warm but not sweet enough for his taste.

'Eight years, nine in April,' said Sweeney.

'What did you do?' Sweeney didn't reply. 'Sorry, I forgot, never ask, right?'

'Can I give you some advice? Be careful who you go around picking fights with.'

'You think I made a mistake with Dragoslav?'

'Some guys you don't mess with. He's one of them. A certified lunatic. You should have kept well clear. You don't know what you've done.'

'He should have stayed away from me. How is he?'

'They moved him to the hospital wing.'

Blake had a recollection of the prisoner with black, slicked back hair running towards the Serb in the cell corridor. Checking to see if he was alive. Feeling for a pulse. He recalled his voice calling for the guards.

'Was it you who came to help him? Called the medics?' said Blake.

'I thought you'd killed him.'

'I did you a favour. All of you. I don't know how many were signed up to that racket but it's over.'

'It's not over,' Sweeney snapped. 'You think just because you've turned up and knocked some heads together that's it? That we'll all just get on with doing our time in peace and harmony? Geezer, were you born yesterday?'

'He's finished. He's a bully, that's all.'

'He's not finished. After this it'll be worse. You humiliated him and when you get back they're going to kill you, for sure.'

'I don't think so.'

'You're a dead man walking.'

'He won't try anything again.'

'You got lucky this time, that's all. But it's not Dragoslav you need to worry about.'

'Those two muscled-up goons? I'm not worried about them. I've cut off the head of the beast.'

'You should be. They're going to catch up with you and then you'll find there's nowhere to run. The screws won't help. Don't think they will. Just watch your back. I've got to go before they send someone to find me. I'll be back in the morning.'

The hatch slammed shut and Blake finished his meal alone, draining the mug of tea and setting the tray at the end of the bed. He eased his aching body onto the mattress and sat with his back resting against the wall staring at the concrete opposite, visualising patterns and pictures in the textured swirls. After a while, he let his eyes close.

He replayed in his mind his arrival in the prison van and of being processed into the high security unit. He recalled in fine detail being led to his cell and the bed with its clean white sheets and pillow. The smell of disinfectant and the sound of water clunking through pipes. He fast-forwarded to the moment he'd had the Mohican and the Neanderthal dump Dragoslav's unconscious body in the middle of the wing. He'd taken a good look at everyone along the corridor. He never forgot a face. Or a name. The trick was simple mnemonics and scanning for three unique features. Three was the most workable number. Any fewer and his memory struggled. Any more and it was too difficult to assess at speed. It might be unusual physical attributes. A hooked nose, crooked teeth, blemishes or birthmarks. He looked at facial shape, lip size and the thickness of eyebrows, tagging each face with a unique name that connected with their features. It was an impressive party trick he'd developed during prolonged surveillance operations.

There had been twenty-four men on the corridor that morning and although he'd not had long, it was a straightforward task to index and file each of them. He shifted and sorted, reinforcing the memory. But something was bothering him. Something that didn't quite add up but that he couldn't put his finger on. The more he puzzled over it, the further it seemed from his grasp.

He replayed the moment he emerged from Dragoslav's cell frame by frame like he was running a roll of cinema acetate through his fingers. He reached the part where he was tasered by the guards and let the memory roll on. He remembered pitching forwards, unable to break his fall as his limbs locked out. The muscles in his neck contracted and forced his head backwards so that he was looking up at a throng of prisoners, jeering and shouting.

He remembered black leather boots with thick rubber soles and navy blue trouser legs. Vibrations of feet through the floor and rapid-response officers in riot gear towering over him, kitted up in dark overalls and full visor helmets, with batons tucked up against clear plastic shields. They were turned away from Blake and facing the other prisoners, formed up into a long line with shoulders tight together and their shields high.

What were they doing?

The guards must have seen the state of Dragoslav and over-reacted. Maybe their panicked arrival had sparked a riot. Blake remembered seeing punches thrown and kicks lashing out, angry voices galvanising into a roar.

But he'd been on the edge of consciousness. Nothing other than his own personal world of hurt had registered at the time. He'd tried to focus on something, anything that would stop him slipping away. His eyes had fallen on an object in the middle distance. A fleeting glimpse of something like a shadow created by the headlights of a passing car. He'd forced his eyes to open wide, trying to fix on it, to make some sense of what he was seeing. But the harder he'd tried to hold onto consciousness, the further it had slipped away. His eyes had closed once, twice and by the third time his lids fluttered shut, his conscious brain had shut down.

Chapter 11

Blake had been sleeping fitfully when the serving hatch crashed open and a tray with gloopy porridge in a bowl was thrust in. He rolled off the mattress but the hatch had slammed shut by the time he reached the door. Sweeney was his only source of information about what was happening on the wing while he was locked-up in solitary confinement and Blake regretted missing him.

He made sure he was waiting by the door when his lunch tray arrived. He grabbed it with both hands.

'Sweeney?'

'What?' an unfamiliar voice replied.

Blake recoiled to his bed with his tray and sat poking the food with a plastic spoon wondering about Sweeney's absence. When he failed to arrive with his evening meal, Blake feared there was something wrong. Maybe the guards had discovered he had been talking to Blake and punished him?

The following day Sweeney returned.

'Blake, are you awake?' he hissed through serving hatch.

Blake scurried across the dirty floor and sat with his ear near the opening. 'Where have you been? I was worried I'd got you into trouble.'

'We've been in lockdown.' Sweeney took Blake's dirty dishes and passed him a bowl and a mug of tea. 'They didn't let us out all day yesterday.'

'Why?'

'One of the lads has gone missing.'

'Escaped?'

'The guards have been going berserk. It happened the night you attacked Dragoslav. His cell was empty when they called lights out. There's no sign of him anywhere.'

'Who is it?'

'Guy called Ricky Vaughn.'

'He's a thin guy, right? Boxer's nose, brown eyes? I saw him.'

'When?'

'After they sent in the riot squad. I was on the ground. I'm sure I saw him before I passed out.'

Blake was convinced of it. A dark figure noticeable because he was standing away from the rioting throng. His back against the wall, hands tucked into his pockets. He peeled away from the others, inching his way towards a staircase while the guards' attentions were otherwise occupied. He made it up the steps in four large bounds and disappeared.

'What's up the stairs at the end of the corridor?'

'The canteen. There're some pool tables and a bit of gym equipment. Not much else.'

'Is there a way out?'

'Not unless he had the keys to a dozen gates. And even if he made it out of the unit, he'd still be inside the perimeter of the main prison.'

'So the chances are he's still inside the High Security Unit?'

'I suppose,' said Sweeney. 'Why do you care so much?'

'I'm curious. Aren't you?'

'I guess. Look I'd better get going. I'll talk to you later,' said Sweeney. The hatch clattered closed and Blake heard his soft footsteps disappearing.

It wasn't long after Sweeney had brought breakfast that a key rattled in the lock and the cell door was heaved open. Two guards appeared with their jackets buttoned up and caps pulled low over their eyes. They clamped cuffs on

Blake's wrists and shackles around his ankles.

'What's going on?' Blake asked.

No reply.

They marched him out of the cell, up two flights of stairs and into an interview room with a table in the middle and two chairs screwed to the floor.

'Sit down, you've got a visitor,' said the first guard, leading him to one of the chairs.

'Who?'

'Who're you expecting? Your mum?' the second man sneered. 'It's your lawyer, stupid. You're on punishment, so you don't get to see anyone else.'

They cuffed him to the chair and clamped his ankles to the legs, before retreating to the back of the room, standing to attention with their eyes fixed ahead. Blake flexed his hands against the cuffs. A mesh-covered window overlooked the exercise yard he'd walked through a few days earlier. It was the first time he'd seen natural light in days and his eyes were drawn to the sky even though it was a grey, gloomy morning. There were splatters of rain on the window and thick cloud enveloped the roof of the red-brick building opposite. He longed to be outside. To taste a fresh breeze and feel the rain on his face.

His attention was snapped back to the room when Alex Mortensen strode in looking every part the smart lawyer. Hair tied back, white blouse buttoned to the neck and a dark-coloured trouser suit. She had a briefcase in one hand and walked with a swagger that bordered on arrogance. He thought she was overplaying it a bit but the guards didn't blink. Her shoulders were back and her chin was up. She shot the guards such a look of disdain that Blake couldn't help himself but smile. He was loving the performance. She hadn't even looked him in the eye. It was like he wasn't there.

Her briefcase landed on the table with a thud and she was unfastening the catches when she noticed the guards still standing at the back of the room. She stopped mid-catch and coughed.

'Thank you, gentlemen,' she said with barely disguised impatience. 'You can leave us now.'

'Ma'am, we can't leave you on your own with the prisoner.'

'Are you being serious?'

'It's against regulations.'

'Firstly, stop calling me 'ma'am'. Secondly, screw your regulations. Lawyer-client privilege means this man is entitled to speak with me in private. So leave. You've cuffed him pretty well, so he's not going to be much of a threat is he? You can wait outside. I'll call if I need you.'

The guards looked at each other and shrugged. 'Your choice. We'll be the other side of the door. If you need us, shout.'

'Very authoritative,' said Blake, as the men closed the door behind them.

Mortensen sat, closed the briefcase and placed it on the floor. 'God, you look like crap,' she said.

He'd not seen a mirror in days but imagined how he must look. A face ravaged by several days' beard growth and his hair a tangled mess. He'd not washed so figured he didn't smell all that great.

'Thanks, you still look pretty amazing. What's in the briefcase?'

'Anything I could find to steal from the stationery cupboard,' she smiled. 'Some paper, a notebook and some pens.'

'Nice touch.' Mortensen's arrival had lifted Blake's mood more than he'd expected. Her suit jacket was pinched in at the waist and tailored trousers emphasised her long legs. Her eyes sparkled green, picking up a hint of the gemstones she wore around her neck.

'I didn't get to say thanks for a great evening the other night,' he said.

'Just doing my job.'

'Seducing and drugging me? And I thought we were on the same side.'

'I didn't seduce you. As I remember, you were the one making all the moves. Besides, we had to make your arrest look convincing. I might have encouraged you back to the apartment but you didn't take much persuading.'

'And the drugs?'

'We couldn't have had you putting up a fight and making a scene.'

'Or we could have worked through a plan together.'

'We thought your reaction would be more genuine if the arrest came as a surprise. Think of it as helping you get into character.'

Blake shuffled on the hard, wooden chair but found it difficult to find a comfortable position with his arms and legs immobilised.

'How are you settling in?' Mortensen asked after a strained silence. 'All the other boys being nice to you?'

'What do you think?'

'I hear you have your own cell.'

'It's better than that, I have solitary confinement. But sadly, as you can see, and probably smell, the washing facilities are in short supply.'

'Solitary confinement?'

'It's a long story.'

'So you've not made any progress on the case?' she asked.

'It's been a bit tricky while I've been in a punishment cell.'

'I thought you were used to working covert ops and keeping a low profile? You've only been in five minutes. What did you do?'

'I needed to acquire some credentials, so I took down the toughest guy on the wing. Anyway, he was trying to tap me up for some kind of protection racket.'

'And there was me thinking that blending in and living with the enemy was your field of expertise.'

'Don't start lecturing me on how to do my job. I needed to establish a status otherwise no one's going to take me seriously. Now I've made my point, I can talk to a few people about Rahimi. What about you?'

'The lab came back with details of the phone you found under Rahimi's floorboards.'

'And?'

'The SIM card's interesting. A number of calls were made from it from inside Marshside.'

'Not the phone?'

'We think Rahimi smuggled in the SIM on its own,' said Mortensen.

'But he still needed a phone to use it.'

'And that still leaves the question of why he bothered smuggling it out again, doubling his chances of being caught. None of it makes a great deal of sense.'

'So I need to crack on with finding out who Rahimi was associating with,' said Blake.

'That's the other thing. I've checked and he didn't have clearance for the High Security Unit.'

'So what the hell am I doing in here?'

'It's where the calls were made from. The Americans are adamant.'

'They've made a mistake,' said Blake.

'I don't think so. They were very precise about the location. Once they'd determined the number the calls were made from, they were able to accurately track the device. And it was in the HSU, no doubt. You need to concentrate on finding out who made the calls.'

'How?'

'I thought you'd be able to use some of your mind-control stuff,' said Mortensen.

'What are you talking about?'

'Come on, I know all about it. Coercive hypnotism, right?'

A trickle of sweat ran down the back of Blake's neck, soaking into his collar. The room was uncomfortably warm. 'You've read the files,' he said. 'You tell me.'

'You developed it to help in the interrogation of hostile witnesses. I know that much,' said Mortensen. 'I also know that Echo 17 specialised in the extraction of information from high value targets from inside non-friendly states and that your role was invaluable. Unique even. The files say you can bend people's minds to your will. Is it true?'

'Within reason. It can certainly help to loosen tongues.'

'Show me. Put me under,' said Mortensen, leaning forwards in her chair and resting her arms on the table. She looked at Blake with wide, doe eyes.

'Tempting right now but no, it wouldn't be ethical.'

'Don't be like that. How are those cuffs?' she said, nodding at his wrists. 'Tight enough? I bet you could make the guards remove them if you wanted to. Shall I call them?'

'This isn't a game.'

Mortensen was already on her feet. 'Guards!' she shouted.

'Alex, don't do this,' said Blake.

The two prison officers crashed through the door at the same instant an ear-splitting alarm, like an air-raid siren, sounded. A red light screwed into the ceiling flashed and radios clipped to the officers' belts crackled with distorted shouts. They stopped on the spot, torn between the alarm and Mortensen's cries for help. They looked first to Blake, then finding he was securely restrained, glanced at Mortensen. Finally their eyes were caught by something outside the window.

'Bloody hell,' said Mortensen, her jaw falling open.

The arm of a crane had been extended over the top of the outer wall of the prison. Beneath it an open-sided bucket dangled from a hook with a figure dressed in black overalls standing inside. His face was hidden by a balaclava. The bucket came to rest on top of the wire ceiling above the exercise yard and the man inside produced an industrial-sized pair of wire cutters. He leaned out and cut open a circular section, peeling it open with gloved hands. He shouted into a radio handset he snatched from his hip, and the pulley rope snapped taut. It lifted the container fractionally off the mesh and lowered it through the hole. Within a few seconds it had vanished from view, plunging to the ground below.

Nobody in the interview room moved. Four pairs of eyes were fixed on the drama outside, their brains unsure what to make of it. A shouted command over their radios jolted the two guards out of their inaction.

'Stay here with them,' the first shouted over the alarm. He turned and sprinted out of the door, slamming and bolting it behind him.

'Ma'am, the prison's going into lockdown. You'll need to stay here for the time being while we resolve matters,' said the second guard.

'What about him?' She nodded at Blake.

'He stays too. I'll keep him cuffed to the chair,' he said. 'You'll be safe, don't worry.'

Blake said nothing. He sat back in his chair and tried to make himself comfortable. Mortensen moved to the window.

'Ma'am, please sit down.' The guard stepped towards her but the look she gave him stopped him in his tracks.

The crane arm was fully extended at a sixty degree angle over razor wire that topped the perimeter wall. As they watched, the lifting cable snapped taut and the bucket reappeared with three people inside. Two prisoners had joined the balaclava-clad man in their distinctive regulation grey jogging trousers and t-shirts. The taller of the two had his arm clamped around his chest and a knife against his neck. The shorter man stood wide-eyed and motionless as the container swung up into the air.

Sirens sounded in the distance as the bucket rose. It ascended high above the roof of the adjacent buildings, swung over the top of wall and dropped out of view while the alarms continued to ring at an ear-splitting volume.

'Hey, buddy, any chance of loosening these cuffs?' Blake gave the guard an encouraging smile. He was losing precious minutes to act while chained to the chair. The chances the escape wasn't somehow connected with Rahimi's murder were too slim to contemplate.

'Stay where you are, Blake. We'll get you back on the block as soon as we can but try to relax, okay?'

'Okay,' said Blake. 'I understand.' His head dropped and the guard turned his attention back to the window. 'Maybe I could talk to you privately for a moment?'

'I said relax, we'll get you back onto the wing as soon as we can.'

'I really need to speak to you. It's important.'

'For God's sake, what is it, Blake?' A frown clouded the guard's face.

'It's a bit awkward. I don't really want to say in front of the lady.'

The guard stepped closer, his hand on a baton in his belt, wary of the tricks the prisoners played. He knew to keep his distance even from someone secured to a chair. His was particularly cautious of Blake's head, knew the damage a skull could cause used as a weapon. A flex of the neck muscles was all it would take.

'What is it?' he said with a huff.

'I've got a really bad itch,' said Blake.

'What?'

'Top of my leg. It's driving me insane.'

'For God's sake.' The guard leaned forwards, arm outstretched, his eyes never leaving Blake's face.

At the moment his fingers brushed past Blake's hand, he snatched the guard's wrist like a viper pouncing on a mouse. 'Sleep,' said Blake, pulling the guard closer.

The man's eyes fluttered and closed. His shoulders relaxed and his head fell to one side. Blake spoke slowly and deliberately as if from a well-rehearsed script, his tone soft. His words were designed to burrow into the core of the guard's subconscious and reach the deepest depths of his psyche.

'You're going to do exactly as I tell you. I'm not a genuine prisoner so there's nothing for you to fear. I need your help, so you'll follow my instructions without question or hesitation. Do you understand?'

The guard nodded. Mortensen had turned from the window and was watching intently with her head tilted to one side.

'Still sceptical?' said Blake.

'It's really as easy as that?'

'When you know what you're doing. I don't normally work with an audience but needs must. Now grab your briefcase, I'm going to get us out of here.'

'Is he okay?'

'He's fine.'

'And he'll do anything you tell him?'

'I can't make him do anything that would inherently put him in danger but I can override his conscious decisions to an extent. He'll stop if I try to overstep his natural boundaries.'

'Which are what?'

Blake shrugged. 'Who knows? We're all different, different compulsions and different urges. No two people's boundaries are the same.'

'So what now?'

'Time to get out of this chair.'

Blake instructed the guard to release his cuffs and the restraints around his ankles, then stood and stretched his cramped muscles.

'And your next trick? A rabbit out of a hat?' said Mortensen.

'You said you wanted to see what I do. Now you know.'

A sudden silence. Someone had cut the alarm although the red light continued to flash.

'Did you recognise the men who escaped?' asked

Mortensen.

'Only one of them. The tall guy with the knife was on my block. I didn't recognise the other one.'

'Name?'

Blake was certain it was the same man he'd seen disappearing during the riot. The prisoner who'd been missing for the last two days. Even from a distance he recognised his build and his flattened nose.

'Ricky Vaughn,' he said. 'I saw him on the morning they put me in solitary. Now come on, we need to get out of here.'

On his command the guard unlocked the visitor's door and Blake and Mortensen followed him into the corridor.

'Quickly, there's someone we need to pay a visit to,' said Blake.

Chapter 12

It was turning out to be a bad day for Jim Mullins. He'd left his wife sitting at the breakfast table clutching the letter that had turned their lives upside down. Now he wondered if he should have stayed. They'd sat for a while lost in their own thoughts, that single sheet of paper between them like a hideous pustule. What was he supposed to have said? That everything was going to be fine? The toast had remained untouched in the silver rack and their mugs of tea had eventually gone cold. He'd made uncertain claims about the advances in modern medicine, partly to ease her concerns but mostly to reassure himself. He didn't dare think of a life without her. He'd never be able to cope. He didn't even know how the dishwasher worked. Margaret was one of life's copers, there in everyone's hour of need. After twenty five years of marriage he'd never seen anything shake her so badly.

He'd convinced himself he'd be no use at home. She'd be better off calling her sister. She'd have the right words to say. That was the thing about women. They were born with an empathic gene most men lacked. It would be better all-round if he carried on as normal. Besides, the prison wouldn't run itself. He had staff to lead and prisoners' welfare to consider. She was still in her dressing gown when he'd left, her eyes red and her cheeks streaked with tears. He'd kissed her on the head and told her he'd be home by seven. Then he'd left. Like any other working day.

As he'd driven, he couldn't shake the image of her

sitting at home, ashen-faced, staring at the words and numbers as if by reading the letter over and over she could change their meaning. There would have to be an operation, of course, and treatment to poison her insides and make her sick. He knew that much. He'd wondered if she'd lose her hair. He'd pictured her wearing one of those brightly-coloured scarves.

He'd driven on auto-pilot, barely registering his route and had arrived at his office looking and feeling weary. His face was hollow and grey. He'd tried to busy himself with the routine of the morning, checking e-mails and signing off the overnight reports but his heart hadn't been in it. He'd tried to concentrate on the final details of a parole board report but hadn't found the focus.

When the alarm sounded, it was a welcome distraction. He looked up from his desk as if expecting someone to come bursting in with news. The wailing siren cut through walls and ceilings accompanied by the distant sound of pounding boots and strangulated cries. He couldn't remember if there was a scheduled drill but he wasn't unduly worried. He was confident his officers knew what they were doing. The procedure was standard for any incident. Prisoners would be locked in their cells and the jail would go into lockdown with the control room remotely sealing doors and gates.

Mullins prided himself on his record. There'd never been a break-out or any significant trouble in the five years he'd been governor. He suspected a minor incident which, under the rules he'd implemented to tighten security, necessitated the alarm to be raised. He'd know soon enough. Protocol dictated the duty control officer would contact him as soon as the details could be verified.

Realising the futility of trying to continue with his report while the sirens were raging in his ears, he swung his chair around to face the window behind. His usual view was of the exercise yard and the barred windows of the cells opposite, a scene he normally viewed with a certain satisfaction. But not that morning. He stood slowly and stepped closer to the glass. The bright, yellow arm of a crane spanned the top of the perimeter wall and was lowering an open capsule into the grounds. As it landed on the protective wire screen above the yard and a figure in dark overalls leaned out with a pair of wire cutters, Mullins snatched up the phone on his desk. He punched in a three-digit number and was connected instantly to the control room.

'What the hell's going on?' He tried to keep his voice even. No point panicking until he knew the facts, but he heard his words waver as he spoke them.

'Guv, there's an attempted break-out.'

'I can see that.'

'Sir, we also have a hostage situation.'

They were the words Mullins had dreaded to hear. 'An officer?'

'No, one of the men on the HSU's taken another inmate.'

'Right,' said Mullins with relief. 'Names?'

'We're still trying to find out.'

'And the situation, is it contained?' There was a pause on the other end of the line. 'Please tell me we have this under control.'

'We can't get to them. Not without putting the hostage in danger. One of the prisoners has a knife and he's making threats.'

Mullins turned back to the window as the bucket was winched up through the mangled wire ceiling. He had an obscured view of the three men inside but couldn't make out their faces.

'Have the police been notified?'

'On their way, Sir.'

The capsule swung into the air and over the top of the razor-wire capped wall, before disappearing from view.

'Shit!' Mullins slammed down the phone and immediately his mobile phone rang. He checked the number and dumped the call.

He knew the standard procedure. His next step should have been to alert the Home Office. They'd want the identities of the two escapees and an assessment of their danger to the public. It would determine not only the level of response but how much to reveal to the press. The recriminations and inquiries would come later. It wasn't something to worry about for the time being.

Mullins slipped his glasses from his nose and rubbed his eyes. He wondered if the day could get any worse. He dialled another number on his desk phone and reached the senior warden on the HSU.

'I need the names,' he said, as calmly as he could. It suddenly felt very warm in his office, the collar of his shirt tight around his neck.

'Ricky Vaughn, Sir,' he said. Mullins picked up a hesitancy in his voice.

'Are you sure?'

'Absolutely.'

'Who else?'

'A guy from A Block. Elias Pitts.'

'Christ, what a mess.'

Mullins hung up, rocked back in his chair and tried to compose himself. He needed to think carefully about his words before making the next call. He'd just become the first governor in the prison's thirty year history to have allowed a successful break-out. Not a record that was going to do his career much good. Someone silenced the alarms. He took a deep breath and picked up the phone.

Chapter 13

Blake and Mortensen found the governor's office at the top of a staircase pungent with the aroma of disinfectant and polish. A brass plaque engraved with Jim Mullins' name had been screwed to the door. Blake knocked and walked in without waiting for a reply. He left the prison officer on guard outside.

Mullins glanced up. He was on the phone and stopped speaking mid-sentence. Mortensen pushed in front of Blake fearful his appearance unwashed and unshaven in his prison uniform might provoke some alarm. She flashed an identity card in a leather wallet.

'Sorry for the intrusion, Governor.'

Mullin's left hand had already disappeared under his desk, reaching for a panic button. It was no surprise. Blake couldn't have looked any less like an MI5 agent. His clothes were dirty and dishevelled and his knuckles grazed and bloodied.

'Please don't do anything rash,' said Mortensen. 'If you put the phone down, I can explain.'

Mullins took the receiver from his ear and looked at it as if he'd forgotten he'd been on a call. 'I'll call you straight back,' he said, hanging up.

Mortensen pulled up a chair. Blake remained at the back of the office, leaning against a row of metal filing cabinets.

'MI5?' Mullins' eyes narrowed. 'Did you know this break-out was being planned?'

'We're investigating another matter but it could be

connected,' said Mortensen. She crossed her legs and placed her hands in her lap.

'Tell me what you know about a man called Javid Rahimi,' said Blake. 'You employed him as a cleaner.'

Mullins threw up his hands in an exaggerated gesture of exasperation. 'We have lots of ancillary staff. I don't know them all. Why?'

'He was a political refugee from Iran.'

'So?'

'Rahimi was found dead a few days ago,' said Mortensen. 'We think he'd been murdered.'

Mullins fell back in his chair deflated, like a balloon pricked by a pin. 'How?'

'Poisoned, possibly because of something that happened in Marshside. We can't elaborate on the details but Blake's been inside the HSU trying to establish the circumstances.'

'On whose authority?' Mullins' tone hardened.

'I'm sorry, we had to keep you in the dark to make sure his arrival raised no suspicion.'

'Look, we have to assume the break-out was linked with Rahimi's death. It's vital we get as much background on the men involved,' said Blake. 'We need details of their convictions, names of their associates and everything else you have on record about them.'

'I can't give out that information. Not until I can confirm who you are.' Mullins reached for his phone.

'I don't suppose this escape is going to look great on your record, is it? Of course, if you were to help us recapture of these men, that could go some way towards mitigating what's happened. I'm sure the inevitable inquiry will take that into consideration,' Mortensen said.

Mullins withdrew his hand from the phone and put his fingers to his lips. He studied the two agents, his eyes moving from one to the other as if he was working out whether he could trust them.

'The men you're looking for are Ricky Vaughn and

Elias Pitts,' he said at last, rising from his desk. He approached Blake who stood to one side and let him open a drawer in one of the filing cabinets. He pulled out two cardboard files. 'Vaughn's your main concern. You might have met him in the HSU?' He peered at Blake through finger-smudged lenses.

'What's he's in for?'

'Murder and armed robbery. It was a well-documented case in the press.' Mortensen raised her eyebrows, encouraging Mullins to continue. 'He was the mastermind behind a jewellery raid in central London,' said Mullins, sitting back at his desk and opening the file. He smoothed down a sheet of paper pinned inside the front cover. 'It ended in a shoot-out with police at a farmhouse in Wales.'

'I remember it,' said Mortensen. 'Remind me of his background?'

'He grew up on an East London housing estate. His mother's an alcoholic. He has a brother and sister, both from different fathers. His criminal career began when he was around thirteen with some low-level drug dealing, cannabis mostly but there was nothing significant until he was caught dealing steroids at a gym where he'd developed some talent as a boxer. He could have made something of himself there. By all accounts he had some talent in the ring but he became involved with a gang with some serious form for assault, robbery and firearms offences. At some point they came up with an idea to rob a jewellers in Bond Street. It was supposed to be a one-off big-time hit that was going to fund their early retirement.

'Four of them stormed the shop just before closing time, dressed in boiler suits and ski masks and armed to the teeth with handguns and semi-automatics. Vaughn was the ringleader. They held the staff hostage, forced them to open display cabinets and safes and when they were done wiped the CCTV footage. Then they walked out of a back entrance with several million pounds worth of gemstones, gold and silver stuffed in holdalls.

'The alarm wasn't raised for nearly four hours when one of the shop workers managed to free himself but by then the gang had split their spoils and vanished. They should have got clean away but someone couldn't keep his mouth shut and word started to spread among the criminal underworld. Eventually someone coughed a name to the police and after that it didn't take them long to piece together who was responsible. They picked them up one-by-one until there was only Vaughn left.

'They tracked him to Wales where they think he was lying low before attempting a ferry crossing to Ireland. He found a remote farmhouse, broke in and murdered the elderly owners in their kitchen. The alarm was raised by a postman who was concerned when he saw the post piling up. Two police officers from the local constabulary who went to investigate were shot dead by Vaughn on the doorstep, and when armed response teams were scrambled, there was a long stand off. Three more officers were wounded and Vaughn was only finally apprehended when he'd spent all his ammunition.'

'What about his hostage, Pitts?' asked Blake.

Mullins closed Vaughn's file and opened the other. 'I take a special interest in our inmates in the HSU but Pitts was in the main wing so I don't know so much about him. He's serving eight years for fraud, so in many respects he couldn't be any more different than Vaughn. He's Oxford-educated and a banker by profession but lost a lot of money in 2008 during the global financial crash. Not only was he made redundant but discovered that many of his investments were worth next to nothing. That's when he became wrapped up in a sophisticated international pump-and-dump fraud scheme.'

'What's that?' asked Mortensen.

'With the money he had left, he and a number of associates invested heavily in worthless penny stocks, often taking control of the companies involved. By announcing fictitious business ventures and mergers they were able to artificially bump up the share prices, then dump their stock. Tens of thousands of smaller investors lost millions while they creamed off massive profits.'

'And Pitts was housed in the main prison?' asked Blake.

Mullins nodded. He ran a finger along a sheet of paper in Pitts' file. 'He's been with us for three years.'

'And the prison and the HSU are operated completely independently?'

'Absolutely,' said Mullins.

'And there's no way inmates in the two blocks could have any contact with each other?

'Security in and out of the HSU is incredibly tight, as I'm sure you've seen for yourselves,' said Mullins.

'So if the HSU prisoners couldn't get out and the inmates in the main block couldn't get in, how did Ricky Vaughn manage to take Elias Pitts hostage?'

'That's a very good question.'

Chapter 14

The thudding clunk of bolts being slid into place heralded Blake's return to incarceration. It was a sound that set his nerves on edge and made him wonder why he'd argued so hard to be allowed back onto the wing. Standing in the middle of his cell, the walls closed in. The block remained on lockdown and the frustrated screams and angry banging from inmates furious at their prolonged imprisonment carried through the thick walls. The window, with bars cemented into the brickwork above the head of the bed, served only to tease him with temptation of the freedom beyond.

He tried to find distractions. Firstly he washed, rinsed his stubbly face and the back of his neck, lathered his hands and rubbed the dirt from his forearms. He really needed a shower and shave but he had to make do. He ran wet fingers through his hair, flattening it where he could feel tufts standing on end, and dried with a thin towel. He hauled himself up to the window, and tried to snatch a glimpse outside but saw only the top of a wall and a patch of cloud-splattered sky. He dropped to the floor and dragged his body through enough press-ups and sit-ups to make his muscles weak, then collapsed on the bed.

The mattress was thicker than the soiled and lumpy makeshift bed in the punishment cell, and smelled clean by comparison. The sheets were unsoiled and the pillow full enough to support his head. He stretched out his legs, kicked off his shoes and lay staring at a patch on the ceiling where the paint was flaking.

They'd bullied Mullins into letting Blake back into the High Security Unit but he'd agreed only to a twenty-four hour window. It was hardly long enough to make headway into Rahimi's death but it was the best deal they could hope for in the circumstances. Mullins had wanted Blake thrown out of the jail immediately, fearful of allowing an MI5 operative into the HSU with the liability of his identity being discovered. If the inmates found out, they'd string him up, he'd warned them, and he wasn't prepared to risk it. But Mortensen had been most persuasive, flirting and flattering to win him over, promising the service would clear Mullins' name with the Home Office and ensure no disciplinary action would follow for the escape of two prisoners under the noses of his guards.

It was late afternoon when the lockdown was finally relaxed and the cell doors unlocked. Blake followed a stream of prisoners filing their way up a flight of stairs and joined the back of a queue for food in the canteen. Blake was pleased to see Sweeney standing behind a stainless steel serving counter, his black, gelled hair glistening under unforgiving lights. He was ladling meat and gravy onto plates from metallic bowls.

'So you're back,' he said to Blake, passing him a plate under a heat lamp.

'For now.'

The canteen was alive with the murmur of insignificant chatter. Groups of men were sitting around tables eating, talking and laughing, their relief to be out of their cells palpable. No one made eye contact with Blake, so he found an empty table in a corner and tucked into his meal with the relish of a man who'd not eaten for three days.

He glanced up when a tray clattered onto the table and Sweeney swung himself into a seat opposite with lithe energy.

'How is it?' He nodded to a fork that was halfway to Blake's mouth.

'Okay,' said Blake.

'So you missed all the excitement.'

'The break-out?'

'It was a-maz-ing.' Sweeney elongated the word so that it sounded like three. 'Apparently they came in over the wall with a crane. Can you believe it?'

'I saw it, from the interview room. I was meeting my brief.'

'So? What happened?'

Blake gave a blow-by-blow account of the escape. 'You must have heard about it being planned?'

'Uh-uh,' Sweeney shook his head. 'Nothing. Not a peep.'

'Tell me about Vaughn.'

'Not much to tell.' Sweeney shrugged. 'Thinks he's better than the rest of us. Nobody's sad to see him go.'

'What's he in for?'

'Armed robbery. He fancied himself as a player but there's not much going on up here.' Sweeney tapped his forehead with two fingers. His ragged fingernails had been chewed down beyond the tips of his fingers. 'Mind you, they say he took down a few coppers when they caught him, so he can't be all bad, eh?'

Sweeney pushed away his empty plate and dug in his pocket for a pouch of tobacco. He rolled a skinny cigarette, lit it and exhaled a vapour trail of smoke.

'What about the guy he took hostage?'

'Elias Pitts?'

'Know him?'

'Yeah,' Sweeney said with a knowing grin. 'Some guy from the main wing.'

'So how did Vaughn get to him?'

'Maybe he was already inside the HSU?' Sweeney sat back in his chair, folded an arm across his chest and let Blake puzzle it out.

'But how? The security around here's tighter than Fort Knox.'

'Not for everyone. Not for a librarian, say.'

'I don't understand.'

'Pitts was in charge of the library. We get to visit once a week. Didn't they tell you? It's a very popular service,' Sweeney said with a conspiratorial wink. 'And as the prison librarian he had certain privileges, like being able to move around the different wings to restock their books.'

'So he's the one prisoner from outside who's allowed in?'

'The only one.'

'So what's he like?'

'Don't know. Never met him. None of us are allowed in while he's changing the books. He always supervised and we're always locked out. Supposed to be for his own protection. He's some kind of hotshot banker who got caught with his fingers in the till. Good bloke though.'

'Why'd you say that?'

Sweeney shot a glance over his shoulder and waited for one of the prison officers to pass. 'He was our bagman,' he said, grinning from ear to ear and then breaking out into a chesty laugh when he saw Blake's confused frown.

'A courier?'

'You wanted it, Pitts could get it for you. For a price, you know.'

'He was smuggling stuff in? How?'

Sweeney crushed the remnants of his cigarette under his heel, picked up the butt and dropped it onto his plate. 'We leave requests in the books and a week later the stuff arrives. He leaves it hidden on the shelves.'

'What sort of stuff?'

'Snout mostly but smack if you want.'

'Phones?'

'No problem. He could get you pretty much anything you wanted.' Sweeney leaned across the table. 'And now he's gone which is a complete bummer.'

'But you said he was always supervised. So how did he manage to get the gear in?'

Sweeney shrugged. 'You ask a lot of questions.'

'I'm curious,' said Blake, holding Sweeney's stare. 'That's all.'

'I don't know, mate. As far as I'm concerned he got it, no questions. Reckon one of the screws must have been in on it but, who cares? Right, washing-up duty calls.' Sweeney stood and swept up his tray. He was halfway across the canteen when he turned back to Blake. 'You know, Vaughn's not done us any favours you know,' he said.

After the meal, most of the inmates remained on the upper floor, watching television, playing pool, table tennis or cards. A few of the younger men were lifting weights. Some drifted away to make calls from the payphones mounted on a pillar. Blake sat on his own, observing the others for a while. When he was certain no one was watching, he slipped back to the cells.

The doors were all open but the corridor was deserted. He walked lightly, carrying his weight on the balls of his feet, counting the cells off on his right. Vaughn's was almost exactly halfway along the corridor. It was a mirror image of his own with the same stainless steel sink, toilet bowl and concrete bed set against the side wall. The sheets had been pulled roughly over the mattress under a woollen blanket while a greasy, brown dent cratered the centre of a pillow at the head of the bed. A vague hint of disinfectant and the odour of another man's sweat hung in the air. One of the fluorescent bulbs flickered and strobed and a stream of burnt amber flooded through the window at the top of the far wall, signalling the departure of the late afternoon sun as it faded beyond an unseen horizon. A toothbrush and paste were lined up on the edge of the sink, next to a bar of soap crusted with dried foam. Against a wall by the door was a square-topped wooden table where a book and an empty mug had been set. The book was a novel by Dostoyevsky, wrapped in a protective, clear plastic cover. On the inside first page, Blake found a faded blue stamp identifying it as belonging to HMP Marshside. The pages had turned brown and stiff like baking paper and gave off a musty smell as Blake flicked through them with his thumb. He turned it over, smiling at Vaughn's choice of reading matter. He wondered if 'Crime and Punishment' was Pitts' idea of a joke. But there was no obvious communication inside, so he set it down and turned his attention to the rest of the cell.

With one hand he lifted the mattress, pulled back the sheets and ripped off the blanket but found nothing. He checked under the bed and shuffled around the room tapping the walls with his knuckles, checking for any hollow sounds that might reveal a cavity.

Next he turned his attention to a number of pages ripped from magazines stuck to the wall above the bed. They were mostly pornographic images of surgically enhanced women pouting at the camera with sultry eyes and arching backs. The centrepiece was the image of a sports car parked in a harvested cornfield in front of a rising sun. Below it, a key fob decorated with a blue and white chequered BMW emblem hung from a lump of blue putty. Blake grabbed it, weighed it in his hand and puzzled at why a prisoner would keep a car key in his cell. It sat comfortably in his palm, beautifully weighted and designed. Typical of German engineers to extend their ergonomic skills to the key fob, he thought. It was about six centimetres long with two silver buttons on one side. Blake turned it over and noticed a catch which seemed to serve no discernible purpose. When he pressed it, a plate opened with a click. He flipped it up with one finger and found the miniature keypad and LCD screen of a cleverly disguised mobile phone. With the nail of his thumb, Blake held down the green call button and the screen flickered to life. A message on the display flashed up: 'Please insert SIM'.

'Bingo,' said Blake to himself, powering the phone down and slipping it into the pocket of his trousers.

He barely registered the sharp blow that caught him at the back of his neck as he was turning to leave. He legs collapsed and his vision blurred as his brain shut down. The last thing he saw was the cold, hard floor rushing up to meet him.

Chapter 15

A doctor checked his watch, noted the time and snatched a clipboard from the end of the bed. He bit on his lower lip and nodded his satisfaction at the notes. The man lying motionless before him was lucky. Blake appeared to have suffered no lasting damage but was unrecognisable. His face had blown up like a ball, discoloured by a vibrant patchwork of purples, blues and reds. His eyes were swollen closed, his lips split open and there were cuts across his forehead, cheeks and chin. The bruising had spread down his neck onto his chest and arms, leaking from black into all the colours of the rainbow like ink spots spreading through blotting paper. After ten years at the prison hospital, the injuries were familiar to the doctor, the contusions and abrasions consistent with a serious physical beating. Remarkably there were no broken bones or internal organ damage.

Blake's breathing came in rasps, slightly out of time with the metronomic pulse of the machine he was plugged into recording his vital signs. A colourless tube looped into his arm from a bag of fluid suspended above his head. The doctor moved around to the side of the bed and checked Blake's pupils, peeling open each eye and dazzling him with a penlight torch.

Blake stirred and winced. He tried to shift his weight but his muscles screamed that he'd be better off remaining still. His mouth was dry and his head was pounding. He tried forcing open his eyes but could only see through narrow slits. Everything around him glowed white and, for a confused moment, he wondered if he'd died. Only the throbbing ache that ran from his legs, through his torso and into his arms dissuaded him of the idea. Slowly his vision came into focus and he saw he was in a narrow room painted white. There were no windows or furniture other than the bed in which he lay but the room seemed to be filled with people staring at him.

'You're awake. How're you feeling?' the doctor asked. He had a bald, domed head and a stethoscope draped over the shoulders of his white coat. He was leaning over Blake so closely he could make out pimples on the doctor's cheek and the whites of his eyes tinged yellow against his ebony skin.

'Sore,' Blake whispered, the word rising from the back of his throat. He struggled to remember what had happened to him. He wasn't sure he was still in the prison.

'You're lucky,' said the doctor. 'Nothing broken. I think you'll live.' He smiled and straightened up.

'I don't feel lucky,' said Blake.

'Given the beating you took, I'd say you're very lucky indeed.' Blake remembered being in Vaughn's cell and the mobile phone that looked like a key fob. 'I heard they had to drag them off you.'

'I don't remember…'

'Any nausea? Dizziness?'

'No.'

'That's a positive sign but to be sure I'd like to get an MRI scan. You've taken a number of blows, possibly kicks to the head.'

'That won't be possible.' Jim Mullins stepped into Blake's line of sight from behind the doctor.

'Governor, there's a high probability…'

'I said that won't be possible,' Mullins raised his voice to cut off the doctor. 'I want this prisoner prepared for transfer as soon as possible.'

'I have to protest. There could be any number of complications we don't know about until we get a scan.'

'In which case, I'll find another doctor and you can start looking for a new job. I want him out of here.'

Mullins and the doctor stood toe-to-toe, facing each other down.

'He needs at least forty-eight hours more bed rest before we even contemplate moving him,' said the doctor.

'He's got twenty-four.'

For a moment it looked like the doctor would protest, then thought better of it. 'Then that's your decision and on your head,' he said as he shepherded the nurse from of the room.

Mullins waited for the door to close before turning to Blake. 'I warned you this would happen. They nearly killed you.'

'Who?'

'Dragoslav's men. Who do you think? You were followed to Vaughn's cell and they found you alone. Fortunately, two of my officers noticed they were missing. Like the doctor said, they had to be dragged off you.'

'I didn't hear them coming. I should have been more careful.'

'Damn right, you're a liability. I knew this would happen if they found out about you.'

'They didn't. It was retribution for what I did to Dragoslav, I'm sure of it. I promise they have no idea. I humiliated their boss while they stood outside and let it happen. It was their way of evening the score and I was careless. It won't happen again.'

'That's right, because by tonight you're out. I can't put my officers in any more danger. I won't have it on my conscience.' Mullins pulled a phone from his jacket and tossed it onto the bed. 'Call your people and make the arrangements. We'll provide an ambulance but after that you're on your own.'

It was dark when they came. Two porters in short-sleeved shirts arrived just after three in the morning, threw on a light and woke Blake with a start. He'd been in a deep but restless sleep, his head full of nightmarish visions, until an adrenaline shot hot-wired his heart.

'What's going on?' he grumbled, briefly unable to make sense of his surroundings.

'Time to leave, mate,' said one of the porters pushing a wheelchair. He grabbed a linen bag from the seat and threw it at Blake. 'Get dressed.'

The doctor who'd examined Blake followed the porters into the room. His cheeks were shadowed by stubble and there were bags under his eyes. Blake looked for a name badge but saw only red and blue ink stains above a pocket where he'd kept his pens.

'I apologise for the sudden intrusion. Governor's orders,' he said, striding towards the bed. 'Let's get you as comfortable as we can.'

He set down a kidney-shaped dish and picked out a syringe and a vial of clear liquid.

'What is it?' asked Blake, his voice hoarse.

'Something to help with the pain.'

'No more drugs.'

'It's only a little morphine. Honestly, it will make your move a lot more bearable.'

'I said I don't want it.'

The doctor shrugged and dropped the syringe back into the dish. 'Your choice.'

Blake struggled to sit up, gritting his teeth against the agony of movement. He opened the linen bag and found his old clothes laundered and pressed. He swung his legs out of bed, letting his feet drop onto the cold floor. He tried reaching the ties that held his surgical gown in place but his arms were stiff and uncooperative.

It took a twenty minute effort to finish dressing with the porters' help. Then, determined to show some independence, he insisted on making it to the wheelchair unaided. He fell into the seat and waved away a blanket they tried to drape across his legs. It was humiliating enough to be wheeled out without being wrapped up like a geriatric on a day out to the coast. They took him past a nurses' station lit up by the glow of a desk lamp and into a service lift panelled in stainless steel.

They descended two floors into a vehicle bay heavy with diesel fumes where an ambulance was waiting with its engine running. A fresh-faced paramedic stepped forwards, guided Blake into the back of the vehicle and made him lie down on a stretcher.

With a degree of effort, Blake hauled up his legs and lay flat, allowing the paramedic to secure him with two straps across his chest and thighs. He pulled them tight, maybe a little too tightly, so Blake was immobilised. It was all part of the plan, he told himself, fighting the claustrophobia of being able to move only his head, hands and feet. The worst part of it was a sense he had no control over what was happening to him or where he was being taken. The arrangements had been made by his former unit commander and he trusted Harry Patterson with his life. He took a deep breath and reminded himself Patterson had it all under control and there was nothing to worry about.

The paramedic pulled the doors shut and took a jump-seat as the ambulance rolled forwards. It slowed to negotiate a series of security gates and then picked up speed, accelerating away hard from the prison with a siren blaring. Blake exhaled a long breath and let his shoulders relax. He had no regrets about leaving HMP Marshside. His eyes fell closed and he fantasised about taking a warm shower, drying with soft towels, and enjoying a bottle of cold beer with freshly baked pizza. Soon the comforting tendrils of slumber began to wrap themselves around his mind as his conscious thoughts melded into dreams.

He was jolted awake as the ambulance bumped through a tight turn that sent it rolling on its soft suspension and pinned Blake's bruised arms against the straps. He howled in pain but his screams were lost amid the screech of tyres and the whine of the engine being thrashed. The paramedic had braced himself with one hand on the stretcher and another on a cabinet. He was staring out of a window wide-eyed and tense. Blake struggled against the straps biting into his arms as a knot of panic tightened in his stomach. What the hell was going on?

Things progressed from bad to worse in a millisecond. The wheels squealed under the heavy load of braking and the ambulance slewed across the road. Thin rubber tyres burned and shredded, leaving dirty black trails across the asphalt. In the back, packets, boxes and plastic tubes flew into the air, rising like seeds scattered on a gentle breeze and Blake sensed the vehicle listing. It pitched further and further towards its tipping point until there was a moment of weightlessness before the five-ton, out-of-control lump of metal crashed down in a spray of sparks on its side. The paramedic's body was thrown across the cabin, his arms and legs sprawling in all directions. An appalling scraping sound was accompanied by the acrid stench of burning metal.

The ambulance came to rest amid the hiss of ruptured radiator pipes. The siren slurred, faded and stopped. Blake was suspended on his side with his aching muscles bearing the strain of the straps, the pain temporarily dulled by adrenaline. There was carnage below him. The paramedic was lying in an awkward heap, semi-conscious and groaning with a bloody gash across the side of his head. He was covered in detritus dislodged from cupboards and cubbyholes. Blake tried shouting for help but the words choked in his throat. Not that he expected anyone to hear his cries. At that time of the morning it was unlikely to be anyone around.

But he was wrong. He heard the rumble of tyres, the murmur of an engine and heavy footsteps. Two, maybe three people approaching the stricken ambulance.

'Help!' he called. He stopped struggling. Lay still to listen.

Someone tried the handle of the back doors, now horizontal to the ground. They rattled and popped. The sound of someone forcing their way in. Blake's spirits lifted. He arched his neck to see but as the doors creaked open he was blinded by a powerful beam of light.

'Get down! Don't move!' a voice screamed to no one in particular.

Two figures scrambled over the debris of medical equipment behind shafts of white torchlight that tunnelled through a swirling pall of smoke filling the interior. In the gloom Blake saw the unmistakable shape of a Heckler and Koch MP5 sub-machinegun, a torch integrated into the barrel of the weapon and a finger poised over the trigger. The gunman's face was hidden behind a ski mask. He levelled his weapon at the paramedic's head while a second man approached Blake, slung his weapon over his shoulder and with a flick of his wrists released the straps holding Blake to the stretcher. Blake fell onto the floor that had once been the side of the ambulance, his weight crumpling onto the legs of the paramedic.

'Time to get out of here, sport,' a gruff voice said, his accent muffled through his mask. He hauled Blake up by his collar.

Trust Patterson to send in the boys from the Regiment to add a sense of drama, thought Blake with a smile. A little over the top but a nice touch.

Blake limped his way into the street towards a black Range Rover Sport with tinted windows. Its headlights were blazing and its engine running. Between the two soldiers, he was half-dragged and half-shoved towards the car.

'Get in, quickly!' the first soldier shouted, pushing him through an open rear door.

Blake perched on the middle seat, the cream leather creaking as he settled in. The two troopers joined him on either side. A third man who he realised had been covering the rear of the ambulance hopped in beside the driver. His door had barely closed before they took off to the fanfare of a throaty V6 roar.

They headed away from the crash scene with impolite speed, their seats punching them in their backs. Nobody spoke. The only sound over the road noise was the laboured breathing of the three soldiers rasping through their masks. They sat with their weapons locked and loaded on their laps.

Blake twisted to look out of the rear window. The ambulance was a mangled wreck, lying on its side and straddling the road with its blue lights still pulsing. The carriageway was littered with the shards of metal and plastic wrenched from the vehicle as it had skidded across the road.

'What the hell happened back there?' Blake asked.

The Range Rover slowed as it turned into a back road, assuming a more respectable speed that wouldn't attract attention.

'Your driver was an idiot.' The man behind the wheel caught Blake's eye in the rear-view mirror. 'I thought they were supposed to be professionals?'

'You ran him off the road?' asked Blake.

The two assault troopers in the back with him had pulled off their masks. The man on his left ran a hand through a crop of sweat-soaked black hair. He checked his MP5, unclipped its magazine and handed the weapon and ammunition to the soldier in the front seat to stow in the foot well.

'They were only meant to pull over, not crash the bloody thing,' said the driver, a cold fury in his eyes. Blake understood his anger. He could see it should have been a straightforward job, jeopardised by the ambulance driver's inability to control his vehicle when confronted with a Range Rover trying to force him to stop. Now there was a mess to be cleared up and questions to be answered.

'So where now?' Blake asked. No one replied.

He didn't recognise anything of the network of streets

and couldn't tell if they were even heading north or south. Empty offices and shops flashed past. Traffic was light apart from the occasional black cab and the odd early morning delivery van. Eventually they pulled into an ugly housing estate where high-rise tower blocks rose into the amber-tinged night sky. They slowed to a crawl, passing a children's play area behind wrought-iron railings. The driver stopped in a residents-only car park beneath a high-rise block.

And suddenly Blake knew exactly where they were. It was a location he knew well. The car had barely stopped when the rear door was thrown open from outside.

'Hello, Blake,' said a voice he wasn't expecting to hear.

Chapter 16

'You look terrible,' said Mortensen, giving Blake the once over.

'It's good to see you too,' Blake replied, easing himself out of the car. It was the twilight hour between the dead of night and the start of the new day but Mortensen looked fresh and alert. Her eyes sparkled and her skin had a rosy glow, as if she'd just stepped out of the shower. She thumped the tailgate twice to dismiss the vehicle and marched into a leafy pocket-square with mature oaks and a neat lawn enclosed by a wrought-iron fence. She halted abruptly in the middle of a sweeping path.

'Patterson said to wait here,' she said. 'Don't ask me why we couldn't meet at the office.'

'Because he knows it brings me out in a rash.' Thames House, the headquarters of MI5 since the late 1980s, was an unobtrusive building on the corner of Millbank and Horseferry Road, overlooking Lambeth Bridge on the north bank of the Thames. But Blake refused to step inside. 'It's full of stuffed shirts and Oxbridge toffs,' he said.

'Like me, you mean?' She wrapped her arms around herself and stamped her feet to ward off the chill.

'I'm guessing King's, Cambridge?'

Mortensen gave Blake a wry smile. 'Wrong colours. I'm a dark-blue girl through and through. Lincoln College, actually.'

'As if to prove my point. Come on, this way.' Blake headed for a densely overgrown tangle of shrubs had overrun a nearby flower bed. With his feet sinking into the damp earth, he cleared a path through the branches to reveal a steel door set into a low, concrete building hidden by vegetation. The walls were a dirty algae green and the door defaced by scrawls of faded graffiti. Blake grinned as if he was a magician producing a dove from thin air. The door, as he had expected, was unlocked. The handle was stiff and the hinges rusty but it opened wide enough for them to squeeze through.

'Come on, you don't want everyone to see, do you?'

'What is this place?'

Mortensen stepped into a narrow hallway with a low ceiling. It was illuminated by the flickering light of an ancient fluorescent bulb. The air was stagnant and damp, the grey concrete walls stained by rivulets of water that had accumulated in pools on the floor.

'A nuclear bunker. A legacy of the Cold War. It's rather cool, don't you think?' said Blake.

'It's a bit grim.'

'It was supposed to have been used by Government officials if there was a nuclear strike on London. It would have been a command and control centre but since the thawing of the East they've forgotten it's here. Patterson requisitioned the key from the Ministry of Defence and now it's a useful meeting point away from prying eyes and ears.'

Blake pulled the door closed and headed for a set of steps that spiralled below ground. Harry Patterson was waiting for them in an airless round room. He was pacing up and down with his hands stuffed in his trouser pockets. Metal plates on the heels of his expensive brogues tapped out a rhythm on the hard floor. His mousey hair, receding at the temples, was sleep-ruffled and there were dark bags under his eyes.

'Everything okay?' he asked, watching with only mild concern as Blake hobbled down the stairs, his battered body stiff and his face a patchwork of coloured bruises.

'A few aches and pains. Nothing that won't mend.'

'He was attacked when he returned to the cells,' said Mortensen. 'The Governor reckons he's lucky to be alive, let alone to suffer no lasting damage.'

'I wouldn't worry about him too much, Alex. He has extraordinary powers of recovery.' Patterson had seen Blake put his life and body on the line more times than he could care to recall. 'It'll take more than a few bruises to keep him down. So, what progress?'

'You know about the escape, I presume?' said Blake.

'Alex briefed me and besides, it's all over the news. What's the significance?'

'I think one of the guys who escaped was Rahimi's contact on the inside.' Patterson raised an eyebrow. 'His name's Ricky Vaughn, an armed robber serving multiple life sentences for murder. I searched his cell and found a mobile phone missing a SIM card. My bet is he was using the SIM we found at Rahimi's flat to communicate with the Iranians.'

'Rahimi was smuggling the SIM in and out of the High Security Unit? How?'

'Through the second escapee, a guy called Elias Pitts,' said Blake. 'He was the prison librarian and the only Category A prisoner who had access into the HSU. It gave him a unique opportunity to operate a smuggling racket. Mostly he was dealing in tobacco and cannabis but I was told he could lay his hands on most items, for a price.'

'So there are two of them involved?'

'Pitts is innocent collateral, a means for Vaughn's escape and an easy hostage. He's a former banker serving time for fraud. I don't suppose he even put up any resistance.'

'So assuming he's dumped Pitts somewhere, what's Vaughn's next move?'

'It depends on the deal he cut with the Iranians. It seems logical to assume that his Iranian contacts organised the logistics of the escape, which means whatever he was offering was worth the trouble.'

'The crane was hired by a bogus building firm, paid for in cash,' said Patterson. 'It was picked up by a guy called Whittaker on a fake driver's licence. We've got a description but to be honest it's so vague it matches a quarter of the population of London. Witnesses say there was a gang of four, including the crane driver. They disappeared in two stolen cars, both found burned out. Forensics are going over them but they don't hold out much hope of pulling anything useful from either vehicle. Whoever it was knew what they were doing and covered their tracks.'

'So what's our next step?' asked Blake. 'What about Vaughn's gym?'

'The Met sent a couple of officers to speak with the owners and we've put surveillance on it but nothing yet,' said Mortensen.

'I'll go in,' said Blake, 'see what I can dig up. I bet there's someone there who knows what's going on.'

'My thoughts exactly,' said Patterson. He pulled a slim paper file from a briefcase and passed it to Blake. It contained a single sheet of paper with an address, brief background notes on the gym and a list of names. Clipped to it were a dozen grainy images shot on a long lens of men walking in and out of the building. 'Some of the characters we suspect have connections with Vaughn,' Patterson explained.

'I'll get up there straightaway, sign myself up,' said Blake, tucking the file under his arm.

'You certainly look the part. Get back to me as soon as you have anything,' said Patterson.

Blake touched his face under his eye where the skin was purple and swollen. He was sporting cuts on his cheek and forehead. At least it would give him credibility at the gym. He turned for the stairs and had taken three steps when Patterson called after him.

'How are you two getting on, by the way?' Blake

stopped in his tracks. 'Alex is one of the agency's rising stars, you know. You're lucky to be working with her.'

'I work alone.'

'I need the two of you co-operating. The PM's spitting feathers. It's bad enough it took the Americans to intercept those calls from Marshside. The breakout's added a whole new level of complication. There's real pressure coming from Downing Street. We're all under increased scrutiny. I've promised them we can deliver a result, but the deal is that you have to make it work with Mortensen. Is that clear?'

'I work with people I trust, Harry. You authorised her to have me drugged and arrested at gunpoint.'

'It was in your best interests, Blake,' said Mortensen.

'And Sir Richard personally asked for your involvement,' added Patterson. 'Let's get on with it shall we? You need each other. You bring different sets of skills. Work out a way of getting along, and quickly.'

Patterson unclipped his briefcase and pulled out Blake's Browning Hi-Power nine millimetre with two ammunition clips. Blake begrudgingly stepped back into the room and snatched the gun. He checked the chamber was clear, snapped a clip into the handgrip and loaded a bullet into the breach. The other clip went into the back pocket of his trousers, the Browning into his waistband behind his back.

'I'm serious, Blake. Cut her some slack.' But Blake was already halfway up the stairs.

Mortensen caught up with him as he reached the upper hallway. She followed him through the reinforced steel door, emerging into the park under a lightening sky.

'I thought I was doing the right thing, Blake,' she said.

'You should have talked to me about getting into Marshside.'

'Okay, I get it. I'm sorry. It won't happen again.'

'Damn right it won't. From now on, I work on my own.'

'You heard Patterson; he wants us to work together.'

Mortensen was struggling to keep up with Blake's long strides.

'Fine, that's exactly what we'll tell him. Don't worry, I'll give you a glowing report.'

'Don't patronise me, Blake. I know what this is about.' They reached a deserted main road and stopped on the pavement. Blake scanned both ways looking for a taxi.

'Really?'

'Your pathetic masculine ego. I've put a dent in it because you thought I was trying to seduce you. Not used to women saying no, is that it? Can't they usually resist the green eyes and the silky charms?'

'That's what you think this is about?' He spat the words out with venom, staring at Mortensen with narrow eyes and flattened brows.

'Close to the mark, aren't I?'

'You're not even in the arena.'

A black cab trundled towards them, an amber light shimmering on its roof like a beacon. Blake shot out his arm.

'Where are we going?' Mortensen asked, climbing in behind Blake as the car pulled to a halt.

'We're not going anywhere. I'm going to Vaughn's gym. You can please yourself.' Blake gave the address to the driver who swung the cab around.

'Come on, Blake, we need to work this out. Can we start over?'

Blake settled into his seat and stared out of the window at the dull grey streets zipping past. Despite everything he enjoyed Mortensen's company. The prospect of spending more time in her company was appealing. His head told him to accept her apology but his heart remained stony. He knew he was acting like a petulant teenager and blamed it on his male pride. He came to a decision, took a deep breath and was about to speak when Mortensen's phone rang. She held a finger up to stop him as she plucked the mobile from her pocket.

She listened for a few minutes and frowned. 'Are you sure?' She checked her watch. 'Okay, we're on our way. We should make it by late morning. Lunchtime at the latest.'

'What is it?' asked Blake as she hung up.

Mortensen held the phone in her lap, staring at it with thin lips. 'That was Patterson. He's just picked up a message from Scottish police. A family was abducted at gunpoint last night. They took the husband, wife and two young kids.'

'What does that have to do with anything?'

'Forget Vaughn's gym, we need to get up there as soon as possible.'

Mortensen leant forwards in her seat. 'Sorry, change of plan, driver. Can you get us to Biggin Hill airport as soon as you can?'

Chapter 17

A Cessna Mustang was prepared and waiting when Blake and Mortensen arrived at the airport, its engines idling with a low whine. They buckled into cold, leather seats and watched the pilot going through a pre-flight check-list.

'We have a provisional slot for take-off in five minutes,' he said, turning in his seat. 'The weather's looking fine so we should make Oban in a little over an hour.'

A few minutes later they rolled to the end of the runway and paused momentarily before the engines roared and the aircraft accelerated into a steep take-off. As its nose lifted, Blake's blood drained into his boots and his head swam. Through the narrow portal windows they watched a patchwork of fields and ribbon roads disappearing while weak, auburn rays of light from the early morning sun poured into the cabin. They banked hard right through a veil of low cloud and swiftly reached a cruising altitude of 30,000 feet. Blake stretched out his legs, tilted back his seat and closed his eyes, his body relaxing into the cushioned leather.

He was woken an hour later by Mortensen shaking his arm. They were passing snow-peaked mountains that rose up with ice-crystal caps sparkling like glitter balls. Below, the ink-blue waters of an icy-loch were looming closer as the Cessna descended through wisps of altocumulus. They bumped down on a short airstrip and rolled up to an arrivals hall with a corrugated tin roof adjacent to a rudimentary control tower.

A hire car was waiting for them. Mortensen took the

keys and jumped into the driver's seat. She checked her watch, fired up the engine and pulled away, waiting until they were out of sight of the rental agent before flooring the accelerator. They stopped an hour later at a roadside filling station where they grabbed a stale sandwich and metallic-tasting vending-machine coffee. They ate sitting on the bonnet of the car, filling their lungs with the clean Scottish air.

'How much further?' asked Blake.

'We should make Skye by late morning. I spoke to the senior investigating officer while you were asleep and warned him we were on our way.'

'Did he tell you what happened?'

'A neighbour raised the alarm. She saw everything, apparently. Two men arrived in a dark-coloured 4x4 sometime between eight-thirty and nine last night.'

'Two men?' Blake raised an eyebrow.

'That's what he said.'

'Descriptions?'

'Not yet.'

'What about the family?'

'Benjamin and Sophie Pitts.'

'Pitts?'

'Benjamin is Elias' brother. He's three years older. They've got two young children, Ellie and Charlie. The girl's eleven, the boy's eight. They've lived on the island for about six years.'

Blake fixed his gaze on a patch of rock on a distant mountain slope. 'Do they have a theory for the abduction?'

'I had the distinct impression they're completely in the dark. I got all the guff about following a number of lines of inquiry.'

'But they know about Elias escaping from Marshside?'

'They're not convinced the two incidents are connected.'

'Fair enough. So how was the copper you spoke to? Co-operative?'

'He was okay, a detective superintendent they've sent from Inverness. Wasn't too happy about our involvement but what do you expect? I'd be the same if they'd sent someone up from London to trample all over my case.'

'Trample?'

'You know what I mean. Just trying to see it from his perspective.'

'It sounds like the sooner we get there, the better. Let's go. This time I'll drive.'

They found the house off a narrow track in a desolate spot exposed to the elements, overlooking the Sound of Raasay. It was an unremarkable building constructed in a traditional style with white rendered walls and a slate roof surrounded by ragged fir trees and scrubby fields. A steep driveway led into a gravelled courtyard packed with police vehicles and a bustle of activity. A constable with ruddy cheeks posted at the top of the drive stopped them as they approached. Mortensen flashed her identity card. 'We're here to see the SIO,' she said.

'You'll need Detective Superintendent Douglas. He's down there,' the PC pointed in a vague direction towards the house and ushered them through.

Blake parked alongside a mobile incident van where uniformed officers were mingling with white-suited crime scene investigators. From the far side of the courtyard, a scraggy figure in a pinstriped suit and heavy overcoat watched them. He combed his fingers through fine, grey hair and sauntered over as they spilled out of the car.

'Ms Mortensen? We spoke on the phone earlier,' he said with an outstretched hand. Mortensen took it and noted his firm shake. 'Superintendent Torquil Douglas. It's a long way for British Intelligence to travel. What am I missing?'

Mortensen ignored his question with an apologetic smile. 'This is my colleague Blake.' The two men exchanged a cautious nod. 'We need to know what happened last night.'

The detective peered down his aquiline nose as Blake regarded him over Mortensen's shoulder. His face was grey and creased, the skin sagging from under his eyes and cheeks as though the muscle had wasted away and allowed gravity to take hold. It gave him a melancholic countenance. Not a man for many laughs, Blake thought.

'I can't tell you much more.' Blake struggled to tune into his thick brogue. 'The emergency call was made late yesterday evening. The house was empty when the first response team arrived, and the back door was wide open.'

'Any sign of a break-in or a struggle?'

'The door's intact so we think the family let them in willingly. There's nothing to indicate any violence and nothing seems to have been taken from the property either.'

'Other than the family,' said Mortensen.

Douglas gave her a wan smile. 'Of course, other than the family.'

'Who reported the abduction?' asked Blake.

'The woman next door.' Douglas nodded towards a second house about twenty metres away. It was built in a similar style but closer to the cliff and in a depression in the ground so from the courtyard only the upper floor and roof were visible. 'She saw what we think was a 4x4 pull up at around eight thirty. A short while later two men marched the family out of the house at gunpoint. They were driven off in the car they arrived in.'

'Is she sure? It must be as dark as Hades here at that time of night?'

'Security light.' Douglas pointed above the door at the back of the Pitts' house. 'Lights it up like Christmas.'

'Did she give you a description?'

'They were both white, one taller than the other, both wearing dark clothing. She's helping with a photo-fit but that could take a little while.'

'What about the car?'

'Dark-coloured, possibly blue or black. She didn't get the number plate but she thinks it was a new model.'

'Can we see inside?' asked Mortensen.

Douglas shrugged. He dug his hands into his pockets and trudged towards the house with Blake and Mortensen trailing behind. As they reached the door, they stepped aside for two crime scene investigators carrying clear, sealed plastic bags containing an assortment of objects neither Blake nor Mortensen could make out.

'See for yourself, no sign of a forced entry.' Douglas indicated to the doorframe as they passed through.

'You think they knew their attackers?' said Mortensen.

'You mean was it Benjamin's brother? I don't know. This is a quiet island. Crime is low and folks don't tend to keep their doors locked. The intruders could have let themselves in. We're keeping an open mind.'

The entrance led into a kitchen where the worktops were cluttered with plates, pans and cooking utensils, as though someone had been in the middle of preparing a meal. Blake was struck by the bitter stench of burnt food.

'The pans had boiled dry and whatever was in the oven was burned to a crisp,' said Douglas.

In a room that led from the kitchen, an oblong table was set for two and a bottle of wine had been opened. On the other side of the room were two faded sofas, a television on a grey stand and toys strewn across a patterned rug in front of a wood burning stove, a few embers still glowing faintly through the carbon-stained glass. A staircase coiled up behind the chimney breast and light flooded in through a window overlooking the cliffs and the bay beyond. A mantelpiece was crowded with ornaments and an assortment of photographs in frames. In one, a smiling couple peered into the room with faces fixed in wedding-day grins. Others showed the children at various ages, from birth to school.

The image that caught Blake's attention was a group shot. He stepped over dolls, toy cars and assorted coloured plastic bands, to look more closely. It was framed in dark wood behind a sheet of glass smudged with finger marks. The family was posing in front of a sandstone-cottage with pale blue shutters. A woman, who he assumed was Sophie Pitts, was sitting with a young boy on her lap. Her hair was cut in a boyish bob and her eyes sparkled. The boy was little more than a toddler, grabbing his mother's chin in a pudgy hand oblivious to the camera. An older girl was standing at the woman's side, her arms crossed and she was pouting coquettishly. Her free flowing blonde locks tumbled over her shoulders. Behind them and leaning into the lens was the man Blake took to be Benjamin Pitts. He was peering through a pair of glasses that would have been fashionable five years earlier. It was a portrait of a perfect family. Happy, relaxed and without a care in the world.

'What do you think happened to them?' Blake asked, holding up the photograph.

'Best guess? They were the victims of a robbery that went wrong.'

'But you said nothing was taken.'

'They've not ransacked the house, which is unusual but it's possible they came looking for something in particular, something they thought was in the house. The fact is, we don't know.'

'So why abduct the family?' asked Mortensen.

'If we knew that, we'd be closer to catching them. There's also the possibility of extortion or blackmail. We're checking the Pitts' financial records and we've frozen their accounts for good measure.'

Blake shot Mortensen a look that Douglas missed. 'How much was in their accounts?' he asked.

'Not a fortune. Enough for a rainy day,' said Douglas.

'And what do you know about Benjamin's brother?'

'Elias? I know he was doing time for fraud and that he escaped from prison a few days ago but there's not much evidence he and Benjamin had had any contact in recent years, which is why I'm not jumping to any assumptions.'

'Elias was a successful banker who lost everything in the global financial crash,' said Mortensen. 'He wasn't only made redundant but lost millions as his personal investments nosedived. He was involved in a complex fraud conning thousands of people out of their savings. We don't think he planned his own escape. He was an unwitting victim of a hostage situation but now he's free we think he might be trying to lay his hands on some easy money. His brother might have been his best option. But if Benjamin was unwilling to help, maybe Elias was desperate enough to try to force him to hand over his savings?'

'The woman next door is sure two men were involved.'

'In which case, he could still be with the man he escaped with,' said Mortensen, glancing at Blake.

'His name's Ricky Vaughn. He's an armed robber who was serving his sentence for multiple murders in Marshside's high security unit. He's extremely dangerous. Your officers need to know he should be approached with extreme caution. He won't think twice about shooting if he's cornered.'

'I see,' said Douglas, rubbing a finger across his bottom lip. 'And nobody thought to mention this earlier?'

'We're mentioning it to you now,' said Mortensen.

Chapter 18

The woman who answered the door of the adjacent house wasn't elderly at all. She appeared to be no more than in her early thirties although she had the demeanour of someone older.

'Yes?' she asked, in a tone that suggested she was surprised to see strangers on the doorstep.

'Mrs Aitchison?' Mortensen asked.

'No. Who are you?' Her hair was scraped back severely in a bun. Her eyes were hawkishly sharp.

Mortensen produced her identity card, held it at head height for a second and snapped it shut. 'British Intelligence. We're investigating a prison break we believe is connected to the abduction. We need to speak with Mrs Aitchison about what she saw last night. Are you a family member?'

'Family liaison officer.' The woman stepped to one side. 'She's in the living room. I'll put the kettle on.'

The old woman was sitting in a threadbare armchair by a window overlooking the cliffs. Her translucent skin barely concealed a network of thread-like veins and her hands were so badly deformed that her fingers were clawed under her palms.

'More questions?' she asked with weary resignation.

'Mrs Aitchison, we understand you had a clear view of what happened last night?' asked Mortensen, leading the questioning without any introductions.

The woman settled back in her seat and tugged her cardigan tightly around her shoulders. 'Like I explained already, I saw headlights in the yard and thought it was a bit strange for visitors at that time of night,' she said, as if she'd rehearsed the line. 'I've been through this several times.'

The sound of a kettle boiling and cups being rattled floated through from the kitchen. 'Just one more time please, Mrs Aitchison. If we're going to find your neighbours we need as much information as you can give us. Now what time did the car arrive?'

'Well, I was upstairs fetching my hot water bottle after my programme had finished, so it must have been after 8.30. There were two men. They came in a fancy car, one of those off-road types.'

'Did you get a clear look at them?'

'Oh yes, they set off the light at the back of the house. They were an odd pair, shifty-looking. You wouldn't have put them together.'

'What do you mean?'

'One was like a boxer, tall with a flat nose and no neck. His head looked like it came straight out of his shoulders. He looked arrogant to me, something in the way he walked.'

Mortensen gave her an encouraging smile. 'And the other man?'

'He was shorter, with scruffy hair that looked like it needed a cut. I don't remember much else about him.'

The family liaison officer carried a tray with mugs and a pot of tea into the room. She set it down on a low table. 'Shout if you need anything. I'll be in the kitchen.'

'And how did they act?'

'They seemed to know exactly what they were doing. They went straight to Ben and Sophie's so I thought they must be friends of theirs.'

'And they went straight in?'

'I don't know, I can't see the back door from my window. I heard raised voices which was odd because I don't usually hear anything from the house, only sometimes if the children are playing outside.'

'Could you hear what was being said?'

The old woman's wet eyes looked off into the distance. She wiped the end of her nose with a crumpled tissue she had clutched in a misshapen hand. 'Not really. It was just voices shouting. Then there was a scream. Sophie, I think, not one of the children but I couldn't be sure, I'm sorry.'

Mortensen rested a hand on the woman's arm. 'Don't worry, every detail you remember could help.'

'I didn't like to go outside but I saw one of them had the children. They were dragging them out of the house and into the car. I could tell they didn't want to go. Ellie was crying. She tripped over on the gravel and one of them raised his hand to hit her.'

'What about Ben and Sophie?'

'They came out behind the children. The tall one was at the back with a gun.'

'Are you sure?'

'I think so.'

'What sort of gun? A handgun?' asked Blake, speaking for the first time, his interest piqued.

The old woman nodded. 'They made Sophie and the children get in the back of the car with the shorter man. Ben sat in the front next to the driver and then they were gone. That's it, that's all I saw.'

'Think carefully, Rhona,' said Mortensen. 'You definitely didn't recognise either of those men?'

'I'm sure I've never seen them before.'

'What about the Pitts family? Do they have relatives nearby?'

'Sophie has a sister who lives abroad, in Canada. Ben mentioned having a brother but I don't think they're close.'

'Friends?'

'They're friendly enough but they keep themselves to themselves on the whole.'

'And they both work?'

'Sophie's a teacher at the local school. Charlie still goes there but Ellie's moved up to the high school. Ben works for a laboratory in Glen Brittle. He did try to explain what he did once but it went over my head. Something to do with testing vaccines. Developing a flu vaccine I think. I'm sure that's what it was.'

Blake set his mug of tea on the tray, his eyes narrowing. 'He's a scientist?'

'He didn't really talk about his work.'

'What about the name of the company?'

'I don't remember. Sorry, is it important?'

'It might be. How far is the laboratory?' Blake asked, retrieving his mobile phone from his jacket.

'I don't know where it is for sure,' the old woman said,' but Glen Brittle is on the other side of the island. It's no more than an hour's drive.'

Blake was staring at his phone. He raised it to head height and when he couldn't find a signal, lifted it higher. 'Is there any mobile signal around here?'

'It's supposed to be bad on this side of the island,' said Mrs Aitchison. 'But I don't know, I don't have one of those phones.'

Blake stood, towering over the diminutive woman hunched in her armchair. 'I'll try outside,' he said. 'Thank you for your time, you've been most helpful.'

He tramped out of the house, leaving Mortensen behind. His face was set in dogged determination as he crunched across the courtyard and up the drive, his eyes never leaving the screen of his phone. He finally picked up a signal as he reached the lane. The connection was slow but it was better than nothing. His thumb flicked across the screen, tapping at a keyboard but the results of his search left him puzzled.

'That was a quick exit. What's up?' said Mortensen as she joined him on a patch of unkempt grass overlooking the two houses.

'I don't know, yet.'

'From her description, that's got to be Vaughn and Pitts.'

'Almost certainly,' said Blake, distracted by his phone.

'So what next? A trip to Glen Brittle? Must be worth a poke around at this laboratory?'

'There might be a problem with that.'

'Why?'

Blake handed her his phone. 'Look at this.'

'What is it?'

'I've been trying to find any labs listed at Glen Brittle. There aren't any. So I widened the search to the Isle of Skye, and guess what?'

'You didn't find anything?'

'There's nothing like that listed on the island at all. It's like it doesn't exist.'

'Meaning what?' asked Mortensen.

Blake switched off his phone. Below them a dozen police officers were milling around like worker ants toiling for crumbs. He watched them for a moment, thinking.

'Blake?' Mortensen prompted.

'There're two possibilities as I see it,' he said. 'Either Rhona Aitchison is lying or that laboratory is supposed to be off the grid.'

'But why?'

'I don't know. Let's find out.'

Chapter 19

First came the broiling black clouds that stole the day of light, then the thick globules of rain exploding on the windscreen in watery splatters warning of an impending downpour. Mortensen flicked on the headlights and wipers without taking her eyes off the road ahead. She was concentrating on the bumpy track with her foot hard on the accelerator and gripping the wheel tightly as the uneven camber threatened to rip it from her grasp. Blake was rocking around in the passenger seat trying to navigate from a map on his mobile phone. Around them a black mountain loomed like a silent giant, its sharp peaks needling the sky.

'Slow down, the turning should be on the left,' he said, looking up into the near distance.

Mortensen lifted her foot a fraction. A kidney-shaped building concealed within a mature woodland at the foot of Cuillin mountain was Blake's best guess for the location of the laboratory. It had stood out among the pixelated green and brown squares of a low resolution satellite image, its unnatural colour and shape a curiosity among the trees. It looked to have been constructed in a clearing at the end of a spindly track and flanked on two sides by what appeared to be a small car park. Blake found it after a little more than fifteen minutes poring over images from the western side of the island. He'd painstakingly scanned section by section, hampered by a painfully slow mobile signal. As they drew near, they shared a sense of anticipation that the net was closing on Vaughn and Pitts.

'There,' said Blake, pointing ahead to a slim gap between the rows of firs.

Mortensen jumped on the brakes. They skidded to a halt on a patch of loose gravel, overshooting the turning into an unmarked driveway barely wide enough for a car. She backed up and rolled the vehicle into the forest where the trees closed in overhead.

'Take it slowly and kill the lights,' said Blake.

'Are you sure this is it?'

'Not really. Let's see where it goes.'

The asphalt drive had been built long and straight, cutting through the forest for a quarter of a mile before opening out into a wide glade. A stark, modern building with white walls and banks of tinted glass rose from the ground behind an eight-foot chain-link fence. The roof was cluttered with metal boxes of ducting and vents. It was an alien blot on the landscape, in marked contrast to its natural surroundings.

'Someone must've had good connections with the council to get that through planning,' said Mortensen.

'Or a very good case for it to be hidden away up here.'

The heavens finally opened as they pulled up in front of padlocked double gates. The deluge beat down on the roof like a hundred tiny hammers. The windscreen wipers, running at double speed, struggled to keep up with the volume of rain that was falling. Mortensen left the engine running and turned up the heating to full blast to clear the fog clouding the glass.

The building appeared to be deserted. The car park was empty and there were only a few perfunctory lights on inside. A dozen 'Keep Out' signs in vibrant yellow were attached to the fence. More warned of CCTV and 24-hour security patrols. Blake counted no less than eight cameras, probably only the ones intended to be noticed, put up as much as a deterrent as for surveillance, like the empty alarm boxes people attached to the front of their houses to discourage burglars. He wondered how many more hidden cameras had recorded their arrival.

A board with a company name printed in blue on a white background alongside a triangular logo was mounted on two metal poles. Skyevax Sciences Laboratories.

'Ever heard of them?' Blake asked.

'No. Is there anything on the internet about them?'

Blake tried his phone but it had lost the weak signal he'd picked up earlier. He slipped it back in his pocket with a shake of his head. As the worst of the cloud-burst passed over, he zipped his jacket up to his chin.

'Time for a closer look,' he said, letting himself out of the car.

Outside the rain hissed noisily through the trees, almost drowning out the sound of the idling engine. Ignoring the rivulets running from his brow into his eyes, Blake stood silently scanning the site. Mortensen appeared at his side gripping a Glock 23 nine millimetre. She'd thrown on a cream raincoat over her suit.

'Looks like someone's been here before us,' she said, nodding at the padlocked chain. It had been cut through leaving two ends hanging loose. A crude attempt had been made to conceal the break-in by pulling the gates closed. They opened with a gentle push and clattered against two concrete posts, disturbing a crow which took off from a nearby tree with a loud cack-aw.

To the right of the entrance was a gatehouse. Blake put his hands to the glass of a window and peered in. The blank screen of a computer monitor sat on a desk alongside a clipboard, assorted pens and a copy of a tabloid newspaper.

'Let's check the main building,' he said, drawing his Browning from the small of his back. He ejected the magazine, cracked it back into place and chambered a round. The gun sat snugly in his palm, its weight reassuring. It was like being reacquainted with an old friend.

They padded across the puddled asphalt to a glazed,

semi-circular vestibule with curved sliding doors. Beyond it was a second glazed door that led into a double-height atrium in semi-darkness that housed a sweeping reception desk surrounded by leafy pot plants.

'I guess no one works at the weekend,' whispered Blake. 'Wait here, I'll check around the back.'

It took him precisely ninety seconds to scout around the outside of the building and conclude there was no other way in. There were no windows on the ground level and a fire exit at the back was locked from the inside. He found Mortensen where he'd left her, with rain dripping from the end of her nose, her hair flattened to her scalp and mascara running down her cheeks.

'Nothing,' said Blake. 'If Vaughn and Pitts got inside it was with Benjamin's help.'

'The security's pretty sophisticated.' Mortensen ran a hand over the glass of the outer sliding doors. 'This one's opened by a basic electronic swipe card but beyond that it looks like there's a retina scanner to access an airlock entry pod.'

A metallic box with a dark screen was mounted on a pillar at head height inside the first door.

'Both doors leading from the reception area have some kind of electronic entry system too. It looks like a number pad with a fingerprint scanner,' Mortensen added. 'If Vaughn and Pitts wanted to get in here, I don't think they could have done it without Benjamin's co-operation.'

'Conclusions?'

'It's the pharmaceutical industry. Standard precautions,' she shrugged. 'The sector's worth billions, so whatever they're working on in there is bound to be commercially sensitive. They're sensible measures to protect their investments.'

'So it's feasible that Benjamin was working on some kind of new drug?'

'In which case, what's Vaughn's interest?'

'Money?'

'I'm not so sure,' said Mortensen. 'It's a bit sophisticated for an armed robber.'

'You're right, this doesn't stack up. And there's something else. If Vaughn and Pitts came to steal pharmaceutical secrets, then Elias' escape from Marshside was no coincidence. He wasn't picked out by Vaughn randomly, he was the key to getting to Benjamin,' Blake said, looking up to the sky as the rain finally stopped.

'Which begs the question, what does this all have to do with Rahimi?'

'Or the Iranians?'

'Maybe nothing at all, in which case we've been chasing a blind lead,' said Mortensen. She holstered her gun under her suit jacket and stepped back to study the building, as if seeing it as a whole might present a solution to the conundrum. 'You know it's entirely possible the breakout was unconnected with Rahimi. The only link to Vaughn so far is a mobile phone missing its SIM.'

Blake's face clouded. It was a long way to have travelled on a wild goose chase. If Mortensen was right, they were back at square one. 'We need to find Benjamin.'

'If he's still alive.'

'My gut instinct says he is and twenty quid says they're all still on the island.'

'But we don't have the remotest idea where to start looking.'

A trickle of rainwater rolled down the back of Blake's neck and inside the collar of his shirt. But he didn't notice. His eyes had fallen on a security camera over the main entrance, trained on them like a beady eye. He turned to another attached to the wall of the gatehouse and two more facing in different directions on a pole secured to the security fence.

Blake jogged back to the gatehouse and tried the handle of the door. It swung open easily. That surprised him. He'd expected to find it locked. What kind of security guard signs off duty and doesn't secure the gatehouse?

Come to think of it, if security was so tight on site, why wasn't there a guard posted twenty-four hours a day? It didn't seem right. Nor did the smell that hit him. The rank and pungent odour of death. He stepped inside, his weapon raised. He saw the feet first. Boots attached to a pair of legs emerging from under the desk. Dark, heavy-duty trousers. Blake dropped to his knees and dragged the crumpled body of the security guard out into the middle of the floor. A bloodied hole in his chest revealed where he'd been shot. His eyes were open, bulging and staring blankly at the ceiling.

Mortensen appeared in the doorway and shrieked.

'Is he dead?'

Blake felt for a pulse under the man's chin but knew he'd long gone. He closed the guard's eyes with his fingers. 'For some time,' he said. 'There's nothing we can do for him. Help me move the body.'

Blake stepped around the lifeless corpse and slid his hands under his arms. Mortensen reluctantly grabbed his ankles and between them, they shifted him to the opposite side of the room.

Blake wiped his hands on the back of his legs and pulled up a chair to the desk. The computer was attached to a dated-looking keyboard made grubby from dirty fingers. He hit a random key and a monitor sparked into life revealing a chequer-board of grainy, monochrome video images.

'What are you doing?' asked Mortensen.

'Looking for unexpected visitors.'

There were feeds from every conceivable angle around the exterior of the building. More cameras covered the inside showing empty offices, gloomy corridors and sterile cloakrooms where white overalls hung from pegs. Blake navigated to the desktop page using a plastic mouse so clogged with dirt that the on-screen pointer jumped and jerked erratically.

He found a document that contained seven sub-folders

labelled with the days of the week and clicked on a file from the previous day. It brought up another set of video images. Twenty feeds, five by four across the screen. The locations were identical to the live feed but the light was different.

'Let's start from nine o'clock last night,' said Blake, tapping in a series of numbers on the keyboard that jumped the videos forwards by twenty-one hours.

The feeds went blank momentarily and reappeared showing a handful of people variously around the laboratory. A cleaner was running a vacuum around one of the offices. Another camera picked up a couple of indistinct figures leaving through the main entrance and walking to cars. No doubt late night workers making their way home.

'Can you speed up the action?' asked Mortensen.

Blake hit another key and they watched in as the cleaner finished her rounds in double-quick time. She left after an hour, driving off in an ancient Ford.

By a little after ten, the security guard, who they'd found dead, was the only person left on site. He fastened the gates with the chain after the cleaner had driven off, and retired to the gatehouse.

When the counter at the bottom of the screen hit midnight, the feeds stopped playing and Blake had to load a new file. It started at a second past midnight with the familiar shots of the empty building.

The timecode was approaching two in the morning when they spotted the glare of headlights illuminate the entrance gates. Blake slowed the footage to real time as the bonnet of a dark-coloured car materialised. It drew to a halt and the driver hopped out. He was a man of medium build in jeans and a leather jacket whose movements were quick and precise. He disappeared behind the vehicle and reappeared with a pair of bolt cutters. In less than half a minute he had cut through the chain.

'Vaughn?' asked Mortensen.

'I'd say so.'

A second figure appeared in shot. The guard emerging from his booth to investigate the disturbance. He was unsteady on his feet as if he'd been woken unexpectedly. Vaughn looked up, pulled a gun from his belt and pointed it at the guard's chest. A second later the guard collapsed, sprawled out on the floor. On the grainy camera footage, a dark, grey patch spread across his front where the bullet had pierced his chest.

Vaughn hauled the body back into the guardhouse, shut the door and returned to opening the gates for the car. A Volkswagen 4X4 rolled into view and pulled up outside the entrance of the laboratory.

Vaughn was first out. He straightened his jacket and looked around as if he was checking they weren't being observed. Blake froze the image and zoomed in on Vaughn's face revealing eyes that were hard and unforgiving. His nose was distinctively misshapen and one side of his mouth was scarred and twisted, giving him a perverse, permanent sneer.

A second man appeared from the passenger side. He was shorter and stockier with lighter coloured hair that fell limply over his ears and collar. His shoulders were rounded and his stomach ballooned with a paunch that looked as though it had been earned from a lifetime of good living. He looked around nervously, scratching the back of his hand.

'Elias Pitts?' said Mortensen, her eyes flicking between the feeds that showed him from various angles.

Vaughn used his gun to persuade a third man from the back seat. Even on the black and white shot, Benjamin Pitts' face was etched with terror, his tired eyes no more than narrow slits behind thick-rimmed glasses. He was as tall as Vaughn but seemed to shrink in his presence. Vaughn shoved him roughly towards the entrance and he fumbled in his pocket for a credit-card sized plastic fob that he used to open the sliding doors. He disappeared inside the vestibule and the doors slid shut.

'Why aren't they following him?' asked Blake.

'They can't get in. Benjamin's about to go through the airlock entry pod which I'm guessing is fitted with an air pressure sensor and probably weight pads too. It's designed so only one person can pass through at a time. If the air displacement's too great, the door won't open. They've got no choice but to trust him. But of course, that's why they've got his wife and kids. Nothing like a little family leverage.'

A camera fixed high above the reception desk in the atrium showed Benjamin turn left towards a solid door, punched a code into a keypad and placed his thumb on a scanner. After passing through the door he disappeared for a brief second, caught between cameras. Mortensen finally spotted him as a distant speck at the far end of a lens in a room filled with rows of desks cluttered with computer monitors, paperwork and phones.

He was wringing his hands, his head jerking to the left and right as if he was looking for something important. He rushed to a desk, snatched up a phone but almost immediately slammed the handset back in its cradle.

'They cut the phone lines,' said Blake. 'It was a fair assumption that he'd try to call for help as soon as he was inside, I guess.'

Benjamin stood by the desk with his head slumped on his chest and his hands hanging by his sides. His shoulders shook and he collapsed to the floor, sobbing.

'Poor guy,' said Mortensen under her breath.

But the tears didn't last long. With one finger he pushed the bridge of his glasses up his nose and lifted his chin. He stood up, spun around and scanned the room as if searching for something he'd lost. His eyes fell on the camera. He stepped closer, staring at the lens. His eyes were wide and focused, his fingers stroking his bushy beard. As he moved closer, the fisheye lens distorted his features, drawing his face into a thin oval.

'What's he doing?' asked Mortensen.

'I don't know.'

Benjamin jumped up and down, waving his arms frantically. His mouth yawned open wide and clamped shut.

'He's trying to call for help,' said Mortensen. 'Except nobody's watching. Until now.' She bit on her finger. Blake touched her arm. They both feared they were watching the final desperate moments of a dead man.

Benjamin kept up his energetic jig for nearly a minute. His chest heaved with the exertion and he squinted at the lens as if trying to work out whether he'd been seen.

Finally, with a dispassionate calm that belied his state of stress, he performed one simple act that would save his life. When Blake and Mortensen realised what he was doing, they looked at each other and grinned like clowns.

'You clever old stick, Benjamin,' said Mortensen, clapping Blake on his shoulder and grabbing a pen and scrap of paper from the desk.

Chapter 20

The corridors blurred as Benjamin Pitts flew through the guts of the building. His heart was racing and beads of sweat pearled on his brow despite the air-conditioned chill. He wasn't sure whether it was from the exertion or his fear. He skidded to a halt at the top of a metal staircase, wiped his forehead with his sleeve and checked his watch. Eight minutes gone already. He'd promised to be out in thirty. *Make it twenty,* said the thug with the broken nose and the twisted grin who'd leered at Sophie with a lascivious glint in his eye. He couldn't risk over-running while his wife and kids were being held hostage. So why had he wasted precious minutes gambling on trying to raise the alarm? As if anyone would be monitoring the security camera feeds at that time of night. He cursed his stupidity.

A short flight of steps took him into a square hallway and he slammed his palm on a button on the wall.

'Come on, come on,' he urged under his breath, rocking impatiently from foot to foot as he waited for the lift.

The doors sighed open sluggishly and an iris scanner took the best part of a minute to confirm his credentials before he was dropped two floors into the concrete-encased bowels of the building where the laboratories were concealed. Running into a storeroom he snatched a set of navy-coloured scrubs, stiff from the laundry, and in an adjacent changing room ripped off his jumper and faded Rolling Stones t-shirt. He kicked off his shoes and jeans and dumped everything in a heap on a bench as he pulled on the cotton top and trousers that were rough against his skin. Not comfortable like cotton should be.

Eleven minutes gone.

The suit room was through two heavy steel doors. Inside, coils of red hoses snaked from the ceiling like giant springs and a row of orange protective suits hung limply from metal hooks. Benjamin grabbed the nearest suit and slid his legs in easily. He found the left arm on the third attempt, twisting to reach behind him and wiggling his fingers into a glove pre-attached to the sleeve. After easing the bucket-hood over his head he grasped a hose from the ceiling and attached it to an umbilical cord at his waist. Two brass connectors clicked together and triggered a noisy hiss of compressed air. He zipped himself in and chose a pair of plastic boots, all the while trying to steady his raging pulse.

'Calm down, Benjamin', he told himself, slowing his breathing as the hazardous materials suit inflated.

A hot flush prickled his face and neck despite the flow of compressed air. A dribble of sweat stung his eyes. He blinked his vision clear and focused on the red light on the door ahead, beckoning to him. Part of his brain screamed for him to leave. He could walk out and tell them he couldn't do it. Be a man. Call their bluff. Without him there was no way into the laboratory and soon enough someone was going to notice they were missing. Or maybe they wouldn't. It was the early hours of Saturday morning. Neither of them were due back to work until Monday morning. Probably the first time anyone would suspect something was wrong. And that was still thirty hours away. Plenty of time for Elias' friend to inflict any manner of suffering on his wife and children to ensure his compliance.

He closed his eyes and, with a grudging acceptance, realised he'd come too far to turn back. He pictured Sophie cradling the children, trying to calm them with soothing words, her wrist shackled to an old gas pipe and her face streaked with tears. And in that moment he hated his brother more than he'd ever done in his life.

Drawing air tainted with the odour of mechanical processes through his nostrils, he punched in a code on a keypad on the door, overriding the lock usually controlled by the lab director. It opened smoothly on oiled hinges and closed behind him with a muted thud. The container he'd come for was on the top shelf of a large refrigerator. No bigger than the jewellery box on his wife's dressing table and unremarkable other than for a white label fixed to the silver lid printed with the identifying code 'HR2T-v'. Five innocuous characters that veiled the true horror of what lay within.

He carried it in two hands, overcompensating for the thick gloves by gripping it too tightly. He set it down in the centre of a glass bio-hazard cabinet cluttered with rows of test-tubes, a stand of pipettes and plastic trays in vivid colours. With trembling fingers he eased open the lid and stared six glass tubes. A Pandora's Box filled with enough deadly virus to wipe out six large cities. A super-strain of bird flu mutated and engineered to pass from human to human as easily as winter flu.

Benjamin steadied his hand as he leaned forwards to pinch one of the test-tubes between his thumb and forefinger, careful not to squeeze too hard. The virus was suspended in an inch of clear liquid that slopped lazily around the bottom of the tube. Ten millilitres of lethal fluid, viscous like a shot of vodka that coated the glass with a thin layer of translucent residue. He placed it in a plastic rack, took a second tube and placed it next to the first.

Elias had been clear. He wanted the lab's entire stock. But that wasn't going to happen. It would be Benjamin's gesture of defiance. Without at least one of the samples it would be impossible to produce a vaccine. Using a pipette he drew off half the liquid from each of the two vials and divided it equally between two empty test-tubes. A small step towards redemption. The loss would set the lab back several months but at least there would be some virus left to continue their work.

Benjamin struggled to screw caps onto each of the test-tubes. His hands were clammy and the hair on the back of his head was soaked through with sweat. He bit his lip as he concentrated, and when he was done threw a glance at the clock on the wall to his left. Five minutes to make it back outside. It was going to be tight but he was banking on them waiting for him.

'Damn it!' he said, realising he needed a case for the tubes. There was one on the other side of the room. Benjamin sprang from the chair and made it across the lab in three strides.

He felt the tug at his waist too late. The connectors attaching the air supply to his suit flew apart. The hiss of air in his ears fell silent and a loud crack of smashing glass echoed around the lab. He turned, fearing the worst, to find the air supply hose had snagged on his seat and was swinging wildly, its brass end bobbing up and down from the ceiling. His eyes flashed to the bio-hazard cabinet. The protective glass screen over the working area was crazed with a thousand cracks. Shattered but intact. He let out an involuntary gasp as his suit began to deflate.

The four tubes he'd lined up in a rack were undamaged. Of the two original glass tubes, one was missing its screw cap. It was also shorter by a centimetre or two. A hairline crack ran down its length. The hose connector had taken the top clean off. It was a miracle it hadn't knocked the case over or spilled any of the liquid.

He found the missing top behind a pipette stand and reached into the cabinet to retrieve it.

'Shit!' he whistled as a sharp edge sliced through his glove and nicked the end of his finger.

He flinched at the shock. A short incision across the pad of his index finger, seeping blood, was visible through a tear in the glove. He stared at it for a second or two, the horror of his own stupidity sinking in. In his panic he was rushing, forgetting the precautions. And now this. Maybe it was rough justice. Bad karma, Sophie would have said. Chances were he'd been infected. Nothing he could do now but to hope.

He grabbed the four test-tubes from the cabinet and packed them into the tight polystyrene lining of a transportation case. He snapped the lid shut, tucked it under his arm and, with a last look back at the mess he'd left, stepped out of the lab and into a decontamination chamber.

Chapter 21

The road to Carbost was a narrow and rutted sliver of asphalt that cut through a barren heath of greens, greys and browns. The landscape pitched and rolled for as far as the eye could see, an unspoiled wilderness where trees struggled for a foothold and only the hardiest grasses flourished. Not that Blake took much notice. He was in the passenger seat clutching his mobile phone while Mortensen, back behind the wheel of the rented Ford, was fixed on the winding route ahead. Blake was looking for a decent signal but didn't find one until the threatening waters of Loch Harport, dark and unforgiving, opened up before them.

'I've found it,' he said finally. He scrolled down the screen, flicking through the internet search returns with one finger.

'Care to enlighten me?'

The words Benjamin had held up to the security camera had been unequivocal. He'd scrawled 'Loch Cill Chriosd' across a blank sheet of paper in a thick felt pen, in capitals, big and bold.

Blake's brow furrowed as he read. 'It's not a loch at all. It's the ruins of an old church.'

Mortensen shot Blake a look, taking her eyes off the road for a split second. 'What?'

'It's a former parish church, although it looks nothing more than rubble and a few walls to me,' he said.

'Do you think that's where they're being held?'

'It doesn't seem right,' said Blake. 'It's like a local

landmark and right on the side of the road. Why would they take them there?'

'Maybe it's the closest point of reference Benjamin had? How far is it?'

'About twelve miles as the crow flies but by road more like thirty. It'll take us at least an hour.'

'I'll have us there in forty,' said Mortensen with a devilish grin. She floored the accelerator as they flew around a blind bend.

'Preferably in one piece,' said Blake, gripping the dashboard with his free hand.

They made it in a little over thirty five minutes, Blake thankful the roads were deserted. Mortensen only slowed when he pointed out the salt and pepper stone remains of a church on a mound approaching on their right. It was a long, roofless building enclosed by a moss-ridden stone wall encircling a graveyard with lichen-covered headstones jutting out of the ground at oblique angles. They pulled up onto a grass verge opposite.

'What now?' Mortensen asked.

Blake peered up at the skeletal ruins of the church, grey and sinister under wide skies heavy with the remnants of the passing storm. 'Drive on slowly but keep your eyes peeled. We're looking for a building, maybe a farmhouse or a disused barn.'

Mortensen drove on for a hundred and fifty metres before they spotted mud on the road. Indistinct trails partially washed away by the rain had stained the asphalt brown. The trails led from a grass track that ran away from the carriageway towards an inland loch.

'Worth checking out?' asked Mortensen.

'Sure.'

The car struggled for traction where the grass had been cut up by the wheels of another vehicle. Their tyres slid and spun, spitting out clods of mud, and after their high-speed flight across the island, their progress was became painfully slow.

A croft house appeared over the crest of a rise, a simple, single-storey building to the south of a copse of dark green firs in the shadow of a black mountain. Bleached beams were exposed through wide holes in its roof where sections of tiles were missing. Along its back wall, two square windows were cut into the stonework.

Mortensen cranked on the handbrake.

'It looks derelict but someone's obviously been here,' said Blake.

Mortensen killed the engine. 'I'm going to take a look,' she said, stepping out and closing the door quietly.

Blake pondered the wide tranches of tyre tracks that led to the building for a moment. They looped around in messy circles where a car had been driven back and forth.

'Wait,' he called, jumping out of the vehicle and jogging the short distance Mortensen had covered. They approached the house in silence together, eyes wide and ears tuned for any sound.

The entrance to the house overlooked the loch. Blake drew his Browning, thumbed off the safety and nodded to Mortensen to approach from the left while he circled the perimeter, stopping only to snatch glimpses through the windows at the rear. The panes were smashed and the frames rotten. Inside was in darkness. The interior comprised of a single room bare and forlorn. Spots of light shafted through the holes in the roof illuminating patches of stone floor where rubble and debris had collected in piles. Too much of the room was in deep shadow to be certain whether there was anyone inside.

Mortensen was waiting for Blake at a paint-flecked wooden door hanging from rusted hinges. On either side, two windows had been sealed with old boards grey with age. Tufts of spiky grass had been trampled into the mud by what looked to be several pairs of feet. Blake urged himself not to jump to conclusions. Maybe local teenagers had hung out here for a smoke or it had been used as a refuge by fishermen caught in a storm. He put his finger to his lips and they listened. But there was only the rush of wind through the branches of the nearby trees and the lap of water on the loch.

An uneasy feeling swelled in Blake's stomach and his hand tightened on his nine millimetre. The croft measured no more than six metres by four, a tight space for a gun fight if Vaughn and Pitts were holed up inside. He already knew how it would play out. Loud and fast. The dizzying disorientation of muzzle flashes lighting up the room and the splintering cracks of gunfire. Blake and Mortensen would hold the initial advantage of surprise but they'd be silhouetted in the door-frame. At best could count on two or three seconds before Vaughn and Pitts grabbed their weapons – the same length of time it would take for their own eyes to adjust to the gloom. But calculations like that were immaterial. It would be madness to storm the croft with guns blazing and four hostages inside. Not unless they fancied a body count on their consciences. Blake preferred the odds to be stacked higher in his favour. A belt-full of stun grenades would have helped that but there was no time to think about the what-ifs.

He stepped back and regarded the grey walls one last time but there was no alternative way in.

'Ready?' he whispered to Mortensen.

She nodded and her long, thin fingers flexed around her Glock. Her breathing was slow and assured.

Blake forced his shoulders to relax and released a violent kicked at the door close to the handle. It crashed open, the desiccated wood fracturing with a loud snap. He rushed inside with Mortensen at his back, sweeping his gun into the darkest recesses of the room. As his pupils adjusted to the murk, he hunted out tell-tale signs of movement. But there were no screams of surprise, nor volleys of gunfire. Just thick motes of dust cannoning into the beams of light shining through exposed rafters.

Mortensen saw them first. Four crumpled figures slumped on the floor and huddled so closely together that at first it was impossible to tell how many there were. Benjamin, recognisable from the security footage at the Skyevax laboratories, was at the back, his eyes dark and tired behind the lenses of his glasses. A woman half-lying in front of him held up her head. Her hair was bedraggled and a wisp of fringe that fell over her face. She possessed a rugged boyishness and a spirit of defiance. She held an arm around two children crouching between her legs, their bare arms trembling with cold.

Mortensen slipped her gun into a holster under her arm. One of the children whimpered.

'It's over,' said Mortensen. 'It's all over,' she repeated softly.

The woman kept her eyes fixed on Blake's gun. He remained standing inside the door, his feet planted and his aim levelled at the family.

'Where's Elias?' he barked.

'Gone,' said Benjamin, squinting.

'And Vaughn?'

'The other guy? He went too. They've not been here for hours.'

'Where did they go?' Benjamin stared back at Blake blankly. 'Where?' Blake repeated, raising his voice.

'I don't know.'

'Blake, for God's sake,' said Mortensen. 'Let's get them out of here first, okay?'

'Who are you?' The woman's voice was calm and measured.

'We're the good guys. Are you hurt?' asked Mortensen.

A spot of blood had congealed below the woman's left nostril and a purple bruise was rising on her cheek. She shook her head.

'And the children?'

The woman tried to speak but the words caught in her throat. Tears welled in her eyes as she shook her head again.

'It's Sophie, isn't it? Let's get you out of here.'

Mortensen draped her coat over the children, noticing the chains that bound their wrists to a pipe running along the wall. She turned to Blake with eyebrows raised. 'Any ideas?'

Blake lowered his gun.

'Hang on,' he said, turning and running out of the house.

He returned with a scissor jack he'd found cocooned inside a spare tyre in the boot of their hire car. He wedged it between the wall and pipe. It took six turns of the crank to wrench the pipe from its fixings that had been weakened by age and rust.

'Get them into the car to warm up,' said Blake. 'And call an ambulance. We should let Douglas know too, put him out of his misery.'

Mortensen helped Sophie and the children to their feet. They rubbed their wrists and stretched, their hollow eyes full of fear.

'The car's just outside. We'll have you home in no time.'

Mortensen ushered them towards the door and they shuffled through the dust and debris, blinking as they emerged into the daylight.

Benjamin tried to follow but Blake stepped across his path. 'Not you,' he said.

They stood eye-to-eye, Blake a little taller, a little broader across the shoulders. A flicker of fear clouded Benjamin's face as he massaged blood back into his arm where the chains had cut off the circulation to his hand. His eyes flitted to the gun at Blake's side.

'We need to talk.' There was no warmth in Blake's voice. His eyes were emotionless orbs.

'I just want to get home…' Benjamin stuttered. He tried to sidestep Blake but was prevented by a muscular arm across his chest.

'Not until I get some answers.'

'How did you find us?' asked Benjamin.

'We saw your message on the Skyevax cameras.'

'Really?' Benjamin's tired face lit up.

'We also saw you leave the laboratories with a silver case which you gave to your brother and his accomplice. Both known criminals, and both currently at large from prison.'

Benjamin's delight vanished in a second. He hung his head and shuffled his feet.

'I need to know where Vaughn and your brother are right now.'

'I told you. I don't know,' said Benjamin.

'I don't believe you.'

'You think I'm involved in this?'

'Are you?'

'Of course not. They had my family. What was I supposed to do? What would you have done?'

Blake's expression was impassive. He wanted to believe Benjamin was an unwitting victim, coerced into breaking into the Skyevax building by threats to his wife and young children. But he needed some convincing.

'Who are you anyway?'

'My name's Blake. I work for the Government. That's all you need to know. I'm here to help but this isn't looking good for you right now. You need to start talking.' He slipped his gun into the waistband of his jeans.

'The Government? Jesus, what a mess.' Benjamin ran his hands through his hair, slipped off his glasses and rubbed his eyes. 'You don't have any idea what I've done.'

Blake clamped Benjamin on the shoulder. 'I need to know the truth. I can't help you otherwise,' he said, his tone softening. 'We saw you disappear into a lift. Wherever you went wasn't covered by cameras, and when you reappeared you had a case which you gave to Elias and Vaughn. What was in it?'

'I'm so sorry. I didn't have a choice…' Benjamin began to sob, his pent up emotions finding a release.

'Benjamin, tell me,' said Blake, removing his hand from

the scientist's shoulder but leaving it hovering behind the back of his head. Benjamin looked up, his eyes red and puffy.

Blake heard the distant sound of a car door slamming shut. Sophie and the children. By now Mortensen would be on the phone to Douglas. He'd be on his way within minutes accompanied by a fleet of wailing squad cars and crime scene investigators. There would be ambulances and paramedics, psychologists and smiling liaison officers to look after the children. Blake's time with Benjamin was running short.

'Turn around,' he ordered, spinning the scientist through ninety degrees and using his boot to kick his feet together so his ankles smashed together. 'Now look at me.'

When Benjamin looked up, he found a hand in front of his face hovering above his eye line, drawing his focus away from Blake's wide-eyed stare. His brow furrowed but his bewilderment lasted only a second as Blake tapped him lightly on the forehead.

'Sleep,' said Blake.

Benjamin's body crumpled. His eyes fell closed and his legs gave way as if someone had flicked an off-switch on his back. Blake caught him under his arms and eased him onto the ground, intoning soothing words into his ear. Benjamin lay still with his arms at his side and his eyes shut.

'You're safe here now,' said Blake, taking a seat on the floor with his back resting against a wall. 'You're in a deep state of relaxation. In a moment I'm going to ask you some questions. I want you to answer truthfully and honestly. Do you understand?'

'Yes,' said Benjamin.

'I want your mind to return to the last time you were at the Skyevax laboratories. Your brother, Elias and a man called Vaughn took you there and asked you to fetch something for them. Do you remember?'

'Yes.'

'You gave them a case.'

'Yes.'

'I need to know what was in it.'

There was a flicker behind Benjamin eyelids and the lines on his forehead tightened. He took a deep breath and started to talk.

Chapter 22

The way Blake viewed it, the procurement of information from someone unwilling to give it up was an art. And like any art form true proficiency took years of practice. He'd found traditional interrogation methods cumbersome and slow; barbiturate truth serums unpredictable and the use of torture not only morally dubious but highly unreliable when it came to weeding out lies and half-truths. But hypnosis guaranteed a hotline to the brain that could bypass any conscious reluctance someone might have to talk.

His first encounter with the possibilities hypnosis could offer had come from a vulgar performance at a party. He'd watched mesmerised as a stage comedian put a handful of willing participants into a trance with a snap of his fingers. Some obligingly grunted around on their hands and knees when told to behave like pigs in a sty, young women were convinced that cleaning mops were handsome young men at a dance and others were persuaded they were standing naked on stage.

They were cheap gimmicks but Blake was fascinated by the apparent ease with which the hypnotist had been able to induce total control over a random selection of people. It was the start of his journey towards the development of rapid hypnotic induction, and the manipulation of someone's mind to reveal secrets they ordinarily wouldn't divulge.

He experimented with its use in his role as chief interrogator with the black-ops Special Forces counter-terrorism unit, Echo 17. And it produced spectacular results. His first success had been with an Al Qaeda commander snatched from a compound on the Afghanistan border with Pakistan after a six day covert stakeout. The Afghan went out like a light and coughed up detailed plans of an imminent attack being planned on an American base. Even Blake had been surprised at how easily he'd reeled off the information. It was like chatting to his grandmother about the weather.

But that was a long time ago. In a different lifetime.

Benjamin's chest rose and fell, his face implacable. Rainwater was dripping from the broken roof and puddling in pools while the wind howled down two chimney stacks that opened up into soot-blackened fireplaces at either end of the room. Blake shifted on the stone floor to make himself more comfortable but it was cold, damp and covered in the dirt from a generation. He stretched his legs and examined mud that had accumulated on the toecaps of his boots.

'Tell me about the laboratory,' he said. 'Why all the security?'

'We're developing a vaccine for a human variant of avian flu.' Benjamin's body was in stasis, his muscles loose.

'I don't understand. What interest would Elias have in a vaccine for bird flu?'

'He doesn't. He wanted the Armageddon Virus.'

'The Armageddon Virus?'

'It's a super virus we engineered so we could develop the vaccine, a strain of avian flu that's just as potent but much more infectious to humans.'

'How infectious exactly?'

'One infected person could spark a global pandemic in a few days. It's passed on by coughing or sneezing. Just like winter flu. You could contract it in exactly the same way.'

'And you've grown this virus in a lab?'

'It's in a secure state-of-the-art bio-hazard unit so it's

impossible for it to escape into the environment.'

'Unless someone deliberately removes it from the building, of course. But why the need for a vaccine for a virus that's only manufactured in a laboratory?'

'Because the avian flu virus will eventually mutate in nature and if we don't have a vaccine ready tens of millions of people could die.'

'That's a bit melodramatic, isn't it?'

'Not at all. Winter flu claims around half a million lives a year, mostly old, young and chronically-ill victims. But avian flu is different. It's highly pathogenic and constantly evolving.'

'You mean there's a possibility of it mutating into a virus that could behave like winter flu?'

'It's not a possibility. It's a certainty. The only doubt is when. We've already had a strain of avian flu that had limited ability to be contracted by humans. And in the late 1990s it wiped out millions of birds.'

'The H5N1 virus, right?' Blake remembered it dominating news bulletins and swathes of newspaper column inches after the first cases of the human strain were reported. The media had become hysterical about the threat, warning of a global catastrophe before it slipped from their consciousness and their attentions switched to the next calamity waiting to befall humanity. 'I thought that had all gone away,' he said.

'The danger is greater than ever. At the moment the avian flu virus is still difficult for humans to contract but the concern is that sixty per cent of those who have, have developed severe symptoms and died.'

'And if avian flu was as easy to catch as winter flu, it would be catastrophic?'

'We've calculated the numbers would be on a massive scale.'

'My God, it could trigger widespread global panic.'

'Our models suggest international borders would close, healthcare systems would be overrun and eventually economies would collapse.'

'But that's just a model, right? Those things are designed to predict the worst case scenario.'

'In 1918 the Spanish Flu killed fifty million people. That was before you could fly around the world in a matter of hours on a jumbo jet. And already the latest mutation, H7N9, is showing signs of being able to transmit between human carriers,' said Benjamin.

Somewhere above an eagle screeched. Blake saw the silhouette through a gaping hole in the roof, a magnificent bird with wings outstretched, soaring on the currents. It was the picture of effortless grace and beauty. Hard to imagine a species so magnificent threatening the existence of mankind.

'So let me get this correct, you've artificially manipulated bird flu to make it behave like winter flu so you can work on a vaccine to protect the world?'

'There's much opposition in the scientific community to what we're doing because people fear the Armageddon Virus. That's why there's so much secrecy around our work.'

'What are the symptoms?'

'Of catching the Armageddon Virus? Much like winter flu at first but death would almost certainly follow, especially for the fit and healthy.'

'But I thought you said flu mostly affects the old, the young and the chronically-ill?'

'Avian flu is different. It causes your immune system to generate killer cells that attack healthy lung tissue and makes the blood vessels leak.'

'So you'd end up drowning in your own blood?' said Blake.

'If you don't suffer any complications like pneumonia or multiple organ failure.'

'In which case the healthier you are, the worse it could be.' Blake sucked in breath through his teeth. 'How long before the vaccine's ready?'

'There were still a few months of testing.' Benjamin hesitated for a beat. 'The loss of some of the control virus will set us back.'

'So, how did Elias find out about the virus, given all the secrecy surrounding the laboratory?'

'I told him,' said Benjamin, without a hint of remorse. People were often detached from their emotions under hypnosis.

'Why would you do that?'

Benjamin didn't have a response to the question so Blake tried another tack. 'Tell me about your relationship with Elias. Are you close?'

'I hate him.'

'Why do you hate him, Ben?'

'He was always the favourite. I was the disappointing sibling with a pointless low-paid job in scientific research.'

'Your parents favoured him because he was more successful? Is that it?'

'He was an A-grade student who went to Cambridge and earned a massive salary working for an investment bank in the City.'

'Who ended up in jail for fraud,' said Blake.

'Only after my parents died. They never knew.'

'So you told him about the virus to prove you were a success too? When did you tell him?'

'After he was convicted.'

'Tell me how it happened. Did you visit him in prison?'

'I despised him for how he'd always treated me but Sophie wanted me to try for a reconciliation after he was convicted. She said it would be good for my peace of mind.'

'I see.'

'I put it off for a long time.'

'What persuaded you to go in the end?'

'I wanted to see him behind bars.'

'As a common convict? How was he?'

Benjamin flinched. 'More arrogant than I'd known. It

was as if he was proud of being in that jail.'

'How did that make you feel?'

'Angry.'

'So you told him about the virus?'

'After he made fun of me. He laughed and said no one should have to wear a white coat and fill test-tubes for a living. So I told him about the laboratory. I knew I wasn't supposed to but I couldn't help it.'

'What exactly did you say?'

'That I'd been risking my life every day working on a super virus that could wipe out humanity.'

'Did he take you seriously?'

'Yes, I think so. He asked lots of questions.'

'What sort of questions?'

'He wanted to know where the laboratory was and what sort of security we had on site.'

'And you told him?'

'Yes.'

'Didn't you think about the consequences?'

'He'd never been interested in my work before and the more questions he asked, the more carried away I became talking about it.'

'Oh, Benjamin. What have you done?' In the distance, Blake caught the wail of sirens. In a few minutes the house and surrounding area would be swarming with police. There wasn't much time. 'Did you know he'd escaped from Marshside?'

'No.'

'Tell me what happened when he turned up at the house.'

'He was with another man who was in charge. They pushed their way in, barged past Sophie. The other man was waving a gun, and started shouting and screaming, ordering us all to get down on our knees.'

'And Elias?'

'He was there too. He kept saying we should do as we were told if we didn't want to get hurt.'

'And they asked you to fetch the virus?'

'They wanted to know how to get into the laboratory.'

'But you told them it wasn't possible because the security systems couldn't be overridden?'

'Yes.'

'So they threatened Sophie and the children?'

'The one in charge kept telling me how pretty Sophie and Ellie were and he could have some fun with them. He held a gun to Sophie's head and told me I had to steal the virus for them if I wanted to see her alive again.'

'How much did you give them?'

'Twenty millilitres.'

'And in real terms, how many people could that infect?'

'Hundreds. You'd only need the smallest dose to develop the virus.'

'And of course it would rapidly spread. Did they tell you what they planned to do with it?'

Benjamin hesitated as though his brain was scanning a bank of memory chips for information. 'No,' he said finally.

Blake sighed, eased himself to his feet and brushed dust from his trousers. The sirens were louder now. It was hard to tell how many there were. Their tones merged into one dulled through the thick stone walls. Blake stepped towards the windows at the rear of the room. Through a cracked pane he counted four police cars forming a lazy semi-circle around the croft house. Two more appeared as he watched, mounting the crest where their rented car was parked.

'Time's nearly up, Benjamin. One last question. Think very carefully. Did you hear either Elias or Vaughn talk about what they were going to do with the virus?'

Benjamin thought about the question for a few moments. Policemen in thick coats emerged from their cars, pulled on gloves and caps and moved in a line towards the building scanning the ground as they walked.

'There was a phone call,' said Benjamin. 'Elias took the

call while the other one chained me up. They were talking in loud voices.'

'Arguing?'

'Yes, I think so.'

'About what? Do you have any idea?'

'I don't know.'

'Think, Benjamin. It's really important. Remember your wrist chained to the pipework, Sophie and the children with you. Think about the cold stone floor, the sound of the wind through the loose tiles. Put yourself back in that moment.'

Benjamin screwed his eyes tight. His breathing became laboured. Outside an unmarked gunmetal grey Volvo bounced over the track and slid to a halt.

'Remember Elias' phone ringing, watching him disappear outside and Vaughn following. Did they leave the door open?'

'Yes,' said Benjamin.

'So you could hear their voices. They started arguing. Remember their words, Benjamin. Dig deep into your memory.'

'I can't,' he said.

'Think. Hear the sound of their voices again.'

Benjamin's lips began to move, like he was mouthing the words in his mind. 'It was where they had to make a rendezvous,' he said, his voice husky. 'I think they were being told where to take the case. The one with the gun didn't want to go. Elias said he had to if he wanted the money.'

'Benjamin, that's great. Stay with the voices and think hard. Did they say where the rendezvous was taking place?'

Benjamin opened his mouth to speak but his words were lost in the sound of the croft house door crashing open. Detective Superintendent Douglas stood framed in the opening. He combed a grey fringe away from his eyes with his fingers.

'What's going on?' he asked, nodding at Benjamin

laying on the ground.

Blake knelt at Benjamin's side, whispered in his ear and helped him to sit up. 'We were just chatting,' said Blake. 'Come on, Ben. Time to get up.'

Benjamin stood slowly, blinking. He looked around the room as if struggling to make sense of his surroundings. A post-hypnosis disorientation clouded his face. It always happened when they came around. Usually lasted no more than a few minutes before they were back to their full consciousness. Blake put an arm around Benjamin's shoulder and guided him out of the door, brushing past Douglas without a second look.

Chapter 23

The delay was out of his control but it didn't make Stijn Bogaert any less anxious. He was paid good money not to ask questions but there was also an expectation he'd keep to schedule. An unspoken part of the deal. Like making sure the plane was fuelled and serviceable. He based his reputation on it and it kept the work coming his way. With an ex-wife and two kids to support, God knows he needed the money. He wiped his palms on the thighs of his jeans, his eyes behind the mirrored aviator sunglasses fixed on the horizon ahead. Visibility was good and the wind was light. He checked the rows of dials on the instrument panel and settled into his seat. The Cessna C340A dipped and rose as it caught a thermal. Bogaert steadied the wings with a slight adjustment on the control wheel and tried to relax. The plane was flying beautifully. Everything was fine. He should still make the pick-up within the hour.

His instructions had been straightforward. Pick up two passengers from an airfield on a place called Skye, a Scottish island he'd never heard of but it fitted his expectations. No doubt a tiny airstrip used predominantly by hobbyist fliers, one of thousands of quiet airfields dotted around Europe that could be dropped into without attracting the attention of border control or customs. Minimal time on the ground. Land, pick-up and take-off. Same as always. There'd be no time to refuel, so he'd taken off with full tanks. The Cessna, with its bulbous wing-tip fuel tanks, could easily cover a thousand miles, more with a favourable wind. Plus its manoeuvrability made it perfect for nipping in and out of even the shortest airstrips. There was comfortably space for five passengers and it could cruise happily at 200mph.

The only departure from his previous assignments was the parcel he'd been asked to stow in the hold. Delivered by courier to his house two days earlier and wrapped in brown paper, sealed with parcel tape. Slightly larger than a shoebox and considerably heavier. No label and no return details. They said it was needed by his passengers when they arrived at their destination in Norway. Bogaert knew better than to be curious about its contents. Curiosity only found you a whole heap of trouble. So he'd tucked it next to the briefcase he always took with him on business trips. Thought nothing more about it.

He checked his charts, then his watch. Opened the throttle a little further, comfortable he could afford to burn more fuel to cut the journey time. It irritated him that he'd allowed plenty of time for the journey and yet he was still going to be late. But really, it wasn't his fault. He could never have predicted the problems at the airfield in Belgium. He'd been manoeuvring towards the end of the airstrip when the voice from the control tower crackled in his headphones, advising him to hold his position. He'd had no choice. An incident with a pilot experiencing medical issues who had to make an emergency landing. Ten minutes passed. Fifteen. Twenty. Finally, after half an hour, a flimsy two-seater popped through the low cloud like a dragonfly on the breeze, bobbing and pitching in the crosswinds. It hit the runway with a bounce that sent its tail sliding one way and then the other. It buzzed past Bogaert with a mosquito-like whine and drew to a halt fifty metres further along the runway. Another twenty minutes passed while the pilot was attended by medical staff in his cockpit. Nearly an hour wasted. But he had no way of warning his passengers. They'd have to wait.

Two paramedics were fussing over Sophie and the children

when Blake returned to the hire car with Benjamin. Mortensen was standing a few feet away with two police officers hovering in the background. She pulled a forced smile at Blake and watched Benjamin smother his family with hugs and kisses as they were reunited.

She walked with them back to the road where two ambulances were parked while Blake struggled to reverse the car along the track. He caught up with her the family were being ushered into the back of one of the vehicles.

'We've got to go,' he shouted through an open window.

She jumped into the passenger seat and Blake navigated around a fleet of emergency vehicles scattered across the road, doubting whether the island had ever seen so many cop cars.

'Did Benjamin tell you anything useful?'

Blake gave Mortensen an abridged version of the events Benjamin had set out. 'There are four vials in the case we saw Benjamin remove from the laboratory, each with enough virus to start a chain reaction that could sweep the globe in a matter of days,' he said. 'We're talking deaths in their tens of millions.'

'So where is it now?'

'We have to assume it's with Vaughn and Pitts and they've made it off the island.'

'The police have put up a roadblock on the bridge so I think it's doubtful they escaped by car.'

'Agreed. So that realistically narrows it down to boat or aircraft. Check your phone. Are there any landing strips nearby?'

Mortensen plucked her phone from her pocket. 'You think aircraft rather than boat?'

'It's what I'd do. They need to get somewhere fast now they have the virus. They can't risk being caught with the test-tubes and I doubt they'd waste time going to sea.'

'Not even on a speedboat?'

'I wouldn't have thought so. A plane or helicopter would be the faster option.'

'Okay, say we narrow it down to an aircraft, what then? We have no idea where they're going.'

'Benjamin overheard Vaughn and Pitts arguing about a rendezvous.'

'With the Iranians? Did he overhear where?'

'He heard a name but wasn't sure. Ever heard of a place called "Stoit"?'

Mortensen's brow knitted. She looked up from her phone and stared at the road ahead without really seeing it. 'It sounds familiar but I'm not sure.'

'It means nothing to me but see what you can find online.'

'Hang on, I think I might know where it is,' she said, diving back into her phone. Her fingers darted across the screen but an intermittent mobile signal meant the results of her search were slow coming. She tapped the dashboard with her fingernails as she waited.

'What are you thinking?' asked Blake.

'I think it's in Norway,' she said. 'Yes, I'm right. It's actually Stord but it's pronounced "Stoit".'

'How did you know that?'

Mortensen shrugged. 'What can I say? Must be something in my Scandinavian blood. I have a vague recollection of it from somewhere.'

'Where is it?'

'South of Bergen. About 450 miles due north east from here, straight out over the North Sea.'

Blake slowed at a junction. 'What's there?' He looked both ways and on a whim turned right, as much as anything to keep driving. While they were moving it seemed like they were making progress.

'It's a municipality and an island. I can't imagine why they'd choose it as a rendezvous though.'

'Something we're not seeing perhaps. What about an airstrip? Anything on Skye?'

'Give me a minute,' said Mortensen as she continued to tap away at her phone. 'There's an airstrip at Broadford.

It's less than seven miles from the ruined church.'

She looked up at the road, glanced left and right and back at her phone again. 'We're on the right road. It's up here on the left.'

Chapter 24

Bogaert began his descent through a woolly blanket of grey cloud. It rushed past his windshield cloaking the wings in droplets of dew. He could see neither land nor sea but an altimeter dial rolled backwards to remind him how rapidly they were racing to meet him. He was never entirely comfortable putting his faith in instruments but accepted it as a necessary evil as he dived through the thick Scottish stratus. The fuselage popped and creaked with each lurch of rising current and swiping side-wind. He felt every bump and jolt of turbulence through his hands resting lightly on the control wheel.

A twinge in his back reminded him how much he longed to stretch his legs and uncurl his spine but he was running late and his instructions had been quite specific. A quick pick up and get airborne as soon as possible. There would be no downtime. Good job he didn't have a weak bladder.

At just under two thousand feet, the Cessna broke through the cloud and Bogaert was relieved to see he was lined up perfectly with a distant airstrip. It was as if a giant ruler had been dropped from a great height and had landed in the middle of a field, abnormally straight like nothing nature could have produced, an anomaly in its craggy surroundings. In the distance dark mountains framed the horizon and beneath him were a dark blue sea ragged with rolling whitecaps and the foaming bow waves of tiny fishing boats.

The airfield had been built on a small peninsula

alongside a sliver of golden sand and a narrow lagoon, which meant any approach had to be from over the water and away from the dwellings that peppered that side of the island. Bogaert peered over the centre console and tried to estimate its length. It looked short. Very short. At best it was a little over two thousand feet. The maths was simple. He could bring the Cessna down in eight hundred at a push but that didn't leave much room for error. He wondered why he hadn't checked the detail before he'd left.

With a flick of a switch and a mechanical groan, the landing gear unwound itself and locked into position. Bogaert checked his airspeed and adjusted the flaps. He reminded himself there was no room for error, his stomach tightening. Not that the landing was weighing particularly on his mind, rather the anticipation of the job ahead. There was only one sort of passenger who required the kind of taxi service he was able to provide. The sort you'd go out of your way to avoid under any other circumstance. But they were paying handsomely for his services and that was all he needed to know. He eased the throttle back a fraction and wiped his hands dry.

The white centre lines loomed large and then he was on top of them, over them, drifting downwards, counting off the distance in his head, careful not to let the nose drop despite his urgency to land. He let the wheels touch down with a gentle bump, pulled back on the throttle and stamped on the brakes, only vaguely aware of fields and fences flashing by as the plane ate up the ground, hurtling towards the end of the runway. He stared at the speed on a dial, urging the aircraft to slow, trying to judge whether he'd overshot. Had he nailed it? If not, he had about two seconds to reapply the power and hope there was enough concrete left to make it back to take-off speed, which in the Cessna's case was precisely 91 knots.

Then directly ahead he saw a car. It had been nothing more than a dark speck before. Now he realised it was 4x4 with its front doors wide open, pointed down the runway, and he was bearing down on it at startling speed. He applied more pressure to the brakes until his calves ached but it was like stopping an oil tanker. The plane was slowing but not quickly enough.

Ricky Vaughn brushed crumbs from his clothes and reached for a pack of Marlborough on the dashboard. He lit one with a plastic lighter he'd picked up with packets of sandwiches and cans of soft drink when they'd stopped at an all-night garage. The tobacco crackled as he inhaled.

'Do you have to smoke in the car?' said Pitts, throwing open his door. They'd been sitting in the stolen VW parked at the end of the runway for the best part of two hours. A rusting steel corrugated hangar had initially provided them with a hiding place but they'd moved, as much for the change of view as to allow them to see their plane arrive. Vaughn took a slow, deliberate drag, turned and blew the smoke in Pitts' face.

'For Christ's sake!' Pitts exploded. 'What the hell's wrong with you?'

'Relax will you?'

'How can I relax? We're sitting in a knocked-off car waiting for a plane that might never turn up on an island that's probably swarming with police.' Elias scratched at a patch of flaky skin on the back of his hand with nails bitten down to the tips.

'It'll be here.'

'You sure?'

'Yes, I'm sure.'

'I wish I had your confidence.'

Vaughn put his cigarette between his lips and snatched the silver case from Pitts' lap. 'Let's check on the booty while we wait shall we?'

Pitts lunged for the case and grabbed it back with both hands. 'They were due an hour ago.'

'You worry too much.'

'You do know there's no other way off the island? Unless you fancy swimming? If that plane doesn't turn up we're stuck here.'

Vaughn shrugged. 'Worse case scenario? We steal a boat. Look they're happy to pay twenty-five million for the contents of that case. That makes them eager beavers. The plane will be here. You ever seen twenty-five million before?'

Elias didn't reply. He knew what twenty-five million pounds looked like. On a computer screen at least. Never in cash. He imagined bundles of notes stacked in a briefcase or loosely thrown into a holdall. Like he'd seen in the films.

'If they're that eager, they're not going to stand us up are they? Have patience,' said Vaughn

'And hope the cops don't turn up first?'

Vaughn flicked the remnants of the smouldering cigarette out of the window and reached into a pocket in the car door. He wrapped his hand around a nine millimetre Berretta. Pulled it out slowly. He made a big deal of ejecting the magazine, checking the exposed parabellum, rolling it with his thumb. 'I wouldn't worry too much about that,' he said.

'Easy for you to say.'

Vaughn twisted in his seat and swung the Berretta into Pitts' face. He pressed the barrel into the gap between his eyes and watched the blood drain from his face. 'Shut up with your moaning will you? I've got the virus thanks to your brother and now I'm struggling to remember why you're still here. No reason why I shouldn't put a bullet in your skull and save myself your share of the fee.'

Pitts swallowed hard. The urge to itch his forearm, where his eczema was red and inflamed, was overwhelming. But a sudden movement to scratch wasn't going to end well.

'We're a team, right?' Pitts mumbled. 'Without me there would be no virus and you'd still be doing sixteen hour stints behind bars in Marshside. You owe me.'

'I don't owe you nothing. Remember who got you out in the first place.'

'All I'm saying is that we need each other.'

'Wrong. I don't need you,' said Vaughn. His finger played over the trigger.

'Listen, you just got really lucky. Twelve million pounds lucky to be precise. Easiest payday you've ever had I reckon, so don't blow it. I could have asked anyone in that prison for help but I asked you. Do you know why? Because I trusted you. Because I recognised you had principles. Maybe you are some hotshot gangster but I heard you were loyal. And honourable. A rare quality among thieves.'

'Don't think you know nothing about me. You're just some rich kid who got caught with his hand in the till. Right now I'm standing in line for twelve million. But I'm not stupid. If I kill you here and now, I take it all. You think anyone will give a shit?'

'It's your conscience,' said Pitts as his attention was caught by a movement in the sky. His eyes darted to the left for a split second. He looked again, longer this time. 'It's here,' he said, quietly.

Vaughn turned while keeping the gun pressed into Pitts' flesh. In the distance he saw the outline of an aircraft drop out of the cloud. It might have been a sea bird other than for the bright landing light mounted in its nose piercing the gloom of the day.

'Now what did I tell you?' said Vaughn, breaking into a grin and lowering the Berretta. 'Looks like our lift's arrived.' He threw open his door and stepped out into the chill air.

The aircraft grew larger, floating towards the concrete runway where tufts of grass poked through wide cracks. To their left a ragged old air sock flapped noisily against a metal post, a relic of when the airport had supported a commercial operation. All that had gone.

Pitts eased himself out of the passenger seat and stood leaning against the door while the Cessna bobbed and dived towards them with its wings dipping and rising as the pilot battled to keep them level. The buzz of its twin engines carried across the emptiness. It took less than two minutes for it to reach the runway where it seemed to hover, suspended in flight over the crumbling concrete. And then it dropped the final few metres, landing with a skittish bounce. Behind the windshield, they saw the outline of the pilot, his expression fixed in concentration. As he hit the brakes and cut the throttle, the nose of the aircraft dipped and its tail rose up, like the exotic bird bowing to a mate Pitts had seen once on a wildlife documentary. But it continued to race towards the VW on a collision course, fast at first but slowing. Slowly.

Pitts shot a concerned look over the top of the VW at Vaughn. 'It's not going to stop,' he said, shuffling away from the vehicle, eyes wide.

Vaughn said nothing. He squinted as he watched but stood still.

The buzz of the twin props became a roar and the dizzying aroma of aviation fuel hit them. The draft of the propellers ruffled their hair but Vaughn remained impassive. Pitts turned and ran, diving for cover, clutching the silver case. He visualised their car being mangled, the thin panels of aluminium ripped and sawn apart.

At the last moment the plane swung away, arcing in a wide loop to their right, missing the car by a clear two metres. Vaughn didn't even blink.

Chapter 25

The road to the airport was an unobtrusive single track off the main A87. It was signposted 'Raon-Adhair' with a helpful image of an aircraft for motorists without an understanding of Gaelic. The entrance was over a cattle grid and through a metal gate which opened up into a wide apron adjacent to a concrete airstrip. There was a distinct lack of facilities. Blake noted a large hangar and two deserted single-storey buildings, like mobile homes set back on the edge of a gravel car park. They looked as if they might be used as office space or a clubhouse for a local flying club. The runway lay on an east to west axis, poorly maintained with tufts of grass growing through cracks in the surface that from a distance looked like green veins. Its eastern approach was obscured by a bank covered by a crop of scrubby vegetation. To the west was the village of Broadford. A narrow ribbon of land beyond the airstrip gave way to icy-looking loch waters and the distant dark mountains of Scalpay which rose up like primordial sleeping giants.

'We should check the hangar,' Mortensen said. 'If they're here, it's the only place you could hide a vehicle.'

Blake nodded, eased his foot off the brake and let the car grind forwards in first gear. The hangar was an ugly structure, constructed around a curved frame with a skin of corrugated steel the elements had turned rusty amber. Where daylight penetrated a wide opening Blake saw sections of aircraft; tail fins, propeller blades and wings. Mortensen was right. There was probably plenty of room to hide a car. He dropped the clutch and let the car freewheel.

The low hum of an idling aircraft engine was quiet at first but grew louder. It was being carried on the breeze. Distinct and familiar, resonating through the air almost in a whisper. It wasn't coming from the hangar, rather from somewhere behind them. Blake hit the brakes throwing Mortensen forwards in her seat. He ignored her scowl. Cocked his head to listen.

He realised he'd been wrong. It wasn't a single engine. It was a twin-prop, the double stuttering ticker of one propeller fused with another and minutely out of sync. He wound down his window and was hit by a cold blast of air. The engine murmur grew louder.

'Listen,' said Blake.

'Maybe we're not too late,' said Mortensen, loosening the seatbelt and turning to look over her shoulder through the rear windshield but seeing nothing beyond the bank which obscured the far end of the airfield.

The murmur wound into a grunt which evolved into a high-pitched whine.

'Whatever it is, it's taking off,' said Blake. He slammed his foot hard on the accelerator but the hired Ford was old and tired. It had been thrashed too often by too many careless drivers. The engine was loose and suffocated with carbon. The best it could offer was a wheezy gasp that set the tyres spinning and squealing. Blake shifted the gear lever, dropping into second and letting the revs jump into the red zone. The worn rubber tyres finally found some traction and the Ford bumped onto the runway.

Like a mirage the Cessna came into view, shimmering in the heat haze from two 300-horsepower Continental engines mounted beneath its wings. It was lined up for take-off with its propellers a blur.

'There's the VW,' said Mortensen pointing to a dark-coloured 4x4 parked behind the plane, the vehicle they recognised from the Skyevax security footage.

'In which case, time to get introduced to Mr Vaughn and Mr Pitts,' said Blake.

With a free hand he yanked on the handbrake, forcing the Ford's back end to slide out so the car ended up facing the Cessna. He crashed into third gear and let the revs build through the asthmatic rasp coming from under the bonnet. Their speed rose slowly. Thirty. Forty. Fifty miles an hour. Not exactly race car acceleration but the best he was going to achieve with four-cylinders of naturally aspirated engineering.

The windscreen was covered in a film of filth but through a clean arc cut by the wipers, he saw the Cessna roll forwards. Slowly at first but quickly building pace. Blake heard the gutsy grunt of the Cessna's props reaching maximum power and pictured the pilot with one hand on the throttle, concentrating on keeping the plane on the centreline. If Blake wasn't able to force the plane off the runway, it would be like hitting a brick wall. But mutually assured destruction wasn't in his game plan. He rammed the gear stick into fifth and placed both hands on the steering wheel, eyes narrowed, focused on the Cessna, watching it grow bigger, the distance between them shortening.

'What the hell are you doing?' Mortensen screamed. She had braced herself against the dashboard. Her body was stiff with tension. Fight or flight responses. Except she had no choice in either. There was nothing to do but watch events play out.

'Rolling the dice,' said Blake.

His father had been no great gambler but was fond of telling Blake nothing worthwhile had ever been achieved without someone having taken a chance. Right now Blake was gambling the pilot would lose his nerve first. A lethal game of chicken. Except the plane continued to accelerate towards them and was showing no sign of giving up the runway.

Blake saw the outline of the pilot's head, his eyes

obscured behind a pair of sunglasses, a headset clamped over his ears. He didn't look at all concerned that there was one-and-a-half tons of metal, plastic and rubber racing towards him.

'It's going to hit us!' Mortensen shouted.

Doubt crept into Blake's mind. If anything, the pilot was still accelerating, holding an unwavering line down the middle of the runway. The engine noise was deafening as the whirling propellers grew closer, giant steel blades that could slice through the Ford's fragile aluminium bodywork like a band-saw through plywood. Blake tried not to think what they could do to flesh and bone.

The plane was almost on top of them, about to reach the point of no return. Blake swore under his breath, jumped on the brakes and pulled the steering wheel hard to the right. The front wheels seized and, as he fought with all his upper body strength to keep the car from spinning, the plane shot past within a hair's width.

Blake's attention was entirely on keeping the car in a straight line but he no longer felt in control. The vehicle screeched off the runway and hit rough ground with a heavy thud. Wheels dug into soft earth and bounced over rocks and divots, the chassis buckling and the suspension coils struggling to keep the car in contact with the ground. Inside their necks snapped and their bodies rolled.

They came to a sudden halt when the car hit an immoveable pile of rock dumped from an earlier construction project. Airbags inflated with a loud bang and the front end of the Ford crumpled like a wet cardboard box. A radiator pipe ruptured in a hiss of steam and the bonnet sprang up over the cracked windscreen.

Blake's brain processed the scene in double quick time. He saw in slow motion the white bags inflate to cushion his head and the drawn out sound of cracking glass and splintering metal. The dashboard shifted towards his knees as the engine block shifted backwards. And somewhere behind him he heard the buzz of the Cessna.

Chapter 26

Stijn Bogaert gripped the throttle levers tightly, feeling the rotors throbbing through his hand and up his arm.

'Do not abort this take-off!' the guy called Vaughn with the ugly grin and the broken nose had shouted when he saw the car racing towards them. The sour stench of his breath filled the cockpit. 'I want this plane in the air now.'

As if to reinforce his words he'd unbuckled his seatbelt, risen from his seat and produced a handgun. He'd jammed the barrel into the base of the pilot's skull.

'But he's heading right for us,' said Bogaert.

Vaughn cut off his protestations with a sharp prod of cold steel.

'I don't care. Shut up and fly!' he yelled over the roar of the engines.

Bogaert planted his feet on the rudder pedals, applying the brakes, his eyes fixed on the Ford. It had appeared from nowhere and was bearing down on them like an Exocet missile, spewing a dirty cloud of exhaust in its wake.

'We'll all die,' said Bogaert, his voice strangulated. 'There's not enough room. We'll hit him before we make fifty knots.' Beads of sweat pearled under his shirt and over his scalp. He wandered about feigning a mechanical fault but dismissed the thought as quickly as it had entered his head.

'Tell me, can you fly without the use of your legs?' said Vaughn. He slid the gun from Bogaert's neck, caressed the pilot's arm and hip and let it come to rest pressed against his thigh. 'I guess you probably can, if you don't pass out with the pain. I'm only going to ask nicely one more time and then I start shooting. First a bullet through your right femur. Then one through the left. I doubt you'll walk again but we can stem the blood flow enough to keep you alive. Isn't that right, Elias?' There was no response from the man at the back of the cabin. 'I want this plane off the ground!' Vaughn's voice rose to a shrill crescendo.

'You're crazy,' said Bogaert, lifting his feet from the pedals.

The Cessna rolled forwards, bumping along the airstrip, slowly at first but rapidly gaining speed. Bogaert's eyes zipped between a dial showing their speed and the view of the advancing car.

'Let's see how good you are,' said Vaughn.

'We're not going to make it. You're going to get us all killed.'

A wide grin spread over Vaughn's face. 'Don't be so dramatic. He'll pull over. You'll see.'

Bogaert wasn't so sure.

They were already up to 45 knots but the car was so close he could see two figures inside. A man was driving and a woman was in the passenger seat, hugging the white centreline and showing no sign of backing down. Bogeart was numb. It was the first time in all his years' flying he hadn't enjoyed the excitement of a take-off. He loved the controlled power of the dual Continental engines pulsating through the fuselage, the kick in the back of the seat and the heady aroma of aviation fuel. But not today. Today he was convinced he was going to die.

Vaughn moved his gun back to Bogaert's head. The Cessna made it to 55 knots and was still accelerating, but not quickly enough.

Ten metres.

Bogaert pictured the ball of flame that would engulf them. He wondered whether he'd feel pain.

Five metres.

At the moment before impact, Bogaert snapped his eyes shut, stamped on one of the rudder pedals and pulled both throttles back. The aircraft veered off the runway and onto the grass verge, narrowly missing the car as it pulled away in the opposite direction. Vaughn fell backwards, catching his shoulder against the back of one of the seats and cracking his head against the fuselage with a satisfying thud. Bogaert was too busy wrestling for control of the plane to pay much attention. The Cessna shook and rattled uncontrollably as it clattered along the scrub. It wasn't designed to run on anything more rugged than rough concrete. Bogaert gritted his teeth, trying not to think of the damage he might have done. Or how much it might cost to put right. At least he was alive. For the moment.

Vaughn hauled himself to his feet as Bogaert brought the aircraft to a standstill and killed the engines.

'You stupid idiot!' he roared, rubbing the back of his head. 'What do you think you're doing?'

Bogaert twisted in his seat. 'I'm sorry. Are you okay?' he asked with genuine concern.

He didn't see Vaughn's punch coming. It caught him squarely in the mouth sending his aviators flying. It cracked two teeth and split his lip. 'I told you to get this plane in the air. Now look what you've done.' Vaughn's eyes burned with rage.

The colour had drained from Bogaert's face and he was trembling from the shock of the unexpected blow. He was used to the company of uncompromising men. It was a peril of the job. But none had ever hit him. Or held a gun to his head as he was trying to fly a plane. He dabbed his nose with the back of his hand and discovered he was bleeding.

'Get yourself cleaned up, get this plane back on the runaway and be ready for take-off in three minutes,' said Vaughn, turning into the cabin.

Pitts was slumped in one of the executive leather seats with his legs crossed. He was scratching at dry skin on the back of his hand, still gripping the silver case. Vaughn followed his gaze out of one of the windows. The Ford had come to rest embedded in a mound of earth with steam rising from its crushed front end.

'Any idea who that was?' asked Pitts. He glanced up briefly at Vaughn and back out of the window.

'Time to find out,' said Vaughn. He grabbed a sports bag from under one of the seats, unzipped it with stubby fingers and pulled out a MAC-10 sub-machine gun. A pray and spray weapon for close quarter combat and a rival to its more famous cousin, the Uzi. It had limited range and dubious accuracy. But none of that was a concern for Vaughn. Not at the distance he planned to use it.

He grabbed two magazines from a side pocket. Long, rectangular boxes filled with thirty two rounds of nine millimetre cartridges. He clipped one into the MAC's grip handle and stowed the other in his back pocket.

'Do what you've got to do but hurry up,' said Pitts. 'Let's get off this miserable island.'

Vaughn glared at him, reached for the door handle and jumped out. He landed heavily on the grass, found his balance and headed directly towards the crashed Ford with the gun swinging in one hand at his side.

Bogaert watched him from the cockpit, nursing his bleeding nose with a handkerchief. Vaughn was taking loping strides, walking with his shoulders square, his head held high. A man with one purpose in life.

He was less than five metres from the car when he swung the gun level and pulled the trigger. It purred as it spewed its deadly load, cutting a ragged line of thumb-sized holes along the length of the driver's side. He unleashed another burst into the boot. Stopped, switched magazines and emptied another round into the passenger door. As the echoes of the gunfire died away, Vaughn reached for the door and pulled it open with his weapon raised, squinting into the interior, ready to finish off the job.

Blake and Mortensen were lying face up with their backs pressed into the soft ground. Mortensen's breathing was hard and laboured in Blake's ear. She had a smear of blood across her cheek and a wild, terrified look in her eye. She was trembling, whether from the cold, the shock of the crash or fear, Blake wasn't sure. A burst of gunfire crackled somewhere behind them on the far side of the mound where they were hidden. Mortensen tensed and drew a sharp intake of breath. Blake squeezed her hand.

He'd had to half-drag her from the car, up the steep bank and down the other side. The first salvo of bullets had made them both jump. Blake put his finger to his lips and Mortensen nodded her understanding. They waited for the firing to stop, praying Vaughn wouldn't come looking for them. As silence settled across the airfield, a car door opened and slammed shut. And then another.

Blake rolled onto his stomach and up onto his elbows. The earth was wet and slippery so he had to dig his toes in to stop himself sliding. He flicked off the safety on his Browning and grimaced at the sound, fearful it had carried. He hauled himself up the bank using his elbows like pickaxes and peered over the top. The wild grass had been crushed flat when they'd scrambled over but it still provided enough cover to hide his face.

He saw Vaughn prowling around the car and kicking at the spent brass cartridges that littered the ground. It was the first time Blake had seen him face-to-face since Marshside, a bruiser with a pumped out chest and arms that swung at his side like an ape. He'd only caught a brief glimpse of Vaughn's face before but his flattened nose and the unnatural curl of his lip that gave him a permanent sneer had stayed with him. His weapon hung loosely from his hand.

The Cessna had come to rest a hundred metres behind Vaughn. Its engines had either stalled or been killed. A figure hung out from a door, and although it was too far to make out his features, Blake was in no doubt who it was. Elias Pitts shouted something Blake didn't catch. Vaughn yelled back.

'I'll be there in a minute. Make yourself useful and get that plane back on the runway.'

Pitts didn't reply. He ducked inside and a moment later the engines coughed and spluttered. With one last despairing appraisal of the car, Vaughn backed away, turned and jogged to the plane.

Blake supported his Browning in two hands and lined up Vaughn in his sights, a laterally shifting target disappearing quickly out of range. He had one shot to make it count, one shot that would give away their position to a man carrying a gun that could unleash a magazine of nine millimetre shells in a split second.

Blake sensed movement at his elbow. Mortensen had clambered up the bank to join him. He took his finger from the trigger and relaxed his grip.

'They're going. We've got to stop them,' she said.

'We're outgunned but if we can draw Vaughn's fire there might be a way to stop them. He's already wasted an entire magazine ripping up our car and I heard him change clips. At best he has sixteen rounds left, assuming he's out of ammo clips. He needs some encouragement to waste the rest of them before we take our chance.'

'How do you know he doesn't have another magazine?'

'Educated guess.'

'Great,' said Mortensen. 'So what do we do?'

'He's furious we disappeared. He was hoping to have vented his anger by pumping us full of lead, so I don't think it will take much to draw his fire. We'll give our position away and his trigger finger should do the rest.'

'That's your plan?'

'Given that we have less than a minute before he makes it back to that aircraft, do you have any better ideas?'

'I just thought you might have come up with something less suicidal than starting a firefight with a guy holding a sub-machine gun.'

'It'll be okay if we can stack the odds in our favour.'

'And how do we do that?'

'There're two of us for a start. But we don't have much time.' Vaughn was already half way back to the Cessna. 'You attract his attention and I'll find an alternative line of sight.'

'How?'

'I'll whistle a signal when I'm in place and you start firing. You won't hit him from this range but make sure he sees you.'

'Oh, terrific.'

Blake scrambled down the bank and scuttled away to the right. He kept his head low, running in a half crouch. Vaughn still had his back to him but the Cessna's engines were running at full throttle and the plane was rolling forwards. It bounced over the soft grass, turning back onto the runway. Blake took his chance and broke cover. He sprinted hard across the verge and fell flat on his stomach on the edge of the runway, halfway between the wreck of their car and the plane.

Vaughn was carrying the MAC-10 in his right hand, so Blake figured it was his dominant side. The odds were he'd spin to his right when he heard Mortensen's shots and hopefully would be so distracted by the fire he wouldn't notice Blake.

Mortensen had climbed to the top of the mound, her hands wrapped around her Glock and her elbows locked out. She was aiming at Vaughn with her head slightly cocked. Blake double-checked Vaughn's position. Thirty metres from the plane, putting Mortensen outside of the effective range of the MAC. Close up it was a nasty gun. Good for gangsters sorting out turf wars. Particularly effective in drive-by shootings. His old unit used them from time to time. But he wasn't a fan. At a distance it was good for nothing. Unless it was fitted with a suppresser which you could use to control the kick-back. Otherwise it was a one-handed weapon with a powerful recoil. At best it would manage seventy metres. No way Vaughn would be able to pick off Mortensen. He'd have to turn, close the gap and walk straight into Blake's line of fire.

Blake pursed his lips and whistled a birdsong trill. Mortensen opened fire with four rapid shots over Vaughn's head. Vaughn ducked and spun around, moving to his right as Blake had predicted.

Mortensen made sure she was seen before cracking off three more shots that echoed along the length of the airfield. Vaughn drew himself to his full height and smirked. He levelled his gun but didn't fire. He stepped forwards, his eyes focused on Mortensen's slight frame silhouetted on top of the mound. She didn't move. He started to march purposefully towards her. He covered ten metres. Fifteen. Twenty. But he held his fire.

'Come on,' Blake urged under his breath. He lifted the Browning, taking its weight through his forearms and pivoting on his elbows. He sized up Vaughn through the sights with one eye squinted closed. He had a reasonable shot but didn't fancy the risk of missing. If the MAC was still loaded, Vaughn could cut him down like mincemeat from that distance.

Blake checked over his shoulder, saw Mortensen raise her gun and squeeze the trigger twice more. Two more harmless shots. And then she stood up, her arms by her side, legs slightly apart, her gun hanging loosely from her hand. A defiant stance like she was willing Vaughn to take a shot. Yanking on his male ego.

Vaughn couldn't resist. His trigger finger twitched and the MAC purred. A short burst of shots. Less than a second. Spent cartridges tinkled onto the concrete. Mortensen stood still. She tossed back her head, the picture of calm serenity. Another angry burst of fire. A half dozen more spent shells hit the ground.

The Cessna bumped onto the runway away to Blake's left, its door wide open and its engines idling on quarter power. Blake was vaguely aware of it moving onto the concrete in a lazy loop behind him as it prepared for a second take-off attempt but he doubted it would leave without Vaughn.

Blake stretched out the tension in his fingers and clasped them around the Browning's grip. He slipped his index finger through the trigger guard and applied a little pressure, took a deep breath and let it go, letting his body sink into the ground as his lungs deflated. His focus was fixed on Vaughn but in his peripheral vision he saw Mortensen raise her gun and take aim for a third time. Vaughn responded with another burst of fire. The bullets whistled through the air and landed harmlessly, buried in the earth mound. Mortensen collapsed, hit the ground and rolled down the bank while Blake concentrated on keeping Vaughn's head in his sights. He hoped she'd not been hit but forced the thought from his mind.

Vaughn's submachine gun fell silent. He tilted the weapon on its side to check the chamber, as if a rogue shell might have blocked the breach. Only Blake seemed to have realised he'd just spent the last of his ammo.

Blake sensed the Cessna drawing closer, tiny vibrations through the concrete and the murmur of the engines becoming louder. He let the tension out of his shoulders and lined up his shot. Vaughn glanced at the approaching plane and saw Blake. His eyes widened and his sneer grew more grotesque.

Blake braced himself and fired.

Chapter 27

The bullet left Blake's gun at close to four hundred metres a second, hitting Vaughn in the beat of a hummingbird's wings. Vaughn predicted the shot and tried to dive to his right, not quick enough to dodge a bullet but fast enough to save his life. The round caught him in the shoulder in an explosion of red mist that knocked him off his feet.

Blake scrambled across the uneven concrete and stood over Vaughn, his Browning aimed between the injured man's eyes. A pool of blood was puddling under Vaughn's shoulder, his useless MAC-10 lying out of reach. Vaughn rolled onto his back and grinned at Blake, his eyes cold and emotionless. He showed no fear and in any other circumstance, Blake would have been impressed. His finger found the trigger and started to squeeze.

'Blake!' Mortensen's shout of alarm caused him to glance over his shoulder. The Cessna was barely a few metres away, its whirling propellers moments from ripping into his flesh.

Blake tumbled onto the grass, rolling on his shoulder under the wing tip and planted himself flat on the floor. The turbulence of the propellers buffeted his back and the noise of the engines left his ears ringing.

Mortensen ran towards him, her clothes streaked with mud and her hair loose, tight curls bobbing around her face. Blake was relieved to see no sign of a gunshot wound.

'Are you okay?' he shouted.

'I'm fine. What happened to Vaughn?' Mortensen

431

asked.

'I shot him.'

'Is he dead?'

'Only a flesh wound sadly,' said Blake sitting up.

From under her belly of the Cessna they saw the movement of shadows. No doubt Vaughn being helped back on board by Pitts. The plane turned in a sharp arc to line-up on the runway again, the engines roaring.

'What now?' Mortensen yelled over the noise. The Cessna was already accelerating along the airstrip, rumbling over the rough concrete.

'We have to stop it taking off. Aim for the engine housings or the landing gear.'

Mortensen didn't need to be told twice. She broke into a sprint alongside Blake with her Glock in her hand. Blake emptied what was left in his ammo clip more in frustration than in any realistic hope of hitting a vital area of mechanics as the Cessna pulled away. It hurtled along the concrete airstrip, building speed until its nose pitched up and it climbed sharply into the air.

Blake pulled up with his lungs burning and his heart racing. There was nothing he could do but watch the aircraft disappear into the low cloud. Mortensen jogged up to him a second or two later. Her breathing was hard and heavy.

'They've gone,' she said, unnecessarily.

'At least we know where they're going. We need to get a flight,' said Blake, retrieving his phone from the front pocket of his jeans. He called up one of the few numbers he stored in a contacts file and waited for a connection.

Harry Patterson answered his mobile after two rings. 'Blake?'

'We've lost them.'

Patterson's voice on the other end of the line was muffled, as if he was juggling the handset between his jaw and shoulder. 'Where?'

'We're still on the Isle of Skye. I presume by now you

know about Elias's brother, Benjamin, and his work at a secret laboratory on the island?'

Patterson hesitated. 'Yes, I've been briefed. He was working on a Government-funded project to stop the spread of avian flu.'

'Harry, he was involved in the creation of a modified super virus.'

'Yes,' said Patterson, matter-of-factly. 'Did Vaughn and Pitts manage to acquire any samples?'

'Four test-tubes, about twenty millilitres. We tracked them to an airport on the island but we weren't able to stop them escaping. They were picked up by a light aircraft. Vaughn's injured but they both escaped I'm afraid.'

'And the Pitts' family?'

'Being looked after by the local emergency services. We think Vaughn and Pitts are heading for a rendezvous in Norway, possibly to meet with their contact. If we can get there we might be able to stop them. Can you track the plane?'

'Give me the details.'

Blake reeled off the registration number of the Cessna that he recalled had been stencilled along the side of its fuselage. 'We think it's heading for a place called Stord.' He pronounced it "Stoit" but spelled it for Patterson. 'It's near Bergen.'

'I'll get our boys onto it.' Blake could hear the rustle of paper as he wrote down everything Blake had told him.

'It's not too late to stop this thing, Harry, but you've got to get us off this island. We're still at the airfield at Broadford. The airstrip's a bit on the short side but it's not in bad condition. If you can get us an aircraft as soon as possible we can pursue.'

'I'll do what I can. Stand-by.'

Twenty minutes later, a police car screamed to a halt in front of the aircraft hangar at Broadford airport and a young-looking constable jumped out of the passenger seat.

'Major Blake?'

Blake nodded. He despised anyone addressing him by his former rank since he'd been discharged from the Army but he let it go.

'We were told you needed a pilot in a hurry.'

The officer opened a rear door. A middle-aged man with a grey beard and glasses appeared with a smile that lacked assurance.

'Meeson Heath,' he said, extending a hand. 'They told me you need a plane?'

'We thought a plane was being sent for us,' said Mortensen as Heath headed off in the direction of the hangar. She traded Blake a puzzled look.

'Oh, I see.' Heath stopped in his tracks. 'I was told there was an emergency. They asked if I could help out,' he said, indicating to the police officer who remained standing by the car. 'He said you needed to get off the island as a matter of urgency? Government business?' He whispered the last sentence as if he'd been made privy to some kind of conspiracy. 'I wasn't doing much so I thought, what the hell. Now give me a minute or two and I'll get our ride sorted.'

The pilot disappeared inside the hangar while Blake and Mortensen waited on the apron.

'They've sent you to fly us?' Mortensen called after him.

Heath reappeared with an oily rag in his hands. 'I'm sorry, I assumed you were expecting me?'

'Not exactly,' said Blake, reaching for his phone again. He jabbed at the screen with his index finger, found Patterson's number and redialled. It only rang once.

'Harry, what's going on? I said arrange a flight off the island, not send a weekend pilot from the local flying club.'

'It's the best we could do at short notice,' said Patterson. 'Try to show some appreciation. Now, the good news is the Navy are tracking the Cessna and just as you said it looks like the plane's en route for Scandinavia. There's a destroyer on exercise in the North Atlantic not far from where you are. They have a radar locked on it.'

'Are they going to bring it down?'

Patterson sighed. A drawn-out breath. 'Blake, we're not contemplating shooting it down. That would be…' he struggled for the right word, '…inappropriate at this stage.'

'Inappropriate? You understand what happens if they make that rendezvous?'

'It's complicated.'

'They're over international waters. Shoot down the Goddamn plane before it's too late. Make it look like an accident.'

Blake watched Heath haul a single-prop Piper Arrow onto the apron, duck under its short wings and begin a series of pre-flight checks around the exterior of the aircraft.

'And when crash investigators find the wreckage and piece together that the plane was taken out by a British missile? What then? How's that going to look?'

'A whole lot better than when they find out that the British military had a chance to stop the virus being sold to terrorists and they did nothing.'

'It's not as simple as that. The aircraft's registered in Belgium, for a start. They'll want their own investigation.'

'Then tell them the truth. The pilot's unavoidable collateral.'

'It's not an option,' said Patterson firmly. 'And besides, there's no guarantee the virus would be destroyed.'

'A high altitude explosion over the North Atlantic? I think the odds would be pretty good.'

'It's not going to happen.'

'Why? I don't get it.'

Meeson Heath sprung up onto one of the Piper's wings with the energy of a younger man and jumped into the cockpit to continue his preparations.

'Look, if you're right and the rendezvous with the

435

Iranians is at this place in Norway, then there's still a chance to intercept them,' said Patterson.

'Sounds to me like you're trying to cover up the theft.'

'I've made arrangements for you to be flown to Inverness airport where you can pick up a direct flight to Bergen,' Patterson continued.

'The question is why. Who's arse are you trying to cover?'

'We're not trying to cover anyone's arse. We're trying to locate a virus before it falls into the wrong hands.'

'Of course, if the virus was illegally manufactured in the face of an international ban, that would explain everything. Certainly it would account for the secrecy surrounding the Skyelab laboratories.'

'The Norwegian authorities have been alerted. We've asked for them to provide surveillance on Vaughn and Pitts but not to intervene until we get there. They seem happy to co-operate and will allow us to make the arrests.'

'You told them about the virus?'

'Of course not. No sense in causing them to panic. A senior team from the Norwegian Police Service will pick you up when you get to Bergen. The rest is up to you. Good luck.'

Heath was finishing up when Blake ended the call.

'Hop in,' he said, opening a door over the wing.

Mortensen climbed into the back, settling into a well-worn leather seat. Blake took his place in the front next to the pilot and strapped himself in as the plane rolled onto the runway, past the bullet-ridden hire car that remained embedded in a bank. Heath stared at the wreck but said nothing.

They came to rest at the end of the airstrip while Heath conducted a brief conversation with air traffic control.

'Ready?' asked Heath.

When Blake nodded, they pitched forwards, accelerating along the bumpy concrete with the engine racing. Before they knew it they were levelling out over the top of a thin layer of stratus and into bright sunshine and blue skies.

The vibration of his phone ringing in his pocket surprised Blake. He hadn't anticipated he'd pick up a signal while they were airborne. Heath shot him a look.

'You can't use that up here,' his voice crackled in Blake's ears. 'It'll interfere with the navigation systems.'

'It's urgent. I won't be long,' said Blake, knocking his headset from one ear to answer the call. He'd recognised Harry Patterson's number.

Patterson's voice was distant and distorted. It dropped in and out as they reached the limit of a signal that wasn't designed to be picked up in the skies.

'Harry, we should make Inverness in less than half an hour. What's up?'

'Bad news, I'm afraid. The Navy say they've lost the Cessna.'

'What? How did they manage to lose it?'

'I mean it's vanished. One minute it was there, the next it was gone. I've just had word. We're trying to find out exactly what happened but it looks as though there was a mid-air explosion. It seems they've been blown clean out of the sky.'

Chapter 28

A dwarfish grey Westland Lynx helicopter with pumped-up muscular lines was waiting for them at Inverness. Its navigator was a tall, lean airman with perfect teeth. He met Blake and Mortensen in a pre-fabricated hut that passed as a heliport lounge, tucked away behind the main airport terminal building. He introduced himself as Lieutenant Peter Hawkes.

'Major Blake?' he said, approaching them with a chipped flight helmet tucked under his arm. Blake shook his hand and introduced Mortensen. 'We're planning to fly you straight to the crash site if that's okay?'

'I thought Patterson was arranging a direct flight to Norway?' said Mortensen.

'That's fine,' said Blake. 'We need to find out what happened to that plane and whether the virus survived. Has the Coastguard been notified?'

'Yes, Sir,' said Hawkes. 'Their rescue chopper was scrambled from Shetland.'

'As eyes only?'

'They're under strict instructions to keep out of the water. We've also imposed a five mile exclusion zone. Fishing vessels in the area have been told to keep clear.'

Hawkes had them pull on olive-coloured flight suits and handed them tough black boots made of cracked leather.

'The chopper's ready to go when you are,' he said, then waited patiently as they pulled on lifejackets and stuffed foam noise defenders into their ears. 'Hopefully we can eyeball the wreck site before returning to HMS Dashing.'

438

They fastened on helmets and the airman led them from the building, around the back of an enormous hangar and onto a helipad where the Lynx was waiting. They were struck by the potent fumes of hot exhaust gases and aviation fuel, the bone-rattling noise of the engines and the rhythmic beat of its rotor blades.

The Lynx was one of the Royal Navy's favoured aircraft, a jack-of-all trades that could be fitted with air-to-surface missiles, torpedoes and submarine-busting depth charges but was also compact enough to operate from a fleet of frigates and destroyers. Blake and Mortensen took seats in the rear bay on opposite sides of a central canvas bench. Strapped themselves in and plugged communication cables into their helmets

The pilot, his face obscured by a mirrored visor, turned in his seat and gave them the thumbs-up. The aircraft shuddered violently as he opened the rotor throttle and a moment later they were lifting off, rotating through ninety degrees as the pilot concentrated on working the collective control and foot pedals. He swung to a north-easterly direction and zipped across the airport runway. A blue and white passenger aircraft was stationary at one end, its take-off held up by their departure.

They flew low and fast, the land quickly giving way to a sea of dark and uninviting waters with white caps whipped up on the surface by the turbulence of the rotors. Ahead the cloud hung over the horizon as a thick, grey soup making it difficult to determine where the sky ended and the sea began.

'We should be over the wreck site within fifty minutes,' Hawkes' voice hissed over the intercom system.

Blake closed his eyes. The noise and vibration helped him to fall asleep almost instantly, his mind drifting into an oblivion of emptiness he was so tired.

He woke to the sound of Hawkes' distorted voice almost an hour later. 'The Coastguard helo has found some debris. They've sent us co-ordinates. We should be there in a few minutes,' he said.

Blake sat upright and leaned forwards to peer out at the sea below. Mortensen shuffled in her seat behind him.

The darkness of the early evening was drawing in but there was no mistaking the remains of the aircraft scattered in the rolling waters. It was as though someone had torn a sheet of paper into a thousand shards and thrown them to the wind. Some unidentifiable scraps of metal were still burning. Others bobbed aimlessly on the swell. It was hard to believe that all the fragments had once fitted together to form an aircraft.

'Can you give us a wide sweep of the area?' Blake asked the pilot.

The helicopter banked sharply upwards until they had a panoramic view of the site. On the horizon, Blake spotted flashing red and white lights he presumed was the Coastguard.

'There's the tail,' said Blake. A large section of metal that had largely retained its shape was semi-submerged in the dark seas. Nearby a chunk of white aluminium with ragged edges rolled on the current. Two letters in dark paint were clearly visible. They matched a section of the registration number Blake had noted earlier on the fuselage of the Cessna.

'That's definitely our plane,' he said to no one in particular. 'Has the Coastguard identified any survivors?'

'Negative,' said Hawkes. 'It's unlikely anyone survived. The best we can hope for is bodies but there's not going to be much left to find if the plane disintegrated in mid-air.'

'Is it possible the plane was damaged before it took off?' asked Mortensen.

'If we'd managed a lucky shot in Skye, the plane wouldn't have taken off, let alone have travelled half-way across the North Atlantic,' said Blake. 'And I doubt that a nine millimetre round could have done this much damage anyway.'

'So what then?'

'I don't know. It's one for the crash investigators. Let's worry about what happened to Vaughn and Pitts? If they're dead, I want proof.'

'And the virus?'

'Let's hope it was obliterated.'

'I'm afraid we're going to need to return to the ship shortly, Sir,' said Hawkes. 'We're running low on fuel.'

'That's fine. I've seen enough from up here. I need to take a closer look anyway.'

The helicopter banked away from the flotsam and set a heading directly north, skimming low over the waves. After fifteen minutes the shape of a warship loomed on the horizon. It had a sleek silhouette with steep angular lines conceived to generate a low radar signature. HMS Dashing was one of the Royal Navy's newest Type-45 destroyers, a modern generation of stealth ships that wasn't pretty but was effective at hiding from the enemy. It was crammed with technology, most of it in the ugly one hundred foot tower and domed radar unit perched above the bridge and which allowed it to track more than a thousand targets from up to 250 miles away – good enough to single-handedly defend London from an aerial attack.

The helicopter landed with a gentle bump on a narrow deck. Blake and Mortensen jumped out and were escorted into an aircraft hangar busy with mechanics and hardware where they were greeted by a young lieutenant commander with a wide smile and a warm welcome.

'If you'd like to follow me I'll take you to your quarters to freshen up,' he said.

'I need to visit the crash site before we lose the last of the light. Can you find me a boat?' Blake asked. He wasn't keen on waiting until the morning when the seas would have had a chance to disperse the wreckage far and wide.

The officer hesitated for a moment. 'Yes, of course,' he said with a forced smile.

'I'll stay,' said Mortensen. 'I'd like to talk to the team

who were tracking the plane.'

'We can arrange that.' The officer summoned a rating who led her inside the vessel, and then shouted orders for a rigid inflatable boat to be made ready for immediate departure.

The only way onto the RIB was by clambering down a cargo net attached to the side of the ship and jumping on board as it rose and fell several metres under a heavy swell. Half a dozen men wearing blue overalls, helmets and serious expressions were waiting for Blake. He landed heavily, losing his footing as the boat rocked on a rising wave he hadn't seen coming. He grabbed the back of a seat to keep himself from falling.

The bosun didn't wait for Blake to compose himself. He backed the RIB away from the warship and, as soon as there was clear water between them, threw the throttles forwards, the Yanmar engine responding with a powerful urgency.

The boat rode the waves like a marlin chasing a school of fish, jumping from the water on every rising swell and crashing back down on its belly with a jarring thud when gravity regained its grip. As they approached the crash zone, the gloom of the night sky was already descending, making the job of finding anything significant in the debris even more difficult.

'We're looking for bodies and a silver case,' Blake shouted over the din of the engine and the crashing bow-wave. 'But don't touch anything. If you see something, shout. Is that clear?'

There was a general muttering from the grim-faced sailors. None seemed particularly pleased to have been volunteered for an unplanned early evening trip. The bosun cut the power as they approached and evidence of the wrecked plane soon became apparent. High-powered searchlights penetrated the murk, sending bright beams of white light reflecting over the surface of the water. As they drifted through scraps of plastic, foam and wood, Blake clambered into the bow and flattened himself on the rubber tubing. Others took up positions to create a 360-degree lookout.

With the engine idling, Blake was struck by the eerie silence of the North Atlantic. The wind had unexpectedly dropped and the sea quelled. There was hardly any sound over the men's breathing other than the slap of waves against the hull. They picked their way through the flotsam, identifying nylon straps, cardboard, insulating fleece and twisted fragments of metal from the fuselage, but nothing that remotely resembled the silver case containing the four test-tubes.

After forty minutes the crew became restless. It was cold and almost dark. Blake was thinking about calling off the search for the night when the RIB brushed against a long shard of aluminium the size of a scaffold plank. It looked as though it was probably from a wing. Its edges were torn and ragged. In places the paint was blackened and chipped. Blake reached over the hull and grabbed one end. It struck him as odd that it was sitting so high in the water. It lifted easily and when Blake saw what had been propping it up, he tossed it to one side.

An organic mass bobbed to the surface. A human body lying face down in the water with a mop of black hair spread out around its skull in an almost perfect circle. One arm was twisted from the elbow at an unnatural angle. The other was missing, torn from its shoulder socket. It took three of them to pull the corpse on board and as they lifted it from the water they saw its legs were missing too. Both limbs had been cleanly amputated above the knee leaving fleshy stumps of muscle and bone.

The corpse thudded into the bottom of the boat and the crew crowded around. Someone shone a torch over Blake's shoulder lighting up an unfamiliar face. Most of the man's forehead and one of his eye sockets was missing. In its place was an ugly star-shaped wound where flesh and bone had been blown away.

Chapter 29

Mortensen was sitting at a table in the officers' mess with the ship's commander when Blake returned. He stooped through a low entrance hatch, reminding himself why the Royal Navy had never been a career option for someone of his height. All the low beams and watertight hatches would have meant a lifetime of bumped heads and mild concussion.

The officer jumped from his seat. He was a small man with a shock of black hair tinged with grey and two gold epaulettes on the shoulders of his black sweater.

'Commander John Saxby,' he said, gripping Blake's hand firmly. Blake caught the aroma of strong aftershave, an old-fashioned scent that reminded him of his grandfather. The commander ushered him to a seat next to Mortensen and beckoned to a steward to bring them coffee.

Mortensen had stripped out of her flying overalls but still wore the heavy black boots with her business suit. 'Did you find anything?' she asked, as Blake slumped into a chair.

'A body but no sign of the case.'

'Pitts?'

Blake shook his head. The steward approached their table with a silver pot and thick white cups and saucers balanced on a tray. He laid them out with a jug of cream and a pot of brown sugar rocks.

'It's the pilot,' Blake said when the steward retreated. 'Shot before the crash and with half his face missing.'

Mortensen was about to take a sip of coffee. Her hand stopped half way to her mouth. 'Shot?'

'A bullet in the back of the head. Not much of an entry wound, so probably fired at close range.'

'An execution? But why shoot the pilot?'

Blake had no answer. He took a mouthful of coffee. It was strong and hot.

'At least that explains the crash,' Mortensen continued. 'They had an argument, killed the pilot and the Cessna ditched into the sea.'

'It doesn't explain the explosion though. And who in their right mind shoots the pilot of a plane mid-way across the North Atlantic, argument or not?'

'Maybe the pilot was threatening to blackmail them? Or was demanding more money? What about the case? Any sign of it?'

Blake shook his head. Saxby had been listening with interest. He leaned forwards with his arms on the table juddering from the power of the two 25-megawatt gas turbine engines in the belly of the warship.

'Could you kindly explain what's going? I was given orders to track a light aircraft from Scotland supposedly because it was carrying two escaped British prisoners. Why the interest from MI5?'

Blake set his cup down on a saucer. 'It's a sensitive issue,' he said.

'And I signed the Official Secrets Act too,' said Saxby.

'There were two escaped prisoners on that plane.' Blake lowered his voice. He was conscious the mess hatch was open and there was a constant flow of people passing. 'Our interest is in an experimental virus they stole from a laboratory on the Isle of Skye. It was developed by British scientists researching a vaccine for a bird flu mutation. If it's released into the environment it has the potential to infect millions of people. The men who stole it were on their way to trade it with an Iranian terrorist.'

'I see,' said Saxby. 'And the virus was on the plane?'

Blake nodded. 'So you can understand our urgency to search the crash site as soon as possible.'

'And what were you hoping to find? This virus couldn't possibly have survived an explosion.'

'Ideally? A couple of bodies and a silver case containing four test-tubes. So far we have the body of the pilot and a hell of a mess. The best outcome is our escapees have been killed and the virus vaporised, but I'd like some proof.'

'And if you can't find it?'

Blake shrugged. 'I guess we keep looking.'

'The Coastguard has been using thermal imaging to look for any survivors. If your prisoners haven't been found by now then it's safe to assume they're dead but you may never recover their bodies. The ocean is a cruel mistress. As for the case, it's more than likely on the seabed. That's about two thousand metres below us, about the safest place it could be. No one's going to find it down there.'

'I hope you're right,' said Mortensen.

Saxby's eyes drifted to the door. Blake subconsciously followed his gaze and saw another officer waiting patiently to attract the captain's attention.

Saxby beckoned him in. 'Ms Mortensen, I think you've met our principal warfare officer, Lieutenant Commander Hughes?'

'He kindly talked me through the radar operations and how you tracked the Cessna before it disappeared,' she said with a smile in his direction.

'I'm sorry to interrupt, Sir, but there's something I thought you should know,' he said, stepping across the room and hovering by the table. 'I've had the operators review the radar imagery in case there was something we missed.' He turned his attention to Blake and Mortensen. 'Advanced technology means our systems can store a large amount of radar images that we constantly record from a 250-mile radius around the ship. It's all kept on a hard drive. It's a lot of data and sometimes things get overlooked,' he explained.

'And?' said Saxby.

'We concentrated specifically on the immediate crash zone and rolled back to an hour before we lost contact with the plane. There was a boat, Sir, within half a mile of where the wreckage was found. It had been anchored in the same location for several hours.'

'A fishing boat?'

'I don't think so. The signature was all wrong and, besides, fishing boats don't tend to weigh anchor in the middle of the North Atlantic.'

'What are you trying to say?' asked Blake.

'Well, within minutes of the plane disappearing the boat was gone. The radar imaging shows it set off at high speed on a north-easterly bearing.'

'Are you still tracking it?' asked Blake.

'Of course,' said Hughes. 'It appears to be making a direct course for the Norwegian coast.'

Chapter 30

The Princess V56 was skimming across the ocean in excess of thirty knots. Rolling and pitching, its fibreglass hull thudding through the swell. Below deck, a nauseous wave rose from the pit of Ricky Vaughn's stomach. His face flushed and a hot sweat broke over his brow. Closing his eyes only made it worse. He'd remembered from somewhere that focusing on a single point was a good way of overcoming sea sickness. He tried fixing on a light fitting in the galley opposite and inhaled lungfuls of air through his nose. It didn't make any difference. His head was thick and fuzzy and he had to concentrate hard on keeping the contents of his stomach down. And every time the vessel crashed over the top of a wave, a dagger of pain exploded down his arm and across his chest. A handful of pills had taken the edge off but he wasn't going to get better with a bullet lodged in his shoulder. The crew had done their best to patch him up. They'd cleaned and bandaged the wound and hung his arm in a sling around his neck. But he needed a surgeon, anaesthetic and a few weeks' recovery. None of which was an imminent prospect. Still, there'd be plenty of time to worry about his health when they'd delivered the virus.

It was all right for Pitts. As soon as they'd been hauled on board he'd found a cabin below deck and fallen into a deep slumber on one of the king-size beds below deck. The thunderous reverberation of his snoring reminded Vaughn that he was suffering no ill-effects from the journey.

A judder from the engines was the first sign of a problem. It was as though they were running low on diesel or there was dirt in the fuel lines. Vaughn knew he should have been concerned. They were in the middle of the ocean and a good two hours away from the coast. But as the powerboat slowed he was relieved. His nausea eased a little as the pitching and rolling subsided. Eventually the engines died completely and the vessel was left bobbing gently on the rolling swell.

One of the Norwegian crew members stuck his blond head through a hatch.

'Small mechanical problem. Engine is overheating. Soon have it fixed,' he said.

Vaughn heard footsteps clattering over the deck. He raised his good arm, gave a thumbs-up and the Norwegian disappeared. He struggled to sit upright, dragged his feet together and felt the hard edge of the silver case he'd stowed on the floor. He reached for it, set it on the table and flicked open its metal catches. Inside four glass test-tubes sealed with orange plastic caps were lined up in their tight-fitting polystyrene lining. He plucked one out between a thumb and forefinger, rolled it on its side and watched the viscous liquid flow lazily along the glass.

'What are you doing?'

He hadn't heard Pitts emerge from his cabin. His lank hair looked even more unkempt than usual. His eyes were bleary with sleep.

'I was curious to know what twenty five million pounds looks like,' said Vaughn.

Pitts shrugged. He knew exactly what twenty five million pounds looked like. It looked like green numbers flashing on a computer screen. In the good old days. Before the crash. 'Put it back,' he said.

'What?'

'I said put it back.'

'Screw you.'

'I'm not joking. You don't know what you're doing.'

Vaughn's eyes burned. 'Don't tell me what to do.'

'Smash that tube and you sign our death warrants. Weren't you listening to Benjamin? A couple of drops and we'll both be infected. Then it's an inevitable, slow death. Like the sound of that? Now put it back.'

'I don't like your tone,' said Vaughn, setting the vial on the table. It rolled across the polished surface. Pitts held his breath as it came to rest with a gentle chink on a raised lip. 'Speak to me like that again and I'll blow your brains out, you jumped-up public-school prick.'

Vaughn had reached for his handgun. He aimed for the centre of Pitts' forehead, right between his piggy eyes. He stared at Pitts' face, puffy and bloated, feeling something between pity and revulsion. Even incarcerated within the confines of a maximum security prison he'd kept to a strict exercise regime that maintained his muscle tone. Pitts' body was a corpulent disgrace. He had a physique that had grown fat on a lifestyle of riches. His skin was pasty and his stomach bloated.

'Ricky, come on,' Pitts said softly. 'We're partners aren't we?'

When Pitts started scratching the back of his hand, Vaughn felt his trigger-finger twitch. 'Partners in crime? Don't make me laugh you fat freak. I don't need you any more.'

The test-tube rolled across the table. Pitts' eyes darted between the gun and the virus. His pupils were full and black.

'Not looking good for you right now, is it?' Vaughn was enjoying Pitts' obvious discomfort.

'You need me.'

'I don't need you.'

'It's my deal.'

'Correction. It was your deal.'

'My plan. My deal. My virus.'

'Not any more, sunshine. It was a good plan but we all have to adapt to survive. Didn't they teach you that at university?'

It was true. It was a decent plan that had largely worked out, apart from the incident at the airport in Skye. But a flesh wound to Vaughn's shoulder was a small price to pay for a twenty five million pound jackpot. And they were almost home and dry. It had been easy to persuade the lily-livered pilot to reduce the Cessna's cruising speed and altitude as they headed out into the Atlantic. A nudge in the back of his neck with the cold steel of Vaughn's nine millimetre Sig Sauer had done the trick. He'd put up little resistance when they'd demanded he depressurised the cabin. That was Pitts' idea. No good killing the pilot and finding the air pressure had sealed the door closed. Vaughn had made him switch on the auto-pilot and then shot him. The bullet barely left a mark in the back of his skull. It made a mess of the dashboard though. A pebble dash of blood, bone and brains that splattered the dials and peppered the windscreen.

The Norwegian powerboat crew were waiting exactly where they said they'd be. Two giant men with forearms like girders had dragged Vaughn and Pitts on board after they'd parachuted into the sea. The captain of the vessel had put himself in charge of detonating the bomb, using a mobile phone to trigger a device hidden in the parcel that Bogaert had unwittingly stowed in the hold.

'You want more money? Is that it?' asked Pitts.

'I don't want more money. I'm taking all the money.'

'You know I could have asked anyone in that stinking jail to get me out. But I chose you. I trusted you. I offered you a fair deal, half the money for helping me get the virus and deliver it safely.'

'Maybe you're a bad judge of character. The thing is you needed my help but now I don't need you. I have the virus and you have nothing,' said Vaughn.

'Think you're smarter than me? So go ahead, shoot me. Let's finish it here and now.'

Pitts lifted his chin and threw up his arms. Vaughn's

finger twitched again. The knuckles on his gun-hand were white.

'But first let me ask one question.' Vaughn let the barrel of his gun drop a fraction. 'Where is the rendezvous with Khan? I assume you must know if you feel confident enough to kill me? I mean you might have the virus but do you have the contacts to sell it?'

Vaughn's twisted mouth turned up in an ugly smile. 'You already told me, you fool. It's a place called "Stort".'

'The island or somewhere in the municipality?'

Vaughn's grin fell from his face.

'The fact is you have no idea and without knowing where the rendezvous is that virus is worthless. No deal, no cash.'

'Tell me,' demanded Vaughn.

'And if I do? What then? You'll shoot me. Not much of an incentive. And don't think the crew have any idea either. They're under instructions to deliver us into harbour and that's it.'

Vaughn lowered his gun. 'I could make this very painful for you. Are you a Tarantino fan?'

'What?'

'Quentin Tarantino? Reservoir Dogs? I love that film. Remember how it starts with Mr Orange shot in the stomach and bleeding, a lot, after a robbery's that's gone tits up? He knows he's dying but Mr White tells him that although it's painful to be hit in the stomach, it's not as painful as being shot in the knee.'

Pitts' eyes followed the barrel of Vaughn's gun as it came to rest aimed at his legs.

'It's called kneecapping. It's supposed to be the most painful place to be shot without killing someone. Something to do with the bone and cartilage and muscle fibres or something. But mostly it's about the bone. So, where's the rendezvous?'

A defiant smile crept over Pitts' lips. 'Screw you.'

'Problem?' said a voice.

The captain had appeared from the deck above, an MP5 slung over his shoulder. He ran a hand through the thick black beard that covered most of his face.

Vaughn glanced over his shoulder without lowering his weapon. 'No problem,' he said, as the engines coughed and growled back into life.

'Problem's been fixed,' said the captain. 'We're about to get going again.'

Vaughn saw his eyes were focused on the silver case lying open with the tops of the test-tubes exposed. Vaughn dropped his gun in his lap and snatched the loose tube from the table. He slipped it back into its slot in the polystyrene.

'Thank you,' he said, as the bow of the vessel rose up under the power of the twin 900hp engines and a spasm made an unwelcome return in his stomach.

Chapter 31

The ship was alive with the quiet efficiency of a crew who knew intuitively what they were doing, a slick operation produced from years of training. Blake was standing alongside Commander Saxby on the bridge watching a radar screen glowing green. The white blip that interested them was on the far edge of the circle, moving at speed towards the Norwegian coast. The vessel had stopped briefly, for some unknown reason, but was back at full velocity.

'I think it's unlikely we'll be able to head her off,' said Saxby, frowning as he glanced up from the screen to peer out into the void of darkness beyond the Dashing's bow. Her Rolls Royce gas turbines had her cutting through the water like a dagger through silk, a foamy trail churned up in her wake. 'They're managing at least 30 knots. We don't have much more than that and we're running at full speed.'

Blake moved away from the radar and stepped between a gap in a bank of screens that stretched across the front of the bridge. An officer at each position was focusing on their various displays. Blake grabbed a pair of binoculars and directed them at a point he guessed was the horizon, searching for lights or a sign of the boat they were pursuing. Mortensen came up behind him.

'We're not to going make it,' she said. 'Time to start thinking about a Plan B.'

'I'm not sure I had much to offer in the way of a Plan A,' said Blake, chewing his lip.

'We still have time to cut them off before they make it to Stord. Could we intercept them by helicopter?'

'Sir, we're approaching the two mile mark,' one of the

455

officers sitting near Saxby called out.

Saxby acknowledged the information and issued a quietly-spoken order. 'Hard on starboard on my command,' he said. 'Standby for my mark.'

'What are you doing? You're calling off the chase?' said Blake.

'We're on the limit of Norwegian territorial waters. We can't go any further.'

'We're NATO allies. We have an agreement to operate in each other's waters.'

'Yes, and I'm sure our Norwegian friends would be very happy to see us. But we can't just drop in unannounced. They'll want to know why. Do you want to tell them?'

Blake stared at the commander, who met his eye and held it.

'No,' said Blake at last.

'I thought not.'

'So what now?' said Mortensen. 'We can't just give up.'

Blake mulled over the possibilities. There was no way the commander was going to allow his ship to cross into Norwegian waters and any other visible encroachment was going to require an explanation they didn't want to give.

'We'll sneak in,' said Blake.

'How?'

'Commander, how would you feel about lending us your RIB again?'

The ride was cold and wet. Blake sat on the floor in the bow next to Mortensen, resting his back against the engine housing and clinging to a rope that looped around the boat's rubber hull. Behind them a grim-faced helmsman perched on the edge of his seat gripping a chrome steering wheel in both hands. Two Royal Marines Saxby had insisted on sending had taken up positions aft with SA80 rifles resting in their laps.

They made quick time crashing over the lumpy sea and

soon the hull of the warship faded into the inky night. The Pacific 22 rigid inflatable was designed for speed and manoeuvrability, not for protecting its passengers from the elements. Blake was soon drenched by a shower of salty spray. Ahead a dark outcrop took shape jutting into the water where the coast loomed. Beyond the headland twinkling lights of towns and villages appeared.

They sped into a wide inlet cut into a shadowy landscape shaped by steep cliffs and illuminated by the ghostly light of a half-moon. The helmsman kept them close to the shore, avoiding the shipping channels but where razor-sharp rocks peaked dangerously out of the water. When he shouted to Blake his words were inaudible over the buzz of the engine. Blake stood and leaned closer.

'It looks like the boat's made harbour,' the helmsman said, easing back the throttles. The RIB slowed to swimming pace. He tapped a screen that was taking a direct feed from HMS Dashing's radar. A white dot blipped in the centre of a series of contracting circles.

'How quickly can we get there?'

'In no time at all.'

The harbour turned out to be a natural cove, an almost perfectly symmetrical horseshoe at the foot of a hill peppered with houses. Red and grey roofs of traditional Norwegian homes were visible in tiers among the vegetation. Two short piers came into view as they drifted around a peninsula. A small fleet of pleasure craft and fishing boats was moored up. One vessel stood out among the others. The Princess motor cruiser was tied up alongside the nearest pier. It was four times the size of the next biggest vessel, all sleek lines, sharp curves and tinted windows. Its hull had been finished in pearl white and trimmed with sparkling chrome handrails.

'I guess that's it,' Blake whispered to Mortensen, fearful the sound of his voice would carry.

'They're certainly not skimping on style.'

The sweet pungency of pine fused with the salt of the

sea floated on the breeze. Blake drew a deep breath and listened hard. Every sound registered loudly, from the slap of the current against the hull to the cry of a nocturnal creature from the woodland in the hills. A familiar tension tightened the muscles of his stomach. A reaction to the fear of the unknown. He drew his gun and directed the helmsman to take them closer.

They approached the stern of the Princess where a teak-decked platform protruded like a jutting bottom lip. It was either a low-level terrace for swimming or a landing stage for smaller craft. Or maybe both. Whatever its purpose it provided quick and easy access from the sea, which suited Blake perfectly. A light was on in an area Blake imagined was the main living quarters but there was no other sign of life on board. He stood in the bow of the RIB with one foot on the inflatable hull.

One of the Marines grabbed a mooring post on the pier and they came to rest within a couple of metres of the boat. Blake readied himself. He rocked on one leg, trying to judge the distance of his leap. He was about to jump when a sliding door opened on a deck above. A bearded man sloped out into the open and palmed a cigarette between his lips with a nonchalant cool.

Blake froze with his Browning levelled. He was close enough to put a bullet between the man's eyes. A match flared loud and bright in the silent darkness, lighting up a craggy face lined by age and exposure to the sun. The man drew hard on the tobacco and blew out the flame with a lungful of smoke. His shoulders relaxed with the hit of nicotine. He flicked the spent match over the side.

He stared into the distance, his attention on nothing in particular. A lazy disinterest in the village built into the hill. His gaze shifted to the pier and the fishing boats bobbing on the current. Which was when he saw an arm clinging to a mooring post and found it attached to the body of a Royal Marine with a rifle cocked in his direction. Four more faces were staring at him. For a split second nobody reacted.

Then everything happened at once.

First came the man's shout of alarm. A cry somewhere between an exclamation of surprise and a hollered order. In the same instant he snatched at an MP5 sub-machine gun hidden in the folds of his coat. He swung it in a fluid arc from a strap over his shoulder, firing a rapid volley of shots that somehow missed the RIB and hissed into the water. Muzzle flashes lit up the night. Blake stumbled backwards, knocking Mortensen off her feet.

The helmsman had seen the danger, threw the throttles into reverse and a surge from the two hundred horsepower engine pulled them out of the line of fire. A staccato crack of rifles opened up over Blake's head but the shots flew harmlessly into the air as the Marines were thrown off balance by the sudden acceleration.

Someone fired up the Princess' engines. They snarled with a resonant gurgle like the rumbling digestive system of a giant sea monster. Blake raised his head over the RIB's hull and saw a broiling froth emerge from under the teak platform. The shadow of a figure ran the length of a lower deck freeing the mooring lines and the boat heaved forwards. Its bow rose up and the vessel leapt forwards, charging for open water and spewing a foaming trail in its wake.

'Don't let them get away!' Blake shouted.

The helmsman reversed the thrust and after a brief moment where they seemed to tread water, the RIB shot forwards. It hit the Princess' choppy wake with a thud. The motor cruiser had already made some distance and was pulling away around a headland.

'Can we catch her?' Blake yelled over the din of the engines.

'We can make 27 knots, maybe more with a far wind but she'll be able to max out nearer 35. Best I can do is try to keep her in sight,' said the helmsman.

A quick calculation in Blake's head suggested that in

less than seven minutes the crew of the Princess would be able to pull out a lead of around a mile. Unless by some miracle she developed a mechanical problem. Blake tucked himself low into the bow. He squinted at the vanishing Princess. There had to be a way to stop her. He rose into a crouch and shuffled to the rear of the RIB. His progress was hampered by the instability of the vessel. He grabbed the sleeve of one of the Marines as the RIB was pitched sideways threatening to knock him off his feet.

'What's the effective range of your rifle?' Blake shouted in the Marine's ear.

'Around three hundred meters. Why?'

'How good's your shooting?'

The Marine had comic-book heroic features. A square jaw and steely, grey eyes. Clean cut and with a trace of acne that suggested he was barely out of his teens. Not that Blake underestimated his abilities. He knew the type. A man who knew no fear. A professional who'd stop at nothing to get his job done.

'If you're going to ask for a clean shot at that boat while we're bouncing around in this RIB, that's a tough challenge.'

'You have to try.' Blake stumbled as they hit a rogue wave at an oblique angle. 'It's the only way of stopping her. She's outrunning us by five to seven knots.'

'I'll give it my best,' he said but the look in his eye suggested he thought his chances were slim.

'Aim for the stern, above the waterline. Her engines are probably well protected within the hull but there's a chance you could hit a fuel line.'

The Marine crabbed past Blake with his green beret pulled low over his brow and took up a position on one knee with his rifle jammed into his shoulder. He squinted through an optic sight and wrapped a finger around the trigger. But every time he steadied himself for a shot his rifle was thrown askew by a jolt of the hull catching the heavy swell. So he opted to lay down a barrage of rapid fire, banking on the law of chance that at least one of the rounds might find its mark. He emptied his magazine, lowered his rifle and peered across the fjord. In the gloom it was impossible to tell whether the Princess had been hit. She certainly showed no sign of any ballistics damage.

The Marine turned to Blake with an apologetic look. 'I can't be sure I even came close,' he said.

The spluttering cough of one of the engines juddered through the hull.

'We're losing speed,' said a dark-haired Norwegian sitting at the helm.

The captain's eyes narrowed. They were almost out of sight of the chasing RIB. A few more minutes and they'd be clean away. It was poor timing. They should have concentrated on fixing the mechanical problem as soon as they made land. But then they hadn't anticipated this.

'Arnesen, go and fix it,' he said to a third man who nodded and disappeared down a flight of steps.

Jonas Lanvik turned up the collar of his coat against the cold and slotted a new magazine into his MP5. He had no idea who their pursuers were and he wasn't planning on waiting to find out. They'd made their intentions clear and if he'd not happened to step outside for a cigarette as they were preparing to board the Princess, they might all now be in custody. Whether it was a police or military patrol didn't really matter. The fact was they'd been discovered and his priority was to vanish. He'd make some enquiries later about how they'd been rumbled. It was no random patrol. Whoever was in the RIB had been acting on intelligence.

Arnesen reappeared out of breath, cleaning his hands on an oil-stained rag. 'It's the same engine, running too hot. A problem with the water filter or the impeller. Nothing I can fix while we're in the water. We'll have to make do on one engine.'

'Go look at it again,' said Lanvik. 'We'll be dead before

we get to a dry dock. Find a way.'

Arnesen rolled his eyes and dropped back below deck. The high-pitched engine hum of the RIB sounded a way off, behind them and slightly to their port side. Then an explosive starburst caught Lanvik's eye followed a fraction of a second later by a loud pop. Three long bursts of rifle fire followed but not a single round came remotely close. It was a desperate act. Lanvik fished in a pocket for a packet of cigarettes. He lit one and exhaled slowly.

'Look,' shouted Mortensen, 'I think we're gaining on them.' Her hair was crusted with salt and her cheeks vibrant with a ruddy glow.

Blake grabbed a pair of binoculars from the helmsman. Mortensen was right. Even from a distance, and through the darkness of the fjord, he could see the Princess's bow was riding lower in the water. She wasn't limping but someone had definitely cut her speed.

'Something's wrong,' said Blake.

'Did we hit her?'

'I can't see any damage but it's difficult to be sure.'

He had a good view of her broadside. One man was at the helm on an exposed fly bridge. He never once looked back. Kept his eyes on the way ahead. The window in the deck below was smoked for privacy and offered no view inside. It was more like a mirror than a window, reflecting the boat's foaming bow wave. Blake swept the binoculars along the vessel's sleek lines and found the bearded figure they'd surprised in the cove. He was standing with an arm gripping a gun and the other looped around a metal rail. A reminder that even if they were able to close the distance to the Princess they remained horribly exposed in the inflatable. The boat was quick and agile but its rubber tubing that kept them afloat was susceptible to bullet holes. Blake knew an attempt to draw alongside the Princess with its crew armed with sub-machine guns was nothing short of suicidal.

Mortensen tapped him on the elbow. 'Blake, look,' she said, pointing away to their left. Both boats were heading for a rocky mass that loomed out of the water. A row of flashing lights snaked their way in a long line across the horizon high above the land. At first Blake wondered if they might be the landing lights from planes. But they were static. Too low and too close together.

Through the binoculars he focused on one of the nearest lights. Indistinct against the night sky he saw the top of a towering concrete column. It was easily a hundred metres tall supporting a thick cable looping from the top and falling into the blackness below.

A bridge. Or more accurately a series of bridges.

They weren't heading towards a single land mass at all but a collection of islands spanning the fjord.

A buzz of machine gun fire crackled through the chill air. The bearded man in the stern of the Princess had opened fire as the RIB drew close. The star-shaped muzzle blasts briefly illuminated his upper body and revealed a face set with a determined grimace. The helmsman yanked hard on the wheel and flipped the RIB onto its port side veering clear of the deadly hail of bullets.

'Keep us just out of range of that gun but don't lose her whatever you do,' Blake shouted.

The helmsman nodded and manoeuvred the RIB. A third man appeared on the Princess and took up position on the bow deck with his arms over the silver railings and a weapon aimed in their direction.

'Stalemate,' said Mortensen.

'Not quite,' said Blake. 'Hold your position and whatever you do don't deviate from this course,' he said to the helmsman as the seed of a plan formed in his mind. Mortensen was right. They'd reached a stand-off. Unless they could regain the element of surprise.

An arrowhead of rock rose out of the water directly in their path. A peninsula that divided the fjord in two. On their current bearing, the RIB was heading for a passage to the east of the island. The Princess was steaming towards a channel on the opposite side and within minutes would disappear from view.

'Give it full throttle, everything you've got,' said Blake.

'We're going to lose them,' said Mortensen. She glanced at the approaching land mass.

'Let them see us racing ahead.'

The helmsman pushed the throttles to their stops and the RIB surged forwards past the first outcrop of rock. A moment later they lost sight of the Princess as it veered away to the west of the island.

'Now kill the engines and bring us around slowly,' said Blake.

The helmsman obeyed the instruction without question. He closed the throttles and the RIB slowed. He threw the wheel hard to the right and tickled the engine to bring the boat around to face the way they'd come.

'Follow the shoreline but don't break cover of the rock,' said Blake.

'Are you insane?' said Mortensen. 'We're losing them.'

'They're expecting us to appear on the other side of the island.'

'Where we can intercept them if we can get ahead.'

'And then what? They'll gun us down. Besides it's what they'll expect us to do. They can't outrun us so their best hope is to slip away in the darkness. If it was me, I'd wait until I was out of sight behind the island, turn around and head back. Hopefully I'd be able to find a sheltered cove to hide.'

'And if you're wrong?'

Blake moved behind the helmsman and tapped the radar screen on his console. 'Which one's the Princess?' The helmsman pointed to a bright white pixel. 'You mean the one that's turning and reversing course?' he said, looking at Mortensen with a triumphant smile.

'So you were right. We're still out-gunned.'

'But now we have the element of surprise.'

They heard the roar of an engine first. Then a flash of white emerged from the other side of a spine of rocks they were hidden behind, racing back along the channel in the direction of the cove where they had found the Princess moored.

'After her!' yelled Blake.

The helmsman had already opened the throttles and they shot into open water, hitting the Princess' wake with a thud that rolled them from one side to the other. Blake was grateful to see the bearded gunman had moved from the stern. There were now three figures standing together on the fly bridge with their backs to the RIB.

Blake waited in the bow with his foot on the hull urging the inflatable on. If they could make it to within a few metres of the motor cruiser he was confident he could leap onto the low stern deck. The helmsman was using all his years of experience to hold the inflatable steady against the turbulent, choppy water. Blake was coiled to spring when the Princess veered sharply away. At the same instant he was startled by a sharp crack of gunfire fired over his head by one of the Marines. The RIB broke to the right. Blake was thrown sideways and grabbed a handful of rope to stop himself falling overboard. Then the night lit up with a burst of automatic fire from the bridge of the Princess.

'Turn around and get back after them,' Blake shouted to the helmsman.

They'd lost their element of surprise. Time to throw caution to the wind. The RIB turned in a tight arc heading back towards the motor cruiser.

'Ride in her wake and get as close as you can.' The two Marines had their rifles primed, jammed into their shoulders and levelled at the Princess. 'Put down some covering fire.'

The RIB dropped back into the Princess' wake and quickly closed the distance. Blake settled himself in the bow with the wind in his hair and sea spray stinging his eyes. He concentrated on the teak-decked platform riding low over the waves, looking for a handhold to grab when he pounced. In the periphery of his vision he saw movement on the bridge. One of the Marines fired a controlled burst of three rounds and the Princess turned sharply off course, heading for the shore.

'I think I zapped one, Sir,' said the Marine with steely grey eyes. 'Target at the wheel went down.'

The Princess had been put on a collision course with a stony beach less than half a kilometre away. And kept going. No one on the boat reacted. It kept hurtling onwards, arcing gently to the left, eating up the water towards the shore. It hit the beach hard and flew straight out of the water. Her hull hissed through the wet shingle and came to an abrupt halt with her functioning propeller revolving at full speed, digging a hole in the ground and spitting stones and coarse sand into the air.

Chapter 32

Two men were sprawled in ugly contortions across the fly bridge. Blake wondered for a moment if they were both dead. Certainly the blond giant slumped over the wheel with the side of his head missing was showing no signs of life. His body was twisted and limp, thrown out of his chair onto a console of dials and screens. A second man was in a heap on the floor. The dark-haired captain, Jonas Lanvik, was lying face down with his coat crumpled around his body and the barrel of his MP5 protruding from under his arm.

Lanvik stirred as Blake approached. A groan slipped from somewhere at the back of his throat. Alive but unconscious. The bridge was covered with blood and brain matter. A viscous coating clung and dripped from the seats, deck and navigating console. But Blake was pretty sure the man on the floor hadn't been hit. More likely he'd been thrown off his feet when the Princess veered and been knocked unconscious as he fell.

Blake found a key still in the ignition lock and killed the engine. He wiped blood-sticky fingers on the back of his legs, failed to find a pulse on the man hanging over the steering wheel and turned his attention to Lanvik. He leant over him with his Browning aimed under his chin and pulled the MP5 clear of his body. The muzzle was still hot and the magazine spent. He tossed to one of the Marines who'd followed him on board.

'Nice shot,' said Blake, nodding to the dead blond at the wheel.

'He stood up and put his head in my sights,' the Marine

explained, as if justifying why he'd removed part of the man's skull.

'Good job.'

'What about him?' The Marine kicked Lanvik's feet with his boot.

'Concussed. Looks like he caught his head on the table on his way down but I think he'll be fine.'

Blake swept a patch of hair away from Lanvik's face looking for a head wound. He found nothing. He was about to search the captain's pockets for identity papers when his body twitched and Lanvik rolled groggily onto his back. His eyes sprung open and his expression twisted into a mixture of horror and surprise. He opened his mouth to speak but thought better of it when he saw the Browning in his face.

'Easy does it, sunshine. Now sit up, slowly.' Blake waved the gun in an upwards motion.

Lanvik's eyes fell on the Marine and the SA80 lined up with his chest as he eased himself into a sitting position.

'What's your name?' asked Blake.

Dark, resolute pupils stared back at him. The man's skin was like leather, tanned and lined from a life lived outdoors. Puffy bags sagged under his eyes but his beard was lustrously black and lacking any sign of grey.

Either he didn't understand the question or, as Blake suspected, he was being obdurate.

'Name?' Blake repeated.

The man jutted out his chin but kept his mouth shut.

'Let's not waste time with petty pleasantries then.' Blake raised his gun under Lanvik's nose. He didn't have time to play games. 'The two men you picked up earlier this afternoon, where are they?'

Lanvik's eyes flickered upwards for a fraction of a second. An involuntary tell that he'd just visualised the moment. 'I don't know what you're talking about,' he said.

'Don't lie. I need to know where Vaughn and Pitts are.'

No response.

'They had a small case with them. Did you see it?'

Another involuntary glance over Blake's shoulder.

'You took them to the harbour where we found you moored.' Blake said it more as a statement than a question. 'Where were they going?' Blake raised his voice.

No response.

'You want to do this the hard way?' Blake said lowering his Browning. He snatched Lanvik's wrist. He tugged it from his lap and forced it palm flat against the deck, pinning it down with the barrel of his gun. 'Where are Vaughn and Pitts?'

Lanvik drew a deep breath through his nose. His lips pursed tightly closed and his eyes widened.

'Blake!' Mortensen's voice echoed through the boat from the deck below. 'Blake, you need to see this.'

'I'll be right there,' he shouted back. He turned to the Marine standing with his rifle at his hip. 'Go and check she's all right.'

Blake watched him go, listening to his heavy footsteps before continuing. 'Just you and me now. Do you understand? Let's try a different approach.' His tone was softer. Calming.

He grabbed the man by his shoulders, swung him through ninety degrees and tapped his forehead with two fingers. 'Sleep,' he said, and instantly Lenvik's eyes fell closed and his body went limp. Blake intoned soothing words into his ear until he was satisfied Lanvik was completely under. He laid the flaccid body on the deck and crossed the captain's hands over his stomach.

'Blake? You need to come see this.' Mortensen's head peeked through the stairwell. 'What are you doing?'

'Finding out where Vaughn and Pitts are.'

'Blake, this really can't wait.'

'I'll be there in a minute,' he said. Mortensen caught the sharpness in his tone. 'What's your name?' he asked the soporific Norwegian.

'Jonas Lenvik.'

'And you're the skipper?'

'Yes.'

'Do you know the two Englishmen Ricky Vaughn and Elias Pitts?'

'We picked them up after they jumped from their plane.'

'Why did they jump?'

'To make it look like they'd been killed, in case the British authorities were following them.'

'So they blew up their own plane to cover their tracks? How?'

'A bomb in the hold that was detonated by a mobile phone call.'

Blake glanced at Mortensen who was standing motionless halfway up the stairs. 'And you did that from the boat?'

'Yes,' said Lenvik.

'Did Vaughn and Pitts have a silver case with them?'

'Yes.'

'Do you know what was in it?'

'They said it was important and they needed to deliver it to Khan.'

'Who's Khan?'

'The contact they're meeting.'

'Our Iranian agent,' said Blake, raising his eyes at Mortensen. 'Did you see what was in the case?'

'Four test-tubes. The two Englishmen were arguing about them.'

'What did they say?'

'The man called Vaughn was threatening to kill the other one.'

'Where's the meeting with Khan?'

'A house at Mortjorna.'

'Where's that?'

'By a fjord, a few miles inland.'

'When's it happening?' Blake glanced at his watch.

'I don't know.'

'You must know. Think hard.'

'No one told me anything about the meeting.'

Blake stood. 'Okay, sleep deeply, Mr Lenvik.' He stepped over the captain's body and followed Mortensen to the lower deck.

'What's the urgency?'

'There's a body,' she said.

She led him through a sliding door into an opulent lounge fitted out with polished dark wood surfaces, cream carpet and leather sofas. One of the Marines was standing with his rifle aimed at a crewman slumped on a sofa. His hands were bound behind his back. Shoulder-length straw-coloured hair fell over his eyes. Mortensen ignored them both, striding into a sleek galley with marble worktops and shiny stainless-steel fittings. She led Blake down a set of steps into a wood-panelled lobby. She pushed at a door and stood to one side.

Blake squeezed past and saw the body on the bed, its feet on the floor and arms stretched out wide. A head lolled to one side. Rivulets of blood dribbled from the mouth, nose and ears. An engorged tongue protruded from between blue lips and bulbous eyes stared lifelessly from their sockets at the ceiling. Blake walked around the bed. A dark, red ring encircled the neck.

'He's been garrotted,' said Blake. He put a hand on the side of the pale face. It was cold to the touch. 'He's been dead for at least a couple of hours. Any sign of the case?'

Mortensen shook her head and let her eyes fall on the twisted smile that was fixed on the man's face. A loose bandage wrapped around one of his shoulders had leaked onto the bed and stained it crimson.

'I don't understand,' she said. 'Why did they kill Ricky Vaughn?'

Chapter 33

They returned to the horseshoe cove and moored alongside a pier on the far side of the harbour. It was deserted. Blake had been worried the noise of gunfire from the Princess may have woken the village. But they had either dismissed the noise or decided to keep their heads down. Either way it suited Blake. The last thing he needed was a neighbourhood of overly-curious locals asking awkward questions.

The pier extended into the bay from a shingle beach of blue-grey flat stones. There were no houses nearby and the only building was a red tin-roofed boathouse set back from the water's edge. Blake helped Mortensen out of the RIB and onto the pier.

'Persuade you boys to join us?' said Blake.

'Would love to but the Commander was quite clear. We're not allowed to step foot on Norwegian soil. Can't go starting a diplomatic incident. We'll have to leave you to it, I'm afraid,' said the young Marine with the grey eyes.

'Shame,' said Blake. 'We'd have been grateful for the help.'

The helmsman reversed the RIB away from the pier. He gave a one-handed wave and sped away into the shadows of the night leaving Blake and Mortensen alone.

'Next stop, Mortjorna. Any ideas?' said Blake. He stepped off the pier onto a worn patch of ground where the earth had been scrubbed away by hundreds of pairs of feet.

'I could hitch up my skirt and try to flag down the next

passing vehicle.'

'You're not wearing a skirt.'

'I think you're missing the point,' she said. 'Or we could find a car to hotwire.'

'They teach you that at spook school?'

'They teach us lots of things,' Mortensen said with a sly grin. 'So which is it to be?'

'I think I prefer plan B given the lack of traffic at this time in the morning.'

'Good choice,' she said Mortensen setting off along a dusty track that ran up through a hillside of pines. It was the only way in or out of the cove and climbed steeply for several hundred metres before flattening out where the first houses appeared. The car they found was an old four-wheel drive Toyota pick-up parked on the side of the road. A vehicle favoured by African rebel gangs and Middle-Eastern jihadists, minus a heavy machine-gun mounted in the flatbed. Its paintwork was faded and covered in a film of dirt. Mortensen let out a triumphant squeak when the handle of the driver's door clicked open in her hand.

'Your carriage awaits,' she said with a victorious glint in her eye.

The fabric of the driver's seat was badly worn. In places yellow foam was visible through it. Mortensen ducked under the dashboard while Blake leaned against the back of the truck trying to look casual. He surveyed the road left and right. A small crescent of houses had been built into the hillside ahead on their left but there were no lights on in any of the homes. The owner of the truck was unlikely to miss it for several hours.

'Did they leave the keys?' Blake asked in a loud whisper.

'No such luck.'

The click of a starter motor was followed by the sound of the engine spluttering, coughing and finally turning over. It belched a plume of black diesel smoke.

'Get in,' said Mortensen, leaning out of the door.

Blake jumped to attention and hopped into the passenger seat. 'That's an impressive skill,' he said. A bundle of wires like multi-coloured spaghetti hung from under the dash by Mortensen's knee where she'd disembowelled the ignition's electrics. He watched her tickle the accelerator, trying to counter the cold engine stutter.

'A little trick my dad taught me.'

'What was he, a mechanic?'

'No, a car thief.' She turned to see Blake's reaction. 'I'm kidding. Never mind. See if you can find Mortjorna on your phone.'

Blake held up his mobile between a finger and thumb. 'Dead,' he said. The screen was blank and unresponsive. 'Yours?'

'The same. Not sure I'd get a signal here anyway. So back to the old-fashioned methods. Have a look for a map.'

Blake fumbled around in the glovebox. He found a pair of oil-stained leather gloves and a set of screwdrivers. Underneath a pile of cracked CD cases he found a creased map that looked as though it hadn't been opened in years. The kind that folds up like a concertina and is almost always impossible to refold the way it's supposed to. The paper had worn and ripped where the folds had been worked open and closed too many times. He spread it out on his lap. Flicked on an overhead light and twisted it around trying to find his bearings.

'We must be here,' Mortensen said, jabbing her finger near the bottom of the map.

It was difficult to tell. The coastline looked as though it had been ripped roughly out of the sea. It was made up entirely of ragged coves, inlets, islands and fjords, like the country had been constructed of thin tissue paper and the waters surrounding it were corrosive acid that had eaten away at its edges.

'You might be right,' said Blake, holding the map to his

face. 'Saetrevik,' he read.

'Can you see Mortjorna?'

'It's north east from here. I'd say less than four miles away.'

Mortensen crashed the gears into first and pulled away with a lurch. Only when they were clear of the village did she turn on the headlights.

'There's only one building on the fjord marked on the map,' said Blake, squinting to see the tiny print.

'So guide me there.'

Out of the village they turned onto a main road, followed it for less than a mile and took a narrow tree-lined track that meandered forever upwards. Progress was frustratingly slow. The Toyota chugged along obediently like a faithful old dog used to the familiar paths around its home, happiest meandering at low speed. Unsure of the roads, Mortensen approached each turn cautiously, fighting with the wheel over an uneven camber. At one point the shimmering waters of a fjord opened up through a gap in the trees, capturing the reflection of the moon but Blake urged Mortensen on.

'It's about half a mile further on,' he said, staring through the grime-encrusted windscreen.

Mortensen rolled her neck to ease the tension in her shoulders. 'I'll be glad of a decent bath when this is all over,' she said.

'I'd settle for a warm shower and a beer right now.'

'A cold glass of Sauvignon…' She didn't have the chance to finish the sentence.

Blake grabbed the steering wheel and pulled it hard to the left. 'Pull in! Quickly!' he shouted.

Mortensen wrenched back control and crashed off the road through a bush. They came to a violent halt under a canopy of trees.

'Kill the engine and the lights,' Blake hissed.

'What is it?' Mortensen asked, deliberately stalling the engine.

'Listen.' Blake cocked his head and opened his door a fraction.

The whirling buzz of a helicopter washed through the branches overhead. Faintly at first but progressively louder. He peered at the tops of the pines towering above them and through a narrow gap that exposed the sky.

The noise grew louder until it was a deafening roar. The powerful glare from a searchlight hit them. It turned night into day for a second. The hulk of a hovering helicopter followed. It flashed overhead and was gone as soon as it had appeared. The whining drone of rotor blades and gas turbine engines tore off into the distance and silence enveloped them.

'Do you think it was looking for us?' asked Mortensen.

'They don't know we're here.'

'Unless the crew of the Princess alerted someone.'

'I doubt it. One of them's dead and I left another one out cold. As for the captain, I made sure he'll have no memory of us. It'll be a routine patrol securing a perimeter, which is good news.'

'How's that good news?'

'It means we must be close to the rendezvous point. Let's lose the truck. We're best off on foot. It looks like a short hop down through this wooded area to the edge of the fjord,' said Blake, passing the map to Mortensen. 'The cabin should be easy to locate from there.'

Blake tried to put out of his mind the thought that they were heading into the unknown with no intelligence and no back-up. It went against everything his training had taught him. A senior Iranian agent was on his way to negotiate for the Armageddon Virus which meant the place would be swarming with security. The helicopter was probably the least of their worries. He set his Browning on the dashboard and emptied his pockets. One spare magazine. Thirteen rounds. Good job he wasn't a superstitious man.

'How many rounds do you have left?'

'Two magazines and one half-full clip locked and loaded,' said Mortensen.

'Not exactly armed to the teeth are we?'

Mortensen shrugged. 'No time to call in the cavalry now.'

'We are the cavalry. You ready?'

The hop down to the fjord turned into a mad scramble. They slid down slick mud, trying to control their descent by clutching at sharp branches that scratched their hands. They crashed noisily out onto a narrow plateau ten metres above the sparkling blue waters of the fjord. They dropped into a crouch as they stumbled out into the open, eyes wide, scanning to see if they'd been spotted, or more likely overheard.

'Okay?' Blake mouthed.

Mortensen nodded as she straightened out her suit.

They were perched on the top of a rock protruding from the hillside. It provided a natural viewing platform to take in the length and breadth of the fjord and the verdant forest that enclosed it.

'It's beautiful,' whispered Mortensen. The first glimmer of the new day had already broken the horizon although the sun remained out of sight.

Blake put a finger to his lips and pointed along the shore to a solitary building. It looked more like a Swiss ski lodge than a Scandinavian cabin, partially clad in wooden weatherboards with a grey slate roof, wide eaves and balconies on the upper floor. Just like on the cuckoo clock Blake's grandfather had owned. A wooden pier extended from a deck at the front of the house. Behind it, Blake counted at least a dozen cars. Mostly black. Highly polished. Tinted glass. Range Rovers and Mercedes mostly.

'Looks like someone's having a party,' he said.

Two men in dark suits and shirts appeared, picked out by a halogen security light. Short-barrelled sub-machine guns were slung casually across their stomachs. They walked lazily. Two bored guards on perimeter duties who looked as though they'd rather be anywhere else. Blake and Mortensen watched silently as they sauntered around the back of a squat outhouse and dropped onto a pebble beach. Their shadows disappeared under the darkness of the wood deck and eventually their voices drifted into the distance.

'The map showed a drive leading from the main road on the other side of the house. If their patrol route takes that in, it should give us at least ten minutes to find a way in before they return,' said Blake.

'What if there are more guards?'

Blake caught the edge in Mortensen's voice. 'Let's deal with that eventuality when it arises. We'll be fine,' he tried to assure her.

Blake pulled his pistol from his belt, loaded a round in the breach and prepared to move.

'Don't you ever get scared?'

Mortensen's question stopped him in his tracks. He reached out for her hand. It was icy cold. 'Keep your head down and follow me. You'll be fine,' he repeated.

'You didn't answer my question.'

'It's all a state of mind. Something in your head that needs to be controlled. The trick is to ignore what your head is telling you sometimes. Concentrate on the job.'

'Blake, we don't stand a chance if they start shooting.'

'I'm not here on a suicide mission. We get into the house, locate the virus and get the hell out.'

'How?'

'We'll find some leverage. But my biggest worry right now is that Pitts manages to offload that virus to some crackpot terrorist who'll do God knows what with it. We're the only hope of stopping that happening and I can't do it on my own. I need you, fully functioning. Understand?'

Mortensen nodded but there was sadness in her eyes. No, maybe not sadness. Fear perhaps.

'You're going to be just fine.' He squeezed her hand.

'We've got to hurry. Let's move,' he said, scrambling to his left, into the woods and down to the back of the house. His feet almost ran away from him on the steep incline and he had to concentrate hard on avoiding the craggy tree trunks that sprouted from the ground. His shins burned from the effort of staying upright.

He reached the bottom, breathing heavily, and turned to catch Mortensen as she hurtled out into the open. She narrowly avoided crashing into the rear end of a Mercedes. Blake pulled her close, feeling her ribcage rise and fall. The pounding of her heart.

'I'm okay,' she breathed.

'Keep your eyes open. I'm going to check the house. Stay here.'

He left Mortensen hidden between two vehicles while he scuttled across a gravel parking area and fell against a stone wall. It was cool. Cold almost. Moss mottled the wall where it met the ground. Four windows on the lower floor were in darkness. Made sense. Everyone would be at the front of the house with its views across the fjord. All the living areas would have been constructed around that vista. The rear of the property, where the sun rarely shone, was where the utilitarian rooms would be. Storerooms. Pantry. Kitchen. Bathrooms.

Blake stole around the side of the house, tried a door but found it locked. He snatched a glimpse through the glass into an empty hallway that told him nothing. He needed a better vantage point, somewhere to assess the layout of the house and see how many men were inside. He scooted back to Mortensen and ducked down to her level so they were concealed behind the bodywork of a gleaming Range Rover.

'I need to see what's going on at the front,' he whispered. 'We'll skirt around that outhouse, drop onto the beach and come up under the deck.'

With the sun below the horizon he figured they could snatch a look through the windows without much risk of being seen. There were lights on inside and the reflective properties of the glass should keep them from being spotted. As long as they didn't stray too close.

Blake checked for guards and seeing the area was clear, darted out of the cover of the cars. He winced as his boots crunched on the gravel. Mortensen kept close behind but froze when a bright light lit them up.

'Security light,' said Blake, pointing at a lamp above the locked door he'd tried. 'There's nobody there.' He grabbed her arm and propelled her forwards.

She stumbled, lost her footing and half-fell to the floor.

At the same moment Blake heard the drone of a helicopter somewhere in the near distance. No doubt the same aircraft that had spooked them earlier, still on its patrol loop, coming over the hill from behind the house. And closing fast. The unmistakable whump of rotor blades grew louder until it made their ears pulsate. They were caught in no-mans-land with nowhere to hide.

Blake pulled Mortensen forwards so roughly that she squealed in shock. The helicopter shot out over the trees and buzzed the roof of the house. Its powerful searchlight picked out the landscape below. Blake and Mortensen threw themselves flat on the ground. The downdraught whipped up their clothing and covered them in a cloud of dust and debris. When Blake looked up, the chopper was soaring skywards, turning a wide, slow loop over the fjord. Coming around for another pass. They must have been spotted, caught in the open under the brilliance of the security light.

It was a Hughes 500, a variant of the helicopter the military was so fond of for observational duties. Light and highly manoeuvrable with a distinctive shape that reminded him of a giant dragonfly. Its fuselage was painted matt black with no markings. No insignia. Not even a registration number. Legs dangled from each side of an opening where the rear doors had been removed. Feet propped on the skids. That wasn't a good sign. With the weak rays of morning sunshine growing stronger, he caught a fleeting glimpse of a dark figure silhouetted in the doorway. And with a sickening dread noticed the long-barrelled rifle mounted with a high-power sight.

'Get up! Run!' shouted Blake.

He was beyond caring whether his voice would be heard by anyone inside the house.

Chapter 34

The outbuilding was less than thirty metres away by Blake's estimation. It looked like a garage but with no obvious entrance for a vehicle. It had a slate roof and walls constructed of the same grey stone used on the lodge. Whatever it was for, it was their best hope of evasion.

Blake scrambled to his feet, dragging Mortensen with him. His legs pumped in an all-out sprint, hoping Mortensen was close behind but knowing there was nothing he could do to make her run faster. He reached the far corner of the building and looked for a door. When he found one, it was locked.

Mortensen joined him a second later, panting hard. Her eyes wide and her chest heaving. Blake gave her a 'what now?' look.

'Over there.' She pointed to the upturned hull of a decrepit rowing boat. It was propped up on bricks in the middle of a scrubby lawn and partially hidden behind a barren bush. The wood had been bleached grey-green by age and exposure to the elements. It wasn't quite what Blake had in mind but, in a list of options that numbered one, it was going to have to do. Mortensen turned and ran.

Blake glanced over his shoulder. The chopper had completed its turn. It was heading back in their direction with its nose dipped. The beam of its searchlight was a translucent shaft hunting them down.

Mortensen skidded on the wet grass, deliberately falling feet first. Her body disappeared under the boat. Blake scrabbled in behind her as the growl of the helicopter swelled. They sat with their knees up to their chests, holding their breath, waiting for an explosion of gunfire to rip the boat apart. A standard .308 NATO round from a sniper rifle at close range would cut the flimsy boat to shreds as if it was balsawood. Flesh and bone would fare little better but Blake pushed the thought from his mind.

The helicopter approached so low it caused the hull to vibrate. Its downdraught kicked up through the gap they'd dived through. As Blake's vision became accustomed to the dark he saw Mortensen's eyes wide and her jaw slack. Her breathing was shallow. He tried smiling because he didn't know what else to do. It seemed a silly gesture when their lives were hanging on a thread and he gave it up.

The roar of the rotor blades enveloped them so completely that Blake sensed the aircraft was directly overhead. He braced himself for a gunshot, hoping that if this was their moment to die then at least it would be a clean shot to a vital organ. The worst he could imagine was a deep flesh wound that left them to bleed out in agony. Not that he was worried for himself. He just couldn't contemplate the thought of Mortensen suffering. Of dying an ignominious death. His grip on his Browning tightened. He contemplated rolling out onto the grass to take a shot at the chopper. A couple of well-placed rounds near the engine housing or at the windshield could be enough to bring it down. He was close enough that there was a chance he could make the rounds count. The beam of a searchlight bled under the boat and partially illuminated their pallid faces.

'Is this it?'

'No,' said Blake with as much confidence as he could muster. 'I don't think they saw us.' He wasn't sure he believed it but it might be true.

Mortensen screwed her eyes tightly closed and they waited.

But as soon as it had come, the light was gone.

The pitch of the rotor blades changed and half a

minute later the sound of the helicopter had vanished completely.

'It's gone,' said Mortensen. Her face broke into a grin of relief.

'For now.' Blake peeked out from under the hull to make sure. There was no sign of it.

'Do you think it's coming back?'

'It'll keep sweeping the area at least until Khan arrives. The sooner we can get into the house the better.'

'What makes you so sure Khan's not here yet?'

'I'm not, it's only a feeling. The way the guards were behaving. They looked way too relaxed. You can usually spot a subtle change in body language when the head of an organisation arrives. It's always the same. Prime minister, president or a commander-in-chief. They all have the same effect. It's like there's a tension in the air, the moment they've been planning for and it's time to step up. My guess is Khan's expected at around first light.'

'So how do we get into the house?'

'I haven't figured that out yet. Stay here while I see if I can get a view through the front windows. I'll be a couple of minutes. No more. You'll be safe, but if anyone comes do what you have to,' said Blake nodding at Mortensen's Glock.

She lifted her gun as if realising for the first time she was holding it. 'Okay, but be quick.'

Blake pulled a wan smile and rolled out onto the lawn. He rose in a crouch, looked left and right and listened hard. He wondered how long he had before the two guards on patrol reappeared.

He jogged to the outbuilding and sidled along a wall towards the fjord where he found a slipway rolling down to the lapping waters. It spilled out from a set of double doors set into the narrow end of the building. A boathouse, he realised. He snatched a darting look around the corner and heard the dull voices of men in casual conversation. Artificial light was spilling from the house onto the wooden deck but no one was out in the open. He turned back the way he'd come and halted at a small window alongside the locked door.

Inside was in darkness but, by holding his hands to his eyes, he was able to make out the shape of a boat. It was a sleek-looking speedboat with a polished hardwood hull and a seating booth that had been cut into the body. Fixed on the far wall behind the vessel were shelves heaving with cans, bottles, boxes and tools. But what intrigued him was what he saw on the floor on the far side of the room. It looked like a quadrangular halo. Four thin lines of light each about a metre long in a perfect square. He squinted to see better and was hit by a dawning realisation.

He turned and ran back to the inverted hull of the old rowing boat.

'Alex, it's me,' he hissed, barely able to conceal his excitement.

Mortensen's head appeared followed by her shoulders and the rest of her body. She snaked her way out onto the lawn.

'What is it?'

'I've just found a way into the house,' he said.

Chapter 35

Blake pointed through the window of the boathouse. 'Do you see it?' he said.

Mortensen jammed her face up against the glass. 'What am I looking for?'

'A hatch in the floor, in the far corner.'

'Oh, right.'

Blake was deflated by the disappointment in her voice. 'There's a light on behind it.'

'So?'

'I bet that it leads to the house.'

'Or down to a basement storage room. Anyway the door's locked.' As if to make her point Mortensen grabbed the handle and tried to pull it open.

'It can't be that difficult to break in.'

'Really? With a house full of bad guys less than a stone's throw away? What are you going to do? Kick the door in? Smash the window and reach in for the key? That's a double-glazed window, by the way. Any idea how difficult they are to smash?'

'Not with this,' he said, holding up his Browning.

'So what's the plan? Shoot it out or smash it with the stock? Either way you'll have a small army on us before we've made it inside.'

'Well, okay Miss Smartarse. Do you have a better idea?'

Mortensen gave him a withering look, reached into her hair and pulled out two thin pins. She bit off a rubber end from one and bent the other in half around her finger. She dropped to her knees and inserted the metal prongs into the barrel like a surgeon beginning a lifesaving operation.

'You pick locks too?' said Blake.

'Of course,' she said, throwing him a surprised frown. 'Basic training. It's more subtle and less likely to get us shot. Now shut up and let me concentrate.'

'I thought that only worked in films.'

'You thought wrong.' She bit the end of her tongue as she concentrated. 'It's not quite as easy as I'd hoped.'

'What's wrong?'

'Someone's left a key in the other side, but if I can just - there, got it.'

Blake heard the tinkle of a key fall to the concrete floor. Then, with her head cocked to one side listening to the tiny clicks of pins lifting in the locking barrel, Mortensen set back to work with a series of delicate pokes and tweaks. In less than twenty seconds she had the door open. She stood with a triumphant grin.

'Impressive work, Miss Mortensen. Shall we?' Blake held the door open. He ushered her inside and pulled it closed behind them.

'Wow, someone has some panache.'

An Italian-designed Saetta sat gleaming on a trailer. A modern retro-styled nineteen-foot speedboat that would have looked more at home cruising the Italian lakes. Mortensen ran a finger along its finely-varnished African mahogany hull and sucked her breath through her teeth. The grain of the timbers ebbed light and dark like the closely-clipped flank of a pedigree racehorse. It was set off against a silver trim and fixtures. Opulent leather seats had been hand-stitched and its flowing curves gave more than a passing nod to 1950s chic.

Blake was unimpressed. He gave the boat only a cursory glance as he headed for the hatch in the floor. He found a recessed brass ring-pull and heaved it open. He aimed his Browning through the gap but saw only steep concrete stairs leading into a narrow passageway lit by florescent lamps on the walls.

'Listen!' hissed Mortensen.

From the corner of his eye, Blake saw her stiffen. He froze and listened hard.

Voices. A low chatter. Drawing closer. Blake checked his watch. Eight minutes since they'd seen the two guards patrolling around the house. More than likely the same pair on their way around again.

'Get behind the boat,' Blake whispered.

Mortensen snapped into action, squeezing between the bow and the double doors at the front of the building. She took up a position crouched down behind the Saetta. Blake lowered the hatch and joined her.

The voices grew louder until they could distinguish individual tones. Blake thought he recognised the language although he couldn't understand the words. He was reasonably sure they were speaking Farsi. One man was doing the majority of the talking, as though he was telling a long story. The other was encouraging him with the odd grunt and occasional interjection. Blake peered over the top of the boat and saw their shadows through the window. A flame flared as one of the men lit a cigarette. Their conversation became more animated, both voices rising. They were close. Maybe right outside the door.

And then silence.

'Come on, move away,' Blake urged under his breath.

A face appeared in the window so suddenly that it made him jump. An unearthly visage with thick brows, dark lips and coal black pupils that swam in milky pools. A cloud of condensation from the guard's warm breath formed where he pressed his nose against the glass. He raised his hands to cover his brow and squinted into the shadows just as Blake had done.

Blake ducked behind the speedboat trying to hold his adrenaline in check. He turned to Mortensen and put his finger to his lips. He listened for the door handle opening. Seconds passed like minutes, painfully slowly. One of the voices piped up in a short burst of unintelligible garble followed by a throaty laugh. When Blake looked over the boat again the face in the window was gone.

'All clear,' he said when he was certain the guards had moved on.

He returned to the hatch, threw it open and dropped through the space in the floor. Mortensen followed. It took them into a passageway with a low roof and white painted walls that ran in the direction of the house for around thirty metres and ended in a flight of steps. Halfway along, it opened out into a small room that served as a wine cellar. Hundreds of dusty bottles were stacked on their sides in racks.

Blake stopped to grab a random bottle.

'A 1990 French burgundy,' he said examining the faded label by the weak light. 'Do you think it's any good?'

'Get us out of here in one piece and you can take one as a souvenir,' said Mortensen, pushing past. 'But for now, put it back.'

Blake returned the bottle with a reluctant shrug and followed her towards the stairs at the end of the passageway. They were built of wood worn smooth and spiralled up to a heavy oak door pulled shut.

Mortensen went first. She put her ear against the door and listened.

'I can hear voices. But they're muffled. I don't think there's anyone on the other side.'

'Only one way to find out for sure. Ready?' said Blake.

Mortensen nodded and eased the door open a fraction. She put her eye up to the gap and looked both ways.

'It leads into a hallway. There's a flight of stairs opposite and a closed door to the right,' she relayed to Blake.

She pulled the door open and they emerged into a dark hallway, just as Mortensen had described. An unlit staircase led to an upper floor. A door to their right was pulled shut. The murmur of conversation was coming from behind it. Deep masculine voices speaking casually. Not the incessant chatter of a party but the refrained dialogue of people killing time. Like strangers chatting in an airport departure lounge. Blake put his ear to it and realised the sound was also travelling down the stairs from somewhere above. He took a step back and pondered the enigma.

Only one way to find out what was going on. He took the steps two at a time, with Mortensen following. His back brushed against one of the walls and he kept his feet away from the obvious weak points in the middle of the boards where a creak might give them away.

He wasn't surprised to find the stairs rotated through ninety degrees and led to a mezzanine floor where a line of doors opened into what he presumed were bedrooms and bathrooms. A balustrade ran along the length of the landing overlooking a lounge below. It explained how the sound had carried more clearly down the stairs than through the heavy door.

Blake counted seven men. All but one of them was dark-skinned and dressed in cheap black suits and shirts, like the guards they'd seen patrolling outside. For the most part they were armed with sub-machine guns. Some wore them slung over their shoulders, others had set them down near to hand on tables and surfaces. Bulges in their jackets hinted they were also carrying small arms. A few were sitting, others drifted around the room aimlessly, kicking their feet on the varnished floor. They exchanged brief words as though they were waiting for something to happen.

A man who Blake immediately recognised as Elias Pitts was sitting in the middle of the room in an armchair near a blazing open fire. He looked exhausted. His skin was pale and his eyes puffy. He was absentmindedly chewing his fingernails. His shoulders were tense and his thighs bobbed rhythmically as he bounced his feet on the floor. Mortensen nudged Blake's elbow and pointed to a stippled silver case lying on a low coffee table within Pitts' reach. It was no bigger than a child's lunchbox secured closed with two clasps.

'The Armageddon Virus,' Mortensen breathed.

Chapter 36

The plane dropped through the early morning haze as an indistinct blur against the low rising sun. The drone of its propeller cut through the silence like an angry mosquito in the humid heat of summer. Its wings bobbed as it glided through shifting thermals rising from the fjord. For a moment it seemed to hang in the air as if suspended on a strand of elastic. Behind the controls, a pilot in shirt-sleeves was concentrating on keeping the aircraft level. He sensed the man in the seat behind was growing restless.

Khan pulled his coat tightly around his body and stared at the icy waters below. He shuddered. He hated northern Europe for its grey, dreary days and long nights. Most of all he hated the bitter cold. Scandinavia, he thought, was the worst with its tedious snow-capped mountains, endless fjords and rolling pine forests. He wondered how anyone put up with it. He'd rather be back in Iran. At least the mountains were tempered by a climate of dusty heat, even if the cities were choked by smog.

Beside him, Tariq Shahidi was fussing with his .45 handgun.

'Put it away,' Khan encouraged with a light hand on his arm. 'Have the men secured the house?'

Shahida holstered his gun and shrugged. Khan liked to call him his PA. He thought it fitted better with his cover as a businessman. In reality Shahida was a close protection officer who knew far more about inflicting pain with his bare hands than he did about spreadsheets and appointments diaries.

'A team's had the house locked down since yesterday. Everything's okay,' he said.

The lodge appeared through a light mist at the foot of a dense forest of pines. The plane hit the water and skimmed across the surface on buoyant skis, startling half a dozen men into action. They ran from all directions like spooked sheep to take up positions around the jetty with their weapons poised. Shahidi was out of the door and onto the jetty before the plane had barely come to rest. He stood with his back to the aircraft. He crossed his hands over his stomach and scanned for threats.

Khan stood and smoothed the creases from his trousers. He had chosen one of his favourite powder-blue suits, tailored by his man in London. He set it off with an open-necked white shirt with double cuffs protruding from his jacket sleeves by a regulation half inch. He adjusted his aviator sunglasses, checked the time on a gold Rolex and ran a hand through a handsome head of jet black hair.

He bent down to pick up a briefcase from the floor and was almost knocked off his feet by the unexpected turbulence of a low-flying helicopter that rocked the plane. Khan steadied himself and scowled through a window at the aircraft banking hard over the fjord. Two snipers were hanging from the back door. He regained his composure and stepped onto the jetty. A man whose face he recognised but whose name eluded him was on hand to greet him. One of his security detail.

'Is he here?' Khan asked. He brushed past the man with barely an acknowledgement.

'He's in the house.'

Khan took long strides towards the house with his overcoat flowing behind him like a cape. A set of folding glass doors opened up into the lounge from the outside deck. He clipped his sunglasses onto the front of his shirt and saw Pitts slumped in an armchair near an open fire. He was fiddling with his fingers like a naughty child about to be chastised. His breath rasped loudly in the silence. Not what Khan had expected at all. Pitts looked up, rose from his seat and flinched as a log on the fire popped loudly. Khan suppressed a smile.

'Ricky Vaughn?'

Pitts approached Khan with his hand outstretched. 'Elias Pitts. Ricky Vaughn's been unavoidably and permanently delayed,' he said.

'Dead?'

'Yes.'

'Sit down,' said Khan. His gaze fell on the silver case. 'Is that the virus?'

'Four test-tubes. Twenty millilitres of Armageddon Virus. It's everything the laboratory has produced.'

Khan lowered himself in a chair opposite Pitts. He laid his briefcase flat on the table with its handle facing towards him.

'You'd only need a few drops to start a worldwide pandemic,' Pitts added, filling an awkward silence.

'May I?' asked Khan.

Pitts pushed the case across the table. Khan flicked the catches open to reveal four glass tubes in a protective bed of polystyrene. He prised out one of the tubes and lifted it to the light between his finger and thumb. He let the liquid roll along the glass, mesmerised by its lazy progress from one end to the other.

'It looks like water,' said Khan.

'Looks can be deceiving.'

Khan glanced over the top of the tube at Pitts. 'Is it water?'

'No, of course not. Don't be ridiculous.'

'You're sure?'

'Of course I'm sure. It's come straight from the laboratory in Scotland, as we agreed.'

'Your brother is the bio-chemist who helped produce the virus?'

'That's right.'

'And he was working on a vaccine?'

'You're well informed.'

'How close are they to completing the vaccine?'

'It doesn't matter. That's everything the lab produced and without it they can't carry on with the research. They'd need to start from scratch and that could take years. They can't even admit it's been stolen because under international law they weren't supposed to have been developing it in the first place. It's too dangerous.'

'And you're happy to sell it? No regrets and no doubts?'

'I expect to be paid well for my efforts. We agreed twenty five million which I think is more than fair price given that it could secure Iran's place on the international stage of superpowers. If your country wants to go nose-to-nose with the US and Europe, if it wants real power, you're holding it right there in your hand. That test-tube is more potent than any nuclear weapon or army. That's world domination in twenty millilitres.'

'Once our scientists have produced a vaccine.'

'Which shouldn't take long. The British have done the hard work. As soon as the vaccine is complete and your country is inoculated, the rest of the world will be at your feet. When you threaten to unleash that virus every Western regime you despise will be on their knees begging you not to do it.'

'And my guarantee that I have the genuine virus?'

'You have my word.'

'Your word? I don't even know you. My deal was with Ricky Vaughn.'

'He was a hired hand, a bit of muscle, that's all. He was useful in helping to get the virus but he was a liability.'

'So you killed him?'

'Is that a problem?'

'And now you won't have to share the money, of course.'

'The thought hadn't crossed my mind,' said Pitts with a

sickly smile.

'What about your brother. Silenced?'

'Yes, of course,' he lied.

'And I can trust you, can I?'

'Absolutely.'

'Because you know it wouldn't be wise to lie to me.'

'I understand.'

'I'm not sure do. I know all about you, Mr Pitts, and when it comes to money there's not an honest bone in your body.'

'I don't know what you mean,' said Pitts.

'You met Ricky Vaughn in prison, didn't you?'

'Yes, but that's nothing to do with - '

'What were you jailed for?'

Pitts stayed silent. A scab on the back of his hand started to itch. He fought the desire to scratch.

'I know who you are and I know what you've done. You're a conman, Mr Pitts. You trick people out of money.'

'That's not true - ' Pitts protested.

'Not so long ago you surrounded yourself with every luxury your wealth could afford. But when you lost everything you turned to crime, conning people out of their money.'

'The market crash ruined everything. One day I was earning more money than I knew what to do with, the next it was running out of my hands like sand. I was out of a job, redundant to requirements and left with nothing.'

'So you thought you'd trick people out of their money instead.'

'We do what we have to to survive. Isn't that what you do?'

'My honesty isn't in question here, Mr Pitts. You're trying to strike a deal with me for twenty five million pounds and you're fundamentally untrustworthy. That's not my opinion. That is fact.'

'This is different,' said Pitts.

'You're a born liar. I think you have difficulty knowing yourself when you're lying. So how can I be sure you're telling the truth now? You give me your word but we've established it's next to worthless. I need something more tangible.'

'One test-tube alone contains more than enough virus to cause an international meltdown. It's been engineered to be as contagious as winter flu and as deadly as the plague. One week of that in your system and you'll be drowning in your own blood. Imagine the fear that's going to cause.'

'I know exactly what the virus is capable of. That's not in doubt. What I need is proof these test-tubes contain what you say.'

Pitts wiped a sheen of sweat from his brow. 'What sort of proof?'

'Twenty five million pounds worth of proof. I need to know our investment is sound.'

'I have no proof, for God's sake.'

'So we have a problem.'

Khan let Pitts stew. He watched him squirm in his chair, scratching at the skin on his hand until his nails drew blood.

'Of course, there's one way to prove beyond any doubt whether you're lying to me,' said Khan eventually.

Pitts stopped scratching. 'There is?'

Khan slotted the test-tube back in its case, closed the lid and put it on the table. He beckoned to Shahida who was standing on the far side of the room. For a man who was more bulk than brain he moved with fluid ease. He came up behind Pitts' chair. Slipped a meaty arm around his neck and pinned him to the seat.

'What are you doing?' Pitts gasped.

'Just relax, Mr Pitts,' said Khan. He flicked open the catches of his briefcase. The box he pulled out was long and thin. Hinged on one side. He placed it on the table and plucked one of the test-tubes from the silver case. It happened to be the one second from the right. A random choice. He unscrewed the orange cap.

'What's going on?' Pitts eyes opened wide.

Khan took out a medical syringe from the box, removed a cap from the needle and plunged it into the liquid. He drew off a small quantity.

'Time to find out if you've been telling the truth.'

He grabbed Pitts' arm. Pulled back the sleeve to expose bare flesh. Traced the line of a faint vein with the syringe needle.

'For God's sake, are you crazy?' Pitts' eyes bulged in their sockets.

'It's the only way we'll be able to tell for sure if this is the virus. If it's a harmless liquid you have nothing to worry about. At least from the injection.'

'If you infect me, everyone in this lodge is at risk of contracting it too. That includes you,' said Pitts through clenched teeth.

'How long's the incubation period?'

'I don't know. About the same as winter flu.'

'And how long do you think you'd take to die?' Khan applied a little pressure to the needle so it bowed the skin without puncturing it.

'Christ, I don't know! Please put the needle down. I swear to you that's the Armageddon Virus.'

'You're sure?'

Tears had welled in Pitts eyes and his body was rigid.

'Yes, it's the goddamn virus. Stick that needle in my arm and I'm as good as dead – and you'll be next. Please, don't do this. I'm begging you.'

Khan pressed the syringe a little harder. The needle punctured the skin and a drop of blood pooled on Pitts' arm.

'Okay, I believe you,' said Khan. Nobody was that good at faking fear. He stepped away and returned to his chair. 'Let him go, Tariq.'

Pitts' relief was palpable, like a smell in the air. Shahidi relaxed his grip and Pitts slumped into his seat. He rubbed his throat where his windpipe had been constricted.

'Satisfied?' asked Pitts.

'Twenty five million is a lot of money. You'll understand I had to be sure about the purity of the sample.' Khan squirted the contents of the syringe back into the test-tube and sealed the cap.

'So we have a deal?'

Khan smiled thinly. He replaced the syringe in its case and flipped open his briefcase.

'We have an understanding?' Pitts repeated.

'Yes, we have an understanding, Mr Pitts.'

Pitts didn't have time to register that Khan had produced a gun from his briefcase. A Beretta 92 with the unmistakably long barrel of a silencer. Khan squeezed the trigger and a single bullet pierced Pitts' forehead just above his right eye, killing him instantly.

Chapter 37

There had been an inevitability about Elias Pitts' death, Blake realised, watching from the shadows of the mezzanine landing. He'd sealed his fate the moment he'd tried to strike a deal with the Iranians. No reason to let him live after he'd delivered the virus. Not that it made his execution any less shocking.

Blake nudged Mortensen's elbow and guided her down the stairs and into the underground passageway. They raced through the tunnel and bounded up the concrete stairs into the boathouse.

'See if there's any fuel in those canisters,' said Blake, indicating to a row of fuel tanks stacked against the wall alongside the Saetta.

He ransacked a workbench and found solvent in a can on a shelf. He grabbed a handful of oily rags from a drawer.

'Two of them are full,' said Mortensen.

'Throw them in the boat and look for some matches. There were some candles in the wine cellar we passed. Have a look down there.'

Mortensen vanished down the hatch while Blake doused the rags in solvent. He tossed them into the boat with the fuel tanks and poured the remains of the can over the front seats.

'Sorry, old girl,' he said. She was a stunning vessel and part of him felt a sentimental regret.

'Matches,' announced Mortensen. She reappeared out of breath. Blake caught the box one-handed. From outside they heard the whine and cough of the seaplane's engine being turned over. It stuttered three times and finally caught.

'Help me with the doors,' said Blake.

Two metal bolts that held the doors in place slid open easily. Mortensen pushed one open a fraction and risked a look outside. Two guards with weapons slung over their backs were carrying what she presumed to be Pitts' body wrapped in a sheet. It looked as if they were going to load it on the seaplane but they walked straight past to the end of the jetty and threw it into fjord. It hit the water with a loud splash and sank almost immediately suggesting it had been weighted down.

'Give me a hand,' said Blake.

He was standing at the stern of the speedboat. He struck a match and touched it to the edge of one of the solvent-soaked rags. The fumes exploded in a puff ball of fire which rapidly consumed the inside of the vessel.

'Push!' Blake yelled, putting all his weight into moving the boat.

The trailer crept forwards slowly on heavy rubber tyres. Flames that had engulfed the leather seats were giving off choking fumes. It would be only a matter of seconds before the heat caused the fuel tanks to explode. Blake pushed harder, his legs pounding on the concrete floor. He concentrated his effort through his thighs, back and shoulders. The trailer gained some momentum. Crashed through the double doors and picked up speed when it hit the ramp. With one final effort they sent it on its way. The trailer hit the water with a surging splash and disappeared to the bottom while the Saetta bobbed onto the surface. It drifted away from the shoreline with curling fingers of flame licking the air.

Blake and Mortensen ran back inside the boathouse and dived onto the floor. The first fuel tank exploded with a roar that echoed across the fjord. It was followed by a second explosion which rattled the boathouse doors and prompted a flurry of panic-stricken shouts from the guards.

'Let's get out of here.' Blake rose to his feet and dragged Mortensen up by her arm. His ears were ringing from the blast. It was an uncomfortable sensation that left him feeling disorientated.

They ran with their heads down around the back of the house. Blake trusted the guards' attention would be focused on the front of the lodge and trying to fathom out the cause of the explosion. It gave them a limited window of opportunity.

Their luck was in. When they rounded the far side of the building they discovered Khan isolated and alone on the wooden deck with his back to them. He was watching the chaos unfold with the silver case in one hand and his briefcase in the other. Shahidi was by the seaplane. His gaze was fixed on the burning remains of the Saetta. The explosions had broken her back and her charred remains were lying half out of the water. Three guards were standing at the end of the pier shouting and waving orders to the others. Some were out of sight on the beach below. Two more had clambered onto the concrete slipway and were approaching the boathouse with weapons cocked.

As far as Blake could tell most of the guards were accounted for. He sprinted to the deck and vaulted a balustrade. He landed square on his feet behind Khan. He shoved the barrel of his Browning behind the base of his skull and wrapped a hand over his mouth.

'Quiet or I'll blow your head off,' Blake whispered in his ear.

Mortensen fell in beside Blake with her Glock trained on Shahidi. She snatched the silver case from Khan's right hand and, for good measure, wrestled his briefcase from his left.

'Start moving slowly towards the plane,' Blake instructed Khan. He encouraged him forwards with a nudge of cold steel in the bone behind his ear. 'Nice and easy. No sudden movements.'

With their bodies pressed together, Blake used Khan as a human shield. It was an added insurance in the eventuality that one of the guards should fancy taking a pot-shot. Shahidi heard their approach too late. He whirled around with his .45 drawn. His eyes popped open wide when he saw Khan with a gun to his head.

'Drop it!' Mortensen screamed.

Shahidi was momentarily paralysed. His eyes shuttled between the three figures.

'Do as she says,' said Blake, 'unless you want to see your boss die.'

Blake needed the bodyguard disarmed before he could think about his options. They were hopelessly outnumbered by the guards and there were far too many weapons in too many hands for his comfort. Shahidi released his grip on his gun. He let it swing around his finger on the trigger guard before dropping it.

'Kick it away,' said Mortensen, edging forwards. The gun skidded across the wooden planks. 'Now, down on the floor.'

Shahidi was a big man. He collapsed heavily to his knees. Mortensen stooped for his gun and stowed it in the waistband of her trousers as he lowered himself onto his stomach.

'Put your hands on your back where I can see them. If you so much as twitch I'll put a bullet through your neck,' she said.

Three guards at the end of the jetty had turned at the sound of the commotion. They held their sub-machine guns loosely in front of their bodies, unsure how to react to seeing Khan and Shahidi overwhelmed by two strangers who'd appeared from nowhere.

'Throw down your weapons,' Blake shouted at them. They glanced at each other and, after a brief hesitation, did what he asked.

In the distance, the faint drone of helicopter rotor

blades grew louder in the natural bowl created by the fjord. It was no doubt on its way to circle the lodge and grounds once again. Time was in short supply.

'Who are you?' Khan asked with ill-concealed venom as Blake let his hand slip from his mouth.

'Funny you should ask. I had the same question for you. Iranian Intelligence?'

Khan said nothing.

'And you're here to buy four test-tubes of a virus stolen from a British lab? Let me know if I've got any of this wrong. The problem is the virus isn't for sale, so I'm here to collect it on behalf of its rightful owners.'

'British Secret Service?' said Khan.

'Strictly speaking I work for MI5.'

'Then I hope you're prepared to die for your country.'

'I'm not the one with the gun at my head.'

'You're surrounded and outnumbered. You have no hope of getting out of here alive, with or without the virus.'

'If they shoot, then you die. Are they trained to deal with that kind of dilemma? I didn't think so. They're here for one reason and that's to protect you. They're not going to risk your death.'

'In which case we have an impasse,' said Khan.

'I think it's more a Mexican stand-off,' said Blake, with no trace of humour. 'Get down and put your hands on your head.'

Khan fell to his knees. 'So what next? You can't kill me . I'm the only reason you're still alive.'

'I thought we might borrow your plane for a short trip.'

'And where did you have in mind for us to go?' Khan shuffled around, twisting towards Blake so the muzzle of the Browning was level with his nose.

'There are people back in the UK who'd like a chat,' said Blake. 'They have some questions about a number of attacks we have reason to believe were sponsored by the Iranian regime.'

'It's not going to happen.' Khan spoke impeccable English with barely a trace of an accent. The benefit of a Cambridge education. His eyes were emotionless. A man with a gun to his head should show some fear. But there was nothing. Maybe a touch of defiance. His expression certainly didn't giveaway what he saw behind Blake.

The first Blake knew about it was a sharp prod in his back.

'Put the gun down,' the voice said in a heavy accent. A guard who had slipped unseen under the jetty had emerged behind them. 'I said drop the gun,' the voice repeated.

Blake pressed the Browning into Khan's forehead and took up the play in the trigger.

'If I drop this gun you'll kill me. That's not going to happen so it leaves a couple of choices. You could shoot me, in which case there's a high chance the first round from that high-powered sub-machine gun in my back will pass straight through my body and kill the man you're supposed to be protecting. You could aim high but I should warn you my finger is a hair's width from activating this trigger. If you shoot, my body will tense and the weapon will fire. Your best option right now is to step away, put the gun down and I'll give you an assurance no one dies here today.'

No response. Blake let the silence hang. He'd made his offer. The ball was out of his court. Decision time for the other guy.

Khan laughed. A suppressed chortle which developed into a full-bodied howl that swelled from the pit of his stomach. He stood up and stared Blake in the eye. 'Is that the best you can do?'

The growl of the helicopter surged from behind the lodge. Blake forced himself not to blink. He held Khan's gaze until his eyes watered.

'Blake, for Christ's sake put the bloody gun down, will you?' Mortensen's voice was thick with emotion. She'd stepped away from Shahidi and was moving towards him with her back to the bodyguard.

'Alex? What are you doing?'

'Put the gun down or you're going to get us both killed.' Shahidi was picking himself up.

'Perhaps you should listen to the lady. Maybe we can come to some arrangement. Give me the virus and we can all get on our way. No harm done,' said Khan.

'No,' said Blake.

'That's the muzzle of a T9K light sub-machine gun in your back. Are you really this stupid?'

'I wouldn't be so confident with a nine millimetre lined up with your frontal lobe.'

'The cards are still stacked in my favour.'

'And my finger tends to get a little twitchy when people start to threaten me.'

'But we've already established that if you pull that trigger, we'll both die. The difference is that my men will have the virus.'

'You want it that much you're prepared to die for it?'

'Of course. It's a weapon of unimaginable power. Too long we've suffered because of the West's sanctions. You treat us like a Third World country and stop us developing even basic nuclear power plants, afraid we might use the technology for weapons. But with the virus, who needs a nuclear bomb? The four test-tubes in that silver case are a thousand times more terrifying than an arsenal of nuclear warheads. That case represents more power than you can imagine.'

'You're insane. You and your country. You'd threaten the world's entire population because of a perceived slight against Iran by the West?'

'We're not insane. We're tired. And we're hungry. And we're sick of your anti-Iranian rhetoric. We have planes falling out of the sky because our airlines can't buy parts for maintenance. Inflation is out of control and meat and fruit is so expensive families can't afford them. Unemployment is rising and the economy is being strangled. All this because of the West's trade sanctions. So don't preach to me about right and wrong.'

'And you think this virus is the answer?'

'We have a team of scientists ready to begin work on a vaccine. As soon as our population is inoculated we have a rather interesting situation, wouldn't you say? Let's see how long America is prepared to maintain its stranglehold on my country when the threat of a worldwide pandemic is hanging over their heads.'

'Which is why I can't let you take it. Too many lives are at stake.'

'You can't stop me. But I know you're only trying to do your job. I'm prepared to compromise so we all might walk away from this awkward situation. Let me back on my plane with the virus and I give you my word I'll let you leave here safely.'

'I'll remind you again that I have a gun aimed at your forehead. You're not in a position to compromise.'

'Blake, it's over. Lower your gun,' said Mortensen. She was at his side with her Glock levelled at his waist.

'What?'

She gripped his wrist. Squeezed but didn't try to force his gun down. Her face was blank. 'I'm sorry it has to end this way,' she said. She jammed her Glock into the tight muscles of his neck. Blake's eyes almost popped out. What the hell was she playing at?

'Alex?'

'I'm sorry, Blake.'

'I have a new deal for you,' she said to Khan. 'Ten million pounds and I'll guarantee your safe passage home, with the virus.'

'A deal? I don't need to negotiate with you,' said Khan.

'Really?'

Mortensen's arm moved in a flash. She pulled the trigger and shot the gunman behind Blake through the temple. He dropped like a stone with his eyes rolling in his head.

507

'I think you do,' she said. 'I think for all your bravado you still value your life. The suit, the hand-stitched leather shoes, the Rolex watch. They all tell me you're a man enjoying his taste of Western freedom. And who's paying for it all, by the way? The Iranian Ministry of Intelligence, I suppose? Are you their man on the outside, doing the deals?'

Khan said nothing.

'And if you die? Who cares? You won't be remembered. Tehran will deny your existence. Your family will be disgraced and for what? I can offer a better way out of this for both of us.'

'Who are you?'

'My name's Alex Mortensen. I'm a field agent with British MI5. I set you up with Javid Rahimi.'

'What are you saying?' Blake took his eyes off Khan for a second to study her face.

'You don't think a prison cleaner managed to make contact with one of Iran's intelligence agents without some help, do you? He came to us when he was approached by Pitts inside Marshside. Pitts had found out about the Armageddon Virus from his brother and calculated he could sell it at a massive profit if he could find a buyer. When he discovered Rahimi's Iranian background, he figured that Tehran was as likely to be as interested as anyone else. In return, he was offering Rahimi a deal to be reunited with his family. But Rahimi got scared and had the sense to report what had happened. It was too good an opportunity for us to miss.'

'A juicy bait to hang out for one of Iran's top intelligence agents?' said Blake.

'We knew there was someone based in Europe, an Iranian-sponsored terrorist but his identity had eluded us. Khan might not have been planting bombs but he's the one orchestrating the attacks in the West. We were desperate to discover his identity. Rahimi was an unexpected Godsend. We circulated information that the virus was for sale and within days Khan's people had made contact with Rahimi, who in turn put him in touch with Ricky Vaughn. He was the front for Pitts, the guy who could arrange the prison break and put the frighteners on his brother.'

'So why are you offering me a deal to return home?' Khan asked.

'There's no other option left. My choices are somewhat limited to death or retirement. I've had enough of dealing with scumbags like you and honestly, ten million will let me disappear. I can see out my days in the sun sipping chilled wine by the sea.'

'Alex, don't be so stupid,' said Blake.

'Shut up, Blake. We did our best but we lost. Time to adapt the plan. You might be prepared to take a bullet for your country but I don't intend to die today. Not here and not like this. We're operating illegally in a foreign jurisdiction and you know the game. The agency will deny our existence. Our lives will count for nothing.'

'Not if we can stop the virus leaving for Tehran. Think for a minute about what you're doing. You're signing the death warrant on a generation. You know what that virus is capable of. It's our duty to stop that happening. At any cost.'

'Stuff our duty, Blake. Do we have a deal?'

Khan drew a deep breath and closed his eyes.

'I need some guarantees you're not playing me. Proof of your intentions.'

'I'm not here to bargain. Straight deal, yes or no?'

'Then we all die. Prove to me you mean what you say, that you're prepared to turn your back on your country to save your skin.'

'How?'

Khan's dark eyes fell on Blake. 'If you're serious, kill him.'

Chapter 38

The pupils of Blake's eyes grew full and round. 'Alex?'

'Put the gun down, Blake.'

'Are you serious?'

'Put the gun down!' She jabbed her Glock into his neck so sharply that he winced. His arm fell and he dropped the Browning. Khan stepped away with a victorious grin.

'Tell your bodyguard to go back to the house, then walk slowly to the plane with your hands where I can see them,' Mortensen told him.

'Alex, he'll kill you the moment you take your eye off him.'

'I don't want to hear anymore, Blake. Button it.'

Khan shouted something in Persian to Shahidi. His bodyguard shrugged and trudged off the jetty. Mortensen watched him disappear into the house.

'Good, now hands on your head and get into the plane. Tell the pilot I want to be ready for take-off in two minutes.'

'Whatever stunt you're trying to pull, you'd better start thinking again, Alex,' said Blake. 'This doesn't end well. The moment you're on that plane you're as good as dead. We can work this out. Let me come with you.'

'I'm sorry. Time to say goodbye, Blake.'

'Alex, please?'

'Let's not drag this out. Start walking.' Mortensen jabbed him in the neck to force him along the jetty.

Blake wondered if she was playing some kind of clever bluff but with every step he took, the less convinced he became. There was a deadly look in her eye. How had he misread her so completely? He considered trying to disarm her. She'd left herself vulnerable. Too close. With a flick of his elbow and a twist from his waist, he could easily knock her gun away and overpower her. But with three armed guards watching it didn't seem such a good idea. If he put her down they'd kill them both without hesitation. The only thing keeping them alive right now was their confusion. They could see she had the case with the virus and was now doing their job for them by taking care of Blake.

'Jump!' she shouted at the guards as they approached. They stared at her with puzzled expressions. 'I said jump. Get in the water.'

The three men looked at one another. They'd seen her murder one of their colleagues in cold blood so knew she was capable of violence. So when the first man plunged into the fjord, the others quickly followed.

Mortensen pushed Blake into the space they'd vacated. He stumbled forwards. Stopped at the jetty's edge and looked down at the water. It was crystal clear. A crazed pattern of rocks and stones was visible under the gentle swell. He closed his eyes and waited. The bitter stench of the smouldering Saetta filled the air and a cool breeze chilled his cheek. He took a deep breath.

'Just do it clean,' he said.

Khan leaned forwards in his seat. Through the insect-splattered windshield he watched Mortensen order his men to jump from the jetty. Fools, he thought, although he admired her audacity. He allowed the faintest hint of a smile to creep across his face. He never ceased to be amazed at the influence that could be asserted with the lure of cash and the threat of death. Individually they were seductive forces. Combined they were compulsive. How easily Mortensen had abandoned her loyalties to her country and a fellow agent when she was staring down the barrel of a bloody death. He respected her ability to change position when she realised the inevitable. Not only had she negotiated for her life but for a multi-million pound pay-off too. Not that he had any intention of fulfilling his side of the deal or sparing her life. She couldn't be trusted. Not now she knew his identity. It would have to be taken care of. Maybe when they were back in Russia.

The pilot was finishing his pre-flight checks with the single-prop engine running idly in preparation for take-off. Khan checked his watch. The complication MI5 had thrown up had delayed his schedule but not significantly. They could make up the time in the air. Right now he was more interested in Blake's execution. Mortensen had shown some steel. It was a fascinating development. His palms were moist with anticipation. He guessed Blake was ex-military. Maybe even Special Forces. He had that manner. An easy confidence in the face of unlikely odds and an icy, dead look in his eye. A man who'd faced down death before. He hadn't anticipated it would be this easy to see him off. Khan willed Mortensen to hurry.

He was on the edge of his seat when Blake reached the end of the jetty. The perverse side of his nature would have liked to have listened to the final words exchanged between the two agents. But as it was, he could only watch and imagine. Mortensen took a step backwards and raised her gun. To Khan's frustration she partially obscured his view of Blake. He was looking forwards to watching the gory detail, the sight of Blake's body crumpling as his brains were blown out.

The hollow crack of a single gunshot echoed across the water, piercing the throb of the whining seaplane's engine. Mortensen's arm jerked from the recoil of the shot and Blake's body pitched forwards into the water. A ruthless and efficient killing. Mortensen spun on her heel and marched back to the plane without a second look. Her face was deadpan. Not a flicker of emotion. She climbed in next to Khan and pulled the door closed. Khan caught the lingering trace of burning gunpowder.

'Let's get out of here,' she said.

Khan issued the order to the pilot. 'I didn't think you had it in you,' he said. 'I'm impressed.'

Mortensen settled into her seat and placed the silver case on her lap. She crossed her arm over it protectively so her semi-automatic was aimed at Khan's stomach. 'So it turns out that cold-blooded murder isn't such a big deal. And now you know I won't hesitate to kill you if you give me cause.'

Khan snatched a glance at the weapon in her hand. He liked the way her bony fingers wrapped around its curves as if she was caressing it. She was an attractive woman and he was surprised that being under her control excited him. There was nothing like a strong-willed woman who knew exactly what she wanted.

'Where are we going?' Mortensen asked. The plane bobbed into position for take-off on its inflatable skis. The fjord opened up ahead of them framed on all sides by towering green pines.

'St Petersburg,' said Khan.

The pilot increased the power to the engines and the plane accelerated over the water. The fuselage rattled with violent vibrations as they skimmed over the choppy surface and Mortensen struggled to hold her gun steady. Halfway along the length of the fjord, the pilot pulled back on his controls and the plane soared effortless into the air and calm was restored.

'Russia?' said Mortensen. She screwed up her face.

Khan stared into her eyes. Piercing pale emeralds that sparkled with a sorrowfulness. Several corkscrews of red hair had fallen loose over her forehead. He resisted the temptation to sweep them away, imagining how it would feel to brush her cheek with the back of his hand. 'Russia's always been a good ally to my country. We have a common distrust of the West.'

'My enemy's enemy? How quaint.'

'An anti-West alliance. Russia has been true to Iran while the rest of the world shunned us. They've helped us build nuclear reactors and traded with us in the face of the West's sanctions.'

'Not to mention supplying arms. From Russia I suppose you intend to fly to Tehran with the virus?'

'There's a connecting flight to Moscow where I can pick up a plane direct to Iran.'

'And the Russians are happy with these arrangements?'

Khan said nothing.

'The Russians don't know, do they? You're planning to smuggle the virus through two Russian airports. But how?'

'Diplomatic bags,' said Khan, with a knowing smile. 'The Iranian ambassador will accompany me on the flights. The virus will be stowed in his luggage.'

'Which is exempt from custom checks. What about my money? This case stays with me until the cash is wired to my account. It sounds like you're in a hurry, so you'll want to sort that out soon.'

'Don't worry about the money,' said Khan, gazing out of the window. The coast of Norway disappeared below them. 'I give you my absolute word you'll be taken care of.'

Chapter 39

No one took the slightest notice of the woman who strode through Leningardsky railway station trailing a small flight case. She was tall and thin and walked with her head held high. Her lips were painted bright red and her eyes were hidden behind a pair of Audrey Hepburn sunglasses. A pure white ushanka perched on her head contrasted with the wisps of raven-black hair that spilled down her neck.

She disappeared among the bustling crowds, heading directly for the luggage lockers lined up in the shadows off a cavernous hall. She fetched a key from her pocket and rattled open one of the doors, relieved to find the silver case was still there. She snatched it by its handle. Zipped it into her flight case and walked away without a backwards glance.

It had been a long three days. Mortensen had last seen Khan in St Petersburg where she'd hijacked the private jet he'd laid on from the airport. She'd left him to make his own way to Moscow, promising to rendezvous with him in thirty-six hours. She told him she'd have the virus, assuming he'd transferred her money. She'd found a crummy hotel in a downtown area of the city and waited.

She'd done little but sleep for the first twenty-four hours having arrived in the city exhausted and with her nerves frayed. The eight-hour flight in the seaplane from Norway had been bumpy and uncomfortable. They had landed in the Gulf of Finland and been collected from a dreary coastal town by a chauffeur in a black saloon who had driven them straight to the waiting jet. It had only been a ninety-minute flight to Moscow but it had given her a head-start on Khan. Time enough to find somewhere suitable to lay low.

The hotel was as cheap and as anonymous as she'd been able to find, set between two apartment blocks with a hand-painted sign above the door. For a small cash deposit a woman with two stumps for teeth had handed over a key on a wooden fob. The building was thick with cooking smells and the sounds of raised voices and slamming doors. The room they'd given her was dirty and small, accessible by a metal lift that rattled and screeched through the core of the building. The room had hideously garish papered walls and stained carpets but the sheets had been clean even if the mattress was thin. More importantly it had had good views over the main street. Mortensen had barricaded herself inside with a chest of drawers pulled across the door. She'd kept her semi-automatic under the pillow and had spent her time listening for the creak of floorboards in the corridor.

On the second day, she'd coloured her hair with a bottle of dye from a nearby pharmacy. She'd shaded her eyebrows to match and ironed out her corkscrew curls with a clothes iron. She'd completed the look with the brightest red lipstick she could find. She'd hardly recognised the woman who stared back at her in the cracked mirror above the bathroom basin.

She'd left on the third day, wrapped in a newly-purchased overcoat over a plain, grey suit. The cut wasn't flattering but under the coat it hardly seemed to matter. The ushanka was a flamboyant touch but helped her to blend in with the locals. She'd taken a series of taxis through Moscow's congested streets, changing vehicles in the busiest parts of the city confident she'd done enough to lose any of Khan's men if they'd tried to follow her.

Mortensen walked out of the station with her heart pounding. She was more vulnerable now she had the silver case back in her possession. She hailed the first cab she saw.

'To the airport,' she said to the driver, settling into the rear seat and trying to calm her nerves.

She arrived an hour early, true to her plans. It gave her enough time to put a few details in place. Khan had suggested meeting in a cheap diner in a quiet corner of the airport. She chose a table with a chequered vinyl tablecloth near the back and sat with a clear view of the door. She ordered a Bloody Mary, with ice, and waited. She watched the natural ebb and flow of families, couples and businessmen, snatching meals ahead of flights. Three men entered separately over the course of the hour and took seats at tables. Each went out of their way to avoid eye contact with her. They ordered coffees, smoked cigarettes and read newspapers. Tough looking guys with gaudy gold chains, tattooed necks and sports clothing. Killing time. None showed the unsettled impatience of passengers waiting for boarding gates to be called. They were in no rush to be anywhere. Khan's men, for sure, sent to secure the location.

Outside a rowdy gaggle of soldiers had gathered. Fresh-faced boys in grey uniforms passing around a bottle of vodka. They were in high spirits, emboldened by the alcohol. Mortensen was caught watching by one of the men who turned to look through the window. She checked her watch pretending not to have seen them. Khan was late. She hadn't expected that.

He appeared ten minutes later in a charcoal grey suit with a sharp, white shirt and a dark tie. He drew up a seat opposite Mortensen. A waiter in a stained apron slid a menu under his nose.

'Have you eaten?' asked Khan.

Mortensen shook her head. He ordered shashlik with rice for two. The waiter gave a deferential nod, scribbled on his pad and scurried away.

'That was presumptuous,' said Mortensen.

'I'm sorry. Would you prefer something else?'

'I'm not used to other people making decisions for me,' she said.

'In Iran, a woman is grateful to be led by her husband.'

'I'm not your wife.'

A loud bang on the window. A soldier had fallen against the glass. It reduced the rest of the group to a hysteria of laughter.

'Damned drunks,' Khan muttered. He took a sip of sparkling water. 'How was your stay in Moscow?'

'You didn't find me, so I suppose it was as good as could be expected.'

'You think I was looking?'

'Of course. And if you'd have found me and located the virus, you'd have had me killed.'

'I'm disappointed you think so poorly of me.'

'You deny it?'

Khan smiled. 'I had three of my best men trying to locate you but you're most resourceful. Of course, I'd expect no less from a British MI5 agent. I almost didn't recognise you when I walked in.' He indicated to her hair. 'For my benefit I assume?'

'Sometimes a girl needs a change,' she said, running a hand over her head, feeling the straightened strands and reminding herself of her radical new look. 'Do you have my money?'

'The virus first.'

'It'll be delivered as soon as the funds clear my account.'

A flash of anger flickered across Khan's face. 'We had a deal.'

'We both know that as soon as you have your hands on that virus my life becomes worthless to you. So you'll understand I've made arrangements to ensure my safety.'

'I've given you my word. No harm will come to you.'

'Your word?'

'You don't trust me?'

'I think you're worried I'm still working for MI5, and

that I've seen your face. Not great for someone who relies on their anonymity.'

Mortensen watched Khan's eyes reading her face. She worked hard to ensure her expression gave nothing away.

'You don't make a compelling case for me to spare you.'

'My death would serve you no purpose. I told you, all I want to do is disappear.'

'And if you're lying?'

Mortensen shrugged. 'Then kill me. Except you'll never see the virus again. Your choice. I'm sure Tehran will understand.' She let Khan consider that possibility for a moment. 'Let's cut the crap and do the deal. Ten million is a small price to pay. I want to live out my days in obscurity, preferably somewhere hot, where the agency can't find me. So let's get over the trust issues and move on.'

Mortensen slid a slip of paper across the table. Khan raised an eyebrow.

'Details of my account,' she said. 'The bank has instructions to confirm the moment the money has been deposited. As soon as I receive that call you'll get the virus.'

The restaurant door flew open and a man with a thick thatch of grey hair that contrasted with his bushy black eyebrows swept into the room. He scanned the tables and picked out Khan in the corner.

'Damn traffic,' he muttered in accented English. He grabbed a chair and waved a finger to attract the waiter. He ordered a coffee and shrugged off his coat.

'I presume this is our defector,' he said. He extended a limp hand across the table.

'Less a defector and more a businesswoman with a keen eye for a deal,' said Mortensen taking his hand. It was soft and clammy. 'You must be the Ambassador?'

He regarded her across the table with penetrating eyes behind a pair of rimless glasses. His voice was barely audible above the background hubbub. 'But you were a British agent? Why the change of heart?'

'I've been looking for a chance to bail out. The opportunity came up in Norway when it was either die or negotiate a healthy pension.'

'How very fortunate.'

'I know this may be difficult for you to believe but I had my reasons for wanting to get out. Now, I have the virus and I'm asking a fair price. Pay the money and you can hop on the next plane home to a fanfare from the Ayatollah. Or I can walk away.'

'You've checked her background?' the Ambassador asked.

'She's an MI5 agent. There's no background to check,' said Khan, scanning her face.

'Do you trust her?'

Khan thought about the question before answering. 'Yes,' he said.

'Then make the payment. Our plane leaves in a little over an hour.'

Khan snatched Mortensen's slip of paper. 'Is the virus here, in the airport?'

'Make the transfer and you'll have it soon enough.'

Khan produced a slim laptop from a case at his side. It came to life with a chirrup. He tapped in a series of passwords while Mortensen's attention was distracted by the soldiers outside. Their mood had darkened. Earlier horseplay was developing into a quarrel. Men were squaring up to each other. Someone was shoved in the chest and sides were being taken.

Khan plugged the sequence of numbers from the paper slip into the computer.

'There,' he said, 'the money's in your account.' He showed her the screen.

'When confirmation comes through from my bank I'll fetch your case.' She gave him a wan smile and set her mobile phone on the table between them. Less than a minute later it rang. She answered, holding it to her ear without speaking.

'Thank you,' she said.

'Everything in order?' asked Khan.

'The Swiss are so efficient when it comes to banking. They've confirmed ten million pounds has been transferred from an unnumbered Lebanese account.'

'And my case?'

'In luggage storage on the underground level.' She pulled a credit card-sized token from her pocket. 'Give this to the attendant.'

The Ambassador snatched it from her hand. He rose from his seat and turned for the door. The noise of the squabbling soldiers filled the restaurant as he left. Their alcohol-fuelled shouts drowned out the sound of clattering cutlery and casual chatter.

Mortensen gathered up her hat and coat and stood to leave.

'Sit down please, Miss Mortensen,' said Khan. 'We also need confirmation you've been true to your word. You should know I have a gun under the table. You'll be free to leave when the Ambassador confirms he has the virus safely in his possession.'

Mortensen sat back down. 'Of course,' she said, forcing a smile that was belied by the fear in her eyes.

'Nothing to worry about is there?'

'Not at all,' she said.

Khan ordered coffee. It was hot and so intensely bitter that Mortensen had to drop three rocks of sugar into her cup to make it palatable. They sat in an uncomfortable silence until Khan's phone rang. He answered in Persian, listened briefly and hung up.

'The Ambassador has the case,' he said, scraping his chair backwards and pocketing a pistol. 'I hope you have a good day.'

'Good luck,' she said. She pulled on her coat but she wasn't foolish enough to think he was going to let her walk away. She'd made a fool of him. Not only had she unmasked his identity but she'd managed to negotiate a small fortune for the virus. And he hated her for that. She could tell by the way he looked at her. No doubt he intended to have her followed and killed at the first opportunity.

She let him make it half-way to the door before she threw a final taunt. 'I'll be thinking of you as I spend my money.' She couldn't help herself. The words just fell from her lips.

Khan spun around to respond. He hadn't seen the waiter coming from the other direction with a tray of drinks and whose attention was taken up by a table at the far side of the room where a couple were waving for their bill. The two men collided. Glasses spilled and drenched the front of Khan's suit.

'You idiot!' he screamed.

The waiter tried to dab Khan's clothes dry with a cloth while Khan shooed him away. A man who'd been sitting at a table alone with a newspaper since Mortensen had arrived jumped up. He shoved the waiter away and guided Khan outside. Mortensen left some cash on the table hoping it would be enough to cover the meal, and slipped out of the restaurant.

The concourse was busy but not overcrowded. Dead-eyed passengers burdened with luggage were wandering in random directions past shops, bars and cafes. Mortensen stopped in the entrance of a store selling magazines and unfamiliar-looking confectionary. She adjusted her ushanka and found her sunglasses in the bag slung over her shoulder. She made a pretence of scanning a rack of newspapers to check if she was being watched. It occurred to her that the soldiers who'd been fighting outside the restaurant had vanished. In the drama of Khan colliding with the waiter, she hadn't noticed them disappear.

On a bench across the other side of the concourse was a man she recognised. He'd been in the restaurant. He'd arrived before Khan, taken a table and ordered coffee. His arm was draped casually over the back of the bench and he was checking his phone. He never once looked in Mortensen's direction. Her pulse quickened. It was one of Khan's men. How many others were there? Her eyes darted around the hall looking for lone men. They'd be loitering, pretending not to watch her.

A languorous gaggle of students engaged in casual chatter approached the shop. All jeans and boots and greasy skin. Mortensen whipped off her hat as they passed. She turned from the newspaper stand and stepped in line with them, hoping from a distance the intermingling of arms and legs and bodies would make her invisible.

The group slowed as they approached a fast-food burger bar with its ubiquitous golden logo like a shining mecca seducing the youth. Their faces turned up to study the menu boards and Mortensen peeled away, looking for signs for the exit.

She was almost immediately surrounded by a flying fury of grey coats and noise. The soldiers from outside the restaurant had appeared from nowhere, swarming in a sweaty clamour. She couldn't make out their faces, only the blur of whirling limbs and heavy bodies, knocking her off balance as they barged their way through the concourse. A fist flew in front of her face, narrowly missing a jaw. Two men fell to the ground, wrestling like lion cubs scrapping.

Mortensen snapped to her senses. She attempted to push her way out of the throng. But the harder she tried to escape, the tighter they knitted together. Their bodies formed an immoveable barrier that held her in place.

She saw a boot fly, connecting with one of the body of one of the soldiers sprawling on the floor. He howled in pain. Hands fell on the perpetrator, clawing, grabbing and punching. The maul tightened until Mortensen couldn't breathe. Panic clouded her brain.

'Stop it! Stop it!' she yelled, but her voice was drowned

out.

Her bag was wrenched off her shoulder. She'd already lost her ushanka, trodden into the ground by a dozen pairs of army boots. She was finally taken off her feet by the weight of a collapsing soldier. His legs buckled and as he dropped to the ground the group parted for a second. Mortensen went down hard. There was nothing she could do. He landed unconscious on top of her with his face in her ear. She felt the heat from his muscles and the foul stench of his breath on her skin. A heady cocktail of vodka and garlic that made her gag. She screamed. She bucked and kicked but she was pinned down by the soldier's dead weight with her ribcage compressed against her lungs.

And then everything stopped.

Short, sharp blasts of a whistle pierced the air. A stunned hush descended over the soldiers. The thud of boots running vibrated through the floor. Mortensen tried turning her head but found the stubbly chin of the soldier on her neck.

The soldiers moved apart. Men with great coats, long boots and black ushankas appeared among them. Shouting. Authority in their voices. Like policemen, she thought. Military police. A wave of panic. She had no identity papers and no passport. She was in the country illegally and that was going to take some explaining.

The body that had fallen on top of her rolled away and she took a grateful lungful of air.

'Are you okay, Ma'am?' said a voice in English.

A pair of green eyes peered down. A man offered his hand and helped her to her feet.

'Yes, I'm fine.' She smiled.

'We need to get you out of here. Come with me, quickly.'

Chapter 40

In a washroom near the restaurant, Khan had made the stain on his shirt look worse. He tried dabbing at it with wet paper towels but the damp patch grew larger and more distinct. He hadn't even started on the splatters on his jacket and trousers. For a man who took care of his appearance, it was a slight to his pride. He refused to turn up on a plane in Tehran looking like a tramp who'd spilled his dinner, so he'd dispatched one of his henchmen to buy a new suit and shirt.

Khan threw a pad of disintegrating wet towels into a bin and gave it a sharp kick. It resonated with a thud that masked the sound of the door opening. Two cleaners in dark overalls entered pushing a metal trolley. Khan was too caught up in his own rage to pay any attention.

The first man, broad and lean, approached the line of basins and stared at Khan in the mirror. He spoke in garbled Russian, pointing and gesticulating.

'What are you saying? I don't understand,' said Khan, turning to face him.

The cleaner spat the words out like bullets in a language Khan only had the faintest grasp of. He pointed and prodded at the wet patch on the Iranian's shirt. Khan batted his hand away.

'Get away from me,' he said. His hand wrapped around the pistol in his pocket.

The cleaner was undeterred. He grabbed a clutch of paper towels from a dispenser and tried to wipe Khan's chest.

'Stop it!' he said.

Distracted by the first man, Khan didn't see the second cleaner move silently behind him. He was a giant with a receding hairline and dashes of grey around his temples. He wrapped his arm around Khan's neck like a giant anaconda. The pressure on Khan's throat left him gasping for air and he was gripped by the horrifying terror of his windpipe constricting. His eyes bulged in their sockets and pinpricks of light danced across his vision. He wrestled with the material of his coat for his gun but it was kicked from his hand and clattered to the ground.

The arm around his neck squeezed and lifted him from his feet. He grasped at the thick muscle, rising to the tips of his toes. Eventually his feet cleared the floor. His vision faded and, as his panic set in, he became a writhing mass with his legs kicking helplessly in the air.

And then he was still.

His brain shut down. He convulsed twice before his body went limp. The cleaner dropped him to the floor in a messy heap.

They picked him up by his arms and legs and bundled him into the trolley. Covered him with a crumpled sheet, retrieved his gun and wheeled the trolley out.

Mortensen couldn't see. The Englishman with the green eyes had thrown his heavy overcoat over her head and marched her out among the soldiers. They seem to have been put under arrest but beyond that she had no idea what was going on. Boots pounded the ground and she watched her own feet scuttle along. They moved tightly together. The military policemen flanked the group. They were being herded out of the airport. But to where she had no idea. To waiting vehicles she presumed.

Her mind whirled, searching for a means of escape. She couldn't risk ending up in a Russian military prison. Not a chance. But at that moment, her situation looked grim. Her Glock was in the handbag that had been ripped from her shoulder and she was blind under the coat.

The swish of glass doors sliding open preceded a blast of icy air. Marble floor tiles disappeared under dark mats and suddenly they were outside, jogging over worn paving slabs mottled by the elements. They slowed and stopped by an enormous wheel that Mortensen guessed belonged to some kind of troop transporter. Its throbbing diesel engine was idling and she could taste the metallic fumes from its exhaust. She was guided to the back of the truck and saw the rungs of a ladder.

'Get in, quickly,' a voice said.

Someone removed the coat from her head and urged her up the ladder with a hand on her lower back. She looked left and right for somewhere to run but the light was bright and hurt her eyes. As her pupils adjusted she saw she was surrounded by stoic-looking Russians in black uniforms and fur-lined collars. The AK-103s they carried were a convincing deterrent against making a break for it. A hand shoved her forwards with an urgent insistence.

'Hurry,' a voice hissed.

Mortensen didn't have much choice. She climbed the ladder into the back of an olive-coloured military lorry with a canvas awning that provided little protection against the freezing temperatures. She sat on a wooden bench between soldiers with hand-cuffed wrists in their laps. The military policemen flanked them at the ends of the rows with their rifles between their knees.

The lorry lurched forwards. It chugged along slowly at first and stopped frequently as it negotiated its way through traffic around the airport. At last it settled into a steady speed as they moved onto an open carriageway.

The soldiers sat in silence, staring at the ground or at their hands. They shifted restlessly on the hard bench and stifled coughs. There was an uneasy tension in the air but no one paid Mortensen any attention. The presence of a foreign civilian woman rounded up with a group of drunken soldiers misbehaving at an airport should surely have elicited some curiosity. It was odd they all seemed so accepting of her presence.

She studied their faces expecting to see regular conscripts fresh out of military training. But they were much older than she'd imagined when she'd first noticed them squabbling outside the restaurant in the airport. They all had tanned, leathery skin and crows-feet around their eyes. They were broad-chested and broad-shouldered. Soldiers in the peak of physical condition.

After a little over fifteen minutes, one of the policemen stole a look through the canvas out of the back of the truck.

'All clear,' he said. His accent sounded to Mortensen like a thick Glaswegian brogue.

A collective sigh punctured the tense atmosphere. The police officers put down their guns and worked their way down the truck releasing the handcuffs. The faces of the soldiers broke into broad smiles.

'What's going on? Who are you?' asked Mortensen, as the green-eyed officer who'd escorted her from the airport stepped past.

'The rescue party.'

'You're not Russian?'

'No.'

'Special Forces?' He ignored the question. 'It's not what I was expecting.'

'If you'd have been expecting it, it wouldn't have looked so convincing.'

'What about Khan? Did you get him?'

'I can't answer your questions, I'm afraid. I'm sure they'll be a full briefing in due course. In the meantime, try to make yourself comfortable. We have a long journey ahead.'

The truck ploughed onwards until the light began to fade and it became too dark to pick out the features of the men opposite. Most were trying to sleep, their bodies hunched over with their chins resting on their chests. Mortensen's legs were numb and she was beginning to feel the chill. She pulled her overcoat more tightly around her shoulders and wished she'd managed to hold onto her ushanka.

When the truck slowed and bumped onto an uneven surface, the soldiers stirred with anticipation. It came to a grinding halt with a squeal of brakes not a moment too soon as far as Mortensen was concerned. She was cold, tired and feeling a little sick from the nauseous exhaust fumes.

Men stood stiffly, stretching their backs, arms and legs. Someone rolled up a canvas flap that had been pulled down over the back of the truck. They were surrounded by the dark outline of tall trees under a rising moon. They were at the edge of a forest.

The soldiers poured out of the truck, landing heavily on rough ground. They gathered in small pockets, exchanging jokes and cigarettes. Some used the time to check their small arms.

'Hello, Alex,' said a familiar voice. 'Fancy seeing you here.'

A distinctive figure walked towards her. She recognised his gait. A slight limp in his right leg, shoulders back, a self-confident coolness oozing from his pores.

'You're supposed to be dead.'

'You need to learn to shoot straight,' said Blake.

'I was worried.'

'That I didn't know what you were playing at?'

'I had to do something. They were going to kill us both.'

'It's okay – just next time don't shoot quite so close to my head,' he said, rubbing a hand over his ear where he'd been partially deafened by the gunshot Mortensen had fired.

'I'm sorry.'

'It was a good plan as far as it went.'

'Did you doubt me?'

'No.'

'It's good to see you again, Blake.'

She caught his smile in the moonlight. 'I'm not sure I like what you've done with your hair,' he said.

Mortensen touched her head. 'Maybe I'll shave it off when we get home.'

'That might be a little over-the-top.'

'So, what's the plan?'

Blake opened his mouth to answer but was interrupted by the arrival of a white van. It rolled into the clearing with its bright headlights bobbing over the bumpy ground. The soldiers took up positions with weapons raised.

'They're with us,' said Blake. 'Don't worry.'

The van pulled up behind the truck. Two soldiers threw open the rear doors and wheeled out a laundry trolley. They reached in and hauled out a dishevelled figure. Khan stood unsteadily with his arms tied behind his back and a strip of tape across his mouth. His suit was a crumpled mess. His hair was tousled.

Blake pushed through the soldiers. 'Khan. You remember me, don't you?'

A moment passed as Khan struggled to place Blake's face. His eyes narrowed, then widened in surprise.

'That's right, back from the dead. And no, Mortensen didn't betray her country. Far from it. She led us directly to you because we couldn't let you get away with that virus. I told you before, it doesn't belong to you.'

Khan tried to speak. Blake ripped the tape from his mouth. 'You're too late. It's already on a plane to Tehran.' Khan gave Blake a supercilious grin.

'Oh, the silver case that left Moscow with the Iranian Ambassador? I'm afraid not. We switched the test-tubes.' Khan stared at Blake with an ill-concealed hatred. 'There's no virus in that case. We filled them with vodka. Only the cheap stuff though. The problem is you really are too trusting.'

'So what now? Are you going to kill me?'

'That would be an easy way out, wouldn't it? I was thinking maybe we could hand you over to the Americans. I hear they're desperate to get their hands on you. They have quite a few questions about a number of attacks on US assets they have reason to believe you orchestrated.'

Mortensen saw the flash of fear. The idea of being gifted to the Americans appeared to hold a greater terror to Khan than death.

'I expect the President will be beside himself. They'll probably leak it to the media too. It would be a terrific coup for them. Can you imagine the headlines? Iran's secret agent exposed. Ayatollah's Armageddon Virus plot foiled. After they've made you confess to your crimes, they'll probably let you rot in Guantanamo. That would be my guess. Meanwhile, the British Government will be able to bask in the glory of capturing you.'

'We can do a deal,' said Khan, suddenly. 'I have money. Lots of it. Name your price. She'll tell you. I transferred ten million into her account. There's plenty more. You have the virus back. You could let me go.'

'Where would you go? You've failed and humiliated the Ayatollah. They'll hunt you down. Europe's out for sure. And America. Russia would sell you back to Iran in an instant.'

'I know how to disappear. Please, I'm begging you.'

'Begging?'

'Yes.'

'Then you'd better get down on your knees.'

'What?'

'Get down on your knees and beg.'

Khan collapsed to the ground.

'Blake? You can't seriously be thinking about letting him go,' said Mortensen with a note of alarm in her voice.

'Shut up!' he barked with a venom that made her draw breath.

'Beg,' said Blake. There was a cruel edge to his tone.

'Please,' said Khan. 'I beg you, let me go.'

'Don't be ridiculous. Bag him.'

Blake nodded at one of the soldiers who lifted his rifle and struck Khan's head a glancing blow with the stock of the weapon. It knocked him out cold. The Iranian slumped to the floor and a second soldier pulled a sack over his head.

'Put him in the back of the truck,' said Blake. 'And get rid of that van. Everyone ready to roll in two minutes.'

'Where are we going?' asked Mortensen, as soldiers around them snapped into action.

'A rendezvous on the Latvian border,' he said. He turned from her with no other explanation and jogged back to the cab of the truck.

Mortensen clambered into the back with the soldiers. She was at the top of the ladder when a massive explosion rocked the night. A pluming fireball erupted in the forest. Two men came running from out of the trees. They hauled themselves on board the truck and stepped over the unconscious body of Khan to find spaces on one of the wooden benches. The engine rattled to life and they settled in for the long haul.

Blake gave the order for the driver to move on. The Russian-built Kamaz gathered speed slowly but even when it made it back onto the open road its top speed barely touched 50mph. Blake checked his watch and stared with tired eyes at the ribbon of road picked out ahead by the yellow headlights. If the driver kept his foot down they'd be at the border by the early hours of the morning. That was several hours of solid driving during which they remained vulnerable to being stopped and discovered by Russian security forces. They were going to need a lot of luck.

Not that that was at the top of Blake's list of worries. There was another big problem looming and time was running out to find a solution.

Chapter 41

The E22 superhighway, stretching from Dublin in the west to the Russian trading town of Ishim in the east, is one of the most strategically important roads in Europe. It's a three thousand mile narrow strip of asphalt that carries millions of tonnes of freight every year. And yet for the last thirty minutes Blake hadn't seen another vehicle.

They'd rumbled on for mile after mile catching only the occasional glimpse of headlights in the distance. Beams would appear on the horizon as pinpricks of light, dancing a hypnotic jig as they grew larger, and flashed past in a blinding glare that stung Blake's sore eyes. The weak headlights of their own truck barely illuminated the immediate patch of road ahead and threw only a faint glow over the trees of the rolling forests around them.

Blake would have normally taken the opportunity to sleep. It was an old Army habit. Banking sleep whenever he could. But it had been impossible. His mind was working overtime. And he wanted to keep an eye on the driver. It would have been a disaster if he'd nodded off.

'How are you feeling?' Blake asked.

'Fine, thank you, Sir,' said the young corporal. He glanced briefly at Blake before setting his eyes back on the road.

He was a quietly-spoken Liverpudlian with thick eyebrows and hairy arms. Lean and lithe. Much smaller than the tough, fighting men in the back. Not that Blake doubted his credentials. He'd trust with his life anyone who'd won the coveted winged-dagger of the SAS.

'I don't want you falling asleep on me.'

'I'm as fresh as a daisy. I only wish we could get on a bit faster.'

He'd driven for hour after hour without a hint of fatigue. Blake knew his own eyes would have been rolling into the back of his head a long time ago.

'What's your name?'

'Toller, Sir.'

'Do you have a first name?'

'Danny.'

'Volunteer for this mission?'

'Of course. Without hesitation.'

'Why?'

'Why not?'

The operation had been put together with barely twenty-four hours' notice when Blake had raised the alarm from Norway. With the Armageddon Virus heading for Russia and on to the Middle East, a plan had been hastily convened for an audacious Special Forces mission into the heart of the Russian capital, although not without resistance from some quarters of the Government. Committing troops to Russia without the Kremlin's knowledge was like waving a match at a petrol-soaked rag. It might pass off without incident, but there was a fair chance it would blow up in their faces. If the Kremlin discovered British Special Forces were operating under their noses in Moscow, it would go way beyond a diplomatic incident. Wars had been started over less. But there were precious few other options. Mortensen presented them with a narrow window to retrieve the virus and capture Khan, and Blake had been determined to take it.

A team had been rapidly put together and dispatched into Russia in pairs to avoid suspicion. They'd posed as tourists and businessmen and travelled by plane, coach and train across the border. Their rendezvous was on the outskirts of Moscow where arrangements had been made with well-placed contacts to supply them with Russian Army uniforms and military vehicles.

So far the operation had run without a hitch. The test-tubes Mortensen had hidden at the railway station had been switched. Two of the team had taken a train to Poland with the virus, and been evacuated by helicopter back to the UK.

'No reservations? It's a high-risk mission.'

Toller rubbed his eye with the knuckle of his left hand. 'Not at all, Sir. There aren't many of us Russian language specialists in the Service.'

'You speak Russian?'

'My grandfather came from Vologda.'

'Well, what are the chances?'

They watched the lights of a truck loom large and blaze past on the opposite side of the road. The turbulence from the speeding lorry rocked the Kamza.

'Can I ask a question, Sir?' asked Toller.

'Of course.'

'How are you planning to get us across the border?'

Their rendezvous with the RAF Chinook was in a little more than ninety minutes, on the other side of the Latvian border. An airborne extraction from inside Russia had been dismissed as too risky. Latvia, on the other hand, as a paid-up member of Nato, would turn a blind eye. It had permitted an aircraft into its airspace on the condition it was on a pick-up and recovery op. But no one had resolved how to transport a lorry-load of British soldiers, an MI5 spy and their Iranian prisoner out of Russia through a fully-manned checkpoint. That detail had been left to Blake to work out on the ground and had been taxing him for the last four hours.

'Where's the next truck stop?' Blake asked.

'I'm not sure,' said Toller. He fumbled in the pocket of the door for a creased map. He tried to unfold it over the steering wheel.

'Here, give it to me.' Blake took it and spread it out on

the dashboard. 'Here, in about thirty miles,' he said. He jabbed at it with his finger. 'We'll stop there. We need to lose the truck.'

'Excuse me, Sir?'

'We can't cross the border in this truck. We don't have the papers and a military Kamza packed with Russian soldiers might raise a few eyebrows on the Latvian side, don't you think? Is your Russian good enough to blag your way across?'

'Yes, Sir.'

'Then we need to find alternative transport. A service station's our best and only chance at this time of night.'

'You think it will be open?'

'Better if it's not.'

The service station appeared on their left after a gentle rise in the road. Facilities were basic. A cashier's cabin and two sets of pumps under a wide canopy. Lots of white plastic sitting starkly amid a pine forest and illuminated by the amber glow of down lighters. The cabin was in darkness apart from the strobing red light of an alarm.

Four articulated lorries with paintwork marbled with layers of dust and grime were parked in a line. Toller pulled up alongside the nearest one. Killed the engine and let the rattling die away. It was a Polish-registered truck with a plain white trailer. Ideal for what Blake had in mind. A miniature satellite dish had been mounted to the roof of the cab and curtains drawn around the windscreen.

Blake was out of the Kamza before it had rolled to a halt. Toller joined him and they approached the lorry together. Blake crept up to the driver's door. 'Hey! Hey! Wake up! Quickly!' He banged with a flat palm.

A light came on and the vehicle rocked on its suspension as someone moved about inside.

'Hey! Hey!' Blake shouted again.

The door opened a fraction and a voice heavy with sleep called out in a language Blake didn't understand. He grabbed the door and wrenched it from the hand of a startled truck driver with a looping grey moustache and an off-white vest tight over his pot-belly. His eyes grew wide when he saw Blake in his Russian military uniform pointing a pistol. Toller hauled himself into the passenger seat on the other side of the cab.

'Hello, mate,' said Toller with a cheery smile. He aimed a Sig Sauer P226 at the man's gut.

'Speak English?' asked Blake.

'Of course,' said the driver, rubbing a hand over the bristles of several days' beard growth. His brow furrowed.

'Sorry for the wake-up call but we need your truck,' said Blake. 'Move over.'

The driver looked at Blake blankly.

'What's in the back?'

'Nothing.' The driver shook his head as if he was coming to his senses. 'I carry machine parts but I made the delivery and now I'm on my way home.'

'Not ideal but we'll have to make do,' said Blake looking to Toller. He was keeping watch for approaching traffic. 'Get the men unloaded and into the back.'

Toller slipped out of the cab and when he had disappeared from view, Blake fixed the driver with a penetrating stare.

'What's your name?' he asked softly.

'Oskar Smolak.'

'Been running freight long?'

'About eight years on this route,' he said.

He'd barely managed to speak the words when Blake's left hand flashed towards his head. He tapped the driver's forehead with two fingers. 'Sleep now,' said Blake.

Smolak's eyes rolled into the back of his head and his chin slumped onto his chest. Blake intoned soothing words into the man's ear, watching his breathing slow as he relaxed into a deep trance.

From the corner of his eye Blake saw a trail of soldiers jog around the front of the lorry. He heard their boots thudding into the empty trailer. It took less than three minutes to load all the men, including Mortensen and the captive Khan, from one vehicle to the other. The rear doors clattered closed. Toller hid the Kamza behind the service station, in the shadow of the forest.

'Everything okay?' said Toller. He nodded at the slumbering driver as he hauled himself into the cab.

'Oskar, wake up. I want you drive us to the Latvian border.'

Smolak's eyes peeled open. He looked around his cab with incomprehension, as if he had no idea where he was. Blake threw him a shirt hanging in the rear of the cab and switched seats. Smolak fired up the Scania. Bright headlights illuminated the forecourt and, with a hiss of brakes, they rolled out of the service station, picking up speed as they joined the main carriageway.

The checkpoint appeared in the middle of the road out of nowhere. A blue hut with a striped traffic barrier. Smolak eased off the accelerator and a guard emerged blinking in the glare of the lorry's headlights.

'They won't be expecting me at this time of the night,' said Smolak in a flat tone. 'It will be very suspicious to them.'

Blake ducked under the dashboard. Toller followed.

'Convince them everything's normal,' said Blake. 'Remember we're not here.'

'You trust him not to raise the alarm?' whispered Toller.

'He won't.'

The lorry rolled to a halt at the barrier. Smolak wound down his window. Blake heard a woman's voice speaking in heavily-accented English. 'It's early to be travelling.' She posed the statement like an accusation.

'I'm behind time,' said Smolak. 'I had to replace a wheel and I'm supposed to be back at the depot by the morning.'

'Passport?'

Smolak handed down his documents. The guard

seemed to dwell on them for an age. Longer than she might during the busy parts of the day, Blake suspected.

'Okay, come through. You know the drill.'

Smolak threw the lorry into gear and they trundled forwards.

'Good work, Oskar,' Blake whispered. Despite his concerns, their passage through the checkpoint had been remarkably easy.

'You'd better stay down,' said Smolak.

'What?'

'Keep your head down.'

The lorry was slowing again. It rolled to a halt less than twenty metres on.

'What are you doing?' asked Blake.

'I told you, he can't be trusted,' said Toller.

Smolak pulled on the handbrake and killed the engine. 'That was the first checkpoint. I need to get through customs and immigration,' he said.

'What does that entail?'

'I have to show my papers,' said Smolak. He reached into a glove box for a sheaf of documents. 'Sometimes, if they're bored, they like to search the trucks.'

'Persuade them that's a bad idea. Do you understand? You have to make sure they don't find us.'

Smolak jumped from the cab and slammed the door closed.

'Damn!' Blake cursed. It was strictly against his own code of conduct to let someone under his hypnotic control leave his sight. He considered it professional misconduct. But Smolak had gone before he had a chance to stop him.

'He's going to tell them,' said Toller.

'I don't think so, but there's a chance he might inadvertently raise their suspicions and they could insist on checking the lorry. Have your sidearm ready.'

Blake heard voices. He held his breath but couldn't make out what was being said. He checked his watch and stretched a leg where he could feel cramp setting in.

Minutes passed like hours and without the heat of the engine the cab soon fell cold. Blake was grateful for his Russian greatcoat. He hoped Mortensen and the men in the trailer weren't suffering too much.

Eventually the driver's door swung open and Smolak climbed in.

'Is everything all right?'

'Yes, we're can carry on,' he said, without looking at Blake. He turned the ignition key and the truck rattled into life. Smolak raised a hand to an unseen figure and they moved forwards.

Blake risked raising his head and saw two border guards with dark uniforms and severe expressions clutching SR-2 Veresk sub-machine guns.

'Is that it?' asked Blake.

'I told them I was in a hurry to get back and that the trailer was empty.'

'They believed you?'

'They know me,' said Smolak. His face was expressionless.

'Exceptional work, Oskar. Thank you.'

When Smolak looked down at Blake under the dashboard it was as if he was seeing him for the first time. His eyes were dead. The cab jolted forwards as he selected second gear. His foot hovered over the accelerator and he checked his side mirror.

'Halt! Halt!' One of the guards was screaming at the lorry to stop.

'What's going on?'

'They want us to stop,' said Smolak. He hit the brakes, sending Blake and Toller into the solid plastic of the dashboard with a heavy thud.

The guard caught up with the Scania and approached it with his submachine gun angled across his body. Blake's hand settled on the Browning in his pocket. He eased off the safety with his thumb. 'What do they want?'

'I don't know.'

'Act normally. Smile and get rid of them.'

Smolak wound down his window.

'We can't let you leave,' said a voice in English spoken through a thick accent.

'What's the problem?' asked Smolek.

'You know you really shouldn't be in such a hurry.'

Blake's pulse was racing and his gut tightened. He wondered how it might play out if the guards decided to check the trailer. What if they found British soldiers, dressed as Russians, hiding in the back? He thought of Mortensen and Khan. An MI5 spy and their Iranian prisoner. There was no easy way to explain any of it away.

Smolak said nothing.

'You see, I think you are forgetting something,' the guard continued.

'No, I don't think so.'

'Your passport, Oskar. You left it in the office. You wouldn't have made it far home without it.'

'I'm an idiot. Thank you.' Smolak leaned out and took the passport.

'No problem. Safe journey.'

Smolak tossed the passport onto the dashboard and wound up the window. 'We have one more barrier to clear but we shouldn't have to stop,' he said.

The truck rolled towards a third and final barrier which was raised as they approached. Smolak waved to a guard in a wooden hut and accelerated onto the open road stretching ahead.

Blake waited until he was sure they were clear of the crossing before hauling himself from the floor.

'Can I have my truck back?' said Smolak, without a hint of emotion.

'Of course,' said Blake. 'A little further on and you can pull over.'

'Where's the rendezvous, Sir,' said Toller, dusting himself down.

'Close. You'll know when we get there.'

Smolak drove at a steady 50mph, never letting his eyes stray from the road that stretched ahead straight and true for as far as his headlights would reach. The three men sat in silence until Toller spoke.

'Can you hear that?'

Blake peered through the windshield at the charcoal sky. At first he heard nothing over the drone of the lorry's diesel engine and the hum of a dozen rubber tyres on asphalt.

'A chopper,' said Toller. 'It's close.'

'Slow down,' said Blake. Smolak eased his foot off the accelerator and changed down a gear. 'Slower,' Blake insisted.

The unmistakable throb of helicopter rotor blades resonated through the air and filled the cab. A spectral pulsating that vibrated in their chests. The bulbous hulk of an RAF Chinook materialised over the tops of the trees that lined the carriageway. It came in low and fast, swooping into their path and hovered over the road a quarter of a mile ahead.

'It's landing in the road!' said Smolak.

He jumped on the brakes, locking the wheels in a squealing cloud of burning rubber. The trailer fishtailed, threatening to slide out of control. The truck eventually came to rest with the trailer sideways to the cab.

'Get the men into the chopper,' Blake ordered Toller. 'As quick as you can. And make sure the woman is looked after.'

'Yes, Sir.' Toller nodded and vanished out of the cab.

Smolak sat with his hands on the wheel, staring at the helicopter.

'Oskar, I want you to sleep deeply now.' Blake had to shout to be heard over the noise of the Chinook. 'Let your eyes close and relax.'

Smolak's head lolled to one side and his lids fluttered shut. His hands dropped from the steering wheel into his lap.

'In a moment I want you to start counting from one hundred down to zero. When you reach zero you'll be awake and feeling refreshed. You won't remember anything about what's happened. You'll continue to drive until you find the next rest area where I want you to pull over and sleep until morning. When you wake you'll continue your journey home as if nothing has happened. Do you understand?' Blake took Smolak's slight head movement as a nod.

Through the windscreen Blake watched the soldiers scuttle towards the helicopter with their heads bowed. One of the men carried the limp body of Khan over his shoulder like a sack of flour. He kept a careful eye on Mortensen as she was escorted towards the aircraft by Toller. And when he was sure they were all safely on board, he started Smolak's countdown and jumped out of the cab.

He ran to the rear of the helicopter and up a ramp into its belly where two waiting airmen grabbed his arms to help him on board. The soldiers were strapping themselves into seats with the grins of men sensing the relief of completing a mission unscathed.

Blake sat next to Mortensen as the rear ramp closed and the engines whined into an excited frenzy ready for take-off.

'Everything okay?' he mouthed. Her skin was pallid and there were dark patches under her eyes.

She looked at him for a moment and nodded. 'Yes,' she said and let her head fall on his shoulder. They felt the pull of the giant Chinook lifting them skywards.

'Good,' he said, grabbing her hand. He squeezed it gently. 'We'll be home by morning.'

Chapter 42

THREE MONTHS LATER

A cooling breeze drifted off a glittering sapphire sea and ruffled Blake's hair. The tang of sea salt and the perfume of frankincense whispered through the fronds of date palms growing through squares in a wooden terrace. It was warm like an English summer. Shirt-sleeves weather. Not the stifling heat that Oman likes to cook up in the high season. The cold and wet London Blake had left behind seemed like a different world.

'Blake,' said a voice. Mortensen strode out of a stone villa. 'You came,' she said with a genuine smile.

'I was intrigued.' He was glad to see she'd rinsed her hair back to its natural colour and the tight curls had returned.

She grabbed him by the arms and offered a cheek to kiss. 'I wasn't sure you would. How was your flight?'

'Tiring.' He sipped at a cold beer someone had pressed into his hand.

She led him to a circle of Rattan armchairs around a glass-topped table adjacent to a plunge pool cut into the terrace. They sat opposite each other, the craggy mountain the colour of lion-pelt creating a dramatic backdrop.

'This is an impressive place,' said Blake.

'Our Omani friends make sure we're comfortable.'

The villa was traditionally Arabic with its natural stone walls and soft, bleached wood but it had been designed with luxury in mind. The floors were marbled, the furniture expensive and it was kitted out with the latest technology. It was hidden behind high walls at the end of a long, private drive on the outskirts of Muscat. An expensive holiday retreat for the wealthy and privileged.

'We're handing Khan back,' said Mortensen.

Blake studied her face looking for the glimmer of a smile, a crack in her stony expression. But there was nothing. 'You asked me out here to tell me that?'

'He's no use to us any more.'

'He's a terrorist.'

'He was careful never to get blood on his hands. We know he was involved in at least half a dozen attacks on Western targets but there's nothing to link him to a single incident. We'd never make a prosecution stick. We managed to drag some useful intelligence about the regime out of him but that's it. It's too complicated to detain him in the UK. Besides the Iranians are kicking off.'

'And since when did we start worrying about what Tehran wants?'

'Since it started suiting us.'

'What about the Americans? They had their eye on Khan long before us.'

'They'd like to get him to Guantanamo but the PM's refused extradition. We've given them access in the UK but they've not had much joy either.'

'We risked everything sending a team to Moscow. How can you even think about letting him go?'

'He's already gone. A few hours ago. The Omani Government made the arrangements for the hand-over.'

'Thanks for the heads-up.'

'The Iranians know what happened in Moscow.'

'It was always a risk.'

'They're threatening to expose the operation to the Russians. We know Putin's already jumpy about the West. We don't know how he'll react if he finds out. Worst case scenario is a military retaliation. We can't risk it. The deal was we hand Khan back and they keep quiet.'

'I thought we had good intelligence on Khan? We could have saved ourselves a whole lot of trouble.'

'It was worth the risk. We've eliminated him from the game. He's no use to Iran now, not with his identity blown. At best he'll be punished with a desk job.' She paused for a beat. 'But there's something else I've not told you.'

Mortensen crossed her legs and picked at an imaginary hair on her knee as though she was working out how to phrase her next sentence. Blake pursed his lips.

'I was in contact with Javed Rahimi before his death,' she said. 'I was assigned as his case officer but he was killed before I had the chance to find out what was going on in Marshside.'

Blake drained his glass and watched a beery froth slide to the bottom. He set it down on the table. 'So what you told Khan in Norway was true? Why didn't you tell me before?'

'Rahimi approached the police shortly before he was murdered. The case was referred to Special Branch who alerted the agency. He was terrified about what he'd got himself caught up in. I wanted to tell you, but I needed you untainted. To draw your own conclusions.'

'So what did he say?'

'That he'd struck up a friendship with Elias Pitts.'

'Pitts was grooming him?'

Mortensen frowned at Blake's use of the word. She knew what he meant. 'I don't think so. It was more opportune than that after he found out about the project Benjamin was working on. He realised the potential of the virus as a weapon and was looking for a means to exploit an opportunity.'

'You mean he needed someone to sell it to and Rahimi was his best option?'

'Probably his only option. Rahimi told him about his past in Iran and about how he'd been tortured. He told him he'd fled the country but had to leave his wife and daughters behind. Pitts made him an offer, said he could guarantee the safe passage of his family to Britain.'

'On what condition?'

'That Rahimi found someone in Iran who would negotiate a deal on his behalf.'

'So Pitts told Rahimi about the Armageddon Virus?'

'No, I'm certain he knew nothing about it. Pitts told him he'd acquired some information that would be of interest to the Iranians. That's all. He wanted Rahimi's help to put the word out. When I interviewed him he'd already managed to make contact with someone from the Iranian Ministry of Intelligence. They'd arranged for him to smuggle a phone into the prison so they could speak directly with Pitts.'

'Khan?'

'More likely one of his subordinates. They had no idea what Pitts was offering at that stage but were intrigued enough to find out more.'

'So if you knew what was going on, why did it take the Americans to raise the alarm? You said they intercepted a call from inside the prison. But you already knew a phone had been smuggled in.'

Mortensen squinted at the sea as sunlight sparkled off its surface. 'The truth? We didn't take the threat seriously. What Rahimi was claiming seemed so far-fetched.'

'Until the Americans located the phone signal and Rahimi wound up dead?'

'Yes,' said Mortensen. When she looked back at Blake her eyes were red. 'We let him down, Blake.'

'You couldn't have known.'

'He was murdered because the Iranians found out he'd spoken to me and I did nothing to stop it.' Mortensen wiped the corner of her eye. 'As if that poor man hadn't been through enough.'

'You can't blame yourself,' said Blake, unsure what else to say. He chewed his lip while he waited for her to elaborate.

'He was really scared. He begged me not to send him home and pleaded for my help to get his family out of the country. I was due to meet him the day after his body was found.'

'If we followed up every crack-pot conspiracy theory that came our way we'd never sleep. You made the best judgement you could with the information you had.'

'I should have taken it more seriously. If it wasn't for me, the Armageddon Virus would never have been stolen and Rahimi would still be alive. I messed up. But I'm going to make amends.'

Mortensen flicked a loose corkscrew of hair out of her eyes and sniffed as she composed herself.

'How?'

'There's something I want to show you.' Mortensen rose from her seat and smoothed her skirt over her thighs.

She led Blake inside the villa and out through a main door into a courtyard he'd passed through when he'd arrived. A small group had gathered. Agency staff. All white shirts, dark suits and sunglasses. Patiently waiting among the soft plants and palms in the shade of the towering security walls that surrounded the complex.

A pair of gates buzzed open slowly letting the sunlight stream through a widening gap. A convoy of three black cars swept into the compound along a drive covered by a fine dusting of sand. They came to a halt in a semi-circle. Six men sprang from the cars at the front and rear. Omani Secret Service, Blake guessed. They all wore double-breasted suits, sombre ties and dark glasses.

A Mercedes saloon in the middle of the three was so highly polished that it reflected the stonework of the villa in its bodywork. One of the Omanis stepped up to a rear door and held it open. A middle-aged woman with a purple hijab wrapped around her head and face appeared. She adjusted her clothing and stood blinking in the bright light, staring at the faces watching. Two more women emerged. Young and slim, their eyes bright but furtive.

Mortensen stepped forwards and the older woman pulled them to her chest.

'Welcome,' said Mortensen with a slight bow. 'I hope your journey wasn't too stressful.'

The women said nothing, holding Mortensen's eye with a look of distrust.

'Please, come inside and freshen up. We have a few hours for you to relax before we leave for the airport.'

The three women were ushered into the villa. Two Omani secret servicemen followed behind with bags from the boot of the car.

'Who are they?' said Blake.

'You don't recognise them?'

'Should I?'

'The older woman is Niyoosha. Her daughters are Yasaman and Alaleh. You saw their photo in Rahimi's bedsit.'

'His wife and daughters? What the hell are you playing at Alex?'

'Making amends for what happened to Javed Rahimi. He wanted his family out of Iran and given asylum in the UK. So, we've made it happen.'

'You exchanged them for Khan? And that's your way of fixing this?'

'Don't be so bloody righteous, Blake,' said Mortensen. She pushed past him, brushing his shoulder. She marched into the villa, Blake a few paces behind.

'Makes you feel better, does it?'

'Keep your voice down,' she said.

Blake followed her onto the terrace overlooking the Gulf.

'I can't believe this has been sanctioned. Is Patterson aware?'

'Of course he's aware. Didn't you wonder how a prison cleaner could get access to someone senior enough in the Iranian intelligence services who would sit up and take note of Pitts' claims that he had secrets to sell?'

Blake shrugged. 'I guess it was a little implausible.'

'You want to know how he did it? Well, you just met her.'

'Rahimi's wife? What do you mean?'

'No, not his wife. His daughter, Yasaman. The older girl.'

Blake's mind whirled. He tried to remember how old she was. A girl in her late teens. Maybe still at school. How could she possibly have been involved. 'I still don't understand,' he said.

'She's a chip off the old block. A computer whizzkid.'

Blake shook his head.

'Rahimi was a software engineer, in the private sector working for an oil firm. He was well regarded in the industry until he was caught up in the political unrest. It turns out Yasaman is equally adept around a computer. Except she's put her skills to less legitimate pursuits.'

'A hacker?'

'State-sponsored. She was part of an elite network of so-called black hatter hackers employed by the Iranian intelligence service to develop worms and malware to target systems in the West.'

'A cyberterrorist?'

'Tasked with probing commercial and governmental computer systems looking for weak points to exploit. But they've also been given responsibility for tightening up Iranian systems to prevent attacks like the Stuxnet worm that compromised Iran's nuclear programme.'

'Clever girl. And she was able to get access to someone who would take Rahimi's request seriously?'

'With a little digital subterfuge, we think.'

'And she's worth the trade with Khan?' asked Blake.

'I think she could be worth ten of him.'

They stood with their backs to the villa watching the dark shadow of a cormorant skim across the water, its wing tips almost touching the surface.

'I really hope so, for your sake, Alex.'

For a while they didn't speak, enjoying the warmth of the sun on their necks. The bitter remnant of hops on his tongue made Blake wonder if there was somewhere he could find another beer.

'Blake, I need your help,' said Mortensen, breaking the silence.

She was leaning on a railing on the end of the terrace peering down at the surf foaming onto the rocks below. The sun had flushed her pale skin a shade of red.

'Which is the real reason you've asked me here?'

'We want Yasaman to work for us. She's a bright kid and her skills would be invaluable to our cyber security unit. Plus, she'll be able to give us an insight into Iran's cyber programme.'

'Will she co-operate?'

'When she finds out the truth about what happened to her father, I think we'll be able to persuade her.'

'Why do you need me?'

Mortensen angled her head upwards to look at Blake. 'I want to know if we can trust her.'

'Enough to give her access to Governmental computer systems? That's a lot of trust for someone you've only just met.'

Mortensen stared at Blake as if she was waiting for him to come to a conclusion. Those big, green eyes. Windows on the soul. He noticed a spatter of freckles across her nose. Maybe brought on by the sun. Her lips were pursed tightly, her hair scraped away from her face and cascading down her neck in tight ringlets.

'Alex, don't even think about asking.'

'Blake, please?'

He turned from her and walked away towards the villa, his feet thudding across the deck. She caught up with him, grabbed his elbow and spun him around.

'We have to be sure we can trust her.'

'Then find another way,' said Blake. 'I'm not interrogating a teenage girl. Find someone else to talk to her.'

'There is no other way. We have to be absolutely certain she won't betray us and only you can give us that certainty. You can sow the seeds in her mind that will guarantee her co-operation. I've seen you do it before.'

'No, Alex. She's no more than a girl. Her brain is still developing.'

One of the women Blake had seen earlier appeared from the villa. Another agent. More junior than Mortensen, Blake guessed from her demeanour. She hovered at the edge of the terrace, uncertain whether to interrupt.

'Miss Mortensen, we need you upstairs,' she said at last.

Mortensen shot her a look that left her in no doubt her timing was poor.

'What is it?'

'It's Mrs Rahimi. She's working herself up into a state about everything. I think you need to come and talk to her.'

'Can't you sort it out? I'm busy,' Mortensen barked.

The woman remained rooted to the spot with a pained expression.

'All right, I'm coming.' Mortensen turned and barged past Blake. 'Stay here, I'll be right back.'

Blake watched her glide away, her hips rolling under the tight fabric of her pencil skirt, her heels clicking across the deck. He glanced up at the sky, marvelling at the deepness of blue. There wasn't so much as a wisp of a cloud. It didn't feel much like February. Voices drifted from a room upstairs and he heard muted wailing. It made him shudder. He wasn't much good with emotional women. Was there somewhere to get another beer?

He wandered casually through the villa, retracing his steps to the outer courtyard where the row of black Mercedes was parked. He stepped up to the gates and they clicked open automatically, triggered when he broke an invisible beam. He waited patiently for them to swing apart fully and reveal the sand-dusted drive ahead. They thumped to a halt against rubber stoppers and Blake adjusted his sunglasses. He glanced over his shoulder but no one was watching. He took one step forwards followed by another, onwards towards the city.

It was going to be a long walk in the heat but he knew the first beer in the first bar he found would make the trek worthwhile.

The Viper's Strike

Chapter 1

Tom Blake nudged the cardboard cup across the table. 'Drink,' he said, with a nod and a neutral smile. A small gesture weighted with a ton of psychological significance.

I'm your friend. I'm here to help you out of this mess.

Blake noticed the man's fingernails were chewed down to the flesh. Red raw and ragged. 'What's your name?'

The man set the cup next to a hardback atlas of the world open on the table. A green expanse fringed by sea spilled over two pages. 'Neno Kasun,' he said, with a weary sigh. Sharp incisors toiled at a snag of skin around his thumb.

'I need you to answer some questions.'

Kasun nodded. His tie hung loosely around his neck, and the top two buttons of his shirt were undone, exposing a grubby vest.

'Age?'

'Forty-seven.' His accent was difficult to identify. He could have been from anywhere from central Europe to the Middle East. And he looked tired to the point of collapse. His clothes were crumpled, and his eyes heavy, sunken into dark sockets. He'd been well worked over by interrogators throughout the night, but resolutely stuck to his story, as ridiculous as it sounded.

'Why are you in the U.K.?'

Kasun had been tapping his foot rhythmically on the floor. And then it stopped. 'I've been through this already, many times,' he said. 'When can I go?'

'Tell me again,' said Blake, his tone even and calm. His

good cop voice.

Kasun rolled his eyes to the ceiling, and blinked. The air was dry, and stale with the fug of fear and anxiety. 'I'm a salesman. I have a meeting with a client.'

'What are you selling?'

'Machine parts.'

Blake watched for any subtle giveaways that would confirm Kasun's deceit. 'You're lying to me.'

'No.'

It was clear from the moment he'd been detained that his whole story was a fabrication, which was confirmed when they checked the details. The managing director of the Oxfordshire engineering firm, with whom Kasun claimed to have an appointment, answered his phone through the fog of sleep, and replied testily that he had no appointments scheduled with salesmen at all that week. And no, he'd never heard of anyone called Neno Kasun.

'Are you married?'

'Yes.'

'What's her name?'

Kasun hesitated, and his brow furrowed. 'Elena,' he said, at last.

Blake raised an eyebrow. 'Are you sure?'

'Yes.'

'How long have you been together?'

'Fifteen years.'

'Children?'

'No.'

Blake uncrossed his legs, and leaned forward with his forearms on his thighs. He'd carried out hundreds of interrogations, but the interview room wasn't Blake's natural domain. A table and two chairs in a well-lit, temperate room was a luxury. Usually, he was lucky if he managed to find somewhere with a roof.

'You flew in from Turkey?' Blake asked, at last.

'Yes.'

'And you travelled through Syria.' Not a question. A

statement of fact. It was documented in black and white.

Kasun sat up straight. He obviously knew where this was going. He nodded, and let his gaze fall to his feet. His head lolled to one side as if he no longer had the strength to hold it upright.

'What were you doing there?'

'Business.'

'Who goes to Syria on business? The country's being torn apart by civil war.'

'War doesn't stop machines from breaking,' said Kasun. He reached for the coffee cup. Blake noticed his hand quiver.

'You're a Muslim?'

'Yes.'

'Devout?'

'I try to be.'

'Were you selling parts to Islamic State?'

'Of course not.'

'Weapons?'

'No!'

'But you're sympathetic to their cause?'

'No.'

'You're lying to me,' said Blake.

Tears welled in Kasun's eyes. He sniffed hard, and wiped his nose on his shirt sleeve. Blake sensed the fight ebbing from him.

'I just want to know the truth,' said Blake, his tone softening.

I'm your friend. I'm here to help you out of this mess.

'Why don't you believe me?' Kasun slurred his words, the effect of sleep deprivation finally taking its toll. His will was faltering. 'I want to go home.'

'I don't believe you, because nothing you've said makes sense.' Blake stifled a yawn, struggling with his own fatigue.

'I don't understand what you want.' Kasun's face crumpled, and for a moment, Blake felt a pang of compassion. Until he remembered the passport.

He dragged his chair closer to the table, pushed the atlas to one side, and picked up a blue passport hidden underneath it. It looked like a relic from the colonial past. A little larger than a standard British passport, with thin pages bound between a heavy-duty cardboard cover, and embossed with an intricate gold crest.

'Recognise this?' Blake flicked casually through the pages. They were well thumbed, and filled with a large number of immigration stamps.

'Of course,' said Kasun.

Blake passed the document across the table. 'Tell me what it says under the crest on the front?'

Kasun picked up the passport, and held it in his lap. He read the words out loud.

'And you can't see my problem here?'

Kasun shook his head solemnly; his eyes red and puffy.

Blake rocked back in his chair, and folded his arms across his chest. 'Well then, perhaps you'd like to explain to me exactly where we can find this Republic of Amana?'

Chapter 2

The man claiming to be Neno Kasun had arrived under grey skies at London's Heathrow airport on the 17:55 Turkish Airlines flight from Istanbul. He had attracted little attention on the uneventful four-hour flight, nor as he drifted through the labyrinth of airport corridors towards immigration control carrying a brown leather overnight bag, a battered attaché case, and a raincoat over his arm. He'd been able to stow all of his luggage in the overhead cabin lockers so he could circumvent baggage reclaim on his way out. Not that he made it that far.

At first, the dour border agency official suspected an elaborate prank. Without a hint of humour, the grey-haired officer flicked to the back page of Kasun's passport and checked the photo. It was a recent picture, and a decent facsimile.

'Where have you travelled from, sir?'

'Turkey,' said Kasun.

'Your country of origin?' said the officer, raising an eyebrow.

'Amana.'

The officer held Kasun's eye, showing not a flicker of emotion. 'Amana?' The shadow of a frown darkened the officer's face, and his finger drifted towards an alarm button on the underside of his desk. Two agency officials appeared, to escort Kasun out of the queues and into a windowless, sound-proofed interview room.

Kasun was warned that he faced a heavy fine unless he could produce some genuine documentation, but when he

561

didn't waver from his assertion that he was born and bred in a country no one in the world's busiest airport had ever heard of, they brought the matter to the attention of the police. They were equally dumbfounded, and wasted no time in alerting MI5 when it emerged Kasun had travelled through Syria. The inspector who'd inherited the case couldn't wash his hands of it quickly enough. And so, Neno Kasun had found himself departing the airport in the back of a police van heading for the high security cells at Paddington Green police station for questioning on suspicion of terrorism offences.

The agency brought in one of its most experienced interrogators. Myles Harrington had a voice like warm chocolate, and thin lips that seemed to curl both up and down, making it impossible to read his expression. He also possessed an eye for forensic detail, and a superhuman immunity to fatigue. It was gone eleven when he began his initial cross-examination of Kasun, and well past breakfast when he finally emerged from the interview room with a shake of his head and an admission of defeat. Kasun was sticking to his story.

Bringing in Blake was a last resort. His methods were unusual, but the agency was desperate. They had no intelligence on Kasun, and their paranoia was running high. They needed to know what he was doing on the British mainland. And fast.

*

The arrival of two strangers had silenced the greasy spoon café where Blake had been indulging in a cholesterol-laden breakfast. The pair stood awkwardly in the doorway, looking as if they'd landed from Mars. Tall and athletic in expensive tailored suits and with a practised public school confidence.

Blake knew at once that they'd come for him, and did his best to avoid their gaze. He smoothed out a page of the second-hand tabloid that had been left on his table, and stabbed at a watery mushroom. Hopeful that they'd not spotted him, he glanced up, and caught the eye of the younger looking of the pair.

'Tom Blake?' said the man with Joe 90 spectacles as he made a beeline for Blake. 'You need to come with us.'

'I'm eating,' said Blake. He hoped his gruff disdain might be enough to send them packing, but they stood patiently, undeterred by his rudeness.

An old man with a toothless grin and a soiled polyester suit stared at them with rheumy eyes from the next table.

When it became obvious the two strangers weren't going to leave, Blake kicked out a chair from under the table. 'You'd better sit down.'

'This is Agent Bill Sanders,' said the guy with the over-sized glasses, taking a seat. 'My name's Jonathan Green. We've been sent to bring you in.'

Neither man appeared to have hit their thirties. Both clean cut and soft around the edges. Their suits were sharp, and their shirts out-of-the-packet crisp white.

'Is that right?' Blake ran a hand over his chin, shadowed with three day's growth. His hair was an uncombed mess, and his unwashed clothes badly creased.

'It's urgent, sir. The Firm's been trying to reach you.'

'Yeah? Well, I've been busy.'

Busy was an understatement. Blake hadn't slept in over thirty hours. He'd forced himself to stay awake in anticipation of the arrival of two Somali brothers who were due to meet with a sleeper agent he was handling. It should have been the culmination of a six-month operation to infiltrate a weapons trafficking organisation, and the first major step to dismantling their network.

'Perhaps we're not making ourselves clear.' Sanders drew a hand over his shaven scalp, and fixed Blake from under a thick brow. 'This isn't a request.'

Blake slammed a palm against the table so hard his knife and fork jumped off the plate. 'And I told you already, I'm eating.'

'Sir, your phone's been switched off.' Green's eyes had grown wide behind his glasses. 'Nobody's been able to reach you.'

The knot of muscle in Blake's jaw tightened. He wasn't in the mood for this. The night had been a write-off. The brothers hadn't shown, and the lack of sleep had set his temper on a short fuse. His eyes stung, and his head was woolly. He pushed back his chair, and dug in his pocket for some loose change, which he dropped on the table to cover the bill.

'Follow me,' he said.

The two agents trailed him outside, through a series of quiet streets and back alleys, into the dark underbelly of the city, where tower blocks cast long shadows and the doorways stank of stale urine. Blake's temporary home.

He ducked through a metal gate, and vanished among stinking rubbish bins. Green followed first, fast, and urgent, trying to keep up. Blake's thick hands grasped his collar and lifted him off his feet. He slammed the agent into the wall with his forearm across his throat, a short career with MI5 proving no match for the experience of three decades in the military.

'Who the hell do you think you are, barging in like that and trying to blow my cover?'

The agent stammered for an answer, and Blake felt his Adam's apple rise and fall. His foppish hair had fallen loose over his eyes, and he looked even younger than when he'd walked into the café. Sanders came around the corner and froze. Blake shot him a look that persuaded him that intervening wasn't a good idea.

'Who sent you?' Blake loosened the pressure on Green's throat.

'Harry Patterson,' said Green. 'He was insistent that we shouldn't take no for an answer.'

'Patterson? Why?'

'I can't tell you,' said Green.

'You'll have to do better than that. I'm in the middle of an operation here.'

Sanders' feet scuffed on the ground. 'The operation's been burned.'

Blake blinked hard. 'What?'

'Your agent's been extricated, and the operation's been stood down.'

Sanders' words rang hollow around Blake's head. They must be mistaken. It had taken the best part of six months to set up the sting, and finally he was on the cusp of a major breakthrough. Why would they close down the operation when they were so close?

He let Green slip from his grasp. The agent dusted himself down, and ran his fingers through his hair. 'They were worried about his safety,' he said. 'But they got him out.'

'When?'

'I don't know the details. This morning, I think,' said Green.

'And Patterson authorised it? I need to speak with him. Give me your phone, mine's dead.'

Sanders called a pre-programmed number on his mobile, and when it connected offered it to Blake.

'Harry, what are you playing at?'

'Blake, at last. I need you. Get here as soon as you can. There's a car waiting. Something's come up that I think you'll be interested in.'

'But the operation? We've been planning it for months.'

'Don't worry about it. I'll explain everything when you get here.'

'You can't just do that without discussing it with me first,' Blake began, but the line was already dead. Blake stared at the phone in disbelief then tossed it back to Sanders. 'Right, so where's this car?'

Chapter 3

The first time Blake saw Neno Kasun was through a two-way mirror. His feet were crossed at the ankles, and he was rocking gently. Deep-set eyes and sallow cheeks gave his face a haunted expression. A little boy lost, waiting in the headmaster's study to face his punishment.

Blake barged into a darkened office trailed by Sanders and Green. He gave only a cursory glance at the hunched figure behind the glass before turning on his boss.

'What the hell's going on, Harry?'

Harry Patterson pushed himself off a wall. 'Blake, at last.'

'I want to know why you pulled the plug on the operation.'

'Don't worry about it. Rafiq's safe.'

A smell of stale coffee hung in the air.

'We were this close to getting him embedded. What possessed you to pull him out? The meeting was all set for last night.'

'The brothers didn't show, did they? Something spooked them, and I had to make a decision to protect you both,' said Patterson. 'We tried to contact you.'

'My phone died. Doesn't mean you had to burn Rafiq.'

'Look, something else has turned up that I really need your help with.'

'And that's it? Something else has turned up?'

'Don't be so melodramatic.'

Blake clenched his fists into tight balls as a sharp pain caught him behind the eye. 'To cap it all, you sent

Tweedledum and Tweedledumber to bring me in.'

The two agents shuffled awkwardly at the back of the room.

'They're good men, and for your information they've been assigned to the team for a while. Get used to them being around.'

'Don't be ridiculous,' said Blake.

'On the direct orders of the DDG,' said Patterson.

Sir Richard Howard, the deputy director general of MI5, with responsibility for domestic counter-terrorism operations had personally recruited Blake and Patterson when their specialist unit was shut down by the Army. Their continuing careers depended on his support.

'They're hardly old enough to be out of college. We're supposed to be a specialist team. What am I going to do with them?'

'You can start by cutting them some slack. Now look, we're wasting time. Forget Rafiq. We can rebuild the operation. We'll get him a cover story, say his uncle fell ill, or something. Right now, I need you to talk to this guy.' Patterson moved towards the dusky glass of the two-way mirror.

Blake sighed, considered storming out, and thought better of it. He and Patterson went way back and had forged a tight friendship facing hardship and adversity together.

'Who is he?' said Blake. He stepped closer, and took his first proper look at Kasun.

'Truth is, we don't know. He arrived in the country yesterday evening on a false passport, claiming to be on business. He's been thoroughly grilled, but we can't get a word of sense out of him.' Patterson detailed how Kasun had been detained at the airport

Blake raised an eyebrow. 'So he's a fantasist?'

'Who's recently travelled to Syria.'

'Did he say why?'

'Business.'

'You don't believe him?'

'I don't believe anything he's told us so far. The question is whether he's a danger to British security. Talk to him. Find out what the hell's going on.'

*

Blake slid the open atlas across the table. 'Show me on the map.'

Kasun leaned forward and blinked. His eyes settled where his finger landed on the page. It traced its way down the spine of central Europe, and came to rest on a ragged area sandwiched between Romania and Ukraine. 'Here,' he said.

'Read the name.'

Kasun squinted at the tiny black letters. 'Moldova,' he said, struggling with the word. He pronounced it with three syllables like a child encountering a new spelling.

'Close enough,' said Blake. He observed Kasun carefully, watching for any involuntary signs that he was feigning ignorance. 'Or to give it its full name, the Republic of Moldova. Population three million, and an autonomous nation since 1991 when it declared independence from Russia during the disintegration of the Soviet Union. Sound familiar?'

Kasun shook his head, his eyes fixed on the page.

'But absolutely no mention anywhere of this place you call Amana.'

'This is Amana.' Kasun's body language gave nothing away. None of the subtle ticks or tells that people usually displayed when they were evading the truth.

'No,' said Blake. 'Read it again.'

'Moldova,' Kasun repeated.

Blake shot a look at the two-way mirror, and caught a glimpse of his own reflection. He looked haggard and grey. His beard was tinged with silver and crows' feet framed his eyes. Age and too little sleep were taking their toll. He ran a hand over his scalp, and noted his hairline had receded a little bit farther.

On the other side of the glass, he was aware of three pairs of eyes watching, hoping for the answers that had so far eluded Kasun's inquisitors. But he was getting nowhere. It was time for an alternative course of action. The reason Blake had been summoned in the first place.

He stood, and pinched the corners of his eyes. Kasun watched him like a hawk, fearful of what his interrogator might do next. Blake paced around the table, and came up behind him.

'Keep looking at the book,' he said. 'I need to hear the truth. Unless you think this atlas is wrong?'

Kasun's attention returned to the contours of central Europe while Blake pulled up a chair behind him.

'Read some of the names of the major cities,' said Blake. 'See if they sound familiar. Start with the capital.'

Chisinau was marked in bold type, geographically as well as constitutionally at the heart of the country. But it wasn't important whether Kasun could pick it out or not, only that his attention was focussed on the map so that when his chair was pulled violently backwards the surprise rendered him momentarily dumb. The squeal of legs scraping on the tiles cannoned off the walls, and as Kasun spun through ninety degrees, his eyes opened wide. Blake seized on his sudden disorientation, and tapped him twice on the shoulder.

'Sleep,' he said, the warmth of his breath caressing Kasun's ear.

In a few brief seconds, Neno Kasun had fallen under a deep hypnotic trance. His eyes rolled back, and his lashes fluttered closed. His head lolled lazily on his shoulders and collapsed onto his chest, which rose and fell in a steady rhythm as his breathing slowed and his whole body relaxed.

Instant hypnotic induction. A technique Blake had mastered through years of trial and error. It had become his stock in trade, a quick and efficient means of extracting sensitive information from those unwilling to divulge their secrets. He'd discovered that even the most reluctant patient - he'd called them patients in keeping with his status as a fully qualified medical psychologist - could usually be persuaded to impart their darkest confidences under hypnosis.

His skills had been honed while operating within the covert Special Forces unit, Echo 17, where eventually he found he could conduct hypnotic interrogations almost anywhere, given a quiet space. It was clean and effective, and although considered ethically dubious in some medical quarters, Blake thought it far more humane than subjecting detainees to the horrific abuse he'd seen other security services employ to loosen tongues. But most importantly, hypnosis had rarely given rise to the false confessions that other interrogation methods regularly produced.

Not that his skill was unique. Stage hypnotists who used shock hypnosis or rapid hypnotic induction to induce a trance for entertainment had perfected the technique. But Blake had taken it to a new level, applying it in situations where hours, days, or even weeks of interrogation would usually be necessary. Coercive hypnosis, he called it.

Blake imagined Patterson straining to catch his amplified words through the speakers in the observation office, with Green and Sanders, maybe others, watching as the veil was lifted on his secret world. Blake hated being observed. Hypnosis exposed a patient's deepest subconscious, and stripped their soul bare. Blake believed he owed his subjects the dignity of privacy, no matter what secrets they were hiding. It wasn't a stage act for public consumption, and he certainly wasn't putting on a circus freak show.

Not that there was much he could do about it right now, other than keep it brief. He vowed to himself that he'd establish the essential facts of Kasun's story and wake him. With his true identity and purpose for travelling to Britain established, he could hand him back to the regular interrogators.

Blake listened to Kasun's breathing fall into a light and shallow pattern. He took a deep breath, and spoke slowly, close to Kasun's ear, guiding him down the deep tunnel to where his subconscious resided.

Satisfied that Kasun was in a deep trance, and susceptible to any question, Blake began the interrogation. And that's when everything started to unravel.

Chapter 4

Harry Patterson was watching from the interview room with Green and Sanders at his side.

'Hypnosis?' asked Green.

'Watch,' said Patterson. Although he knew Blake couldn't bear to be observed, he found the whole procedure mesmeric. 'He knows what he's doing.'

'How is it possible?' asked Sanders.

'Ethically or physically?'

'Both.'

'It's only ethically dubious if we stop achieving results. Then they'll start asking questions.'

'I thought it was impossible to put someone under if they're unwilling?' said Green.

'Blake's proven the research papers are wrong. He's the only one I'm aware of who's perfected a non-cooperative hypnotic programme,' said Patterson.

Most Western intelligence agencies had dabbled with the idea of hypnosis for interrogation, but none had found a fool-proof method. The CIA had thrown a multi-million dollar budget at it, but with little success. And Israeli Intelligence had encountered similar difficulties, despite a long era of experimentation that had lasted at least a decade.

'It's remarkable,' said Sanders.

'It's also classified. Nothing you see here today is spoken about. Understood?'

Both men nodded vigorously.

'Are his results reliable?' Sanders seemed to have taken

a particular interest in what was going on.

'It's not an exact science, but it's the most reliable interrogation method I've ever seen.'

On the other side of the glass, Blake leaned closer to Kasun.

'My name is Tom Blake. You are in a safe place,' he began. His voice, picked up on hidden microphones, crackled through speakers mounted in the office.

Kasun murmured through a bubble of spittle that had formed at the corner of his mouth. When Blake demanded his name, his response was inaudible nonsense.

'It happens sometimes,' said Patterson, with a shrug. 'It's a disconnect between the muscle that controls the mouth and the synapses in the brain, like when someone's talking in their sleep.'

'What's your name?' Blake repeated.

'Neno Kasun.'

If Blake was surprised, he didn't show it. 'Your real name?'

'Neno Kasun,' he repeated.

'Okay, well you recently arrived in Britain from Turkey, travelling on a fake passport, and told staff at the airport that you'd come from a country called Amana. Do you accept now that that was a lie?'

Kasun screwed his eyes tightly closed. His face crumpled in a twisted agony, and a low groan rose from his throat.

'Do you accept that was a lie?' Blake persisted.

Kasun's head rolled from side to side. His arm twitched violently, and when his body convulsed with an unexpected spasm it rocked the chair.

'What's happening?' asked Green.

'I'm not sure,' said Patterson.

'I'll take your silence as confirmation,' said Blake. 'So tell me the truth. Where have you come from?'

Kasun's low groan amplified into a wail as if he were battling some horrific inner demon. His hands clawed and stiffened. His head thrashed wildly, and convulsions wracked his body.

'He's having a fit,' said Sanders, stepping back from the glass. 'He needs a medic.'

'No,' said Patterson. 'Leave it. Blake knows what he's doing.'

'Mr Kasun, listen to me,' said Blake. 'You're fighting the truth. You have to relax.'

But Kasun's wail grew louder. It rose from deep within his chest like a banshee's scream. When his eyes shot open, his pupils had rolled back into his head, leaving only demonic milky white slits visible.

'Control your breathing. Remember, you're safe here in this room.' Blake's voice rose over the agonised screams that distorted the speakers and penetrated through the thick wall dividing the rooms.

Blake scowled at the two-way mirror, and shook his head slowly like a man admitting defeat.

'I'm going to bring him back around,' he said at last. 'Something's not right.'

Patterson bit his lip. He'd rarely seen Blake fail. He nodded his head with reluctant agreement, even though he knew Blake couldn't see.

Another agonising five minutes passed before Kasun's convulsions abated. Finally, he collapsed in his chair, his energy spent.

Blake stood, tapped on the door, and was let out without a backwards glance.

Chapter 5

The pain behind Blake's eye had settled into a dull ache. He sipped at a cup of insipid coffee from a dispensing machine, in the hope that caffeine might bring some relief. But, if anything it made it worse.

'I can't help,' he said. 'Kasun's delusional. There's a risk I could cause permanent damage to his mental health.'

'That's it?' said Patterson.

Blake sunk into the soft leather chair, and allowed his muscles to relax. 'He's telling the truth. Or at least what he believes is the truth. You saw him. He was turning himself inside out.'

'Terrific. So what am I supposed to report back? That he's some kind of inter-dimensional time traveller who's materialised through a black hole from an alternative universe? This is serious, Blake.'

'You wanted my professional judgement.'

Patterson paced up and down on the far side of the long conference table on the second floor of the police station. 'How can you suggest that someone who's arrived on a badly faked passport is telling the truth?'

'I said he's telling what he believes to be the truth.'

'And what's that supposed to mean?'

'He's confused and disorientated, maybe mentally unstable, but that doesn't make him a terrorist.' Blake rubbed the tips of his fingers across his brow, trying to massage away the pain. 'Put him on the next flight back to Turkey. They let him fly without checking his passport, so return the favour. Make it their problem.'

'You know we can't do that.'

'What other options do you have? Hold him indefinitely without charge?'

A rap on the door interrupted them. Green's head appeared through the gap. Blake tutted and rolled his eyes.

'Sir, the branch commander's demanding a progress report,' said Green, holding up his mobile phone.

'Stall him. Tell him we're still interrogating Kasun, but we're making some progress.'

'Are we?' asked Green.

'No, but no need for them to know that just yet.'

'Very good, sir.' Green eased the door closed behind him.

'Irritating little runt,' said Blake. He rolled his shoulders, crunching out the tension.

'You don't like him?'

'Not much.'

'He'll keep T Branch off our backs for a while, so be grateful for small mercies,' said Patterson.

As the agency's counter-terrorism investigation unit, T Branch had assumed responsibility for Echo 17 since it was brought under the auspices of MI5, and by rights, Blake and Patterson were now answerable to the T Branch commander.

'Keep them off your back, you mean,' said Blake. 'This has nothing to do with me. Not my operation.' He rubbed his eyes with the palms of his hands, and instantly regretted it. It was like smearing sand under his lids. He spun the chair to face the window overlooking the road, and forced his eyes wide.

'It is now.' Patterson pulled out a chair. The leather wheezed under his collapsing weight. 'I promised we could deliver results.'

'Harry, I did my best.'

'Yeah, I know.'

'There must be something else to go on? You've checked his luggage? His briefcase?' Blake stared at the traffic ebbing and flowing on the congested A40.

'He only had one small overnight bag and an attaché case. Nothing out of the ordinary. The case was stuffed with documents and sales invoices that appear to verify his story. A team's going through the names and addresses.'

'Nothing else?'

'His wallet was full of U.S. dollars and sterling. No family pictures. No driving licence. No credit cards.' Patterson paused. 'Although there was an address on a scrap of paper. They're checking that out too.'

'What address?'

'A residential property in Central London.'

'Could be a contact. I'll pay a visit if you like.'

'You just reminded me this isn't your operation.'

'Just trying to help out an old friend, Harry.'

'Thanks, I'll get the address over to you.'

'What about the CCTV from the airport?'

'What about it?'

'Has anyone checked it out? Maybe Kasun was an elaborate distraction?' said Blake.

'Distraction?'

Blake stood, walked to the end of the table, and squeezed past a flat screen television on a stand. 'Stand up,' he said.

Patterson hauled himself from the chair, and stood with his hands hanging loosely by his side.

'Have you ever watched a pickpocket? I mean, really studied what he's up to? It's all about misdirection.'

Blake opened Patterson's jacket with the tips of his fingers, tapped the wallet in his inside pocket.

'What are you doing?'

'No way I could take your wallet without you knowing about it, is there?' Blake's hands and arms moved in a synchronised whirl as he sidestepped Patterson and the men ended up shoulder to shoulder.

'Of course not,' said Patterson.

The colonel's wallet landed with a thud on the table. It

was like taking sweets from a baby.

'What the hell?'

'You had no idea I'd taken it because I'd directed your attention elsewhere. I changed your focus,' said Blake. 'And maybe that's what Kasun was doing. Have someone take a look at the CCTV in the arrivals hall around the time Kasun was detained. Get them to keep a careful eye on the other passengers. It could be that something else was going on while attention was focussed on Kasun.'

'Like what?'

'I don't know, but it's worth a check, isn't it?'

'Fine. I'll get someone to look into it. In the meantime, go home and get some kip. You look terrible.'

Blake tried to stifle a yawn. 'If you're sure?'

'Quite sure - unless you fancy another stab at Kasun?'

Blake shook his head. 'No way. He's too fragile. You'll have to do it the old-fashioned way.'

Chapter 6

The old warehouse appeared derelict; the mortar between the bricks was crumbling, and the paint on the door had blistered so badly a rainbow of faded colours was visible beneath. Metal and glass office blocks had sprung up on either side of the building from when developers had moved in to rejuvenate the area, but Blake had spotted the potential first, and resolutely clung onto his small slice of riverside heritage when they'd tried to buy him out.

Over the course of time, he'd transformed the interior into comfortable but basic accommodation, ripping out worm-ridden timbers, and installing new strip floors and tall windows overlooking the water. It had all the home comforts he needed, while retaining what he described as the building's character. In other words, walls had been left unplastered, ancient cobwebs gathered dust on the rafters, and the only source of heat was a rusty, wood burning stove in a sectioned-off area Blake called his lounge.

Blake threw his coat on a hook, and climbed a short flight of creaky stairs to his living quarters, taking the steps two at a time. The air was musty, but he was glad to be home, even though the fridge was bare apart from a half-empty carton of milk after a week camped out in the mouldy flat on the other side of the city. He sniffed it, recoiled at the curdled stench, and poured the lumpy contents down the sink. It was the all too familiar consequence of living alone. No one took care of home affairs while you were away.

He vowed to stock up later, but decided his need for

sleep was more pressing. He climbed a rickety ladder to his bedroom on a mezzanine floor in the loft, and collapsed fully clothed onto the bed.

When he woke with a start several hours later, the light had faded, and cool air had chilled his skin. It was already late afternoon. His lips were dry and cracked, and his head ached. He was vaguely aware of having been woken by a noise. The phone in his pocket chirruped again. A message from Patterson with the address from Kasun's wallet. At first glance, it seemed to be a random location in a smart area of town that meant nothing to Blake. He remembered his promise to visit, but needed a shower first.

The blast of hot water revived his senses, and a decent shave took at least five years off him. These days his stubble grew like a salt and pepper pebbledash. More grey than black. At first, he thought the five-day beard gave him a distinguished look, but conceded that losing it was an improvement. He tousled his hair dry, and wandered back into the bedroom with a towel around his waist.

He stopped by the shelf he'd built from a reclaimed timber beam, and swept up the dusty photograph of Laura. He wiped it clean with his forearm, and reacquainted himself with her image. Her long, blonde hair was pulled back from her face, and her blue eyes sparkled. She was on the cusp of smiling, captured by a photographer whose words had long been lost to him. So happy. So carefree. A long time before -

He banished the thought.

A younger version of Blake was standing in the background, a little out of focus, awkward and bemused in his formal, military number ones. A blue tunic buttoned up to his neck, his hair cut short under a dark beret. At some wedding or other. He couldn't remember now. Only that he'd been totally eclipsed by her. Somehow, the camera always seemed to bring out the best of her in the same way that it always captured the worst of him.

It was quite possible that she wore her hair short now,

and that the crags and wrinkles of age had altered her appearance beyond recognition. But he was sure he would always recognise her eyes, those scintillating orbs the colour of a warm summer sky.

He angled the frame so he could see it from the bed. It amused him that Laura would never have entertained the idea of living in the warehouse with its uneven, dusty floors and crooked beams. She'd have complained that the salty stench of rotting marine matter that filled the house twice a day made her nauseous, and that it wasn't a sensible place to bring up children. Too dark, too dingy. She'd always wanted children, and they'd talked about starting a family once they were married. Probably she'd have insisted he left the Army too for a safe, reliable job behind a desk. Blake shuddered at the thought.

A hollowness in the pit of his stomach reminded him of his hunger. He threw on clean clothes, and eventually found a can of soup that had lost its label lurking in the back of a cupboard. He warmed it in a pan, and while he waited for a pot of coffee to percolate, stared out the window at the passing river traffic. A string of barges had just stolen into view when three short bangs shattered the silence. Blake scowled. He wasn't used to receiving visitors, particularly as his address was a jealously guarded secret.

He grabbed his Browning from the kitchen worktop, and stuffed it in his waistband. He opened the door cautiously, and was surprised to find Johnnie Green standing on the threshold, his hands stuffed in his pockets, and an apologetic grin on his face. Bill Sanders was behind him, leaning against a Range Rover parked on the pavement.

'What are you doing here?'

'Patterson sent us to pick you up,' said Green.

'Again?'

'He wants us to take you to the address in Kasun's wallet. You promised to pay a visit?'

'Did you find out who lives there?'

'It's government owned, and the current residence of Russian dissident, Alexei Polzin,' said Green.

'The name sounds familiar.'

'He's a human rights campaigner given sanctuary in Britain after he received death threats in Moscow.'

'Any connection to our man from Amana?'

'No. But he does have a full security detail. Apparently, the prime minister was worried he could be the target of a Russian assassination attempt, and after the fiasco with Litvinenko, he doesn't want any more Russian blood spilled in London.'

Blake raised an eyebrow. 'Really?'

'What, you think Kasun might have been sent by the Kremlin?' said Sanders.

Blake shook his head. It was possible that Kasun was an assassin, but it seemed highly improbable. What state-sponsored killer would risk his mission by travelling on a fabricated passport with an immigration stamp that would inevitably be red-flagged at the border? 'Doesn't make sense,' he said.

'What then?' asked Sanders.

'I don't know. Shall we go and find out?' Blake snatched his jacket from a hook, pulled the door closed behind him, and jumped into the passenger seat of the Range Rover. 'Come on, let's go.'

Chapter 7

The receptionist was attractive in an unconventional way. Her suggestive smile held the hint of more fun than her straight-laced uniform promised, but her teeth overcrowded her mouth, and her skin bore the scars of youthful acne under a thick layer of foundation. A flimsy chiffon blouse, buttoned up to her neck, was finished off with a colourful silk scarf. It was almost transparent against her pasty skin, and allowed him to trace the outline of her underwear.

'Room 329.' She handed him a credit card sized key in a cardboard wallet. 'On the third floor. You can take the lift, or the stairs are through the double doors.' She checked the computer screen. 'And it looks like there's a parcel for you too.'

As she tottered into an adjacent office, his eyes wandered over the tight fit of her skirt and down her tan-stockinged legs.

She returned with an oblong box wrapped in plain brown paper.

'There you go.' There was that suggestive smile again.

He tucked the package under his arm, and considered asking when her shift finished. But stopped himself. No time for distractions when he had a job to do.

'What's your name?' He leaned over the counter, and her smile dropped.

She glanced down at the name badge pinned to her chest as if to remind herself, or more likely to break his intense gaze.

'Cara,' she said, uncertainly.

'Well, thank you, Cara. You've been most helpful.' He reached for the badge between his thumb and forefinger, and deliberately let his hand brush against the silky material of her blouse and the swell of her breast. A red blotch flushed under her chin. The poor girl's embarrassment only emboldened him further. He touched her cheek with his fingertips, and his stomach fluttered with the excitement of possibilities as she stared back at him in horror.

Automatic doors at the front entrance sucked open, heralding the arrival of more guests. He withdrew his hand and snapped to attention. He picked up a leather holdall from the floor, and turned for the stairs. He generally avoided lifts. Nothing worse than being crammed in with a bunch of strangers trying to pretend they didn't mind the forced close contact. Besides the exercise kept him fit.

His room was halfway along a narrow corridor, clean and anonymous like a million hotel rooms around the world, with a bed, a desk, a wardrobe, and a kettle. His second room in two days.

He sat on the bed with the package on his lap, and peeled the tape so the paper didn't rip. Inside was a wooden. The gun was packed in a dense ball of wood shavings, stripped into two sections, and wrapped in oiled cloth.

He inspected each component, rolling them around his fingers, savouring the smell of gun oil. The slide slotted onto the grip with a satisfying click. At the bottom of the box he found a fully loaded magazine and the heavy silencer cylinder, which he screwed into the barrel. He turned it over in his hand to admire the craftsmanship, held it at arm's length, and lined up the sights in the mirror. The irony that they'd provided an American Glock wasn't lost on him. At least they'd been able to source a .45. So much better for his purposes than a 9mm. Fully loaded, it weighed a little over a kilogramme. The suppressor added some weight, but overall he liked the feel of it in his hand.

A phone rang in his holdall. A muffled trill. He set the gun on the desk, and pulled a mobile out of a side pocket.

'Da?'

He listened to the instructions, checked his watch, and hung up.

Three hours to kill.

He kicked off his shoes, and slumped onto the bed. It was a little hard and a little lumpy for his tastes. He closed his eyes, and let his mind wander. He imagined an evening's entertainment with the young receptionist, and fell into a light sleep with a smile on his face.

Chapter 8

A pair of heavy duty security gates set into a tall wall secured the entrance to the house. Beyond them, a block-paved driveway rolled up to a smart, Georgian fronted villa with an ornate door and arched windows. Blake let his finger linger on the buzzer of an electronic intercom system fixed onto a brick pillar. The crackle of a phone being answered inside the house followed a short wait. A man's voice answered. Curt and gruff.

'Yes?'

'I need to speak with Alexei Polzin.' Blake put his head close to the speaker to hear above the noise of passing traffic.

'Who's this?'

'My name's Blake, MI5. I need to ask Mr Polzin a few questions.' Blake checked up and down the street. 'It's urgent,' he added.

'You don't have an appointment.'

'Listen to me. I need to speak with him urgently.'

'Nobody sees Mr Polzin without an appointment.'

A loud click signalled that the other man had hung up. Blake was about to hit the buzzer again when Johnnie Green tapped him on the shoulder. Blake tensed from the unexpected physical contact. He'd left strict instructions that the agent should wait in the car.

'Let me have a go,' said Green, with a smug confidence.

'It's okay, I've got it.'

'Really?'

Blake bit hard on his lip. 'I said I've got it.'

'Suit yourself.' Green stepped back.

Blake stared into the pinhole lens of a fisheye camera above a speaker in the intercom panel, and kept his finger on the buzzer for a long minute. 'How quickly can we get a warrant?' he snapped at Green when no one answered.

'Perhaps I could try first?'

Blake ran a hand over his freshly-shaven jaw. A warrant could take several hours, even if they could persuade a magistrate that a hand-written address on a scrap of paper was enough evidence to sanction questioning the Russian dissident. He reluctantly stepped aside.

Green straightened his glasses and cleared his throat. He smiled into the camera, and poked the buzzer with his index finger.

'Good morning. My name's Jonathan Green. I have an appointment with Mr Polzin. I'm a little early, but it's important I speak to him as soon as possible.'

The gates clicked, and swung open with a grinding buzz of hidden motors. Blake scowled, and slipped inside. He marched across the driveway, stomped up three steps, and as he reached for a gleaming brass knocker, the door was thrown open by a police officer in shirt sleeves, a revolver in a holster under his arm. He regarded the lanky figure in dirty jeans and a crumpled jacket with disgust.

Green, who was, as usual, dressed impeccably in a tailored pin-striped suit, nudged past Blake, and extended his hand. 'Jonathan Green,' he said, smiling. 'This is my colleague, Tom Blake. We have reason to believe that Mr Polzin could be in imminent danger. May we speak with him?'

They were shown into a lounge tastefully decorated in neutral shades, but lacking personal touches. Two floral patterned sofas dominated the room, and an eclectic collection of artwork hung on the walls. Mostly originals, but none by artists Blake was familiar with.

'I told you to wait outside,' Blake hissed when the

police officer had withdrawn.

'I thought you could use some help.'

'You thought wrong.'

A small man in glasses, greying hair, and a neatly trimmed beard appeared in the door. 'MI5? How can I help?' he asked politely, but with a hint that their arrival was an unwelcome intrusion.

'We're investigating a man called Neno Kasun,' said Green, before Blake could speak.

The dissident removed a pair of frameless glasses, and rubbed tired-looking eyes with the ball of one hand. He waved the two agents towards the sofas, and sat in an armchair opposite. 'I'm sorry, I've never heard of him,' he said.

'He arrived in the country yesterday evening. We have reason to believe he's known to you,' said Blake. He pulled Kasun's passport from his jacket pocket, and handed it to the Russian. 'Do you recognise him?'

Polzin studied it at arm's length for a moment. 'What is this? A joke?'

'He claims to have come from the Republic of Amana. His passport is obviously a fake, and we're trying to determine his identity. Take a look at his picture, please.' Blake was on the edge of the sofa with his arms resting on his thighs.

'I don't understand what this has to do with me,' said Polzin.

'Your address was in his wallet. Can you think of any reason why?'

'Of course not.'

'Then if you could just take a look at his photograph,' Green said.

'I need my reading glasses. They're in the study.' Polzin jumped up, and left through a door at the back of the room.

Blake stood, and moved to the mantelpiece over a carbon-blackened fireplace to examine two photographs in gilded frames. The larger of the two was a studio portrait of a young woman in profile. She was clutching a dozen red roses, consciously ignoring the camera, and staring enigmatically into the middle-distance. Two loose strands of auburn hair had fallen over her face. The second picture was of the same woman with a younger-looking Polzin by her side. His hair and beard were less grey, and his face was softer. He had his arm around her shoulder, and she was clutching him around the chest. They were both smiling into the camera, eyes squinting into the sun against the backdrop of an anonymous city.

'My daughter, Natasha,' said Polzin, as he returned to the room.

'She's very beautiful. Is she still in Russia?'

'She's dead.'

'I'm sorry.'

Polzin wiped his nose with the back of his hand. 'It was a long time ago. She was only nineteen, with her whole life ahead of her. She was a victim of the Moscow theatre siege.'

Blake knew the incident well. Forty Chechen militants armed with a small arsenal of weapons and explosives had taken more than nine hundred people hostage at the Dubrovka Theatre. After three days, and with the world's media watching, the Russians sent in Special Forces to bring the siege to a rapid conclusion, but at the cost of more than a hundred of the hostages' lives. It had been a dark day in Russian history.

'Ironically, she survived the terrorists, but died at the hands of Spetsnaz,' said Polzin.

Green looked puzzled.

'It's believed they died because of the gas Spetsnaz used against the militants,' said Blake.

'The emergency services weren't warned that the gas was going to be used,' said Polzin. 'Consequently, there weren't enough ambulances to treat the hostages for the effects quickly enough. You know the man responsible for her death was decorated for valour. They called him The Hero of Russia.' He shook his head slowly. 'And not a single official was held accountable for all the fatalities.'

'Is that why you left the country?' asked Blake.

'Ultimately I suppose it was.' He held up his left hand. There were two stumps where the tips of his fingers should have been. 'I embarrassed the Kremlin by asking too many questions. This is the result of a parcel bomb. I had to leave if I was going to live, and Britain was quick to offer sanctuary.'

'Where you've continued to campaign?' asked Blake.

'Russia has descended into a dark place, growing poorer on a diet of corruption, and where dissent is punished punitively. Activists are being harassed and arrested daily, critical online voices blocked, and the police turn a blind eye when vigilantes attack gay-rights protesters. At least here I'm free to write the truth.' Polzin turned the passport over in his lap. 'Has this man been sent to kill me?' he asked, softly.

'It's possible,' said Blake.

'I don't care if I die. There are others who are speaking out. The Kremlin can't silence us all.'

'Did you take a look at the photo?'

'I'm sorry, I don't recognise him.' Polzin returned the passport to Blake.

'You're absolutely sure?'

'I'd like to be able to help, but -'

'And you have no idea why Kasun might have your address in his wallet?' asked Green.

'I'm sorry.' Polzin stood, indicating that the interview was over. 'I've answered your questions as best I can.'

'Of course,' said Blake. 'If anything should occur to you, will you give us a call?'

Polzin took a business card from Green. The dissident slipped it into his pocket without reading it. 'Yes, of course. One of the officers will see you out.'

Chapter 9

The park was in darkness. A chill wind rattled the leafless branches, and ruffled the tips of a roughly trimmed lawn that was divided by a meandering path. After leaving the dissident's house, Blake made his excuses to ditch Green and Sanders, and spent the rest of the day on his own, pondering the mystery of Neno Kasun and his connection with Alexei Polzin. It seemed improbable that Kasun had been sent to kill the dissident, but Blake had a nagging feeling that Polzin hadn't been entirely forthcoming with the truth.

Patterson had wanted a full update, and wouldn't speak on the phone. So they arranged a meeting at their usual haunt in Paddington Green, under the cover of night. Blake headed directly for a clump of evergreen shrubs in a bed in the middle of the park, and pulled back a twisted knot of branches to reveal a small, metal door recessed into a concrete construction not much bigger than a garden shed. The entrance to a disused Cold War bunker.

It had been constructed when fear of a nuclear strike on London was rife. It would have been used as a command and control centre for government officials, but had been long forgotten as the Iron Curtain lifted and the horrific face of Islamic terrorism was revealed as the new bogeyman intent on destroying the West.

Patterson had stumbled on its existence in an old file. He'd requisitioned the key from the Ministry of Defence, and now he and Blake used it as a regular meeting place, away from the oppressive confines of Thames House, the headquarters of MI5 in Millbank.

Blake let the door thud closed behind him, and followed steep steps down to a rectangular room deep underground. It had been designed for maybe a dozen desks, but was a cramped and airless environment with few creature comforts. Cold, dusty and full of stale air.

'So, how did you get on?' Patterson rose from a plastic chair when he heard Blake's footsteps.

'I've had friendlier welcomes.'

'Does he know anything about Kasun?'

'He claims he's never heard of him. He played a decent poker face, but I'm sure he's hiding something.'

'Do you need to go back and exert a bit of pressure?'

By extra pressure, Blake knew that Patterson was suggesting a session of coercive hypnosis. He pulled up a chair, and sat on it the wrong way round. 'A bit heavy-handed for a hunch, don't you think? Anyway, we'd need a decent excuse to get back into the house, especially as he's under twenty-four hour police guard. I can't just march in there.'

'I'll square it if Polzin's hiding something. Don't worry about that.'

'No, let him stew for a bit. I wouldn't mind getting a surveillance team on the house though.'

'Shouldn't be a problem.'

'What about Green and Sanders? That'll keep them out of my hair for a while.'

'Blake, I told you they're part of the team for now. Anyway, there's been a development. I had the lab analyse Kasun's passport. Turns out the Syrian stamp is a fake. It's the wrong kind of ink. Not even a close match. Which means Kasun may never have even travelled to Syria.

'This gets stranger by the minute,' said Blake.

'As if Kasun was waving a red flag as he passed through Heathrow, trying to get noticed.'

'Which strengthens my hypothesis that he was a diversion.'

'But for what?'

'Have you gone through the airport CCTV yet?'

'There's a team going through it frame-by-frame, but on first viewings it seems there was very little fuss when Kasun was detained. Immigration staff followed protocol to the letter. He was quietly removed from the line, and taken to a private interview suite for questioning. No big dramas, and hardly anyone in the queues paid any notice.'

'So back to the theory that he's from an alternative universe?' said Blake.

Patterson smiled. 'Not quite. There's something else. The teams have gone through hours of footage from cameras all around the terminal in the immediate hours before and after Kasun's arrival. And they found this.' Patterson opened a briefcase, and pulled out a brown envelope. 'Take a look.'

Blake slid out a grainy, black and white photo of a passenger walking through the terminal. The focus was soft, and the picture indistinct where it had been zoomed in. The man was casually dressed, with short-cropped fair hair and carrying a dark holdall.

'His name's Nikolay Kozkov,' said Patterson.

'Russian?' Blake raised an eyebrow.

'He arrived on a flight from Turkey an hour after Kasun. He's former KGB, now FSB. In Moscow, they call him Gadyuka.'

'The Viper?'

'He's an assassin. And a very good one. One of our profilers picked him out,' said Patterson.

'A coincidence?'

'What do you think?'

'Well, I don't suppose he's here on holiday. And the fact that he's here at all, regardless of whether he's connected to Kasun, is a concern.'

'He's travelling on an assumed identity,' said Patterson, 'going by the name of Nikolai Lagunov.'

'So maybe he and Kasun are working together?'

'An assassination squad? It still doesn't explain Kasun's passport, or the shoddy Syrian stamp.'

Blake stood, and paced the room, scuffing his feet on the dusty floor. No matter which way he laid out the pieces of the mystery, none of them seemed to fit. Maybe they weren't supposed to fit. It was possible that Kasun's arrival was entirely coincidental to the arrival of the Russian assassin. Improbable, but not impossible.

'Where's Kasun now?' asked Blake.

'The cells at Paddington Green were full for the night, so given there's no evidence of any criminal behaviour beyond the fake passport, he was taken to the hotel he'd already booked into. We've put a police guard outside his door. We thought a decent night's sleep might clear his head.'

'Is that entirely wise?'

'It was the best option we had,' said Patterson.

'I need another chat with him.'

'Not tonight. Doctor's orders. He's been up for over twenty-four hours. Let him sleep, and you can question him again in the morning.'

'That might be too late,' said Blake. Sleep deprivation was one of the most effective tools for breaking a man. Given a comfortable hotel bed, and lulled into a false sense of security, it would be the perfect opportunity to try him again for information. But Blake didn't argue. It was pointless. Once Patterson had made his mind up there was no changing it.

'Tomorrow morning then,' said Blake. 'I'll try him first thing.'

Chapter 10

The twin Victorian pillars of Tower Bridge stood proud like two Gothic towers guarding the dark ribbon of the River Thames as it ebbed and twisted through the city. Blazing uplighters caught drifts of mist rolling on a cool, evening breeze, not the frigid air of a Moscow winter threatening snow, but a biting north easterly chill that had persuaded most people to remain inside. Which suited Nikolay Kozkov just fine.

He was wrapped up warm admiring the magnificence of the architecture from the south bank of the river. He loved its pretentiousness. He especially appreciated its symmetry, elegant lines, and dramatic turrets. He balanced on the edge of the pavement, with one eye closed, trying to line up the arches.

Two black cabs trundled past in slow succession, but there was no one else around apart from a lone figure leaning against the railings half way along the main span, transfixed by the seeping waters below.

The man glanced up as Kozkov approached. His eyes slate grey and framed by creases. His skin pallid, and loose around his cheekbones, his expression neither surprised nor fearful. Kozkov suspected he was one of those hardened men incapable of feeling fear. An emotionless shell, who'd witnessed too much brutality, left exhausted and wrung out.

'Anderson?' Kozkov passed him a piece of paper folded neatly into four.

The detective unfurled the sheet, and looked only

briefly at the image. 'That one's easy. His name's Neno Kasun. He was arrested at the airport.' His voice a gravelly rasp of a forty-a-day smoker.

'Why?'

'Probably because of the cock and bull story he tried to pass off.'

'What story?'

Anderson stuck out his bottom lip. 'He arrived on a fake passport claiming to be from the Republic of Amana. Clearly delusional, the poor beggar. They'll end up chucking him in a psychiatric ward, for sure.'

Kozkov raised an eyebrow. He hadn't expected it to be this straightforward to find out information, even from a corrupt police officer. 'Where is he now?'

Anderson straightened up. 'The cash?'

'Of course.' Gadyuka tapped his jacket pocket.

Anderson lazily scanned the length of the bridge, and found it deserted. Kozkov planted the envelope in his palm.

'He was at Paddington Green nick for questioning. But they've moved him to a hotel for the night.'

Anderson flicked through the notes in the envelope, and satisfied all the money was there, slipped it into the pocket of his overcoat.

'Which hotel?'

The officer reeled off the details. 'I don't know the room number, but it shouldn't be hard to find. They've posted a guard outside his door. But there's something else you should know.'

Kozkov frowned. 'What?'

'The case isn't being handled by the Met. It's been passed over to MI5. Don't ask me why.'

Kozkov nodded. 'Thank you.'

'You're welcome.' Anderson turned up the collar of his coat, and after checking nobody had been watching, turned in the direction of the Tower of London. He walked quickly with his shoes tapping out a rapid patter along the flagstones.

Kozkov counted to five under his breath, and rolled the muscles of his neck. He drew a deep lungful of air through his nose, and set off after the policeman.

Chapter 11

Danny Travis was waiting patiently at a set of lights, drumming the steering wheel, and wondering whether he was getting too old for the game. Business was slow, and he was struggling for fares. The way his night was going, he'd probably end up spending more in fuel than he'd take home.

Maybe it was time to jack it all in. Twenty years amounted to a lot of time sitting in traffic. Besides, things had changed. Congestion charging had eased the roads of the worst logjams, but in turn, it had opened up the streets to more cyclists. Thousands of them. And they were everywhere, jumping red lights and threading through gaps that didn't exist. You had to have eyes in the back of your head these days.

He should be at home with his family. Not spending his twilight years trawling the streets for trade that was increasingly hard to come by. It was different when the kids were young and they struggled to make ends meet. But not now. Why did he put himself through it?

The lights turned green, and the cab chugged forward. Danny waited for a delivery van to pass, and swung through the junction onto Tower Bridge Road. His last fare had taken him into Bermondsey so he thought he'd try the north side of the Thames on his way back into town, through the City of London, looking for the late evening crowds spilling out of the bars and pubs. And if nothing was doing he'd head for the West End and run the gauntlet for the theatre business.

The bridge loomed large, but he hardly even registered it. His eyes were glued to the road. Traffic was unusually light. He shifted his weight, and felt that twinge in his back again. Maggie had been pestering him to book an appointment to see the doctor. But what was the point? He knew the problem. Too much time behind the wheel. Not enough exercise. He pulled a cushion higher up his back, and tried to make himself more comfortable.

Two men were walking along the pavement up ahead. Danny checked his mirrors, and eased off the accelerator. One of the men was dressed in a suit and overcoat, his hands deep in his pockets, and his shoulders bunched up against the cold. Maybe an office worker making his slow way home after an impromptu evening out. The other was more casually dressed, walking close behind. It struck Danny as odd, almost as if he was stalking the first guy.

Half intrigued and half-hopeful of a customer, the cabbie slowed to a crawl and checked his mirrors again. Nothing worse than not paying attention and losing a fare to a driver on your tail. Danny was too canny for that.

He squinted at the lights in the distance, so bright they were haloing. Impossible to tell what type of vehicle it was. Could have been a van or a hansom cab. Its lights bobbled as it hit the bridge.

A sudden thud jolted Danny's attention back to the front of his vehicle. He instinctively hit the brakes. The taxi lurched forward as a shadow bounced over his bonnet, rolled into the middle of the road, and ended up in a tangled heap. Danny fell back into his seat with his heart pounding so hard it felt as though it was trying to break out of his chest.

'Shit!' he hissed under his breath.

He threw open the door, and eased himself out as quickly as his niggling back would allow.

The man in the suit was sprawled out. His arms and legs were twisted at unnatural angles, and his eyes had rolled back in his head.

Danny stood over him helplessly, staring down at the broken body in blind panic. Another cab pulled up behind him. Its light threw a ghostly veil over the horrific scene, and picked out a rivulet of blood running from the back of the man's head.

The driver rushed out, fell to his knees, and looked for signs of life.

'What happened, mate?' he asked.

Danny shook his head. The colour had drained from his face.

'I didn't see him,' Danny heard himself saying. 'He just walked out in front of me. I didn't stand a chance.'

Chapter 12

The hotel was an ugly slab with few redeeming features, thrown up in the Eighties when plain and ugly passed for modern and sophisticated. More like a hospital than a hotel, with rows of tall windows over five storeys. Blake suspected they'd put Kasun on the top floor where the opportunity to escape through a window was nigh on impossible by virtue of the sixty-foot drop to the pavement below. There were probably no more than fifty rooms on each floor, and with an armed guard posted outside Kasun's room, he figured it shouldn't be too hard to locate.

He retreated into a doorway as a young couple scurried past arm-in-arm, chattering conspiratorially. He listened to their voices fade, and stepped out of the shadows. The night was chill, and the air damp with the threat of rain. He pulled up the collar of his jacket, and plunged his hands into his pockets. It was late, but the caffeine in his veins kept him alert.

He'd stumbled on the late-night Soho café by chance, as he was killing time. He'd ordered his coffee black, drank it without sugar, and nursed it until the waiting staff, too polite to ask him to leave, made an exaggerated point of closing up. He'd felt bad for keeping them up, and left a generous tip. An hour later, his heart was still racing from the potent Columbian brew.

He checked his watch. It was a little past midnight.

Blake picked his way towards a glowing neon sign hung over the hotel's main entrance, through a line of parked cars, strolling casually, trying not to draw attention to himself. It wasn't that he'd set out to deliberately disregard Patterson's orders. But the urge to question Kasun had grown stronger with every step as he'd walked away from the underground bunker. Strictly speaking, Patterson had only insisted that Blake waited until the morning, and technically, it was after midnight, so he wasn't directly contravening the instructions. Besides, experience had taught him that waking a man in those first few precious hours of sleep put his defences at their lowest ebb, and often yielded the best results.

A black cab rattled into the square. It swung lazily through two corners, and disappeared down a side street. Blake zeroed in on the hotel's sliding doors and the tiled lobby beyond, adjacent to a bar, which still appeared to be open. Lights from inside were on low, and a couple of indistinct figures were sitting by the window.

He expected no difficulty in reaching Kasun's room. At best there might be a night porter on duty, probably with his feet up at a desk dozing over a late night film. He skipped across a grassed island that divided the street, and checked left and right for traffic. He stepped into the road, but a howling scream stopped him in his tracks. An animalistic cry of fear that pierced the night and raised the hairs on the back of Blake's arms. It was silenced by a sickening thump of flesh and bone, which hit the ground ahead of him. It took a moment to comprehend that the mangled pile of clothes was a body. Twisted and grotesquely deformed. Arms and legs contorted. A swelling pool of crimson seeping into the asphalt from a head bent unnaturally to one side.

The square was swamped by a sudden stillness.

Blake froze as his brain struggled to process what he'd seen, until he became aware of the sound of blood rushing through his ears and a long breath escaping from his lungs. He looked up. Five floors above, a window was tilted, open-wide, and thin gauze curtains billowed out.

A woman's cry of distress snapped Blake to his senses. He jogged across the road, and dropped to his knees by the crumpled form. He glimpsed olive skin, a dark beard, and black hair.

'No, no, no,' Blake hissed, listening for a rasp of breath, and feeling for a pulse in Neno Kasun's neck.

Nothing.

Blood was leaking from one of Kasun's ears, and it was obvious that all sorts of bones were smashed and internal organs obliterated by the force of the fall. The small consolation was that his death would have been instant. No lingering pain. No long drawn out suffering.

'Oh my God! Oh my God!' a woman screamed hysterically.

'Jeez, what happened?' said a man close by.

A curious crowd was closing in, mawkish nighthawks drawn in by the horror.

'Is he dead?' asked another.

'Call an ambulance,' said Blake, to no one in particular. He caught the tremor in his own voice.

The terror of Kasun's final moments as he plunged five storeys to his death was fixed on his face. His mouth was agape, as if in mid-scream, and his eyes open wide. Blake closed them with his fingers, and draped his jacket over Kasun's head and shoulders, trying to give him a little dignity in death. He hadn't deserved to die like this.

'An ambulance is on its way,' said one of the bystanders.

'Stay here with him until they come. Don't let anyone touch him,' Blake said.

Kasun had been delusional, for sure. But he hadn't shown any signs of being suicidal. Blake had a sense that something wasn't right.

He pushed past a shell-shocked young couple, and dived for the hotel lobby. He sprinted for the lifts, banged the call buttons with his fist, but when they failed to arrive rushed for the stairs. He made it to the third floor before his lungs and thighs started to burn, but pushed on to the top floor.

He emerged into a long, carpeted corridor with sweat dampening his shirt. In the distance, he heard the strains of an approaching siren. He drew his Browning from the small of his back, and crept forwards. He'd calculated that Kasun's room was third from the end of the corridor, beyond a dogleg kink. He counted off the doors and approached cautiously.

The door to room 527 was sitting on its latch, not quite closed. Blake pushed it with fingers spread, and let it swing noiselessly into the room. A blast of cold air hit him from the window where curtains and gauze netting were flapping wildly in the breeze. The body of a uniformed police officer was lying on his back in the middle of a whole heap of mess. Drawers had been turned out, clothes scattered, and a miniature fridge wide open. Blake stepped inside, checked the empty bathroom on his left, and approached the body. A bruised hole in the policeman's forehead revealed where he'd been shot at point blank range. It was in line with the bridge of his nose, and barely the width of Blake's little finger.

Avoiding the blood and corporeal matter seeping into the carpet, Blake moved to the window. It had been tilted open horizontally, two safety catches designed to prevent it opening more than a few inches had been snapped off. He leaned out, and peered at Kasun's body at the bottom of a dizzying drop. A police car had arrived, and two young officers were trying to secure the scene by pushing the morbid onlookers back.

Blake eased the window closed without worrying about fingerprints. He doubted the forensics teams would find any physical evidence to link the killers to the scene. He dialled a pre-programmed number on his phone, and sat on the edge of the bed as the call connected.

Patterson answered after two rings.

'Harry, we have a problem.'

Chapter 13

The monochrome images on the monitor were grainy, but clear enough to show two men strolling casually into the lobby and past reception. They were dressed near enough identically in hooded tops, dark trousers, and baseball caps pulled low over their eyes.

Patterson pushed himself away from the desk. 'Looks as if they knew exactly where they were going,' he said.

He'd requisitioned the office behind reception to view the CCTV footage as soon as he'd arrived, while the Metropolitan Police were still swarming over the hotel, securing exits and marshalling guests outside.

'It's a professional hit,' said Blake.

It was the third time they'd watched the short sequence. Two men strode through the main entrance with the confidence of hotel guests who knew their way around.

'What makes you so sure?'

'Look, they knew precisely where the security cameras were positioned. Watch how they dip their heads every time they pass one.'

The camera angle changed to show a view inside the elevator, distorted by a curved lens that made the walls appear rounded. The two men were visible only from above. They stood, heads down, facing the doors without speaking.

'And no sign of stress. They're on their way to kill Kasun and a police officer, but you'd never guess from their body language,' Blake added.

The lift juddered to a halt, and the doors opened. The

men disappeared into the hall where there were no cameras, 'to protect the privacy of guests,' the hotel duty manager had explained.

'Conclusions?'

'A hit squad,' said Blake.

'But who would want Kasun dead?'

'Impossible to tell until we find out who he was, and what he was doing in the U.K.'

'Motive?'

'The room was turned upside down so it's possible they were looking for something.'

'Like what? He arrived with hardly any luggage.'

Blake shrugged.

'And why throw him from the window?'

'To cover their tracks?' suggested Blake.

'But we know they were armed and happy to use their weapons on the police guard, and yet they decided to throw Kasun from a fifth-floor window. It doesn't add up.'

'I think they were trying to scare him. They hung him out of the window to frighten him into talking.'

'Then dropped him?'

'It fits the evidence,' said Blake. He shifted a pile of papers on the desk, and perched on the edge. 'What luggage did he have with him?'

'An overnight bag, that's all. We searched it. There were only some clothes and a washbag.'

'You said he had a briefcase?'

'Still with the investigations team. They're going through the paperwork line by line.'

'Tell them to tear it apart, look for hidden compartments, fake bottoms, anywhere Kasun could have hidden something.'

A knock on the door silenced their conversation. Green walked in.

'Oh great,' said Blake, rolling his eyes.

Patterson shot him a look. 'Any joy with eyewitnesses?'

'There were a couple of businessmen in the bar around the time, but that's it. I'm afraid no one saw a thing.'

'Okay, thanks for trying.'

'Sir, the plods are getting a bit jumpy about us being here. They want to know what MI5 are doing snooping around. I played dumb,' said Green.

'That couldn't have been hard,' said Blake.

Green ignored him. 'They're insisting it's a criminal matter, and want to secure the hotel. I think they'd like to see us gone.'

'Fine. Not much more to see here anyway. Let's make ourselves scarce before the media get wind. You know what the Met's like, leaky as a sieve. The press will be crawling all over the place as soon as word gets out that there's a dead copper involved.' Patterson jumped up from his chair. 'We'll pick this up again in the morning. Blake, go home and get some sleep.'

'Too wired to sleep, Harry. I need to mull this over for a bit, but I'll catch you tomorrow.'

'Right, Johnnie, make sure he doesn't get himself into any trouble will you?'

Blake shot him a withering look, but Patterson was already out of the door.

Chapter 14

The bar was sandwiched between a pizza restaurant and a café. It had a sweeping counter under neon lights, pockets of seating in semi-dark corners, and jazz music humming through hidden speakers. They probably called it a wine bar, or a cocktail lounge. Blake wasn't really sure of the difference. The quiet murmur of late night chatter from a trendy young crowd echoed off the plain, white walls. It wasn't quite what he had in mind, but at least it was still serving beer.

The barman was a smooth Eastern European with a laconic smile. He nodded politely when Blake ordered a lager with a foreign sounding name that came in a tall, skinny glass. Blake took a long draught, and settled on a stool, trying to banish the memory of the crumpled heap of Neno Kasun's body. He was haunted by the sound it made when it hit the ground, the dreadful, hollow thump, and the sudden silence after the scream. He was hoping the alcohol would dull the memory.

He pictured Kasun as he'd first seen him in the interrogation suite. Nervous and twitchy, and completely overwhelmed by the situation. His dark eyes looked as though they were retreating into his skull, and his fingers picked and scratched incessantly. Cheap clothes and scuffed shoes. Neither the demeanour nor the appearance of a terrorist nor an assassin, in Blake's opinion.

The barman slipped a bill on a white saucer across the counter. Blake fished in his jacket for his wallet, and found Kasun's passport. He traced the gold crest on the front cover with his finger, and laid it on the counter.

The Republic of Amana.

He read the words under his breath as if by saying them out loud the truth would reveal itself. The man from Amana. The mystery of the traveller with no home.

Blake slid a note under the bill, and put his wallet away. He paid no attention to the door opening, nor to the man who drew up a stool next to him and ordered something German sounding. On ice. The barman poured a thick, black liquid like molten tar into a tumbler.

'What do you want?' asked Blake.

'You know we're on the same side?' said Green.

'Same side, different teams.'

Green took a sip from his glass, and set it on the bar, squaring up a paper coaster under the tumbler. 'What is it, the look of my face? Or something I've said?'

Blake finished his beer, and ordered another. 'Look, I don't need a young upstart fresh out of spook school interfering. That's all. Nothing personal.'

Green smirked. 'Is that what you think of me?'

Blake shrugged. It was almost two o'clock in the morning, but Green looked freshly groomed. His hair was perfectly combed, and his suit had creases in all the right places. His tie was knotted with a classic Windsor twist, and a waistcoat accentuated his slim torso. He wouldn't have looked out of place on a London Fashion Week catwalk.

'I've no time for babysitting,' said Blake. He felt the muscles in his jaw tightening.

'I was sent to help.'

'I operate on my own,' said Blake. The beer left a bitter taste on his tongue.

'Really? I didn't think there was a place for individuals in the Army.'

'This isn't the Army.'

'But you were an SAS troop commander. And that means you worked in a team.'

'My teams earned my respect.'

'You won't give me the chance to earn your respect.'

'Trust me; you haven't got what it takes.'

'How could you possibly know?' said Green.

'My men put their lives on the line for me. If I'd asked, they'd have marched through the fires of hell. I trusted them implicitly, not because they went to fancy universities, or were recruited in a cosy club on Pall Mall, but because their education came from plumbing the depths of their courage. That's how they earned my respect.'

'You're right, I can't live up to those standards,' said Green. 'Look at me. I'd struggle to break my way out of a paper bag. But I'm good at what I do. And you know, bravery isn't about the biggest gun you can fire on the battlefield. Give me a chance to prove it. That's all I'm asking.'

A young couple who'd been sitting in the shadows brushed past on their way out. She was giggling as he struggled to find the arm of his jacket.

Green swirled his drink around the glass. 'I heard you were the youngest ever Medical Officer recruited by the SAS. Is that true?'

Blake snorted. 'A long time before you were ever thought of. I was in the right place at the time, with the right skills and qualifications. That's all. There weren't too many other candidates who'd passed selection.'

'Still some achievement.'

'Yeah, maybe. But what does it count for? I travelled the world and saw things you can only imagine. But that's gone, and here I am sitting in a bar drinking on my own.'

'What about your family?'

Blake shook his head. 'Don't have one,' he said. 'The Regiment was the only family I've known.'

'Everyone's got a family,' said Green.

'Not me.'

'You never thought of settling down? Getting married?

Kids?'

Blake was silent. It was funny how the memory of Laura's face could appear in his mind so clearly when he wasn't trying to recall the detail of it, only to evaporate the second he concentrated on cementing the image. The familiar wash of regret and sadness filled him. 'Not any more,' he said.

Blake caught the barman's eye, and ordered another beer. 'One for him too,' Blake said. He hooked his thumb in Green's direction.

'It's late. I shouldn't -' Green began.

'You want to earn my respect? Start by having a proper drink with me.'

Green nodded, and adjusted his glasses. They watched silently as the barman poured two beers, and set them down with a chink on the marble counter.

'What about you?' asked Blake. 'What's your story?'

'Not much to tell. I joined the Firm straight from Cambridge,' he said.

'I thought so,' said Blake.

'There you go, judging me again.'

'That's it?,' said Blake.

'That's it,' said Green.

'Married?'

'No.'

'Wedded to the job, eh?'

'Something like that.'

'I saw him fall,' said Blake. 'Right in front of me. He dropped from the sky like a stone, screaming and yelling.'

'Jesus, I didn't know. I'm sorry.'

'Splattered all over the pavement like roadkill.' Blake drank hard and deep. 'And we never did find out his real name. You want to impress me? Tell me what you think's behind all this.' He slid the passport across the bar.

Green flicked through the pages. He paused at the over-exposed picture of the dead man on the back page. 'I think Kasun's a decoy.'

'Why?'

'Nothing about it feels right, does it? I mean, look at this passport. Obviously, it's fake, but it's like a kid knocked it up in his back bedroom. The quality is that poor. There's no watermarking, no bio-data, and no machine readable text. It's as if it's come from the 1950s.'

'So?'

Green turned the passport over in his hands, examining it in detail. 'I don't think it was ever designed to pass close scrutiny.'

'So why go to the trouble of making a fake passport if it stood no chance of getting through border controls?'

'To make some kind of statement?' said Green, thumbing at the edge of passport, and peering at it over the top of his glasses.

'Which makes no sense,' said Blake.

'Maybe not.' Green held the passport under the beam of a spotlight in the ceiling. The tunnel of light caught the dancing motes of dust drifting on the air. 'But I don't think he was capable of killing anyone.'

'Neither do I,' said Blake.

'Why not?'

'Wrong demeanour. He was like a rabbit caught in the headlights in the interview room. Which means we've been barking up the wrong tree.'

'I agree,' said Green. He was pre-occupied with picking at the edges of the passport, holding it close to his face. Suddenly, he sat back in his chair. 'Look. See the back cover here, on the edge of the cardboard?'

Blake held it up, trying to catch the most of the dim light. 'Bloody hell, it's been cut open,' he said. 'Why didn't I notice that?'

'It's only a small slit. Easily overlooked.'

'Well spotted,' said Blake.

'I think there was something hidden inside.' Green looked faintly embarrassed by the oblique praise.

Blake grabbed a cocktail stick from a pot on the bar,

and prodded it through the cut. 'There's nothing there now,' he said.

'In which case, it's already been removed.'

'But the only people to have had access to it -' Blake stopped mid-sentence as the realisation hit him.

Green was staring at him with sharp, bright eyes. 'Which means he wasn't a terrorist.'

'No,' said Blake. 'He wasn't a terrorist. He was a courier.'

Chapter 15

A tree-shaped air freshener danced from the rear view mirror and filled the cab with a sickly sweet smell. Like the scent of cheap perfume, it put Blake in an irritable frame of mind, which wasn't helped by a gasping squeak that came from the springs under his seat. His beer buzz had long since evaporated into an aching weariness, and he barely registered the city landmarks as they rattled through the empty streets.

Green had talked him out of confronting Alexei Polzin that evening. After a lengthy argument, he'd persuaded Blake that the dissident was best tackled in the cold light of day. Not in the small hours after a few beers. Definitely not a good idea. And although it would have given him great pleasure, Blake conceded that nothing would be gained from dragging him out of bed. Instead, he had reluctantly hailed a taxi, and was slumped low in the back seat fighting the urge to sleep.

When Blake's eyes finally flickered shut, Kasun's face returned to him. The man from Amana, sitting in the interrogation suite picking at his fingers. His eyes like black stones. It didn't need an expert to read his body language. Kasun had something to hide, but even now, the truth remained tantalisingly out of reach.

The cab jolted to a sudden halt, and Blake's momentum was arrested by a sharp tug of the seatbelt against his shoulder. His bloodshot eyes sprang open.

The driver swivelled in his seat. 'Where to now, guv?'

Blake glanced out of the window at the familiar church

of St Peter's. 'This'll do,' he said.

When the taxi had driven away, Blake pulled his collar up, took a deep breath, and started walking. The cool night air revived his senses and cleared his head. It was normally a ten-minute stroll to his door from the church, but he hoped to make it in five. Along Wapping Lane, and cut through Bridewell Place, onto the cobbles of Wapping High Street, where the familiar brick warehouses lined the river. He started out at a quick march, past the pizzeria, and the row of bikes clamped by their front wheels waiting for the morning commuters. Blake caught the tangy maritime aroma from the muddy beaches exposed by the retreating river tide. It smelled like home.

He turned onto Brewhouse Lane with his fingers furling around a key in his pocket, and heard the hiss of tyres on asphalt. A car rolling slowly along. Its engine murmuring. The hiss became a rumble as the tyres hit the cobblestones. Blake checked over his shoulder, trying to make it look casual. A fifteen-year-old Jaguar was creeping up behind. An X-Type. Maroon. A smart car in its day. Standard number plates. Clean and well maintained. He counted four heads. All male. Two in the back. Two in the front. Eyes fixed ahead, their expressions grim.

He suspected they'd come for him, hunting him like a pride of lions stalking a lone antelope. He slowed down, and let the car draw level, noting the subtle clicks and rattles from the purring V6 that hinted at a timing issue and an engine that had been around the clock more than once. The nearside window was wound down, but Blake kept his eyes ahead, refusing to meet the challenge of the driver's stare. The Jaguar came to a gentle halt blocking the road. The passenger door opened, and a well-built man spilled out. He eased around the bonnet, and cut off Blake's path.

'Help you?' asked Blake.

The man stood mute. His arms hung loosely by his sides. He was wearing surgical gloves, which struck Blake as a little ominous. Thin, translucent rubber over enormous clubs of meat emerging from the sleeves of a tracksuit top zipped up to his neck under a padded gilet.

Two more men emerged from the vehicle, and took up positions behind Blake. Similar build. Same bad taste in clothing. Cheap polyester and scuffed jeans. Thin rubber gloves. Blake wheeled to his left, putting his back against a metallic up-and-over garage door set into an arch in a brick wall.

The driver ratcheted on the handbrake, and killed the engine. He was last out, and that made him the boss. Henchmen first to secure the area, and the man in charge bringing up the rear. The driver stepped onto the pavement, and squared his shoulders. He had the look of a man recently released from a long jail sentence. Thin lips and a thick head. Eyes filled with a seething resentment, and a way of looking at you as if you'd had the impudence to call his mother a whore.

'You're messing with the wrong guy,' said Blake.

The driver grinned with a mouth full of crooked, yellow teeth. 'I don't think so,' he said, in a thick East London accent that sounded fake.

Blake felt no fear. Not that his adrenaline wasn't flowing, quickening his pulse, and exciting the receptors in his brain. His pupils grew wide, and sweat moistened his palms. Not through fear, but anticipation. He was a child on the night before Christmas, quivering with expectation. His hand trembled in his pocket as he palmed the key between two fingers to fashion a weapon.

'Let me put it another way,' said Blake, fighting to keep his voice even. 'I'm giving you one opportunity to get back in the car and drive away.'

The driver laughed without mirth. 'Are you blind, or just stupid? Count. Four of us, and only one of you, dumbass.'

'The alternative is that someone calls an ambulance to scrape you off the pavement when I've cracked your skulls open.'

'The passport. Give it to me,' the driver said.

'What?' said Blake. If in doubt, play stupid.

'The passport, in your pocket, give it to me.' The driver stretched out a hand.

'I don't know what you're talking about.'

'Listen, don't play dumb with me, mate.'

'I don't have it,' said Blake.

'I saw you put it in your jacket pocket before you left that crappy bar. Now, turn out your pockets.'

'Who are you?' said Blake.

'It's not important.'

'It is if you want the passport.'

The driver's piggy eyes narrowed. 'You really don't want to know?'

'Really I do. I'd like to know who the cowards are who killed Neno Kasun, and more importantly, why they did it. First of all, how did you find him? He was under protective custody.'

'I'm losing patience,' said the driver.

'I guess it doesn't really matter. The fact is you tracked him down and killed him. And a police officer too. So it must have been a real blow when Kasun told you his passport had been confiscated. Not that you believed him.'

'What makes you say that?'

'Why else hang him out of his hotel window? You had to persuade him to talk. But the thing is you didn't have to drop him. You did it anyway. Did that take all four of you? Because, I mean, that's pretty brave. Four against one.'

'Shut up and give it to me,' said the driver. His mouth turned up into snarl. 'Unless you want to go the same way?'

'Are you boys really up for this? You see I'm a different prospect altogether. I doubt that Kasun even put up much of a fight. But if you fancy your chances with me, let's go. Otherwise turn around and clear off. And that's the last time I make that offer.'

'Grab him.'

'Hang on a minute,' said Blake, holding up a hand. 'I'll give you the passport. Just tell me who you're working for.'

The driver nodded to one of his men, who popped open the boot of the car and leaned in. Time to move to plan B. No way Blake was going to wait to discover what delights were in the Jaguar's luggage compartment. He feinted a move to his left, shifted his weight to his right, and dropped his shoulder. Like an Olympic sprinter out of the blocks, he sprung forward, powering through his thighs and calves with an explosive energy. His shoulder landed squarely in the sternum of the guy to his right. It knocked the breath from his lungs, and pitched him backwards. He stumbled, and fell hard on the base of his spine.

Blake had hoped that his own momentum would carry him past, but the man's flailing legs took his feet from under him. He felt himself falling. He scrambled to find his balance, but was already going over, arms outstretched. Beneath him, a face stared up in mute surprise. Blake collapsed onto the man's crumpled body, and although he tried to roll away, their limbs tangled in a fleshy knot.

From behind, Blake heard a shout. Muscles were galvanised into action, and feet thudded on the pavement. The last thing he remembered was driving his elbow hard into the stomach of the man beneath him to make him release his grip on his arm. Adamantine bone plunged deep into soft, vulnerable flesh. He barely registered the sharp blow across his shoulders from a baseball bat swung hard and low, before he collapsed unconscious.

Chapter 16

Bill Sanders straightened his tie, folded back his cuffs, and secured them with a pair of gold-plated links. He grabbed his watch from the bedside table, and slipped it over his wrist.

'You off?' came a sleepy voice from under the duvet.

'Sorry, did I wake you?'

The covers rippled. 'Do you have to go in today, babe?' His girlfriend, Natalie rolled over, pouted, and gave him her best doe-eyed look.

'I'd rather be here with you. Both of you.' Sanders perched on the edge of the bed while she folded a pillow under her head. His hand wriggled under the duvet and found the swell of her stomach.

They hadn't planned on falling pregnant. At least not yet. A happy accident, although his mother said it was carelessness. They'd not ruled out having a family. They'd talked about it occasionally, but Sanders had hoped to have moved them to a bigger house first. They could do with at least another bedroom and some outside space too. The rented flat in Hammersmith, with its poky rooms and steep stairs was far from ideal. But with a crippling monthly rent, trying to save for a deposit on a house in London was tough.

Then there was the job. By its nature, MI5 didn't operate a nine-to-five culture. He was at the service's beck and call twenty-four hours a day, seven days a week, and was regularly away for days on end with no contact with home. He wondered how that would play out with a young baby.

'What are you up to today?' he asked.

'Julie's coming around for coffee later, and mum said she might pop in. What about you?'

He stood and gave her a wry smile. 'You know, the usual.'

It was a ritual they went through every morning. She would ask, and he would avoid the question. He hated not being able to discuss his job, but those were the rules, and they both knew them well enough. He snatched his jacket from a hanger, and shrugged it over his shoulders.

'What time you back?' Natalie propped herself on her elbows to see over the end of the bed.

'Don't know yet. I'll call you later.' Sanders kissed her lightly on her forehead, dropped to one knee, and planted another kiss on her bump before sweeping up his car key and stealing out of the flat.

His Range Rover was parked directly outside. He'd been lucky to find a space so close. The car chirruped as he pressed a button on the key fob. He threw his jacket across the back seat, and was hopping into the driver's seat when his phone vibrated in his pocket.

The message from Green was short and to the point.

'Pick me up from home as soon as you can. J.'

Sanders tapped the keyboard with his thumb as he fumbled with the ignition. *'On my way.'*

With the early morning traffic, it took almost forty-five minutes to cross London to Pimlico with its regency architecture and sweeping white stucco facades. Its close proximity to MI5 headquarters at Thames House made it a popular, if expensive place to live for many spooks. Not that Johnnie Green had to worry about the cost of living. With a father grown fat on a career in the bank, Green hadn't wanted for much in his life. As far as Sanders was aware, Green's parents were still supplementing his meagre MI5 salary with regular top-ups that granted him a more lavish lifestyle than Sanders could ever hope for.

He found Green pacing up and down outside Warwick Square, a green and leafy park surrounded on four sides by terraces of magnificent town houses.

'What's up? You look tired.'

'Late night,' said Green, as he climbed in.

'Oh yeah? What's her name?'

'Nothing like that.' Green pulled on a seatbelt.

'So where are we going?'

'I said we'd pick up Blake.'

'Terrific.'

'He's okay, you know.'

'The man's a total screwball.'

'I had a good chat with him last night,' said Green.

'You spent the evening with Blake?'

'Neno Kasun's dead.' Green's tone was so matter-of-fact that Sanders wondered if he'd heard him correctly. 'Someone threw him out of his hotel window.'

'Slow down. What do you mean he's dead? If that's a joke, it's not very funny.'

'Patterson called late last night. I went over to help with witnesses, not that anyone saw anything.'

'Hang on a minute -'

'It didn't need two of us. I thought with Natalie being, you know, you could do with the night off. Anyway, Blake was there.'

'Oh well, if Blake was there, why would you need me?'

'I thought I was doing you a favour.'

'Sounds like you just saw a good excuse to cosy up to Mr. ex-SAS.'

'He watched Kasun fall from the fifth floor, right in front of him. He was pretty upset.'

Sanders frowned. 'What was he doing at the hotel?'

'He thought he'd have another go at Kasun, see if he could squeeze any more info out of him.'

'In the middle of the night?'

'You know what he's like,' said Green. 'I think he feels we let Kasun down.'

Sanders pulled out of a junction narrowly missing a cyclist who swerved around the bonnet waving an angry fist. 'Any idea who the killers were?'

'It looks like a professional hit. CCTV showed two guys with baseball caps heading for Kasun's room just before midnight. We think they were looking for Kasun's passport because there was something hidden inside. The back cover had been cut open.'

'Whoa, hang on a minute. Are you saying Kasun was a smuggler?'

'More likely a courier, and we may have helped him deliver his package.'

'I don't understand,' said Sanders. He shot Green a quizzical look.

'We think Alexei Polzin must have been the recipient. So Blake wants to see him again. That's where we're going.'

'With us playing chauffeur?'

Traffic lightened as they headed east. Low in the sky, a break in the dense cloud allowed the weak autumnal sun to break through. Sanders pulled up on double yellow lines outside Blake's apartment, and joined Green on the pavement as he banged on the door with his fist.

It was a long while before the door opened a crack.

'Blake?,' said Green.

The door opened wide, and Blake hobbled backwards into the dingy hallway. He looked a mess. His face was puffed and bruised, and his right eye was almost entirely closed up.

'What the hell happened to you?' asked Green.

'I'm fine,' said Blake. He mumbled the words through a swollen lip. 'Looks worse than it is.'

'Who did this?' asked Sanders.

Blake grabbed a jacket, and winced with the movement. He was holding his left arm awkwardly across his stomach. 'Four guys in an old Jag who followed me from the bar.'

'Did you recognise them?' asked Green.

Blake shook his head, and pulled the door closed. 'No, but my bet is it's the same gang who killed Kasun. In fact, I'm sure of it. They were after Kasun's passport.'

'Did you give it to them?' asked Sanders.

'Well, it wasn't in my pocket when I came around.' Blake pushed past the two men. He eased his aching body into the passenger seat of the Range Rover.

'So they knew there was something hidden in it too?' said Sanders.

'I guess so. Hopefully, Alexei Polzin will be able to tell us what it was. Let's find out what he's got to say for himself.'

Chapter 17

Blake left it to Green to negotiate their way back into Alexei Polzin's house. It took him a little under twenty seconds to persuade the police guard that the Russian's life was in immediate danger, and to open the gates. Blake led the way in, and barged through the front door, ignoring a scowling policeman.

'Where's Polzin?' he said.

A second officer rushed into the hallway, but before he could protest, the Russian's voice called from the top of the stairs. 'What's going on?'

'We need to talk,' said Blake.

Polzin descended with a weary languor. 'What is it now? I've told you everything I know.'

'Is that right?' said Blake. He strode into the lounge as he if owned the property. 'Well, then this shouldn't take long.'

The room was as it had been the previous evening. Clean. Tidy. A hint of furniture polish in the air. Cushions plumped up on the sofa, and a spread of aspirational magazines fanned out on a coffee table. No unsightly coffee stains or half-read newspapers strewn across the floor. Like walking into a show home.

Blake collapsed casually onto one of the sofas, and waved Polzin towards the chair opposite. Green remained by the window with his hands in his trouser pockets, while Sanders disappeared through a door at the back of the room, just as they'd arranged on the way over.

'I'm a little busy,' said Polzin. 'Perhaps you could get to

the point.' His eyes followed Sanders out of the room, but he didn't complain.

'This letter explains our authority.' Green stepped forward, and handed the Russian a single sheet of paper. 'It gives us full freedom under the Terrorism Act.'

Polzin took the letter, and studied it briefly. 'Yes, yes,' he said.

'It's important you read it,' said Blake, 'all the way through, to make sure you understand.'

Polzin scanned the letter, and tossed it on the coffee table. 'What can I help you with?' He smiled through gritted teeth.

'You don't need your reading glasses?' said Blake.

'Are you here to play games, or is there a point to this?'

Blake had decided he didn't care much for the Russian with his lofty academic air. 'Tell me about Neno Kasun.'

'I told you, I don't know him.'

'But your address was in his wallet.'

'I don't know him.' Polzin raised his eyebrows, challenging Blake to contradict him.

'I think it was put there deliberately for us to find; Kasun's way of ensuring we paid you a visit.'

Polzin snorted. 'Is that right?'

'Were you expecting us yesterday?'

'No.'

'But you were waiting for someone to deliver Kasun's passport?'

'How many times? I'd never heard of Neno Kasun, until you mentioned his name.'

'The passport was a neat trick to raise the alarm at the airport,' said Blake. 'Kasun knew he'd be arrested, questioned, and if he held out long enough, we'd have to start looking for answers elsewhere. Obviously, we'd check his wallet, and find your address. It was a predictable next step that we'd pay you a visit, bring Kasun's passport to see if you recognised him. A breathtakingly simple plan.'

'What are you talking about?'

'All you had to do was make an excuse to leave the room so you could remove whatever was hidden inside,' Green chipped in.

'That's quite some allegation.' Polzin laughed sardonically.

'What was in the passport?' asked Blake.

Polzin threw up his hands as if he had no idea how to respond to such a ludicrous question.

'You took it into your study last night, because you said you needed your reading glasses. And yet you managed to read the letter I showed you without them.' Green nodded to the sheet of paper on the table.

'I think I've heard enough. I've not done anything wrong. You have no right to barge in here making accusations like this. I'd like you to leave.'

'Neno Kasun was thrown from the window of his hotel last night,' said Blake. 'He died instantly.'

Blake watched the expression on the dissident's face. A flush of anger that had risen from his neck and swamped his cheeks drained away. 'He was murdered.'

'Murdered?' Polzin's hands fell into his lap, and the arrogant jut of his jaw fell away. He removed his glasses, and pinched the bridge of his nose.

'And it's pretty clear that whoever killed Kasun will be coming for you too,' said Blake.

'Tell us what you took from the passport, and we can help you,' said Green.

'I don't need help.'

'The men who murdered Kasun also killed a police officer guarding his room. They shot him between the eyes at point blank range.'

A flicker of fear flashed across Polzin's face.

'So it's best you start talking,' said Green.

'Do you know who killed him?' asked the Russian.

'An hour after Kasun arrived in the U.K., a known FSB assassin, Nikolay Kozkov, entered the country. They call him Gadyuka. He's one of the FSB's best. Our suspicion is that he was sent to intercept whatever Kasun was couriering,' said Blake. 'We think he's hired some local help. At least four men. Maybe more. They turned Kasun's room upside down, and when they couldn't find what they were looking for, killed him and came after me.'

Polzin frowned. 'They did that to you?' He nodded at Blake's bruised face.

'They'll do worse when they find you. So, what's Kozkov looking for?'

Polzin was silent.

'We can stop him, but you have to cooperate with us,' said Green.

'A memory card.' Polzin spoke the words so softly Blake had to strain to hear.

'Go on,' said Blake.

'A dossier of photographs and testimonies.'

'That the Russian government would prefer were kept secret?'

Polzin nodded. 'Enough evidence to prove that the authorities are complicit in the deaths and suffering of thousands of Russians.'

Bill Sanders wandered back into the room, and gave Blake a barely perceptible shake of his head, indicating that he'd found nothing of significance in his search of the dissident's study.

'I need to know the details,' said Blake. 'We have to know what we're dealing with.'

Polzin steepled his fingers, and took a deep breath. He spoke quickly, and without elaboration, detailing the key evidence without emotion. When he had finished, he slumped back into his chair as if the effort of revealing all had drained him.

'Why was the information sent to you?' asked Blake.

'Because I have a reputation for exposing the truth. People listen to what I have to say. I also have the freedom to publish. It would be impossible to make these allegations in Russia without being prosecuted, or worse.'

'Where's the card now? Is it still here in the house?'

'Yes.'

'Right,' Blake turned to Green, 'get hold of Patterson, and tell him we need a safe house.'

'I'm on it.' Green stepped out into the hallway with his phone clamped to his ear.

'Mr Polzin, we need to get you out of here, to somewhere safe.'

'I can't leave.'

'If you stay you'll be dead by tonight. Go and get packed. Grab an overnight bag, and be ready to leave in five minutes. And remember to bring the memory card.'

'It's in my computer.' Polzin swept out of the room.

Blake checked his watch. Everything was beginning to make sense, but the stakes had gone through the roof. Every minute they stayed in the house increased the risk to Polzin's life. They had to move him fast. It wouldn't take long for an assassin like Kozkov to piece the puzzle together.

He moved to the window, and stared out onto the driveway. Beyond the gates and the high brick wall he could see the tops of roofs and chimneys. Occasional flashes of colour revealed cars and vans passing by.

'I'll need a bag from upstairs,' said the Russian, returning to the room.

Blake didn't hear. He was focussed on a vehicle that had pulled up outside. A bright red van. The driver hopped out and approached the intercom. It was followed by a muted buzz from somewhere down the hall. The gates swung open, and a bearded man in a scarlet fleece jacket and shorts skipped into the courtyard whistling. A postman with a small, brown package tucked under his arm, and a clutch of letters in his hand. Blake let out the breath he had been holding.

'I said I need to grab a bag from upstairs,' Polzin repeated. He was standing clutching a laptop computer to his chest.

'Yes, hurry.'

But Polzin didn't move. He was staring through the window over Blake's shoulder. Blake whirled around, and in his peripheral vision, saw one of the police guards breeze along the hallway towards the front door. Blake heard the click of the latch being opened, and through the window saw that a second figure had slipped through the gates, following the postman. In his hand, he carried a silenced gun at his side.

Chapter 18

The staccato sound of gunfire echoed through the house like doors slamming in the wind. Nothing like the wet tissue whimpers in Hollywood films. Bullets ripped through flesh, and deadened screams followed the sound of bodies collapsing. The postman was first to die. An innocent victim shot in the back of the head before he even knew anything was wrong. He tumbled through the door, his face rigid with a puzzled expression. Then the two police guards, gunned down with their hands reaching for their weapons.

Blake went for his Browning, but wasn't planning on trading fire with the assassin. His overriding concern was keeping Alexei Polzin alive. He vaulted the sofa, and manhandled the dissident roughly out of the door at the back of the room. With Sanders leading, they emerged into an open space behind the stairs where Green was crouching with his gun drawn.

'What the hell's going on?' Green hissed over his shoulder.

'Kozkov,' was Blake's one word explanation. 'We need to get out.'

He shoved Polzin into a kitchen that was all sparkling black marble and polished stainless steel. Folding glass doors overlooked a garden, which extended fifty meters through sweeping flowerbeds and ornamental trees. Sanders tugged at the handle, but the doors were locked.

More gunfire. Single shots that ricocheted off walls, louder than the first. Green trying to pin the assassin down.

'Where's the key?' shouted Sanders.

The Russian muttered under his breath, and his gaze dropped. The house fell eerily quiet. The firing stopped, and the screams of the dying men faded away. Green reversed into the room with his gun extended at arm's length. He eased the door closed, grabbed a stool from under a breakfast bar, and jammed it under the handle.

'Come on, Alexei. We don't have all day. The key?' said Blake.

Polzin pointed to a wall-mounted cupboard. 'Up there, I think.'

Sanders pounced on it, diving into tins and jars. He found a solitary silver key, and set to work on the lock. It sprung open with a metallic click, and the doors slid open on well-oiled rollers. The four men spilled out onto a raised patio above a neatly manicured lawn enclosed on three sides by a tall brick wall. There was no obvious escape route.

'What's beyond the wall?' asked Blake, nodding towards the end of the garden.

Polzin looked blank. 'A railway line,' he said.

'Good enough. Let's go.' Blake dragged the Russian by the arm down three stone steps onto the lawn, and cajoled him into a shuffling jog. But the grass was soft and slippery, and twice Blake felt him lose his footing. Twice he hauled him up and urged him on.

The wall, in the shade of a beech tree, was at least two meters tall, and dwarfed the diminutive dissident.

'Over, quickly,' said Blake.

'I can't get over there,' said Polzin.

'You have to, or we'll all die.' Blake holstered his gun, bent over, and laced his fingers.

'What about my computer?' Polzin asked, his laptop cradled across his chest as if he was never going to let it go.

'Drop it. I'll bring it.'

Polzin hesitated, set the computer on the damp ground, and stepped into Blake's cupped hands. He weighed next to nothing, like a baby bird, all skin, bones, and brain. The dissident scrambled up the wall and disappeared over the top, landing on the other side with a muted thud.

At the same moment, two men burst out of the kitchen doors, spraying bullets. Blake recognised the brutal faces and bad haircuts of Kozkov's henchmen. The same men who'd knocked him unconscious and beaten his unresponsive body as he lay on the pavement near his home. A twinge in his ribs reminded him of the kicking, and aroused a burning desire for vengeance that he fought to suppress. His priority was to keep Polzin safe. Retribution would have to wait for another day.

Green and Sanders were on opposite sides of the garden with weapons drawn, in what looked to Blake like a well-drilled defensive position. He was impressed, not least because they'd acted without instruction. Green had found cover behind the slim trunk of a beech tree, but Sanders was more exposed, hunkered down on one knee trying to hide among an explosion of tall grasses.

'Sanders!' Blake shouted.

He jumped at the sound of his name, and sprinted flat out across the lawn. Stepping into Blake's cradled hands, he vaulted the wall in a fluid, athletic movement. Green followed with bullets whistling around his head. With a shove from below, he scrambled up the brickwork and straddled the top of the wall.

'Grab my hand,' he shouted.

Blake scooped up Polzin's computer under one arm, and snatched Green's wrist. His adrenaline and an urgent pull from Green carried both men over the top of the wall, and they collapsed in a tangle as a hail of bullets peppered the brickwork in puffs of rusty coloured dust.

They landed in a wide corridor between rows of houses where a spaghetti network of railway tracks on a dirty, oil-stained bed of ballast curved its way through a gentle corner. Less than fifty metres away, a train was approaching, swaying lazily on its axles. Their options were limited to running along the tracks either east or west. There was no other way out.

'Which way?' asked Green.

The rumble of the train grew louder, shaking the ground under their feet. A pair of hands appeared over the wall, followed by a blond head, and Kozkov's pale blue eyes, which fixed them with an emotionless stare.

A piercing blast from the train's horn made them all jump. The driver's anxious face was visible behind a fly-splattered windscreen. He was sitting ramrod straight and staring at the men as if he feared they were about to jump in front of him. The blast on the horn was a noisy rebuke, and intended to force them to move out of the way.

But Blake did the opposite. He stepped over the track, grabbed Polzin by the arm, and pulled him hard. The Russian stumbled on the loose ballast, and fell to one knee in front of the train. A sickening screech of brakes and a grinding howl of metal on metal followed. Sparks flew from the train's overworked brake blocks, and the Russian's face lost all colour as the engine loomed large. Blake tugged at his arm, but Polzin had become fatalistically immobile, watching the locomotive bear down on him.

Green and Sanders snapped into action in unison, sweeping up Polzin under his arms. They dumped him into a dip between the tracks as a hurricane of hot air bowled them sideways and ripped at their clothes.

'Get up and run,' Blake screamed, hauling Polzin to his feet, and starting out on a furious sprint alongside the coaches as they flashed by.

Polzin followed at a slow jog.

'Faster!' yelled Sanders behind him.

But the ground was hard going. The track ballast was rough and uneven while taut wires, wooden cable reels, and piles of concrete girders littered their way. After less than a hundred metres, Polzin was flagging. His face burned scarlet, and his expression contorted into the agony of a man unused to physical exertion. He couldn't go any faster, and there was every danger his heart might give out if they pushed him on.

Blake trotted to a halt as a seemingly endless number of carriages blazed past with a singsong clackety-clack. Behind the windows, bemused passengers stared at them with lifeless eyes.

'I can't go on,' Polzin panted. He doubled over to catch his breath.

'Once this train passes, there's nothing between us and Kozkov,' yelled Blake. 'We have to go on.'

Polzin shook his head, hands on his knees. 'Take my laptop, make sure it's safe,' he said.

'We're not leaving you.'

'Just go.'

Sanders pointed to a dirt-blackened, Victorian, brick road bridge that spanned the line two hundred metres away. 'What about over there? That should give us some cover if we can make it,' he said.

Blake spun around, and followed Sanders' hand.

'What do you reckon, Alexei? Do you think you can make the bridge?' said Blake.

Polzin's chin dropped onto his heaving chest.

'No chance,' said Green.

Blake weighed up the distance, and made a calculation in his head. 'You're right,' he said. 'I'll carry him. Take the computer.'

Blake swung Polzin up onto his shoulders like a fireman carrying an unconscious body from a burning building. He adjusted Polzin's dead weight across his neck, and snapped into a fast jog, ignoring the protests from his bruised and aching body.

After fifty metres, his thighs and lungs started to burn, and he remembered he wasn't as young as he used to be. But he had a point to prove to the two young agents, and it spurred him on over the rough terrain that threatened to turn his ankle with every uneven step.

Another train hurtled past in the opposite direction, and Blake was almost knocked off his feet by the blast of displaced air. Trapped in a perilously narrow gap between the carriages, Blake fought with every last ounce of energy to stay upright. If he stumbled or fell, he knew Polzin would almost certainly end up under a set of carriage wheels. He gritted his teeth and ploughed on, ignoring the deafening noise and body-shaking turbulence.

And in a flash the train was gone, hurtling away into the distance, granting them instant relief from the assault on their bodies. Blake looked up, and when he saw the bridge less than twenty metres away, put on another turn of speed. They reached it as the final carriage swept past.

Blake stumbled across the track, and fell onto a muddy bank behind a brick pier. Polzin sprawled on his back, grimacing. Blake collapsed beside him with his lungs heaving. He clenched his eyes tightly shut, and waited for the lactic acid to drain from his legs. The bank was cold and muddy, and strewn with the detritus pitched from passing cars. The rattling of exhausts and the rumble of tyres filtered down from above.

It took a minute for Blake to catch his breath. He edged to the bottom of the bank, and snatched a glance back where they'd come. In the distance, Kozkov and two of his men were prowling along the tracks, spread out, checking over walls and fences. Blake allowed a smile to creep across his face.

The three agents helped Polzin up the slippery bank and over a wire fence at the top. They brushed the mud from their knees, and crossed a busy road towards a row of shops bustling with mid-morning trade.

'Where now?' said Polzin. He'd picked up a slight limp.

'We'll find you somewhere safe to lay low,' said Blake.' But you can't go back to the house.'

'Lay low? I'm not going into hiding. I have a story to

tell.'

Chapter 19

Patterson was sitting by the river under a weak autumnal sun overlooking the Houses of Parliament. Across Westminster Bridge, camera-clutching tourists were jostling for pictures, while to the east the chalky stone cornices of the Whitehall buildings stood out imperiously against the azure sky. The sun was unusually warm for an October afternoon. Maybe the last mild day of the year. It wouldn't be long until the cold tentacles of winter would coil around the days.

'Nice view,' said Blake, sliding onto the bench next to Patterson.

A gaggle of chattering foreign students bustled past under the drone of a jet plane growling high overhead.

'How's our Russian guest?'

'Missing his home comforts,' said Blake. 'I've left Sanders and Green babysitting.'

Patterson smiled. 'So you finally managed to offload them?'

'Is that what you think?' Blake feigned outrage.

'And the memory card?'

'We've made back-ups, but the original's with Polzin while he works on the material.'

'Have you seen it?'

'I've seen enough. It looks plausible.'

'Plausible enough to kill for?'

Blake shrugged. 'The Russians have been systemically poisoning their own people over decades,' said Blake.

Patterson raised an eyebrow. 'Where?'

'Bratsbirsk, in the Siberian wastelands, north east of Moscow. It's a town built around the timber trade, but barely a pinprick on the map. It has a population a little over seventeen thousand people, but almost all of them have suffered some kind of ill health. There are extraordinarily high rates of cancer, respiratory problems, allergies, and autism. Way above the national average. Add that to the high levels of diabetes, miscarriages, and birth defects and you've got a medical catastrophe.'

'Caused by?'

'The water supply. Levels of CCA have been recorded at around a thousand times higher than approved safe levels.'

'CCA?'

'Chromated copper arsenate. It's a chemical compound used as an industrial preservative injected into wood. But it's been leaking into the underground aquifers for years from a mill on the outskirts of the town.'

'Arsenate, as in arsenic?' asked Patterson.

'Precisely. The mill was under state ownership until the early 1990s, before most of the country's industry was denationalised, and these health issues date way back,' said Blake.

'Back to when it was run by the state?' said Patterson.

'Absolutely.'

'So the Kremlin knew what was going on?'

'Polzin's been given details of a whistle-blower who says there's been a massive cover up.'

'Where's the information come from?'

'He won't tell me,' said Blake, folding his arms across his chest and stretching his legs. 'He wants to protect his sources, and I can't blame him.'

'And how long before he's able to publish?'

'He's changed his mind about that.' Blake shifted awkwardly. 'He now wants to make a speech.'

'It's out of the question,' said Patterson. 'We can't protect him if he appears in public. Not with Kozkov on the loose.'

'He thinks it will have a greater impact, and that he owes it to Neno Kasun. We owe it to Kasun.'

'So he did know him?'

'Not exactly. He received instructions that the memory card would be concealed inside the cover of a passport, but claims that he had no idea when or how it would arrive. He certainly wasn't expecting MI5 to hand deliver it.'

'We couldn't have known we were doing Polzin's dirty work,' said Patterson.

'Nonetheless, I signed Kasun's death warrant by taking it to Polzin.'

'You can't blame yourself.'

'We're responsible, Harry, like it or not. Any ideas what they're going to do with his body?'

'The coroner won't go ahead with an inquest until they establish his identity. Until then, he stays on a cold slab. Are you sure Polzin doesn't know more than he's letting on? His contacts must have set this up.'

'He's refusing to say anything until after he's made his speech.'

'Well, we know Kasun was a damn good liar, whoever he was. I've never seen anyone hold up under interrogation like that before.'

'He wasn't lying.'

'Of course he was,' spluttered Patterson.

'I questioned him under hypnosis. He was telling the truth, or at least what he believed was the truth. Chances are he was suffering from some kind of personality disorder that made him genuinely believe everything he told us. Perhaps that's even why he was chosen as the courier. We should let Polzin make his speech,' said Blake. 'At least it would give some meaning to Kasun's death.'

Patterson sat forward, and watched a police motor launch power up the river. He'd known Blake a long time and trusted his judgement. But it was a big call. If Polzin was killed by an FSB assassin while in MI5's protective custody, it would be his hide on the line. 'I don't know, Blake,' he said.

'Come on, Harry. We owe it to Kasun. He gave his life for that memory card, and for all those people in Bratsbirsk.'

'And give Kozkov another chance to finish the job?'

'We're supposed to be the good guys. If not for Kasun, then for the sake of the families in that town. We owe them justice. Let Polzin have his one big hurrah, and I'll personally oversee his protection.'

Patterson rubbed his temples with the tips of his fingers. Every fibre of his being was telling him this was a bad idea.

'Harry, it's the right thing to do.'

'Fine. Alright. But it'll be on your head.'

'Thank you,' said Blake, quietly. 'I take it there's been no further news on Kozkov?'

'Nothing yet. We have eyes on the ground, but so far, we've drawn a blank. But we're hopeful we'll flush him out soon. In the meantime, I'm leaving Green and Sanders at your disposal. Make good use of them.'

Blake sighed and stood up. 'You know me, Harry. I work best when I'm alone.'

'You need their help if you're going to keep Polzin alive.'

'I'm done with teamwork, Harry.'

'Don't be so ridiculous. It's how we've always worked. We run teams.'

'Not any more,' said Blake. He dug his hands deep into his pockets.

'You know what? You're turning sour, Blake.'

'Maybe I'm just getting a bit long in the tooth.'

'You should be grateful you still have a job.' Patterson felt his irritation rising. Blake had a rare knack of getting under his skin. 'I saved the unit and your career. You'd do well to remember that.'

'You had me killed.'

'I had to,' said Patterson. He felt the familiar pang of guilt. 'We've been through this.'

MI5 had insisted that Patterson arrange Blake's death before he was recruited. They wanted no trace of the soldier Blake used to be. And so Blake's military records showed he'd been killed on active service by a Taliban sniper. Patterson had even arranged for a coffin to be flown home for a full military burial while Blake sneaked back into the country on a civilian flight under an assumed name.

'Seriously, you have to give Green and Sanders a chance.'

Blake pouted like a petulant child.

'Let's put it this way, they'll be assisting with the security arrangements if you want my blessing for this speech to go ahead. Just try to show them a little respect.'

'I can't perform miracles, Harry.'

'And I'll look forward to hearing your full report on their performance.' Patterson checked his watch. 'I need to get back. Keep me posted, and I'll let you know how we get on with Kozkov.'

Blake was already walking away when Patterson stood. He watched Blake drift off along the river embankment and disappear among the crowds. A ghost walking among men. One of MI5's greatest assets.

Patterson sighed. He had a really bad feeling about this.

Chapter 20

Through a carefully constructed tissue of innuendo and rumour, neighbours had concluded that renovation work on a townhouse in the middle of their street had come to a temporary halt because of a structural issue with the foundations. Some speculated that the unknown owners had run into difficulties trying to extend a basement. Others that the wrong type of supporting steel beams had been used when the internal walls were ripped out. But none suspected the aborted construction work was a front to conceal an MI5 safe house.

Blake's car pulled up on the opposite side of the road. He let himself out, and ran a finger around his collar where his tie constricted his neck. His shirt was fresh out of the packet, and irritated his skin. His new shoes pinched his toes.

Outside the house, thin polythene sheets masked a lattice of scaffolding and stacks of cellophane-wrapped bricks piled up on the pavement alongside sacks of cement and plaster. It looked the real deal. Nobody could possibly suspect there was anything going on inside other than one of thousands of refurbishments across the city.

Checking he'd not been seen, Blake eased through a gap in the security fence, and slipped through a loose-hanging plastic sheet. Even though the house looked deserted, his light tap on the door was answered almost immediately, and he stepped quickly inside.

The ground floor had been stripped bare. Pink plaster walls and exposed dusty floorboards. Blake brushed past a burly guard, and headed straight for the stairs, tiptoeing his way up, conscious of his footsteps echoing through the building.

The first floor was fitted out with a kitchen, thick carpet, sofas, and chairs. A large screen television was on in one corner, opposite a rectangular dining table. Heavy blackout blinds hung over the windows.

Alexei Polzin was pacing the floor, running through his speech, while Green and Sanders lounged in black suits on the sofa, distractedly watching an animal documentary.

'Ready?' said Blake.

Polzin nodded solemnly. He grabbed his jacket from the back of a chair, and shrugged it on. His dinner suit was expensively tailored, accentuating his lean figure.

'Just give me a minute,' he said, disappearing up another flight of stairs to his bedroom.

'How is he?' asked Blake.

'He's spent most of the day slowly winding himself up into a frenzy,' said Sanders.

'But no last minute jitters?'

'No, he says he's still determined to go through with it,' said Green.

Polzin trotted back down the stairs polishing his glasses with a handkerchief. 'Did you find Kozkov yet?' he said.

'Don't worry, the venue's secured. Come on, let's go,' said Blake.

They travelled in silence in an anonymous, chauffeur-driven Mercedes. Blake took the front passenger seat with Polzin sandwiched between Green and Sanders in the back. They turned onto Goodge Street, past the British Museum, and south towards the river, maintaining a constant speed.

As they approached High Holborn, Blake whispered into a radio mic in his sleeve, and a second Mercedes, identical to the first, pulled out in front of them at a junction. Blake checked the side mirrors, and confirmed a third car had slotted in behind. Four passengers in each car. Three in the back, one in the front. Almost impossible to tell them apart.

The convoy rolled through Leicester Square towards the National Gallery, and on towards Trafalgar Square where the statue of Lord Nelson surveyed London from his perch. The lead car pulled up outside St Martin-in-the-Fields, a three hundred-year-old church that looked as if it had been imported from Venice, with an ornate portico supported on a row of Corinthian columns.

Blake directed their driver to keep moving, and turned in his seat to watch as a swarm of television cameramen, curious onlookers and photographers with flash bulbs pulsating swamped the car. A ring of police officers made only a half-hearted effort to hold them back. Blake smiled wryly to himself. A human smoke screen.

'Take the next left,' he said.

The driver swung into Duncannon Street, and pulled over. A voice crackled in Blake's ear. He adjusted the moulded earpiece, and answered into his cuff.

'Roger that. Standby, he said.

Green was first out. He met Blake on the pavement, and they formed a two-man guard around the rear door, watched by two grim-faced police officers armed with Heckler and Koch MP5s. Sanders joined them on the pavement, and Polzin followed nervously. He adjusted his jacket, and ran his fingers through his hair as a helicopter buzzed overhead, sweeping the area with a high-powered spotlight.

'Let's go,' said Blake. Forming a tight net around the dissident, they led him past the armed officers, and down a steep flight of stairs into an underground crypt beneath the church.

The space was used during the day as a café and restaurant. Tables and chairs covered the uneven stone floor, and the smell of stale food and coffee lingered in the air.

'Make yourself comfortable,' said Blake, checking his watch. 'You've got thirty minutes until you're on.'

Polzin stood awestruck. Sixteen stone pillars supporting a vaulted brick ceiling that seemed to defy gravity intersected the room.

'Come on, relax. Take a seat,' said Blake, pulling out a chair at a nearby table, his voice echoing off the walls.

Polzin sat, opened his laptop, and tapped at the keys.

'We need to check everything's okay upstairs,' said Blake. 'The doors are locked, and no one can get down here.'

'I'm fine,' said Polzin. He waved Blake away with a dismissive hand.

Blake pulled Green and Sanders to one side. 'You two, come with me. We need visuals on every guest before we even think about moving him. If Kozkov is here, I want to know about it. Tonight, nothing goes wrong. Understood?'

Chapter 21

The air in the nave was a sweet sweat of perfume and aftershave. Men in suits, and women in expensive dresses, mingled and chatted, swapping air kisses and firm handshakes. Nobody noticed the three MI5 agents emerging from a door by the altar.

Polzin had handpicked the guests. Influential ex-pats including lawyers, doctors, novelists, academics, and scientists. But by far the loudest group was a knot of oligarchs who'd grown wealthy on the carve up of Russia's energy markets, and relocated to Britain to further their interests. All had impossibly full heads of black hair, perfect white teeth, and glamorous younger wives, bleached blonde and squeezed into tight gowns.

A bank of television crews, with their cameras jacked up high on tripods and aimed at a low stage in front of the altar, had set up at the back. The location had been chosen to impress. Sparkling gold chandeliers hung from a vaulted alabaster ceiling, and towering pillars supported two dark mahogany balconies on either side of the room.

'Look for anything suspicious or out of place,' said Blake.

Green and Sanders peeled off on a slow patrol around the edge of the room. Blake took the centre aisle between the two rows of dark wooden pews. He scanned left and right, conscious that he didn't really know what he was looking for. All the guests had been vetted in advance by an MI5 intelligence team, and searched on their way in. It was unthinkable that Kozkov could be inside.

He looked up at the balconies, cordoned off for the evening and occupied by a handful of police marksmen.

Blake tugged at his collar where it pressed against his Adam's apple, and regretted not going for a larger size shirt. In his ear, voices were running through checklists and confirmations. Requests for information and status updates were answered by section commanders positioned throughout the building. Everything was running to plan. Everyone was accounted for, and nothing was out of the ordinary.

And yet Blake had a definite sense of unease.

He checked his watch. Ten minutes before Polzin was due to speak. The last stragglers were passing through the vestibule where their invitations were being scrutinised and their bags searched. Blake squeezed into a corner out of the way, and spoke into his cuff.

'Green? Sanders? Anything?' He'd lost sight of them among the throng finding their seats.

'Nothing, boss.' Sanders answered first.

'Negative,' said Green.

'Right, back down to the crypt. I'm going outside to see what's going on. I'll meet you down there in five.'

Blake eased past two armed guards at the main entrance, and stepped outside. He was surprised that the evening air was a few degrees warmer than in the church. From the top of the steps under the portico, he surveyed Trafalgar Square. It was chaotically busy with a seeping movement of brightly illuminated buses, black cabs, and meandering groups of people. The crowds who'd swarmed around the decoy cars had largely dispersed, disappointed when they realised there wasn't even a minor celebrity to catch a glimpse of, although a few press photographers who'd not been accredited places inside the church, hung around with their cameras dangling over their shoulders, stamping their feet and breathing warm air into their fists.

Blake took a deep breath. In less than an hour his job would be done. Polzin's secret would be out, and the threat from Kozkov over. What could possibly go wrong?

'Blake? Do you copy? It's Sanders.'

'Blake here. Go ahead.' His heart picked up ten beats as he sensed the urgency in Sanders' tone.

'It's Polzin,' he said.

'What's wrong? Is he okay?'

'I don't know,' said Sanders. 'He's disappeared.'

Chapter 22

Colourful balloons floated aimlessly across the screen of Polzin's laptop, and his chair was pushed back at an angle on the stone floor, as if he'd abandoned it in a hurry.

'We shouldn't have left him alone,' said Sanders.

'Let's not jump to conclusions,' said Blake. 'The only way out is up the back stairs to the nave. He's probably gone to see who's here. Anyone checked the toilet block?'

Green shook his head, took the hint, and marched off to investigate.

'Try the stairs,' Blake instructed Sanders.

When he was gone, he leaned over the laptop and tapped the keyboard. A box popped up demanding a password. His finger hovered over the keys, but he thought better of it.

'All sections secure,' a voice hissed in his ear. 'Standby everyone.'

Blake checked his watch again. Three minutes until Polzin was due on stage. He tried to assure himself that there was nothing to worry about. Probably the Russian was stretching his legs, mentally preparing himself for his public appearance.

Green crashed back into the room, his face flustered. 'There's something you need to see.'

Blake's stomach lurched. 'Polzin?'

The toilets were on the south side of the crypt off a narrow hallway. The gents' were tiled in white from floor to ceiling. An overwhelming smell of pine disinfectant masked a more unpleasant odour. A row of urinals ran along one wall, opposite a line of hand basins, and above them, a black and white photograph on an A4 sheet of paper was attached to a mirror with two strips of sticking tape. It was a recent picture of Polzin, with a gun sight superimposed over his face.

Blake tore the sheet down. 'How long has this been here?'

'I don't know,' said Green.

'The building was supposed to have been swept. If Polzin's seen this -' His voice trailed off as he scanned the room. He folded the paper, and slipped it inside his jacket pocket.

'Who do you think it's come from?' asked Green.

'Kozkov playing games.'

They were interrupted by the sound of Sanders shouting. They found him in the hallway.

'Got him,' he said, relief written all over his face. 'He was in the kitchen looking for a glass of water.'

'Is he okay?' asked Blake.

'He's fine, just a little dry mouthed. Must be the nerves.' He frowned. 'What are you two doing in here?'

Blake took the photograph from his jacket. 'This was taped to the mirror.'

Sanders studied the picture. 'Shouldn't we evacuate the building?'

'No, that's exactly what Kozkov wants. He can't get in. So I'm guessing this is an attempt to flush Polzin out. We carry on as planned.'

'I hope you're right.' Sanders ran a hand over his bald head.

'Look, the best we can do for Polzin right now is to get him on that stage in one piece. Once the story's out, Kozkov's mission's failed. Now I need your full support to make that happen.'

Polzin was sitting at the table over his laptop as if nothing had happened. He glanced up, and smiled without humour as the three agents approached.

'Alexei, it's time,' said Blake. He placed a gentle hand on the Russian's shoulder. 'Ready?'

Behind his glasses, Polzin's eyes were wet and rheumy. 'Da.' He closed the lid of his laptop, and scraped the chair back. 'How do I look?'

'Like a man about to shed the weight of the world from his shoulders.'

'And Kozkov?'

'We're operating under maximum security, Alexei. Your guests have been verified and double-checked. There's nothing to worry about. Now, your audience awaits. Shall we go?'

Blake sent Green and Sanders ahead, and then led Polzin up the flight of stairs at the rear of the crypt. They stopped in a hallway behind the altar, where an expectant murmur of hushed voices carried through the walls. Blake took a deep breath, and focussed on slowing his heart rate. He wiped his palms on his thighs. He'd done his best to convince Green and Sanders that the threat from Kozkov was minimal, but wasn't convinced by his own rhetoric. The assassin had been sent from Moscow with one objective - to kill Alexei Polzin. Blake knew that the Kremlin would be unforgiving if he failed.

'You told me he has a nickname,' said Polzin.

'Who?'

'Kozkov.'

'Gadyuka,' said Blake.

'It means "The Viper".'

'Yes, I know.'

'Why do they call him that?'

Blake shook his head. 'Alexei, don't worry about it. Concentrate on your speech. Worry about all those families in Bratsbirsk, and bringing them justice.'

'Maybe it's because he strikes without warning?'

Blake grabbed Polzin by the shoulders with such force that the dissident's eyes widened in surprise. 'Listen to me,

Alexei. He can't touch you in here. The place is surrounded by armed police. The building has been secured, and every one of those guests out there has been vetted and searched. He can't touch you.'

Blake brushed a speck of dust from Polzin's arm, and straightened his bow tie.

'Thank you,' said Polzin. He attempted a smile, but it came out more as a grimace. 'I mean for everything you've done.'

'Just doing my job. Now, wait here while I check they're ready for you.'

'I'm not going anywhere.'

Blake eased through heavy double doors, and stepped into the powerful beam of a spotlight fixed on the balcony and angled towards the low stage where the Russian was due to deliver his speech. Blake felt several hundred pairs of eyes fall on him. He swallowed hard, and took a step back into the shadows.

It occurred to him that none of the guests had the faintest idea what Polzin was going to say. And yet they'd all come, presumably on the strength of the Russian's reputation, and their own vanity at being invited to such an illustrious and mysterious event. The room slowly fell silent. Green and Sanders were at the back alongside the camera crews, their eyes never still, scanning the room for anything that might constitute a threat.

Blake tried to convince himself that everything was set. They couldn't delay it any longer. He turned for the doors, but was distracted by an agitated chatter in his ear. The final orders being issued to make sure the security teams were in place and primed?

'Gold One, I'm going to bring Polzin through. Are your teams all set?' said Blake, into his cuff.

'Negative. Hold your position.' It was the voice of the police commander in charge of co-ordinating the armed security units.

Blake's earpiece clicked and fell silent. Green and

Sanders were staring at him wide-eyed. Green shrugged as if to say 'I don't know what's going on either.'

The drone of a helicopter roared overhead, and a bright wash of light pierced the arched window over the altar.

'What's going on?' Blake hissed.

'Stand down. Do not bring the speaker through,' said the commander in his ear.

'Gold One, repeat please,' said Blake.

'We have a credible threat. Stand the speaker down.'

'What the hell are you talking about? What threat?' Blake marched back to the double doors with his adrenaline rising. It was impossible that Kozkov was inside the building.

'Section commanders to the main exits. Evacuate the building immediately.'

'Hang on a minute,' shouted Blake, as he heard the thud of police boots on the wooden floor above.

The nave filled with armed officers who started clearing the rows of pews quickly and efficiently as the guests stared at them in wide-eyed confusion.

'Will somebody talk to me? I need to know what the hell is happening here,' said Blake, raising his voice over the hubbub.

'We've received a bomb threat, a specific warning that a device has been planted inside the church, under one of the pews.'

'No, no, no,' said Blake. 'This is exactly what he wants. You have to stop them leaving.'

There was a momentary silence in his ear. 'I'm afraid I can't do that.'

'Shit!' Blake crashed through the doors, and grabbed Polzin by the arm.

'Downstairs. Now. There's been a delay.'

'Is it him?'

'No, come on.'

'I'm not going anywhere until you tell me what's going on.' Polzin dug in his heels and refused to move.

Blake sighed. 'They're evacuating the building. It's a hoax bomb threat.'

'How do you know it's a hoax?'

'Look, this church has been on a secure lock down since yesterday evening. It's been swept by sniffer dogs three times. There's no way anyone could have planted a bomb in here. Trust me. It's just a ploy to waste time.'

'So why are they evacuating the building?'

'Standard procedure. We'll soon have it sorted out. But there's no point hanging around up here getting in the way. Come on.'

Polzin's resolve evaporated, and he allowed Blake to escort him back to the crypt where Green and Sanders were already waiting. Blake settled the dissident at a table, and took the agents to one side.

'Shouldn't we be getting Polzin out of here?' asked Sanders.

'Polzin stays here until we find out what's going on.'

'You don't think the threat is serious?' asked Green.

'He couldn't have smuggled a device in here with the security we've had in place.'

'I wish I had your confidence.' Green pushed his glasses into place with a thin finger.

'All right, let's prove it shall we?' said Blake. 'Let's go and find this bomb. If it's really under a pew, it shouldn't be too hard to locate.'

Chapter 23

The nave was filled only with a disquieting silence. The main lights blazed brightly, transforming the space from intimate to functional. Blake regarded the two rows of dark pews, and pondered where to begin.

'Gold One, this is Blake,' he said.

'Go ahead, over,' the police commander responded.

'What are the specifics of the threat?'

'I'm sorry?'

'I assume it was phoned in? What did they say?' Blake didn't try to hide his exasperation.

'Yes, a direct call to the station at Paddington Green warning a bomb had been hidden under a pew, in the third row.'

'They specifically stated it was in the third row?'

'Yes.'

'Anything else I should know?'

'The caller was male. He said the bomb was timed to detonate within the hour, and that Alexei Polzin was the target. He wanted us to clear the building immediately to avoid innocent casualties.'

Blake rolled his eyes. Didn't these people realise that Kozkov was toying with them? If the aim had been to kill Polzin, the bomber wouldn't have called in a warning, or suggested the building should be evacuated.

'Anyone claiming responsibility?'

'No. The caller spoke with an English accent, but didn't claim a connection to any organisation.'

'No, I bet he didn't. The FSB doesn't tend to announce

its covert operations.'

'I beg your pardon?'

'It doesn't matter,' said Blake.

'Are you still inside the church?'

'I'm going to look for this so-called bomb.' Blake wandered into the central aisle, and stopped at the third pew where a prayer book had been knocked to the ground in someone's hurry to leave.

'I would strongly advise against that. The bomb squad's on its way. They should be here any minute.'

'I appreciate the concern, Chief Inspector, but let me remind you that I retain overall responsibility for this operation.

'Yes, but -'

'My decision, my call. Just make sure the building is kept secure. Understood?'

'Affirmative.' It sounded as if the officer was about to choke on his words.

Blake dropped to one knee, and used the light from his mobile phone to illuminate the underside of the pews to his left, but found nothing but dust and cobwebs.

'Look from the other side,' he called to Sanders.

They crabbed their way along the row inspecting every nook and crevice until they met in the middle.

'You were right. It looks like a hoax,' said Sanders.

'Let's check the other side.'

They crossed the aisle, and began on the adjacent row. The dust made Blake's throat dry and his eyes itchy. He rubbed them with the back of his hand, but it only irritated them more. He sniffed, and moved on; going through the motions, playing out Kozkov's game, confident they'd find nothing. It was impossible that any of the guests could have smuggled explosives through the ring of steel the police had set up.

'Blake,' said Sanders, from the opposite end of the row. 'I've found something.'

He was crouched low on the floor, his head craned,

eyes fixed on the underside of the seating. Blake scuffed across the polished floor, and followed the beam of Sanders' light. A small package, roughly the size of a paperback, wrapped in plastic was attached to the underside of the pew with duct tape. Small enough to have been smuggled in a bag. Big enough to cause a devastating explosion, and certainly close enough to the stage to have caused Polzin at least serious injury.

'Maybe not a hoax after all,' said Sanders.

Blake lifted his cuff to speak. 'Gold One. This is Blake. Where are the guests?'

'We've put them in a nearby fast food restaurant, drinking coffee,' the police commander said.

'I want everyone checked against the guest list again. Names and photos.'

'But they've already been -'

'Just do it,' snapped Blake.

'You think it was put there by one of the guests?' asked Sanders.

'It's the only explanation. The nave was thoroughly swept for explosives before anyone arrived. The dogs would have found it.'

'So what do we do with Polzin now?'

'Get him out of here. We can't take the risk of this thing going off. I'm afraid Kozkov has forced our hand. If this device is genuine, it could bring the ceiling of the crypt down. Let's move to the contingency plan, and hope we can sneak Polzin out without being spotted.'

Chapter 24

Alexei Polzin's gaze was fixed on the middle distance, focussed on nothing in particular as Green finished a trite anecdote, his attempt to keep Polzin distracted from the drama going on around them. Not that the Russian had the slightest interest in what he was saying, that much was evident.

'Relax,' said Blake, holding up what he hoped was a reassuring hand. 'Everything's fine.'

'No bomb?' said Polzin.

Blake hesitated a fraction of second, which was probably enough to confirm Polzin's worst fears. 'We're moving to Plan B. We're getting you out.'

'Leaving?'

Blake glanced at Green, who'd stopped talking mid-sentence. 'Find a car and bring it around the back. Quick as you can.'

'Give me ten minutes.'

'Make it five.'

'Where are we going?' asked Polzin.

'Somewhere safe.'

'So there is a bomb?' The Russian's eyes widened, his face taut.

'The chances are it's a dummy device, but my priority is keeping you alive.'

Blake picked up Polzin's laptop, and folded it closed. The Russian's nervous energy had evaporated. He stood like a puppet whose strings had been cut, a look of defeat apparent on his face.

'Do I have a choice?' he said.

'Not if you want to stay alive, Alexei.' Blake extended a comforting hand to touch Polzin's shoulder as Green reached the door to the stairs that led up to the vestibule. He rattled the handle.

'The door's locked,' he called over his shoulder.

'But you just came down that way.'

'I'm telling you it's locked. I can't get out.'

'Let me try.' Sanders was halfway across the room when the crypt was plunged into an impenetrable veil of darkness that rendered them all momentarily silent.

'What's happening?' Blake caught the quiver in Polzin's voice.

'It's nothing to worry about.' Blake's brain went into overdrive, hunting for a plausible explanation. He fell on the first thing that came to mind. 'They've killed the power to prevent the bomb being accidentally detonated. It's a standard procedure.'

'You said it was a fake.'

'It's just a precaution.' Blake forced his eyes wide open, trying to hurry his night vision to kick in. At the back of his mind was the isolating fear that sudden darkness always evoked. A primeval response to being deprived of one his key senses. And this one of the worst kinds of dark. A complete blackout, like falling into treacle. Funny how the old mantra his mother used to recite came back to him.

There's nothing in the dark that wasn't there before.

A bright white light suddenly illuminated Sanders' head and shoulders. Blake let out the breath he'd been holding.

'Everyone okay?' said Sanders, his voice reassuring.

Green had stepped back from the door, looking dazed and bewildered. Blake held up his arm to shield his eyes as Sanders swung the light in his face. He fished in his pocket for his own device, and was fumbling with the buttons when the door at the bottom of the stairs crashed open. Green stumbled back into Sanders who dropped his phone. It beamed a cone of light over the arched brick roof, revealing a grotesque, cumbersome figure standing in the doorway. A full-face plastic visor attached to a heavy round helmet obscured the features behind it.

'Bomb squad.' The voice was muffled behind the mask. 'Are there any others down here?'

The man in the bomb blast suit shuffled stiffly forwards, and raised a powerful torch in his left hand. Its light shone into the shocked faces of the four men in turn, trapping a concert of dancing dust motes in its beam.

Green picked himself up, and dusted down his suit. 'No, this is it,' he said, stepping forward. 'The door was locked -'

He didn't see the torch start on its violent arc through the air. It caught him on the side of his head with a powerful, glancing blow, and from the way his body crumpled into a limp heap, it was clear he was unconscious before he hit the floor.

As Green collapsed, Blake registered that the man was holding a gun in his other hand. The long barrel of a silencer rose almost in slow motion, and Blake was already diving to his left when a muted muzzle flash illuminated the room, and an asthmatic shot echoed off the walls. His arms grappled for Polzin, and they fell together in an inelegant bundle as a bullet embedded itself harmlessly in a far wall.

'Gadyuka?' gasped Polzin.

Blake hauled him upright, and clamped a hand over his mouth. 'Quiet,' he whispered in his ear, reaching for his Browning. He ejected the magazine, and clipped it back into place, unable to disguise the click-clunk as he engaged a round into the barrel.

'Put your weapons down.' Blake detected a Russian accent even from behind the visor. 'Come out with your hands on your heads.'

Long shadows crept along the walls and ceiling from the torchlight. Blake risked peering around a pillar. Sanders had vanished, but Green was lying motionless on the ground with Kozkov standing over his body. The assassin's legs were splayed, and he was working with both hands to remove his helmet. Blake took his chance to guide Polzin across the room, melting into the inky gloom.

They dropped behind another pillar as the hollow metallic thud of Kozkov's heavy helmet being dropped onto the stone floor reverberated around the crypt.

'I don't have much time,' the assassin said. 'Better if we don't play games.'

The irony of his words wasn't lost on Blake. The room was divided by sixteen pillars in rows, four by four, creating a miniature chequerboard of interconnected spaces. He thought of each of the men as living, breathing chess pieces.

Kozkov moved first. The sound of his boots gave him away. Three slow steps forward. And then another sound. Lighter steps. Moving fast. Quick. Urgent. Sanders racing around trying to outflank the assassin in the dark.

Blake and Polzin sat shoulder-to-shoulder, hardly daring to breathe. Blake listened hard, sounds suddenly acute; the hiss of water through pipes, the creak of expanding wood and the rustle of clothing, his hearing compensating for his lack of vision. Loudest of all was Polzin's breath next to him, rapid and shallow as the air whistled through his constricted nasal passages.

They both flinched when two more gunfire cracks ricocheted off the walls, and Polzin's hand squeezed Blake's arm. In the fleeting light of the gun flashes, Blake saw a stainless steel counter running along the eastern wall near the kitchens. A heated worktop where they served lunchtime meals.

Blake pulled Polzin up by his wrist, and dragged him behind the counter, tucking him low into a corner where he would be best protected from loose-flying bullets.

'Wait here,' Blake whispered in his ear. 'And don't make a sound.'

'Don't leave,' Polzin begged.

'I'll be back in a minute. Keep your head down.' Blake peeled the Russian's fingers from his sleeve, and scurried back into the crypt, following the southern wall, picking out the ragged brickwork in the faint overspill light from Kozkov's torch. He kept going until he was level with the assassin on the opposite side of the room, then stepped into an aisle between the pillars.

Kozkov was taking slow steps, less than fifteen metres away. It was an easy shot. Blake steadied himself, one foot slightly in front of the other, his Browning lightly clasped between two hands. His finger hovered over the trigger as he lined up on Kozkov's head, the top of which protruded over a protective collar extending beyond the shoulders of his suit. It was practically impossible to miss at that distance. A gentle squeeze on the trigger, and he could put a marble-sized hole in the back of his head that would obliterate the assassin's brain and rip off his face with the exit wound.

Blake squinted along the gun sights, took a breath, and exhaled, feeling the tightness ease from his shoulders. He squeezed the trigger with a gentle caress, but at the moment the firing pin engaged, a figure darted from the shadows. The blister of gunfire was followed by an agonised howl, and the crash of table and chairs sent flying.

Kozkov immediately extinguished his torch, and the crypt was plunged back into darkness. No time to think. Only time to react. Blake tucked into a roll, tumbled to his left, avoiding a returning volley of fire, which flew harmlessly over his head. Another stone pillar provided the cold comfort of temporary protection. As he waited and listened, his heart pulsing with an adrenaline rush, he heard the rustle of clothing, and a body dragging itself across the floor. A groan. A grunt.

Blake closed his eyes, and silently cursed his bad fortune. He imagined Sanders with a hole gouged in his arm, his shoulder, or worse, his chest. Oozing blood, his life pumping away over the flagstones.

And if Kozkov stumbled across him?

Blake dismissed the thought, and refocussed. Sanders needed treatment quickly. Two options. Break left, or go right. He pondered the indeterminables, and realised it was down to luck which way Kozkov had moved. Blake loosened his tie, and popped open the top two buttons of his shirt. Time to gamble.

He paused to unlace his shoes. The stiff leather had rubbed raw blisters on his toes, and he was conscious that the leather soles clattering over the hard floor were bound to give him away. He'd be better off in socks.

He turned right, and with one hand outstretched, padded forwards, counting as he went. He found the outer wall of the crypt after twenty-three steps, turned right, and keeping the wall against his left shoulder, felt his way forward. He measured out another fifteen paces. Stopped, listened, and heard ragged, rasping breath. He locked onto it like a beacon. The sound of a man bleeding to death.

Blake dropped to his knees, and crawled.

'Sanders?' Blake hissed.

He stumbled on a foot. The agent responded with a murmur.

At least he was alive. Just.

'Where are you hurt?' Blake whispered. He was lying on his back with his head propped against a pillar.

No response. Blake's hands followed the length of his leg and found Sanders' chest. It was rising and falling in a rapid and unpredictable pattern. Not good.

A warm, syrupy puddle had formed under the agent's shoulder and blood had soaked his shirt and jacket. There was every chance the bullet had shattered the bone, but at least it had missed any vital organs. In the dark, Blake did his best to stem the bleeding. He pulled off his tie, and used it to bind the wound around Sander's upper arm. He tugged it tight, and knotted the ends. Sanders needed an intravenous line, but that would have to wait for the paramedics.

When he was done, Blake sat back on his haunches and wiped his bloody hands on his thighs. Then he stood slowly, and listened. Nothing above Sanders' laboured, sticky breath, and the distant drone of passing traffic in the street above.

Left or right? Another fifty-fifty gamble. But one that ultimately he didn't have to make.

The blinding beam of Kozkov's torch suddenly burned his retinas. Blake threw up his arm to protect his eyes.

'Throw down your gun, or I'll finish him,' said the assassin, who'd risen out of the dark, the silenced Glock steady in his hand.

'He needs treatment,' said Blake. 'Urgently.'

'So maybe you shouldn't have shot him. Now throw down your weapon.'

Blake raised his hands. He reached for his Browning with the tips of his fingers, and eased it from its holster. He dropped it on the floor, and kicked it away.

'And your radio.'

Blake unclipped the radio transmitter from his belt, pulled out a lead that coiled up his back and into his ear, and let it fall at his feet.

'Now his gun. Take it out, slowly.'

Kozkov aimed the torch at the figure on the floor. Blake followed the beam and recoiled. The injured man's eyes were closed, and his skin was a ghostly pale. A sheen of sweat had formed over his forehead.

'Do it now, or I'll put a bullet between his eyes.'

Blake looked up at the light, and back again at the dying man.

'Bill,' whispered Blake. 'I'm so sorry.'

Chapter 25

'Last chance, or his death will forever be on your conscience.' Kozkov's face was in shadow, but Blake imagined his cold, blue eyes and enigmatic curl on his lips.

'Go to hell.'

Kozkov sighed. 'Your choice.'

'I can give you immunity from prosecution, and a plane home. But not if you kill him. No one can help you if you murder an MI5 agent.'

'Fetch me his gun, and tell me where you've hidden the traitor.'

Sanders rolled his head to one side, and let out a groggy murmur.

'I can't,' said Blake, quietly.

'You're testing my patience. Don't say I didn't warn you.'

Kozkov's finger tightened on the trigger as he straightened his gun arm.

'Don't do it,' said Blake. He tried to swallow, but his tongue felt as if it had swollen in his mouth.

'Really? You care for his life that much?'

'I told you, you'll never see home if you kill him.'

'Time to say goodbye.'

'Wait!' Blake blurted it out, hoping to find some words that could stall the moment of Sanders' death, but realised he had nothing to say that could delay the inevitable.

The barrel of Kozkov's gun wavered and steadied. Blake considered launching himself at the assassin, but dismissed the idea as too risky. He scrunched up his toes.

The chill from the stone floor had seeped into his feet and ankles, and now he regretted kicking off his shoes. It seemed hopeless. The only way of saving Sanders was to give Polzin up, and deny the possibility of justice to thousands of families. It was an impossible dilemma.

Blake glanced at the motionless figure by his feet, and realised with a sense of shame that he knew precious little about the man bleeding out on the floor. He had a name, but not much else. And in that moment he vowed that if Sanders died tonight he would personally deliver the news to his family. The same promise he'd always made to his men in the hours before an operation. Except, he had no idea if Sanders even had a family.

Blake peered into the surrounding darkness, hoping for a miracle. It arrived unexpectedly from the depths of the gloom as Kozkov's head snapped violently forward, and his legs buckled. His knees hit the floor, and the rest of his body followed as he collapsed at Blake's feet, spilling the torch. Blake gathered up the light, and shone it into the space where the assassin had been standing.

Green was wobbling unsteadily. He dropped Kozkov's bloodied helmet, and it hit the floor with a clanging thud. He stared at the blood-soaked shirt of his partner. 'What happened?'

'I shot him. He walked across my line of fire. We need to get him to hospital. Go and fetch Polzin. He's behind the counter. I'll see to Sanders.'

Bill Sanders was in a bad way. He was hanging onto consciousness by a thread. His skin was clammy, and he was barely responsive. Blake retrieved his Browning from under a table then lifted the agent to his feet. They shuffled across the room, and Blake punched open an emergency exit on the south wall.

Sanders was revived a little by the cool night air, but the steep stairs up to street level proved a challenge and he was grateful when Green joined them, tucking his shoulder under Sanders' free arm. Between them, they carried him to a courtyard at the rear of the church. They sat the agent on a stone bench, but he lacked the strength to support himself, and collapsed onto his back.

Blake called Harry Patterson's number from his mobile. He answered after only one ring. 'Blake, where are you?'

'Sanders has been shot. I need an ambulance.'

'What about Polzin?'

'Kozkov's unconscious inside the church, but I need a fast car to get Polzin away.'

The Russian was staring at Sanders' injured shoulder, his face fixed in an emotionless glaze.

'What happened to Sanders?'

'I'll explain later. Just get some medical help here quickly.' Blake was in no mood for questions. The debrief and recriminations could come later.

'Okay, where is he?' asked Patterson.

Blake searched the surrounding buildings for a road sign. 'Adelaide Street, at the rear of St Martin's. We're in the courtyard at the back.'

He hung up, and slipped the phone in his pocket.

'Are they coming?' said Green, standing over Sanders with his hands on his hips, chewing his lip.

'Shouldn't be long. Stay here with Alexei. I'm going back for Kozkov.'

Chapter 26

The emergency door slammed shut, and Blake was plunged back into darkness. He inhaled through his nose, filling his lungs. The sound of blood pounded in his ears and the fear hit him. Worse this time.

He flicked on the torch on his phone. It threw eerie shadows up the walls, and fell on the blast helmet lying near a congealed puddle of Sanders' blood that had darkened to a deep maroon and run in rivulets between the flagstones.

But there was no sign of Kozkov. Only a pile of discarded clothing. A pair of reinforced trousers, and a thick jacket with padded arms and a protective chest plate.

'The game's up,' Blake shouted. His voice echoed off the walls, and a surge of adrenaline quickened his heart. 'Polzin's gone, and the church is surrounded. They'll shoot before they ask questions. It's all over. But I can still help you.'

Blake waited for a response, but had a sense that he was alone. He turned slowly, completing a full circle. The torchlight penetrated into the far corners of the room, spilling over the craggy brick pillars, the uneven stone floor, and the door Kozkov had crashed through, hanging open on heavy iron hinges. Blake angled the torch up the stairs, and put a foot on the first step, feeling the smoothness of the worn stone through his sock. Blake thought it was unlikely that Kozkov, now divested of his blast suit, would have been able to bluff his way back out through the police cordon at the front of the church. In which case, where had he gone?

Blake holstered his gun, and tried Patterson's number. It was only when the call failed to connect that he remembered the thick walls and brick ceiling proved an impossibly effective shield against mobile phone signals. He took another step up, gathering his balance, and focussed his Browning on the brass-handled door at the top.

The sound that came from somewhere behind him was a barely audible metallic click. It had come from the opposite end of the crypt. Blake launched himself down the stairs, and sprinted across the floor, slipping in his socks and jarring his shins. He skidded to a halt at the far door, and pressed his ear to one of its wooden panels.

Silence.

He eased it open, and peered through the narrow gap with one eye. Black boots at the end of a pair of thin, grey trousers were disappearing up the stairs. Blake shouldered his way into the hallway, and fired twice, more in hope than expectation. Bullets ricocheted off the walls, taking out large chunks of plaster, and missing the legs by some margin.

Blake charged up the stairs after his quarry, but the landing above was empty. He pushed through double doors into the nave where the pews were bathed in the delicate silver of an iridescent harvest moon pouring through the altar window.

'There's no way out,' said Blake, his voice sounding strained as it shattered the reverential silence.

Feet scuffed the floor. The sound of movement to his left. Blake pivoted on his heel. 'You have to give this up,' he said.

'You know I can't do that.' Kozkov's voice came from low down near the back of the room.

Blake tightened his grip on his weapon. His hand was moist with sweat. 'You don't have a choice if you want to walk out alive.'

'I'll take my chances.'

'In which case you'll die.'

'What's your name?'

'You can call me Blake.'

'Police?'

'No. MI5. I'm the guy who can get you on that plane to Moscow, no questions asked. Or asylum and a new identity. It's up to you.'

'You know I can't surrender.'

'Nikolay, listen to me,' said Blake. 'It's time to face facts. It was a suicide mission from the moment the FSB sent you.'

In the grey light, Blake saw Kozkov's head bob up over the tops of the pews. He caught it in the periphery of his vision a fraction of a second before two gun flashes pulsed from the assassin's Glock. Blake dived to his left, rolling behind the cover of a mahogany pulpit. But he hit the floor hard, and the torch on his phone went out as it clattered from his hand and skidded away under the front row of pews.

Blake cursed silently. 'Think about it,' he continued. 'We know exactly who you are. But we also let you into the country. That was a mistake, an embarrassing one. So it's in our mutual interest to sort this out quietly. We can pretend tonight never happened.'

'I don't think so.'

'Then I hope they're paying you well, Nikolay.'

'You're wasting your breath. You know people like us don't quit.'

'Don't compare what we do. You murder people for a living. We're nothing alike.' Blake scuttled on his haunches, squinting along the rows of pews as if he was hunting rabbits. 'Do you even know why you've been sent to kill Polzin?'

'It's immaterial.'

'Seriously, you don't know? Didn't they trust you enough to tell you?'

'It doesn't matter. My job is to silence him, not to ask questions.'

'The Russian government is covering up its involvement in the deaths and suffering of hundreds of men, women, and children in Siberia. Polzin was going to reveal the truth tonight, to make it stop.'

'I told you, I have no interest in that.'

'Then you either have no heart, or no brain,' said Blake.

'I'm not paid to feel, or to think. I'm paid to do a job.'

'So maybe you're inhuman and deserve to die.'

Blake jumped to his feet, and fired a rapid, ear-splitting hail of shots at a cowering body balled up between the pews on the opposite side of the nave. Wood splintered, and the strips of fabric tore apart under the barrage.

Eventually, the Browning clicked empty, even as Blake's finger continued to pulse on the trigger. The deafening echo of 9mm rounds died away, and left his ears ringing. He let his arm drop, and his head sagged onto his chest. Outside, the moon slipped behind a cloud, and darkness stole back into the room.

Chapter 27

Assistant Commissioner Hester Parkes projected her voice loudly. She was sitting at the head of the table with her hands clasped, and her jacket buttoned up to a black and white chequered cravat at her neck. 'Gold One, repeat your message,' she said. Her hair was scraped back from her face, accentuating her piercing, cerulean eyes.

'We're hearing multiple shots, ma'am, from inside the building.'

'But it's been evacuated.' A grim silence fell over the command centre less than five kilometres away from St Martin-in-the-Fields. 'I need eyes inside the building. Find out what's going on.'

'Ma'am, we can't get in. The doors have been locked from the inside,' said the commander at the church.

'So who's in there?' The impatience in Parkes' tone thinly disguised.

'The MI5 agents moved the speaker down into the crypt.' There was an uncertain pause. 'And there was the bomb disposal guy.'

'What bomb disposal guy?'

Another police officer at the table looked up from his notes, raised his eyebrows, and shook his head. 'They're not due for another fifteen minutes,' he mouthed.

'You're mistaken. There's no one currently deployed on the site.'

'Well, he was here in full kit. Who else could it have been?'

'And you let him in without checking his identity?'

The five men around the table shuffled awkwardly in their seats. The assistant commissioner's short fuse was well known. She looked to Patterson, who was doing his best to avoid her eye. 'What about your team? Why are they still in the building?'

Patterson cleared his throat. 'Actually, Alexei Polzin has been safely evacuated. He's en route to a safe house while we assess the situation.'

'I asked about your men. Are they still inside the church?'

All eyes fell on Patterson, grateful that Parkes' irritation had been deflected onto the MI5 man. She studied his face, a picture of innocence, but she had the distinct feeling he was hiding something. God, how she hated spooks muscling in on her operations.

'Mr. Patterson?'

'It's colonel, actually. As I said, they've managed to extract Alexei Polzin safely from the crypt.'

'Yes, so you said. I'm asking you about the location of your men.'

'One of our agents is currently receiving treatment for a minor gunshot wound -'

'He's been shot?'

'Apparently, yes.'

'And the others?'

'Currently unknown, ma'am.'

She didn't like the way he spat out the word "ma'am", as if it had been stuck in his throat. Typical ex-military with a misogynistic aversion to women in authority. She'd seen his sort before, with their public school confidence and clipped tones. All balls and muscle, high on testosterone, and an unwavering belief that the world could be put to rights with bombs and bullets. No wonder the country's incursions into Iraq and Afghanistan had been such a disaster.

'You mean you've lost them?'

'I wouldn't say that exactly.'

'But you've lost communications?'

'Temporarily.'

'And you've no idea what's going on in there?'

Patterson hesitated. He looked down at the pad of paper he'd covered with scrawls and doodles. 'Not exactly. If I had to hazard a guess, I would say your officers have allowed the FSB assassin, Nikolay Kozkov into the church, and he's currently being engaged by two of my agents. I would imagine he made the bomb threat to clear the building so he could target Alexei Polzin. Now he's trying to escape. The best advice I would give is to keep out of the way and let my team get on with apprehending him.'

Chapter 28

Blake ejected the spent magazine. The pungent aroma of cordite filled his nostrils as his diaphragm sucked air deep into his lungs. He focussed on the shredded bundle, and blinked sweat from his eyes, his arms and shoulders trembling, his anger spent.

He'd made a real mess. Splintered chunks of wood had been taken out of the pew, and clothing ripped to rags was strewn across the flagstones. He shuffled along a narrow gap between the pews, and kicked a discarded bullet case. It chased across the floor with a delicate tinkle, a fragile, almost musical sound after the gunfire storm. He reloaded. Another thirteen rounds, but hesitated before racking the slide. What had possessed him to empty an entire magazine into Kozkov's cowering body? It was an unforgivable lapse in discipline.

The moon emerged from behind a fleeting rush of cloud, lighting the interior of the church. Blake looked for blood as he poked a toe at the pile of rags. They were soft and yielding. The remnants of a jacket, but no dead body.

A door squealed on its hinges. Blake spun on his heel, and saw a shadow darting through a swinging door. He vaulted the pew, landed heavily in the aisle, and charged headlong through the leather-panelled door into a windowless vestibule.

But the assassin had vanished.

Dull footsteps clattered up a spiralling, wooden staircase, and Blake set off in pursuit, emerging onto a first floor landing. Finding it empty, and hearing a thud from above, he was encouraged to keep climbing. Emboldened at the thought of cornering the Russian, he took the next flight two steps at a time.

The staircase ended in another narrow landing. With his heart racing, Blake pushed at a door, which opened into a square room lined with tall cupboards and four round windows. A dozen bell ropes hung from the ceiling, fur-handled loops of rope swinging gently as if a breeze had caught them. The bitter tang of new carpet and stale sweat hit him, and he had a vision of the room alive with jolly-faced bell-ringers performing for a Sunday service.

But where the assassin had gone was a puzzle. There was nowhere to hide, unless by some feat of contortion he'd squeezed inside one of the cupboards. Doubt crept into Blake's mind. It was possible that Kozkov had given him the slip somewhere between the vestibule and the bell tower, and that in his hurry Blake had missed him. Maybe the assassin had doubled back and fled the church. He could be a kilometre away by now, blending in with the busy evening crowds, heading underground for the Tube, or disappearing in a taxi. He should warn Patterson.

Blake toyed with his mobile phone, and turned a slow circle with his thumb hovering over the call button. But something was nagging at the back of his mind. He sensed that Kozkov was close.

As he waited for the call to connect, he noticed a red velvet curtain hanging across a wall from a metal rail. A corner of the fabric was turned up, exposing a section of bleached wood. Blake ripped the curtain back, and found an ancient door, aged a silvery grey, and riddled with a million tiny, woodworm holes. It had a twisted metal handle, and a ragged hole for a key.

It opened easily to reveal a stone staircase with dished steps worn smooth, corkscrewing in an anti-clockwise spiral. Blake stooped into the narrow passage, and climbed awkwardly with his head brushing the stone ceiling. At the top, a hazy artificial light shone through an archway.

Beyond it, giant bells were arranged in a wooden rack.

Blake inched up the last few steps, and twisted through the arch, leading with his gun hand and stooping his head so that his chin was on his chest.

Kozkov was waiting for him, out of sight. His foot struck out a vicious kick as Blake emerged, knocking his Browning clean from his hand, and sending it careening across the floorboards. It hit one of the bells with a melodious thunk, and dropped through a gap. The assassin snatched the back of Blake's collar, and dragged the rest of him into the tight space of the belfry. The cold, hard steel of a silencer pressed in the soft flesh under Blake's chin and lifted his head.

'I was beginning to doubt you'd ever find me,' said Kozkov, in Blake's ear. 'Now, tell me where to find Alexei Polzin.'

'You're too late. He's gone.'

'Where have you taken him?'

'Somewhere safe. You missed your chance.'

Blake felt the grip on his collar loosen. He straightened up, and turned to face the Russian. Up close, his eyes were cold and grey, his skin pale, and his nose crooked.

'Too bad for you,' said Kozkov. He aimed the silenced Glock at a spot between Blake's eyes.

'Even if I told you where he is, you couldn't get out of here alive. The area is crawling with armed police who are about to storm the building,' said Blake.

'You should worry less about what's going to happen to me, and consider your own immediate future. Tell me where he is!'

'I can't.'

The stinging blow from Kozkov's free hand caught Blake square on the jaw. It jarred his skull, and split his lip. Blake staggered backwards, and dabbed at the cut with the back of his hand.

'Why do you care so much about protecting him?' said Kozkov, his eyes burning. 'He's not even a British citizen.

He's nothing to you.'

'Because you want to kill him.' Blake made a deliberate play of checking his watch. 'By my reckoning, you've got about five minutes before this tower is overrun with armed officers. Do you want to talk about that immunity deal yet?'

'Five minutes?' said Kozkov. 'That's plenty of time.'

Blake frowned. 'For what?'

Chapter 29

An expectant hush had descended on the command centre as the six figures around the conference table waited for news. Harry Patterson toyed with his mobile, willing it to ring. Blake's phone was either switched off, or had run out of power, and Green's number continually rang out. He twirled the device around his fingers, his leg tapping out a furious rhythm on the floor.

Assistant Commissioner Parkes drew a breath, and broke the tense silence. 'Gold One, this is Parkes. Can you give us a sit rep?'

The radio crackled, and the police commander's voice came through low and urgent. 'No further gunshots, ma'am. We're awaiting your orders.'

'Have you identified the shooters yet?' Parkes eyes fell on Patterson, who pretended to check his phone.

'Not yet, ma'am.'

'Right, time's up, Mr. Patterson. I want that building secured in five minutes. Commander, have your men ready.'

'Yes, ma'am.'

Parkes laid her palms flat on the table, and locked onto Patterson. 'Any word from your man?'

'Blake's phone's dead. I'll keep trying a second agent who's in there with him.' Patterson rocked back on two legs of his chair, and hit the redial button for the umpteenth time. The phone rang five times, and he was about to hang up when it was unexpectedly answered.

'Green here.'

Patterson spoke in a low whisper. 'Where are you?'

'Still inside the church, looking for Blake.'

'What about Polzin? You were supposed to be taking him to the safe house.'

'He's with Sanders. They're on their way.'

'Sanders is supposed to be at the hospital.' Patterson was conscious of five pairs of ears listening in. He turned his back to his unwanted audience, and hunched his shoulders as if that might shield his call.

'The paramedics patched him up, but he refused any more treatment. That's when we heard gunshots, so I came to look for Blake and left Sanders with Polzin.'

Patterson scratched his brow. 'And to be clear, you're inside the church now?'

'Yes, sir.'

'What about Blake? Or Kozkov?'

'I've checked the crypt and the nave, but there's no sign of either of them. I thought I heard a noise in the bell tower. I was about to investigate.'

'What is it?' Parkes asked loudly.

Patterson held the phone away from his ear. 'One of our agents is back inside the building trying to find out what's going on. Stand your men down until I can establish what's happening.'

'Thank you, but I'll decide when and if my men need to be stood down.'

'With all due respect, Assistant Commissioner, all I'm asking for is a few minutes to establish some facts.'

'Let me speak with him,' said Parkes.

Patterson sighed, and put the phone back to his ear. 'I'm going to put you on loudspeaker.'

He placed his phone in the middle of the table, and returned to his seat.

'Agent Green, this is Assistant Commissioner Hester Parkes. What going on in there?'

'I'm not sure. I'm literally in the dark. The power's been cut, and there's no sign of Blake or Kozkov.'

'We're working on the power. It should be restored soon.'

'That would help. The crypt and the nave are clear. I was about to try the bell tower. If you stay on the line I can talk you through.'

Parkes nodded at Patterson.

'Go ahead, Green,' he said. 'Give us as much detail as you can.'

Green floated up the mahogany staircase, keeping to the edges of each step to avoid the creaks and groans of aged wood. His palm was moist on the grip of his 9mm handgun, but his senses were razor sharp, honed by the adrenaline coursing through his veins.

'I'm on the first floor landing. All clear.'

The second flight of steps ended at the narrow landing Blake had passed through less than ten minutes earlier. 'I can see a door. It's partially open. I'm going through it.'

Green edged forwards until the door was within reach, and stepped to one side so he wouldn't be silhouetted in the frame. He steadied himself, weapon at the ready, and was about to nudge the door open when he heard the assistant commissioner's voice again.

'What can you see?' The urgency in her tone did little to calm his nerves. He decided to ignore her and concentrate on what he was doing. Green put his eye to the gap between door and frame, and peered into the darkness beyond.

'Green? What's happening?' Parkes' voice was really beginning to grate. He was about to answer when he heard a muffled shuffling from inside the room.

'There's someone on the other side,' Green whispered as loudly as he dared.

'Can you see Blake?' Patterson asked.

'Negative. Standby, I'm going in.' Green put his shoulder to the door, and flexed his fingers around his gun as his mind played out a hundred scenarios.

There was every chance Kozkov would be waiting for him on the other side. So he dropped to his haunches, and kept his body as low to the ground as possible. The surprise of seeing Green in a duck walk might buy him a precious second or two, especially if the assassin had to adjust his perspective and his line of fire. It wasn't much of a plan, but it was all he had.

He leaned against the door, and it swung slowly open as the power was suddenly restored, flooding the tower with light and revealing a horrifying scene.

'Green? Are you still there? Talk to me.' Patterson's voice drifted into Green' consciousness as if in a dream.

'I've found Blake,' said Green, his finger twitching on the trigger of his gun. 'But we have a major problem.'

Chapter 30

Blake was on a chair with his arms behind his back and his ankles bound with thick tape. A bell rope extended from the ceiling, and was coiled tightly around his neck. Kozkov was standing behind him taking up the strain, keeping the pressure from crushing Blake's throat. In his other hand, his Glock with its unwieldy silencer was aimed at Green's head.

'Drop it, Kozkov,' said Green, with as much conviction as he could summon. He rose slowly from his crouch, and slipped his phone in his pocket.

Blake's eyes were bulging, and his breath came in short, fast snorts through his nose. He stared at Green as if trying to implore him to run.

'I don't think you're in a position to be making demands,' said Kozkov.

'I said drop the gun.'

'Or what? You'll shoot me? If you do, you'll have to live with your friend's death on your conscience.'

'Don't listen,' Blake gasped, his face flushing red. 'Kill him.'

'He's very brave, isn't he?' said Kozkov. His expression remained inscrutable. 'I think you should at least understand the consequences of shooting me, because your colleague's life is currently hanging by a thin thread. The other end of the rope around his neck is attached to a wheel on a bell directly above us. I'm holding the bell upright, but if you shoot me, and I let go of the rope, the bell will fall and take up about three metres of slack, the slack that's currently around Blake's neck. I don't know how good your imagination is, but think what effect that might have on his health.'

Green followed the path of the bell rope up to the ceiling where it disappeared through a narrow gap.

'Well, let me spell it out for you. The bell probably weighs in the region of two to three hundred kilos. Your friend on the other hand is at most, say ninety kilos. The probability is that it will snap his neck. If not, he'll be hoisted up to the ceiling to hang, and die an agonisingly slow death.'

'Take the shot,' Blake hissed.

'What do you want?' growled Green. He lowered his gun.

'Good decision. I need you to tell me where you've taken Alexei Polzin.'

'Not a chance. 'If I tell you where he is, you'll kill him.'

'He's a traitor who deserves to die.'

'He's a refugee, and we promised to take care of him.'

'So be it,' said Kozkov. He let the rope slide a few centimetres through his hand. It tightened around Blake's neck, and a strangulated cough fell from Blake's lips as his pupils darkened. He tried to speak, but mouthed only silence. 'I really don't know how much longer I can hold on.'

'You won't kill him,' said Green.

'Really?'

'He's the only leverage you have.'

'Maybe I didn't explain myself very well.' Kozkov took his hands from the rope, and let it unwind through his arm.

Blake's head and shoulders jerked upwards, and he was lifted clean off the chair. The rope bit into his skin, and the veins on his neck bulged as the room was filled with the deafening noise of a tolling bell resonating deep and low through the tower.

Green watched horrified, unable to react.

Kozkov snatched at the rope as it whistled past his head, and halted its upward momentum. He tugged on it hard, pulling it to his chest, letting Blake's limp body drop gracelessly. His feet hit the floor, and his back thudded into the chair. His eyes fluttered closed, and his head fell limply to one side.

'Now, that address please,' said the Russian.

Chapter 31

A circling blackness loomed at the edge Blake's vision, and every breath through his crushed trachea was agony. He was hanging onto consciousness by a thread, but at the back of his mind a voice was urging him to battle back from the brink.

His injuries could have been worse, but he'd anticipated Kozkov, suspecting the Russian would have to release his hold on the rope to demonstrate to Green the consequences of his non-cooperation. And in the moment he felt the constriction around his throat, he'd powered through his thighs, lifting himself off the chair. It had reduced the sudden force on his body, and although his actions hadn't prevented his airway being crushed, it certainly mitigated the effects. More crucially, it had left his spinal cord intact.

Blake forced his eyes open, but oxygen deprivation had snatched the colour away. He tried to focus on Green, but saw only a blurry monochrome figure.

'How many times do you think he can survive that?' Polzin's voice sounded distant, even though Blake was sure he was standing directly behind him.

'Enough,' said Green.

'Then tell me where you've taken Alexei Polzin.'

Blake lifted his head, and opened his mouth to speak, but couldn't form the sounds. He wanted to yell at Green not to reveal anything.

'And if I tell you, will you let him go?'

'You have my word.'

The room filled with the loud murmur of an approaching helicopter, and Blake's spirits soared. The police chopper returning to the scene. He imagined a sniper hanging from an open door with his sights fixed on the tower. Maybe he'd even be able take a clean shot through a window. He waited for the crack of a high velocity round, the sound of breaking glass, and the wet clout of bullets piercing flesh.

The whine of the helicopter's rotors grew louder, but nothing happened.

'Time's running out,' said Kozkov. 'Maybe we should see how Blake copes a second time.'

Blake straightened his back, and prepared to rise from the chair, but his legs were weak and unresponsive. He wasn't convinced he could summon the energy for a second leap, though his life was depending on it. He sensed the assassin take a step back, and Blake tensed his neck and shoulders.

'Stop!' shouted Green. 'Let him go.'

'The address?'

'The old public library in Limehouse. It's in Tower Hamlets. It's a derelict building owned by MI5.'

'There you see, that wasn't so difficult.'

'Now let him go.'

'With pleasure.' Kozkov swivelled at the hip, and fired twice.

Green dived to the ground as the bell rope tightened around Blake's neck in a deadly stranglehold that stopped his breath. Blake was hauled out of the chair, and sent hurtling towards the ceiling with his diaphragm convulsing, trying to draw air into his lungs. A fearful panic washed over him as his legs, still bound together at the ankles, kicked violently. The single resonant note tolled like a death peal. A fitting announcement of Blake's imminent demise.

His head brushed the ceiling, and for a second, he was suspended in mid-air, counterbalancing the weight of the bell. And then he was plummeting back down to the ground as it rolled back on its axis, and the rope unravelled. His legs kicked away the chair, and they folded beneath him as another deafening bong announced his unceremonious collapse onto the floor. The pressure around his neck eased, and he gratefully sucked in a lungful of air.

Blake's hands were tucked awkwardly behind his back, twisting his arms and shoulders painfully against their joints. But he dismissed the pain, concentrating instead on trying to free his wrists, realising he had a few precious seconds to release the bonds. If he could get his hands free, maybe he could remove the rope from his neck before he was hauled back up again. But Kozkov had used plastic cable ties, and the more he struggled against them, the deeper they cut into his skin. It was hopeless. With a rising urgency, he scanned the room, looking for a foothold. Anything he could hook his feet under to prevent the rolling bell hanging him.

The pulley rope whistled through the gap in the ceiling, and Blake felt the pressure increasing on his neck. His shoeless feet slithered over the carpet, and he managed to suck in one last painful gasp of air before his airway was cut off again.

His head and shoulders were lifted clear from the ground, followed by the rest of his body, taut and twisted, the veins on his neck bulging, his eyes unnaturally bulbous in their sockets.

And then he was floating. Free of pain and enveloped in a beautiful calm. His muscles relaxed, as if he'd slipped into a warm bath. A rush of endorphins hit him with a chemical rush. His body was awash with a euphoric delight so intense the tips of his fingers and toes tingled. And for once he felt truly happy. Religion had never figured in Blake's life, but at that moment, he had the sense of ascending to some higher place where death didn't seem so bad. No stress. No anxiety. No doubts.

Until strong arms snapped around his thighs and shattered the illusion of death. He was being dragged down by a sharp tug on his legs, and the weightlessness he'd been experiencing suddenly evaporated. He tried to fight it. He had no desire to return to the cold horror of reality with its promise of pain and anguish. But he had no choice.

His feet hit the ground, but he lacked the muscle strength to support his body, and he crumpled onto the carpet. Fast-working fingers unwound the rope from his neck, and his lungs drew whistling gasps of air. When he prised open his eyes, Green was kneeling at his side with his brow knitted.

'Thank God,' he said, when he discovered Blake was still alive. He hacked at the cable ties binding Blake's hands with a pocketknife.

Blake sat up slowly, and rubbed sensation back into his wrists. 'Where's Kozkov?' he rasped in a barely audible whisper.

'He disappeared through there.' Green pointed to the stairwell through the old oak door.

Blake dragged himself unsteadily onto his feet. 'We have to stop him.'

'I'll go.'

'I'm fine.' Blake swallowed hard. He had plenty of time to worry about recovering later. He reached for his Browning before remembering he'd lost it earlier. 'You'd better go first.'

Green dived for the narrow door, and took the stairs two at a time with Blake struggling to keep up. When Blake joined him, Green was circling the belfry with bemused puzzlement.

'He's not here,' said Green.

A cold wind blew in a swirl of dead leaves and dust through an arched window open to the elements. Wooden louvered slats had been smashed out of the frame.

'Through there,' said Blake.

Green moved to the window while Blake hunted for his gun. He found it wedged between two joists above a gap where the bell ropes were threaded through the ceiling. By lying flat on the floor, he was able to reach out and grab it with his fingertips, teasing it through the gap where it had fallen.

Outside the hum of a helicopter grew loud again. It was close, circling the tower at low altitude. Blake rolled over onto his back, clutching his gun tightly. Green was halfway out of the window.

'What are you doing?' Blake tried to shout over the noise of the chopper, but the best he could manage was a pathetic rasp.

He checked his Browning. One round still chambered. Safety catch off. He hauled himself up onto his feet, ignoring his screaming muscles, but when he turned to the window, Green had gone.

Chapter 32

'I've had enough of this,' said Assistant Commissioner Parkes. She leaned nearer the radio. 'Gold One, are your men ready?'

Patterson slumped in his chair, staring at his phone. They'd lost the connection to Green, and could only wonder what had happened. 'Give them another minute, please,' pleaded Patterson. 'At least until we can establish what's happening.'

'And how do you propose we do that? You've lost comms with both your agents. As far as we know, they could be dead already.'

'Ma'am, all units standing by, on your command,' the police commander's distorted voice said over the airwaves.

'We believe the Russian target is in the bell tower. Two security agents are also in the building, but unaccounted for,' said Parkes. 'Have your men proceed with caution. I don't want a body count.'

The radio hissed, but there was no response.

'Gold One, do you copy? I said proceed with caution. I am not sending in body bags, understand?'

'Ma'am, we have a new situation.'

'What situation?'

Patterson slipped his phone in his pocket. There was nothing more he could do but hope and pray that Blake and Green would keep their heads down when the bullets started flying.

'A helicopter's circling the church. It doesn't have any identifying markings. It's possibly a news crew, but I'm not sure.'

Parkes pinched face grew dark. A uniformed assistant to her left looked up from his notes. 'I thought we'd imposed a no-fly zone? Get onto air traffic control and find out who the hell owns that aircraft and get it out of there.'

The officer nodded, pushed himself away from the table, and hustled out of the room.

'It may be too late,' said the gold commander. 'I think it's trying to land.'

'Where?' Parkes snapped.

'It's coming down behind the church. I've got to go.' The radio clicked and static hiss filled the room.

From the window, Blake watched the helicopter descend into an impossibly narrow space between the church and a grey-stone building opposite. The McDonnell Douglas MD500 was designed with short rotors and tail that gave it greater flexibility than most commercial aircraft, but it was still going to be a tight squeeze. Like the police commander, Blake initially assumed the chopper belonged to a news organisation, but dismissed the idea when he saw it was missing any gyroscopic camera under the fuselage. Besides, no broadcaster in the world would have risked the manoeuvre the pilot was pulling for pictures.

The blast from the rotor blades threw dust in Blake's eyes, and rattled the remains of the loose slats hanging from the splintered window frame. He leaned out and surveyed the drop to the shallow-pitched roof below, with one hand shielding his face. He estimated it to be around five metres. A risky jump, but not impossible, although an awkward landing could easily result in a turned ankle or a fractured leg.

Kozkov was tucked up against a low, stone balustrade that ran around the edge of the roof, directing the helicopter with furious hand signals. Green, however, had vanished, and the fearful thought crossed Blake's mind that he'd fallen over the edge. Not that there was time to dwell on it. The aircraft rotated through ninety degrees, and hovered low over the church with its tail hanging over the rear courtyard. Kozkov jumped to his feet, and was buffeted by the whirling turbulence of the chopper's down draft. He caught his balance, and staggered towards the aircraft.

Blake raised his Browning, and squinted down the barrel, but the maelstrom of dust and debris made it impossible to hold his aim true. He was never going to make a clean shot. He'd have to gamble the odds. Shoot and hope. Maybe at least one round would find its mark. His finger tightened on the trigger, concentrating on squeezing, not snatching.

Kozkov stumbled, but Blake was distracted by a heavy thud directly below. Green was sprawled on his stomach spread-eagled on the roof. He'd been clinging by his fingertips from the window ledge to lower himself and reduce the drop. He'd landed behind a ridgeline that ran along the apex of the roof, and was hidden from Kozkov. But it also meant he had no idea that the assassin was within a metre or two of escaping. Blake tried to shout a warning, but his voice was strangled and weak, his pathetic squeak lost in the whine of the chopper's idling engines.

The menacing silhouette of a gunner in dark clothing hunched over a mounted machine gun appeared at a rear door of the chopper. He swung the weapon towards the bell tower, and unleashed a pulse of high-calibre rounds that fizzed through the air and tore chunks from the masonry. An arc of bullets traced a ragged line towards the window where Blake was caught in profile, framed, and perfectly lit. Blake saw the danger too late, his reactions lagging with his exhaustion. He fell backwards, but a stray round nicked his arm, and took a chunk of skin and muscle from just below his shoulder. A glancing blow that looked worse than it was. Painful, but not fatal.

Blake ripped a strip of material from his shirt with his

teeth to make an improvised bandage, and wrapped it tightly around his bicep. Outside, the machine gun had fallen silent. Blake hauled himself across the floor, and raised his head. Kozkov was climbing into the chopper, clambering over the body of the gunner slumped over the smoking machine gun with his eyes staring blankly, blood running from his mouth.

Behind the roof's central ridge, Green was on one knee, urgently reloading his weapon. Blake nodded a silent approval. It was a decent shot under the circumstances, but not enough to prevent Kozkov escaping. He could only watch as the assassin dumped the dead body of the gunner out of the aircraft. It fell limply onto the roof, and crumpled in an unnatural heap. Kozkov strapped himself in behind the pilot, and hauled the rear door closed.

Green rose to his feet, and emptied an entire ammunition clip at the fuselage as the helicopter's engines wound up into high-pitched frenzy. The bullets ricocheted harmlessly off fuselage as the aircraft climbed above the tree-tops. Blake knew it was hopeless. Green should have been aiming for the tail, or better still the pilot. Instead, he wasted the few rounds he had left on an ignorant out-pouring of anger and frustration. Blake punched the window frame so hard it grazed the skin of his knuckles.

The helicopter rose rapidly in a vertical ascent, before dropping its nose and arcing away on a rough course along the Strand towards the Thames. Blake watched it accelerate into the cover of darkness until even its flashing red and green anti-collision lights vanished. Blake could do nothing but warn Bill Sanders that Kozkov was on his way.

Chapter 33

The compact mirror magnified and slightly distorted Annie Murthy's face as she checked her make-up and applied a touch-up of lipstick. Good enough to cover the fatigue around her eyes even under the harsh TV lighting. She tucked a strand of hair behind her ear, and smoothed out a crease in her coat. The scarf she'd chosen was bright red, and she had a last minute panic that it was too bold, too distracting. Perhaps she should have grabbed the cream one instead. Oh well, too late now.

'Annie, everything okay? We'll be coming to you in three minutes.' The director spoke quickly in her ear. He sounded hassled, like a man spinning plates without enough hands.

She smiled into the lens, and gave up a thumbs-up with a gloved hand. Her cameraman, Tony, flicked on a top light fixed to the camera, and she was bathed in a ghostly, bright light that burned her eyes. Tony was one of the old hands. There wasn't much he hadn't seen or done in nearly forty years in the business. He stamped his feet to encourage the circulation. It was a chilly night, and they were both keen to wrap up and get back to the car.

'Great, standby. We'll be with you shortly.' In the background, Annie heard the restless chatter of a well-oiled gallery team preparing to go on air.

'Annie,' said another voice. A familiar one. The smooth avuncular voice of assurance that was beamed into homes across the country at ten o'clock every night. 'You look cold.'

Annie grinned. Steve Armstrong, the evening anchor, was at least twice her age, but she loved how he flirted with her in those intimate moments before they went live. His whispered words in her ear made her feel as if she were the only girl in the world. It was silly really.

'It's brass monkeys out here, not that you'd know sitting in your warm studio,' she said.

He laughed at the conspiratorial joke.

'I'm sure Tony can find a way of keeping you warm.'

Annie pulled a face.

'Oi,' said the cameraman. 'I heard that.' He leaned around the camera, and gurned into the lens. 'You're just jealous.'

'Never a truer word, Tony. So, you're top story. I'm throwing straight to you off the opening titles. You happy?'

'Absolutely.'

And then he was gone. Annie checked her notes one more time, familiarising herself with the details and the order she was going to run through the key events. Tony adjusted a radio mic clipped to her coat, and squinted into the viewfinder to check the framing. Not too much headroom. Enough of the cemetery in the background to give a sense of their location.

She heard the title sequence roll. A heavy beat with a dramatic timbre, tinny in her ear, with the bass notes stripped away by the tiny speaker.

Steve Armstrong delivered the main headlines with the sincere calm that had made him a household name, sweetening the bitter pill of bad news. It was always bad news. But then nobody really wanted to hear good news, no matter how much they protested otherwise.

The title music reached a crescendo and faded away. Annie visualised the opening establishing shot of Steve Armstrong at his desk, checking his scripts, and the slow fade to a centrally framed shot of his head and shoulders. He would pause for a moment for effect. Then he would look up, smile, and wish the audience good evening.

Annie cleared her throat, checked her notes one last time. She stared into the camera, and waited for the throw as Armstrong ambled his way through the opening link.

'Our reporter Annie Murthy has been following the story for us, and joins us now live from Central London. Annie?'

'Cue Annie.'

She took a deep breath, and put on her most concerned face. 'Steve, new revelations tonight, revelations that will strike at the core of the Russian government. Documents released to a number of media outlets have revealed, in detail, shocking evidence of what appears to be the systematic poisoning of an entire population in the remote northern Russian region of Siberia. Thousands of people in the small town of Bratsbirsk have been affected, women and children among them, many suffering horrific illnesses and deformities in what is becoming clear is one of the worst humanitarian scandals seen for many years. But what makes this new information so disturbing is that not only was it happening over the course of several decades, but that it was happening with the full knowledge of the Russian authorities. This document,' Annie held up a sheaf of papers, 'details the full extent of the tragedy, and includes many witness statements and photographs. Many are too disturbing to show.'

'Annie, how has this information come to light?'

The reporter nodded solemnly. 'We understand that the documents had been due to be released last week by the Russian dissident, Alexei Polzin. Now you'll remember he was found dead at a house in the city four days ago, and police are treating his death as murder. I understand Mr. Polzin, a fierce critic of President Putin, had been due to reveal the details at a speech in London. But that event was cancelled at short notice for reasons that have yet to become clear. His funeral was held here earlier today.' Annie half turned, and indicated the cemetery behind her.

'On pictures,' the director said in her ear.

'It was a low-key event attended by a small number of friends, and a few members of the Russian ex-pat community.'

Annie paused to check her notepad while they showed the footage they'd filmed of the funeral. The press had been banned from attending, but they'd snatched a long-range shot of the cortege as it swept into the cemetery. The video was a little grainy, but good enough to give the sense of the occasion.

'Then late this evening the documents highlighting the alleged atrocities were released to the press, together with a video-taped message that Mr. Polzin is believed to have recorded shortly before his death.'

'Back on you,' said the director.

Annie was already looking down the barrel of the lens. 'Now, of course, there has been widespread speculation that Mr. Polzin has fallen victim to a Russian assassination plot, a plot designed to silence him and prevent the publication of this information. That seems to be borne out not only by the recording Mr. Polzin made, but by the fact that he'd made arrangements for the documents to be released in the event of his death.'

Annie glanced down to her left as if she was staring at an imaginary monitor. It was the cue for the director to roll a clip from Polzin's video tape.

'My name is Alexei Polzin.' Annie heard the dissident's husky voice through her earpiece, and pictured the shot. The Russian was sitting upright in a chair against an anonymous white sheet. His hands rested lightly on his knees, his face fixed with an earnest expression. 'If you are watching this recording it is because I am already dead, killed by people who don't want you to know the truth. In recent weeks I have come into the possession of indisputable evidence that the Russian government was complicit in a human rights abuse on a scale not seen since the Second World War.'

'Cue Annie.'

Annie looked up from her imaginary monitor, paused for a beat, and continued. 'The rest of the tape, which lasts around ten minutes, details some of the worst atrocities, but which have not been independently verified at this stage.'

'Annie, no doubt that these are very serious allegations?'

'Absolutely, Steve. And they pose some very difficult questions for President Putin and the Russian government. But there has been a deafening silence from the Kremlin. No comment from them so far, although an unnamed source has been quoted dismissing the claims, and describing the allegations as a complete sham. I suspect though, we'll hear more from them within the next twenty-four hours as the pressure grows on Mr. Putin to react.'

'Annie, for now, thank you.'

Annie kept a stoic stare into the camera lens until she was given the all clear from the director. She whipped out her earpiece, and stamped her frozen feet on the ground.

'How was that? Okay?'

'Yeah, it was fine,' said Tony. He was already removing the camera from the tripod and packing up to move on.

Annie pulled her phone from her pocket, and dialled a pre-programmed number. It rang twice before being answered by Marcus Bolton, the broadcaster's white-haired foreign editor.

'Newsroom.'

'Marcus, it's Annie.'

'Great piece, Annie. Good job.'

'Thanks. So are my flights booked?'

'You leave for Moscow at six tomorrow.'

Chapter 34

The bare branches of leafless trees extended over the roof of a converted boathouse, perched at the bottom of a steep bank overlooking a wide river. Across the water, a shroud of grey cloud hung over the horizon, and in the late afternoon, the little sunlight that filtered through the altostratus was already fading.

Blake's boots thudded heavily on the roughly hewn pine steps that descended to the house. He raised his hand to knock at the door, but sensing it was empty let his arm drop. He peered through a swirling glass panel that distorted everything into a mash of shapes and colours, then cocked his head and listened. Somewhere along the river, a bird screeched. A wagtail darted out of the wood, settling on a wooden railing. It regarded Blake with a curious stare, and flew off.

An elevated walkway led to a balcony at the front of the property. Blake squeezed past an alfresco dining table, and shaded his eyes at a set of glass sliding doors. Inside, a sofa and armchair were arranged around a glass-topped coffee table. A television stood in the corner near a wood burning stove in a stone hearth. A crumpled newspaper had been hastily refolded and abandoned on the floor.

Definitely nobody at home.

Blake leaned over the balcony, and inhaled the crisp, clean air. The city and its energy-sapping hubbub seemed a million miles away. The house had been a real find, hidden from passing traffic, and visible only to the occasional yacht or pleasure craft on the river. Not that it had come cheaply. Prices in this part of Devon were on a par with some of the classiest neighbourhoods in London. Most were second homes snapped up by affluent bankers and businessmen whose easy boom-time cash had priced out most of the locals. Still, the government could afford it.

A silky, black cormorant skimmed the river on a determined course for the sea. It kept close to the far bank, with the tips of its wings threatening to break the surface with every dipping beat. Blake followed its path until it was almost out of sight, beyond an angler who was perched on a rock. The fisherman was concentrating on a spot in the middle of the river. Blake watched for a few moments before climbing down to a sandy beach and clambering along the shoreline.

'How's the fishing?' Blake asked.

'Slow,' the angler replied, without taking his eyes from the water.

'And the house?'

'Peaceful.' He jerked his rod upright with a series of rapid tugs, and hurriedly wound in the reel.

He looked different than the last time Blake had seen him. His hair had been dyed black and cut short. His glasses were gone too. The hair alone took fifteen years off him.

'Sounds perfect,' said Blake.

'If you like that sort of thing.' Waders came up to the man's waist, and looped over his shoulders. He had one booted foot on a rock for purchase.

'You made the news.'

'I might be in hiding, but I'm not a recluse.' The angler tugged hard at the rod, and suddenly lost the tension in his line. 'Damn.'

He raised an eyebrow. 'Not much of a turn out to my funeral.' He laid the rod on the rock, and collapsed in a stripy fold-up chair. He rummaged in a plastic cold box, produced two bottles of beer, and offered one to Blake.

'It was only for show, Alexei.'

Polzin shrugged. 'I always used to wonder what it would be like, to see who cared enough to turn up. But honestly, I wouldn't recommend it.'

'It was totally stage managed, including who attended. We had to convince the FSB you were dead. You shouldn't take it so literally.'

'You stole my identity and this -' he waved a hand across the river, '- is all I have now.'

'You're still alive. You should be grateful.'

'Yeah, well where the FSB failed, British MI5 succeeded. Congratulations.' Polzin took a long swig from his bottle, and pointed out a circular ripple in the river where a trout had broken the surface. 'Look, even the fish are laughing at me. What about Kozkov? Did you catch him?'

'Whose body do you think was in your coffin? He took the bait and walked right into the trap at the house where he thought you were hiding. I guess he should have checked his sources more carefully.' Blake set his bottle down on a rock, and wiped his mouth with the back of his hand.

'Won't the Kremlin make a fuss when they find out he was murdered by MI5?'

'He was a state sponsored assassin, Alexei. Death is an occupational hazard. Besides, with all the heat on them following the Siberian scandal, they won't want it known that they sent an agent to Britain to kill you.'

'What happened to your arm?' Polzin nodded at the sling across Blake's chest.

'It's nothing. A flesh wound from a .50 calibre helicopter mounted machine gun. I've had worse,' said Blake, with a sly smile.

'Really? So what happens next? To me, I mean.'

'I don't know.'

'I guess I'll be quietly forgotten. Your lot will deny my existence, and if I'm lucky, a few conspiracy theorists will postulate that I'm still alive. That's what happens to ghosts, isn't it?'

'You'll work things out. It's not as bad as it seems.' Blake stared across the river, watching the ripples and eddies. He thought about the obituary that Patterson had written for him. Short and to the point. Brief details of his death in Afghanistan at the hands of a Taliban sniper. A few perfunctory words about his exemplary service for his country. The end of his Army career. He'd meant to have it framed. A reminder of his own mortality.

'You know, I'm not allowed to speak to anyone, and I'm a hopeless angler,' said Polzin. 'I can't contact any of my old friends. Even my ex-wife thinks I'm dead.'

'You'll build a new life. Think of it as a fresh start,' said Blake.

'They made me dye my hair,' said Polzin, running his fingers over his scalp. 'And sorted out my eyes with a laser.'

'It suits you.'

'It's not me though, is it?'

'It is now.'

A long pause hung in the air as Polzin finished his beer. 'Why did you come?'

'To check how you were coping.'

'Do you really care?'

'What you did took balls. You must have known they'd come after you.'

'Anyone would have done the same.' Polzin rubbed the corners of his eyes. 'But I was only the mouthpiece. It was the others who risked everything collecting the data. They're the real heroes. I've no idea if they're even still alive.'

'We'll probably never know. But without you the risks they took would have been for nothing.'

'I don't even know who they were.'

'What about Neno Kasun? Did you know him?'

Polzin shook his head. 'I told you the truth. I'd never even heard his name until you mentioned it. I was only ever expecting a passport. They said I'd recognise it when I saw it. But I knew nothing of Kasun.'

'In which case, we'll probably never find out who he was.'

'I'm sorry. I wish I could help.'

'No matter. There are always casualties in war.'

'What will happen to his body?'

'I guess they'll keep it safe in a mortuary somewhere in the hope of one day being able to identify him,' said Blake.

'I see,' said Polzin. He began packing away his fishing tackle as the last of the hazy sunlight disappeared. 'Will you stay to eat?'

Blake checked his watch. 'It's getting late. I can't.'

'Another lonely meal for one then, I guess.'

'I promise I'll be back. I'll bring food.'

'And vodka?'

'Only the best.'

Blake stood, and offered his hand. Polzin took it, and squeezed hard. 'Thank you for coming.'

Blake jumped down from the rock, and landed in soft sand. 'Take care of yourself, Alexei.'

He trudged back to the boathouse without a backwards glance, and took the steps up through the wooded hillside two at a time to emerge onto a gravel parking bay. It would be his first and last trip to see Alexei Polzin. The Russian needed time to adjust to his new life without reminders of the past. They both had to let go and move on.

A car was parked with its nose pointing towards the road. Blake pulled open the passenger door and eased himself in.

'How was it?' asked the man behind the wheel.

'Let's get out of here.' The painkillers were wearing off. Blake threw his head back and closed his eyes.

Johnnie Green fired up the engine and eased off the brake. They crunched along the drive, and emerged onto a quiet, tree-lined lane.

'Come on, spill the beans. How was he?' Bill Sanders leaned forward between the two front seats.

'Angry. Frustrated. How do you think?'

'Really?' said Green. He swung the car smoothly through a series of tight bends.

'He blames us for taking away his identity.'

'How ungrateful,' said Sanders, 'after what we did for him.'

'I don't blame him. We took away everything he lived for. First, he lost his daughter, then his marriage, now his identity. He's got nothing left.'

Blake stared out the window at the blur of a passing hedgerow. A monotonous, unending ribbon of green. The car fell silent as they passed through a sleepy village of grey, slate houses. Green eased off the accelerator, and they slowed to a crawl adhering to the speed limit.

Around a corner, a pub appeared at the side of the road. The car park was empty, and a sign hanging from a stone pillar was swinging in a light breeze.

'Pull over here,' said Blake. 'Let's have a drink.'

ABOUT THE AUTHOR

Adrian Wills has been a journalist for 20 years but writing has been in his blood from since he was old enough to put pencil to paper. He is married to fellow author, Amanda Wills. They live in Kent with their two children, Oliver and Thomas, and their two cats.

28141904R00415

Printed in Great Britain
by Amazon